LEON URIS
BATTLE CRY

This is perhaps the greatest novel ever written about the fighting Marines. From the training grounds to the battlefields and deep into the human soul, *Battle Cry* tells the story of one squad of bold, passionate Marines.

DANNY
*He started a private war when he forgot
his hometown sweetheart and took up
with a Navy officer's wife.*

TEX
*He was certain of only one thing:
all foreigners were cowards, especially Levin.*

LEVIN
*Ultimately, he knew what he had to do—
give up his life for his buddies.*

GOMEZ
*A brawling, butchering little man
whose only passion was killing.*

They're all here—and hundreds more—in this big, bloody, unforgettable novel of the fightingest men on earth, the United States Marines.

BATTLE CRY
LEON URIS

BANTAM BOOKS
NEW YORK · TORONTO · LONDON · SYDNEY · AUCKLAND

THIS BOOK IS DEDICATED TO THE UNITED STATES MARINES, AND TO ONE IN PARTICULAR—
STAFF SERGEANT BETTY BECK URIS

ACKNOWLEDGMENTS

I do not see how anyone trying a first novel can do it without sympathy, help, and faith of friends. No one who ever tried has had better friends than I have.

*This edition contains the complete text
of the original hardcover edition.*
NOT ONE WORD HAS BEEN OMITTED.

BATTLE CRY

*A Bantam Book / published by arrangement with
G. P. Putnam's Sons*

PRINTING HISTORY
Putnam edition published April 1953

A complete serial appeared in the Sunday editions of THE SAN FRANCISCO
EXAMINER *during August 1953; An excerpt from the first chapter appeared in
the Sunday edition of* THE NEW YORK POST *April 4, 1954; Danish edition—
Steen Hasselbalchs Forlag, Copenhagen, October 1953; English edition—
Allan Wingate, London, October 1953; French edition—Plon, Paris, October
1954; German edition—Kindler & Schiermeyer Verlag, Munich, August 1956;
Hebrew edition—Massadah, Jerusalem, August 1954; Italian edition—Baldini
& Castoldi, Milan, April 1955; Norwegian edition—Nasionalforlaget, Oslo,
June 1955; Spanish edition—Editorial Freeland, Buenos Aires, March 1956;
Swedish edition—Bokfoerlaget Gothia, Stockholm, September 1955; Dutch
edition—Uitgeverij & Drukkerij Hollandia, Baarn, November 1954*

*Bantam edition / October 1954
58 printings through November 1989*

*Bantam Books are published by Bantam Books, a division of Bantam Double-
day Dell Publishing Group, Inc. Its trademark, consisting of the words
"Bantam Books" and the portrayal of a rooster, is Registered in U.S. Patent
and Trademark Office and in other countries. Marca Registrada. Bantam
Books, 666 Fifth Avenue, New York, New York 10103.*

PRINTED IN THE UNITED STATES OF AMERICA

KR   66 65 64 63 62 61 60 59 58

PART ONE

Prologue

THEY CALL ME MAC. The name's unimportant. You can best identify me by the six chevrons, three up and three down, and by that row of hashmarks. Thirty years in the United States Marine Corps.

I've sailed the Cape and the Horn aboard a battlewagon with a sea so choppy the bow was awash half the time under thirty-foot waves. I've stood Legation guard in Paris and London and Prague. I know every damned port of call and call house in the Mediterranean and the world that shines beneath the Southern Cross like the nomenclature of a rifle.

I've sat behind a machine gun poked through the barbed wire that encircled the International Settlement when the world was supposed to have been at peace, and I've called Jap bluffs on the Yangtze Patrol a decade before Pearl Harbor.

I know the beauty of the Northern Lights that cast their eerie glow on Iceland and I know the rivers and the jungles of Central America. There are few skylines that would fool me: Sugar Loaf, Diamond Head, the Tinokiri Hills or the palms of a Caribbean hellhole.

Yes, I know the slick brown hills of Korea just as the Marines knew them in 1871. Fighting in Korea is an old story for the Corps.

Nothing sounds worse than an old salt blowing his bugle. Anyhow, that isn't my story.

As I look back on those thirty years I think of men and of outfits. I guess I've been in fifty commands and maybe there were a hundred men I've called Skipper. But strangely, there was only one man among them who was really my skipper and only one outfit I think of as mine. Sam Huxley and the battalion he led in World War II, "Huxley's Whores." What made Huxley's Whores different? Hell, I don't know. They were the damnedest bunch of Marines I'd ever laid eyes on. They weren't Marines actually—or even men for that matter. A gang of beardless youths of eighteen, nineteen, and twenty who'd get pickled on two bottles of brew.

Before that war we had men among us who never knew that life existed outside the Corps. Leather lunged and ramrod straight, hard drinkers and fighters and spit-and-polish career men.

Then came the war and the boys—thousands of them. They told us to make Marines out of them. They were kids who should have been home doing whatever the hell eighteen-year-old kids do. God knows we never thought we could do the job with them ... God knows they fooled us.

What made them different? Well, there was one of these kids in my squad who was quite a writer. I wish he was here to help me explain. He had a way reasoning out things to make them look real simple. He could tell you about fighting spirit and the deeper stuff of movements of peoples and the mistakes of generals and issues and of an American Congress that were sometimes as deadly to the Corps as any enemy in the field. He understood those things far better than I do.

A lot of historians write it off as *esprit de corps* and let it go at that. Others think we are fanatics for glory, but when you come right down to bedrock my kids were no different than anyone else. We had the same human strength and weaknesses that any crew of a ship or battalion of an army had.

We had our cowards and our heroes. And we had guys in love and so homesick they near died of it.

There was the company clown, the farmer, the wanderer, the bigot, the boy with the mission, the Texan. Huxley's Whores had its gamblers, its tightfisted quartermaster, its horse-ass officers, its lovers, its drunks, its braggarts, its foul-ups.

And there were the women. The ones who waited and the ones who didn't.

But how many men were there like Sam Huxley and Danny Forrester and Max Shapiro? And what makes these kids who have the normal loves and hates and fears throw their lives away, and what is it they carry within them that makes retreat worse than death? What was it that turned defeat into victory in the dark beginning at Guadalcanal and on the bloodsoaked lagoon at Tarawa and on Red Beach One at Saipan? They went through a wringer of physical and mental hell but still never failed to give each other that wonderful warmth of comradeship.

I do not berate any man who carries a gun in war, no matter what his uniform. But we Marines got the short end of the stick in that war. How many times in World War II were American forces, aside from the Marines, asked to walk into crushing odds with the cold sea behind them and withering fire before them and only raw guts to pull them through? I remember only one other time, at Bastogne.

This is the story of a battalion of invincible boys. And of my kids, the radio squad.

The Corps suffered humiliating defeats following Pearl Harbor and many fine old outfits fell holding outposts whose names were then foreign to the American people—Wake Island was one of them. We had to start from scratch with a couple of proud hardnosed, but ill-equipped regiments that remained in the scattered and wounded force. The new boys came to double and triple the ranks and we began the hard road back.

The Sixth Regiment of the United States Marine Corps, with me included, was sitting on Iceland keeping company with the northern lights when the war broke out, legally, that is. The Regiment was one of those proud outfits that had been settling banana wars for decades.

We got a big reputation in the first World War in a place called Belleau Wood, where we stopped the Hun dead in his tracks. For doing this the French decorated us with a fancy braid, the Fourragère, which all members of the Sixth Marines wear about their left shoulder.

At Château-Thierry, when Allied lines were collapsing, the story goes that one of our officers yelled: "Retreat, Hell! We just got here!" Maybe you've seen that expression in the history books along with some of our other battle cries.

The rest of the Corps is jealous of the Sixth because we happen to be the best regiment. In their spare time they dreamt up a nasty name for us: they call us the Pogey Bait Sixth. The story, and entirely unfounded, is that in 1931 on one of the ships taking us to Shanghai, we had ten thousand bars of candy but only two bars of soap in our ship's store.

It was no sad parting we made from Reykjavik after we entered World War II, because the weather and the women were way below zero and the whisky strictly rotgut. We had sat out at our camp at Baldurshagi like a gang of stir-crazy cons, the monotony driving us insane.

When the Sixth returned from the frigid monotony of Iceland the regiment was split wide open. All personnel were given furloughs and reassignment orders. They spread the men all over the Corps, to form a nucleus for a hundred new outfits being formed. Thousands of boys poured through the boot camps and the oldtimers were urgently needed everywhere.

I had a month-long blowout and then got a ticket to the West Coast with my old buddy, Sergeant Burnside. We were happy to be able to remain in the cadre of the Sixth Marines to help it reorganize again to full complement. I was made battalion communications chief with Burnside, a notch under me, heading the radio squad. When we hit Camp Eliot, a few miles outside

San Diego, it was little more than one long street with immense
barracks lined down it. The place was nearly deserted, but not
for long.

Burny and I were glad to hear that Captain Huxley had
made Major and was to command our battalion. Huxley was
a hell of a good man. An Annapolis graduate and former All-
American end at Ohio State, he was tougher than a cob. He
hung a lean raw-boned hundred and ninety-five pounds on a
towering six-foot-three frame. He sort of kept an arrogant distance from the enlisted men; nevertheless we couldn't help but
respect him. No matter how he drove his men, you would always find old Highpockets at the head of the column.

Burnside and I ran anxiously to meet the truck as it pulled
up in front of our barrack. At last we were to get a look at our
squad. There was only one other radio man, aside from us; a
waylaid character by the name of Joe Gomez who had drifted
in a week before.

The driver handed me a list. They unloaded their seabags. I
scanned them with interest. My face must have dropped ten
inches, Burnside's was down eleven.

"Fall in and sound off when I call your name." It was the
most ill-aligned, saddest-looking excuse for a Marine squad it
had ever been my displeasure to see assembled in so small an
area at one time. "I said fall in and sound off, goddammit!"

"Brown, Cyril!"

"Here." Christ on a crutch! Right off the farm, a barefoot
boy.

"Forrester, Daniel!"

"Here." Not bad looking, but awfully young. A cherry, no
doubt.

"Gray, Mortimer!"

"Yo." Another damned Texan. Gawd almight damned.

"Hodgkiss, Marion!"

"Here." The name fits, Buster. Wait till Gunner Keats takes
a gander at this motheaten crew.

"Hookans, Andrew!"

"Here." A big dumb musclebound Swede with two left feet.
What the hell had they sent me!

I had to look at the next name on the roster twice. Burnside
was staring, dazed-like.

"Lighttower, Shining?" I finally tried it.

"Ugh, I'm an Injun." The squeak came from behind the big
Swede. He stepped out. There, before my eyes was the picture *End of the Trail*. A skinny, hunched over, deflated piece
of redskin with a nose off a buffalo nickel. He grinned at me.

"Zvonski?"

"Zvonski, Constantine. My friends call me——"

"Don't tell me, let me guess," I sneered. This customer couldn't weigh over a hundred and twenty-five pounds with a mortar on his back. A real feathermerchant. How do they expect *him* to pack a TBY?

My legs nearly buckled at the sight of them. Burnside was pale. Huxley would have a hemorrhage when they tried to operate. Gunner Keats would puke.

The one called Hodgkiss fell out of ranks and picked up two suitcases laying beside his seabag. "What do you have there?"

"A phonograph and some records." I walked over to him and opened an album. A little swing music always livens up the barracks. But it was horrible. I flipped the pages: Chopin, Tschaikovsky, Brahms—a whole lot of those guys. . . .

"Show them to quarters, Mac. I'm going to the slop chute and get pissed up," Burnside moaned.

"What you want, chief, eggs in your beer?" The Injun laughed.

To say that the kids coming into Eliot were a change from the beer-drinking, hell-raising professionals of peacetime, was the understatement of the year. They were babies, beardless babies of eighteen and twenty. The Corps sure was shot to hell! Radio men—I'm laughing. An anemic Indian, a music lover, a lumberjack with ten thumbs, a Texan who couldn't move out of his own way, a farmer, a feathermerchant, and the All-American boy. All this and Joe Gomez, a renegade troublemaker.

After our first field problem, Gunner Keats thought seriously of resigning or begging to be shipped out. Huxley, who rarely showed emotion, gagged.

I found them the dirtiest, filthiest work details possible. I went out of my way to be nasty. Shovel garbage at the dump, clean out the crap bowls, dig ditches, swab the decks of officers' quarters, police the entire camp.

Christ! In the old Corps radio operators were something. They stood watches on the battlewagons . . . they were respected. These . . . these *things* that Major Bolger sent us had trouble with the slowest speed field sets. I wanted to go back to Iceland.

It would be hard to say exactly where a Marine story like this should start and where it should end. The kids were there and we weren't happy about it. Where they came from, how they got there, I didn't know. . . .

1.

THE ROOF of the cold, gray, barnlike Pennsylvania Terminal in Baltimore hovered high over the scurrying travelers and the small whispering groups about Gate Three. In clusters of two, three, four and more they stood around stern-faced youths as the moments ticked away. Here a wife and child, there a half dozen pals shouted encouragement. In a corner an aged mother and father and a group of relatives whispered to a sullen lad.

There were many young girls, some weeping, all fighting back tears as they stood by their husbands, their lovers, or their boy friends. The almost buzzing sound of their farewells bounced and echoed off the walls of the ancient terminal.

Danny Forrester zipped up his green and silver jacket with the block letter F and shifted his weight nervously from one foot to the other. Grouped about him were his father, his young brother Bud, his best friend Virgil, and Virgil's girl, Sally.

"Hey, lady, my brother is a Marine," little Bud Forrester shouted to a passer-by.

"Be quiet, Bud," Mr. Forrester demanded.

Kathleen Walker stood at Danny's side. Their hands were clasped tightly. He felt the cold sweat of her palms as a sergeant in dress blues made his way through the throngs, walked to the gate, and began to check a roster sheet.

"I'm sorry about Mother. I'm sorry she didn't want to come."

"She'll be all right, son."

"Gee, Danny," Virgil said, "I wish I was going with you."

"No, you don't," Sally answered.

"I called up Coach Grimes. He was sort of angry you didn't say good-by."

"Heck, Virg, he'd probably've brought the whole team and student body down. I . . . I didn't want that. I'll write and explain to him."

"Sure."

"You've got the sandwiches and cake I packed?" Sally asked.

"Right on top. Thanks, Sally."

Henry Forrester reached in his wallet and took out a ten-dollar bill. "Here, son."

"I've got twenty already, Dad. That's more than enough."

"Well, you'd better take it anyhow. Never can tell, little emergency might come up."

"Thanks, Dad."

6

"Any idea about what's cooking?" Virgil asked.

"Your guess is as good as mine. I've heard a million stories today. They say the Base is nice. We'll be in isolation for a couple weeks at San Diego. Boot camp, they call it."

"Sure sounds like fun."

"You'll write us, when you can?"

"Yes, Dad."

"Hey, Danny, I want a Jap sword. Get a Jap for me, Danny, huh?"

"I don't suppose I'll see any Japs for a while, Bud. I want you to be a good guy and do what Dad tells you—and write to me."

A loud cry cut through the station. A soothing arm went around a mother's shoulder. A long awkward period of silence followed. Danny and Kathy looked at each other sheepishly from the corners of their eyes.

"Maybe you'd like to talk to Kathy alone for a minute," Mr. Forrèster said.

Danny led her to a deserted bench, but neither sat down. She lowered her head as he spoke softly.

"You don't want to change your mind, do you, kitten? I would understand if you did."

"No . . . no."

"Scared, kitten?"

"A little."

"Me too."

"Kiss me, Danny."

They held each other until the public address system rudely shocked them back to earth.

"Attention all Marine enlistees. Report to platform Gate Three at once."

A mutter of relief was heard and one by one the fifty boys and their parties wended their way through the gate and down the long stairs to the snorting, hissing string of cars below. Virgil picked up Danny's overnight bag and Danny, with one arm about Kathy and the other about Bud, shuffled slowly along amid the crowd.

"All right," the sergeant barked. "Fall in."

For the tenth time he droned through the list: "Tatum . . . Soffolus . . . O'Neill . . . Greenberg . . . Weber . . . Forrester . . . Burke . . . Burke, Thomas K . . . answer up."

"Here."

"All right, pay attention. Soffolus will take the roster and be in charge of this detail. You people board the first car and stay together. There will be no defacing or drinking or boisterousness, or Military Police will be put aboard. Fall out—you have three minutes left."

They broke the shoddy formation and rushed to the crowd arched about them.

"You'll be sorrreee!" a sailor yelled from the fringe of the group.

"You'll be sorreee!" his mate echoed.

"I wish I was old enough to be a Marine. I wish I was old enough." Bud raced back, hiding behind his father. Danny knelt by the weeping boy and hugged him.

"Good luck, Danny," Virg said, grasping his hand.

"Take care of yourself, son, take care of yourself."

"Good-by, Dad . . . and don't worry."

Sally kissed his cheek and stepped back. He embraced Kathy and turned. "I love you, Danny." Her voice trailed after him. He boarded the train and ran for a window seat and tugged the glass up. Virg held Bud up for a hug and then Danny reached his arms down and they were grasped by his father and his friend.

The train lurched suddenly. Its powerful electric engine eased it slowly along at first. Then it picked up speed until the platform was filled with trotting and waving and shouting people. The boys in the car pressed faces against the windows. Faster and faster the train went until the ones outside could no longer keep pace and stopped breathlessly and waved. They grew smaller and smaller. And then the train plunged into a long black tunnel and they were gone.

Danny slumped down in his seat and a weird sensation passed through him. Alone now . . . I'm sorry to God I did it. His heart pounded. He felt unable to control a cold clammy sweat. Alone . . . why did I join? . . . why?

The boy next to him held out a pack of cigarettes. Danny declined, then introduced himself.

"Forrester, Danny Forrester."

"Jones, L. Q. You don't want to hear my first name. It drives people mad. I'm from L.A., but I was visiting my uncle here when the war broke out. . . ." His words fell upon deaf ears as the train broke from the tunnel.

Danny looked out of the window. Block after block of attached brick houses with white marble steps flitted by. A wide lawned street and the Johns Hopkins Hospital. Then, tired from the long day of waiting and falling into lines and waiting, he rested back and closed his eyes.

"I'm a Marine . . . I am a Marine," he repeated to himself to the clickety-clack of the wheels. Everything seems so unreal. A thrill passed through him . . . Kathy loves me.

Forest Park High—it seemed so far away already. Forest Park High. . . .

The game was over. The frenzied alma-mater-singing, cheer-calling, goalpost-pulling students had departed from Baltimore Municipal Stadium.

After a slap on the back by Coach Wilbur Grimes, the weary and dejected players of Forest Park left the gear-cluttered dressing room and went into the frosty November air to receive tribute from the remaining loyal fans.

A half hour later Danny Forrester emerged from the shower. The room was empty save for the little equipment manager scurrying about, on a final check. The place had a mixed odor of sweat and steam and the floor was cluttered with misplaced benches and towels. He dressed, slipped into his moccasins and stepped to the mirror and wiped away a circle of mist. He combed his hair and then placed his finger on his right eye which was bruised and quickly swelling.

"Nice game, Danny," the equipment manager said, slapping him on the back and leaving.

He walked to his locker and took out his green and silver jacket. The door opened, sending a gust of cold air in, and Wilbur Grimes entered, turned down the collar of his coat and pulled up a bench. He took out his pipe and loaded up.

"In a hurry?"

"No, sir."

"Good news, Danny. I've got a letter from the Georgia Tech Alumni Association. The scholarship is all set up."

"Oh."

"Come on now, lad—forget the game, it's all over. The kids were disappointed when you didn't come out with Virg and the team."

"I just didn't see anything to cheer about, Coach. We lost. We wanted to put City's head on a platter and give it to you. This is our last game, we wanted to win bad."

The coach smiled. "I'd say we showed pretty good. Losing by one point to a team that hasn't been defeated for five years is certainly no disgrace. At any rate we would have run them off the field if I had ten more boys like you out there."

Danny did not look up from his bowed position at Grimes' compliment, though it was the first he had ever gotten as an individual from the coach, who always praised or berated only the group.

Coach Grimes puffed his pipe. "At least you might be a little happier over the scholarship."

"I don't know, sir. Georgia is a little far from home. I was sort of thinking about going to Maryland instead."

"Oh come now, Danny. You had your heart set on that Civil Engineering course. Why the sudden change?"

Danny just nodded his head.

"Virg didn't get an offer . . . that's it, isn't it?"

"Well, sir."

"So that's it. I smelled it."

"We sort of made a pact, Coach, that we'd go through college together."

The coach arose and stood over the boy. "Look, lad, you've played your last game for me, so I can speak freely to you. I've been coaching at this school fifteen years. I suppose I've had a thousand boys under me at one time or another. And in that time I can honestly say that I've never had more than a half dozen that were as surefire as you."

"But I don't understand it. Virg has scored twice as many points. Why, he's been the star of the team for three years."

"Danny, I like Virg and I certainly don't want to belittle any friendships or pacts or what have you. But I'd rather have a boy that can make two yards when we need it than one who makes fifty when we don't. And I'd rather have a boy who improves with every game and never makes the same mistake twice."

He turned and paced the floor. "I like a boy who plays the game with everything he has for every minute because he can't play any other way. I'm not going to pressure you, Danny, but I hate to see you throw away that career you want so badly. Think it over and let me know."

"Yes, sir." Danny arose and zipped his jacket.

"And, Danny . . . of course I'll never tell Virgil. But if he knew I'm sure he'd say: Georgia Tech."

The train halted in the Philadelphia Thirtieth Street Station.

"Take care of yourself."

"Write to me."

"Don't worry honey, I'll be O.K."

"Get a Jap for me."

"Good-by, Connie darling."

"Susan . . . Susan . . ."

"Philadelphia contingent in cars two and three!"

Virgil Tucker poked his head in the doorway. "Hey Danny, come on, we're waiting—oh, excuse me. I didn't know you were here, Coach."

Danny thrust his hands in his pockets as he stepped out into the cutting, darkening air. Virgil Tucker placed an arm about his shoulder and they walked toward the car. They looked for a moment across the street where Baltimore City College stood on a knoll like a gray impregnable fortress, glowering proudly down on them.

"I was just thinking," Virgil said.

"What?"

"You didn't miss that block in the last quarter. If I had stayed along the sidelines, outside you, instead of cutting back into the middle of the field . . ."

"What's the difference? Old Lawrence would have pulled something out of the bag. City would have scored again."

"Too bad we don't have a coach like Lawrence . . . well, maybe Poly can whip them next week."

Kathleen Walker, Sally Davis and Bud, Danny's eight-year-old brother, awaited them by the car.

"Danny, Danny," cried Bud. "Nice game, Danny."

Virgil shrugged. "Your Dad went home with my folks and left him. He wanted to see you." Virgil handed him the keys.

"You drive," Danny said, smiling at Kathy.

"Naw, you drive," Virgil insisted. "It's your old man's car."

Virg and Sally snuggled into a corner of the rear seat and promptly ordered Bud up in front.

"Aw girls," Bud snorted. "Virg has a girl, Virg has a girl."

"Sit down and be quiet, shrimp." The car whisked away toward the 29th Street bridge.

"I wish I was old enough to go to Forest Park . . . I'll show those City bums."

"Tell him to pipe down, Danny."

"Shut up, Bud. City boys are nice guys."

"Are not either." He bounced down in the seat and looked stormily out of the window. They swung past the Museum of Art. "Dad says he looks like he's sitting on a pot." The youngster pointed to Rodin's "The Thinker" on the lawn.

"Bud!" And the tone of his brother's voice finally quieted him.

They drove over the railroad bridge, the slim shining pencils of rails running far below. He had lived near here once and in the summer he'd walk the concrete ridgeguard on a dare. And with his gang, they played "bombardier," dropping their flavored, ground ice "snowballs" over the side, far down onto the passing cars and trains.

Fringing Druid Hill Park, they cut off at Liberty Heights Avenue towards the Forest Park District.

"Virg is kissing Sally, Virg is kissing Sally. . . ."

"Danny, tell him to be quiet or I'm going to crown him."

They came to a stop on Fairfax Road before a brick and stone house, exactly like fifty other brick and stone houses on the block. Any trace of individuality had long gone from the middle-class dwellings in Baltimore. They were merely blown-up, more comfortable models of the red brick, marble-stepped domains that ran for mile after mile throughout other districts.

Bud was asleep in the back seat. Virgil had been dropped at Sally's house for dinner.

"What's the matter, you mad at me?"

"No," Kathy answered. "Why?"

"You haven't said a word since I got in the car."

She looked at his swollen cheek. "Does it hurt badly?"

"Oh that, that's nothing."

"I suppose I should be proud and make a lot of noise like Sally does. But I'm afraid you're going to break your neck some day."

He smiled teasingly. "Really worries you . . . I like having you worry about me."

"Do you feel like going to the dance tonight?"

"The victory ball," Danny mused. "That sure kills me. We're always having a victory ball after the City game—only we never win."

"Why don't you just come over and we'll play the radio. You look tired."

"I thought you were dying to go to the ball. That's all you've been talking about for two weeks."

"I know, but—"

"Yeah, I'd like to get out of it, but the gang will say we're stuck up."

"We'll leave early then."

"Swell, meet Virg and Sally at the Malt Palace later."

He took her hand and looked at his class ring.

"I put tape around it, so it would fit." He glanced into the back seat and seeing that Bud was fully asleep drew her over to him.

"Not here, Danny. The whole neighborhood will be looking."

"I don't care."

"Don't be silly." She pulled away and opened the door. "I'll see you in an hour."

After a few dances in the decorated gymnasium, they stole away from the well-wishers and back-slappers. As they drove, her soft golden hair brushed against his cheek and he smelled the fresh sweet scent of perfume. She hummed the tune of the last dance softly.

> *Two in love,*
> *Can face the world together,*
> *Hearts that cuddle up,*
> *Can muddle through. . . .*

He turned the ignition key over and tuned in an all-night music station. The car stood by Druid Lake Reservoir between cars parked every few feet circumferencing the lake. She came into his arms and they kissed and she nestled there, tucking her legs beneath her. He sighed as he kissed her cheek again and again.

"Are you chilly, kitten?"

"No." She drew away and leaned against the opposite door. "I was just thinking."

"What? You've sure been acting screwy."

"I don't know exactly. When I was watching the game, it occurred to me that . . . well, I don't know how to say it."

"What, kitten?"

"It was sort of a crisis for us. We'd be apart . . . you'll be going away to college in a few months. It's been an awful lot of fun." Her voice trembled.

"I've been thinking about it a lot too. I guess we've got to grow up sometimes."

"I suppose."

"I'm going to miss you an awful lot. But we'll have Christmas Holidays and all summer. I'll get work here during the summer."

"You've decided, then?"

"I decided that a long time ago. I wanted to go to M.I.T. But they don't give football scholarships and I'm afraid the bill would be a little too steep for Dad."

"You do want to go to Georgia Tech?"

"Yes."

"Have you talked it over with Virg?"

"No. I don't want to back down on a bargain . . . but I'll never get my C.E. at Maryland . . . not the one I want."

"It wouldn't be so bad if you went there. I'll be going in another year."

"That's the trouble. Georgia is so far away from you."

"I wish you didn't have to play football."

"I like football."

"I don't. I think I'll be worried to death the whole time you're gone."

"About football?"

"And some other girl stealing you."

"You're my girl, Kathy. You'll see someday why I want to be an engineer so badly. They go everywhere in the world, see everything. Do all kinds of jobs—tunnels, bridges, dams. It's a real job. A good civil engineer writes his ticket."

"I know how much you want it."

"Kathy?"

"Yes."

"I don't like leaving you. Try to understand."

"Yes." She came back to his arms and he petted her gently.

"I think if another guy ever touched you, I'd kill him."

"Would you . . . honestly?"

"Do you suppose it will be the same, kitten? I want you to go out on dates and all."

"I won't enjoy them."

"It will be best. Five years is a long time before we can make any real plans. I've . . . sometimes wished I could say a lot of things to you . . . and wished we could be serious."

"It's really a problem, Danny. I didn't think people had problems like this."

"I don't guess it could be much worse—anything at all. We sure have problems."

Early morning found the contingent enlarged nearly six-fold. Throughout the night the train had halted restlessly as parting scenes were played out before its steel sides. Dawn in Buffalo. It was freezing as they stepped into the Harvey Restaurant in the monstrous station. A hot breakfast brought him slowly to his senses and for the first time he became eager and anxious to continue the trip. The full sun banished the initial shock and now he was excited about the coming adventure.

"My name is Ted Dwyer and this is Robin Long."

"Forrester, Danny Forrester, and this guy is L.Q. Jones. Don't let him scare you."

"How about you guys pulling over here and let's have a little card game."

"Good idea. The trip along Lake Erie is a killer. We won't hit Chicago till late."

"Train sure is bulging."

"Yeah."

Mile upon mile of monotonous scenery on the never-ending lake shore finally caused the conversation to dwindle and restlessness to set in.

In the lavatory, a blustering character named Shannon O'Hearne had started a crap game. A large and unruly Irishman, he had gotten himself a band of awed followers and along with the crap game a drinking spree soon began. The group made passage to and from the toilet an obstacle course.

The monotony was broken by a further monotony of standing in line for lunch. There were nearly four hundred men aboard now, all wanting to eat simultaneously—except Shannon O'Hearne and his followers, who drank their meal.

At last the train got lost in the maze of rails that ushered it in to Chicago. Numbed and weary they debarked, glad of the layover.

Henry Forrester sat in his overstuffed chair, his feet propped on an ottoman. Bud lay on the floor, the Sunday funnies sprawled out before him. The voice of a nervous football broadcaster broke the tranquillity of the room.

And now we take a thirty-second pause for station identification.

"Danny," Sarah Forrester called from the kitchen. "You'd better drive over and pick up Kathy. Dinner will be ready in a half hour."

"O.K., Mom, it will be half time in a couple minutes."

"Bud!"

"What?"

"Start setting the table."

"Aw, gee whizz, Mom."

Hello again, football fans. This is Rush Holloway, the old Wheaties reporter here in the nation's capital where thirty-five thousand pack Griffith Stadium on this beautiful December afternoon to witness the battle between Steven Owen's New York Giants and the Washington Redskins.

The noise you hear in the background is the public address system paging Admiral Parks. They've been paging several top brass during this second period. . . .

Mickey Parks has just replaced Ki Aldrich at center. Incidentally, Mickey is a distant cousin of Admiral Parks. Great favorite with the Redskin fans. Now in his fourth season with the Skins. . . .

We interrupt this regularly scheduled broadcast to bring you a news bulletin. Airplanes, identified as Japanese, have attacked the American Naval Base at Pearl Harbor. Stay tuned to this station for . . .

First and ten on their own forty-yard line.

"Did you hear that, Dad?"

"Er . . . er, what? I must have been dozing."

The phone rang. Bud raced to it and then turned the receiver over to Sarah Forrester. "Henry," she called, "where is Pearl Harbor?"

Henry Forrester rapped softly on his son's door, then entered. Danny lay on his bed staring at the ceiling. His father sat on the bed's edge.

About the room hung pennants of Forest Park High and a half dozen college teams. The dresser bore a dozen team photographs and there was a larger one on the wall of the Baltimore Orioles. A baseball autographed by Babe Ruth, Jimmy Foxx and Lefty Grove adorned the center of a small desk.

"Son, won't you come down to dinner?"

"I'm not hungry."

"Your mother is awfully upset. Cigarette?"

"No thanks."

"Don't you suppose we should talk this over?"

"Every time I try to make sense Mom starts bawling."

Henry Forrester walked slowly to the dresser and studied a trophy atop it. Danny had run the last twenty-five yards of a relay race on a cinder track after losing one of his spikes.

"Maybe we could talk between ourselves. You owe me that much."

"I don't understand it myself, Dad."

"Wilbur Grimes told me yesterday. They'll take you at Georgia Tech right after February commencement."

"It just doesn't seem right. Me going off to college to play football with a war going on."

"But Danny, you're only seventeen. They don't want you. If they need you, they'll call you."

"We've been over it fifty times already."

"Yes, and we've got to have a showdown. Neither your mother nor I can go on with this daily sulking. And I'm not signing any papers until I know a reason why."

"Have it your way."

"I could understand it if you weren't happy here or if you were a rattle-brained kid. You've wanted to be an engineer since you were Bud's age. You've got everything now, a home, friends, I let you drive the car . . . Mother and I talked it over. We decided that you could go to M.I.T. if that would help change your mind."

"It isn't that I'm not happy, Dad."

"Then why the Marine Corps?"

"Don't keep asking me."

"What about Virgil?"

"He wants to go too, Dad . . . but with his mother so sick."

The balding man snuffed out his cigarette. "This whole damned thing makes me feel like a miserable failure."

"Cut it out."

"I don't think we'd better pull any punches, Danny. We've done that too often. I feel like one of those fathers who is a star boarder in his own home. I've really never given you and Bud the companionship you've needed."

"You don't have to go blaming yourself because you have to beat yourself out to keep the business going."

"I've envied you, son. You've turned out to be all the things I wished I could have been. Yes, I suppose I'm jealous of my own boy. Ever since you were a little bugger you haven't needed me. I remember how you'd come in from peddling papers when we lived in that flat on North Avenue. You'd be bloodied up from the big boys on your corner. But you always went back and slugged it out."

He sighed and lit another cigarette. "And you wanted to play football. Mother locked you in your room and you'd jump from the second story. You've had the guts to stand up to her. I never have."

"What are you saying?"

"I wanted you to play ball. But I took her side—I always have. Still, I guess, inside me, I'm the proudest man alive that you want to join the Marine Corps. Don't think losing a boy is easy to take. I think . . . this once, son . . . I'll have to carry the ball for you."

"Dad, Dad . . . I don't know what to say."

"Have you told Kathy yet?"

"No, sir."

"I think you'd better go over there and see her."

2.

CONSTANTINE ZVONSKI lay back on the creaky bed and watched the pall of blue smoke drift to the ceiling. From where he lay he could see the garish sign of light bulbs flick off and on. HOTEL, it read, ROOMS $1.50 AND UP. A shift in position caused the ancient bedsprings to groan. The dim yellowish light within partly hid the cobwebs and the faded carpet with its accumulated grit and dirt of the years.

The silence in the street outside was broken by a sharp clicking of heels against the cobblestone pavement. He darted quickly to the window and drew aside the threadbare curtain. It must be Susan.

He snuffed his cigarette nervously as the sound faded and was then reheard coming quickly up the steps. He unbolted the safety lock and opened the door a crack. As she approached the head of the stairs he beckoned her softly. She entered the room breathlessly. He shut and relocked the door.

He took her in his arms. She was fresh and cold from the crisp January air.

"Honey you're shaking like a leaf," he said.

"I'll be all right in a minute, it was cold outside."

"No, you're scared."

She pulled herself away gently and took off her coat, then sat slowly on a hard-backed chair and hid her face in her hands.

"Your old man again?" She nodded. "Dammit, why can't he leave us alone."

"I'll be all right in a minute, Connie." He lit a cigarette and handed it to her. "Thanks, darling."

"Was it bad?"

She managed to steady herself but her eyes watered as she spoke. "The usual. He called us names. He threatened me. I'm here now, everything is all right."

Connie smashed his fist hard into an open hand. "He's right. I'm no good. I'm no damned good or I wouldn't have you come to a dump like this. He's only trying to do what's right for you. If I was any kind of a guy . . ."

"You don't hear me complaining."

"That's the trouble, I wish you'd complain. No, I don't—I don't know what I mean."

He turned and leaned against the dresser. Susan came up behind him and put her arms over his shoulders and rested a cheek on the back of his neck. "No kiss for me, Connie?"

He spun about and grasped her tightly. "I love you so much, sometimes I think I'm going to bust wide open."

They kissed. "I love you too, Connie," Susan said.

She walked to the bed, kicked off her shoes and sat back, resting against the headboard, and drew deeply and contentedly on her cigarette. He seated himself on the edge and took her hand and stroked it.

"I've got something important to tell you. Look, honey— we've talked a hundred times. Your old man will never leave us in peace as long as we are here. We got to get away from Philly."

He began a catlike pace about the room, sputtering to find the right words. "He's got no use for me, maybe he's right. Sure, I got a record and reform school and all . . . but that was before I met you, honey. I'd do anything for you . . . you know that."

"I know, Connie."

"I finished high school, so what? None of the colleges give scholarships for a hundred-and-forty-pound guards. I . . . I just can't get squared away here. Just can't get a decent job— can't save a damned dime. And your old man hounding and calling you dirty names. I can't take that!"

"Don't get yourself worked up, darling."

"Sure, I'm a dumb Polack . . . eighteen-year-old punk. What's he care if my old man died in a charity T.B. ward in a stinking coal town? I've been busted in the ass plenty."

"I wish you wouldn't curse, Connie."

"I'm sorry, honey. See, you just say something and I'm sorry." He smiled and sat beside her once more. "Susan." He ran his hand over her cheek gently. "Susan . . . I'm so crazy about you, you're just like living to me."

She kissed his hand and smiled. "I kind of like you a little bit too, mister."

He reached for an ashtray and lit up. "Like I said, this is important. We've got to end this meeting in dives and sneaking around. You're too good for that—no, let me finish. I figured real hard how to get away from here. Susan, I joined the Marine Corps yesterday."

"You . . . what?"

"Look." He grabbed her by the shoulders. "I got it straight, they're sending us to California to train. California, do you hear? I can get out there and save. I'll put every nickel away and I'll get a place for us and send for you. We can start out there, away from your old man, away from this stinking town. Just you and me, married, all the way out in California, honey." And then he released her from his grasp slowly. "What's the matter, Susan, you don't look like you're happy about it."

"I don't know, darling, you hit me kind of suddenly."

"What is it, don't you want to come to California?"

"Let me think a minute, Connie, let me think."

Off and on the gaudy light bulbs flicked, sending a glare, then a shadow, across the room. In the quiet, the faint smell of the mustiness set in.

"The Marine Corps," she repeated, "the Marine Corps."

"It's the best way," he pleaded. "There will be plenty of time. I'll save hard and there's lots of jobs out there."

"What about your mother and Wanda?"

The words made him flinch inside. "She signed the papers to let me go. My mother is used to suffering. She wants to do what's right by us. She knows it'll never make it here. Wanda has only a year left of school. Uncle Ed will see they get their three squares and have a roof. Dammit! It's *us* I'm thinking about. What's the matter . . . what's the matter?"

"I'm frightened, Connie."

"There's nothing to be scared about."

"I can't help it, I'm frightened. My father is afraid to lay a hand on me as long as you are here. I'll be alone . . . I'll be without you. Oh Connie, so many things can happen. What if you can't get me to California?"

"I will! It's our only chance. I'll rot here. I can't take it any more." He reached for her tenderly and rocked her in his arms as though she were a little girl. "If we keep up this way, you'll grow to hate me. You're all I've got to live for."

His lips bussed her cheek and his hand stroked her hair softly. "Honey, you're so cold."

"I'm afraid of your plan . . . something's going to happen."

"Hush now. Nothing can come between us."

"No . . . nothing," she repeated, and relaxed in his embrace.

"This will be our last time for a while, Susan." His fingers groped out as he slowly unbuttoned her blouse.

"Yes, Connie . . . yes."

Constantine Zvonski walked from the Harvey Restaurant in the Chicago depot. There was a five-hour layover before the Rock Island Line took over the trek. He watched as the boys and men left in pairs and threes, heading for the nearest bar or moving picture house.

"Hey, haven't I seen you someplace?" someone said. Zvonski turned and looked at the boy in front of him. He scratched his head.

"Yeah," he finally answered. "You look awful familiar, too. Did you enlist in Philly?"

"No, I'm from Baltimore. Say, I got it. You played for Central High?"

"Don't tell me. You're that damned halfback from Baltimore that gave us such a bad time. My name's Zvonski."

"Sure, the little guard with the name. Talk about bad times, you spent the whole doggone game in our backfield."

The little Polack's face was wreathed in smiles. "Well, you birds licked us, didn't you? I played a good game, huh?"

"You sure did. We talked about it all the way back to Baltimore. Darned good for being so light. My name's Danny Forrester. Heading for San Diego, I guess?"

"Yeah."

"What's your name again?"

"You can call me Ski or whatever you want. Glad to meet you, too."

"Say, I got a couple, three guys waiting out there. There's a burlesque joint a few blocks down. Care to join us?"

"Don't mind if I do."

Later, the train sped through the night over the plains of Illinois, blinds drawn. From the washroom came the clacking of dice. Wild whoops and dropping bottles and the pungent smell of whisky. It was fortunate that Constantine Zvonski was so slight. Two in an upper were crowded at best.

"Come on little Joe." The dice crackled off the wall.

"Little Joe for poppa, once dice."

"Just one mile south, dice, be nice to me."

"Six to five, no Joe."

"Got you covered."

"Aw, piss or get off the pot."

Danny tried to straighten out his legs without shoving them in Ski's face. The train rounded a curve and he rolled against the wall.

"You asleep?" Ski asked.

"Who can sleep with that racket."

"Me neither, I can't sleep, I'm too excited."

"I wonder what it's like in San Diego?"

"We'll soon find out."

"Hey, Danny."

"Yes."

"You got a girl?"

"Yes."

"Me, too, I got one."

"I was just thinking about her."

"Me, too. I always think about my girl."

"It feels kind of funny. The whole thing is so mixed up. Last week we were at the bowling alley with the gang."

"Yeah, I know what you mean. I feel funny inside too. But I ain't got much to be homesick for. Nothing but Susan."

"Who said I was homesick?"

"Maybe not homesick, but alone." Ski snapped on the light and sat up, hitting his head on the abbreviated ceiling. "Dammit, I'm always doing things like that." He reached for his pants and took out his wallet. "Here's a picture of my girl."

Danny propped up on an elbow. It wasn't a very good picture. He looked at the small dark girl called Susan Boccaccio and emitted a polite, long low whistle.

"Nice, huh?" Ski beamed.

"Darned nice."

"Let me see your girl."

Ski returned Danny's compliment, then he turned off the light and lay back again.

"As soon as we finish with this boot camp thing, I'm going to send for her. We got it all figured. I'm going to save up and get her out here and get married. You going to marry your girl?"

"No, it's nothing like that."

"Oh, kid stuff, huh?"

"I don't think a guy should ask a girl anything like that in these times. Who knows where we're going or what's going to happen? I don't think it would be fair to Kathy. I even heard some fellows say that we're going right on a ship and retake Wake Island."

"Bullcrap."

"Just the same, who knows anything?"

"It's different with us, Danny. We . . . well, we are almost like married now. I haven't got much but Susan."

"I guess I see."

"I'm glad I met you, Danny. I hope we land in the same outfit."

"Me, too."

The train rolled on. The shouting from the washroom became louder. Someone kicked an empty bottle and sent it scuttering up the aisle. Ski swung the curtain open and slipped into his pants.

"Where you going?"

"I'm all jumpy inside. I'm going to smoke a cigarette."

Danny stretched his cramped position and for several moments lay in the darkness listening to the clattering dice and the fascinating clicking of the wheels. And then the noise faded and he thought about her as he had thought about her a thousand times.

The brown and white saddle shoes, plaid skirt and sweater on backwards. The cute flip of her head and the sway of her skirt as she swung past. The stag line at the weekly gym dance, the first date at a neighborhood show. Bowling after school, Friday night rugcutting sessions to Glenn Miller records at the house of one of the gang, ice skating at Carlin's Park, after-game thick corned-beef sandwiches at the Malt Palace and summer ferry excursions to Tolchester Beach.

The fight to find courage for the first kiss. And kissing her and tripping over the milk bottles on her porch and falling down the steps into the rose bushes.

Her dates with other fellows that hurt past all pain. And his spite dates with Alice, the school tramp.

Arguments about him cutting classes to go to the burlesque. Then came the autumn of 1941 and college plans loomed larger and larger. He drove the family car now and there were the nights at the reservoir. He slipped his class ring on her finger and she nodded yes . . . and the night they were together and, almost without intending it, he felt her breast. . . .

The wonderful sensation thinking of her . . . and rehearsing the speech he would say on the day he would return from college and tell her he loved her.

And he thought of how wonderful it would be to sleep with her. But if a fellow felt the way he did about a girl—that wasn't right.

Ski struggled back into the berth and Danny shoved himself against the wall.

"Jesus, I wish those bastards would break it up. How the hell we supposed to sleep?"

"Yeah, yeah . . ."

Marvin Walker lay on the sofa, his nose buried in a magazine. He muttered something about taxes. Sybil Walker sat in her armchair by the lamp, a mending basket in her lap. The rays of light caught a far wall from the kitchen where Kathy studied her lessons.

"Marvin."

"Hmph . . . this administration is nothing but a bunch of Commies . . ."

"Marvin!"

"Getting so a working man—"

"Marvin, put that magazine down."

"Oh yes, dear, what is it?"

"I want to talk to you." He came to a sitting position, stretched his pudgy little body, and took off his reading glasses. "What's on your mind, Sybil?"

"Marvin, don't you think it's time we sat Kathleen down and had a good heart to heart talk with her?"

"That's your job."

"I don't mean that."

"Well, what do you mean?"

"I mean about her and Danny."

"Oh, that again."

"You don't have to take his side all the time."

"I like Danny."

"So do I. He's a fine boy. But . . . well, don't you feel that Kathleen is just a little too young to be going steady?"

"Pissh, woman. You're making a mountain out of a molehill. Just a phase. If we make an issue out of it you'd really make trouble. You seem to forget past experience."

"Nevertheless, she could be seeing other boys. You can never tell just how serious they are."

"Oh come now. The boy is going off to college in another month."

"Just what I mean. I don't want to see her tied down."

"I think they're sensible enough to reach an understanding between themselves on that score."

"I still feel, Marvin . . ."

"See here, Sybil. If the specimens of drips she used to drag home are an example of your so called 'field,' I think she's done right well by herself. My God, I nearly lost my mind with some of those morons she went out with before she met Danny. He's a damned good lad. Clean cut, came up the hard way, and knows his values. I just hope that some other girl doesn't snatch him off before he gets his degree. Furthermore, they'll both be dating when he's gone and I think it would be very unwise to meddle."

"It's just—with a war on—if he goes away."

"He's only seventeen years old. They aren't taking babies."

Sybil Walker sighed and returned to her mending. The doorbell rang, Marvin buttoned the top of his trousers, looped the suspenders over his shoulders and advanced to the door.

"Hello, Danny."

"Good evening, Mr. Walker, hello, Mrs. Walker." Kathy had

already come to the living room with the sound of the bell. "I
know it's a school night, sir, but something rather important
came up and I wondered if I could talk to Kathy for a few
minutes."

"Don't stand there, come on in."

"Hello, Danny."

"Hello, Kathy. Come on out on the porch . . . I want to tell
you something."

"Rambling wreck from Georgia Tech, eh Danny?"

"Now don't keep her too long," Mrs. Walker ordered.

"No, ma'am," he answered, closing the door.

"Fine boy," Marvin said. "Fine boy."

Kathy buttoned her coat and followed him across the porch
to the glider. For a time he sat studying the perfect cubes made
by the long row of porches down the block. Each in the same
design and as they grew farther away they looked like one box
inside another. Each with the porch light in the same place. All
void of life. He shoved his feet and set the glider into motion. It
creaked as it swayed. Kathy tucked her legs beneath her to
keep them warm.

"What is it, Danny?" Her breath caused a little cloud of
steam.

"I—don't know where to start."

He turned and looked into her face. She was beautiful. Her
brow over her blue eyes was furrowed in a frown. "You're going
away, aren't you?"

He nodded.

"You've enlisted in the Marine Corps." Her voice trailed
off to inaudibility.

"How did you know?"

She turned from him. "I suppose I've known ever since Pearl
Harbor. I knew it would be the Marines . . . I remember how
you looked at them at the Fireman-Marine Game. . . . I suppose I knew when the news about Wake Island came over . . . I
suppose I knew for sure on New Year's Eve. You kissed me . . .
like . . . like you were going away for a long, long time. I knew
it would only be a matter of days until you told me."

The swing stopped.

"When are you leaving?"

"In a few days."

"What about college and . . . everyone."

"Everyone and everything is just going to have to wait."

"What about us?"

He did not answer.

"Danny, do you have to go?"

"Yes, I have to."

"Why?"

"Don't ask me why. I've asked myself why, a hundred times. Just that something inside me is eating. Can't you understand?"

"You're going because you're Danny. I guess you'd be someone else if you didn't."

"Kitten."

"Yes?"

"I . . . I want you to give me back my class ring."

Her face turned ashen. She pulled her coat about her.

"I'm not trying to make a grandstand play. College is one thing . . . this is different. I don't know how long I'll be gone. Maybe two or three years. There's a rumor that I'll be sent to the West Coast."

"But . . . but . . . I thought we were going steady?"

"I don't want to drag you into this mess, Kathy. Maybe it was just kid stuff. I just can't go with us making any plans or promises. Something might happen and we might change our minds and we'd be awfully hurt then."

"I won't change my mind," she whispered.

"After all, kitten, we're just a couple of kids—and there really isn't anything set between us."

He took up the gentle rock of the glider and blew into his cold hands. There was silence for several moments, broken only by a neighbor tramping wearily up the stone steps to his door.

"Well, say something, Kathy."

Her lips trembled. "I knew this was going to happen, I knew it." She arose and walked to the rail and bit her lip to hold off the tears. But they came, nevertheless.

"Aw, for Christ sake, don't cry. Please, you know I can't stand it." His hands took her shoulders tightly. "We're worked up . . . let's don't do anything we'll be sorry for later. You'll see, I'll be gone and it will wear off—you'll date some other fellows and. . . ."

"I don't want any other fellows—I just want you," she sobbed, turning into his arms.

"Holy smoke, `you're going to mess up everything." He stroked her soft golden hair. "Holy smoke . . . what are we going to do now?"

"Don't be angry, Danny."

"For what?"

"Crying."

"No, I'm not angry."

"Maybe we're too young . . . I just want to go on being your girl."

"Don't start crying again."

"I can't help it."

"I guess you know what you're letting yourself in for?"

"I don't care."

"What will your parents say?"

"I don't care what they say."

"Gosh . . . I feel kind of shaky all over."

"Me too."

"You'll write all the time?"

"Yes."

"I'll let you know my address as soon as I can."

"I'll wait for you, Danny. No matter how long it takes."

"If you want to change your mind . . . I mean it, honest."

"You really don't want me to."

"No."

He wiped her tears away as she managed a weak little smile. "I guess . . . this sort of makes us engaged."

She nodded.

"A lot of nights I used to think how wonderful you are, Kathy. I used to dream about the time I'd be able to say what I've wanted to."

"I've thought about it a lot too, Danny."

"Do girls think about that?"

"Uh-huh."

"Honest, I mean do they think about it the way fellows do?"

"Yes."

"I . . . I guess it's all right to say it now."

"Yes."

"I love you, Kathy."

"Me too. I love you very much, Danny."

Morning in Kansas City and another contingent of recruits. A diagonal trek through an elongated wheat field filled the day's monotony. Rumors, dirty jokes, conversation, and mounting tension. The long line to the dining car. The train bulged with over eight hundred boys and men.

O'Hearne, down to his last bottle, made a personal call on each one in the car for refinancing. He was only moderately successful. He filled the afternoon with a personal history of himself as boxer, football player, drinker and lurid-lurid lover. He provoked two fights with lesser competition and as night fell the crap game was on again.

Day again and a crazy course still southward from Texas to New Mexico and back into Texas for a stop at El Paso. A mad rush for the postcard counter. Several bedsheets hung from the windows now, announcing that this was a trainload of Marines heading for San Diego.

O'Hearne attempted to lure a young awed girl flushed with patriotism aboard. For several hours past El Paso he reckoned that he could have sold her services at least two hundred times at five dollars apiece and set her up in business in San Diego.

Hot and sticky Arizona. O'Hearne's mob took to defacing the train until M.P.s boarded at Douglas. And so, into the last night.

Bursting tension and sheer spectacle as two steam engines lugged the train up the steep embankments of the Sierras. Wild anticipation. Handbags packed and ready. A collection for the overworked porter. Wilder rumors as the train dipped below the Mexican border and stopped for inspection at Tijuana.

Small boys ran alongside peddling cigarettes and bilking the novelty seekers. The tin soldiers from the Romberg operetta depart.

"I wonder if they got a band to meet us."

"Yeah, after all, we're the first battalion from the East to ever train here."

"I hope they got my dress blues ready. I want to look over the town."

"I hear we'll be in isolation for a couple weeks."

"Don't worry, I'll get into San Diego tonight."

Outside, a few palm trees came excitingly into view. Also, a long line of trucks and a host of green-uniformed sergeants and corporals milling about with roster sheets. The green uniforms struck the first sour note in the new recruits.

"Philadelphia and Baltimore contingent, start loading in truck sixty-eight. Answer up when your name is called."

The convoy moved towards the Marine Corps Base and was greeted by shouts of "You'll be sorreee!" from the streets.

The lazy hot day was a wonderment for the people who had left the midwinter of the East. Past the huge camouflaged aircraft plant they rolled and then into the spotless military base, over the enormous parade ground and toward a sandy area of tents at a far isolated end.

They debarked and answered roll again by an arched sign which read; RECRUIT TRAINING DEPOT, MARINE CORPS BASE, SAN DIEGO, CALIF.

And the gates of mercy closed behind them.

3.

"ALL RIGHT, you people. We have a long row to hoe tonight so I don't want to see anybody goofing off. Drop your gear and follow me." They tagged after him to the mess hall.

Danny was amazed. From earliest recollections he had understood that soldiers ate nothing but hardtack and beans and the like. It was a surprise to find a tray filling with roast beef, potatoes, slaw, jello, ice cream, and the tables lined with pitchers of coffee and milk. Somewhere along the serving line, however, the ice cream got lost under the potatoes and gravy.

After the meal they were split into groups of sixty men and led to the large reception barracks. L.Q., Danny and Ski bemoaned the fact that O'Hearne had fallen into their group. A sharp blast of a whistle brought them scurrying to the center of the room around a starched corporal.

"All right, you people. Nobody leaves the barracks. I'll be back for you when they're ready to take you. When I re-enter, the first person that spots me yells 'Attention.'"

"Are you going to be our instructor?"

"You'll meet your instructor in the morning."

Before they could turn a barrage of questions loose, the corporal spun about and left, with a curt, "You people will find out all the answers soon enough."

Danny and Ski strolled over to several charts hanging from the wall. One read: *Rocks and Shoals: Regulations and Customs Governing the United States Navy.* It was in small print and too long and double-worded to keep their attention. Another chart contained rank and insignia of the Navy and comparable Marine Corps rating. A third chart proved more interesting: *Common Naval and Marine Corps Expressions.*

BLOUSE	— *coat*
BOOT	— *recruit*
BULKHEAD	— *wall*
CHOW	— *food*
DECK	— *floor*
D.I.	— *drill instructor*
GALLEY	— *kitchen*
HEAD	— *toilet*
HATCHWAY	— *doorway*
LADDER	— *stairway* (and so on down the list.)

Catching on quickly, Ski announced proudly, "I got to go to the head." In a moment he ran back and grabbed Danny and towed him into the lavatory. He raced past a long row of toilets to the final one and pointed to a sign. It read *Venereal Disease Only.*

They gaped, then retreated from the place. Danny checked his watch. It was a quarter to ten. He slipped out of the door to a small porch and zipped his jacket. It was chilly, but the sky was clear and filled with stars. A far cry from the icy January of Baltimore. Then he saw a strange sight. He counted sixty baldheaded boys running through the night in underwear with a corporal behind them shouting out curses.

It slowly sunk in that he was going to lose his too. With a tinge of panic he pushed his fingers through his hair. Something phoney about this place. He spotted the form of the reception corporal cutting up the tarred walk and raced inside ahead of him screaming "Attention!"

"Fall in and follow me. Leave your handbags here. You won't need anything in them any more."

Danny's group fell in line somewhere about the middle of the other seven hundred and forty men who made up the new battalion. They ran a half mile to the dispensary and then stood for over an hour.

"Peel down to the waist," a sailor corpsman ordered as he walked the line with a bucket of mercurochrome in one hand and a paint brush in the other. He painted a number on each chest and the name was recorded by a following corpsman.

Midnight brought them to the steps of the dispensary.

"Oh man," L.Q. moaned, "my lil ole pappy tole me not to leave our magnolia plantation. Oh man, I'd just love to be a settin' and a sippin' mint juleps . . . oh man!"

"Shut up in that line, goddamit!" The tempers of the corporals grew progressively worse with each passing minute.

At last they entered the building. In quick succession they were pricked in the finger for a blood smear, blood was taken from the arm for a Wassermann, and eyes, ears, nose, heart, and reflexes checked. Followed a hernia check, blood pressure, balance, and a chest X-ray. As the last man left they were herded to another building.

"When you enter, take off all your clothing."

"Oh . . . oh," Jones moaned. "Oh . . . oh."

An assembly line of needle men awaited them. Vaccination, tetanus shot in the right arm, two others in the left and a grand finale in the buttocks.

For the last shot a well-oiled team worked. One corpsman painted the butt cheek and popped in a needle as though he was tossing darts. The next corpsman worked in flawless motion filling the hypodermic, screwing it into the needle, shooting, and removing the needle into a boiling tray.

An exhausted Shannon O'Hearne fidgeted in the line. As the needle entered the man in front of him, a bead of perspiration formed on O'Hearne's brow and his stomach felt queasy. The corpsman screwed in the holder and pushed in the serum. As he went to withdraw the needle it stuck in the lad's flesh, leaving a slow drip oozing from it. O'Hearne passed out and had to be dragged back into line by two stronger-hearted friends.

Two-thirty in the morning. They limped into the barracks

and fell into their bunks. Danny tried laying on his back, then on each side. But he was swollen from blunt needles and dubious techniques. He found solace flat on his stomach and closed his eyes, too worn to feel sorry for himself.

"Hit the deck!" The lights went on. Danny rolled. It must be a joke. He had just fallen asleep. He struggled his eyes open, his body ached from the plunging. He steadied his head long enough to catch the time: four-thirty. He placed his watch against his ear and assured it was still ticking, lay down again.

The scream of a whistle split his ears and he realized it was no dream or joke. It was still dark and the sky still flooded with stars. Straining, he eased himself from the upper bunk and staggered in behind the other disheveled, half-asleep men who cursed and mumbled their way to the head. He lined up behind Jones at one of the sinks which had a six-deep waiting list.

"My lil ole mammy told me . . ." L.Q. moaned hoarsely.

The splash of cold water failed to clear the cobwebs, but another blast of the whistle did. Half undressed, they fell in outside in the darkness. Chow, but too sore and tired to remember eating, and they trudged back to the barracks, packed and fell out once more.

With heavy eyelids and disheveled persons they awaited the next process. Their wait was not long. A tall, leathery, red-headed corporal dressed in stiff khakis, pith helmet, and glossy shined shoes stepped before them with roster in hand.

"Ten-shun!" he snarled. The sun slowly cast light on the motley-looking recruits. The corporal's face was freckled and his eyes steel blue and cutting. He walked the line, hands on hips. From one hand dangled a stick thirty inches long with a leather-laced thong hanging from it.

"From now on this is platoon One Forty Three. My name is Corporal Whitlock. You'll hate the day you met me."

"Hey, corporal. How about letting us get some sleep."

"Who said that?"

"I did," Dwyer answered.

A path cleared as the corporal walked to Dwyer. For a full minute Whitlock cut him down with an icy glare. "What's your name, son?"

"Ted Dwyer."

"My name is Private Theodore Dwyer, sir," Whitlock corrected.

"P . . . private . . . Theo . . . dore . . . Dwyer . . . sir."

"Are you chewing gum?"

"Yessir."

"Swallow it."

Gulp.

He paraded before the new platoon, which stood frozen.

"Goddam Yankees," he finally hissed. "Goddamyankee is one word in my book. All right, you people. My name is Whitlock . . . you address me as sir. You sonofabitches aren't human beings any more. I don't want any of you lily-livered bastards getting the idea you are Marines either. You're boots! Crapheads! The lowest, stinking, scummiest form of animal life in the universe. I'm supposed to attempt to make Marines out of you in the next three months. I doubt it. You goddamyankees are the most putrid-looking specimens of slime I have ever laid eyes on. . . . Remember this, you sonofabitches—your soul may belong to Jesus, but your ass belongs to me."

The drill instructor's cordial welcome to the Corps thunderstruck them. They were all awake now. And the dawn came up like thunder out of Coronado 'cross the bay.

"Answer up when your name is called, goddammit." He ran down the roster. "O'Hearne . . . O'Hearne!"

"Here," a voice whispered. Whitlock advanced on the husky, curly-haired Irishman.

"What's the matter? Lose your voice, craphead?"

"Been on a drunk—my voice is gone." He dropped a cigarette butt on the deck.

"Pick up that butt, craphead."

"Don't you call me craphead."

O'Hearne balled his fists. Whitlock poked his little stick under Shannon's chin. "We got special treatment for tough guys. Pick up that butt." The stick lifted O'Hearne's chin slowly. Shannon unballed his hands and reached to the ground. As he bent, Whitlock's glossed shoe met him squarely and sent him sprawling. Shannon arose and charged, then pulled up short and fell meekly back into the formation.

The corporal launched another tirade. He cursed for ten minutes, seldom repeating an obscenity. He expanded on the group's future status in life. Isolation from the outside world . . . loss of all trace of individuality . . . no candy . . . no gum . . . no newspapers . . . no radios . . . no magazines. . . speak only when spoken to . . . salute . . . address as sir and obey all men within the confines of boot camp above the rank of private.

With each new word they slumped into increasing acceptance of the snare they now realized they were utterly trapped in. Never before had they heard such a collection of words thrown together. So this was palm-treed, blue-uniformed San Diego.

The corporal ran them past the permanent structures to their new quarters. It was a tent city bordering a gravel parade ground on one side, with vast expanses of sunbaked sand stretching to the bay on the other. Danny, Ski, and L.Q. Jones drew a three-man tent. Then they were introduced to Platoon

Sergeant Beller, a Texan also, and no less a ranter than the corporal.

Beller cursed them for another ten solid minutes, then sent them off on a whirlwind procedure of hurry and wait. Double time, then stand in line.

They drew seabags and passed down counters stacked high with articles of clothing. The items were hurled at their heads. Everyone was angry and every few moments the recruits picked up a new curse word to add to a fast growing vocabulary.

The seabags became crowded with a barrage of skivvies, socks, overcoat, belts, boondockers, high-top dress shoes, field scarfs, and the rest of the wardrobe of a Marine. Everything was fitted hastily and with obvious disregard for the size of the man involved. The new gear was pocked with stickers and white tags.

For shoes, the recruit jumped up on a platform and held a pair of twenty-pound weights. As his feet flattened on the measure an NCO hurled them at him.

Double time. Draw cots, pads, ammo belts, shelter halves, and the rest of the field gear. They sagged under the cumbersome weight as they tried to keep up the racehorse gait.

Now to the canteen, where a book of chits was issued, its value to be deducted from the first pay call. Regulation purchases were required. A bucket soon carried a scrub brush, laundry soap, shaving gear, and a battle pin—an item once known merely as a collar clasp. Then came steel wool, Blitz cloth, seabag lock, toothbrush, cigarettes, steel mirror, shine kit, a tin of Kiwi polish and finally a blue volume labeled *The Marine's Handbook*. Then they ran home with buckets swinging.

After chow the whistle shrilled. "All right, you people. The uniform of the day from now on will be: boondockers, green trousers, khaki shirts, field scarf and battle pin—and pith helmet. There are a couple of goddam irons in the pressing tent and you bastards make use of them. When you fall in tomorrow I want you looking like something. Get into uniform and pack your civilian gear . . . two minutes to dress and a minute to weep over your civvies . . . fall out!"

A headlong dive into the seabags and they emerged, their attire a long way from a recruiting poster. Overlooked tags, iron-stiff shoes, uniforms too long or too short, too loose or too tight. Canvas belts large enough to encompass a baby elephant. The pith helmets either perched high or fell over the eyes.

Whitlock looked at them. He lifted his eyes skyward. "Gawd!" he cried in anguish. "Gawd!" he cried again. "Square away that helmet!" His fist smashed the sun hat down over

O'Hearne's ears and eyes from its jaunty angle. Throughout the ranks there was a quick movement to adjust them.

"Gawd!"

After bidding adieu to their civvies they drew stencils and the remainder of the first momentous day was spent marking every belonging.

"I'll give you crapheads till eighteen hundred to square away your uniform of the day. Fall out!"

"I never sewed in my life," moaned L. Q., running a needle into his finger.

"Sure could use my mother now," Ski added.

"Ya know, I don't know just why I feel this way. But I got a sneaking suspicion that I'm not going to like this place."

"Christ—two and a half months."

"How about that Texan?"

"Oh, he's a great kid. I remember where I saw him. It was his picture hanging in a post office. Where does the Marine Corps find these gems?"

"Goddammit!"

"What happened?"

"I stuck myself again."

"I wonder what that quartermaster was thinking of?" Ski buttoned his trousers and looked down at the bottoms which draped over his shoes and onto the floor for a full ten inches.

"I guess I'm squared away," Danny said, wiping his battle pin clean with the Blitz cloth. "Better get in line for that iron."

The whistle blew. "Fall in. Bring your topcoats! All right, line up and dress down. Cover down—try to make it look like a formation. We're going to the movies."

"Corporal Whitlock . . . sir."

The long Texan strode to Jones. "Sir, Private Jones requests permission to speak with the drill instructor," he hissed, smashing the helmet over L.Q.'s eyes.

"S . . . sir, Private Jones requests permission to speak with the drill instructor, your majesty."

"You don't talk in ranks, craphead, but what is it?"

"Sir, did I understand you to say we are going to the movies?"

"Correct."

"Well sir. Is it all right if you want to stay in the tent, sir?"

"You got to have entertainment," he explained to the men, who could think of nothing more entertaining than to lay their weary bodies on a cot. "It's good for your morale. However, Private Jones, if you'd rather stay in, that's O.K. with me."

"Oh . . . thank you sir, thank you sir."

"Sergeant Beller," the D.I. called. Beller, built low to the ground and solid as a tank, rumbled from his tent. "Sergeant, Private Jones doesn't want to go to the movies."

"Is that correct, Private Jones?"

"Oh no sir. Not at all sir. I think movies will be just double peachy."

"Are you calling me a liar?" Whitlock spat.

"Oh no sir. The fact is that I didn't want to go, but I do now. I'm sorry."

"You're never sorry for anything you do in the Corps, craphead."

"Oh no sir, I'm not sorry."

"Well, corporal, if Private Jones doesn't want to go to the movies he doesn't want to."

"You're absolutely right, sergeant. I don't think he should go."

"Correct. Instead we'll give him a little detail."

"Oh . . . oh."

"Do you know where the bay is?"

"No sir."

"It's three miles—thataway."

"Thataway, suh?"

"Thataway. Private Jones, get your bucket and another one and double time to the bay. Bring me back two buckets of salt water. I want them full or you'll be drinking them."

"Yes sir, two buckets of salt water, coming up sir." A swift kick sent him hurrying to the tent and then off into the darkness as the platoon double timed toward the theater.

Danny slumped forward on the hard wooden bench and drew his coat about him. He remembered little of the picture. Only something about Orson Welles shouting, "Rosebud." Each time he dozed he felt Dwyer's elbow in his ribs.

"Stay awake for Chrisake, Danny. Whitlock is watching us."

A bugle blasted reveille through the loudspeaker. It was followed by a record that soon became the hated symbol of four-thirty in the morning.

Forty-five minutes to shower, shave, dress, make up the cot, police the area and fall in for rollcall. In darkness to the mess hall to stand and wait. It was here that Danny first learned to sleep while standing and leaning on Ski. The meals were solid and plentiful as they had to be to sustain the men through the ordeal of the day.

Back to the tents and clean up. Mop, squeeze, pick up cigarette butts and bits of paper. The policing buckets were always nearly empty and it was a rare prize when a boot found a stray fruit peel to pounce upon.

"A helluva way to fight the war."

"Yeah, I got a letter saying how proud they are of me. They should see me, now."

"This is the bible from now on," the corporal said, holding up *The Marine's Handbook.* "The other one may save your soul, but this one is going to save your ass. We want you alive! Let the other son of a bitch die for his country, we want you alive!"

"All right, you goddamyankees. We got a date with the barber."

"Barbershop," whispered Chernik, the farmer from Pennsylvania. "They should call it a wool-shearing station."

"And we got to pay two bits for it yet."

There was only one instrument used, an electric clipper. In groups of five they ran from formation to the waiting chairs within.

"Shampoo, shave and light neck trim," sighed L.Q. as he flopped into the chair.

"Prevents lice, makes every man in boot camp the same. Makes no difference what you once was. You're a craphead when you come out of the barbershop."

For the first time the D.I. laughed as the men without names came from the shack. And they laughed at their own misery. Everyone looked ridiculous. Feeling naked and branded they once more trotted to their area and lined up in formation.

Beller took over. He marched the line of hairless men. It was hard to tell the banker from the baker now.

"What's your name, son?"

"Private Forrester, sir."

"Did you shave this morning?"

"No sir."

"Why?"

"The head was crowded, sir. Besides, sir, I only shaved twice a week in civilian life."

"Is that so?"

"Yes sir."

Beller hunted out another non-shaver. O'Hearne was his man. He called the pair in front of the formation. "You people were told to shave. The Marine Corps says you need a shave every day! Private Jones!"

"I shaved sir, twice."

"Private Jones, go to the head and get two razor blades. I want old rusty ones. Then go get two razors."

"Two old rusty blades coming up, sir."

Danny and Shannon stood before the platoon, which was rigid and warned not to laugh. Without soap or lather the two offenders shaved each other simultaneously. The worn blades pulled and tore skin from each other's face until Beller was satisfied they were smooth.

"You people shave every morning!" he yelled again.

The neat, squat, starched man in front of the platoon contrasted strangely with the raggedy-ann men before him.

"You people have a lot to learn. From the looks of you, you'll be a long time learning. The first thing is how to fall into a formation and stand at attention. I want the lard asses to my left and the feathermerchants to my right. Line up by height."

Danny, O'Hearne, and Chernik headed the three columns while Ski, Dwyer, and a lad named Ziltch brought up the rear. After shuffling the platoon around Beller said, "Remember who is on your right and always fall in at the same place."

The lessons began. Hard-learned. Drilled-in a thousand times. A Marine at attention: hour after hour they stood at attention. Heels together, feet at a forty-five degree angle, knees straight but not rigid, hips equally balanced and drawn back slightly, stomach in, chest out but not exaggerated, neck straight, head parallel, eyes forward, arms at sides, thumbs along seams of trousers, palms in, fingers fall away naturally.

"Zounds, I curled a toe when he wasn't looking."

"Goddam, I didn't think there was so much to learn when we was standing still. What about when we start walking!"

"Jones!"

"Yes sir."

"What the hell you think you are? A Prussian general? Relax."

"Relax sir, yes sir."

"Forrester!"

"Yes sir."

"Front and center. Here is one craphead that seems to get the idea. Look at him. You can drop a plumb line from his chin down. . . . Return to ranks . . . all right, you people, let's try it again."

"I'll be a sad bastard," the D.I.s mumbled over again and again during the day as they caught errors. "Jones, where the hell is your chest? Palms in, dammit—stop curling your fingers."

"Now we'll try at ease and parade rest."

For three days they fell in, stood at attention, at ease, back to attention, to parade rest, to attention, fell out (one step backwards say "Aye aye sir" . . . about face) fell in and stood at attention for a change.

"Make your bunk by the book!" Morning inspection found fifty-seven beds torn up and thrown from the tent to be remade. A wrinkle, an improperly laid corner, a seabag that wasn't square at the corner, was enough to outlaw a bunk. Seabags were overturned and the contents strewn and then repacked. Several recruits made their cots nine times until the instructors were satisfied.

Each day found a lesser number of overturned cots, but one morning a cigarette butt was discovered on the catwalk. The platoon double timed through the ankle deep sand of the boondocks until after an hour four men had dropped from exhaustion.

> *Dear Kitten,*
> *This is the first time I've had to write since we've arrived. You'll find my address on the back of the envelope. They sure keep us busy here and the instructors are a couple rough characters. It would be useless to try to go into a lot of detail....*
> *A couple of swell fellows, Ski, and a jokester named L. Q. Jones. Honey, as each day passes I seem to wonder a little more about why I'm here. I don't know how long it will take or where I'm going. If you've changed your mind, let's have it now before it becomes too involved.*
> *I'm thankful that they keep us busy ... I'm afraid if I thought about you too much I'd go crazy....*

"Lep face ... right face, lep face ... right face. Ten shun! At ease. Ten shun! About face ... about face ..."

"I can't get this shirt on."

"Why not, L.Q.?"

"Nobody done tole me you ain't supposed to use a box of starch with a bucket of water. Whitlock is gonna hang me."

"Fall in and dress that goddam line down. Come on, Chernik, get with the living. Goddammit, ain't you people ever going to learn? As I pass down the line, hold up your washing for inspection." The corporal's gimlet eyes scanned the newly scrubbed clothes. "Belt dirty, do it over. Sox dirty—shirt dirty, do it over."

"Jones!"

"Yes, sir."

"You call this a wash?"

"Oh ... oh, sir."

"Lookit them goddam nicotine stains on your skivvy drawers." The bucket of clean clothes was turned over and dumped into the dirt and ground in under Whitlock's heel. "Whole thing over ... you people gonna ever learn?"

"Pay attention, you stupid bastards. I don't know why I'm

rushing you so, but I'm going to try to teach you crapheads to march. You always start off on your left foot. O'Hearne, point to your left foot . . . if you can. Remember it. You hold your normal interval. Steps are thirty inches—not twenty-nine, not thirty-one." He paused a moment.

"For'd harch! Your other left, goddammit . . . lep . . . lep . . . lep two three po . . . lep right lep. Halt by the numbers . . . one . . . two.

"Don't anticipate the command of execution. Forward. . . ." Several men lurched up on their toes in readiness to step off. "Fall on your faces, you stupid bastards. Don't anticipate the command of execution."

Hour after hour the platoon stepped along to the broken-record droning of the D.I.s "Left flank po . . . straighten up that goddam line . . . column right po . . . reah harch . . . reah harch . . . fall on your faces . . ." Another helmet smashed down. The stick jabs a rib. . . .

"In cadence, count."

"One, two, three, four," the platoon shouted back.

"Louder, dammit, louder . . . in cadence, count."

"ONE, TWO, THREE, FOUR!"

"That's the way I want to hear it . . . in cadence count."

"ONE! TWO! THREE! FOUR!" (The goddam Marine Corps.)

"Lep . . . to your lep." (You left a girl behind you when you left, you left.)

"Chernik, stop thinking about that broad. Some dogface is probably in her britches . . . lep, two, three, four . . . lep, two, three, po."

4.

THE BALDHEADED recruits of One Forty Three could move together reasonably well at the end of a week. A few always decided to take off in another direction at a flank command but the majority of the main body hung on.

The end of the week also found a scratch on every boot's forehead from the ornament screw where his pith helmet had been smashed over his face. Whacked fannies, poked ribs, and fingers cracked by the stick the sergeant carried were other helpful reminders of lessons forgotten. The stick, originally designed for measuring, had found other uses in the Corps. When it wasn't heavy enough, the instructor's boot was.

The days were broken by lectures. Field sanitation, personal hygiene, sex in San Diego and a hundred other subjects on which the Marine must be fully informed. The Manual was studied till taps in "spare time" and recited word perfect. But mainly it was drill, drill, drill!

An hour before taps found Danny's tent jammed with visitors. Chernik, Dwyer, and another fellow called Milton Norton. Norton was unusually quiet, studious, and quite a bit older than the rest. He was very likable, though, and popular throughout the platoon.

Danny returned from Whitlock's quarters.

"Did you pass?" Ski asked as he entered.

"Yes."

"How do you like that for learning—Christ, he recites the Eleven General Orders and Rank and Insignia all in one day."

"Quiet," L.Q. snorted. "I'm trying to figure out who I hate the most, Beller or Whitlock." He thumbed through the Manual. "To walk my post from flank to flank and salute all bastards above my rank . . . I know them . . . I know them."

"You better learn them, L.Q., by tomorrow."

Jones pulled a long comb from his pocket and ran it through the tenth of an inch fuzz on his head. "I washed it today and I simply can't do a thing with it."

"I hear tell," Dwyer said, "that Whitlock is one of the easiest D.I.s in boot camp. I was talking to a guy from One Fifty today and he really got a tough one."

"Oh yeah, that's a crock—what's his name, Hitler?"

"How about it, farmer?"

"Oh, I don't know," Chernik answered. "I sort of like the extra hour sleep I get here."

There was a loud noise from the other tent.

"O'Hearne," Dwyer spat. "Of all the crapheads in the Marine Corps, I got to draw a tent with him. Our D.I. away from the field."

"Yeah, he sure gripes me."

"Say, Norton, I heard they been feeding us saltpeter. Is it a fact?"

"What makes you think so?"

"I ain't had a hard on since I been here."

"Just overworked," Norton explained.

"Ha-ha, dirty Ted Dwyer. You were the guy who was going to San Diego the night we got here."

"Yeah, Ted, how do you like your dress blues?"

"Hey, Norton, what did you used to do in civilian life?"

"Teacher."

"I thought it was something special."

"There isn't a thing in the world special about teachers," the quiet fellow retorted.

"I mean, you're not like most of the yardbirds here, fresh out of high school. Where did you used to teach?"

"University of Pennsylvania."

"Penn! We got a celebrity in the tent, men."

"Jesus Christ, what are you doing here?"

"Taking boot camp like the rest of the crapheads."

"But—a teacher at Penn. . . ."

"I don't see any sign barring us." Norton smiled.

"I'll be go to hell, how about that?"

L.Q. picked up his skin-tight green trousers. "In another goddam week I'll fit them if that Texas keeps drilling us like he has."

"I had a dream last night. I dreamed I was in San Diego with a beautiful broad. I was making time with her and I woke up laughing and laughing."

"Why?"

"She was Whitlock's wife."

"I won't have you speaking of my old friend that way."

"All I dream is lep two, lep two—fall in, fall out."

Jones sprang to his feet. "All right you goddamyankees . . ." he aped Whitlock's shrill voice, "ain't you goddam crapheads ever gonna learn . . . Gawd . . . Jones, your other left . . . saddest bunch of boots I've ever seen . . . eh, Mister Christian . . . Mister Christian . . . what is the matter with Jones . . . where the deuce is his chest . . . hup two . . . I'll be a sad bastard . . . goddamyankees . . . can't you people understand American when it's spoke . . . on your feet, featbermerchant . . . stand on your head . . . run to the bay . . . lick the floor clean." The men doubled in laughter did not see the tent flap swing open. "Mister Christian, ten lashes for the goddamyankees." L.Q. spun around and his eyes met Corporal Whitlock's. "Oh . . . oh . . . *Tenshun!*"

They continued laughing, not seeing the D.I.

"TENSHUN!" Jones shrieked.

Cots and seabags overturned in a race to get to their feet.

"Outside, all of you," the Texan hissed. "And bring your buckets."

They stood in front of the D.I.'s tent, stiff as ramrods. The other men of the platoon peeked adventurously from their tents. The corporal paraded in front of them. "What are you people?"

"Crapheads," they answered in unison.

"Goddamyankees too," L.Q. added.

"Keep repeating what you are."

"I'm a craphead . . . I'm a craphead . . . I'm a craphead."

"Now put the buckets on your heads and keep talking."

"I'm a craphead," came the muffled sound beneath the scrub buckets.

"Left face . . . for'd harch."

For an hour he paraded the seven offenders throughout the entire boot camp area. The platoons of boots gawked in amusement. With a pair of D.I. sticks he beat a drum roll on the buckets to their chant "I'm a craphead."

In the darkness, he ordered them into buildings, ditches, clotheslines, heads, and light poles until they reeled like punch drunk fighters. Then the chant was changed to, "I love my Drill Instructor."

During the hours of drill the voices of Beller and Whitlock alternately droned cadence and shouted corrections. It was as though the two men had eyes on their feet, in back of their heads, and on both hands. The smallest flaw was always discovered.

"Straighten up that goddam line. You ain't a bunch of soldiers."

"Get your mind off that broad."

"When you do 'eyes right' I want to hear the eyeballs click."

"Stop swinging those arms. You ain't gonna fly outa here."

"When you come to 'attention' I want to hear leather pop."

"Your other left, dammit."

"Fall on your faces, you sad bastards."

"Don't you know the difference between a column and a flank? Gawd!"

"There's nicotine stains, wash them over."

"You got three specks of dust under your cot."

"Stop scratching in ranks. Them crabs got to eat too."

"Sound off!"

"Sick, lame, and lazy out for sick call."

"Whatsamatter, Ski, did they make the pants too long?"

"Goddamyankees! Ain't you people ever going to learn?"

A voice from the ranks: "Sir, Private Jones requests permission to speak with the—"

"You don't talk in ranks, ain't you ever going to learn?"

"But sir, I got to take a piss something awful."

"Piss in your pants, Private Jones."

"In my pants sir, right away sir."

"Mail Call!"

Those two electric words. A word from home. For the first time in a thousand to come, the hungry scene played itself.

Not even Whitlock's sneering at the Northern addresses and postmarks could dim the happy fire that burned inside them.

> *Dearest Danny,*
>
> *You sound confused. I know that this boot camp is tougher than you are letting on. . . .*
>
> *The coach said he understood why you didn't call. He sort of figured you would do something like join the Marines. He is going to write and send the school paper (I'm an editor on it now) and also a subscription to* Esquire. . . .
>
> *It's lonesome here without you. Sometimes I jump out of my skin when the phone rings . . . the folks have been very understanding. . . .*
>
> *Sometimes though, I can't help but feel that you really don't love me, the way you write. I think about us all the time. It will never wear off for me, Danny.*
>
> *I'll write again tomorrow,*
>
> > *I love you,*
> > *K.*

He read it once more before turning to the other stack of envelopes. Then, he hid his face with his hands. *I've told myself a thousand times that it isn't right and it won't work. But what would it be like if I didn't have her? So far away. I knew it would be lonely, but not like this.*

"Nice, huh?" Jones startled him by thrusting a picture under his nose. He looked at a homely girl, fat as L.Q., with a toothy grin.

Danny whistled. "Wow."

"Nice huh, Ski?"

"Yeah, some dish."

"No cussin' now. I'm putting this picture in my wallet. Confidentially I know she looks like a beast, but me and Heddy had a split-up."

"Good news, Ski?"

"Yeah . . . yeah, it will be all right. We'll make it."

"I hope so."

Jones took to calculating when the war would be over as Danny read through the rest of his mail. "Just think," Jones babbled, "I gave up a nice warm bed in a flophouse for all this."

"Get a T.S. chit from the chaplain. In the Russian Marines they call it a toughski chitski."

"I was just thinking," L.Q. continued, "of the best way to murder Beller. I already got it for Whitlock. Hang him by his balls."

"You should be at the ass end of the line, like I am," Ski said, "and try keeping up with the lard asses double-timing."

The bitching session faded as Danny pulled a sheet of paper from his portfolio. It had a Marine emblem on the letterhead. He toyed with his pen several moments.

> *Dear Kitten,*
> *Let's put an end to this doubting. I love you and with each passing hour I love you more. The thought of losing you now . . .*

He tore up the sheet and began again.

> *Dear Kathy,*
> *Well, only nine more weeks of boot camp left and I'll be a free . . .*

He sealed the envelope and put MMRLH (Marine mail, rush like hell) on the back and walked the catwalk to the mailbox. Disgusted, yet glad. In the distance he heard the curse of a drill instructor. He smiled with little satisfaction that One Forty Three was drilling better than the other platoons. And his mind wandered back to Kathy. Then he ran for his tent to find a laugh from L.Q. As he entered, Ski was lying on his sack.

"Hey, Ski. Get off your cot. You know we aren't supposed to lay on it before taps. Want to get us murdered?"

"He isn't feeling good."

"Looks like you got a fever, Ski."

"Holy Christ, we got to go to the movies tonight."

"I'll go see Whitlock."

"That's O.K. Don't go getting the rebel mad, Danny."

Danny cut up the catwalk and stopped before the D.I.'s tent. "Sir, Private Forrester requests permission to speak with the drill instructor."

"At ease, Forrester, what is it?"

"Sir, Private Zvonski appears to be sick." He followed Danny back to the tent. Danny shouted, "Tenshun."

"That's all right, son, lay down." The corporal bent over and felt Ski's forehead. "You've got the Cat Fever, nothing serious. Lay in during the show and if you don't feel better by reveille, go to sick bay."

"Thank you, sir." He left.

"Phew," Jones sighed, "I thought he was going to boondock us for sure. What did you say?"

"I told him if he didn't let my old buddy take the night off I'd start punching holes in him."

"Gee, thanks, Danny. I'm your slave."

The whistle blasted. "Fall out, Top coats."

"Here we go to get our morale built up."

The four-thirty bugle found Ski's fever gone and he wobbled to the head. As he advanced to the sink he asked Jones, in the next line, "How was the picture?"

"Great," L.Q. answered, "great. They marched us clean over to the Base Theater. People were there, even women. Even saw a real Marine in dress blues. I said to myself right there and then that if I got to go into this war, I'm gonna join the Marine Corps."

"What was the picture about?"

"Called *To the Shores of Tripoli*," L.Q. answered, opening his shaving kit. "Well, this here guy is a horse's ass like Beller and Whitlock and he joins the Corps because his old man was a Marine."

"Gee, a picture about Marines."

"Well, he gets to boot camp and first thing he does is read off his D.I."

"Just like real life."

"Yeah. After giving the D.I. the word he beats the hell out of the whole platoon. Nice guy, only nobody likes him. There's a kid in boot camp who wants to make Sea School but he washes out and he's heartbroken."

"No blue uniform for that boy."

"In the next scene he's makin' time with this Navy nurse. He's a private and she's a looey."

"Just like real. Sorry I missed it."

"Anyhow, he squares himself by saving the life of the D.I."

"What he want to do that for?"

"Don't interrupt . . . the picture ends with the war starting and the whole outfit marching down to the docks to ship out. Bands are playing and people waving flags and everyone singing the Marine's Hymn, and they board ship and who do you think is waiting for him?"

"The nurse."

"How did you guess?"

"Just like real life."

"Hey, you guys, how about getting your ass in gear? We got to shave too," an irate boot shouted.

L.Q. washed the soap from his face and replaced the razor in the kit. "Tomorrow is my day to put a blade in, don't let me forget it."

4:30 Reveille and the cursed record over the loudspeaker. Mad dash to the head. Dark and cold. Shower and shave.
4:50 Roll call. Make up bunks, square away seabags, police up area. By mop, by broom, by police bucket, by squeegee.
5:15 Run to mess hall. Daily game of trying not to be the last to drink from a pitcher of coffee or milk or you have to take it to

be refilled. L.Q. always seems to be anchor man on the milk pitcher. Plunge the mess gear into steaming buckets of boiling water and the slow walk back to the tents with a welcome cigarette and the rising sun. Clean up mess gear with steel wool. Dirty gear causes dysentery. A final touch-up on the area.

6:00 Sick, lame and lazy call. A straggling line of the sick and the imagined sick. The sad line outside sick bay. Their stories fall on unsympathetic ears. A day off for cat fever. Scorching tonic for crabs. Quick knife and back to duty for a blister.

Crap details to clean heads or ride the garbage trucks.

Fall out and be inspected. Growls and curses and punishment. Tent inspection and a wake of overturned cots.

6:30 Drill. Drill and double time in the company area, the parade ground, the ankle deep sand of the boondocks.

9:30 Lecture: How to stand seabag inspection. How to scout enemy terrain. The proper way to take a prophylactic after sexual intercourse. How to salute an officer. How to recognize ships of the fleet.

10:30 Drill.

12:00 Chow. Noon chow is getting monotonous. Three times a week ground beef with gravy on toast. A Marine Corps standby. SOS, they call it. Shit on shingle.

1:00 Paper work. Take your picture for the record book. How much insurance do you want? Take ten thousand.

2:00 Drill.

5:00 Chow. The walk back is slower this time of day, but there is work to be done. Personal gear to be shined, mended, pressed. Clothes to be washed. The uniforms are beginning to fit and show vague signs of losing their newness.

6:00 Laundry call and wash inspection. Do it over.

6:45 Drill.

8:00 Rest period. Study lessons from the Manual. Recite them word perfect or the platoon goes to the bay. Help a buddy.

"Come on, Ski, try those half steps again on the column."

"I can't get it, I tell you."

"You can. That Ziltch is a feathermerchant too, but he gets it."

"I'll . . . try."

Mail call. Funny sounding word—"home."

"Fall out for the movies, you got to have recreation."

10:00 A whistle. No, not reveille already. Beller in from liberty, drunk. He thinks a moonlight trot to the bay might be good exercise.

Sunday, thank God for Sunday. Didn't think the Marines recognized Sunday. Thought the D.I.'s were Jesus here. "Don't belong to a church? Well, you belong to one now. Take your pick. The Corps says you need religion."

All day to clean gear and write letters. Read the ones from home over a hundred times. All day to feel sorry for yourself. To ask what the hell am I doing here?

> *Dear Mom,*
>   *Everything is going swell. They keep us busy. . . .*

Danny and Milton Norton worked down the long row of sinks, scrubbing them clean after the morning's rush. Shannon O'Hearne leaned in the doorway warbling "Mother Machree."

"Professor," Danny said.

Although the modest man emphasized he was merely an instructor, the platoon persisted in promoting him. Norton was liked and respected. For most of them, little had been surrendered in the way of a career to join. Norton's stature as a learned man seemed to make them feel, at times, that their plight was worth while.

"Yes," he answered softly.

"I've been wondering, Milt, what made you join up?"

He smiled at his young friend. "That's a funny question, Danny. Why pick on me?"

"I know the war and all that, but what I mean is, couldn't you have gotten a commission?"

"I suppose."

"See, after all you shouldn't be going through all this. Hell, a teacher of economics—that's somebody."

"Is it? I didn't know."

"Don't give me a snow job, professor. Seriously, I feel sort of silly cleaning out sinks, next to you. Why, you know more in your little finger than those two Texans will ever know."

"You're quite wrong, Danny. I'm learning a lot from them."

"You're an idealist, Milt. I mean a real one. One of those guys who keeps it inside him and doesn't blow hot and cold."

"Ideals are one thing, Danny. If we don't get this head cleaned in an hour, that's another."

"You know . . . pass me the brush, thanks . . . for a long time I've been trying to figure it out. I guess I don't know the answer. But I'll say one thing. I'm glad I landed with you."

They stepped back from the sinks, and then put final touches on an overlooked speck or spot before they turned and faced the urinals. Danny cast a leer in the direction of O'Hearne. "We could get through a lot quicker if you turned to."

"Below my stature," Shannon answered.

Norton tugged Forrester away from any further argument. Danny calmed and returned to work.

"What about this boot camp, professor? It's over my head."

"It seems we've joined an exclusive club and we aren't going to get our membership card till we've served the initiation."

"You make it sound simple."

"Not that simple. I suppose the Marines are all they're cracked up to be. This gives us a common bond, very democratic."

"Democratic?"

"Maybe that's a bad word. What I suggest is that we're all the same here." He plunged the long-handled brush into a urinal.

"I see what you mean."

"According to the book every Marine is basically a rifleman. That is the basic difference with the other services."

"What about all this damned drill. We haven't seen a rifle yet."

"A divorce from civilian life. The first thing is to let you know that you are a part of a group and that the group moves together. Discipline, immediate reaction to command. Very good psychology."

"It might be good, but I sure wish it was over."

"Me too."

They went about their work finishing up the urinals. Then Danny arose and walked to O'Hearne and dropped the bucket and brushes at his feet. "I saved the toilets for you."

O'Hearne grinned and commenced singing.

"Who the hell you think *you* are? Come on, professor, let's shove. He's got fifteen minutes to finish up."

"Come back here, wise guy, or I'll knock the crap out of you."

"Take it easy, fellows," Norton crooned. "You know the penalty for fighting."

"Forrester, I don't like you or your crowd. Square away before I get mad."

"You don't like us because we don't kiss your ass like the rest of the boots."

"Take it easy, fellows."

"O'Hearne, you're a craphead like the rest of us. If it is going to make you happy to swing, go on and swing. At least you'll go boondocking with us if this head isn't finished."

Shannon poised and Danny walked past him to the outside. Then he turned to Norton. "I suppose you'll have to finish up, Shannon." To attack Norton would mean ostracism from the platoon. He snarled a moment then reached for a long-handled brush with the promise to settle the score later.

"Fall out!"

"Aye aye, sir."

"Gather around on the deck. The smoking lamp is lit." The squat sergeant stood in the semicircle of sweating recruits. "Today is the most important day in your lives. You people are going to draw rifles. You've got yourselves a new girl now. Forget that broad back home! This girl is the most faithful, truest woman in the world if you give her a fair shake. She won't sleep with no swab jockies the minute your back is turned. Keep her clean and she'll save your life."

They laughed politely at Beller's recitation. Smiling content, he continued. "You can take tanks, artillery, planes and any other goof ball invention and jam it. The rifle is going to win this war like it's been winning them ever since we whipped you goddamyankees at Antietam. The Marines are the best goddam riflemen in the world." Beller took off his pith helmet and wiped his forehead. "Learn to shoot straight and the Corps will pay you extra for it. But before you ever squeeze off a shot, you're going to know every part and every part of a part of the rifle. Get your buckets, change to dungarees and fall in, in three minutes."

"Sergeant Beller, sir."

"What is it, Dwyer?"

"What kind of guns are we going to get? Springfields or Garands?"

Beller's leathery face became a mass of wrinkled snarls. "Dwyer, God help you or any other craphead that calls his rifle a 'gun'!"

Danny felt a tinge of excitement as his hands reached for the weapon. He felt powerful. The guns came from cases which had held them silent between two wars. Awaiting a warrior's hand to grasp them again, as they knew it must.

He took the grease-packed weapon and bayonet and marched to an open-air cleaning stall. Instructors raced up and down issuing screw drivers, brushes, and cans of gasoline as they barked instructions on how to dismantle the piece. The entire day was spent elbow deep in gasoline, brushing cosmoline from the parts. Twenty years to get it in and one day to clean it out. So they scrubbed and scrubbed under dire threats of Beller.

"Private Forrester."

"Yes sir."

"What is the name of your piece?"

"United States Rifle, Caliber .30, model 1903."

"Jones."

"Yes sir."

"What is the serial number of your rifle?"

"1748834632 . . . sir."

"Private Chernik."

"Yes sir."

"Describe your rifle."

"It is a breech-loaded, magazine-fed, bolt-operated shoulder weapon, sir. It holds five rounds in a clip and the weight is 8.69 pounds without bayonet."

"Private Zvonski."

"Yes sir."

"What is the effective range?"

"Six hundred yards, sir."

"Private Dwyer."

"Yes sir."

"What is the muzzle velocity....?"

Danny put down his manual, sighed and crossed his fingers.

"Going to take the test, Danny?"

"Yes."

"Man, I ain't got past the butt plate yet."

"Sir, Private Forrester requests permission to speak with the drill instructor."

"At ease. What is it?"

"Sir, I'd like to take the test for nomenclature of the rifle."

"Go ahead."

He held up his rifle, drew a breath and began pointing out the parts. "Butt plate, butt plate screw, stock, oil and thong well . . ." Methodically he worked up to the barrel, calling out a hundred parts, then came to attention.

"Is that all?"

"Yes sir."

"You forgot the lower band spring, Forrester."

Danny's face reddened. "Get some canvas, tie the rifle to your leg and sleep with it tonight."

"Yes, sir."

The platoon started from scratch once more to learn the manual of arms. The positions were pounded in with the same mercilessness of the other lessons.

Every day after morning chow now, there was exercise with the rifle, by the numbers. From extended order they lunged in unison to Whitlock's count.

"Side lunge . . . left side first . . . one two, three four . . . up and out by the numbers . . . up and on shoulders by the numbers. . . ."

They exercised till they felt their arms would fall off, till numbness set in. A minute's rest and through the exercises once again, until they staggered from formation. Then once more.

One day Dwyer dropped his rifle. In the middle of the parade ground he knelt, bowed and kissed the weapon for three hours, declaring, "I love my rifle . . . I love my rifle."

"Up and on shoulders" from the exercises was a standard punishment. When one roamed the Recruit Depot, he was sure to see at least a dozen boots standing before their D.I.s shoving the rifle up in the air and to the back of their necks. Until they swooned from exhaustion, but fought to keep from dropping it—the cardinal sin.

Platoon punishment. Standing at attention, arms extended forward. Palms down and rifles on fingertips. They stood till every muscle danced and trembled, red-faced and sweating, praying some other man might drop his rifle first.

Mr. Dickey the principal of Forest Park High, walked to the rostrum of the flower-decked stage. Behind him were the black capped and gowned boys and the white capped and gowned girls of the graduation class. Before him sat the sniffling mothers and the straight-necked fathers of the seniors. He took the pince-nez from his nose and held them dramatically as he spoke slowly into the microphone beside the long table filled with rolled diplomas.

He babbled seriously of the task that lay before them, then turned to the empty chair on the stage. "He could not wait. We all knew him, we all loved him. Student, athlete, credit to his school. Would Mr. Henry Forrester please step forward and receive the diploma for his son Danny?"

Henry took a deep breath. Kathy squeezed his hand for courage and as he stepped into the aisle the orchestra struck up the Marine's Hymn to the rising applause of the audience and students. Martha dabbed her eyes.

Mr. Dickey grasped Henry Forrester's hand. "We are proud sir, proud. Our hearts . . . our deepest thoughts of Godspeed go out to him tonight, wherever he may be."

"Your eyes are like . . . hey, professor. How do you spell limpid?"

"l-i-m-p-i-d."

"Limpid pools, whatever that means. She'll like it, anyhow."

"Not very original."

"That's all right, she isn't very bright."

Danny eased the bolt back into his rifle and muttered, "I'll never get all the cosmoline out of this piece."

"Christ, I thought I'd go in my skivvies during inspection. Old Bellers steps up to me and I see the stuff oozing through the butt plate swivel. I think it's the first time he ever missed."

"Say, did you hear about the kid in One Sixty One, slugged the D.I."

"Bull crap."

"Honest."

"For why?"

"He didn't take a shower—so they gave him one. Used a bucket of sand and a scrub brush. He was a bloody mess when they got through with him. Anyhow, he took a punch at the D.I."

"Yeah, where is he now?"

"In the brig."

"Hey, professor, what did you think of them reading off that prisoner on the parade ground?"

"Kind of gives you the creeps, the way they do it. March ten thousand guys out and walk him up to a platform with his head shaved. Thirty days bread and water for stealing a couple skivvy shirts."

"Almost like a lynching."

"Tradition," Norton mused, thinking of the gruesome ceremony.

"Just don't get caught, Dwyer."

A booming voice sounded from O'Hearne's tent.

> *"Put on your old red bustle,*
> *Get your tail out and hustle,*
> *For tomorrow the room rent is due,*
> *Lay it down in the clover,*
> *Let the boys look it over,*
> *If you can't get five, take two."*

"Nice kid, that O'Hearne."

"I want to be around the day we quit here. He swears he's going to kick the hell out of Beller and Whitlock."

"Say, where is L.Q."

"With Ski, doing their wash over."

"Zounds," popped Dwyer, "I think I can do a Queen Anne salute."

"For Christ sake, don't we get enough drill without you practicing with that goddam rifle in here."

"We looked pretty sharp today on the monkey march and wind marches. One Forty Four hasn't even learned the marching manual yet."

"Lend me some linseed oil for my stock."

"I wonder if there's a lineup for the iron?"

"Yeah, three deep."

"How about that, even old L.Q. got the monkey march."

"We're sure getting fancy—fo' goddamyankees, that is."

Danny worked the bolt several times and looked his rifle over from butt to muzzle and placed it on the canvas straps under his cot. Dwyer went "Bang, bang, you're dead," and slipped the bolt on his.

"Christ, clothing inspection again tomorrow."

L.Q. and Ski entered with their buckets. "Hey, fat boy. You're going to ruin them clothes, scrubbing them so much."

"Jones put a whole bottle of bleach in them today to make sure he got them white."

"Oh no."

L.Q. shoved his way to his cot, edged Chernik and flopped down. He was pale.

"Hey lard, you sick?"

"I got woes, I got woes," the stout one lamented.

"What's the matter, blubber butt?"

"I'm a craphead from One Forty Three. Woe is me, Woe is me."

"I saw Beller talking to you after drill. What happened?"

"I . . . I . . . called my rifle a gun today."

The tent became deathly silent. Murder or rape, yes. But your rifle a gun—good Lord have mercy. Sympathetic eyes focused on him. He was on the brink of tears.

"I gotta report to Beller after the wash."

"Don't worry, L.Q. He'll probably just march you with a bucket on your head."

"Or a hundred 'up and on shoulders.'"

"Or send you to the bay."

"Or make you sleep with it."

"Or make you scrub the catwalk with a toothbrush."

"Or make you stand at attention in front of the water fountain for a couple hours in midday sun."

"Or make you balance it on your fingertips."

The consoling of his friends had little effect. He trudged out. They slapped his back and sighed as he headed for Beller's quarters.

"Sir, Private Jones reporting."

The barrel-chested sergeant looked up from a letter he was reading. "Just stand there." He finished it with a fiendish slowness and replaced it in its envelope. "I believe you called your rifle a gun today, at inspection."

"Yes sir."

"But it isn't a gun, is it, Jones?"

"No sir, it's a United States Rifle, M-1903, thirty caliber, breach-loading, bolt-operated shoulder weapon, sir."

"Then why did you call it a gun?"

"I forgot, sir."

"Do you think you can remember?"

"Oh yes sir, infinitely and eternally."

"I believe we can help you remember it."

"I'm sure you can, sir."

Beller arose and put on his duty NCO belt and led Jones

from the tent. Heads peered out down the row.

"Private Jones, unbutton your fly."

"Yes sir."

"That's your gun."

"Yes sir."

He led Jones through the entire tent area. At each street he blew his whistle and a platoon of boots came flying from their tents. Jones then stood there, holding his "gun" in his right hand and his rifle in his left and recited:

> *"This is my rifle,*
> *This is my gun,*
> *This is for fighting,*
> *This is for fun."*

Days slugged by. One Forty Three moved to a prefabricated barrack in a new area to make way for the increasing flow of recruits. With each day Whitlock and Beller were able to discover less dirt and fewer errors. They marched smartly and did their other work well. With the lessening of errors, the slack in wrath was taken up by pouring on more and more drill.

"Hit those pieces when you change shoulders. If you break them we'll buy you new ones." And hands, at first tender, grew leathery and calloused.

The punishments of the early days decreased. Only O'Hearne, who was late for rollcall one day, received an especially stiff one. He was discovered in the head, shaving in leisurely fashion and singing "When Irish Eyes Are Smiling." For this crime, O'Hearne stood at attention one entire night in front of the D.I.s' barracks serenading them with Irish ballads. Each time he weakened, a bucket of water and the one-word command "Sing!" greeted him. The loss of his voice was generally welcomed by the rest of the outfit.

There were many aggravating, to say the least, tricks that Whitlock constantly pulled from his grab-bag. A favorite was to march the platoon back and forth before a water fountain at Port Arms. As the sun blistered down, he would take a sip of the cool stuff and march them in rear marches until they were dizzy, their tongues hanging out, and their arms falling off from the weight of their rifles.

When they were at the point of collapse he would give them three minutes rest, then double time them through the ankle deep sand of the boondocks. Then, carrying their pieces at an arm-breaking Trail Arms he would run them clear back to the barracks.

It was about this time that they began to get a little proud of themselves. They firmly believed they could outdrill any other outfit in the Depot. Whitlock arranged to have their ego deflated.

It came the day they went to the edge of the Depot to receive booster shots. They "stacked arms," received the shots and fell in for the exercise they knew was coming, to work out the stiffness. As they prepared to depart, a platoon of Sea School Marines doing close order drill on the Base grounds marched by.

"At ease, I want you guys to watch this."

The Sea School Marines were a sight to make any boot cringe. Six feet tall, husky and tanned, they were the men who manned the guard of battleships and cruisers of the fleet. The air was alive with the color of their dress blues. Their sergeant rippled cadence from his tongue and in his hand he swung a beautiful golden saber. The polish of their golden buttons and buckles, the mirror of their shoes and cap brims, the white of their belts and gloves and the magnificent unison of movement was a sight to behold.

"Tenshun," Whitlock barked. "Right shoulder arms! For'd harch! Lep . . . two three po . . . pick up the step Forrester, straighten out that piece Norton . . . you ain't carrying a broom. Ain't you people *ever* gonna learn?"

"When you run the bayonet course, I want to hear some rebel yells. Scream! If you can't whip them, scare them to death. Use that rifle butt . . . knock his goddam head off . . . twist when you lunge. If it sticks in his guts, blow off a shot and knock it loose."

Danny didn't like the looks of a bayonet. He let out a blood-curdling yell as he raced into the straw dummies. . . . "Crouch, Forrester, get him in the neck, rip his jugular vein out. . . ." His stomach turned over. He thought he would vomit. "Get mad at him . . . yell, Forrester, yell!"

Then there was the obstacle course. It was a quagmire of pit-falls. Underground tunnels with dead ends, barbed wire, scaling walls, ditches, hurdles, rope ladders, tires to dive through, and a huge well. The latter was twenty feet in diameter and ten feet deep. Over dead center hung a slippery rope which led to the slimy well bottom.

To get over this obstacle the boot had to be running full force and leap ten feet with rifle and pack and hit the rope perfectly to swing over to the opposite side. The ones who had successfully completed the last obstacle gathered around the well for a little sport.

They laughed uproariously as some missed the rope and tumbled into the quagmire or grabbed the rope and slid down. The funniest ones were the danglers. Barely missing the safe side, then swinging back to the middle, they squirmed, wiggled, and struggled. Then inched into the miserable muck and succumbed to the mud bath. Their reward was to keep attempting it till they made it.

It was not the damage to themselves they minded—it was hell on rifles.

One day, five weeks after boot camp started, Danny Forrester had a strange sensation. He looked at L.Q., and Jones resembled someone he had met on a train. He took his mirror from his seabag and studied himself. There was a quarter of an inch of hair on his head. He rubbed it over and over again. And the feathermerchant, Ski, was looking filled out and hard. Not half so puny. "By God," he whispered, "we're becoming Marines."

That afternoon at drill he had the same sensation. As Beller chanted cadence, the rifle felt like a toothpick in his hands. In the quiet of the remote corner of the grounds he could hear the unison of hands smacking their rifles as they changed shoulder positions. Then Beller's monotone cadence began to resemble music. There was melody here. . . . "Lep two three po . . . to your reah po . . . reah po."

During a break he stared at his hands. They were like leather. The cramps and blisters that harassed him a month ago were gone. *Funny, I ironed my shirt perfect last night and made up for inspection in ten minutes today—and Whitlock hasn't said "I'll be a sad bastard" for almost a week.*

5.

SIX WEEKS were gone and the recruit battalion prepared for the final step in basic training. They moved to the rifle range at Camp Matthews, several hours from San Diego, for a three-week small arms course under great and near great marksmen.

Friction within the platoon, centered around Danny and O'Hearne, increased. Shannon's heft and bluster gave him forceful leadership of most of the men. In the closeness of the barracks he kept up a constant harping on his lurid sex and fighting and drinking feats. Most everyone smiled respectfully —except Danny and his group of friends. This made O'Hearne boil. He could not bear being ignored.

O'Hearne plotted his course carefully. To fight Norton or Ski would add little luster to his reputation. Chernik he didn't care to tangle with. L.Q. would not fight, would merely say something funny; and Dwyer had been transferred to the Base Hospital with an extreme case of cat fever. This left Danny to hold the fort. Danny, long resigned to the fact that he would get slugged eventually by O'Hearne, merely shrugged and decided to do the best he could.

It finally blew up on a rainy afternoon. Although Beller and Whitlock would have taken pleasure in marching them in mud, there were powers even more almighty than the almighty D.I.s who banned drilling in the rain. Instead, they ran the platoon through six harrowing hours of inspections and recitations from the blue book. Finding nothing left to inspect, they let the men alone after noon chow.

Everyone was nervous from the rain, the closeness and the morning workout. O'Hearne's boisterousness lent no comfort. He slipped into the sack next to Danny, who was writing a letter.

"Did I ever tell you about the time I was in bed with three broads?"

"The last time I heard it, it was six."

The big Irishman smiled and slapped Danny across the back, overly hard. "Hear you used to play football."

"Some."

"Me too. Bartram High and semi-pro. Played tackle and fullback, just like Nagurski. Let me tell you about the game I played against . . . what the hell was the name of that team . . . doesn't matter. Anyhow, I remember the score." He then launched into a modest volume on how he crossed up the opponent's offense and smashed its defense. Ski, in the upper bunk, was content reading over several old letters until O'Hearne's booming voice overrode his train of thought.

"Hey," he yelled down, "seems to me they had a dumb quarterback on the other team. I would have run a tackle trap right over you, the way you said you was rushing that passer."

Shannon winked and nudged Danny in the ribs, then held his nose.

"I played ball," Ski said swinging to a sitting position.

"Get this, men—he played ball. What grammar school?"

Ski bounced down. Everyone edged in, sensing a fight.

"I played for Central."

"What, in your dreams, feathermerchant?"

"Guard."

"Oh, spare me."

"Bet?"

"You say you played guard?"

"You can hear."

"O.K., sonny. Just for kicks, I want you to block me out of a play." Ski looked to Danny, and Danny nodded and smiled.

O'Hearne assumed the position of a charging lineman. The feathermerchant immediately saw the product of poor coaching—if O'Hearne ever did play. His angle was too high and he was off balance. The little lad crouched. "Hike," sneered O'Hearne as he raised his arm to slap the feathermerchant down. Shannon didn't have a chance. Ski's uncoiled body drove upwards, his shoulder sinking into the big man's stomach a full six inches. O'Hearne thudded against the bulkhead and sank to his backside. He heard a roar of laughter.

His face turned crimson. He sprang to his feet and hit Ski in the mouth. Danny was up and dived and both went careening into a doubledeck bunk which toppled under the impact. He wrestled Danny's grip free, just in time to catch a punch on the jaw from Chernik, then something dropped on him. It was L.Q. Jones. Ski bounced back into the melee and the four of them pinned down O'Hearne quickly. It was gentle Milton Norton who spoke.

"Shannon O'Hearne, you've been asking for this. Let this be a lesson to you. Any more hooliganism on your part and we won't let you off this easily—is that clear?"

"Clear?" Chernik repeated, grabbing O'Hearne by the short hair and batting his head on the deck.

"Clear," he croaked. He wobbled to his feet, red and shaking. For an instant he tensed for a second try, then sagged and shoved his way toward his bunk.

"Tenshun!"

"Well, well," Whitlock hissed, "what have we here, a little grabass?" He spotted the offenders. "O'Hearne, Feathermerchant, Chernik, Forrester, Norton, Jones . . . come to my quarters."

They went.

"All right, stand at ease. You first, Ski."

"We was practicing some football plays, sir."

"Forrester?"

"That's right, sir."

"Norton?"

"Yes sir?"

"Don't tell me you played football, Norton?"

"No sir, but at Penn, sir, University of Pennsylvania, I used to watch practice all the time. Er, Coach Munger is a personal friend, sir—I was naturally interested."

"I think you're all lying, Jones! I know—I know, you were practicing football." The freckled corporal turned to O'Hearne. Shannon had them cold turkey . . . brig for the whole bunch. Now was his chance. Six to one.

"That's right, sir, football. I guess we got too enthusiastic, sir."

A sigh of relief went up. The corporal snarled and dismissed them. Sergeant Beller turned to Whitlock after they left.

"You ain't buying that story, Tex, are you?"

Whitlock smiled. "Looks like they worked him over. He had it coming."

"Should we haul them all in?"

"What for, acting like Marines? Maybe we made us another good gyrene today. We could use us some good fighting Irishmen like O'Hearne. You know something, that's one hell of a platoon, best we've ever trained. I bet they can outdrill any bunch of crapheads in the Depot."

"Dammit, Whitlock, better survey you to the FMF, you're getting plumb sentimental."

"I'll drill their goddamyankee asses off, soon as this rain stops," Whitlock answered.

They walked to Shannon O'Hearne's bunk. He had been sitting silently for an hour.

"O'Hearne."

"That was a noble gesture," Norton said.

Danny extended his hand. Shannon looked up slowly, then arose. He lowered his head and thrust his hand forward into Danny's. Then they all began laughing.

"Say, did I ever tell you about the time I was walking down Market Street and this here broad comes up to me . . ."

At Camp Matthews, the rifle range, like the Depot, was overcrowded by the sudden shift from peace to war. Barracks were being constructed at breakneck speed and new platoons were placed wherever space could be found. Right off the highway were the main buildings. Their aging paint seemed to blend with the rustic setting of tall pines and hills and gulleys of the camp.

The five main ranges worked away from the highway. The ranges were cut into the ravines to give the minimum of wind disturbance. Firing lines were placed two hundred, three hundred, five hundred, and six hundred yards from the targets. Targets were run up on pulleys from pits made of concrete. Behind the targets was a hill to stop the slugs.

Targets were manned by recruits, with more permanent personnel to oversee and co-ordinate the firing. At either end of the targets small flags were flown to indicate wind strength and direction.

The firing lines had numbered posts corresponding with each target. Behind the firing line were smudgepots to blacken gunsights and cut the sun glare, and large buckets to hold expended shells.

Megaphone-bearing NCOs ran up and down the line relaying messages telephoned from the pits. In the pits the target workers worked in two-man teams, using paste buckets and patches to cover target holes. Long poles with signal markers were raised over the pits to give the scoring to the men firing from the lines. In the pits there was also a red flag, the nemesis of a rifleman. "Maggie's Drawers," it was called— the signal for a complete miss.

Every target on every range was tutored by a Marine who had shot *expert*. They wore shooting jackets and old Marine campaign hats. Although these hats were long out of issue they were badges of honor, and the expert marksmen of the range were permitted to wear them at cocksure and jaunty angles.

The various ranges held targets in numbers varying from twenty to E Range's enormous breadth of a hundred.

There were other ranges at Matthews, twenty-two caliber, forty-five pistol, BAR, and machine gun ranges. Every man who entered the Corps went to boot camp and every boot went to the rifle range. Every man had to have intimate knowledge of how to fire and strip each basic infantry weapon.

Before a recruit was allowed to fire a shot, he lay at a dummy range for over a week, snapping in. Here was the monotony of learning to drill, all over. The lessons pounded in, till you knew them in your sleep. By the time the boot fired a round, he knew what he was doing. His position was as perfect as the haranguing instructors could make it.

"The Corps pays extra for its marksmen. Qualify as a Sharpshooter, three bucks a month; qualify as Expert, five bucks." In the days of twenty-one dollars a month, this was a small fortune.

Platoon One Forty Three drew quarters past E Range, the furthermost point of Camp Matthews—a knoll overlooking the firing range, some two miles from the main buildings. No electricity, running water, head, or toilets. Taps was automatic at darkness on the cold, windswept hill.

Working conditions were far better than at the Base. In sharp contrast to the cursing, the punishments, the drill, and the misery of boot camp. Although the rifle instructors were no less exacting, their tactics were different. The lessons were personalized and given with firm but kindly words. They were the most important weeks in the life of a Marine, his rifle training.

"Squeeze the trigger, don't jerk it," a thousand times over.

"All right you people, gather around. All right, you are out of boot camp. You go to Dago on liberty and this here luscious blonde picks you up. You go to her apartment and she fills you with liquor. Next thing you know, you are in bed with her. You get ahold of her tit. Would you jerk it or would you squeeze it?"

"Squeeze it!"

"Remember that. Equal pressure throughout the right hand, squeeze like a lemon."

From sunup to sundown they lay on the dummy range, snapping in.

"Line up your sights at six o'clock. Your sling is wrong . . . don't hold your thumb up . . . it will push right back in your eye."

Prone, kneeling, sitting and offhand. Who concocted the positions? They must be crazy. No one can shoot with their body twisted up like a pretzel. *The Marine Corps says you can, son.*

"Lay those ankles flat, spread your legs, assume a forty-five degree angle to the target, spine straight, move that elbow in closer, thumb down, cheek against the stock."

Hours of instruction and muscles stretched into the contortionist's nightmare of positions. It ain't human.

Sitting position, worst of all.

"I can't move forward," L.Q. cried, "my stomach is in the way."

The instructor sat on L.Q.'s neck and jammed his body down. "Like that—I'll sit here and you snap in."

"I'm dying—I'm dying."

Live ammunition! Twenty-two caliber, forty-five automatics, BARs, machine guns. Not long now till you get to the big range with your rifle, Marine.

"Next relay to the firing line." Danny Forrester buttoned his shooting jacket and placed the cotton plugs in his ears. He walked to the smudgepot, blackened the sights of his piece and lay down beside the sergeant on the firing line.

He tipped his campaign hat back, "My name is Sergeant Piper, son. Adjust your sights for three hundred yards. Put two points left windage and we'll get your rifle zeroed in."

The fire master at a midway point along the alley of a hundred shooters held the field phone to his ear. He picked up a huge megaphone. "All ready on the right! All ready on the left! All ready on the firing line! Load and lock! Shoot at will, ten rounds slow fire, prone position!"

"Go on, son, let's see if you remember your snapping in lessons." Danny gritted his teeth. "Relax, boy—calm down," the mentor soothed.

He forgot everything.

Rigid, he jerked the trigger with his right thumb up. The rifle recoiled meanly and smashed into his stiffened shoulder, his thumb jammed his eye. He was shaken. The target setters in the pits looked for a puff of dust from the hill behind them to indicate a round had been fired; instead they were greeted with a shower of dirt from the pilings up front. They happily waved a Maggie's Drawers in retaliation for the bath. Target missed.

Danny lay there crimson faced and trembling.

"Ever fire a rifle before, son?"

"No sir, just the stuff out here."

"Forget everything?"

"Kind of looks like it, sir."

"Let's try another round. Real easy . . . that's right . . . got it lined up at six o'clock . . . get that thumb down . . . take a breath and hold it . . . squeeze her off easy like."

BLAM! "A four at nine o'clock, that's better, take another shot, lad. Another four at nine . . . now you're shooting . . . take two more." The target was lowered and raised after each round, the last two shots going into the same group.

Piper took the rifle from his student and Danny studied, in awe, the flawless position of the master. The sergeant laid five shots in quick succession. All fell into a neat little group . . . four at nine o'clock. "Nine shots laying in the same place, know what that means, lad?"

"I think we need just a shade of right windage for zero, sir."

"That's right, half a point, maybe lower your elevation ten yards and I think we have it."

He adjusted his sights and fired more rounds. The initial fear gone . . . and he saw the thrill of a cartwheel, a bullseye, flash over his target. He looked at his rifle, patted it and grinned from ear to ear.

"Feels good, doesn't it, lad?"

"It sure does."

"About a week and you'll be doing it in your sleep. All right, pick your brass up and stand by. Next relay to the firing line."

They pumped lead from dawn to dusk. Under Piper and a hundred others like him, the recruits soon turned the firing line into a deadeye duck shoot. More cartwheels, more happy grins. The last phase. Clean it, march with it, kiss it, sleep with it, exercise with it, bayonet with—and now, shoot it.

Each day they ran the course:

Five Hundred Yards:	Ten rounds slow fire, prone.
Three Hundred Yards:	Ten rounds rapid fire, prone.
	Five rounds slow fire, kneeling.
	Five rounds slow fire, sitting.
Two Hundred Yards:	Ten rounds rapid fire, sitting.
	Ten rounds slow fire, offhand.

Possible score of five points on each round. Two hundred and fifty points for the "perfect possible." It had never been done.

To qualify for the Marksman's Badge: a hundred and ninety points. Sharpshooter's Cross: two hundred and fifteen points. Expert: two hundred and twenty-five points.

The rivalry was on as thousands of rounds poured down the gulley. Evenings they practiced positions until darkness fell, in the tents.

The cleaning chore after firing. Hot soapy water . . . steel brush . . . dry . . . lighter bore brush . . . oil . . . linseed the stock . . . Lay her under the bunk with loving hands.

A rain halted firing one day. By evening, after late chow, it had gone. L.Q. Jones approached Corporal Whitlock's tent, stepped in, and snapped to attention.

"Sir, Private Jones requests permission to speak with the drill instructor."

"At ease, what is it?"

"Sir, it is too late for firing and still light. We've all cleaned our rifles . . . er . . . er . . . several fellows suggested I speak to you because they feel I'm the only one crazy enough to bring you such a strange request."

"For Chrisake, Jones, get off the pot. What is it?"

"We'd like some close order drill, sir."

"You'd WHAT!"

"Well sir. We've been here over two weeks and we haven't drilled. With graduation coming up we feel as though we have a good chance of being the honor platoon and we'd like to brush up. Maybe some fancy stuff . . . we aren't too good on rear marches from left and right obliques."

"I'll be a sad bastard—all right. Tell them to fall out."

"Thank you, sir."

The tent area was pitched in darkness. Danny, Ski, and L.Q. lay under the deluge of cover, enjoying a late cigarette.

"It won't be long now. One more week of boot camp."

"Yeah, one happy Polack is going to kiss this goddam place good-by."

"How did the practice round go?"

"I shot one ninety. Jesus, I got to qualify, Danny. Three extra bucks a month is going to help a lot."

"How did you go, L. Q.?"

"My stomach still gets in the way on sitting position."

"I got to make at least Sharpshooter," Ski repeated.

"Try and relax more," Danny said. "You can't shoot when all you're thinking about is getting her out here. It makes you too nervous."

"I got to get her out here, Danny. It's going rough back there. She ain't saying much, but I can tell."

"You can't help her much by shooting Maggie's Drawers."

"Yeah, you're right. I got to relax. Trouble is, Danny, every damned thing I do is hard for me. I just can't pick up stuff like some guys. When I was playing football it was the same. The same in everything I do. I got to practice like hell."

"Anyway," Danny said, "we were sure lucky to get Piper for an instructor. He's one of the best in the Corps. Even got his picture in the blue book." He reached to the deck and snuffed out his cigarette and pulled his arm back under cover quickly. "Colder than a well digger's butt out here."

"Yeah," L.Q. moaned. "I've had to take a piss for an hour, but I'll be damned if I can get up enough guts to get out of the sack."

"Will you shut your mouth? You'll have me thinking about it now."

"How do you like that Whitlock? He gave me the detail again; emptying piss buckets. Third time." Jones scratched. "I think they got all the crabs, but one. The bastard is driving me crazy."

Silence.

"Danny," Ski said.

"Yeah."

"Know something?"

"What?"

"I'm sure lucky I got lashed up with you and L.Q."

"Go to sleep."

"No, I mean it. If you hadn't been helping me out I'd be a screwed goose. They'd probably made me start all over. I just don't catch on fast."

L.Q. threw off his blankets and dashed for the tent flap. "I can't hold it, my back teeth are floating!" He returned and flung himself into his sack and buried himself, shivering.

Several moments passed.

"Danny," Ski said.

"Aren't you asleep yet?"

"What do you figure after boot camp?"

"I don't know. Scuttlebutt has us going from Truk to Tokyo."

"Yeah, got to take scuttlebutt lightly. But I did hear on good authority it might be Wake Island."

"Could be."

"What are you going out for when we get back to Dago?"

"Not much choice in the Corps. We'll all wind up packing a rifle in the FMF sooner or later."

"Yeah, ain't a hell of a lot to choose from."

"Maybe I'll take a crack at the test for radio school."

"Radio, why?"

"Oh, I don't know. Just something a little different. Not that I mind packing a rifle. Just something a little special."

"I'd like to get into aviation. Fifty per cent more pay. I could get her out here faster."

"Sure rough to try saving on twenty-one dollars a month, Ski."

"Yeah, but it will be twenty-eight soon. Jesus, I'd never make aviation."

"Why don't you quit pushing so hard, Ski?"

"Can't help it, Danny. I just can't rest with her in that lousy town. It eats me all the time. Her there with that bastard old man of hers."

"I know."

"Danny."

"Yeah?"

"Do you think I can get into radio? I'd sure like to stick with you."

"Why not take a crack at it?"

"Radio guys wear them lightning flashes on their sleeves, huh?"

"They call them 'sparks.' "

"Yeah, I'd like that. But Christ, I'd never pass the test."

"Rub your nuts for luck."

A voice boomed from the next tent.

"Hey, you guys, knock off the crap! Let's get some fart sack drill."

"Yeah," another added. "Ain't you crapheads heard we're shooting for record tomorrow?"

"I guess they mean us," Danny said.

"Blow it," Ski called back as he crawled deeper into his sack and drew the blankets over his ears.

Then there was quiet.

"Jesus H. Christ," L.Q. cried.

"What's the matter now?"

"I got to piss again."

It came to pass that the platoon belied Beller's prediction that none of them would ever learn to shoot straight. On record day, the goddamyankees qualified with an astounding total of eighty-six per cent. Of these, six entered the golden circle of Experts; O'Hearne and Forrester were among them. Even L.Q. managed to get his stomach low enough to fire a Marksman and receive a badge on his basic medal.

The basic medal worn by Marines told the deadly qualifications of each man: BAR, pistol, bayonet, chemical warfare, and the almighty rifle.

Firing on the last relay, the whole platoon gathered around

to support the professor. Ideals and all, Norton saw not much more than Maggie's Drawers. Several of his shots went into the target next to his.

Happy and reeking with the cockiness of a platoon in its last week, they left Matthews for the Marine Corps Base sporting an inch or more of hair.

Exams filled the final week. Openings for the few specialists schools. Some ventured to take the tests; others merely waited for the axe of fate to fall. Yet others, like Milton Norton, volunteered into the newly forming Pioneer Battalion.

Nervous, bursting with excitement, the sharply pressed and shined men scampered about putting on the final touches for the graduation.

"Christ, wonder where I'm going from here?"

"You'll find out soon."

"Come on, fellows, no pooping on the poop deck. We got to fall out in a couple of minutes."

"Just think, tomorrow I wake up, the sun is shining. I look at myself and say . . . hey Jones, what are you? And I answer, why pardner, I'm a yonited states gyrene. This ole fat boy ain't no craphead."

"Sure will be sorry to leave all this."

"You can say that again."

"Danny," Norton asked quietly, "will you square away my field scarf? Never could get these knots right."

"Sure, professor." Danny worked with the earnestness of a French hairdresser, until he was satisfied the knot was perfect. They sat on the edge of his bunk and lit up, nervously. "Sure feel shaky, professor. Gosh, I never thought this day was coming. Suppose we've changed any?"

"An understatement, Danny." He smiled.

"Wonder where we're going?"

"Oh, I wouldn't worry. I think you passed your radio test."

"Not so much me. I'd like to see Ski and L.Q. make it. At least I hope we all flunk out together."

"Why?"

"I don't know really. Just that you make a buddy—and, well, I think it's more important we stick together than we make it alone."

Norton thought carefully. "Funny, Danny, how people from different worlds, different lives, people who wouldn't much bother to talk to each other before the war, are drawn together in such fine friendships in such a short time."

"Yeah. I think that myself sometimes, how you get attached to a guy."

"I suppose the word 'buddy' is something far removed from

anything we ever knew before. Say, I'm off on a tangent."

"I wish you were going with us, professor."

"I sort of hate leaving the gang, myself."

"Why did you volunteer into the Pioneers? It's a rough outfit."

"I want to go home, Danny. I want to be where I can do the most to get me home the quickest."

"I understand, professor."

Whitlock's whistle blew them to assembly for the last unlamented time. As they had done a thousand times before, they poured through the door, almost taking the sash with them. They fell in. The D.I.s looked sharp as tin soldiers. From Beller's glistening fair leather belt hung a silver saber. He and Whitlock paced the ranks nervously, adjusting a field scarf here, a shoelace there, a cap at the correct angle, an ornament that had slipped. They scanned their charges from stem to stern and back to stem again.

"At ease. You goddamyankees have been chosen as the honor platoon. Gawd alone knows why. After the colonel's inspection, we fall in behind the color guard and band to pass in review. For Chrisake don't march like a bunch of dogfaces. O'Hearne, Chernik, you know how to bear your standards and salute?"

"Yes sir."

"Yes sir."

"Now don't forget, when I give Eyes Right I want to hear them eyeballs click."

Down the huge parade ground they marched, erect as one man. For the first time, they felt the full thrill of the title they would carry for the rest of their lives. Past the reviewing stand Beller barked "Eyes Right!" and he flashed his silver saber to a salute. The band struck up the Marine's Hymn. The standards of the battalion and platoon dipped and the colonel returned the salute. To a man their hearts thumped, bursting with pride beneath the neat green uniforms. They had paid with sweat, with humiliation, and a few tears for the name they had. They were Marines now . . . and would be to the day they died.

6.

BACK AT the barracks the pent-up joy broke loose after the final piece of gear was stowed and they were ready to leave the cursed grounds of the Recruit Depot. Happy hugs and back slaps—then terrible anxiety as Beller and Whitlock entered with disposition lists.

"Tenshun!"

"At ease, fellows. All right, gather around," the squat sergeant said. "I know you boys want to get the hell out of here just as fast as you can. But I want to say just a couple of words, and goddamit, I mean it from the heart. You guys are the best bunch of boots I've ever had. It was all in a day's work for me . . . maybe sometimes, not such a happy day's work. We all do what the Corps tells us but I hope what you guys learned here will help you out later some day. I reckon that's about all the thanks me and Whitlock got coming. Best of luck to all of you . . . if any of you guys are still on the Base tonight, come over to the slop shute and have a beer on me."

They cheered.

"Anything you want to add, Whitlock?"

"Fellows, just call me Tex."

For an instant all eyes turned to Shannon O'Hearne, the vengeance-sworn hellion. He stepped forward and extended his hand. "Put her there, Tex."

Beller relieved their anxiety. The majority of the platoon was assigned to a guard company. Norton to Pioneers. O'Hearne to Matthews as a rifle instructor, Chernik to North Island, aviation. A few got mess duty for a month.

"All right, you three—stop pissing in your pants. Forrester, Jones, and Ski—radio school!"

A last round of backslaps, handshakes and farewells; they lifted their seabags and walked from the barracks into a new day.

"You'll be on the Base for a while, professor. I'll look you up as soon as we get squared away."

"Take her easy, Danny."

"All right, you three fellows from this platoon for radio school. Fall in over there," a corporal admonished.

Danny, Ski, and L.Q. wended with their load, rifle and seabag, to the waiting group. Danny laid his seabag down and walked over to a husky lad wearing glasses.

"Hi," the fellow said in a friendly manner.

"My name's Forrester. This is my buddy Zvonski. him Ski. Old blubber butt there is L. Q. Jones."

"Glad to meet you. My name is Marion Hodgkiss a Andy Hookans. We're out of platoon One Thirty F

They all shook hands.

The corporal with the roster called roll and t' load to their shoulders and trudged over the ground of tents, past the administration buildings to t' cruit Depot. Before them lay the sprawli the Base. Running along its edge were long arched yellow buildings.

"Where is the school?"

"At the other end of the parade ground."

"It would be."

A new boot with slick-shaved dome passed between them. In his hand he held a bucket as he searched vainly for cigarette butts. He bumped into L.Q. Jones.

"Hey, you craphead," L.Q. barked.

The boot snapped to attention.

"What's the matter with you, can't you look where you're going?"

"I'm sorry, sir."

"You ain't ever sorry for nothing you do in the Marine Corps."

"Yes sir."

L.Q. slammed the pith helmet over the boot's ears. "Carry on."

"Yes sir."

They moved down the endless grounds shifting their seabags from one shoulder to the other.

"What did you do that for?" Danny finally asked.

"Do what?"

"Chew out that boot."

"Just wanted to see how it felt. Felt fine—and from the looks of him I'd say he'll never learn—no sir, that boot will never learn."

After several moments they reached the far end of the grounds, dropped their loads and awaited the stragglers. The last of the long row of buildings bore the sign: SIGNAL SCHOOL. Over the width of the parade ground was a temporary set of eight-man tents facing an isolated building marked FIELD MUSIC SCHOOL.

"All right, fellows, my name is Corporal Farinsky. You people will stay in these tents until a new class is formed in about a week. Find an empty spot and grab it. When you dump your gear, fall in for a pay call and draw cots and pads. Uniform of day is dungarees. For Base liberty you wear greens, field scarfs and you must be covered at all times away from the school area. You have liberty every other night and every other squad. On duty nights you may have Base liberty. Any questions?"

"Sir. What do we do until a class is formed?"

"First of all, Marine, don't call me sir. You're out of boot camp. Mostly you'll have a few hours a day on work parties and working details. If you behave, you'll have plenty of time to burn to when there's work and we'll get along.

Find an empty spot, drop your gear and fall out in ten minutes."

"How about seeing if we can get together," Marion suggested to Danny.

"Swell."

The five entered a tent midway along the row. There were just three men there, all lying prone on their cots. One arose.

"Ah," he said, "enter our humble domicile. Up, you crumbs, we got visitors."

"Hi," Danny retorted, "got room for five small ones?"

"Why sure. My name is Brown, they call me Seabags. You'll love it here, love it. Just wait till you hear the sound of fifty bugles blowing reveille outside the tent from that field music school. Do nothing but crap out all day."

"My name's Forrester. This here is Ski, L.Q. Jones, Marion Hodgkiss and Andy Hookans. Just left that wonderful place at the other end of the grounds."

"Charmed. That thing there trying to crawl to his feet is Speedy Gray. You'll have to forgive him, he's a Texan. That . . . is Shining Lighttower, pride of the all-Navajo platoon. He's an Injun."

"How, white man."

"He's a card," Brown explained.

"Ugh."

As promised, the wait till the new class was one of easy duty. For a few hours in the morning they performed menial tasks in the nearby barracks, mainly consisting of the eternal search for cigarette butts. For the most part they caught up on rest and found it hard to become accustomed to the new mantle of freedom and respectability they wore. The scars of boot camp were slow in healing They walked and acted as though they were treading on hot coals, expecting to have their heads torn off at any moment. They ventured out and walked about the base with the timidity of curious puppies.

Each morning the student buglers and drummers fell out opposite their tents to blow reveille. The fifty field musics blasting at one time nearly blew the tents down. The din was awful. Then they'd parade the length of the base and return to the tents to blow for another ten minutes as the recipients lay shaken.

"More, more!" L.Q. would scream each morning in anguish. And the buglers generally obliged as the tents nearly buckled. They soon stopped calling for more.

Danny was content to remain on the base, take in a movie, write letters, or bat the breeze. He did look up Beller at the beer hall for the promised brew, but returned to his tent early. The beer had the same sour taste it had had the last time he

tried it a year before. Many evenings after chow he donned
his greens, as prescribed at this military showplace, and visited
Norton, who lived in a tent area not too far away.

One night, a week after boot camp, he felt a siege of loneliness falling over him. This feeling had become more and
more severe with each passing day. He showered after late
chow, dressed, and picked up a liberty card at the First Sergeant's office.

"Where you going, Danny?" Ski asked.

"Into Dago, how about coming?"

"Naw," the feathermerchant lamented, "got to save my
dough. Besides, there's nothing there. The guys all say it's
lousy."

"I just feel jumpy. I've got to see somebody but a gyrene.
We been locked in for three months. Besides, I want to get my
blouse cut down, buy a barracks cap and get some pictures
taken. My folks are riding me for a picture."

"You know something, Danny?"

"What?"

"I'd be a little scared of going into town."

"Scared?"

"Kinda. We been away from people so long, I mean other
people . . . and women. You know, strange town, strange uniform."

"Yeah, it does feel funny at that. Want anything in Dago?"

"You could get my basic medal and pistol, bayonet, and BAR
bars. Also a sharpshooter's medal."

"O.K."

"Take it easy."

"How do I look?"

"Like a dream. I'll wait up for you so you can tell me what
it's like."

Danny crossed the parade grounds, passed the long line of
yellow buildings, and down the road of palmed and lawned
streets to the main gate. He rubbed the sleeve of his blouse
over the buckle on his fair leather belt and squared away his
cap a dozen times. He approached a guard and handed him
the liberty card.

"Where is your battle pin, Marine?"

Danny jumped like a startled fawn, flushed, and dug it from
his pocket. He put the tie pin on and passed through the gate.
His heart thumped as he made it to a bus stop and inquired the
way into San Diego. As the bus moved past the aircraft
plants, an uneasy sensation took hold of him. Although there
were several Marines on the bus, he felt alone, as though he
were either naked or dressed in some outlandish costume and
everyone was staring at him.

After he had debarked and walked down the gaudy tin-plated Broadway the feeling became more apparent. He couldn't understand it. What was there to be afraid of? Almost like the tightness he had known before the opening kickoff in a big game.

Blinding, blinking lights. Hawkers. Dim lights and soft music of the hundred bars. The sea of white-capped sailor hats bobbing up and down, the drunks, the noise, the litter. It all blended into a symphony of discord that set his head reeling.

They say it is easy to spot a new Marine. He has that boot camp stare. They knew the stare in San Diego and had become rich on it. It takes a year of wear for the wool nap of Marine greens to wear down and acquire the knifelike sharpness of a veteran. The boot's uniform wrinkles easily and fits badly. It is easy to see the awe of a boy who has never been away from home. You can spot him in a minute.

The merchant who sold him his basic medal and barracks cap and the photographer who literally jerked him in off the sidewalk had well-oiled tongues and open palms. After an hour a gum-popping floozy took his pictures and he hastened to return to the base.

He walked through the gate disgusted, with himself and with San Diego. As he retraced his steps and crossed the dark parade ground he felt more alone and confused than ever. He trudged toward his tent. Baltimore . . . she had run down the platform waving and stopped as the train took up speed . . . Danny gritted his teeth. He halted before his tent and drew a deep breath and smiled at his buddies. They were gathered about L.Q.'s sack playing poker.

"Back so early?"

"Yeah, not much doing."

"How was Dago?"

"Oh, not bad . . . not bad. Got an open hand there?"

"Step right up, Cousin Dan. Your money is good."

"Er . . . I never played poker before, so you guys will have to sort of help me along."

The course at radio school was divided into four parts: code, Naval procedure, theory, and field practice. When Class 34 formed and moved into the barracks of Signal School, it was a relief to Danny's restlessness. The course wasn't particularly difficult, but he found it fascinating. His day was full and the evenings were largely given to helping the Indian and Ski with studies that seemed to throw them.

As in all Marine schools, the teachers were experts. Radiomen who compared in their way with the illustrious rifle teachers at Matthews. Old salts from the Fleet, all were Tech or

Master Tech Sergeants who could read and transmit code in their sleep. As in boot camp and on the rifle range, the lessons were drilled home with hours of practice and study.

Major Bolger's Signal School taught a shorter course than that given the prewar men. Old-timers were stationed aboard ships and large land stations that required high speed operators. The new men learned low speed field operation. A mere eighteen words of code and twenty-two in English to pass. In the expanding Corps the slant was for men to work the sets they'd use in battle.

With each eventful day, a lonely night. Soon Danny Forrester knew the loneliness of soldiering. Cigarettes and poker. Lonely men need diversion from work and the hours of talk about women and home. He could not clarify the riddle of Kathy. Was it love or circumstances? Was it right or wrong to hold on to her? His letters were almost as impersonal as hers were endearing. He dared not speak of the hunger in his heart —she might drift from him. This thought chilled him. His mother, father, his home and friends all seemed hazy. Only Kathy filled his thoughts. He wondered if this worship wasn't out of proportion. Taps—and men without women slipped between sheets of their empty beds and thought.

Sunday afternoon. Weekend liberty. Danny returned from the usual Sunday chow of fried chicken to the deserted barracks. On the veranda, a line of mattresses lay over the rail being aired. Other Marines lay in swim trunks sunning in the quiet, lazy dog, their muscled torsos reflecting the light. In the barracks two fellows went about fixing "short sheets" to snarl their returning buddies.

At one end of the enormous room Marion's record player spun on. The music haunted the empty place. Danny crushed out a cigarette, threw it into the sandbox beside a dozen others he had smoked. He lay back on his bunk and stared aimlessly at the ceiling, melancholy sweeping into every pore of his body. A pain of loneliness almost sent him screaming. He rushed to his locker, dressed, and left the cursed barracks. He walked the length of the hot, empty parade ground until he came to the tents of the Pioneer battalion. Thank God Norton was there and alone.

"Hello, Danny."

"Hello, professor. I . . . sure am glad to catch you in." He sat on a cot, wiped the sweat from his face and reached for a cigarette.

"See anything new?" Norton said, proudly throwing out his left arm.

"I'll be go to hell. You made Pfc."

"How about that. How's that for promotion?"

Danny rose and halfheartedly punched Norton's arm to "tag on" the new stripe. "You should be an officer, professor."

"Going ashore?"

"Yeah—that damned barracks gives me the creeps on Sunday."

"Anything on your mind, kid?" Norton smiled.

Danny sat silently for several moments. "Christ, Nort, I don't know what's coming over me . . . I . . . I get so goddam lonesome," he blurted.

Norton put an arm around his friend's shoulder. "We're in a lonely business, Danny."

"Do you ever get that way?"

"Sometimes I think I'm going to bust, Danny."

"Jesus, it must be rough on you. Having a wife and all that."

"It's rough on everyone."

"Funny thing, Nort, I never used to be this way. There's a swell bunch at school. I told you about the Indian and Andy and Marion—best bunch I ever met. Oh hell, I don't know."

"Everything all right back home?"

"Sure . . . sure. Look, I got a picture of her yesterday in the mail."

Norton studied the young girl. Golden hair that fell to her shoulders and laughing eyes. Ivory clear skin, a young body, round and firm and tender. "She's very beautiful, Danny. No wonder you're lonely here."

"Nort, could a guy like me—I mean a guy just eighteen and a girl seventeen fall in love? I mean fall in love the same way you feel about your wife?"

"How does she feel about it?"

"She says she loves me, but it's going to be a long time. Too damned long . . . I don't want it to wear off and have her being faithful just because she feels sorry for me—she's like that Nort. She'll stick even if she doesn't want me."

"Hell, Danny, what do I know? How old does a fellow have to be to go through what you're going through right now? You're old enough to be here and wear a green uniform."

"And her?"

"I guess people grow old fast in wars. Nature's way of trying to compensate for the things that young people are asked to do."

"I've tried to fight it off, Nort. If she ever quit me, there wouldn't be any use of living."

"Then stop wading in like a punch-drunk fighter. Ride with the punch as best you can. You're both in a war, clean up to your necks and you can't get out of it. Tell her how you feel."

"I . . . I don't know."

"I sometimes wonder, Danny, if we all aren't a bunch of wild, crazy animals. I guess we all wonder that. But we've got to try to go on living and loving and hating and feeling and touching and smelling whether there's a war, or not."

"Professor."

"Yes."

"Would you lend me your I.D. card?"

"Why?"

"I want to get crocked."

Norton put out his cigarette and shrugged. "Is it going to make it easier by going out and getting drunk?"

"I've got to do something or I'll blow my stack. Don't give me a lecture."

"Have you ever gotten drunk before?"

"No."

"Ever had a drink before?"

"A bottle of beer, once."

"Oh, the hell with it. Here . . . take my card."

Danny forged an air of indifference as he passed through the open portals of a quiet-looking saloon, off the main drag. He propped a foot on the bar rail between two sailors and stared into the mirror back of the bar.

"What'll you have, Marine?"

"What have you got?" he countered with the innocence of a child asking the flavors in an ice cream parlor.

"Humm, let me see your I.D. card."

He flipped the card over the bar and the bartender paid scant notice to the dissimilarity of the boy before him and the picture of Milton Norton. "Just fix me something up. Er . . . a Tom Collins," he said. "Yeah, a Tom Collins . . . double."

He was surprised—it tasted like lemonade. Not at all like the vile smell of a buddy returning from a weekend of liberty. He dipped his fingers into the glass and withdrew the cherry and with a straw stirred the concoction. Three or four quick draws and the drink disappeared. "Survey," he ordered.

"Better take her slow, son," the bartender warned.

"If you've got any good advice, don't give it away, sell it." Danny studied the selections for the jukebox. He picked up a quarter which lay with his change and pushed five buttons. The Sunday serenity of the place was broken by a scratchy needle and a lilty voice, Frank Sinatra, crooning a favorite of his and Kathy's:

> *I'll never smile again,*
> *Until I smile at you . . .*

Always cut school twice a year anyhow. Once when Tommy Dorsey came to the Hippodrome; the other for Glenn Miller . . .

For tears would fill my eyes,
My heart would realize . . .

He guzzled the second drink and felt nothing. Maybe he had the capacity like he had heard others brag about in endless hours in the barracks. He stepped up the pace. Six drinks and he still stood in his original position loading the jukebox.

I don't want to set the world on fire, sung out the high voice of Billy Jordan, Ink Spot.

I just want to start, a flame in your heart.

"W-where . . . is the men's room?"

"End of the bar and to your right." Dammit, he thought, sure is funny trying to talk. Hard time getting it out. He withdrew his foot from the rail and his leg buckled. He grasped the bar quickly and steadied himself, fumbled for a smoke. It seemed his fingers had no sense of feel as they groped through his pocket. After a struggle he finally got one lit and started his trek. "Hey, Marine!"

He turned slowly. "You left some money on the bar."

"Oh . . . sure . . . silly me." Wasn't that a damned fool thing to say, silly me. "Better give me another drink . . . make me one like that guy has," he pointed to a soldier's glass which he had been admiring.

"That's a Singapore Sling, son. Better not mix them like that."

"Give me a Slingapore Sing . . ." He climbed on a barstool and wavered. Hell, I'm not drunk. I know who I am. I'm Forrester, 359195, USMCR . . . he repeated to himself. I'm not drunk . . . I know what the score is . . . isn't much of a drink. Who is that sonofabitch staring at—oh, that's me in the mirror. Better get to the men's room.

O.K., Danny Forrester, don't look like one of those goddam drunken Marines you hate. Easy off the chair, boy. Watch that goddam table there, don't trip . . . why feels like I'm not even walking . . . like being on a cloud . . . there's the door. "Adam," it says. Who's drunk, I can read . . . Adam means man, I'm not drunk.

He doused his face in cold water and studied himself in the mirror. Oh-oh, you silly bastard . . . I guess you are drunk. He shook his head and laughed. So this is being drunk . . . isn't so hot . . . Danny Forrester . . . 359 . . . did I say 359 or 358? Forrester . . . no eights in it . . . that's my rifle number. Rifle, not gun . . . Oh buddy, you're loaded. He laughed again. Mother should see me now. He roared a laugh. He shoved the door open and then sprung back into the lavatory. Forgot to button my fly ... slippery ole buttons ... damned.

A sailor crowded in. "Scuse me, Marine." He edged past Danny. Bet I could whip that swabjockey. "Hi mate," Danny roared, slapping the sailor on the back. "Quite a rig you guys got there, suppose you got to go in hurry?"

The sailor, an elderly sea dog, smiled casually at the young lad. "Easy, Marine, you've got a full load on."

Before Danny could swing he found he had been eased back into the saloon. He studied the long way to the door. The whole room was an obstacle course, a moving obstacle course. He flopped into the first chair he could find, almost taking it over with him. *Danny Forrester ... 35 ... 36 ... no eight ...*

"You'd better move on, Marine."

"Shaddup."

"Come on, boy, go quiet like."

"Gimme a drunk, I ain't drink."

Faint voices. Where the hell am I? Oh Jesus, I'm getting sick. Talk louder, you guys ... I can't hear you...

"Better call the Shore Patrol, Joe."

"Aw, leave him alone. He ain't bothering nobody. Just let him sit there till he comes around."

"I'm ... I'm ... a rifle ... hup ... hup ..."

"Did he come in with a buddy?"

"Leave the guy alone."

"Hey, Marine! Wake up!"

"Oh ... gawd ... I'm sick."

His head fell flat on the table and his new barracks cap rolled to the floor. "Get the Shore Patrol."

"No, don't. I'll take care of him."

"Are you a friend of his, lady?"

"Yes ... yes."

"Hey, Burnside, looks like that broad is going to roll him."

"Yeah, McQuade. Here we been sitting in Iceland all these months and we got to come home to something like this. Come on Gunny, let's have a talk with her."

"Take your mits off him, lady."

"Cut out the heroics, boys. He's just a kid. I feel sorry for him ... or would you rather the Shore Patrol picked him up?"

"Well ..."

This love of mine,
Goes on and on,
Though life is empty,
Since you've been gone. ...

7.

*Rock of ages,
    Cleft for me,
Let me lose myself in thee. . . .*

HYMNS! They're singing hymns. I'm dead . . . I'm in heaven. Danny forced his eyes open. He was in a huge, high-ceilinged room and it was filled with voices singing. He forced his eyes to focus the place into view. Far away . . . almost out of sight he made out the forms of servicemen and girls standing with books in their hands. "Oh Jesus," he moaned, "come and get me."

"How do you feel, Marine?" He caught a whiff of enchanting perfume and felt the nearness of someone. "How do you feel?" It was a soft, sweet voice. An angel.

He rubbed his eyes. She was tall, very dark and about thirty. He glanced from her toes upwards, studying the expensive drapery of her dress . . . and her figure. Class, definitely class, he thought. Well groomed, well heeled, and lovely.

"Who are you?" he groaned.

"Mrs. Yarborough. You're in the Salvation Army Canteen." He smacked his lips; his throat was dry and there was a terrible taste in his mouth. He sat erect, studied the place, and tried to recall the events that preceded his trip to heaven.

"Oh brother, how did I get here?"

"I brought you."

"Why?"

"I stopped to have a cooling drink. I became fascinated watching you pour down those doubles. I wanted to see what would happen when you took your foot off the bar rail."

"Why?"

"I felt sorry for you. Just an impulse."

"Who hit me?"

She laughed. "No one hit you, you passed out."

"Tell them to stop singing, I've seen the light."

"How about a cup of black coffee?"

"Black . . . I'll puke . . . I'm sorry . . . I mean my stomach has been upset lately."

She took a chair next to him. "You really hung one on."

"I do it all the time. This makes an even once."

"Feel any better about it?"

"Next time, I'll try prayer. It's cheaper and easier."

"How old are you?"

"Twenty-four."

"*How* old?"

"Eighteen."

She watched him as he fought his way to complete consciousness. He felt sorry for himself, he admitted it and he was better now. No need for further conversation. "Be a good boy now and I promise not to tell Kathy," she said as she arose to leave.

"Oh Christ, did I drag her into it?"

"I'll say you did."

"Please, Mrs. . . . er . . . er."

"Yarborough."

"Just a moment."

"What do you want?"

"I just want to say thanks. I guess I put on a good show. It was nice of you, I could have gotten into a lot of trouble."

"I usually don't make a habit of stopping in bars. Just a bit of odd luck and hot weather. Now see if you can enjoy yourself, I must go on duty."

It was the first time that he had spoken to a woman in many months. The voice that was not gruff, cursing, or commanding sounded like something he'd almost forgotten. He wanted to go on talking to her.

"Mrs. Yarborough."

"Yes?"

"I feel that you're entitled to know the entire story that led to my downfall, that's the least I could do."

"I listen to them all day. I'll take a raincheck."

"If you don't . . . I'll go out and get drunk."

She laughed. "You'd better not, Marine."

Danny took her hand gently. It felt wonderfully soft and smooth. "I'm an orphan, Mrs. Yarborough."

"Oh."

"You see, my mom died in a fire when I was four . . . trying to save me. Dad did the best he could to raise me . . . but . . . but you know, whisky. He started beating me . . . I was just a tot. He was sorry for it when he was sober . . . I'm . . . I'm sorry."

"No, go on," she said, sliding to the seat next to him.

"I ran away from home when I was fourteen, rode the rails. Hobo camps, odd jobs. Then I met Kathy." He held her hand as he spoke.

"Yes?"

"If you want to really know what happened, I'll tell you."

"You mean you were just pulling my leg?"

"Uh-huh."

"Stinker. I'll never believe another Marine again."

"Mrs. Yarborough. Would you take a walk with me? I'd like to get my head cleared. Now don't tell me how busy you are. Look . . . Marine . . . I mean scout's honor. Walk me to the bus station at the Red Cross Club, put me on the bus and I'll pass from your life forever. Really, I'd like to talk to someone . . . a girl. Would you?"

It was foolish in the first place, she told herself. She should have left him cold in the bar. The strange thing that originally attracted her seemed to grab hard now. For an instant she began to ward off this second mad idea and send him along. "Really, Danny . . ." She made the mistake of looking into his eyes. They pleaded as did a thousand pairs of eyes in the canteen; for a moment of talk, a moment of possession. "This is silly."

"Where is your coat?"

"I didn't bring one."

He had her arm and led her over the long room past the singers, who were now deep in prayer. She caught herself at the head of the stairs, then looked up at him. He was very handsome, standing upright. "I'll get my purse."

He sucked in a deep breath as they stepped into the darkened street, the fresh air nearly sweeping him off his feet. "How do you feel now?" she asked. His first steps were not too steady, then she found trouble keeping in step with his long, easy strides. Vernon Yarborough took short steps, he was easy to walk with.

"I feel like a couple of two-hundred-pound tackles just converged on me."

"Are you a football player?"

"Use to, just high school. Funny thing happened yesterday. I got a letter from the Georgia Tech Alumni Association accepting my application for a scholarship. My buddies nearly died laughing."

Elaine laughed. He took her arm unconcernedly and assisted her across a street. "I used to have a crush on a football player," she said.

"But he wasn't as good as me."

"He was much better looking. Every girl in the school was crazy about him. Of course, I kept the torch to myself."

"Of course," Danny repeated.

"Why do you say of course, that way?"

"Oh, I don't know. You don't seem one to follow impulses. You look well planned."

"For instance?"

"For instance. You are probably wondering what you are doing walking down the street with me. You must be crazy,

you're saying to yourself. You're really robbing the cradle. By
the way, Mrs. Yarborough, I didn't catch your first name."

"Elaine."

"Elaine the fair, Elaine the beautiful, Elaine the lily maid of
Astelot."

"That's funny."

"What's funny about it? Tennyson, required reading—I suffered."

"I know. But no one has said that to me for an awful long
time." They shoved through a crowded group of sailors. She
held his arm tightly. He was strong. Vernon was strong too—in
another way. Vernon was security.

"Why did you help me out, Elaine?"

"Oh, I suppose you reminded me of my kid brother."

"Know something, I'll bet you you don't have a kid brother."

"Keep going, you're doing fine."

"Well, you are a big wheel at the canteen . . . probably head
of a committee. You're the wife of an officer, I'd say a Navy
officer."

"What makes you think so?"

"Something about a Navy officer."

"Snob?"

"No, just that holy reserve."

"Go on, you're a very interesting young man."

"Well, let me see. You're not regular Navy, you're reserve.
Your husband is probably a lawyer, corporation. Maybe a
banker or an advertising exec."

"You're not so smart, he's a certified public accountant."

"Same category, ulcer man."

"Really."

"Yep." She began to feel uneasy, but he continued. "You
probably belong to a clique, immaculate housekeeper with
maid. Social ambitions."

"Really."

"You're repeating yourself. Say listen, I'm getting rude and
you've been damned nice to me."

"I must be wearing a sign."

"No, it shows in your eyes, your dress, the way you talk, the
way you choose words. You've trained yourself."

She changed the subject.

Yes, I've trained myself. The only one of the Gursky girls
who had the guts to go out and get what I wanted. Five daugh-
ters . . . four married, poverty, misery, failure. I trained myself
to get Vernon Yarborough and be his wife. The family didn't
like him; he didn't sit in his shirtsleeves and drink beer on the
front porch and argue baseball like the other sons-in-law. I've
groomed myself . . . his clubs, his parents. To learn to have.

Planned life, plan the next step. People must know where they are going.

"You were saying, Danny, about Georgia Tech and the war came . . ."

They walked for many blocks and then turned from the main street to a quiet, shadowed one. As they strolled he told her about Baltimore, Kathy, Forest Park . . . the wanting to become an engineer. "Funny," he said, "people sure make friends fast. I've just known you a little while and I'm babbling my life's story . . . want a cigarette?"

"I shouldn't smoke . . . on the street."

"Here."

"Thanks."

"Look, Elaine."

"What?"

"Across the street. An ice rink. Let's go skating."

"Goodness, no."

"Why not?"

"Why, I haven't been in years."

"There you go, fighting off impulses."

"Seems like I followed enough of them for one day. Besides, if you are going to continue to accuse me . . . then tell me why I'm in San Diego?"

"That's easy. You're here because it's the thing to do."

"Exactly what do you mean!"

"Look, I'm not trying to be nasty, stop egging me."

"I want to know what you meant by that."

"All right. To uproot and stay here and wait faithfully for ships to come in, it looks good to the clique. Probably the same reason your husband joined up. I'll bet he weighed the best deal for himself very carefully. Look, I don't know what's gotten into me. I shouldn't be angry with you, but I am . . . did that last one hurt?"

Yes, it hurt. She was clever. A clever hostess, a clever pusher for the dull husband. Respectable. A complete divorce from the round oak table and the rye bread and borscht. A small, select circle, do the proper thing at the proper time. She didn't like being stripped naked by a boy she had only known a few hours. Why didn't she just slap his face and leave?

"I guess if you stay around officers' wives long enough, you'll get nauseated enough to try anything. Like join the USO to get away from them. And find out there are a lot of little punks, not wearing gold braid, who are pretty good guys."

"That's enough, Danny."

"I used to go skating in Carlin's Arena all the time, back home. During a real cold winter the rowboat lake in Druid Hill Park froze. Ever play crack-the-whip? Anyhow, there's a little island in the center of the lake with a boathouse on it and a big fireplace. You'd come in half chilled and stand in front of the fire and drink hot chocolate."

"It—it sounds like lots of fun." And then that strange twinge again. A thrill of adventure in walking alongside him. His cocky words, sure manner. Calm and sure of himself. For the first time in many years she felt as though a veil had been lifted from before her. She felt like the young reckless girl who had lived in a big, shingled house on the South Side of Chicago. And then she became frightened of the way he was completely twisting her.

She felt tired and for a moment nearly slipped her arm about his waist and laid her head on his shoulder. "Danny."

"Yes?"

"We'd better go back. We've walked way off our course."

"All right—look, there's a carnival a couple blocks down. . . ."

"I really must go back."

"I've got six bits left. Look, I'm a dead-eye at throwing baseballs at the bottles. I'll win you a kewpie doll. I owe you a present anyhow." He led her to the ticket window and they passed into the aura of twirling lights, sawdust, barkers, a quagmire of bobbing white hats and green and khaki uniforms. He shoved a cotton candy cone in her hand. She took a bite and smiled.

"Come on, Elaine."

"Step right up. Ah there, there's a Marine. Come on sport . . . win the little lady a prize. Three balls for a thin dime. . . ."

"Hold my blouse." He winked. "They don't call me rifle arm Forrester for nothing." He went into an elongated wind-up and tossed the soft ball at the pyramid of iron bottles. He missed the works by a foot. "Hum, first time that's ever happened." She tilted her head back and laughed. One bottle fell, grudgingly, in three tries.

"It's rigged," he whispered, "magnets."

"Hold this," Elaine said, handing him back his blouse and two cones.

"That's right, step right up little lady and show him how." She did and jumped from the ground screaming, "A winner!"

"Yes sir, everybody wins. You there, sailor . . . win a prize. . . ."

Elaine tucked the plaster doll under her arm and walked off still laughing. "I played on a girl's team ten years ago. They don't call me rifle arm Gursky—Yarborough for nothing."

"Very funny, very funny."

"I want a hot dog."

"I'm broke."

"This is on me."

"Oh, look over there."

"What?"

"A ferris wheel. No . . . no, on second thought it is rather high."

"Come on," Danny said.

They whirled up and then looked down. On the crazy city. She grasped the guard tightly and slipped over close to him. "Don't crawl all over me," he said, "I'm just as scared as you are."

"I haven't had so much fun in years."

"What did you say?"

"I said . . . it sure takes the breath out of you."

The wheel stopped suddenly. They were high above the crowd. Their seat swayed back and forth. She gasped and he placed his arm about her. It seemed as though he could reach out and touch a star . . . it was quiet and the world far away. A crazy day, and ending in the clouds. His other arm went about her and she lifted her face. The wheel came to earth. He kissed her and they spun in a giddy circle. Her fingers dug into his arm. She drew back. He kissed her again. The flashing lights . . . the muffled sounds of people below . . . rising and then falling, sent them dizzy. Then the wheel stopped suddenly.

They walked silently from the white way. The maze of sound and light was deaf to them. She turned, her face very pale.

"I . . . I always wanted to kiss a girl on a ferris wheel."

"Good night, Danny."

"I'm not sorry and neither are you."

She was afraid . . . of herself.

"I saw on the bulletin board at the canteen—a hayride next Friday. I have liberty—I'll bet you look swell in slacks."

"I don't want to see you again, Danny."

"Come on, I'll take you back to the canteen."

"No, no. . . ."

"I'll see you Friday, then." She spun around and raced into darkness. Danny withdrew his last dime from his pocket. He flipped it in the air and walked away from the carnival, whistling.

Elaine Yarborough filled a pair of slacks nicely. The wife of Vernon Yarborough made it a point to keep her figure attractive.

She paced the line of hay-filled trucks as laughing men and girls piled aboard, and a sound of starting motors filled the air. She checked her watch, then sighed despondently.

"Hi, Elaine." She started and spun about. He was standing behind her. "I almost didn't make it." They looked at each other long and hard. He took her hand and led her to the last truck. Her hand was trembling. In a quick effortless motion, he took her in his arms and gently lifted her into the truck and hopped aboard. They settled back in the straw, she nestled in his arms.

The beach at La Jolla: a campfire, songs, tangy tasting hot dogs. The surf pounding the shore and a blanket of stars overhead. They walked along the water line. She was lost in his green blouse, which she wore to keep out the chill. And during the evening, hardly a word passed between them.

Afterward, her car stopped before her apartment in the neat court of the motel full of officers' wives. Danny eased it into its port and followed her to the door. She unlocked it, switched on the light of the living room and he closed the door behind him. The room was Elaine, he thought. A miniature of her home in Arlington Heights. Expensive, stiff, cold mementos from the clique, the select circle. A row of books, beautifully bound, well chosen. Danny walked to them and opened one. As he suspected, a neat bookplate on the inside cover: *Ex Libris Vernon Yarborough*. He wondered if they had ever been read.

"It was a wonderful evening," she said. "Shall I fix you a drink?"

"I gave it up for Lent," he answered, recalling his one episode with liquor. He thumbed through the book. "*Cyrano*. I have a friend, Marion Hodgkiss. He reads all the time—talked me into this one. He says there is nothing in modern writing as beautiful as *Cyrano*."

"I'm fond of it . . . I haven't read it in years."

"I had a teacher once. The guy used to read us Shakespeare. You never saw anything like it, the way he could make forty kids sit and listen to him, entranced. A good teacher is like a good doctor, I suppose—as close to real goodness as anything we have on earth. I don't know what made me think of him." His eyes caught a picture atop the book case, a naval officer. Immaculate and impeccable in his uniform. Clean shaven, groomed—stuffy, stiff, studious, and dull. He looked at her. She was the wife of another man. It felt eerie. He was in this man's living room . . . he had kissed his wife. Danny reached up and turned the picture to the wall.

"That wasn't funny. You shouldn't have done that."

"I couldn't stand to have him staring at me when I kissed you."

"Don't."

"I'm sorry."

"Danny," she whispered, "what are you thinking about?"

"I don't think you'd like to know."

"Tell me."

"I was thinking of how I pictured my wife. I always thought of being on a construction job; a tunnel or maybe a highway up in the mountains. Alaska maybe, maybe the Andes. I thought of coming out of a blinding snow and cold into a cozy warm cabin. Not a fancy place. But comfortable, like a woman can make it, with a big fire and her standing there in jeans and a heavy wool shirt. I'd take her in my arms and say, 'Isn't it great we aren't like other people? Next year we'll be on that job in China—after that Mexico or the new oil fields . . . the world is our oyster and we come and go as we damned please. No social conventions . . . nothing to make us stale. Maybe build a little home back in Baltimore and take out time for some kids and when they're old enough to crawl, out we go again. Let them learn to live in freedom!' I'm sorry, Elaine, that campfire got me into a mood."

"It . . . it sounds wonderful, she's a lucky girl."

"It's a long war."

"I feel as if I had a bale of hay down my back," she said. "Do you mind if I change?"

"Go on ahead."

They spoke through the door ajar as he glanced through some other books. Some straw was sticking into him under his shirt. He took off his blouse and shirt and skivvy and wiped the hay away from his body. Elaine Yarborough stood in the doorway. A dressing gown, sheer, white—it flowed like a billow to the floor. Her black hair hung to her tanned shoulders. He held his shirt in his fists still, and gazed at her. Across the room each heard the other's deep breath. She was another man's wife . . . it felt strange, strange. She walked towards him. He could see the nipples of her breasts through the film of silk net.

"I had some hay down my back . . . I . . . I . . ."

Her hand reached up and touched the bare skin of his shoulder and moved gently over his chest. His shirt fell from his hands and he embraced her.

"You're strong, darling."

"Don't talk."

They exchanged fiery kisses. She put her head on his chest. He lifted her into his arms and held her, and she became faint with passion. "Danny . . . Danny," she sobbed.

He walked to the bedroom door and kicked it open. And slowly lowered her to the bed, then lay at her side and once more crushed her against his body. Violently, she tore the gown from her body and tugged at the buckle of his trousers. Their bodies seemed to melt together; she sunk her fingernails into his flesh. "Oh God . . . God . . . God . . ." she said in a dull, interminable rhythm.

8.

THE CODE began to sound like an inescapable whine in Danny's ears during the ensuing weeks. Lessons, once easily learned, became difficult and the fascination of radio grew to boredom. A haze fell over him. An irresistible urge drove him to her arms . . . yet at the same time a constant irking guilt wanted him to break away. It was wrong. Wrong for both of them. Everything he knew told him so. Yet he automatically dressed and passed through the main gate to the waiting car. Like a magnet. Every other night Ski lay in Danny's bunk to cover him during bed check. Ski treated the affair with passive silence. He hated Danny for not finding the strength or the will to remain faithful, as he had done to Susan. Yet they were buddies and he quietly surrendered his liberty card to Danny and protected his absences. There were no bull sessions with the fellows now. No wrestling about or slinging insults. He spoke little to anyone.

Elaine Yarborough quit the USO. She stiffened and turned deaf ears to the icy whispers of the Navy wives. Let them scorn her and her lover. Perhaps it was envy, perhaps it was. She succumbed to him, enraptured, like a hero worshiper. Piecemeal the stiff clandestine tradition of caste built in her marriage to Vernon wilted in his arms. The young Marine dominated her every thought, her every move. The past faded or failed to penetrate to the cloud she lived on. In a nightclub, a roadside rendezvous, the beach, her apartment, she studied him enthralled.

> *Dear Son,*
> *I realize how busy you must be and I promised that I wouldn't make too many demands upon you. But it has been two weeks since we have gotten a letter. Are you ill or have you been transferred from school?*
> *I know there must be some logical reason, son. I hate to harp but you must realize how important your letters are.*
> *Why don't you call us, collect of course. You should be free around six at night—that will be nine, our time. Friday night we will all be standing by. . . .*
> *If you are in any kind of trouble, I'd feel a lot better if you cared to confide in me. . . .*

Danny sat up slowly in bed, yawned and stretched. She lay cuddled under the blankets and peeked one eye open. She

saw the ripple of muscle over his back and purred like a contented cat.

"Holy Christ," he said, "I'm late. Hey Elaine, wake up."

"Leave me alone, I'm going to sleep all day."

"Like hell you are. You're going to drive me to the base.
Get up."

"Oh, must I?" she whined. She rolled over on her back and
looked at him. "Come here, Danny boy," she whispered, holding up the covers.

"Don't call me Danny boy."

"Come here to mommy." She eased him down beside her and
held his cheek against her breast."

"Don't call me Danny boy."

"I like to tease you." He kissed her hand and closed his
eyes. She sighed and ran her fingers over his hard flesh. Vernon
was soft and pudgy. So dull, so without imagination, so routine,
so dutiful. The mornings she lay cold and angry, unsatisfied,
taken for granted. He was soft. He tried to exercise at the club
but there was an ugly ring of fat around his middle.

Danny flung the covers off, rolled her over and slapped her
backside. "Come on, woman, get up and make me some breakfast." He nudged her from the bed to the floor. She stood up,
grabbed a blanket and covered herself quickly.

"You shouldn't do that, Danny."

"Do what?"

"Look at me."

"Why not?"

"It embarrasses me."

"Hell, if I was built like you, I'd walk down Broadway naked
as a jaybird."

"Danny, stop that this minute."

"Hurry up, will you, I'll miss reveille."

He walked into the barracks and opened his locker as the rest
of the men worked slowly into their clothes.

"Aha," cried L.Q. Jones. "Here comes big Dan Forrester.
SOS, the breakfast food of Marines, brings you another chap-
ter in the thrilling adventures of Big Dan Forrester, SUPER-
MARINE!"

"Very funny, very goddam funny," Danny spat as he flung
his towel over his shoulder and stomped off to the head. Behind him there was a sound of laughter.

"What's the matter, Danny, got the red ass?" Andy Hookans
pulled up to the sink next to his.

"I don't see anything funny, that's all."

"Can't blame them for being jealous. That is a damned nice
car. Besides, they're getting frustrated. They've fixed your bed

to catch you in a 'short sheet' for a week, and you never get in till reveille."

Danny lathered his face quietly.

"Forget it, they're only kidding."

"Maybe a good clout on the mouth and L.Q. might keep it shut."

"I wouldn't be sore at L.Q. He answered for you at rollcall."

"What do you mean? Rollcall isn't for twenty minutes."

"Last night, we had an air raid drill. The Sarge was watching Ski. L.Q. answered up for you."

"I . . . I'm sorry. I guess I blew my lid, Andy."

"Better slow down, Danny," Hookans continued. His big Swedish face was clouded and concerned. "We don't want to see you shipped out of school."

"Yeah, thanks . . . dammit to hell." He nicked his chin.

"Forget it when you're in class."

"I can't."

"I know what you're thinking. It's wrong. Well, if you wasn't shacking up with her, there'd be another guy in her bed."

"She isn't a tramp."

"Yeah, I know. None of them are. But they all got to have it."

"I sure want to be there when you fall, Andy."

"Save your breath. They haven't made the broad yet that can make old Andy go down for the count."

Tech Sergeant Hale sat at his desk at the head of the class. His head rested upon one arm as he gazed down into the book. His right hand worked the key, sending dots and dashes into the earphones of the thirty men at the desks before him.

ASPFK KMTJW URITF LZOCC KPZXG HNMKI LOQEI
TZCOV DERAP NOWSS DEBZO

Working some fifteen words slower than his accustomed speed he opened his eyes to fight off the monotony. As his fist sent code, the room was filled with the clicks of typewriters, almost in unison. He turned the page and looked down the rows of men. Stiff ironed khaki and field scarfs and glistening battle pins. Young faces with crew cuts; a slow recovery from the stripping of boot camp.

The Sergeant yawned. "O.K., we'll try numbers now, six words a minute."

20034 38765 23477 88196 . . . the bell sounded, ending classes for the day. A sigh of relief arose as the men doffed their earphones, rubbed their ears and shook their heads to erase the dots and dashes. They arose and stretched.

"Zvonski and Lighttower, report back after chow. You fel-

lows will have to take an extra hour of code each night this
week to make up the test."

"Goddam," the Indian opined, "got a heap nice squaw in
Dago, sarge."

"If you don't learn this code, Lighttower, we're going to send
you to the happy hunting grounds."

Danny slapped Ski across the back. "Come on, you weren't
going any place anyhow. Let's clean up for chow." Marion
Hodgkiss joined them as they left the building.

"Tough luck, Ski." Danny and Ski lit up as they passed
along the arcade toward their barracks.

"I know what's coming through. But every time I go to
type it, I hit the wrong key or something. You don't think they'll
ship me out, do you?"

"For Chrisake, stop worrying," Danny said. "We'll skip the
movie tonight and work in the head after taps."

"I'll help if you like," Marion offered.

They rounded the corner at the far end of the base and
caught sight of a platoon of Sea School drillers. The blue
dressed men whipped their rifles about like button-controlled
robots. Everyone stopped to look at them.

"Look at them bastards," Ski said, "all over six feet tall."

"I guess that's where all the dress blues in the Corps are."

"They sure can drill."

"Funny," Danny said opening the barracks door, "I didn't
even know Marines wore green until I got to San Diego."

"Seriously?" Marion asked.

"Hell of a thing to admit. When I was a kid in Baltimore,
the Marines from Quantico came up to play the firemen every
year. They gave the whole base weekend shore leave for the
game. Those guys were real giants, the peacetime guys. I remember how they looked all decked out in their blues—like
some kind of gods, I guess. All the kids used to stand outside
the stadium and watch them leave, with a girl on each arm and
a half dozen following them. The Corps sure has changed."

Ski threw his books on his bunk and lay down. "I got to relax more with the earphones on."

"I've got to study after chow," Danny said. "I'll meet you
after your late class. Need a few things at ship's store. I . . . I'm
going to phone Baltimore, too."

"You going to blow a whole pay?"

"My dad wrote to me to reverse charges."

Marion passed them with his washing gear. "Come on, let's
get cleaned up before chow call."

Danny and Marion leaned against the wall outside Ski's class,
waiting for the evening session to end. Danny walked to a vend-

ing machine, inserted a nickel and caught a large, moist, juicy apple as it came tumbling out of the slot. An officer passed. They came to attention and snapped a salute. It was returned.

"This place is too damned GI," Danny said.

"The Marine Base is a showplace for them," Marion answered.

The base was built around a long, arcade-type construction, with Spanish archways and a walk which ran a mile alongside the parade ground. Beyond the parade ground, temporary tents and the sandy boondocks stretched to the bay. Along the archways, the barracks and buildings of the Base. Beyond these buildings was officers' country, the PX, sports grounds and administration buildings laid out lazily in curved streets, in immaculately groomed lawns, palms, and gardens. At one end of the parade ground stood the Signal School and near it, the Field Music School. At the opposite end, the entrance to boot camp. Boot camp was a restricted area and no one cared. The base was the epitome of military custom and courtesy. A Marine there had to be starched, pressed, shiny, and cut his corners squarely.

Shining Lighttower and Ski walked slowly from the building, shaking the latest barrage of code out of their heads.

"Christ, I'm dizzy."

"Come on, we've been waiting for you."

"Damned if I can understand this white man's way to send a message. Me and Major Bolger got to talk . . . I'll show him how much easier smoke signals are," the Indian said.

"We're heading for the PX. You coming?" Marion asked.

"No, I'm going to the movies. They got a cowboy and Indian picture." Lighttower cut down to the parade ground. "See you palefaces by the light of the rising sun."

"That guy fractures me," Ski said. "Always trying to make like an Injun."

They fell in step and paced down the archway keeping their right arms loose for immediate action in the event of a passing officer. They strolled into the PX, made their purchases, and found three empty stools at the fountain.

"Order for me. I'm going to place my call," Danny said, stepping into a nearby phone booth. He returned. "It will be a few minutes for a line to Baltimore." They sipped their sodas.

Then all eyes in the PX turned and stuck to the tall, gaunt man who had entered. There was a hush. His gray eyes pierced and darted about as he walked to the counter and asked for some shaving gear.

"That's Colonel Coleman, the boss of the Raiders," Danny whispered.

"I hear he's forming a new battalion," Marion added.

"Brother, I sure hope he don't look this way. I don't want no part of them crazy bastards."

"You can say that again."

"Lucky Lighttower didn't come," Marion mused. "Coleman would have gotten himself an Indian scout for sure."

"I hear them Raiders sleep on the floor. They don't give them no bedding."

"I came in from liberty last night about one o'clock and they were out boondocking. They don't get shore leave, either."

"Man, when a Raider walks toward me, I step aside. Ever see the knives and strangling gear they carry?"

"A guy would have to be nuts to volunteer into that outfit."

Colonel Ed Coleman received his change and walked to the soda fountain. Marion, Ski, and Danny plunged into their sodas. He seated himself on a stool next to Hodgkiss.

"Evening, Marine," he said slowly.

"Good evening, sir," Marion muttered. "Well, I'll see you fellows later." He beat a hasty retreat from the PX.

Coleman gulped down a Coke and walked to the phone booth.

"Excuse me, sir," Danny said, "but I have a long distance call coming on that phone."

"Beg your pardon." Coleman stepped around him toward another booth.

"What the hell you talk like that for, you nuts?"

"All I said was . . ."

"Don't talk to that Raider like that, it makes me nervous."

The phone rang. Danny entered the booth.

"Hello . . . yes, this is Forrester."

"Your call to Baltimore, Maryland, is ready." He shut the door.

"Hello, hello, son. Danny, can you hear me?"

"Yes, Dad."

"Are you all right, son? Are you in any kind of trouble?"

"No, I've just been busy. I'll get a letter off tonight."

"Are you all right?"

"I'm fine, sir."

"We let Bud stay up. He's hanging on my arm."

"Hello, Buddy."

"Danny . . . Danny . . . Danny!"

"Hi punk. You being a good guy?"

"Danny, I got the cap you sent me. I wear it. Get me a Jap sword soon. I told my teacher I'd bring one to class."

"I'll do my best."

"Hello, son. That's all now, Bud, all right . . . just one word."

"Danny, good night."

"Good night, punk. Behave yourself."

"Hello, son . . . this is Mother."

"Hi, Mom."

"Are they treating you all right, son? I'm chairman of the War Mothers' chapter. Do they march you in the rain, son? I hear such awful stories about the way they treat our boys."

"Everything is fine. Don't worry, they treat me swell."

"Have you lost weight, Danny?"

"I've gained."

"We all miss you so much, Danny. Be a good boy and write more often."

"O.K., Mom."

"Here's a kiss, son."

"Good night, Mom."

"Hello, Danny—Dad again. How is everything going?"

"Fine."

"Sure?"

"Yes, sir."

"Any chance of getting a furlough?"

"I won't know till I'm finished school and in a regular outfit, Dad."

"Chin up, boy, we're all behind you, son."

"Yes."

"I've got a little surprise . . ." Danny could hear the noise of people moving around. There was a faint click of a door closing.

"Hello . . . Danny?" His heart pounded wildly.

"Kathy," he whispered.

"I . . . I . . . are you all right?" He closed his eyes and bit his lip. "I haven't had a letter for so long."

"Kathy . . . Kathy, I love you."

"Oh, Danny, I miss you so much."

"Look . . . kitten . . . I had a little problem . . . but it's gone now."

"It's still on between us, isn't it, Danny?"

"Yes, yes! You've got to know it now, kitten. I love you with everything I've got . . . you've got to understand how I mean it now."

"I love you too . . . I love you very much."

"Your time is up. Please signal when through."

"Take care of yourself, darling."

"Don't worry, honey."

"Not—not any more. Say it once more, Danny."

"I love you, Kathy."

"Good night, my darling." He touched his cheek as the sound of her kiss came.

"Good night, kitten."

Ski leaned against the booth and stared in. He watched

Danny's eyes grow soft as he whispered into the phone. The door opened; he stepped out and stood silently. Then he returned to his friend.

"Why don't you call Susan up?"

"How much will it cost?"

"About three bucks."

"I'd like to, but I . . . I better just save it."

"I'll lend you the dough."

"No."

"Look, Ski. We're buddies, aren't we?"

"Yeah."

"Why don't you let me write my dad, like I said before."

"No."

"I tell you it would just be a loan. She'll get work when she gets out here and you can pay it back then."

"I don't want it that way. We'll have time."

"I hate to see you eating your heart out, Ski. You don't go to Dago, you just sit around and think about it all the time. It makes your work lousy."

"You don't understand, Danny."

"For Chrisake. You think I like to see you shining shoes for a dime, cleaning rifles and ironing shirts for pennies?"

"Lay off."

"O.K., it's your life."

"Don't be sore. I just don't want no charity."

Danny slapped him across the back. "Let's get back to the barracks and study."

They stepped from the PX and took off up the arched arcade again. A wind whistled over the parade ground.

"Getting chilly."

"I'm thinking," Ski said as they paced briskly. "Maybe I can get into the paratroopers. There's fifty per cent more pay."

"I wish you'd let me write my dad."

"No."

Marion ran breathless up to them. "Ski, Ski! The word just came through. Congress has passed the pay bill—retroactive!"

"From the halls of no mazuma, to the shores of triple pay! What did I tell you, Danny—what did I tell you. I'll have her out here in no time."

"I got to find L.Q. and tell him," Marion raced on.

"Christ, fifty-four scooties a month. Man, we're millionaires!" They saluted a passing officer.

"Figure out how much I've got coming with the retroactive, Danny. Figure it out."

"Let's see . . ."

"Danny . . . Ski!" They spun about. It was Milton Norton. "Hey, professor, did you hear about the pay bill passing?"

"Yes, great, isn't it? I was looking for you fellows all over. I wanted to say good-bye. The Pioneers are shipping out."

"Honest?"

"Yes, just got the word. We're on twenty-four-hour stand-by now."

"Hell," Danny said, "that might mean a week."

"I don't think so."

"I guess that means no furlough, Nort."

"I guess so."

"That's the way the ball bounces, Danny," Norton said, shrugging his shoulders.

"Well, good luck, professor—give them hell." Ski extended his hand.

"Ski."

"Yeah."

"That offer I made. About having Susan stay with my wife. It still goes."

"Thanks, anyhow. I figure just a couple of months now and I'll have enough saved to send for her."

"Any idea where you're going?"

"No use trying to second guess the Corps. They probably don't know themselves. I've got a hunch we may try a strike to stem any further advance toward Australia. Scuttlebutt says the First Division is on the move already."

"An invasion. . . ."

"Well, we won't worry about it now."

"Come on, Nort. I'll buy you a soda."

"I'll sail for that."

"Count me out," Ski said. "I'd better hit those books before taps. Good luck again, professor." They shook hands warmly and Ski marched off down the long arcade.

Danny and Nort found an empty booth. "How do you feel, excited?" Danny asked.

"Sort of."

"I . . . I was kind of hoping the Pioneers would stick around long enough for me to get out of school. I thought maybe I could get in."

"I thought you wanted the Sixth Marines? Now that they are back from Iceland."

"Well, it would have been nice with us shipping out in the same outfit, Nort." He drew on his straw. "If we get split up on addresses, you can always get mine from Baltimore. I want to stay in touch."

"That's a deal."

Danny emptied the bottom of his glass and dug his spoon into the ice cream and chewed on it, disinterestedly.

"Anything wrong, Danny?"

"Hell, you've got enough on your mind without hearing my T.S. story."

"What is it, kid?"

"Nort," he sputtered, "I talked to Kathy tonight. With the way things have been going the past couple of weeks, I was glad. I was beginning to feel that I was throwing her off. I didn't like getting like I did that Sunday I borrowed your I.D. card. But I heard her voice, and it hit me. I'm just kidding myself, Nort. I love her too much to ever stop loving her." He lowered his eyes and flipped the spoon on the table.

"I see," Norton whispered.

"I just can't fight it any more, Nort."

"I'm glad, Danny."

"But this Elaine's got me twisted up."

"Why?"

"I could understand it if she was a tramp. But dammit, Nort, any guy would be proud to have a wife like her. She came up from scratch, poor family, houseful of girls, she married money. Sure, she's pretty cold and calculating . . . but she's got a head on her shoulders. Besides everything in the world a woman could ask for—money, looks, ambition, position."

"And what has that to do with it?"

"Everything. She might be Kathy or . . ."

"Or my wife?"

"Yes."

Norton drew on his cigarette. "Yes, she may well be."

"Nort, did you ever think of another guy in bed with your wife?"

"A man doesn't like to think about that, but he can't keep it from flashing through his mind sometimes, I suppose."

"When I'm with her, I think to myself, suppose it was Kathy? If it could be Elaine, it could be Kathy. The thought of another guy . . . I tell you, it can drive you crazy."

"Danny, wait. Do you really believe it of Kathy? Do you?"

"No," he said. "No."

"Can't you see Elaine?"

"Maybe I can't."

"It doesn't make any difference how much money her husband made or where she went to school or who her friends are. Why, the whorehouses are filled with college girls. Elaine Yarborough is like a million wives. She's lived in a ghetto, in a circle of boredom. Subconscious or conscious, she wants to escape. Some women do it through cheap love stories in women's magazines, some live in a world of fantasy, some join women's clubs, some drive their husbands beyond their capabilities. Just an age-old frustration, Danny. They look at their stagnant lives and the compromise they call a husband. And they look at the years they have ahead, going on existing when all the promise life held has gone . . . and a war comes, Danny. A woman like Elaine Yarborough runs away from the vicious cycle and comes to a city full of chaos and hysteria. For a moment she finds herself free—and in comes the fairy prince."

"Damned if I feel like a fairy prince."

"Oh, very funny. A young handsome lover, then. And all the frustration years burst out. For a flash, a wild moment, she forgets her years of falseness and she is herself. . . . Hell, kid, it's an old pattern. She'll go back to Vernon Yarborough. She's used to comfort."

"So I'm just a pawn in a frustration complex. Or as Andy says, some other guy would be in her pants if it wasn't me."

"Just an interlude. Families, once stable and solid, are undergoing an upheaval and women like Elaine are bound to act crazily."

"And your wife, and Kathy?"

"The strong find courage. I pray, and you do too, that we have a little more to offer. That we can build on mutual interest and something deeper than money or sex. In plain English, loving her every minute of every day and telling her so and letting her know that she is the most important one in your life. Never take your love for granted, kid. Work at it. Oh sure, I say it couldn't happen to me. But I suppose it could. Frankly, I think Gib and I are too much a part of each other to let a little thing like a war hurt our marriage."

"She'd have to be off her rocker to hurt a guy like you, Nort. So to hell with the Vernon Yarboroughs and three cheers for you and me."

Danny smiled and they arose from the booth. He put his arm about Nort's thin shoulder as they walked slowly over the parade ground toward the Pioneer tents.

"What's the payoff, Nort?"

"What am I fighting for, Danny? That's easy—peace of mind."

"Peace of mind," Danny whispered. "Peace of mind. You make everything sound so damned simple. That's what I like about you."

"It sounds simple, but sometimes it isn't so simple to get."

"Nort?"

"Yes."

"Do they have an engineering course at Penn?"

"I suppose so, why?"

"Oh, sounds kind of a long way off, but I was thinking that

I'd like to sit in a classroom and listen to your brand of bullcrap by the hour after the war."

"What do you mean, bullcrap? I'll have you know I teach only by the latest, approved methods."

Danny spun his glass so the ice cubes tinkled against its sides. He gazed out of the window, down on San Diego from the Skyroom Cocktail Lounge. It was quiet, plushy, and nestled on the top floor of a tall hotel.

"I should be angry, Danny," Elaine said. "I waited for over an hour at the gate."

"I phoned, but you had already left. It was impossible for me to get liberty last night." He drew a leg up on the leather seat and continued gazing below.

"Is anything wrong?"

He didn't answer. She reached nervously for a cigarette and studied him for a long spell.

"Why didn't you come last night?"

"I had to study . . . besides, I was broke."

"You know that doesn't make any difference."

"It does to me."

"Danny?"

"Yes."

"We're washed up, aren't we?" she asked softly. He turned, looked into her anxious eyes and nodded. She crushed out her cigarette and bit her lip. "It sort of completes the circle. Danny Forrester, All-American boy. I knew you'd catch up with yourself sooner or later." He emptied the glass and set it down on the table slowly and fiddled with it. "The little girl . . . Kathy?"

"Yes."

"What would you say if I told you I was going to have a baby?"

"You're too smart for that, Elaine. We both knew it was going to kiss off sooner or later. You're not going to make it rough, are you?"

"Of course not, darling," she answered stiffly.

"I don't guess there's much of anything to say?"

"You think I'm a tramp, don't you, Danny?"

"No."

"Don't be nice."

"Any guy in the world would be lucky to have you for a wife. I guess it's just one of those things that happened that wouldn't have happened if the world was in its right senses."

"Do you know what I was going to do when you told me this? I was going to make a fight, Danny. I was going to make it rough for you. For a while nothing mattered, Vernon, Arlington Heights—nothing. I wanted to be the girl in the Andes cabin. I suppose all women want that type of thing. . . ."

"Elaine, please don't."

"Could you see me in a snowbound shack in the mountains? No, I don't suppose either of us can . . . I . . . want to go home now and wait. Get away from this rotten town."

"Want another drink? The waiter is looking at us."

"No."

He drummed his fingers on the table restlessly.

"Danny, tonight—farewell?"

He shook his head. She turned away, reached into her purse for a handkerchief and hid her eyes. "Maybe I should go out and get drunk. Maybe some other Marine will take pity on me."

She felt his strong young hand on her shoulder. He squeezed it, and in spite of herself it sent a thrill through her body. She dabbed her eyes and looked up. He was gone.

PART TWO

Prologue

MAJOR HUXLEY called us into his office after a few weeks—all the old-timers. It was none too soon.

Burnside, Keats and I had been a bit more hopeful about the communicators at first. We felt we would at least get the cream of the crop, if there was any cream. We stood by anxiously as the word passed down that Class 34 was graduating from Radio School at the base, and that part of it was being sent to us. The only other radioman we had on hand was Spanish Joe Gomez. We had him tabbed as a troublemaker.

Well, they turned out to be a bitter disappointment. The task that lay ahead of us old-timers seemed impossible. There they were, poor excuses for Marines, much less for radiomen. The whole gang couldn't send or receive with my speed, and I'm not good any more.

What did we get? A drawling Texan, a big Swede, the Forrester kid, the Feathermerchant, L.Q. the Clown, Marion Hodgkiss with his fancy music, Seabags the farmer, and that Injun. What a bunch! Burnside stayed drunk for a week. Gunner Keats tried to get a transfer. Sam Huxley groaned openly when the first field problems turned out to be a mess.

"You fellows are probably thinking the same as I am," he said. "How the hell are we going to win the war with these eightballs?"

We murmured in agreement. "They don't look like Marines, they don't act like Marines." We again agreed.

"But remember this, men. They are here because they want to be here, the same as you and me. The Corps, as we once knew it, is gone forever. We might as well reconcile ourselves to that fact. It's getting big, bigger every minute. I visualize three, maybe four divisions of Marines before this war is over."

The estimate seemed impossible. Why, that would be over a hundred thousand men!

"I know what we are up against, we have a lot of work to do. You men know me well enough to understand that when I say work, I mean work. You old-timers have to help me. Curse at them, take them to a saloon, show them what the inside of a whorehouse looks like. Make Marines out of them!

"We all had buddies on Wake, the Philippines, in Shanghai. We don't like what happened to the Corps. We don't like losing. So remember, men, it is going to be a long road back and we can't get back without these kids. Er . . . er, one more thing. You staff NCOs, Mac, Burnside, McQuade, Paris and the rest of you—What I want to say now isn't for publication. We're liable to be getting some officers, too, that, well, may be a little green. Help them along."

1.

IT DIDN'T take me long to discover that Spanish Joe Gomez was the biggest thief, liar, and goldbricker in the Marine Corps. We had a hot potato on our hands. He had a mean streak in him, a mile wide. The first time we realized how ornery he was came shortly after he joined the outfit at Eliot.

We were on liberty, making a round of the slopshutes in Dago and had just entered the Porthole. I was half tanked and trying to make time with a barfly when Gomez poked me in the ribs and said, "I'm gonna have me some fun, Mac. Pick out the biggest swab jockey in the joint." I pointed to a two-hundred-and-twenty-pound sailor bending over a beer a few feet away. Spanish Joe edged his way next to him. "Got a match, mate?"

The unconcerned and unsuspecting victim slid a light down the bar. Joe lit up and put the lighter into his pocket.

"Hey, my lighter."

Joe looked amazed. "What lighter?"

"I said give back my lighter."

"I ain't got no lighter of yours. You accusing me of stealing?"

"You looking for a beef, Marine?"

Gomez was aghast, then sheepish. He fumbled through his pockets and handed the lighter over.

"I oughta bust you one in the teeth," the sailor sneered.

"Gee . . . I . . . I'm sorry, mate. I ain't looking for no trouble."

"I oughta bust you in the teeth," he repeated loudly.

Three bouncers moved up quickly to the scene of trouble.

"This here swab jockey accused me of stealing his lighter," Joe pleaded.

"I oughta . . ." The sailor cocked his fist. A flying squad caught him quickly and moved him toward the door. Spanish

Joe shoved his way through the drinking mob after him. Outside, he approached the very irked gob.

"Say, deck ape. I'm really sorry. . . ."

The sailor turned purple. "I ain't looking for no fight," Joe begged, backing away. The gob wound up and let a right hand fly from the boondocks. Joe deftly dodged the punch a quarter inch from his jaw, the momentum of the swing sending the man in blue whirling to the deck. Gomez bent over and assisted him to his feet, brushing him off. "I ain't looking for no fight."

Enraged, the sailor lurched out again, missing again, again falling down. Joe picked up the man's little white hat. "Gee, you'll get it all dirty."

Again and again he swung, each time catching nothing more solid than the evening air, after coming tantalizingly close to his tormentor's jaw. At last he gave up. "Let's shake, mate, so's there ain't no hard feelings," Joe offered. Realizing the futility of his attempts, the bewildered sailor extended his hand.

At this point Spanish Joe unleashed a lightning pair of punches, knocking the man senseless to the sidewalk. "Imagine the nerve of that guy—accusing me of stealing his lighter. Just for that I'm going to take it." And he did.

It is said that on a good night, Spanish Joe left a trail of ten or perhaps a round dozen prostrate bodies of sailors and dogfaces littered about San Diego.

We were catching up on sack drill and letter writing after evening chow, having knocked off a stiff ten-mile hike with full combat pack. To my surprise, not one of the squad had fallen flat on his face.

In a far corner, by himself, Marion Hodgkiss lay on his sack engrossed in a book by some fellow called Plato. Speedy Gray, the Texan, slowly shined up his battle pin with a blitz cloth and mournfully sang:

> "Send me a letter
>   Send it by mail,
>   Send it in care of,
>   The Birmingham jail."

Now this Hodgkiss fellow was one for the books. I had never quite met a guy like him in four hitches in this lash-up. He did his work well, but he was the only Marine in captivity who neither smoked, drank, gambled, cursed, or chased the broads. On liberty call, when the rest were champing at the bit, Hodgkiss just lay there poring through those books and listening to classical music on his record player. In a gang of sex-mad gyrenes, it isn't easy to stick to stuff like that. But they all had to admire Marion. When the nightly arguments came and bets were on the table, Marion proved himself to be a walking encyclopedia. He was final authority on whatever subject we happened to differ about—the population of Kalamazoo in 1896, or the number of hairs on the human head. Marion knew everything. And he was sweet, polite, and as decent as Spanish Joe Gomez wasn't.

Joe, having stolen a skivvy shirt from L.Q. Jones and given it to someone else for getting his shoes shined, sauntered up to Marion with trouble brewing in his gait.

"Hey, you."

Marion did not look up from his book.

"Hey, I'm talking to you, Sister Mary."

"What do you want?"

"I hear you used to box in school."

"A little."

"Well, I'm learning to box and I'd like a couple of pointers. Let's step out to the ring and spar a few rounds."

"The hike tired me out, I'd rather not."

"You aren't chicken, are you, Sister Mary?"

Marion carefully marked his book, placed it in his seabag, took off his glasses and set them carefully in his breast pocket. "Let's go," he said.

Spanish Joe winked to us and followed him to the door. We all dropped our business and poured out after them.

The gloves were laced on Sister Mary and I whispered in his ear, "This guy fought professional. Why don't you just fall down after the first time he hits you? Nobody will think you're chicken." Marion gazed at the ring mat, deaf to my plea. We all saw, though, that he had some muscles of his own, with shoulders like a medium tank.

"Take it easy on me, Sister Mary," Gomez called across the ring.

"The bastard," I sneered between my teeth.

We gathered close about the apron of the ring as L.Q. called "Time!" This was going to be awful. It was. Spanish Joe was the two-round world's champ light heavyweight. His rapier left jab flicked out at Marion a hundred times from a hundred different angles. The broad-shouldered book reader moved after him with the grace of a pregnant elephant. His wild blows never even dented Joe's shadowy form. He backed Joe into a corner, Joe spun him around and clobbered him. Hooks, jabs, uppercuts, but Marion kept coming on. His ribs were red and his face starting to look like a hunk of raw liver. I said a Hail Mary, wondering what was holding him up. Toward the end of the round Joe's left came in slower and Marion's punches got closer.

The content of an entire gin mill was finding its way through Spanish Joe's pores.

"Time!"

I wiped the blood from Marion's face. He sat there staring at the deck. Joe leaned on the ropes breathing heavily. "I guess that's about it for today, huh kid. Unlace my gloves, Danny."

Marion Hodgkiss arose and walked over to Gomez. "I'm just getting warmed up, let's go."

A smile lit up Joe's face. "O.K., the joke's over, I don't want to hurt you. That's enough."

"Yellow?" Sister Mary asked softly.

Gomez looked stunned. He gazed from the corner of his eyes at the men gathered around the ring. He rolled his tongue about the top of his sweat-beaded lip. "O.K., kid," he said viciously, "let's go."

We clung to the bottom strand of the ropes. "Time," Jones croaked.

Spanish Joe moved slowly to the center of the ring, the sweat making him shine like a panther stalking for the kill. He mustered every ounce of his whisky-soaked strength and lashed out with a right hand. It caught Sister Mary in the mouth with a sharp snapping echo. Joe dropped his hands, his face wreathed in a victor's smile, and stepped back to make room for Marion to fall.

Not only was Marion Hodgkiss upright, but he uncorked a right uppercut from the top of his boondockers, powerful enough to sink the U.S.S. *Pennsylvania*. Gomez, caught flush on the button, was lifted six inches off the deck and landed in a crumpled heap. We all jumped into the ring, showering hugs and kisses on Marion's swollen face and lovingly escorted him back to the barracks. We just let Spanish Joe lay there.

Fifteen minutes later, Gomez had rejoined the living. We were still gathered about his sack; Marion playing coy, engrossed in his Plato. We eyed Spanish Joe stalking into the barracks and cleared a path. Sister Mary turned a page and adjusted his glasses.

"Hey, kid." No answer. "Hey kid, that was a lucky punch, you know that!" Marion withdrew a handkerchief and blew his nose. "To show you there ain't no hard feelings, let's shake hands."

Sister Mary again lay his book down and arose. Spanish Joe extended his hand. Marion let fly a punch sinking almost elbow deep into Joe's guts. Gomez groaned, clutched his belly and sank to the deck.

"Now what the hell did you do that for?" he cried.

Marion bent over and assisted him to his wobbly feet. "I'm sorry, Gomez, but I don't go around shaking hands with rattlesnakes until I'm sure all the poison has been removed."

Gomez scratched his head in an attempt to digest the remark. Mary went back to his book as Joe slipped onto the edge of the sack.

"What you reading?"

"Plato."

"You mean they wrote a whole book like that about Mickey Mouse's dog, huh?" The white teeth of Gomez showed themselves in a smile. "Hey kid, I like you. What you think of Spanish Joe?"

"I think you are the most obnoxious person I've ever met."

"What's this obnoxious?"

"You stink."

Spanish Joe Gomez threw his arms about Marion. "Hey kid, you sure got guts to talk to ole Joe that way. Me and you is going to be buddy-buddies."

Sister Mary turned the page.

Politics and war make strange bedfellows. That's how it began. The buddy-buddy relationship of the most one-way bastard in creation and the guy who was most likely to win sainthood. We all liked this friendship because Marion kept Joe in line and out of our seabags. Hodgkiss took over Gomez's money at pay call and squared away his accumulated debts. The two went on liberty call together, Joe tanking up, Mary usually in an empty booth pouring down the classics of literature. When Joe got boisterous, Marion stepped in, averted the clash and moved him on. More than once we saw Joe trudge home dejected, head bowed and hands in pockets.

"What's the scoop, Joe?"

"I got my ass in a sling," he'd answer sheepishly.

"Why?"

"I borrowed an overseas cap from the Indian and forgot to return it, and Marion caught me." It was hard to keep from laughing. "Mary read the Rocks and Shoals to me, he really give me the word. No liberty for a week and I got to go to church Sunday."

"Maybe I'd better tell him about the way you doped off on that ditch digging detail yesterday."

"You wouldn't rat on me, Mac, would you, buddy? I can't stand another lecture today."

"We'll see."

"Jesus H. Christ on a crutch. I'm a bad hombre, I'm just a bad hombre."

I had finished guard rounds with Gunner Keats and returned to the S.G. tent. Sister Mary, on Corporal of the Guard, was on the edge of his sack, crouched close to the dim light in the center of the tent, reading the *Saturday Review of Literature.*

"All the planes tucked in safe?" he greeted me.

"Where the hell did they dig up this crap detail, guarding them goddam egg crates. Haven't they ever heard of communicators in this goddam outfit? Why, in the old Corps, Marion . . ."

"Only four more days." He laughed at my anger.

"Gets colder than a well digger's ass out on this prairie," I said, blowing into my hands, kneeling and turning up the kerosene stove.

"There's some hot coffee there, Mac."

I tilted my canteen cup, took a long swig, and smacked my lips. "Say, Mary, it's three o'clock. You'd better get some sack drill."

He flipped the magazine to the deck, yawned, and took the cup from me. "I didn't realize it was so late."

"Marion."

"Yes, Mac."

"It isn't any of my business, but could you tell me something?"

"If I can."

"Well, er, what about all those books?"

"The books?"

"Yeah, the books."

I could hear the cold wind whistle, flapping our tent. He unbuckled his duty NCO belt, unclipped the pistol and laid it on an empty cot.

"Mac, someday I'm going to be a writer. I guess you think it's kind of silly."

"Hell no. No ambition is silly. Have you got talent?"

"I don't know, Mac."

"You've got something scrambled up in your head. Something that's nixing you all the time. I spotted it right away. I guess when you've been around men as long as I have, you can almost read their minds." Marion looked at me hard, then seemed to loosen up. I lay back watching the weird shadows being tossed by the bare lightbulb gently swinging from the tent top.

"I came from a small town," Marion went on. "My dad is a retired railroad man. You might say nothing has ever really happened to me," he fumbled.

"And you've wanted to write ever since you were a kid?"

"Yes. But . . . but when I try to, or even talk sometimes, I get tied up into knots. I'm living wonderful things to write about now. But I just can't seem to find the right key. Like Andy says when they have a log jam. There is one key log that will turn the whole thing loose and float them down the river. You've got to take your peavey pole and loosen the key log. . . . I don't suppose you understand."

"I think maybe I do."

"You see what kind of a guy I am. I can't even talk to people without stuttering." He sat down and blushed at his outburst.

"You have a girl, Marion?"

"No."

"Ever been in bed with a woman?"

"No."

"Look here, kid. I don't read Plato, that stuff is a little over me. But there's nothing the matter with you that . . . hell, it's late. Let's get some sack drill."

Major Malcowitz, the huge ex-wrestler in charge of Judo training at Eliot, called us in close about the mats. He spoke through beaten lips.

"All right, youse guys has already loined in past lessons the fine arts of disarming, surprising, breaking ju-jitsu holds, and applying your own tactics. I want one sizable volunteer for the last lesson." We all shied back. He smiled. "You," he said, pointing to the gangly Shining Lighttower, whom Seabags Brown shoved on the mat before he could turn tail.

"Lay down," the major requested, tripping the Indian to the deck with a thud. "Thank you." Lighttower lay prone, looking rather dubiously at the wrestler, who had now propped a foot on his chest. "The last lesson is the most important, so you birds pay attention. Once you got your enemy off his feet, you gotta finish him off quick and quiet."

"I want to go back to the reservation," Private Lighttower moaned.

"The foist step is falling, knees first, onto the Jap's chest, thereby crushing in his ribs." He demonstrated gently on the shaking redskin. "You next bring the heels of both hands over his ears, thereby cracking the base of his skull." A dull murmur sounded throughout the platoon. "Youse guys then take two quick swipes with the flat of your hand, first over the bridge of his nose, busting in his face and blinding him. Second, at the base of his neck, thusly cracking the bastard's spinal column."

The major glanced about at the awed faces. "For neatness, use both thumbs, jamming down into his Adam's apple, thereby choking him. To polish the job you may kick him between the legs, square in the balls, a couple or three times." Malcowitz stood up. "You may then admire your masterpiece—but if that son of a bitch gets up you'd better take off like a stripe-assed ape."

2.

SPANISH JOE had a heavy load on. Sister Mary dragged him from the College Inn down back streets to the YMCA at the foot of Broadway. The Camp Eliot bus pulled in and Marion poured Gomez across the back seat and left him.

He crossed the main drag and walked along the docks until he came to the Coronado ferry slip. He purchased a ticket and boarded the boat. Quickly climbing the ladder from the auto deck, he found a seat by the rail. The whistle screamed as the ferry slid from her moorings. Marion Hodgkiss propped his feet on the rail, loosened his field scarf, unhooked his fair leather belt and ran it through a shoulder epaulet. He gazed down into the gently lapping water as the ferry chugged for Coronado Island.

Out there, in the quiet and dark, a guy could organize his thoughts better. Away from the sweating, swearing, griping, groaning, back-breaking chores of soldiering. Away from the city gone mad. The tin-plated main street where the sharpies and the filchers passed out watered-up liquor and sticky songs to deaden the loneliness of the hordes of men in khaki, blue, and forest green. Away from the dumps where an ugly wench was the sought-after prize for men who closed their eyes and pretended she was someone else. Away from the lights of the aircraft factories burning twenty-four hours a day at a crazed pace—and from the out of bounds hotels where only the plentiful dollars of the officers were solicited. Away too from the blistering hot feet from a hike in Rose Canyon, from the hum of the generator and the eternal whine of dots and dashes beating through your earphones.

Out here, he thought, just a gentle old boat, a kind moon and the water. . . . A guy can organize his thoughts.

"Do you have a match, Marine?"

Corporal Hodgkiss looked up. A girl leaned against the rail, a redhead. Long flaming locks and very pale blue lifeless eyes with dark, but soft, lines under them. She had that milky white, redhead skin. She was the most beautiful woman he had ever seen. He fumbled for the matches he carried for Spanish Joe. The girl sat down next to him and dragged on her cigarette, making her face glow in the darkness.

"Thanks, Marine." The engine of the ferry seemed to chug

louder. "I've seen you here before, lots of times," she said. The corporal's heart beat very fast. He tried to say something but held up for fear the words would twist up coming out.

"Don't think I'm being forward but I was curious. I travel to Coronado almost every night. You've gotten to be a fixture."

"It's quiet out here, I can think," he said.

"Lonesome?"

"No, not really."

"Thinking of your girl, I'll bet."

"I haven't got a girl."

She smiled. "No one has a girl back home when he's talking to a woman in San Diego."

"I'm not one of those hungry guys who'd make a damned fool of himself to buy a few minutes' conversation, if that's what the insinuation is. I like it out here. I can get a rest from ... that rat race."

"Say—I'll bet you really don't have a girl."

"I said I didn't."

"Please, mister, don't bite my head off. All I wanted was a match."

Marion blushed. "I'm sorry, miss, I'm sorry if I raised my voice. I guess I'm a dull character, but there isn't much that excites me in town. I like it better here."

The redhead snuffed her cigarette out on the rail and flipped it overboard and watched it swirl crazily to the water.

"What do you think about, Marine?"

"I'm thinking about how I'd like to write about all the things happening around me. The war, this city, my outfit ... I guess you think I'm off my trolley." He didn't know why he'd said that, but it just seemed to come out natural like.

"How old are you?"

"Nineteen."

"A completely honest gyrene. You are one for the books. You should have said twenty-five to impress me."

"Is it a crime to be nineteen?"

The boat creaked against the dock. She arose. Marion stumbled from his seat as she turned to leave. "My ... my name's Marion, Marion Hodgkiss ... you ... you said you took the boat often ... so do I ... maybe I'll see you again?"

"Could be." She turned and walked away. His eyes followed her until she disappeared into the darkness of Coronado.

Corporal Hodgkiss took a time check for the fifth time as the ferry pulled into San Diego. It was twelve-thirty. An ear-to-ear grin lit his face as he spotted the slim redhead coming up the gangplank.

"Hello, Rae," he beamed.

"Hello, Marion," she answered.

"You look tired. I'll get you a cup of coffee."

"Thanks. I am beat."

"I've got two seats by the rail." She flipped her fiery locks over her shoulder and took a cigarette from her purse. Marion quickly reached over and lit it for her.

"Rae."

"Yes."

"I . . . uh, brought something. I . . . thought you might like it."

"What?"

"A book. Would you like me to read you something?"

"What is it?"

Marion fidgeted. "Sonnets of Shakespeare."

"Shakespeare?"

"Yes, Shakespeare."

"But I don't understand that stuff very well."

"Maybe, if you'd like, I could sort of explain it as we went along."

Rae stretched out, easy like, her face towards the sky. She closed her eyes and drew from her cigarette. Marion opened the book.

The next weeks they worked hard and grueling hours learning their new trade. Learning that every man is a rifleman and must know every job in the battalion. They crawled through and under double-strand barbed wire, drilled for speed in breaking and setting their field radios, learned to cut blisters, and the arts of camouflage, map reading, and pole skinning, as well as telephone operation, message center work, codes, the use of all weapons and grenade throwing, crawling under live ammunition cover, battle tactics, judo and hand to hand, and knife throwing.

They were thrown from ten-foot platforms into the swimming pool with full packs on and they were sent into tents full of live tear gas and made to sing the Marine Hymn before being let out. When they weren't learning they were marching.

And the eternal ring in their ears: "On the double! We ain't got no place for stragglers in the Marine Corps! Hi di hi for Semper Fi!"

They'd answer, "Semper Fi! Hooray for me and screw you!"

Seabags Brown slammed his Reising gun down on his bunk angrily. "Dirty no good armpit-smelling son of a bitch. These goddam pieces are worthless as tits on a boar hog," the farmer ranted.

"Yeah," Ski agreed.

"Yeah," Andy added.

"I shot 'expert' at the range," Danny said, "and look at this goddam thing. I never hit a bullseye all day, even inside fifty yards."

"The bastard that sold them to the Marines ought to have his balls cut off."

"Semi-automatic machine gun," Danny continued. "Christ, my kid brother's Daisy air rifle is deadlier than this thing."

"Lookit, cousin," Seabags said, showing his clips, "rusted. I just cleaned them yesterday and oiled them down and lookit, rusted."

"How about that, Mary?"

"They aren't what you might call the finest weapons in the world," Marion sighed.

"Look at that blueing job on the barrel," Speedy Gray said. "I can damn near rub it off with my fingernail—and them sights, jumping Jesus. How they expect us to protect ourselves with this goddam thing?"

"How about that wire stock? Mother, I've come home to die."

"Maybe," Marion mused, "that's why they teach us so much knife and Ju-do."

"I'd like to see the guy that can hold one of these down firing automatic. Bursts of three, Mac says. Step on the sling so the gun won't jump. The first shot and the goddam gun is pointing up in the sky and I'm sitting on my ass."

"Maybe they were designed for antiaircraft."

"Mine clogged four times today."

I moved over to the bitching session. "Gunner Keats says you guys better learn to shoot these pieces," I said.

"They ain't no fugging good, Mac!"

"I don't give a big rat's ass what you guys think! Maybe if we hike to Rose Canyon for target practice, your aim might get sharper."

"Mac," Danny said, "how did *you* shoot today?" I turned and walked away.

"I guess I need a little practice too," I said as I picked up my gun and shook my head sadly.

Saturday inspection! We stood restlessly by our bunks and looked them over for a fiftieth time, flicking away a stray speck of dust or smoothing out a minute wrinkle.

"Tenshun," First Sergeant Pucchi barked and there was a popping of leather heels as Major Huxley and his staff marched into the room. Pucchi followed with a pad and pencil to take the Major's notations on any fault his X-ray eyes found.

He passed them slowly, looking us over from head to toe—

then our bunks. He wore white gloves and ran them over the windowsills seeking dust.

"Open your seabag, corporal." Marion obeyed. "Very good, corporal."

"Thank you, sir."

There is a way to do everything and it is written in the book and Huxley inspected by the book.

"Lift your trousers," he ordered of Zvonski. "Your socks are not rolled in a regulation manner, Marine."

"Yes, sir."

"Receive instructions from your sergeant."

"Yes, sir."

A hush as he moved slowly down the aisle. Huxley's gimlet eyes scanned every nook and corner. The few minutes seemed hours and he walked to the door. "Generally, very good, Sergeant Pucchi. Take care of the notations I ordered." He turned and left and a big sigh went up and the tenseness relaxed into a mass of lit cigarettes.

The whistle blew. "Fall in for rifle inspection." We donned our blouses, strapped on our fair leather belts and put on our overseas caps. Each man looked over another man, straightening a field scarf, adjusting the angle of the cap, or brushing a spot of lint from the blouse.

We checked our weapons again and moved out to the company street and stepped softly over the dirt lest we ruin the mirror shine on our shoes.

"Fall in and dress down the ranks!" Right arms shot out sidewards and heads left to straighten the line. Mac walked through his platoon and then to the front. He was satisfied.

"Ready . . . front!" They came to attention. "At Ease."

Exchanges of salutes, roll call, more salutes and a rigid man-by-man inspection.

"Little too much oil on the barrel, Marine."

"Yes, sir."

"Stock looks fine. Keep it up."

Each officer had a trick method of tossing the weapon about as he inspected it. The classier ones handled the pieces as though they were batons. The Marine accepted his weapon in the prescribed military manner, snapping the chamber shut, squeezing the trigger, and returning to the order.

After inspection, an hour of close order drill. More, if the inspection was bad. Then, weekend liberty.

In a book I had once read, by a dogface, he wrote that the Marines spent all week shining up for a ten-hour liberty, or something to that effect. Looking back over the years, I felt his observation was an understatement. How they looked going out and how they looked coming back in, of course, was two different matters.

I always got that good feeling when I passed a Marine in town. He had that sharp shine and gait, like he was something special and knew it. Lots of times I felt sick looking at some of the dogfaces. There is a certain dignity, I think, that comes with a uniform and it must be rotten to belong to an outfit that doesn't have enough pride to keep that dignity up. I hated to see a man slouching, cap cocked back, in need of a haircut, shoes unshined . . . maybe, it was because the price of Marine greens came so high to a man that he never let himself get that way.

"O.K., men! Off your dead asses and on your dying feet! Hit the road!"

They dragged themselves up, cursing the day they entered the Corps. The first twenty-mile hike was always rough. I watched the sweat pouring into their eyes and soaking their dungarees as they strained at the handles of the equipment cart. Their rifles hung from the gun sling like lead weights. The two-pound helmets shot unbearable aches down the neck, the tongues were swollen with thirst under water discipline, the pack straps cut into the armpits like machete knives, the ammo belts hung like ropes pulling them into the deck.

L.Q. Jones pulled alongside Danny. "I walked into this here recruiting station. Drunk, mind you," he puffed. "The sergeant is measuring me with a tailor's tape and calling out my measurements to a corporal, who is writing all this down." Seabags Brown and Andy Hookans crossed the road and joined them. "Yes sir, this bastard says, when you get to San Diego, Mr. Jones, your dress blues will be waiting for you. I'll telegraph your measurements tonight. Just tell them who you are when you get there . . . now MISTER Jones, just sign here." You just had to laugh when L.Q. told a story. "I tell you men, if I ever get my meathooks on that bastard I'll rip him open from asshole to appetite. I'll give him a G.I. bath. Dress blues. Ha, I'm laughing."

"All right, you guys," I barked. "Knock off the skylarking and file up those ranks!"

L.Q. Jones began singing:

> *"Oh, the sergeant, the sergeant,*
> *The bastard of them all,*
> *He gets you up in the morning,*
> *Before the bugle call,*
> *Squads right, squads left,*

Front face in that line,
And then the dirty son of a bitch,
Will give you double time."

The whole platoon joined in the chorus:

"Oh, hidy tidy, Christ almighty,
Who in the hell are we,
Zim, zam, GOD DAMN,
The fighting Sixth Marines!"

I hated to admit it, but this gang of kids was beginning to shape up. It was a damned good thing that the earth was two thirds water, I thought, because before Highpockets Huxley got through with them, there weren't many routes they'd miss.

"Straighten up that line," I yelled, "and knock off the singing!"

Marion hadn't taken his eyes off Rae all evening. They had been riding back and forth nearly five hours. The first struggling rays of daylight fought their way up on the horizon. He hummed a tune, softly. "That's how it ends, Gilda had taken the Duke's place and was stabbed. The old hunchback bends over, holding her in his arms as he cries that the curse has been fulfilled, and the curtain falls."

"Just like a man," Rae sighed. "It's a beautiful opera and so many pretty songs. I didn't know one person could write so many." She looked at him lazily. "It's almost daybreak, Marion; don't you have to be back in camp?"

"I have a little time," he answered. "It's Friday—that means field day. Clean up for Saturday inspection. Old Man Huxley inspects the barracks with white gloves on."

"Sam Huxley?"

"That's right, how did you know?"

"I've heard of him."

"Rae."

"Yes, Marion."

"Well—look, Rae, couldn't we meet in San Diego next liberty and you and I go to dinner and a show or something?"

The redhead bit her lip. "I like it here on the boat, same as you do. Couldn't we just go on meeting and . . . oh, now I've hurt your feelings."

"I thought that . . . well, it's been over a month and I kind of felt you liked me."

"Marion, I do like you. I like you a lot."

"I'm just a nice kid, is that it?"

"Golly, fellow, do you think I'd sit here with you till five in the morning if . . . well, honestly, Marion, you said yourself you hated the city. Couldn't we just go on meeting here?"

"If you want to make it a big mystery."

"I want to see you, I really do. I like it here with you." The boat creaked against the wharf. The weary hands roped her up.

"I'd better shove off."

"Will I see you Saturday night?" she called after him.

He looked over his shoulder. "Maybe."

I marched my squad past the last barracks in camp into the sand dunes towards the practice landing nets. The rig-up consisted of a sheer wooden wall thirty-five feet high representing the side of a ship. From the top platform hung a heavy cargo net ending in a Higgins boat, nestled in the sand below. The men struggled over the sand with the communications cart bogging down under the weight of a full load of radios.

"If we got to do mules' work, they could at least give us mules' rating. I hear them animals are at least corporals. I think I'll bang ears for a transfer."

"Come on, jackass, turn off the air and pull."

"O.K., you meatheads, take off your packs and stand at ease," I ordered. "If you don't learn anything else in this lash-up, for Chrisake learn how to get up and down these nets and in and out of the assault boats." They were looking up thirty-five feet to the top of the platform, unhappily. "This is simple. Wait till you hit the bow net of a live ship on a choppy sea."

"I want to go back to the reservation, me no like white man's war."

"I ought to run him up one of them sixty-foot redwoods," Andy, the lumberjack, ribbed.

"Mother, I've come home to die."

"Teamwork is essential. Fubar on the nets and you can louse up an entire landing team." I jumped into the boat. "We'll start the problem backwards. Andy, knock off the grab ass and pay attention!" They gathered about. "To get out of this contraption, you place your hands on the guardrail and spring away from the boat, like this." I shot myself clear, tumbling over and chewing up a mouthful of sand. They roared.

"Encore," L.Q. said.

"It isn't funny egghead. It isn't going to hurt to get your panties wet, but it's sure as hell going to hurt if you don't clear the boat and it bounces back on one of your legs . . . besides, I hear they've got new LCTs with drop ramps in the front. Load the gear and cart and we'll practice hitting shore and charging up the beach." I drilled them till their fannies dragged. "Move, you bastards! We got no place for stragglers in the Marine

Corps! Come on, Andy, not head first! Grab that battery case, hang on to it . . . hit the deck, Injun! When going up the net, use your legs and not your arms or you'll be bearing too much weight. Let your legs carry the load. Keep your eyes on your hands at all times . . . four abreast, up the net, let's go."

They tried it. Then I went on, "If you are on the bow net of the ship, you'll have no support from the side of the ship. The net will be swinging free and your pack and gear will pull you upside down. If you feel like you're going to fall, lock your arms in the net and call for help." I led them to the top, climbed the rail to the platform and watched them struggle up, shouting out corrections. Even Andy, an old timer in the timber, didn't find clumsy rope to his liking.

The squad fidgeted uncomfortably on the platform. "O.K. fellows, here we are, on the poop of the U.S.S. *Tuscarora*. All we have to do is get down into the boat with our radios." There was a feeble ripple of laughter. I showed them how to tie and lash guide lines on the heavy gear.

"Line up four abreast at the rail and go over right leg first. That's important because it will set you all in the same position. Unstrap your helmets, put your rifle muzzles down, unfasten your ammo belt and if you fall, dump your gear the way we practiced in the pool. Unless you throw it off, the weight is going to pull you under faster than a stripe-assed gazelle." I went to the rail. "Always keep your hands on the vertical rope so they won't be stepped on by the man above you."

"What's the vertical?" Lighttower queried.

"The rope going this way."

"Oh, that's vertical?"

I climbed back onto the platform. "Finally, and the most important phase, is getting from the net into the landing craft. On open water the boat is going to be bouncing around like a cork. You approach to a point near the boat and wait until it rises on a swell and then jump in. There will be swabbies to hold the nets as rigid as possible. If you go down too low and the boat rises suddenly and slams the side of the ship with you in the middle, you are apt to get a survey out of this outfit—feet first. On your feet. Andy, Mary, Joe, Tex, hit the side. When you get into the boat grab the nets and hold them fast. Next two men take the guide lines as we lower the gear."

They paused a second and then went over the rail, promptly kicking each other's fannies.

"Right leg first, dammit!"

I watched them descend. "Let that goddam helmet drop— we'll buy you another one."

Brown screamed. "Keep those hands on the vertical and they won't get stomped on. Jump into the boat . . . grab the net,

Andy . . . lower the guide lines . . . lash the ropes on the rail so
the radio won't go down on their heads. . . . Over the side, the
rest of you."

I hit the net last and scampered down a free side ahead of
the last relay. L.Q. Jones almost came on top of me with a loud
thud. The puffing squad ran over and helped him to his feet.

"What the hell happened?" I asked.

"My foot got tangled, so I reached down to loosen it," he
groaned.

"With which hand?"

"With both hands." He smiled meekly.

"Give me strength. O.K., girls, back up to the platform."

Corporal Hodgkiss circled anxiously around the promenade
deck of the Coronado ferry. He spotted her sipping a lonely cup
of coffee at the snack counter.

"Hi, Rae." The redhead turned quickly at his voice, smiled,
then looked away from him.

"I ought not to talk to you. You stood me up."

"I know." He grabbed her by the arm and led her outside.
"It's been two weeks, Marion, don't you think . . ."

"I want to show you something." He half dragged her to a
deck chair and sat her down and strutted about in front of her.

"Golly, fellow, what is it?"

"Look."

"What is it?"

"Go on, open it up to the first page, what do you see?"

Her slim fingers unwound the cord about the flap of a large
Manila envelope. She opened it and read slowly, almost spelling
out the words in the dim light. *"Mister Branshly's Retreat, a
short story by Corporal Marion Hodgkiss, USMCR . . .* oh,
Marion!"

He sprang down beside her. "I didn't want to see you till I
finished it. It's about San Diego, the city gone mad . . . about a
banker who had retired and come to San Diego to roll over and
die in the sun. And then the war comes along and upsets his
pretty palm trees and his serene static existence . . . and he finally wakes up and . . ."

"Darling, it sounds wonderful."

"Rae, you called me . . ." He grabbed his cap from his head
and wrung it around. "When I left you the last time, Rae, I was
angry. Then all of a sudden . . ."

"Marion, don't . . ."

"Please let me say it, Rae. I don't get this brave very often.
All the things that were tied up seemed to come out. I began
writing. I realized that it was being able to just talk to you,
like I never have to anyone before . . . someone who listened

and was interested in the way I feel." He slapped his cap against his knee. "Well, you know what I mean." He brought his eyes up to meet hers.

"I almost wish you hadn't of come back," she whispered. "I didn't want this to happen."

"You aren't happy about it? What is it, Rae, tell me . . . please."

Her eyes brimmed with tears. "Yes, I'm happy, really happy. Read it to me, Marion."

He loosened his field scarf, took off his belt and ran it through a shoulder strap. *"Mister Branshly's Retreat, a short story by Corporal Marion Hodgkiss, USMCR."*

3.

I RETURNED to the barrack after morning chow. Feverish preparations were on, preceding the first overnight hike. Danny Forrester approached me.

"The comm cart's all loaded and ready to go, Mac," he said.

"Did you tell the telephone squad to load their crap in the number two cart? That damned switchboard and wires unbalance our load."

"All taken care of. They tried to slip a spool of heavy wire in on us, but I dumped it."

I walked over to my squad and inspected their packs. I opened up Spanish Joe's. "Just like I thought, Gomez. You got it filled with cardboard. Let me see your ammunition clips."

"Aw Jesus, Mac," he whined. I snapped open one of the pockets on his ammo belt. It was empty.

"This stuff too heavy for you, Gomez?"

"I must have forgot to load them up when I cleaned the clips for inspection, Mac."

"You didn't do a very good job of cleaning them. Load them up on the double. What the hell you think this is, a church outing?" I ripped open the top of his seabag, grabbed the forty-five slugs hidden there and threw them on his sack. "And load up that pack."

As I walked away, another item occurred to me. "Let me see your canteen."

"My what?"

"Stand up." He did. I unsnapped the clip, withdrew one, and unscrewed the top. "Dago red!"

"Pardon?"

"Dago red," I repeated, pouring the wine down the front of his shirt. "In five miles you'll be begging water off the squad."

"It must be a trick, Mac, I just filled them with water."

"Gomez, you march directly in front of me. You're going to pull the communications cart from here to Rose Canyon and back and you'd better not ask for a relief, because you aren't getting one. And every time the TBX goes into operation you crank the generator and furthermore, don't forget you're going to have a four-hour watch on the regimental net. Got it!"

"You're picking on me!" he cried. "Wait till I get my hands on the craphead that filled my canteens with Dago red."

I passed on down the squad. Seabags Brown was struggling with his ass pack. The ass pack is a weird innovation for the radio men. They have to carry the large and cumbersome TBY, the walkie-talkie, plus their normal field gear. In order to handle both, the combat pack is rigged so it hangs from suspenders on a level with a man's backside, thus leaving room on his back for the radio. As he walks, the pack slaps against his rear end. On a march with TBY communications, a two-man team was necessary. One to carry the set, the other to walk behind and operate it.

Andy Hookans was dumping a can of footpowder into his boondockers. "You better get over to How Company on the double." I sent the other walkie-talkie men to their infantry companies and went outside to check the cart again.

Marion Hodgkiss and the Feathermerchant, working the command post TBY, waddled out to the company street. Ski was all but lost under the quantity of gear: steel helmet, Reising gun, radio, two canteens of water, machete knife, first-aid pack, two hundred and twenty rounds of ammunition. His ass pack sagged nearly to the ground and was topped by a trenching tool, poncho, and shelter half. He looked sad.

I checked the time. "O.K., Marion, check in with the line outfits, channel fifty-four." He turned the Feathermerchant around, unsnapped the cover of the radio, and twisted the controls. He donned the earphones and mike and plugged them into the set.

"Fresno White to Easy, Fresno White to Easy . . . how do you read me?"

"Easy to Fresno White, five and five . . . over," Speedy Gray drawled from the E Company station.

"Fox to Fresno White, five and five, over," Danny Forrester said.

"George to Fresno White, five and five, over. At the sound of the chimes you shall hear the golden voice of Lamont Quincy Jones, the Sinatra of the Corps, who shall render for you . . ."

"Fresno White to Jones. One of these days somebody is going to be listening to your military procedure and you're going to be pot walloping the rest of the cruise."

I walked over to Marion. "Fat boy Jones cutting up again?"

"No, just giving him a test count," he lied. He test counted Andy in from How Company. Andy's set was on the bum and the reading was poor, but the best that could be gotten.

A sharp blast of First Sergeant Pucchi's whistle sent the Marines of Headquarters tumbling from the barrack into the street. "Fall in!"

Lieutenant Bryce, the new company commander, rounded the barracks.

"Tenshun!" barked Pucchi. A sharp pop of heels. Pucchi saluted Bryce. Bryce saluted Pucchi.

"Report!" ordered Bryce.

Again a salute and about face to us.

"Comm platoon present and accounted for," I said, cutting away my salute.

"Two Section present and accounted for," Sergeant Paris of Bn 2 barked as he saluted.

"Corpsman present and accounted for," Pharmacist Mate Pedro Rojas said, giving the usual tired sailor's salute.

"Bn 4 and utilities present and accounted for," Sergeant Herman, the quartermaster and most popular man of the outfit, said.

The first sergeant about faced to Lieutenant Bryce. "All present and accounted for, sir." They saluted each other.

"At ease." We shifted about trying to ease the weight . . . and there we stood waiting for fifteen minutes.

"Goddammit," the Feathermerchant moaned, lowering the radio from his back, "didn't anybody kiss Huxley and wake him up?"

"There's a right way and a Marine way."

"Me no like um white man's war. Injuns travel light."

"Fresno White from George. My goddam radio is getting heavy . . . tell that goddam Major to start the goddam hike before my goddam back breaks."

"Fresno White from How . . . ditto."

Another fifteen minutes passed. Then the jeeps came flying up the main street and pulled to a sudden stop before us.

"Ah, we can start the war. The brass has arrived."

Major Sam Huxley and his staff debarked from the jeeps. The parade of gold and silver in the morning sun reflected against our eyes: Marine Gunner Keats, the communications officer; Captain Marlin, operations and training; Doc Kyser, the battalion surgeon; Major Wellman, the exec officer; the intelligence officer; and the one and only Major Sam Huxley.

They arrayed themselves before us. Well . . . as long as we

have to have officers to fight a war, I thought, the Marine officers were the best of the lot.

We once again went through the procedure of reporting and saluting. Keats then marched over to Marion. "Message center," he called. Corporal Banks trotted over and handed him a message pad. Gunner Keats wrote out a message and handed it to Sister Mary.

"All companies from Fresno White. Stand by to move out. George Company assume the point of march, over."

"Roger . . . and it's about time . . . out."

In a moment the Marines of George Company moved past us, cut left to the boondocks and the skipper barked an order. "Second platoon, take the advance party . . . first squad take the point!" The men of the second platoon double timed ahead of the rest of the company and fanned out. Far out in front, the battalion scout held up his rifle for them to halt as the advance party took up its position, forming an arrowhead around the battalion. The scout turned and dropped his right arm in the signal 'Forward' and George Company moved out.

"Fox from Fresno White . . . move out, over."

"Fresno White from Fox, Roger, out."

In open route formation, Fox moved past us, led by the skipper, the exec and the first sergeant. Then came the officer of the platoon, pack swinging on his back and his automatic on his hip; beside him, the platoon sergeant, armed with the Reising gun. Then the corporals of each squad of riflemen. Their raw, gaunt muscles leaned them forward to catch the cadence of the march. They were young men, these riflemen, boys of eighteen, nineteen, and twenty. They were the Marines of the Second World War.

Heavy Weapons passed, How Company. This was the bush league artillery support that each battalion carried. Eighty-millimeter mortars, wicked-looking .50-caliber machine guns, a communications cart filled with telephone equipment to link a line between mortars and the battalion command. These were larger boys. They had to be—to bear the weight of the machine gun barrels, the bandoliers and boxes of ammunition, the mortar plates and barrels.

Major Huxley nodded to Bryce.

"Left face." We turned. "Forward harch!" And we fell in line and moved over the boondocks.

"Easy from Fresno White," Marion called, "bring up the rear, over."

"Roger, out."

"All companies from Fresno White, throw out flank guards."

The feet of eight hundred men, Huxley's Whores, shuffled a slow cadence toward the gate that led them to the highway.

The gate swung open, the advance party passed through. M.P.s stopped the flow of vehicles on the highway as the long line of double-filed men passed through. We took up place on either side of the road and as the rear guard closed the gate, the march was on.

Spanish Joe looked at me hopefully as I called for the first relief on the carts. No dice. He was going to get a gut full this trip, if never again.

We turned off the highway onto a dirt road that had led ten thousand Marines before us on a grind that would end twenty miles away in the wooden canyon. We were soon enshrouded in a cloud of dust. Then came the sweat, the eternal sweat which entices the heavy clay dust to stick to our faces. The first goddam mile is always the worst. That's the mile when you're fresh and alert and can feel the weight and the pain, before the numbness sets in.

Time check. Forty-six minutes down, fourteen to go. We were moving about two and a half miles an hour. A pretty good clip for full battalion in heavy marching order. Huxley must be out to find who are the sickbay soldiers and who are the Marines. I felt sorry for the rear guard; probably double timing to keep up.

I looked at Ziltch, the Major's orderly. It was funny to watch the five-foot six-inch puppy taking three steps to his six-foot three-inch master's one. He worshipped Huxley—he could have chosen a worse idol. The strange relation that existed between this man and this boy seemed something more than that of major to private—more like father and son. Huxley didn't have any kids of his own. When he was a first looey in Iceland he had once told me of the feeling he had when he entered the ward of the crippled children's hospital in San Francisco. He was playing in the Shrine East-West Game. The little kids were pretty swell, even with warped bones and casted bodies. Huxley told about his adopted girl friend, who waved an Ohio State pennant. She had given her hero a large red handkerchief on which she had embroidered the name: Sam Huxley, Ohio State. It wasn't a very good job, but the best her crippled hands could do. . . .

Huxley checked his watch. He took out his large red handkerchief, his good luck piece, and wiped some of the grime from his face.

Marion took the TBY from the Feathermerchant and put it on his own back. Ski almost left the ground when he lost the fifty pounds. Marion wavered a moment and fell into step again. Ski took the earphones, wiped out Marion's sweat and put them on his own dripping face.

Sister Mary was a damned good man. We had the best walkie-talkie combination in the regiment. The ancient and dilapidated and nearly unworkable radios seemed to come alive under his hand and somehow, when he was on the command radio, every company was in touch with the other.

Corporal Banks of message center handed him a message. Ski read out the glad tidings. "Fresno White to all Companies, take ten."

"Fall out!" I ordered. "Communications . . . Burnside, set up the TBX and get in with regiment! Hodgkiss, help me lay out the panels for air identification! Let's go! Gomez, get on that generator!"

As they flopped to the roadside a crescendo of cursing and bitching arose. Marion and I laid out the panels and I advanced towards the party of officers kneeling around Huxley. Ski came up to me.

"Hey, Mac. How is gone. He's using set number fifty-two. It's on the blink."

"Dammit anyhow!"

There was shouting up and down the line. "Easy on the rainjuice! All men crapping, get away from the area and cover it up with your trenching tool!"

I saluted Marine Gunner Keats, the comm officer. "Panels out, sir, for aircraft. The walkie-talkie to How Company is shot."

"Did you try them on CW?"

"No, sir, but I don't think the key will work either."

"O.K.," Keats moaned, "use the alternate set."

"The alternate set is no good either."

"Aw piss." Keats turned to Huxley. "Major, the radio to How is out of operation."

"Can you use semaphore?"

"Not very well while we're marching, sir."

"Well, have message center keep two runners working," he said angrily.

"Major Huxley," Keats said, "those TBYs aren't worth the crap they're made of. They were designed by some goddam sailor for use over water. Every time we pass a good-sized tree it blocks reception. I think we should jam them up the Navy's ass sideways . . . sir."

Huxley arose and faced the fiery warrant officer. Keats, an old mustang from the ranks, generally expressed his thoughts in plain English, which the Major admired—at times.

"Mister Keats," he said, "do you feel you are incapable of operation with the present equipment?"

"Major Huxley, sir. My switchboard was outdated in the Civil War. My men are rolling hundred-pound reels of motheaten wire while the Army has ten-pound spools of combat wire. My coding machine was discarded by General Pershing and my goddam radios couldn't have helped Custer at the Little Big Horn."

The rest of the officers stood back at a safe distance. I was washing out my mouth, trying to pick up as much grit as possible. I spit a swig out, drank a swallow, snuck another, replaced my canteen, and edged in closer.

"Mister Keats! The United States Army also carries Garand rifles and we carry 03s from World War I. The Army flies P-38s and we fly F4Fs. I'm not going to read the roster of combat gear at this time. However, Mister Keats, keep this in mind at all future outbursts: the Marine Corps has managed to get by, and damned well, on the crap we buy with leftover Navy appropriations. Until such time as we can execute this war on the grandiose scale of the Army we shall develop men in such manner that their personal conduct and training will overcome any fault in equipment. We will get a hundred per cent efficiency out of every last piece of gear we have. Is that clear, Mister Keats?"

"Yes, sir."

"You are the communications officer—start communicating!"

"Yes, sir."

Lieutenant Bryce, the company commander, stepped up. "Begging the Major's pardon, could I advance the Major a suggestion?"

"No!"

"Beg your pardon, sir." Huxley brushed past him in a huff.

Keats turned to me. "You are the sergeant in charge of communications. Communicate," he said.

Blow it out, Jack Keats, I thought. "Yes sir," I said.

Sam Huxley paced the road followed by his puppy dog, Ziltch. "Dammit," he muttered, "the air cover was supposed to be here fifteen minutes ago. They can't get anything straight."

That is correct, I thought. The sharp blast of a whistle pierced the air.

"Aircraft!" We scattered from the roadside. Five thousand feet above, a squadron of Gruman F4Fs droned in, in elements of threes. They were slow, clumsy little ships, packing little punch as fighters go. But the snubnosed Wildcats were manned by men, the same as those on the ground, who had to do the best they could with what they had and would probably give a good account of themselves.

We could almost see the squadron leader, a grizzly-faced man, shift the cigar stub in his mouth from left to right and come in lower. He spotted the white identification panels laid out on the deck below him. He peeled off and soared down almost to shootop level, then tipped his wings and barrel-rolled in recognition of friendly troops.

"Headquarters! Hit the road! Off your dead asses and on your dying feet!"

"Fresno White to all companies. Move out. Easy move up and assume the point. George, bring up the rear, over and out."

Pick them up and lay them down, pick them up and lay them down. Into a cloud of dust again. A second break and we stole another extra sip of water. A third break and we guzzled two or three swallows.

Huxley kept his Whores moving briskly, blowing at every minor failure along the line of march. Numbness sets in and it starts getting easier . . . another three miles and it will be just like on a cloud.

Every now and then we passed an exhausted form at the side of the road, hiked into the ground. He'd shake his head sadly with a look of defeat and apology in his eyes. I could read Huxley's mind as he glared fiercely. *There is no place for stragglers in the Marine Corps. Survey to cooks and bakers— but my cooks and bakers must hike too, by God, or my name isn't Sam Huxley. This is only the beginning, lad.*

Lieutenant Bryce was griping to Doc Kyser about his feet and starting a phony limp. I would have given a night at the slop shute to see again the expression on Huxley's face when they told him his new officer was an assistant professor at Stanford. Bryce didn't fit into the picture. He had only been with us a week, but his unpopularity had already spread like wildfire. You can't teach a bunch of gyrenes the articles of war by quoting Bacon and Ben Jonson. It was different with Sister Mary. He was sincere. Bryce was just using it to show how goddam smart and superior he was. I've seen officers come and go in this lash-up and the good ones respected their men, and got respect in return. Guys like Huxley knew that it would be the privates who finally settled this or any other war.

Pick them up and lay them down. The full sun was on us now. The sweat gushed. I peered anxiously ahead to a grove of trees and a wooded area ahead . . . about two miles, I judged. Sensing an hour break for chow, the point bore down on the area and in an almost double time surge we hit it before break time.

"Fall out! Chow time! Easy on the water."

"All right!" I shouted. "Let's go on that TBX, get in with regiment. Gomez! On that generator!"

The weary crew found a clump of trees, eased the weight, and sank to the deck stretching, bitching, and groaning with relief. We opened our packs and took out chow. Two cans of

C ration. One can contained three hardtack biscuits, two pieces of hard candy, a lump of sugar, and some soluble coffee. The second can had either hash, stew, or pork and beans. The hash was foul; the stew was vile. Only the pork and beans tasted almost edible. Theoretically, every third ration was supposed to be pork and beans, but it seemed that the gods were against us. It was a rare day in June when any man was lucky enough to draw pork and beans.

Spanish Joe rested against a tree. He opened his dungaree shirt and let a small breeze take some heat of his wet body. He opened his can of pork and beans and smiled at us. He always managed.

"Think Highpockets is just a little rough for the first forced march, huh, Mac?" Burnside said, taking a spoon of hash and screwing up his face in pain.

"Maybe he's got a broad waiting in Rose Canyon," Seabags offered.

"He's got plenty more where this came from," I warned.

"Man, I done thought I was a goner when that damned point started running to the woods. That ass pack near beat me to death." Seabags rubbed his sides. "Looks like I been beat with a bull whip. I hear say, cousin, they got a new-fangled ration in the Army, K-Rations, they call them. Come in a wax box. Got ham, cheese and even chewing gum and cigarettes."

"Cigarettes and gum! Honest to God?" Gomez said.

"Man," Speedy Gray said, "that Army goes first cabin."

"That ain't all," Seabags added. "Some of them even got lemonade powder."

"Well, kiss my moneymaking ass. Lemonade! Wonder if General Holcomb ever heard of them there rations?"

"I think we got a warehouse full of C rations left over from Belleau Wood and the General wants to use them up before he goes pissing the taxpayers' money away on stuff like lemonade."

Pharmacist's Mate Pedro Rojas, the corpsman, moved into our group passing out salt pills. He dropped one on Speedy's lap. "Give it to the new looey, looks like he can use something the way he's crying to Doc Kyser."

"Take the damned thing, Tex, they're good for what is ailing you."

"Can't use your action, Pedro, they make me puke."

"Suck them slow."

"They still make me puke." Pedro took the salt pill back, shrugged and walked away.

"Hey, shanker mechanic!" Speedy called. "I got a couple of crabs for you to pick."

"You better not let me get too close with my knife. You're

liable to lose a little, and from what I hear, you can't spare any."

"You ought to know."

"Hey, cousin!" Seabags called. "First on blister call tonight."

"Hokay, Seabags."

"You know," Speedy said as the corpsman left, "I like that guy."

"Best blister man in the outfit and notice how easy and sweet he is with that needle."

"Yeah, most of them pill rollers act like they're taking bayonet practice."

"Damned nice guy for a Mexican," Speedy said.

"Just a damned nice guy," I corrected. "He's a Texan too, you know."

"Mexicans ain't the same, Mac. . . ."

I dropped the subject.

We moved out again. What we lost in speed, we more than made up on the trails moving up and down stiff little ridges. The break for chow gave our dogs a good chance to start yapping. Even I, fortified with three pair of sox and good broken-in boondockers, could still feel a blister popping up. Around the turns and drops, the comm cart began giving us trouble. We worked hard to keep the line of march from slowing and at the same time keep in contact with the line outfits.

We hit a clearing and the whistle blew. "Air raid!"

A second squadron acting as the "enemy" droned into earshot. Soon our covering squadron and the enemy were in a mock dog fight. We took off the main road and grouped ourselves in small circles, backs inward, and took a kneeling position. It seemed common logic that under air attack we should find cover. However, the Marine Corps said we had to shoot at them. A plane broke from the pack and dived at us feigning machine gun fire from his wings. We answered him with clicks of empty rifles. He bore down, flashing just over our heads, sending a strong wind through us.

"Crazy bastard! Almost ran into us!"

"Don't worry none, cousin, I got him right between the eyes!"

Legend has it that a Marine at Pearl Harbor downed a Jap Zero with his rifle and so, ever after, we were supposed to fight back and not hide in a ditch. The planes grew tired of their play and drifted off and we took up the march again.

Pick them up and lay them down. On and on we moved until the sun's brightness faded, taking some of its sting from our bodies.

"Rose Canyon!"

"O.K., don't drop dead! Get the TBX in with regiment! Secure the TBY set. Telephone squad, get wires into the companies! On the double, dammit!" Far from resting, the command post became a beehive of activity. Messages flew and orders were barked.

The chow trucks and bedrolls were fouled up and late. There were slit trenches, foxholes to be dug and shelters to be pitched. My squad laid out their two-man pup tents in the wrong direction and failed to cover them with a protective mound of dirt. I made them set the whole bivouac over.

At long last the field music blew recall and we battened down and lit a final cigarette before taps. It was cold outside. We snuck inside our blankets as close as we could and moved next to our bunkies. Our site was on a rocky deck and the stones dug into us through the thin pads.

"Danny."

"Go to sleep."

"I'm thinking, I'm going to see the paratroops tomorrow. Pucchi said they'd O.K. the interview. Fifty per cent more pay. I got almost two hundred saved now. The way I figure, it's about a hundred and fifty for expenses . . . and, well, I can make it in a month. I'll have her here."

"I think you've got rocks in your head trying for paratroops."

"Yeah, I'd hate to leave this outfit. We sure got a nice bunch of guys. Well, I made up my mind. I got to have the dough. Scuttlebutt says we ain't gonna be in the States too long . . ."

A deathly stillness hit the camp. Tired men, too tired to even think about the long walk back, fell into deep slumber. An occasional snore or a whisper from one man to another broke the silence. Andy Hookans moved past a still sentry and picked up the earphones of the radio and made out his log entry.

I like these guys, he thought. It's a swell outfit . . . like the guys in the camps, sticking together. I'm in better shape than most, lumberjacking . . . I'm lucky. We'll all be tough before the cruise is out. Only, I don't like San Diego. The women there are like the rest, after a quick buck and a good time. Maybe I shouldn't ought to think like that. Some of these guys got sweethearts. Maybe some day I'll meet a broad that I can feel that way about. . . . hell, how did I get stuck on this early watch?

The field music stepped into the middle of the command post area. He raised his bugle to his lips. The sound of taps drifted through the still night air and echoed from the walls of the canyon.

"Company, dismissed!"

We took one step backwards, about faced, shouted "Aye, aye, sir," and disappeared into the barracks.

"All right, let's go on this goddam gear and get it stashed in the radio shack before you do any daydreaming."

Forty miles under heavy pack on a forced march was finished and weary bodies flopped on their sacks, trying to work up enough energy to take a shower and clean their filthy equipment. Sergeant Pucchi stepped into the barrack and blew his whistle. "Pay attention. You have one hour to clean up for inspection."

"Inspection? I thought we was going to knock off inspection because of the hike."

"You missed field day yesterday, what you want, eggs in your beer?"

"Jesus H. Christ!"

"Sonofabitch Huxley!"

"Also," added Pucchi, "there will be no liberty call. The Major thinks you guys were skylarking on the hike."

"I'll be a dirty bastard."

"Yeah, Pucchi, Semper Fi, hooray for me and fugg you."

"Come on," I snapped, "you heard the sergeant. Get them goddam pieces cleaned, on the double, dammit, on the double. Off your dead asses and on your dying feet."

4.

SKI WALKED into the barracks dejectedly, went over to Danny's bunk and slumped down.

"How'd you make out, Ski?"

"They wouldn't take me. The paratroopers say I'm too goddam little. I ain't nothing but a feathermerchant."

"That's too bad. Well maybe . . . aw come on, Ski, I'm glad you flunked out. You can stay here now."

"Have we had mail call yet?"

"Yes," Danny answered slowly.

"Anything for me?"

"No." The Feathermerchant stood and turned away.

"Something's gone wrong. I know it. I ain't got a letter in two weeks."

"Don't get yourself riled, Ski. It's probably her old man."

"He didn't break her hands, dammit."

"Take it easy. Better get ready, we got Judo practice."

Ski walked towards his own bunk. "Where the hell is my sack?"

"They changed around this morning while you were gone.

New guys came in from motor transport. I moved your stuff over. You can bunk with me," Andy Hookans said.

"I had a lower, dammit," Ski shouted, "and you moved me to an upper! Get your crap off!"

"Hey, Ski, take it easy, you'll wake the neighbors." Andy smiled.

"Take your crap off, I said!"

Danny came over quickly. "You can take my bunk, Ski. I've got a lower," Danny said.

"No, I want this one. This sneaky bastard is trying to pull a fast one."

"What's biting his ass?" Andy asked.

"He isn't feeling good," Danny said.

"You going to take your stuff off or I'm going to clout the piss out of you!" Ski nosed up to the giant lumberjack.

"Aw Jesus, Ski. I ain't gonna hit you. You're just a little guy."

"Yellow bastard!"

"Hey, Danny, make him knock it off. I don't want to hit him."

"Behave yourself, Ski," Danny said, spinning him around. "If you take a punch at Andy, he'll kill you . . . besides you're going to have to whip me too. Now knock it off quick before you get all our asses in a sling."

The little fellow simmered down and dropped his hands slowly, then extended one to Andy. Andy shook it. "I'm sorry, Andy, I just got . . . I'm sorry." He turned and walked from the room.

"Jesus, he sure got a wild hair up him," Andy said.

"It's that girl, Andy. He hasn't heard from her in two weeks. He's going nuts."

"Poor little bastard," Andy muttered. He took his pad and laid it on the deck and moved Ski's down. "Them broads is all alike . . . I guess I don't want a lower nohow."

Speedy Gray, the Texan, and Seabags Brown, the farmer, wavered precariously on their bar stools. Gray broke into song:

> *"Tired of my hoss,*
> *Tired of my saddle,*
> *Tired of rounding up,*
> *Crappy old cattle,*
> *Come a ki yi yippie, yippie ya, yippie ya. . . ."*

The bartender leaned over to them. "You two guys have had enough, you'd better get going."

"Did you hear the man, cousin?"

"The hell you say."

"Let us not stay in this den of iniquity."

"Yeah, let us not tarry." With each other's aid they managed to navigate from the stool to the deck without incident. Speedy then began to collapse. He fell into Brown, who was falling into him. They braced each other and with arms locked staggered to the street.

The fresh air nearly floored them. They moved backwards and forwards, managing to gain a few feet toward their objective, which was nowhere in particular.

Seabags came to a halt against a building. "Can't go another step, cousin . . . I'm plum tuckered."

He took off his blouse, dropped to his knees, and made a pillow of it on the sidewalk. Then he lay down. Speedy shrugged and lay down beside him.

A huge M.P. leaped from the paddy wagon and went over to the prostrate pair. He poked his billy club into Speedy's ribs.

"What are you doing down there?"

The Texan looked at him through almost shut eyes and answered, "What the hell you think I'm doing? I'm trying to get this bastard home."

It was ten o'clock. Spanish Joe turned his eyes from a floor-show of dubious wartime quality. Sister Mary glanced at his watch and then back to his book. Joe reached across the table and tugged Marion's sleeve.

"Look, Marion," he said, "put down the book for a minute."

"What's on your mind?"

"That fifty bucks I won in the poker game last night—you took?"

Marion withdrew his little notebook. "You owe out thirty dollars and fifteen cents of it."

Gomez downed a double shot of rye and wiped his lips with his sleeve. "It's like this, old buddy, I got the number of a joint . . . and well, look . . . Christ on a crutch, don't give me a sermon. Could I go, huh?"

Marion slammed the book down mentioning something about Satan. Spanish Joe bent close to him, pleading. "I tell you it's a high class joint."

"Doesn't *anything* soak into that renegade skull of yours?"

"Aw come on, Marion, be a real shipmate. Ain't I been to church two Sundays in a row? And I ain't borrowed a thing from the guys all month."

"No!"

"But these girls are sensational . . . Jesus, all guys ain't like you. We're only human."

"I'll bet they're sensational," Marion sneered. "Did you ever stop to think of the consequences that might follow? I mean other than moral." He pointed a finger under Gomez's nose. "Suppose you get a dose and they throw you in the clap shack and make you do G.O. time, without pay."

"Just one of the chances in the game."

Marion reopened his book.

"Most of us are only human. Aw come on, Marion, don't be a wedgeass all your life."

"I'm not going to give you fifty dollars, Joe, and see you get rolled."

"Just a tenspot is all I need, just a sawbuck."

"From what I understand, ten dollars is too much."

"Yeah, but Marion, this is Dago and there's a war on. Broads are hard to import."

Marion eyed his pleading pal and weighed the pros and cons of human weaknesses. Finally he chalked up another round to the devil. "I'll have to go along, understand, or you'll never get back to camp."

Gomez pumped Marion's hand wildly. "That's a real understanding pal. Let's shove."

They found the establishment. Spanish Joe rapped softly on the door. About thirty seconds passed, it opened a crack. "Moe sent us," Joe whispered. The door opened, they entered quickly into a dimly lit, drably furnished living room. They were ushered in by a prune-faced madam.

"There is only one girl working tonight, honey," she rasped. "You'll have to wait a few minutes. Who wants to go first?"

Marion had comforted himself by sitting in a deep chair by a lamp and was already concerning himself with *Gibbons Decline and Fall of the Roman Empire*.

"Just me tonight, momma," Joe answered. The madam leaned over Marion, a set of triple-strand pearls flapping against his face. "How about it, honey? I'm sure you'll like the girl." Sister Mary answered her with a fierce grunt. The madam looked at Spanish Joe, who merely shrugged.

"He's like that all the time, never seen anything like it," he explained as she showed him into a bedroom down the hall.

Marion struggled through several pages of his book, looking often at his watch and trying to play deaf to the muffled noises of the place. A ray of light cracked, heralding an open door. He drew the book in front of his face, quickly turning an unread page and another one. Spanish Joe entered, his arm draped about the kimono-clad whore, gently slapping her buttocks. "Give the little lady a sawbuck, Marion."

Marion reached into his wallet, withdrew ten dollars and stood up. His eyes met those of the prostitute. They were pale blue and sad-looking . . . he saw a flow of flaming red hair and a small trembling body. He clutched the lamp table for support, growing dizzy. A silence . . . so deathly he could hear the tick of a clock down the hall and the thump of Rae's heart. He stumbled from the room.

A blast of cool night air stung his wet eyes. He staggered aimlessly for block after block until he became exhausted. Then he sat down on the curbstone and cried.

It was raining hard. I had the squad locked up in the radio shack, drilling on practice keys. "O.K., take ten." They stood up from their benches, stretched and doffed their earphones.

"Mighty slick corncobs they have in this here outfit," Seabags Brown, the Iowa farmer, mused looking out of the window. "Only trouble is you got to unroll so damned much paper to get to them." He peered at the rain and let a wad of tobacco juice fly out the window. "My gawd, it's raining harder than a cow pissin' on a flat rock."

"You ain't just a whistling through your buckteeth, Spike," Speedy commented.

"Come on, Mac, have a heart and let's knock off. I'm going dit happy at this damned key," L.Q. moaned.

"Highpockets has the red ass," I said, "and I don't blame him. You guys have been fouling up those field problems like a Chinese firedrill."

"What you want, chief, eggs in your beer?" Lighttower grinned.

"Mac," Forrester said, "I think you're bucking for warrant officer."

"I hear tell, cousins, he's been playing drop the soap with Bryce," Seabags said, banging his forefinger against his ear in a familiar gesture.

"Why you boots, you wouldn't last ten minutes in the old Corps with this kind of operating."

"Tell us about how good you guys were in the o-ould Corps," Andy snickered.

"Why in the o-oould Corps," Jones took up the rallying, "now let me tell you recruits something. I've worn out more seabags than you have socks."

"I think Mac is going Asiatic on us."

"Yep, pore old boy is cracking up bigger than hell. Survey him to field music." Seabags let another spit fly out the window.

"Give me a coffin nail," L.Q. asked Lighttower.

"You palefaces ever buy your own cigarettes?"

"Butts on that cigarette," Andy called ahead of Gray.

Forrester took a bar of pogey bait and peeled off the wrapper. "What's the matter with Sister Mary? He's sure had a wild hair up his ass lately."

"Yeah," Andy said, "somebody better give him the word. He's getting awful one way."

"Is it true they're going to survey him to artillery?" L.Q. asked.

Gomez sprang to his feet. "Knock it off."

"Just scuttlebutt, old man. Freedom of speech, you know."

"I said knock off the crap!"

"Don't you dare talk to me like that, Joe—I'm a lover, not an athlete."

I changed the subject. "Back on those keys. I'm shoving off and I don't want any of you bums sneaking out until seventeen hundred." I went to the door, put on my poncho and pith helmet. "Forrester, check into barracks in fifteen minutes and relieve Marion on the C.Q. and take these sickbay soldiers to chow."

I entered the lifeless barracks and scanned the long row of neatly made bunks. In his corner, Marion Hodgkiss on C.Q. duty lay back staring blankly at the ceiling. The phonograph spun a piece of his classical music. It bounced, haunted like, off the empty bulkheads. I shook the rain off and moseyed over to him.

"Damned pretty piece, what's its nomenclature?"

"I told you a hundred times," he recited in monotone. "The last movement of Brahms First Symphony."

"Yeah, that's right, Brahms, damned pretty." I circled around his sack. "Sure is raining out, yep, sure is raining." The record ran out, the player arm going around in crazy circles. I reached over and cut it off.

"I didn't tell you to do that!" Marion snapped.

"Look, Marion, you're going to crack up if you keep this up. There's even scuttlebutt of transferring you to artillery."

He gritted his teeth and looked out of the window. A wind whirred the rain hard against the windowpane, sending the little drops flying and swirling in a million crazy directions. "I happened to be going to Coronado the other night and—"

"Mind your own goddam business."

This type of language from Sister Mary could well mean I might be on the receiving end of a fractured jaw. I turned to go.

"Mac," whispered Marion.

"Yeah."

"Mac, I'm sorry. I'm ... I'm ..."

"Come on, kid, put on your rain stuff and let's go down to the slop shute and talk. The guys will be in here in a few minutes."

"The C.Q.?" he asked.

"Forrester will take it."

He slipped the poncho over his head, buttoned it down and donned his pith helmet. We walked slowly down the slippery, rain-soaked street, the water squishing under our boondockers, past Barracks One to the catwalk over the sand, and entered the slop shute. I brushed the water off and sauntered up to the bar. "Two beers."

"Coke for me."

"Beer and a coke." We took the bottles and sailed for an empty table.

At the end of the bar we spied Gunnery Sergeant McQuade and Burnside tossing down brews. McQuade was surrounded by a gang of his boys from Fox Company. His huge gut hung far below his belt. He leaned on the bar and through sea-hardened lips he bellowed for a survey on the beer. He spotted me.

"Hi Mac," he shouted.

"Hi Mac," I called back.

"This here reecruit is nine beers behind me."

"Line up ten beers," Burnside ordered. "I'd like to see the day that a washed-up mick can outdrink Burnside." McQuade threw back his big red face and roared. They both had reputations as human beerkegs and they'd been having a drinking bout for six years. The "Gunny" turned to his boys.

"Why, I've passed more ship masts than this guy has passed telephone poles," he bellowed as Burnside chuggalugged his third bottle down. "Did I ever tell you men about the all-Marine ship, the old U.S.S. *Tuscarora*? Yes, sir, what a ship! Forty decks deep and a straw bottom to feed the sea horses. Why, one time we was going up the Yangtze River and there were so many bends in it that the aft guard was playing pinochle with the forward guard." He tilted a bottle to his lips, "Here's to the next man that dies," and downed it in two swallows.

Burnside lifted his voice in song:

> *"Glorious, glorious!*
> *One keg of beer for the four of us,*
> *Glory be to God that there are no more of us,*
> *Cause one of us could drink it all alone. . . ."*

I turned to Corporal Hodgkiss. "Think you'd like to bat the breeze, Marion?"

"I'd like to write a story about Burnside and McQuade some day."

"They are a couple for the book."

"Mac," he said, "I don't understand about those women."

"Whores . . . I mean prostitutes?" He nodded. "I don't know, Marion, it's hard to say. When we were over in Shanghai in thirty-one, they had a lot of White Russian girls. I know a couple of the guys who married them. They seemed happy enough."

"Can one of them . . . I mean, Mac, well . . . I never asked her much about herself . . . I always thought they were rough and hard, like the books make them."

"They're women just like any other women. You'll find all kinds, same as there are all kinds of Marines."

"She's so gentle and ladylike, and she likes to learn about things. I . . . just couldn't picture her with . . . Mac, it doesn't add up. She's wonderful . . . why would she be doing that?"

"The first time I went to a joint, Marion, I was just about your age and just about as innocent. The girl had a copy of some high-tone book on a stand beside the bed. I forgot the name of it. The thing that I always remembered about her was the fact that I was so surprised that she read a book. It happened that she was a very nice girl, a college graduate. She had her story. Everyone does—like I said, there's all kinds."

"What would you do if you were in my shoes, Mac?"

"You're the only guy that can answer that, Marion." I lit the smoking lamp and thought hard. "They're funny kind of women, I've known lots of them. A good many of them have been kicked around . . . and men, well—just so many pigs after the same thing. They know all the angles, all the answers. Maybe that's why Rae fell in love with you. You were something new for her." I nursed my beer and fought hard to find the right words. "When a guy gives them a decent shake they get a loyalty like a hound dog. Those girls don't care to look around or cheat. Their man is something special to them. They've got a tenderness that maybe all of us want but few guys are lucky enough to find. But you've got to pay a price for it, you've got to be pretty big and erase a lot of ugly pictures from your mind. . . ." I fumbled and floundered.

"You've met Rae, Mac," he said.

"Rae is a lady, she has class—and she loves you."

"Remember that night at the airstrip?" I nodded. Marion took a letter from his pocket. It was from the magazine that had accepted the story called *Mr. Branshly's Retreat* and wanted more of the same.

"I don't know how it started, Mac. Just a few words at first. She came on the boat tired and we'd talk, mostly about me and writing . . . and then all of the things I've had inside me seemed to come out. I could talk to her without being afraid . . . I could say things I've never been able to say before, and she'd close her eyes and listen to my ideas and we'd talk them over. It was easy . . . she seemed to understand that I was trying to reach for something."

"I think I understand."

"And Mac, I read to her . . . sometimes all night."

I peered outside. The rain was beginning to let up.

"Rae's more than a woman to me. She isn't really bad—I know it. She's wonderful and kind and gentle. I couldn't write without her."

"Haven't you answered your own questions, Marion?"

He forced a little smile. "I don't guess anything else matters, Mac."

"Why don't you do me a favor, Marion? Start running your network the way you're supposed to."

"I'll be all right now—and thanks, Mac."

A loud chorus of ten drunken Marines boomed from the bar.

> *"As we go marching,*
>   *And the band begins to PLAY,*
> *You can hear them shouting,*
>   *The raggedy assed Marines are on parade."*

McQuade and Burnside finally fell on the deck, the duel ending in another draw.

Corporal Hodgkiss ran up the gangplank on the dot of twelve-thirty. He grabbed her and held her so tight she almost broke in half. She clung to him, trembling like a scared little puppy.

"Marion, Marion, don't leave me again."

"I love you, Rae."

"Look," she said, opening her purse, "I've got a present for you." She handed him a pair of socks. "I knitted them myself. Not very good, the first pair. I didn't know your foot size or anything."

Later, Rae entered her apartment first. He followed her slowly. Rae flicked on the light, closed the door, and threw her coat across the divan. He stood there, his back against the door, fumbling his barracks cap awkwardly.

"What's the matter, Marion?"

"I . . . I've never been like this, with a girl . . . before." She smiled, patted his cheek and turned away.

"Take off your blouse and make yourself comfortable. I'll put on some coffee."

He relaxed in a big chair and reached for a book; it was *Sonnets from the Portuguese*. She sat on the chair's arm. "I was hoping you'd come back," she said. "I wanted you to read it to me." She kissed his forehead and disappeared into the kitchen. His eyes followed her from the room.

Rae left San Diego the next morning for Marion's home.

> *Dearest Rae,*
>
> *I'm happy that you like the folks. They wrote and they adore you just as much as I do. I'm glad we decided for you to leave quickly, it is better this way. One of the fellows brought his wife to San Diego and now that we are expecting to leave the States, their life is one climax after another. She is half crazy by the time he gets home each night. Anyhow, we have a wonderful memory to keep us going. I can't yet realize that you are mine.*
>
> *I'm doing a lot of writing. All the spare time I get. One of these days we'll have a lot of wonderful things to do and see a lot of wonderful places together . . . we are going to be so happy.*
>
> *Darling Rae, what you said in your last letter . . . don't think about it any more. It doesn't matter. The past is the past and only tomorrow counts. You are my girl and I love you.*
>
> *Marion*

5.

WE had dispensed with field day and inspection because of an overnight field problem in the brush outside the main barracks area. All night we crawled, practicing infiltration to sharpen ears and eyes in darkness. The squad had a rough time. It was imperative that we send our messages short and fast because the noise of the generator could arouse the dead in such stillness. We had to move quickly after each transmission, lest the "enemy" capture us. After stumbling around in the night for eight hours we returned to barracks dead tired.

"I'm dundee," L.Q. Jones sighed. "Here I got a weekend ashore, that broad all lined up in El Cajon, and I can't get off the sack."

"You know what they call that in the Russian Marines—toughi shitski," his pal Lighttower prodded.

"Yeah, write him out a T.S. chit for the chaplain."

"She's picking me up at the gate, dammit, how about going down and telling her I'm in the brig or something, Injun?"

"Ain't you got that broad, yet, L.Q.?"

"The way I figure, tonight's the night. Her old man has this here ranch and I'm in for the weekend, but this lil ole fat boy is plumb tuckered out . . . I don't think I got the energy." He dragged to his feet. "Recktum I've got to keep up the morale on the home front." He trudged to the head to clean up.

"Is that the same broad that sang over the radio on that church hour," Danny asked Lighttower, "the night he loaded his Reising gun and made us all listen and write letters to the radio station?"

"Yeah, same squaw."

"Hasn't he got none of that yet?"

"Naw, she's giving him the business. I told L.Q. to watch that woman, she's foxy. And she's so damned homely that if she doesn't get herself a husband with twenty thousand gyrenes around, she'll be prune picking on that ranch for the rest of her life. That set up in El Cajon is a trap. . . ."

L.Q. was held up at the main gate and made to enter the guard shack to shine his shoes. He entered the parked convertible amid wolf calls from the Marines heading for liberty. Ninety per cent of the catcalls were for the convertible with white sidewalls, and very few for poor Nancy East, who slid over as L.Q. took the wheel and whisked away.

L.Q. Jones, by the time they reached El Cajon, was a very tired young man. The night problem had left him limp with exhaustion. However, this appeared to be the opportune moment in the cat and mouse game he had been playing with Nancy East. On each succeeding liberty he had made a slight gain toward his objective.

Nancy, on the other hand, granted each gain managing to wheedle a further verbal confession from L.Q. He was armed with a weekend pass, poppa away on business and the blue chips were down.

The homely little girl was well aware of L.Q.'s physical condition. She planned a man-killing itinerary, with teasing promise of better things to come with the night. In this way, she reasoned, she could weaken his mental and physical state to a point where further resistance would be futile. With the aid of her mother, she could pounce in for the kill and thus gain herself a husband. It was dirty poker.

L.Q. had no more than peeled off his greens in exchange for khakis before Nancy slapped a tennis racquet in his hand and rushed him to the courts. She needled him as she trounced him the first set. Now, it is O.K. to kid a guy about his listless game when he is tired and doesn't feel like playing. But to insist that this exemplifies the entire character of the Marine Corps is unfair. L.Q. became very angry. Calling on the reserve that all good Marines carry, he became a one-man tornado and smashed himself to victory in the next two sets—thus preserving the honor of the Corps.

However, before he could reward himself with a well-earned rest he found himself in the saddle of a fierce-looking beast who bounced him across hills and fields for the next two hours. L.Q. hated horses.

Starvation set in. Nancy had the romantic idea of a picnic lunch in a spot about four miles from the ranch. The rugged rancher's daughter hiked him briskly, he under the load of a large basket and thermos jug. Springtime being springtime, Nancy insisted that her lover chase her through the woods as all lovers must, in the woods, in springtime. Now, L.Q. wasn't what one would call a track star. He never caught her. He never had a fighting chance.

Before dinner the young Amazon rounded out a perfect day by challenging him to a game of handball and a quick swim. L.Q. for once thanked God he was fat and could float easily, or he would have surely sunk at this stage.

He collapsed into a chair at the table. Before him Nancy and her mother paraded some fifteen courses, ranging from two-inch-thick steaks covered with mushrooms to a topper of apple pie and Monterey Jack cheese. The meal was a gourmet's dream and L.Q. was the boy who could do justice to it. And Nancy East appeared to have whipped it up with her own little hands in an idle moment. It never occurred to L.Q. that she hadn't had an idle moment since he arrived.

After the feast, the fattened hog was primed for slaughter. He was too stuffed with the epicurean delights to budge. He just sat. And listened to Mrs. East babble and babble and babble. Then, the whole plot dawned on him. TRAPPED! The door, he thought. No, I'll never make it alive, I can't move!

Mrs. East rarely stopped talking. She and her homely daughter seemed to L.Q. to be looking at him with catlike smiles, as if they were licking their chops at the thought of the tasty plump little mouse they had cornered.

He lifted his head and prayed silently. Then, with the blood pounding through his veins, and renewed strength, such as a man fighting for freedom often finds, he uttered his first words of the evening: "Let's make some fudge."

He and Nancy went to the kitchen. Away, at last, from the singsong rhythm of her mother's endless chatter.

As she stood there by the stove, pot in hand, he moved in and spun her about and kissed her.

"Not here, silly," she giggled. He held her close and over his shoulder he saw her mother peeking through the doorway. There was no alternative. They returned to the living room with a plate of fudge. Mrs. East laid down her knitting, reached for a piece of the candy, saying she really shouldn't, and smacked her lips.

"You know," she purred, "Mr. East and I were married during the last war. He was a captain . . . but," she added quickly, "a private makes almost as much as a captain did then." She nodded sweetly at L.Q., who had a look of terror in his eyes.

The hours weighed heavily upon the young Marine. After many more had passed in pleasant conversation, with Mrs. East doing all the conversing, she excused herself and went to bed. He and Nancy had more fudge, and then followed her example.

L.Q. dropped like a dead man to his bed. In the split second between being awake and asleep, a soft rap came on his chamber door. Nancy East entered, clad only in a thin and lacy gown. L.Q. scanned the walls and ceilings for hidden microphones, alarms, and booby traps. On second thought, she didn't look so bad, in the half-dark at least. This was it!

"I brought you an extra blanket," she said, "it gets cold." She seated herself gently on the edge of his bed. The scent of Chanel No. 5 drifted into his nostrils. What can a man do? He brought her down beside him and kissed her.

"No, I must get back."

"Stay a minute," he pleaded.

She kissed him sweetly and suddenly pulled away.

"What is it?"

"You're just like the rest of the Marines. You are all alike."

"Me? Like a Marine? Why baby, I'm maaad for you."

She kissed him again, once more withdrew. L.Q. wheezed very hard. "Tell me you love me, L.Q."

"For Chrisake, I love you," he panted.

"Can't you say it sweeter?"

"I'm maaad for you."

"How much?"

(Chin up boy, she's moving in.)

"Very much," he parried and drew her down beside him and held her tightly.

"No! I'm afraid you're just like the rest of them."

There was a long, long silence. She snuggled into his arms. He did not stir. There were times when a man has to be firm.

At last Nancy East gave in. "I'm yours, L.Q.," she said.

L.Q. Jones answered her with a long, loud snore. He was fast asleep.

"Mail Call!" The men flocked about the duty NCO. As he shouted the names on the envelopes you could see a smile light up on a face. You could see the anxious strain of those waiting for the sound of their names. The Feathermerchant stood on the fringe as Corporal Banks passed the mail from hand to hand. Then it was over, always too soon. And those with word from home drifted to their bunks smiling in eager anticipation. Ski walked away quickly, hands in pockets. There was no letter for him, again.

"Don't talk so much and deal." We were playing poker in the barrack.

"The name of this game, gentlemen, is five-card-draw. Ante up a dime, jacks or better to open."

"How do you like that Bryce, what an asshole."

"Ninety-day blunder if I ever seen one."

"Openers?"

"Beats the hell out of me."

"Up to you, Andy."

"Open for two bits."

"I'll call that bluff."

"Cards for the gamblers?"

"Holding a kicker, Andy?"

"Maybe."

"Two bits."

"Call and raise you a half."

"What you got you're so proud of? Call you."

"Three whores."

"Talk about craphouse luck, here's my openers."

"How about a little studhorse, gentlemen?"

"What about Bryce, Mac, ain't he a pisscutter?"

"I'm not supposed to give my views on the elite," I parried.

"Sonofabitch better stop with that Stanford stuff and talk like we was people."

"Pair of treys is boss."

"The price of poker goes up . . . fifteen cents."

"I fold."

"Bastard is going to end up with a hole in his back, him and his big education."

"Trey's still boss."

"Two bits."

"Beats me."

"Seven . . . pair of deuces . . . trey's still boss."

"Check."

"Two bits."

"Nothing and nothing . . . trey's boss."

"Check."

"Two bits."

"Raise you two bits."

"Right back at you."

"Call . . . what you got you're proud of?"

"Deuces and sixes."

"Three treys . . . had them wired."

"Talk about craphouse luck . . . well that cleans me. Lend me a finsky till payday."

"O.K."

Sister Mary and the Feathermerchant kibitzed in for a moment.

"We got an open seat, gentlemen."

"No thanks," Marion said, "I don't indulge."

"Not for me. One more pay call and I'll have her out here, boys," Ski said.

"They got a USO show and a dance . . . anybody want to come?"

"Naw, I feel sorry for them damned USO troupes. They feel so sorry for themselves because they feel sorry for us. Besides, most of that crap is pretty old."

"Aw, they're just trying to build your morale."

"Yeah, cousin, my morale's shot. Why don't they go to a dogface camp? They feel sorry for themselves, too."

"Why, the last time I seen a USO show I plumb cried myself to sleep."

"Give me a weed."

"Butts on that cigarette."

"Deal."

"Seven-card stud."

"Everytime you get the deal you pull that crap. Next time it will be all red cards wild."

"You know what they call it in the Mexican Marines—el tougho shito."

"A bullet, another bullet, six, whore, jack . . . first bullet bets."

"One thin dime."

"Once, just once."

"They got a dance after the show. Any of you guys going?"

"Can't stand them bitches they haul in."

"Yeah, stick around them long enough and they'll have you going to church."

"The part that makes me scream, is when they look at you with them baby blue eyes and tell you how much they give up to do this horrible hard work—anything for our boys in uniform."

" 'Momma doesn't usually let me go out with Marines and sailors.' "

"Yeah, anything for the war effort . . . ace jack bets."

"Fifteen centavos."

"Yeah, they act like a bunch of goddam martyrs. Back home they'd be dying on the vine."

"Deal, cousin, and you won't have so many cards."

"Where you figure we're going, Mac? They must have something special picked out for the Sixth."

"Scuttlebutt says Wake Island."

"I'd sure like to hit Wake."

"Holcomb was in the Sixth in the last war."

"You mean the BIG war?"

"Yeah, the commandant is keeping his eye out for the Sixth."

"Two bits."

"Call."

"One card down."

"Chicken crap, huh, a little straight."

"Beats my two pairs."

"A little progressive poker, gentlemen, dime ante. Somebody's light . . . Seabags."

"Pawdon."

"Jacks or better to open."

"I sure hope Ski gets that woman out here. I offered him a sawbuck last pay call but he turned me down cold."

"Proud little bastard. Works around the clock. I don't think he's been ashore since we've hit Eliot."

"Yeah, I try to give him a couple odd jobs to throw a couple of bucks his way."

Andy Hookans threw his cards in and stood up. "I'm going down to the slop shute. Lend me a couple bucks, Mac."

I pushed a deuce over to him.

"I hope Ski doesn't get it broken off in him. He's too nice a kid. He oughta lay off them goddam broads." Andy stomped from the barrack.

"What's biting his ass?"

"I think he's just got it in for all broads in general."

"Got an open seat, men?" Sergeant Barry, of the telephone squad, slipped in between the sacks and purchased some matchsticks.

"Cost you twenty cents to get in, Barry. Progressive. Whores or better to open."

"Cut them deep and weep, cut them thin and win."

"Go on, deal . . . you couldn't stack crap with a shovel."

It was near 2400 hours when I got back to the barrack. I had cut the beer bout short as there was another Huxley Special coming up the next day. I left McQuade and Burnside to battle it out.

I entered and walked to the head. As I came into the room I spotted Ski standing at the far end of the long row of sinks. I moved towards him and Ski turned his back. Ski had begged off running the obstacle course that day to take sick call. The

Feathermerchant was no sick-bay soldier by a long shot. What he lacked in size, he more than made up with plain old piss and vinegar. I figured he was upset because he hadn't heard from his girl. Nothing tears a guy down so fast as no news or bad news from home. So, I had let him have the day off and didn't press him about it.

Ski shied away from me. I thought he was acting a little strange. "You O.K., Ski?" I asked.

"Yes," he whispered, still with his back turned, and quickly slipped a little bottle into his trouser pocket.

"Sure you aren't sick?"

"Leave me alone, will ya?" Ski's voice was shaky and cracked. I moved over to him.

"What you got in that bottle?"

"Leave me alone."

"I said what have you got in that bottle?"

"Mind your own goddam business," he hissed and brushed past me. I caught him by the shoulders and spun him around. Before I could utter another word he pounced on me like a wildcat. I was loaded with beer, and he caught me one in the guts. I went to the deck. As he turned to go I put a flying tackle on him and brought him down.

I didn't want to lower the boom on him, but Ski was clouting me all over the joint. I tried holding him off, but he was like crazy. I let a right fly and landed square on his mouth, but he kept coming, kicking and winging in from all angles. He hooked me against the bulkhead and brought one up from the boon-dockers. . . . I felt numb . . . my head cracked against the wall. Finally I clutched him and spun him into a corner and went to work on his guts. Two . . . three . . . four . . . five . . . six . . . square in the belly, with all I had. Finally, Ski started to buckle. Then I let him have it in the nose . . . another one in the chops. He started bleeding like a stuck pig. He gritted his teeth and came at me again . . . but I wouldn't let him out of the corner.

"Cut it!" I yelled, busting him in his smeared face. "For Chrisake cut it!"

Ski grabbed my blouse, dazed, but still tried to pound his fists into me. "Quit!" I begged, hitting his jaw. He spun and sagged to his hands and knees, shaking his head. I jumped him and pinned his arm behind him, and as he tried to struggle loose reached into his pocket. "Stay still or I'll bust your arm off," I warned. Ski stiffened for one more try; then as I found the bottle he grew limp. I let him go. He fell against the bulkhead and buried his hands in his bloody face and sobbed.

"Where did you get this stuff?"

Andy came into the head. "Christ on a crutch, what's the matter with you, Mac? You'll get busted for this."

"The little sonofabitch tried to kill himself." I panted for breath. My stomach felt all floppy. "Get Danny and Marion in here, on the double. And be quiet—don't wake up the barracks."

They raced back in their skivvies, followed by Andy.

"Guard that door, Marion. Don't let anybody in. Give me your skivvy shirt, Forrester." Danny peeled it off and I went to a sink and soaked it with cold water. I grabbed the crying boy by the hair and lifted his face and swabbed off the blood as easily as I could.

"He had a bottle of sleeping pills. Must have lifted them from sick bay."

"Oh, God," Danny whispered.

"Wring this goddam thing out and put more cold water on it. I didn't mean to hit him so hard, the little bastard went berserk."

We slowly brought Ski to his senses. His eyes were glassy and his head hung limp. He stared blankly at the deck. Danny knelt beside him.

"It's me, Danny—your buddy. Can you hear me?"

Ski nodded.

"What did you try to kill yourself for?"

He lifted his head slowly and looked at us. His eyes filled with tears and he tried to open his mouth to speak. His lips quivered, a groan came out. He dropped his head again and shook it slowly.

"Was it Susan?"

He nodded.

"Did you get a letter?"

He nodded again.

Danny frisked his pocket and came up with an envelope. He stood up and moved under a light. His hand trembled and a deathly hush came over us. All we could hear was the uneven breathing of the slumped boy. Danny bit his lip and closed his eyes and stared down at Ski.

"What is it?" Andy asked, at last.

"She's going to have a baby, another guy's. They're going to be married . . . the rest of it is just . . . apologies . . ."

We were too shaken to move. There wasn't much anybody could say now.

"A Dear John letter," Andy hissed. "Them goddam women, them dirty no good bitches!"

"Pipe down, Andy."

"He needed a break, dammit. What's he got now."

"That won't help, Andy," I said, kneeling by the Feathermerchant. "Ski, we're your buddies, you know that."

"Yeah . . ."

"If we turn you in, they'll send you to the psycho ward. You want to stay with us, don't you?"

He nodded.

"We'll take care of you, Ski," Danny pleaded.

"You won't try this again—promise?"

"No," he croaked. "I won't try it no more."

"Try to get some sleep." I aided him to his feet. "I'm sorry I had to work you over."

"It ain't your fault, Mac," he mumbled, walking slowly into the barrack.

"We'd better keep an eye on him," Andy said. "I'll take a two-hour watch." He followed Ski out.

"I'll stand the next one," Marion said.

"You guys all better hit the sack," Danny said. "I don't think I can sleep anyhow."

Before evening chow the next day, First Sergeant Pucchi called me into the company office.

"Hey, what's up, Mac? The Feathermerchant just came in and took out all the money he had riding on the books. Finally getting that broad out here?"

"What!"

"Yeah, almost three hundred bucks. Say, what did he do, run into a tank? His face is sure chopped up."

"He got a Dear John letter yesterday, Pucchi."

"That's too bad, nice kid. Can't predict them women. Well, just thought I'd ask. It seemed kind of funny. He picked up a liberty pass. Think that's the first time he ever asked for one."

"He's going into Dago with that load," I said. "He'll get sharp-shooted for sure. Pucchi, you got to give me a pass tonight."

"You got more crap than a Christmas turkey. I can't give you a pass, you had one last night."

"Listen, Pucchi, he's going to get his ass in a sling with all that dough."

"That's a problem for Chaplain Peterson."

"Be a buddy."

"Christ, Mac, the way that Bryce watches me, I'd be up crap creek without a paddle if I gave you a pass, no dice."

"Thanks, Pucchi," I said, "that's a real buddy. Somehow, I remember a time in Reykjavik when you beat the hell out of that Limey captain, and the Iceland police force and half the Limey army was closing in on you. You didn't mind a favor from me then. I still got a scar on my scalp where I was hit with a beer bottle."

"How many favors you going to ask for one little brawl? You been riding on that one for a year."

"When did I ask you for a favor?"

"Aw, look, Mac, don't be a wedgeass."

"What would you do, Pucchi, if it was one of your boys?"

Pucchi reached in the drawer, pulled out a card and swung around to his typewriter. "Don't forget this, you no good bastard. And for Chrisake don't get picked up by the shore patrol or we'll both be on cake and wine for a month."

"While you're at it," I added, "you'd better make out passes for Sister Mary, Andy, and Danny, too. I might need help."

We followed the Feathermerchant out of the main gate. Three buses lined up to take the first rush of liberty-bound Marines into Dago. Ski boarded the first one, we got into the second.

We landed in Dago forty-five minutes later, dropping anchor in front of the YMCA on Broadway. He lit out for the first slop shute he could find. We stayed a distance behind him. He was turned down at the door of the first three bars when they asked for his I.D. card. He was still under age and they refused him admittance.

He crossed the main drag to a side street. We held our breath as he headed straight for the Dragon's Den. It was the worst clip joint in a city of clip joints. He had wised up; he passed a bill to the door checker and was granted admittance.

I called the boys about me for a quick conference.

"We'll slip in there and take a booth," I said.

"We won't be able to get in," Marion offered. "We're all under twenty-one."

"That's right," I said. "Well, I'll go in and you guys stand fast. Keep a sharp eye, this joint has two or three exits."

"Check, Mac."

I crossed the street and entered the Dragon's Den. It was a rowdy, smoke-filled bar, jammed with tough waterfront characters and stronger elements of the armed forces. There was a three-piece Negro combo slapping out cloud sixteen jazz on the bandstand at one end. I cut through the fog of smoke and saw Ski draped on a bar-stool with a twenty-dollar bill laying on the counter in front of him. I edged into a seat at a table so I was partly turned away from Ski.

"Line 'em up as I squeeze them off, and when this twenty runs out, just whistle like a bird. There's plenty more where that came from."

The bartender, a wiry man with a scarred cheek, eyed him carefully, then looked at the door checker, who gave him the high sign that the little Marine was loaded.

"Sure, Marine," he answered, putting a shot glass on the counter with a thud, "Drink up."

I looked up a little to see what he was pouring. It was O.K. so far, just bar whisky.

The Feathermerchant was no drinker. If he ever was, he had been too long out of practice to last. I ordered a beer and nursed it as Ski downed three quick ones, shook his head and coughed. He slammed his fist on the counter for a survey. It was dished up quickly.

A drunken sailor fell across my table. I was about to push him to the deck when I thought better of it. I didn't want to start anything then. I picked up my glass and moved to another table.

"Hey, bartender, come here!" Ski said.

He poured another shot, which Ski downed. It was his fifth fast one. He was out to bury himself quick-like. I saw beads of perspiration form on his brow. He loosened his battle pin and his field scarf, panting for air. Another shot went down.

As the man next to him moved off his stool, the bartender gave a signal. It was only a moment before a heavily made up, sleazy-looking bitch sauntered over and perched herself next to Ski.

"Hello, honey," she said. The fun would be starting soon. I eyed the room for a quick exit. Ski turned his eyes slowly to her. He was wavering a little.

"Lonely, Marine?"

"Yeah, I'm lonely . . . yeah, I'm lonely."

"Buy me a drink, honey?"

"Sure . . . got plenty, got plenty." He turned to shove some change from the twenty across the bar. There was none. He reached in his wallet and from the fat roll peeled another bill and put it down. "Give the lady a drink and give me a survey. Make mine a double."

The last one made his eyes do a little wild dance, then they started getting bleary. "You Susan?"

"Susan?"

"Yeah, Susan—you don't look like Susan," he said.

"Do you want me to be Susan, Marine?"

"Yeah . . . be Susan, will you? Please be Susan, lady."

"Sure, Marine, I go for you, you're sweet. What's your name?"

"Ski . . . Ski . . . I'm a Feathermerchant . . . you Susan?"

"Sure, Ski, I'm Susan, drink up."

"Why don't you call me Connie if you're Susan? She always calls me Connie . . . all the time, Connie, she says."

I saw a tear trickle down his face. Even dead drunk it was hard for Ski to pretend that bawdy-looking whore was the girl he loved. There was a burst of laughter and screams of joy as the combo broke into a hot number. I felt myself getting sick of these stinking vultures, cashing in on the misery and loneliness of a lost kid. I wanted to start ripping the joint apart. I downed my beer and steadied for the move.

"Why don't you finish that drink, Connie, and come up to my place?"

Ski leaned very close to her. "You . . . we . . . go someplace . . . alone . . . and turn off the lights and I could pretend you were Susan . . . would you hold me real tight, lady, and call me . . . Connie?"

"Sure, finish up your drink." She nodded to the bartender, who deftly slipped the shot glass from the bar. I saw him empty a powder into it before he put it back in front of Ski.

"O.K., sister, that's the ball game," I said. "Come on, Ski, we're going back to camp."

"You can't call me that!" she screamed at me in what was an obvious signal for a bum's rush to get me out of there.

"Knock off the funny business, I'm taking him home—with his money."

"I heard you, Marine," the scarfaced bartender shouted at me. "That kind of talk to a lady don't go in this place!"

I spun about quickly in time to feel something crash against my head. They sure worked neat. I was dazed, but they didn't have me out. I felt several pairs of strange hands pick me up and rush me across the room. I tried to shake the fuzz from my brain but all I could hear was the wild beating of the combo. I was getting numb, fast . . . then it felt like I was sailing on a cloud. . . .

Next I knew, Danny was standing over me, slapping my face. "Snap out of it, Mac."

"Jesus! Look around the back on the double!"

Sister Mary took off at high port, then returned. "I saw them shoving off in a cab just as I got there. Ski was out cold," he said.

I reeled to my feet. "Goddammit, I fouled up the detail. Let me think, let me think." I steadied myself, trying to keep everything from spinning around.

"Let's rush the goddam place and take it apart," Andy said.

"No, we're A.W.O.L.," I said. "Andy, you look the oldest. Take my I.D. card and get in there. Get that bartender alone. The skinny one on the far end. Find out where they took Ski."

Andy wasted no time. We fell back into the shadows as he moved to the door. We stood by restlessly for about ten minutes and then he came barreling out. "Come on, men, Ritz Hotel, Cannon and Clay."

"Yeah," I said, "I know the joint from the old days. Let's grab a cab at the corner."

We sped toward the waterfront.

"How on earth did you do it, Andy?" Marion asked.

"Easy," Andy answered, rubbing his bruised knuckles, "easy. Anybody dealing in whores would deal in hot watches. I got him in the back room where they store beer cases. He thought he was going to look at some hot jewelry."

"Very resourceful," Marion mused.

"He be around to tip them off at the hotel?" Danny asked.

"Naw, he won't be around for a while."

"You didn't kill him?"

"Naw, just worked him over. When he comes around he ain't going to be able to get out of the room." Andy flipped a key out of the window. "They'll never hear him pounding over that band and the racket in that joint."

Minutes later we stormed into the empty lobby of the third-rate hotel. The night clerk was caught off balance. I backed him up against the wall, holding him by the stacking swivel. "Real quick, friend—a little Marine and a brunette?"

Danny cocked his fist. The stunned man began shaking.

"What room, or do we start belting?"

"I ain't looking for no trouble, Marines, I only work here."

"You ain't going to be living in about two minutes. Start whistling Dixie, Junior."

"Room two-twenty, end of the hall on the right. Please, fellows, I got a family."

I turned to Marion. "Sit here and keep this gentleman company, Mary. Sing out if anything comes through that lobby."

Sister Mary placed a hand on the frightened clerk's shoulder and sat him down. "Tell me, friend," he said, "I would value your opinion in the eternal controversy on the relative merits of Brahms and Wagner. I'm a Brahms man myself, but I'm always ready to listen to a good argument."

We dashed up the stairs, got oriented, and slipped the fair leather belts from about our waists. We rolled them around our fists, leaving about four inches of belt swinging free, with the heavy brass buckle at the end. We crept down the dim lit hall and faced the door of Room 220.

Andy waved us aside. He took a run, leaped off his feet and hit the door, jumping Swede style, with the heels of his shoes. It buckled, then gave as Danny followed it up with a crash of his shoulder.

Ski lay prostrate over a bed. Standing over him, thumbing through his roll, stood a man, the whore's pimp. The woman leaned against the dresser with a drink in her hand.

"Watch it!" A chair came down on Andy's skull, dropping him to his knees. The woman made a dash for the door. Danny grabbed her and flung her down, hard. She started sobbing.

"Look out, Mac—he's pulling a knife!"

I inched toward the man who had raised a knife in one hand while clutching Ski's roll of bills in the other. The steel blade lashed out.

The man picked himself up, slowly. "Like I said, Danny, most people attack wrong with a knife." I kicked him, lifted him, and polished him off quick, and took the money from his hand.

Andy was on his feet again. The woman crawled at our feet. "Mercy, Marine!" she cried in a foreign accent.

"I'll give you mercy!" Andy spat. "Stand up, bitch!"

We didn't like the look on Andy's face. It had *kill* written all over it. We calmed him down. "We've already had enough fun for one night, Swede . . . let's hustle."

I grabbed the woman and flung her against the wall. She collapsed to the deck. "If I see your face in this town again, sister, you won't get off this easy."

Marion burst into the room. "Shore Patrol coming up. You fellows are sure noisy."

Andy threw Ski over his broad shoulder and we scuttled for the fire escape as the sound of whistles heralded the arrival of the law.

"Poor little bastard," Andy said, as he passed Ski's body through the window to me.

6.

THE PROGRESS of the battalion was slow, painful, and riddled with mistakes. Every now and then a ray of light broke through. Little by little the begrudging attitude of the old salts lessened.

What really snapped us up was the news that came through on August 7, 1942. The first step on the long road back had been taken. The First Marine Division and attached units had landed on an island called Guadalcanal, in the Solomons . . . wherever the hell that was. We were all mighty proud that the Marines had been chosen to make the first American offensive of the war.

We were in the barracks when the news broke. First by radio, then a paper boy came through and quickly sold out. Danny was lying on his sack. He had a tortured expression on his face. It was twisted like, to hold off tears. His newspaper fell to the deck and he left the room quickly and went to the porch outside. The list was on the first page. There, in a short column on the bottom, he saw it.

FIRST CASUALTY REPORT FROM SOLOMONS' FIGHTING

August 8, 1942 (AP) Guadalcanal, BSI with the First Marine Division: Although fighting on Guadalcanal was comparatively free of casualties, sharp resistance was met by attached units landing on the islands across the waters of Skylark Channel; on Tulagi, Gavutu, and Tanembogo. The Navy Department makes this first American casualty list public:

KILLED IN ACTION:

Aarons, Jacob, Cpl., Newbury, Conn.
Burns, Joseph, Pvt., San Francisco, Calif.
Martinelli, Gino., Cpl., Monterey, Calif.
Nix, James B., Lt., Little Rock, Ark.
Norton, Milton, Pfc., Philadelphia, Penna. ....

WOUNDED IN ACTION: ....

I, too, read the list and saw the light. The Marine Corps had not changed. War was still war and they would be dying, no matter what.

I gathered the squad about my bunk. "I just came from the First Sergeant's office and here is the scoop you fellows have been pestering me about. We have four furloughs open for the squad."

A murmur of a special kind of excitement passed through them. "There are nine of you fellows. Burnside and me don't count. There will be two shifts. Two weeks and no travel time. There is only one fair way to do it, draw numbers."

"Just a minute," Andy interrupted. "Count me out. I . . . I ain't got no special place to go. I just ain't interested."

"Me, too," said Ski. The two walked away.

"All right," I said. "I'll make slips up and number them from one to seven. Low numbers are in. Numbers one and two will leave this Saturday." I dropped the folded papers into my canteen cup and shook it up. I didn't like it—someone was going to be left out. They tensely reached in and sat almost afraid to unroll their slips.

Lighttower's face lit up. "I'm going back to the reservation," he sighed.

"Number one," L.Q. said.

"Iowa, here I come," announced Seabags.

"I'm in," Speedy Gray said.

"Number eight." Spanish Joe said and shrugged and walked away. "Don't make no difference, I'd of sold my trip."

Marion and Danny managed a grin. "Lucky seven," Danny said. "I guess you and me are it," he said to Marion.

Just a bad break. Everyone wanted to go home. Danny and Marion went to Danny's bunk. He began cleaning his Reising gun. In a few moments, L.Q. Jones walked over.

"Hey, Big Dan and Mary."

"What?"

"Why don't you two guys fight over my place? I live in L.A. and get home almost every weekend."

"Naw," Danny said, "I couldn't take your furlough."

"Mac, Pucchi, and Keats already said it is O.K."

Danny turned to Marion.

"Look, Danny," Marion said, "I know you won't believe this, but I don't want to go back until it is all over. I mean that."

"I ... I don't know what to say?"

"Better start packing, Danny," Marion said.

"But ... but ..."

"Just say we're big and easy," L.Q. said and slapped his back.

Danny arrived in Philadelphia from the airport. He went directly to the Thirtieth Street station and purchased a ticket for Baltimore and checked his canvas officer's bag in a locker. He caught a cab at the stand outside the huge marble monument to travel.

"Where to, soldier?" the driver asked.

"I'm a Marine," Danny barked.

"Scuse me, didn't notice. You guys are sure touchy about it. All the same country and the same war."

"Three-fifty College Way," Danny directed.

The cabbie's incessant chatter fell on dumb ears. Danny felt uneasy as they whisked past the ancient brick walls and ivy covered buildings of what obviously was the University of Pennsylvania. In a side street, just a short walk from the school, the taxi pulled to a stop.

He found himself standing on the sidewalk looking up at a Victorian structure. The boards creaked beneath his feet as he slowly walked to the porch and into the lobby. He looked down the row of mailboxes and found the name: *Mr. and Mrs. Milton Norton*. He hesitated a moment, then read a sign under the bell: *Out of Order*. He shoved the heavy door open and began to go up a carpeted stairway with a big mahogany rail. He walked to the third floor, along the row of massive doors and squinted to make out the nameplates. He stopped at the end of the hall a moment.

What can I say? What can I tell her? He took off his gloves and knocked. For a long period he stood there. Then the door opened slowly. A frail, pale-faced woman stood before him. She was plain but neat and had a wonderful calm about her. Twenty-seven or twenty-eight, Danny thought.

"Yes?" she asked softly.

"Mrs. Norton?"

"Yes."

"I was a friend of your husband's. I'm Danny Forrester."

"Won't you come in?"

She ushered him into the small apartment. It was modestly but well furnished. Untidy, but untidy in a very neat way. Untidy as a college professor might be. It was like Milton Norton. A large leather chair beneath a floor lamp, a desk littered with papers, shelves of books, including many whose covers were faded and aged beyond reading their titles. A bed without a backboard nestled in an alcove. It was covered with a spread and filled with colored cushions to serve as a couch in the daytime. A comfortable and homey room. Snug and friendly. The walls were covered with pictures of former students.

The room was full of peace of mind. The pale woman who stood in its center was peace of mind. Danny took off his cap and fidgeted.

"Won't you sit down?"

"I can only stay a moment, Mrs. Norton. I'm on furlough from the coast, on the way to Baltimore."

"It was very nice of you to take time to look me up. Do call me Gib. All of Milt's friends do. I'll put on some coffee." She disappeared into the kitchen. Danny walked over to a picture of Nort. He was wearing his uniform. Nort didn't look good in a uniform. It sort of hung on him. He wore his overseas cap straight on top of his head as if he were balancing a basket. Danny studied the picture till she returned.

"The cake is two days old, but I'm told that you fellows have cast-iron stomachs."

Danny smiled. His inner tension had been relieved.

"Let's see now, you're Danny. He wrote about you. He was very fond of you."

"I was fond of the professor . . . I mean Nort. Everybody was, Gib. He had a slow, easy way of looking at things that sort of made a fellow feel like—well, like he was talking to his dad."

She lit a cigarette. "Milt was like that, Danny. This room used to be a madhouse, a dozen kids a night dropped in. People always felt at home around him, especially young people."

"He . . . he was a great guy. I know how much of a loss it was."

She managed a sad little smile and leaned back on the cushions. She spoke of Nort as though he were right this moment teaching at the university and she might expect to hear his footsteps coming up the stairs with the voice of laughing students trailing behind him.

"Gib, these bums followed me home, do you suppose we could feed them?" he would say; or "Gib, I'm worried about the Weber girl. She's got all the brains in the world, but with her family trouble she's liable not to come back to school next year. It would be a shame."

Danny, now relaxed, spoke of their humorous adventures in boot camp with the two Texan drill instructors. Gib laughed and repeated a dozen times, "Poor Milt. Poor dear, I suppose he was a terrible Marine."

Then they ran out of words. The quiet of the room fell over Danny. Nort was still here, in every book, in every messed-up paper.

"Milt told me about you, Danny, and your problem."

"It is awful nice of you to think about me at a time like this. You're a lot like Milt. He was always trying to give somebody a lift."

He stood up and walked slowly towards the door, then turned. "Gib," he said, "are you sorry—are you sorry, now?"

"What do you think, Danny?"

He shook his head.

She took his hand. "Thanks again for coming. It was very nice of you. Would you like to drop me a line once in a while and let me know how you are? All Milt's boys keep in touch."

"He loved you very much, Gib. I can see why." Danny walked through the door.

"Good luck, Marine," she said after him.

A feeling of warmth passed through his body. She was wonderful, like Nort was. She was him and he was her. Then, the warmth passed to a cold chill as he walked down the steps. He had left her alone. She was alone in that room. She would never hear Nort's soft voice speak again. Never again would she anticipate the footsteps and the voices of the students. Dark nights . . . dark cold nights she must lie awake, fearing sleep, and mornings she must awaken and reach for him. He was gone. Nort was dead, under the ground on an island six thousand miles away. He was never coming back. . . .

The lobby door shut and Danny paced quickly away from the place. He wanted to get on a plane and fly back to San Diego. He must not see Kathy . . . no, it wasn't going to happen to her. A terrifying picture flashed through his mind. . . Mac

was standing there in the living room, he was telling Kathy
what a swell guy Danny used to be.

At last next day the moment came when his family was fully
satisfied he was well and safe, and he could take leave of them.
He backed the car from the garage and nervously headed
for Kathy's house.

The night had that sticky East Coast warmth. Wet heat. As
he turned the car into Fairfax Avenue, he felt a strange sensation all over. The nights of dreaming, the days of waiting, the
endless yearning would soon be over. He pulled the car into
the curb and turned off the ignition. Only her house was as he
had pictured it. Everything else in Baltimore—North Avenue,
Garrison Junior High School, the park—seemed small and out
of shape. Had he been gone only seven months? Strange, the
vision and the reality were so far apart. He stepped from the
car and put on his blouse. He must look right.

He stamped out an unfinished cigarette and wiped the dust
from his shoes with the back of his trouser leg. He breathed
deeply and walked to the steps, moving to the porch. He pushed
the doorbell. The house was dark except for a dim light in the
hallway. The emptiness gave him courage for a second, long
ring. No one was home. Danny studied the situation, glanced
at his watch. A foolish thought struck him. Maybe she is out
on a date? No, crazy idea.

He walked to the porch glider, sat, and lit another cigarette.
The heat was stifling. He took off his barracks cap, laid it carefully beside him and unbuttoned his blouse. His foot moved
the glider into a slow creaky sway. Moments, seeming hours,
passed. A car moving down the quiet street gave him a start
... it passed by. Moments more ... it was near ten o'clock.

Then, through the shadows beyond the reach of the street
light came a faint clicking of footsteps. They were Kathy's.
They grew louder in rhythm with the wild pumping of his
heart. He arose and saw her come into view. He tingled all over
... he could see her ... it was no dream. Beautiful Kathy ...
he wanted to rush down and seize her, but he stood frozen, like
a numbed galoot, entranced and speechless.

He watched her move up the steps to the door. Then, as
though there were voices in the night calling to her, she
turned. Their eyes met and neither spoke.

"Danny," she finally whispered.

"Hello, Kathy."

"Danny . . . Danny." And they stood in their places and
gazed at each other. "I . . . we didn't expect you till Tuesday.
Why didn't you phone?"

"I got a forty-eight-hour pass for a head start. Caught a plane. I wanted to surprise you."

"I was at Sally's. I . . . I . . ."

There was another period of awkward wordlessness. A strange tension inside them told them not to speak or the words would choke coming out.

"Would you . . . would you like to take a drive?" he said at last in a half whisper.

"Yes, I'll leave a note for Mother."

The car seemed to find its way over the familiar streets and into Druid Hill Park.

What was it that made me hold onto him, she thought. A sense of duty? Selfishness? Curiosity? What made me write those things to him in my letters? I told him things I knew I shouldn't have, that no decent girl should write. What if my parents knew what I had written? What if Danny knew what I've been thinking? Why didn't I try to stifle those thoughts. It has been an adventure, almost like a fairy tale . . . like make-believe, until now. He is here, beside me. He came so quickly . . . why didn't he let me know?

They drove through the dark tree-bound roads and climbed toward an isolated little hill where lovers often went.

Gib, Nort, Elaine, Eliot, Ski . . . that damn crazy San Diego . . . the damn cursing barracks, he thought. I've been trying to find the right answer to all this but I've let myself slip further and further from her. Maybe it isn't love, maybe I don't know what it is, but I know the feeling inside me now. Maybe I'm afraid—that could be it. I'm afraid of the unknown and I've got to take her with me into it. Could needing her this way be love? All the thinking doesn't seem to make sense now . . . her breathing is hard and I can feel her leaning up against me. We've been here before, but not like this. . . .

The purr of the motor growled a little as the car shifted into second. A muffled voice spoke on the radio. A warm breeze rustled the trees and a quarter moon floated from behind a cloud to turn a dim golden light on the windshield.

The car stopped and he turned off the radio.

They were in each other's arms, exchanging kisses and caresses quietly, their faces pressed together. He felt her tears on his cheek.

(It's no use. It's no use trying to think any more. I can't help myself . . . I can't speak . . . anything. I love him . . . I can't stop myself.)

He held her tightly and the only words were her name over and over.

(Why can't I tell you? Why can't I say I've thought about this till it has nearly driven me crazy? Can it be true that you want me now like I've wanted you? Why don't you stop me? Kathy, stop me . . . stop me . . . I don't want to hurt you. . . .)

His arm reached over her shoulders and his hand went beneath her blouse. She closed her eyes as he touched her breast.

"Danny, Danny, I do love you! Please, darling . . ."

For a moment they calmed, tottering on the brink, as their flashing thoughts tried to stabilize their mounting passion. Then, all reason was drowned in a surging swell of feeling.

Good God, it's no use fighting. . . .

His hand traced the line of her hips and slid down her thigh and he reached beneath her skirt. She raised her body to him so they were crushed against each other. Slowly he lowered her down on the seat of the car.

"Kathy. . . ."

"It's all right, darling, it's all right."

His body became rigid. She could feel his muscles straining and quivering as he clenched his teeth and his fists, then shook his head. He sat bolt upright, grasped the steering wheel, and flicked on the radio.

The sweat poured off his body. It took several moments for his breathing to return to normal. The spell had been shattered. Calmly he reached for a cigarette. "I'm sorry Kathy, I didn't mean to . . . go that far."

She leaned against the opposite door, curled away from him. Her eyes were misty. "I suppose you think I'm . . . no good."

"Don't say that . . . don't ever say that. Don't you know how I feel about you? It was my fault. I should have my teeth kicked out." He took a long puff of his smoke. "We were just carried away, we'll just have to be more careful. I'm sorry, Kathy."

"I'm not," she whispered.

He turned, amazed. "When you went away," she said, "I didn't really know how I felt. I suppose I was selfish. I didn't want to give you up. Maybe it was the glamor of it. I don't know . . . but when you were gone I felt something inside me that I never felt before. Something eating away at me all the time. All I knew was that I wanted you back—all I could think of was you. Maybe . . . maybe we're awfully young, maybe we don't know what love is. I only know that when a girl feels the way I do . . . if it isn't loving someone, then no girl was ever in love."

She turned her eyes away from him. He wanted to reach out once more and take her in his arms, but he knew he dare not touch her again.

"Can't you see? We haven't any right . . . Kathy, do you think I love you so little that I'd do anything to hurt you?"

She stiffened and faced him again. He had never seen her look as she did this moment. There was something grim, fiery, something far removed from her usual calm sweetness. Her voice was mature and filled with authority—the voice of a woman, not a girl. "I'm going to tell you something. It's hard for me to say, but I must. When you went away, neither of us really knew how it would turn out. But we fell in love . . . you love me, don't you, Danny?"

"You know I do."

"When I found out you were coming home, I thought hard about it. What would happen? I decided, a long time ago, that when you came back . . . that . . . that I had nothing that wasn't yours."

Her words knifed through him. It must be hard for her to say this, think this.

"What do you think of me now, Danny?"

"I think you're the most wonderful girl that ever lived. Kathy, if things were different, if there were no war . . . don't you see?"

"No, I don't! I only see that we love each other and in two weeks you'll be gone and I'll start wondering and waiting and lying awake nights."

"We can't, Kathy, I want to be fair to you."

"Then be fair. You owe it to me to love me. I only want to try to make you happy."

"Kathy, Kathy . . . I'm all mixed up."

"Oh, Lord," she cried, "I don't know what made me talk like this. It's only that I love you so."

"Dammit! We've got to get ahold of ourselves. It isn't right. Do you think I don't want to? Look, honey, don't you understand that if it were any other girl in the world . . . but not you, not you."

"And what are we going to do? Hide from each other for two weeks?"

He slumped down in the seat and tried to think. She had offered herself . . . in Dago he had dreamed of it till he was nearly crazy. He had longed for it. Everything was out of balance—it didn't add up to happen like this. "Suppose you have a baby?"

"Danny, you love me, the way I love you?"

"Yes, darling."

"Then, let's get married. Let's get married tomorrow."

"No no, no no!" Why didn't he go back to San Diego? Why did he have to look at her and touch her? "I've got nothing, no roof, no job, nothing . . . what can I give you?"

"Two weeks," she said, "that's more than a lot of people have."

He grabbed her shoulders tightly. "Kathy, it may be two, three, four years. Think! I might never come back . . . remember that. I might never come back."

"I don't care. You're here now, I love you. I love you."

"Did you ever see a girl whose husband got killed? I did, just yesterday. It tears the gut out of you. Do you want to swap a lifetime of grief for two lousy weeks?"

"And suppose you leave, Danny . . . and we don't love each other, and you don't come back? And you leave me to a lifetime of wondering. All my life I'll say: We had two weeks, I could have loved him, I could have made him happy. Give me that, Danny, I have to have it . . . oh God, tell me what's right and what's wrong. I don't know any more, I just don't know."

"Don't look at me that way, Kathy, I didn't start this goddam war."

An unclimbable wall all around them. Two weeks . . . then years . . . maybe forever. He had to go back. Why? Why?

They were limp and silent from spent tension. He softly took her to him and felt her warmth. His lips touched her cheek. They held each other, their eyes closed. He was only human, there was no other way.

"Your parents are going to kick up a fuss."

"They can't stop us."

"Do you realize . . . you're going to be my wife?"

"Yes, Danny."

"Sounds kind of funny, doesn't it?"

"We won't be sorry, Danny."

"It's crazy."

"No crazier than the rest of the world. Let's promise now. We won't count days. We'll just act like you're going to stay forever. We won't think about a thing in the world but us."

"We'll have our lifetime now, Kathy."

"We can try."

"Kathy?"

"Yes, darling."

"As long as we've decided . . . I mean, do you think it will be all right if we find a place? A motel. . . ."

"Yes, Danny."

She nestled her head against his shoulder as they raced from the park toward the waterfront along Hanover Street, then over the city line to the quiet of Annapolis Boulevard.

"Mrs. Forrester," he whispered. "It sounds so strange."

"It sounds wonderful."

"Are you sure, kit?"

"Who is sure of anything? I'm only sure of the way I feel this moment."

They turned left at Glen Burnie and skirted the Chesapeake

Bay, soon leaving the city far behind. A blinking neon sign: AUTO COURT, *Vacancy*, brought them to a stop.

"Wait a minute, I'll be back," he said. He stepped from the car into a noisy bar and went on to the office.

The flickering light and the noise froze Kathy in her seat. In an instant she found herself bewildered. A lonely road, a noisy, full saloon ... shouting ... singing. ...

Danny returned, followed by a short, old, baldheaded man. He took her hand and they followed the man, shuffling in his bedroom slippers along the gravel driveway. He stopped midway in a row of attached rooms and placed a key in the door.

"I'm taking a chance, young fellow. The military is pretty rough about this sort of thing."

The ugly old man made it sound so cheap, Kathy thought. *Taking a chance. This sort of thing.* What kind of a girl does he think I am? Clammy sweat formed on her hands. The door swung open. Danny flicked on the light and shut the door behind him.

It was cold and dank, dingy. The light from the sign sent a red glow off and on, off and on. The headlights from the speeding cars of the highway flashed against the wall as they swept past the court. A loud jukebox blasted from the bar through the paper-thin walls:

> *There's a burlesque theater,*
> *Where the gang likes to go,*
> *To see Queenie, the cutie of the burlesque show. ...*

The hungry months of waiting, the burst of passion on the hill, the pent-up words that had poured from her—they were gone now. She looked at the tall, tanned man in the center of the room. He stood up straight and wore a green uniform. No, it wasn't Danny ... it wasn't he. Danny wore a silver jacket, he slouched when he walked. She tried to correct it ... Danny wasn't dark ... he had fair skin.

He lit a cigarette. It wasn't Danny, it wasn't; Danny didn't smoke. He was young and his eyes were full of mischief. They were not the serious, grim eyes of this man.

What have I done, what have I said? This room ... this dirty room.

> *Take it off, take it off,*
> *Cried the boys in the rear,*
> *Down in front, down in front. ...*

I want to go home. I want to go to my mother ... oh Lord, he's coming to me. She gritted her teeth. He wants to take me

to bed. She became faint with fright. Run! No, it was impossible.
He was near her, he was reaching for her. . . .

"It's all right, Kathy, I understand. Come on, I'll take you
home."

She felt as though she were drunk. Nothing was real. A
car door slammed. A motor sounded. The song and the noise
faded.

> *Queenie, queen of them all,*
> *Queenie, some day you'll fall. . . .*

Again they drove the darkened road. She rolled the window
down to catch some relief from the stifling heat. Slowly her
senses returned. She didn't dare look at him now. What must
he think? She didn't want to see the hurt look. What a miserable mess she had made. She tried to speak, but her words were
gone now.

The road swung close to the shoreline of the bay. A shower
of stars covered the quiet sky. The moon was hidden behind a
row of cypress trees. Then the gentle splashing water came
into view, beating against the moon-silver sand.

"Danny," she cried softly.

He did not answer.

"I'm so ashamed, I'm so terribly ashamed." The tears poured
out. He slowed the car to a stop and sat as she wept it out.

"It wasn't very nice, I'm sorry. We should have never . . .
maybe it is a lot better it happened."

"I don't know what got into me, I don't know."

"You don't have to explain." His voice sounded sad and tired.
He passed his handkerchief; she dried her eyes and blew her
nose and sighed deeply in relief.

"I'm sorry."

"Shhh."

"You look wonderful in your uniform, I didn't tell you."

He didn't want to talk any more. The sudden drop from
heaven to hell left him empty. "I'm all right, now," she said.

He turned the key, then felt her hand on his. "Let's not
drive off, just yet."

"Kathy, we'd better not start up again."

"It was so strange," she whispered, "as if I didn't even know
you. Funny, I never pictured you in uniform. I always sort of
remembered how you looked in school, walking down the hall.
You smoke an awful lot."

"I suppose I've picked up a lot of bad habits. I guess I've
changed."

"No, not really. Danny! Remember the night that you and
me and Sally and Virg drove out this way and went swim-

ming in the moonlight . . . gosh, I guess it was just last summer. Come on, let's take a walk on the beach, it looks scrumptious." She was out of the door before he could protest. They stepped on the sand and she reached down and kicked off her shoes and laughed. "I like to walk on sand."

"Aw, for Christ sake, this is silly."

"Go on, take off your shoes. It feels wonderful."

"Don't be a baby."

"You know who you sound like?"

"No, who?"

"Danny."

Funny, he thought, for the first time during the night she seemed like Kathy. First, the wrought-up, impassioned woman, then, a scared little girl. She skipped through the sand and there was a happy ring to her voice. And at that moment there wasn't any war or any Marines. He was Danny Forrester and she was his girl . . . like it used to be.

"Kathy, come on back here before I drop you."

"Oh, yeah. Big football star, afraid of getting sand on his itsy bitsy feet?"

"Nuts." He sat down and removed his shoes and ran up alongside her.

"I'm going in the water." She ran along the surf's edge where the sand was hard and made crazy little fading footprints. A trickle caught her feet and she jumped back. "It's cold." She held her skirt up and waded in. Danny sat on the beach and watched her.

"Aw, for Christ sake, act your age."

"It's wonderful, come on in."

"Nuts."

"Sissy."

"Come out, will you? I'm not going to sit here all night." He rolled up his pants' legs and dashed to the water's edge and jumped back as it splashed against him. Kathy laughed. "Water too cold for the big halfback?"

"I'll show you." He waded next to her; she kicked a splash up all over him. "I'm going to brain you! You messed up my uniform."

"You'll have to catch me first."

She ran up the beach laughing. Then zigzagged breathlessly and finally bogged down in the sand. He tackled her from behind, gently, as he always did when they were playing.

"I'm going to make you eat sand." She squirmed and tried to wrestle from his grip.

"Danny! Danny! Don't . . . don't . . . uncle . . . uncle!" she laughed.

He pinned her on her back till she was unable to move. Straddling her stomach, he held her down. "Now, one good handful of nice wet sand."

"Danny—don't."

Then, their eyes met. They became motionless. Slowly he released his grip. No words were needed now. It was silent on the beach . . . each could hear only the other's tense breathing. His eyes asked the question. She nodded and drew him down beside her.

Danny buckled up his trousers and walked to the car. He took a blanket from the trunk and made his way down the beach to where she lay. He knelt beside her and gazed. In the trickle of light from the stars her body looked like an ivory statue. Her skin had a dull, satiny look, her hair lay in long waves around her head. A soft wisp of a breeze passed. She stirred, sighed and moved slightly. He leaned over and touched her to make sure that she was real. Gently he spread the blanket over her.

"Yes, darling."

She sighed once more and closed her eyes and opened her arms for him. She held his cheek against her breast and her fingers ran softly over his shoulder. She drew him close. "Oh, Kathy . . . Kathy."

"Sweet."

"There's a little abandoned shack down the beach."

"All right."

"I'll move the car off the road."

The first rays of light caught his eye through the glassless window. Her head lay on his chest. He reached his arm down and with his finger traced the long, graceful line of her back. How wonderful she felt. He pressed her body against his and kissed her cheek. "Kathy," he said softly.

She smiled and hugged him. "It's almost daylight, Kathy. We'd better go now."

She drew herself up, kneeling, and bent down to kiss his lips.

"You're so beautiful. I just like looking at you."

She blushed.

"Do you mind?"

"Not if it makes you happy, darling."

He propped himself against the wall and she rested in his arms. He studied the rickety, dusty, crumbling one-room shack. "Not much of a wedding. No church, no flowers, no presents. I've cheated you already."

She took his hand, kissed it, and placed it on her breast. "I've got you. And I've had a honeymoon that no girl ever had."

"Kathy?"

"What?"

"Did I hurt you?"

"Not much. I . . . I talked to Doctor Abrams. He told me about a lot of things. I'm shameless, I suppose."

"You rat. You never gave me a fighting chance."

"I knew what I wanted. Oh, Danny, I'm so happy. You were so understanding."

"Royal suite, Waldorf, for Mr. and Mrs. Forrester."

"And breakfast in bed."

"Of course, breakfast in bed."

"Danny."

"What?"

"I'm hungry."

They dressed, unwillingly, and walked slowly to the car. She cuddled in his free arm, closed her eyes, and they took off up the road.

"I'm going to make you happy," she said.

"Be quiet, woman."

"Am I any good, Danny?"

"What kind of talk is that from you?"

"Am I any good? I want to be, for you."

"Will you shut up?"

"Tell me, I want to know."

"Well, I suppose you'd bring three bucks in a joint."

"Danny!"

"I shouldn't have said that. Anybody can see you're a five-buck piece."

"Danny?"

"What do you want now?"

"Am I really beautiful? Look at my hair. It's all wet and stringy. I want to look nice for you all the time."

"Go to sleep, will you?"

"Danny?"

"What?"

"Am I as good as that girl in San Diego?"

He almost veered the car into a light pole. Kathy smiled like a little kitten. "I knew all the time. I knew when you didn't write. I don't care . . . I've got you now."

"There'll never be another girl, Kathy . . . never anyone but you."

At a drive-in on the outskirts of the city they ate a sizzling plate of bacon and eggs, and had coffee. As they reached the city limits, the magic spell of the night turned into a cold reality of what lay before them.

"Kathy."

"Yes, darling?"

"We're in for a rough time."

"I know."

"Are you frightened?"

"A little."

"Stick by me."

"They can't stop us, Danny, they can't."

He stopped before her home and slowly emerged from the car. Taking her hand and squeezing it tightly, he winked at her as they trudged up the steps. She smiled and winked back and opened the door.

The four parents were there. Sybil Walker sat sobbing, as did Martha Forrester. The two men were upright and haggard from the all-night vigil. As they entered the room, there was an instant of electric silence.

"Kathy, darling . . . are you all right?"

"Yes, Mother."

"Oh, thank God!" Martha cried. "We were afraid you'd been in an accident."

Another period of silence as they studied their children.

"Where the hell have you been?" Marvin Walker finally roared.

"My goodness, look at you, Kathy."

"We can explain," Danny said softly.

"You're damned right you're going to explain!" The young lovers backed up a step, still holding hands tightly. "We almost lost our minds."

"What have you done, Kathleen?" her mother said, now assured her daughter was alive and safe.

"If we'll all lower our voices," Henry Forrester offered, "I think we can get to the bottom of this much better, Marvin."

"Lower my voice, hell! It's my daughter, Henry—don't forget that. It's my daughter!"

"Kathleen, did . . . did you?"

There was no answer. Martha Forrester wailed. "Oh, Danny, shame, shame, shame. How could you?" she wept.

"You son of a bitch!" Her red-faced father in anger shook his fist beneath Danny's nose.

"What have you done, son?"

"Wait a minute. Wait a minute all of you," Kathy said. "Mother, don't you understand. I love him . . . Dad, please."

"Go to your room, Kathleen!"

"No!"

"Young lady, you're going to be punished so you'll never forget it. As for you—I'll see that the military authorities take care of you!"

"How could you do this to us, Kathleen?"

"Hang on, dammit!" Danny ended his silence. "We love each other. We want to get married."

"Married! You bastard, you! And you . . . this is what I raised you for—to spend the night in the bushes!"

"Danny, they don't understand—they don't want to listen."

The room became still. Only a broken sob came from Danny's hysterical mother.

"Marvin, Sybil—we'd better calm down and talk this over like normal humans. These kids are serious. Martha, dammit! Stop that confounded sniveling or get out of here."

"How dare you speak to me like that."

"Shut up. I've seen that dying swan act too many times to be impressed. Your son has gotten himself into trouble. Either try to help or get out!" She slumped back ashen faced.

Marvin Walker's rage had turned him a sallow white. He stood shaken. The parents all glared at their children.

"What have you to say, son?" Henry asked more calmly.

"Nothing . . . nor any excuses to make," Kathy answered.

"That's it, Dad."

"You're . . . you're not sorry?" Sybil asked.

Kathy shook her head. "We did nothing to be sorry for."

"You were right, Sybil. You told me a long time ago to break this up—I didn't listen. Henry, I think you and your son had better leave my house."

Kathy put her arms about Danny tightly. "I won't stay here . . . take me away, Danny."

"Are you game, Kathy?"

"Yes," she whispered.

"I won't be a party to this," Henry said.

"We don't need your help," Danny answered.

Kathy walked to her mother and knelt before her. "Mother, I love him. I've loved him an awfully long time. I . . . I don't want to hurt you, but can't you see how we feel?" She arose and looked to her father with pleading eyes.

"Get out," he said.

"I'll just be a few minutes, Danny." She ran upstairs.

Danny's eyes were fierce. "Thanks," he spat, "you're grand people. We don't care if the whole damned world is against us—we'll make out."

"Marvin, stop her," her mother cried.

"They're bluffing, Sybil. Let her go. She'll come crawling back. He hasn't got a dime."

Danny walked to the phone. "Western Union, please . . . I want to send a telegram to First Sergeant Pucchi, Headquarters Company, Second Battalion, Sixth Regiment . . . Camp Eliot, California . . . yes, that's correct. Urgent. Have two hundred dollars riding on the books. Wire to Western Union, Balti-

more, at once. Have Mac raise another two hundred from the
squad and round up an apartment or room in Dago. Line up a
job for my wife at North American. . . . Sign it Danny." He con-
firmed the reading and gave Walker's number for the charge.
He threw a bill on the phone stand. "That's for the telegram."

Kathy came downstairs with a suitcase and a coat over her
arm.

"Son, son . . ." his father pleaded.

"Ready, honey?" He winked.

She winked back bravely.

"Kathleen! No! Don't leave us!"

She turned at the door. "What's the answer, Mother?" she
said coldly.

"Anything."

"Dad?"

Marvin Walker's arched back sagged. "You win, Kathleen
. . . God help us."

Henry walked to the girl and placed his arm about her. "Welcome to the family, Mrs. Forrester . . . dammit, I'm glad!"

"Thanks, Dad," she said.

They exchanged vows in an empty, flowerless church, with
only Danny's father and Sally Davis present. The remainder of
his furlough they stayed in an apartment loaned them by Kathy's
spinster aunt.

They grasped desperately for their moment, their outward
actions trying to smother the turmoil inside them, but each new
dawn was greeted with clutching terror. One day less . . . one
day less. . .

Kathy bolted to a sitting position in bed! She was cold and
clammy and her heart pounded wildly. Danny stirred for a moment and reached out and pulled her down close beside him and
she calmed in his arms.

Sleep was impossible for her but he was tired and she must
not let him know. It was the fourth night in a row of the fright-
ening awakenings. Her hand slipped under his pajama top and
she held him tightly. What was this price she must go on paying
and what was their sin?

Danny's eyes opened, he kissed her cheek softly and stroked
her hair and she was again unafraid and happy for the moment.

The sands ran on. . . .

He shook Wilbur Grimes' hand and led her back to the car.
"Nice guy, the coach. I hope you didn't mind me seeing him."

"Of course not, darling." He started the car and she tucked
her feet beneath her and curled up against him.

"Too bad Virg is gone, we could have had a double date with him and Sally, just for kicks. Haunt the old places and get real mushy."

"That would have been fun."

"Light me a cigarette."

"You smoke too much, Danny."

"Nag, nag, nag. Just like a wife. Get home from a hard day at the office . . . five brats climbing all over me and then the old lady starts griping."

"Shut up or I'll deck you."

"Kathy, where did you learn that talk?"

"From you."

They rode, trying to avoid the heavy hearted, sick feeling inside them. The walls were closing in. The invisible hand was pulling him away. A wild notion, yet too clear for comfort—desert, go over the hill.

"Danny?"

"Huh?"

"I want to go to San Diego with you."

He didn't answer.

"I know it sounds crazy, but we can do it. Maybe we'll have another month, even two."

"No," he answered, "that's it . . . don't try to get around me, please."

"Why, darling, why?"

"Don't you see. Kathy? We'll be grabbing at straws."

"But darling . . ."

"Kathy wait. I guess we both know what we are thinking. No use trying to kid ourselves. There's no time left. But honey, if I took you to San Diego it would be . . . desperation. You'd be alone in a room, maybe even one like that motel. You'd sit alone and wait, wondering if every night was the last one. . . ."

"I'm not afraid."

"I know we promised, but we have a lot of things to talk about. We have to try to plan something for the future. It's going to be rough, but one of these days everything will be worth it all. Till that time, this is your home. I want to remember you here . . . safe. It would bust the bubble. If I took you back there, we'd be just another desperate couple in a desperate city."

"I understand," she said. "I'm going to quit school and get a job. With what you'll be sending, I'll be able to set up a little apartment. I want a place, just ours, for you when you come back."

"No!" The sharpness of his voice startled her.

"Danny!"

"I didn't mean to shout. That is out, absolutely. If your folks get too rough, my dad will stand by you. You'll always have a home."

"But why, Danny? I thought you'd be so happy about it."

His mind wandered back two weeks. A lonely haunted room in a third floor walkup. A pale, sad girl there. Alone—alone with the ghost of Nort. If something should happen, if he didn't come back, she must not be alone.

"Why?" she repeated.

"Don't ask me . . . don't ask me."

The airport was asleep at four in the morning. A few tired travelers sat dozing on the hard wooden benches. Danny bent over and mussed his brother's hair. The little boy squinted one eye open and put his arm about his brother.

"Flight Sixty, for Chicago, Cheyenne, Salt Lake, and Los Angeles. Gate Ten."

"Dad, you don't know how much your help . . ."

"Have a good trip, son. Write to us."

"Yes, sir." Henry smiled at the note of respect.

"Don't worry about the home front, son, I'll take good care of her." Their hands clasped tightly. His father stood back as the young couple walked into the night. A sharp wind howled over the runway. The silver monster waited at the gate. They stopped and she became rigid. *He must not see me cry . . . he must not.* She forced a grin on her white face.

"I'll make it up to you, Kathy, some day."

She nodded for fear speaking would bring tears. He held her a moment, then turned and walked away. He turned again at the door and then he disappeared.

A burst of wind, a deafening roar, and the silver wings were swallowed up in the black night.

"Danny! Danny! I love you!" Henry Forrester placed his arm about the girl tenderly and led her back to the car.

7.

I SLEPT with one eye open, an old Marine trick. I had seen plenty of them come back from furlough. Sometimes it took a week, sometimes a month, sometimes they never snapped out of it. It helped if they had someone to talk to when they came in. I always waited up when one of my boys was due back.

That night, a tall, good-looking Marine passed the sentry box at the gate of Camp Eliot. He trudged down the dimly lit, long street, past the row of quiet barracks, leaning slightly under the weight of his heavy officer's bag. The door opened and he stood for a moment. A snore, a grunt, a turn by a restless sleeper. The clicking heels of a marching sentry outside. He walked slowly to his bunk and sat. It was empty. He felt the same way inside. He lit a cigarette and just sat.

"Hello, Danny," I whispered.

"Hi, Mac."

"Have a good furlough?"

"Yes."

"Hey, you guys knock off the crap. Can't a guy get no sleep around this joint?"

"Come on to the head and let's bat the breeze. I can't sleep." I was lying. I wanted to talk.

I led Danny into the toilet room and slapped him across the shoulders. "Twenty miles tomorrow and you'll be good as new."

"Yeah . . . sure."

"Everything all right?"

"Sure, sure. Did the guys get the money back?"

"Yes."

"Sorry I put you to so much trouble, Mac."

"Hell, it wasn't any trouble."

"Mac, I got married."

"The little blonde?"

"Yes."

"I'll be go to hell, that's great."

"Sure, sure."

"Don't go feeling sorry for yourself, Danny."

"I'll be O.K., Mac. Don't worry about me. I just don't feel like going to sleep right now."

"Hell, I almost forgot. I got a letter here for you."

"A letter? That's funny, I just left last night."

"It came a couple days ago." I handed him the special delivery air mail envelope. A grim look came over him.

"Her father. Looks like trouble . . . he's got me over a barrel now."

He ripped the envelope open. Danny was too nervous to read, so I read it to him.

Dear Danny,

I hardly know what to say or where to start. I wanted this letter to reach camp before you got back, because I know how uneasy you must feel.

First of all, I'm not going to apologize for my actions on the morning you brought Kathleen home. I doubt whether you would have acted differently under the same circumstances.

You see, Kathy is an only child and I suppose we've been over-protective with her. We've tried to give her everything in our power, including guidance. It was a shock, to say the least. Too much of a shock to realize that in the last seven months she has changed from adolescence to womanhood. I should have seen it and helped her in her problem, but none of us knew what would happen when you came home.

I am not so bullheaded as to not be able to sit down in the light of a new day and try to reason a problem out. Sybil and I have talked of this a great deal. There is only one reality to face now. My daughter loves you; and her happiness is still the fore-most thing in my mind.

Danny, when the war broke out I was pretty smug about it. I was damned complacent. I had no sons to go off to fight and I knew I'd never live to see the day that Baltimore would be laid open by enemy bombs. It was bonds and the blood bank for me, a superficial aid at best. Yes, I was happy that the war wouldn't reach me. How foolish I was. There is no escaping war, for any of us. And I'm in it, just as my daughter is. You kids have your own life and must make your own decisions. I humbly admit I can't wear your uniform.

You and Kathleen have a tough row to hoe. I suppose you know that. But I feel that you both have the stuff to see it through. I was always fond of you and I do not disapprove of my son-in-law. Only, his methods.

You have a lot on your mind. You've got a war to fight for the old bastards like me. The least I can do is give you the peace of mind of knowing that your wife is safe and that we are with you, all the way.

Sybil is planning a shopping spree with Kathleen for a bunch of silly junk that women look for. Sort of a delayed wedding present.

I hope you talk her out of this idea of quitting school. I know you feel the same as I do about it. College is another thing. We'll come to that next year. I don't want to influence your marriage in any way, but, perhaps you can write to her about this one thing. She's very hardheaded, you know. Takes after her mother.

Well, son, I'd like to hear from you once in a while. You know, just personal between us. If you run short of money (I understand how those things are in the service) feel free to put the bite on me anytime.

"I'll be damned," Danny said. "Think I'll hit the sack, Mac. Better grab an hour before reveille." He folded the letter, smiled, and walked to the barrack room.

Danny did snap back fast. In a corner of his heart, he tucked away the memory of his furlough and drew it out only in an hour of solitude.

During these days, I watched the squad develop, slowly, into a good radio team. Not like the old Corps, mind you—I could still send code faster with my feet than they could with their fists. But they had developed in a competent way that pushed the ancient equipment to its maximum effort.

Danny wasn't a flashy operator, but he was steady. Reliable. I felt good, knowing there would be no trouble as long as he was at the earphones. Marion had the same cool efficiency and it wasn't long before I singled the pair out as a step ahead of the rest of the squad for added duties and responsibilities. Promotion is slow in the Marine Corps, but when the stripe did come, those two would have a jump on the field.

Shortly after Danny's return we began the slow tedious task of packing to ship out. None of us wanted to leave the States, but yet it was welcome when the word was passed down that we were earmarked for overseas. The quicker we got out, the quicker we'd get back.

We all felt that something special was in store for the Sixth Marines. After all, we were a stalwart outfit; our name had been synonymous with trouble for many decades.

With full complement of troops aboard and all gear issued, we began crating up. On each box a white square was stenciled with the figures 2/6 on it, to identify our battalion. (White was always used for the second battalion.) On the piles of crates, too, we stenciled the two mysterious words *Spooner* and *Bobo*. *Spooner* would be our destination and *Bobo*, our ship.

Soon the camp was a mountain of boxes labeled *Spooner Bobo* and for the other battalions of the Sixth *Spooner Lolo* and *Spooner Mumu*. Then the loading and dock parties started.

In true Marine tradition, I found my platoon were first class goof-offs. To flush them out of hiding for the working parties was a full time job. They could find the damnedest excuses and the meanest hiding places that could be conceived. In this respect they matched the old Corps to a T. The platoon was doubly irked when they had to carry the load for the entire Headquarters Company. The corpsmen did no loading, the cooks none; the other sections, very little.

Burnside and me were pissed to the point of blowing our gaskets. Every time a truck pulled in to be loaded we had to go on a safari for the men. At last we commandeered an eight-man tent and put the whole squad in it and either Burnside or me stood watch on them all the time. As the pace picked up, the working parties ran around the clock.

Spanish Joe Gomez, a past master at goldbricking, got out of camp somehow and in San Diego purchased and brought back twenty gallons of Dago Red in a "borrowed" jeep. For three days and nights the squad staggered back and forth between loading details. When the wine ran out, Joe got into town again and in spite of the scrutiny of the camp guards, returned with more of the two-bit-a-gallon poison. They drank themselves into terrible shape. Only Sister Mary remained sober enough to organize a working party.

Throughout the night, awaiting another truck to come for the gear, they lay on unmade cots in the working party tent and guzzled Dago Red. They didn't even bother to eat. Mornings found the deck spotted with pale crimson vomit. A night of wine drinking and they were burning with thirst in the morning. One drink of water to quench the thirst and they were drunk again. I was glad to see the last crate aboard the last truck and heading for the docks. We moved back to the barracks, packed our personal gear, and waited.

A pay call came in the nick of time. We were given liberty and a chance to say farewell in good Marine style. The battalion went out and got plastered.

Then we staggered back to camp and waited. We did not move out. Another liberty—another wait—another liberty. Each nervewracking day we stood by to move out and each night found us in San Diego toasting eternal friendships.

At the end of the week there was no money left to go ashore on. Not a loose nickel in the battalion. Then we began wiring home for money to buy "essentials"—meaning, of course, for one last fling.

Almost as anticlimax, we boarded buses and trucks and moved into the city to the docks. All the crates marked *Spooner Bobo* were there to greet us. They had to be loaded aboard the ship. It meant another few days, and the trouble with working parties started all over. Only here they had more room to hide.

Then I set foot on the *Bobo*. If ever a gyrene wanted to drown his sorrows, I did. I had been in this Corps for more hitches than I cared to mention; I'd been on a lot of troop transports in my time. None of them were luxury liners . . . but the *Bobo* was the filthiest, grimiest, stinkingest pigboat that ever hauled bananas or cows to Havana. I prayed the trip would be a short run. I tried to conceal my displeasure at this floating coffin manned by the merchant marine, but it wasn't easy. Although we had been hitting the bottle heavy for over a week, when we saw her we were ready to go and really get drunk.

Andy, Speedy, L.Q., Seabags, and Danny hit the first bar on Broadway, determined to drink their way, slop shute by slop shute, to the other end of the long street. I wanted to keep an eye on them but got caught in the middle of a Burnside vs.

McQuade bout and I was in a mood to put them both under the table. So I lost contact with the squad in the second bar, and just hoped that morning would find them all aboard ship.

The warriors in forest green sat, bleary eyed, around a table in a cocktail lounge in Crescent City, on the outskirts of San Diego. None of them could coherently tell how they had arrived there. A subdued light played soft shadows on the walls of the place. On a platform, a sleepy-eyed organist trickled her fingers to fill the room with soothing melody.

"Too bad old Mary ain't here."

"Yeah, too bad."

"Yeah."

"Let's drink to old Mary."

"Good idea."

"Yeah."

"Hey, Andy—you still keep track, cousin?"

"Yeah, this is the twenty-third round for me. The eighteenth for the rest of you cherries."

"Hey, L.Q.—you gonna start crying again?"

"I don't want to cry . . . but I just gotta . . . I can't help it. . . ."

"Aw, gee, L.Q., if you cry, I'm gonna cry. Don't cry, buddy." Andy wept too.

"L.Q., Danny, ole' cousins. I ain't gonna let no Jap get you. You the best cousins I ever had. We stick together, we do."

"You ain't got to cry, just cause we're crying, Seabags."

"Can't help myself . . . I love you so much."

"Hey, Andy, why you crying?"

"Ain't no law that says I can't."

Heads turned, some in disgust, some in pity, some laughing at the five husky Marines bawling at the table.

The drinks arrived.

"Who the hell was we gonna toast?"

"Ole Mac."

"Naw, we was gonna toast our pal, Lootenant Bryce."

"Fugg Bryce."

"Let's all toast our beautiful love."

"Yeah."

"Here, L.Q., take my hanky and blow yer nose."

"Thanks, old buddy."

"Hurry, L.Q., we're already done."

"How many does that make, Andy?"

"Eighty-six for me . . . eighty twenty-three for you cherries."

"Phew."

"Burp."

"Anybody here still read the clock?"

"We got fifteen minutes more. Hey waitress, survey!"

Andy wended a wary course to the organist and chatted and staggered back to the table.

In a moment "The Eyes of Texas Are Upon You" blared out. They looked at Speedy. He sucked in a deep breath and fought to his feet and stood at attention. The others arose and wavered until the song was done.

Then the girl at the organ played, "I'll Take Your Home Again, Kathleen" and their eyes turned to Danny. He lowered his head, a tear trickled down his cheek. He felt four sympathetic hands on his shoulders, slapping them knowingly. "Andy, ole buddy . . . that was nice, seeing as you hate women."

"Buck up, Danny ole cousin . . . ain't no Jap gonna get you, buddy buddy."

"Thata mose beautiful thing I ever heard in my life."

It was three in the morning when I found them again. They were doing close order drill right up the middle of Broadway. Fortunately the Shore Patrol wasn't around. Speedy Gray sat on the curbstone blurting out commands and the other four staggered back and forth over the car tracks, resembling a drill team in their first day of boot camp. They were taking off in every direction.

"Hup two, hup two, reah po, reah po," stuttered the waylaid Texan.

"For Chrisake you guys, get off the street," I called.

"Hi, Mac. Lep right lep . . . lep flank . . . po."

"Dammit, you guys get in here before the Shore Patrol brigs you all."

A crowd of late watchers began to gather to observe the precision drill. A civilian standing next to me decided to give me a hand.

"Why don't you fellows do like your sergeant says?" he shouted.

"Never mind," I answered angrily, "if they want to drill, they can drill."

"I was only trying to help you," the civvy said.

"This is strictly an affair of the military, see?"

Speedy had gotten to his feet with the aid of a handy lamppost, and he leaned against the civilian. "Ain't no goddam civvy going to tell us what to do," he said, flipping the man's silk tie up with his finger. He flipped it again and giggled, apparently amused.

"Don't do that again," the man snarled.

Speedy reached up and shoved the man's hat down over his eyes and spun him about. Andy, who had sneaked up from the rear, clouted him and knocked him into my arms. He was out cold. I laid the poor fellow tenderly down on the sidewalk.

"Let's get the hell out of here."

We ran for several blocks, then were slowed by having to drag Seabags, who decided he did not wish to go any further. A few more moments found us catching our breath in the lobby of the plush Lincoln Hotel.

"What you hit that civvy for?" I demanded of Andy.

"Aw, gee, Mac, a guy can't have no fun when you're around." He pouted.

"Come on, let's go out and wreck a bar," Speedy suggested. "Aw, L.Q., now stop crying."

"The bars are closed," I said. "I'm taking you guys back to the ship."

They groaned. Danny arose and looked across the lobby. An all-night long distance operator was on duty at a counter beside a row of phone booths.

"Hey, wait a minute, wait a minute, men. I'm . . . I'm gonna phone Kathy. Come on, fellows, I want you all to meet my kitten." He staggered to the counter. "Hey, lady," he said, "I want to talk to Kathy."

"Do you know the number, Marine?"

"Kathy, in Baltimore. . . ."

"Kathy who?"

"Kathy Walker . . . I mean Forrester. The phone is Liberty 6056 or 5065. Her old man's name is Marvin. Isn't that a hot one—Marvin, Marvin Walker."

"Do you know the street, sir?"

"What do you mean *sir?* I'm just a buck-assed private, lady." He reached in his wallet, it was empty. "Reverse the charges, Marvin is a buddy of mine."

"Hello," a drowsy voice grunted.

"I have a long distance call from San Diego. Will you accept charges?"

"Who in the hell would be calling at five in the—San Diego, yes, of course."

"Here is your party, sir."

"All right you guys, stop shoving. Hello, Marvin!"

"Danny!"

"Hi, Marvin, old pal. Let me speak with my spouse."

"You're drunk."

"Correct."

"Dad, who is it?"

"It's your husband, that's who it is! He's cockeyed drunk and it sounds like he has the whole Marine Corps in the phone booth with him."

"Danny! Danny darling."

"Hi."

"Danny . . . Danny!"

"Hey look, honey. You know all the guys I wrote you about? Most of them are here. Old Mary is reading the Bible so you can't meet him. I want you to meet—stop shoving, dammit."

"Hi, cousin, my name is Seabags."

"Hello, Seabags."

"One at a time."

"Hello, Kathy, I look at you all's picture all the time. You sure are pretty."

"Which one are you?"

"I'm Speedy, mam."

"Oh, hello, Tex."

"Come on, Andy, say something."

"I don't want to."

"Honey, old Andy hates broads and L.Q. is crying. You wouldn't want to talk to L.Q. when he's crying."

I shoved them all out of the booth and closed the door. "Hello, Kathy, this is Mac, Danny's sergeant."

"Hello, Mac." Two words and I could understand the hunger that was inside Danny's heart. It sounded like an angel's voice.

"Look, honey . . . the boys are a little . . . tight. I tried to talk them out of doing this."

"I understand."

"Kathy."

"Yes, Mac."

"You've got a nice boy, we all like him."

"Are . . . are you leaving soon?"

"Yes."

"Oh."

"Look, Kathy . . . don't worry."

"Keep an eye on him, will you?"

"I'll do my best."

I shoved Danny into the booth again and whispered into his ear, "Say something nice, you bastard." A dim sobriety seemed to cut through his alcoholic fog.

"Kitten, you're not sore at me?"

"No, darling, of course not."

"Kathy, Kathy. I . . . I love you."

"I love you too, my darling."

"Good . . . good-by, Kathy."

"Good-by, Danny . . . good luck to all of you."

PART THREE

Prologue

TROOPSHIPS are not designed for comfort, unless you happen to be an officer. I've been on plenty of them but never found worse than the *Bobo*. Whoever converted this freighter must have thrown the drawing board away. Sadists had designed the quarters. There were four holes, two forward and two aft. Each was two decks deep. We were at the bottom of the well. Canvas cots six and seven high, spaced just about as far apart as flapjacks on a platter. You had to lay on your back or stomach, flat. A roll sideways and you'd hit the cot over you.

Lighting was almost nil. The ventilation was a laugh—if you could call it funny. Space between the tiers of cots was so narrow you were forced to walk sideways, over crammed aisles of seabags and packs, to your miserable piece of canvas. The covered section of each hold was massed with crates. It was terrible, even for an old-timer like me.

At long last we saw green hills looming over the horizon one morning. The horrible journey was over. The hated *Bobo* slipped into the bay and we looked, in awe, at the rolling hills, the quaint, brightly colored houses and the still, beautiful calm of the land. We had reached Spooner, New Zealand!

There were about four thousand of us in New Zealand and the land was ours. Our chow was beefsteak, eggs, ice cream, and all the milk a man could hold. And the people opened their homes to us.

That was one of the wonderful things about being a Marine. The feel of a new land under your feet. As you marched down Lambdon Quay in step with a buddy, your greens sharp and your leather shiny, you saw them turn and smile. The strange smell of foreign cooking and the new and wonderful odors of ale and tobacco; the funny way of talking and the funny money, and the honest merchants who gave baffled Marines a square shake. The beauty of the rolling hills and the gentle summer and the quaintness of the Victorian buildings, matching the slow, uneventful way of life. We were happy in

179

New Zealand. As happy as a man can be six thousand miles away from his home. And my boys were tough and ready. Huxley's Whores—the whole Sixth Marines were like nails.

My squad was fast beoming radio men, like the speed merchants of the old Corps. Their fists were certain as they handled the keys. Our walkie-talkie net amazed the entire regiment. Mary knew his business. If I could only stop them from sending dirty messages—someday we'd be intercepted and the boom would be lowered on us for fair.

Our skins were turning yellow from the daily dosages of atabrine, but I kept close track to see that it wasn't ditched. I had had malaria on the islands ten years before when I was in Manila and I'd have been damned glad to have had atabrine, turn yellow or not.

1.

IN NO time at all, the word was all over Wellington and the sidewalks were lined with smiling gawkers as the Sixth went by.

"Hi, Limey!"

"We aren't Limeys. We're New Zealanders."

"Let me see that penny. Man, look at the size of it."

"Hi, Yank," a girl called from an office window.

"Toss your name and phone number down, honey. I'll give you a ring."

"Fine, Yank—and I have some girl friends."

"You boys from the Fifth Regiment of Marines?"

"Naw, we're the Sixth."

"You wear the same braid."

"Them guys is just cashing in on our glory," we said of the boys who were even then fighting for the life of New Zealand on Guadalcanal. Yes, they were glad to see us. The tentacles of the Japanese Empire were reaching down to snatch at their country. Every man and woman had been organized to fight to the bitter end. Their own men were a long way away and a long time gone. In the Middle East.

The Fifth Marines had come and left for Guadalcanal. And then we had come, and the Kiwi's gave a happy sigh, like they could get a good night's sleep. A gang of cocky, spoiled Yanks —but they loved us.

And after the *Bobo*, how we loved them!

"Fall in, godammit, on the double!"

We were off on our first hike in New Zealand. A half mile

to the camp gate, then two miles down the highway and a right turn up the slowly winding dirt road. It twisted in a slow rise for nearly four miles. We called it the Little Burma road. From the top, fifteen hundred feet up, we could see the rolling green hills, small dotted farms, and in the distance the ocean.

Then we raced over the hills, through ravines and gulleys, over wire fences, along sheer sheep trails, sliding and falling in sheep drop. Through the woods until we wound up in back of Camp McKay, and Paekakaraki, which we could see far below us. Then down a treacherous cliff on our backs and guts until we descended into camp.

On alternate days we reversed the course. Climbing the cliff in the rear of camp first and through the hills and trails and sheep farms to reach the top of the Little Burma. Then, down hill for four miles, to the highway and back to the camp gate.

The Little Burma run was only twelve to fifteen miles, depending on what route was taken, but I felt it was the meanest course I'd ever gone. It was November in New Zealand and the middle of summer and it was hot. The long stretch up the Little Burma was plain wicked. The slow rise sapped the juice out of our legs and the weight of the gear hung like a heavy burden. Then came the sweat, the eternal sweat. Soggy, drenching sweat —and plenty of bitching from the men. Sweat from the feet irritated the blisters.

We'd pause to eat C-Rations at the top where the road leveled off. You had to keep an eye on the water. It was a long way back to camp and we didn't have any place for stragglers in this outfit. A sweating Marine who drinks too much pukes, and can't hike.

If the climb up Little Burma was rugged, the hike down her was worse. Going downhill the impact hits you with every goddam step. Your legs act like brakes for four miles and the weight of the pack slams into you with every pace. The downhill runs were the ones that make your knees buckle and your legs feel like they were turning to jelly.

Salt pills. I could never figure how a little pill could replace ten gallons of sweat. Suck them slow or you'll puke. And lay off the water. Salt makes you thirsty, and too much water will fold you like an accordion.

On the days we carried heavy equipment we'd pull hard on the awkward carts till our hands cracked. We'd throw our bodies against them to keep them from running down the trails. The walkie-talkies made fifty more pounds to lug. Downhill we'd strain and dig our heels into the deck to keep from running away.

On the days we went with just combat packs, Burnside set a murderous pace. He was a hiking fool. The case of beer he had drunk the day before worked out of every pore, till he looked like he was floating. As we hit the camp gate he'd yell, "Double time!" We'd run a hundred yards, then quick pace a hundred and run another hundred till we reached the foot of Little Burma.

One day, we went clear from camp to the peak of the road without stopping. And downhill too, we'd hit the bottom of the road and run all the way into camp, straight to the parade ground.

"There go Huxley's Whores!"

Huxley had the time he had bid for; he had the conditions he wanted and he spared no rods on us. And then we began to pass outfits along the route, crapped out and exhausted. "Candy-ass Marines," our boys would shout as we flashed past them.

Highpockets Huxley, for reasons known only to himself, went on trying to make a Marine out of our company commander, Lieutenant Bryce. There was an intense rivalry between the Intelligence Squad and our platoon. On alternate days Bryce was assigned to hike with us. On the other days, he'd go with Sergeant Paris' boys. Many a case of beer was bet on who would hike him into the deck first. When Bryce was with us, we'd scorch the road until we saw his ass starting to drag, then Burnside would open a mile-long burst on the uphill pull. If Bryce wasn't on his knees yet, we'd wait until he had that far away look as if he was going to quote Shakespeare, then we'd double time. Bryce knew he'd get his ass burned out by the Major if he fell out and he sometimes made it rough on us to finally put him away.

Huxley made everyone in the battalion hike. From time to time cooks, field musics, corpsmen, and other dead weight were assigned to go along with us. For the most part they didn't hold up too well. We left them littered about here and there along the route to limp back to camp on their own.

"Tenshun!"

"All present and accounted for, sir."

"At ease."

Lieutenant Bryce opened the document and read the usual birthday greetings of the Corps from the Commandant. His letter had the flavor of glory, duty, and honor and recalled great feats of the past and the task of the future. In accordance with tradition a day of rest was declared and two bottles of beer were issued to all enlisted men. After a rousing "Semper Fidelis" the formation broke and we entered into our hundred and sixty-seventh year.

"Dibs on your beer, Mary."

"Two lousy bottles, can they spare it?"

"Aw shaddup, ain't you got no sentiment, cousin?"

The garbage truck finished its pickup of large cans of slop from each company mess hall. Hanging on the back for dear life as it sped along the bumpy dirt road toward the dump were Shining Lighttower and L.Q. Jones. As the truck bounced, the contents of the cans splattered all over the two men. Soon they were standing ankle deep in garbage and then the cans began sliding about on the slick iron deck of the truck. It was difficult to hang on, much less try to be nimble as a ballet dancer to avoid the cans, to say nothing of the showers of slush being rained on them.

"Radio men—haha, I'm laughing," L.Q. groaned.

"I want to go back to the reservation."

"Naaa . . . naaaa," sneered Speedy Gray from the chow line.

"Naaaaaa," repeated Seabags at Burnside, who was up ahead of him.

"Naaa," said L.Q.

"Naaaa," said Lighttower.

The inference in their calls to Sergeant Burnside was that he was more goat than human when he hiked them along the mountainside trails. Burnside spun around quickly as the last bleat came out and the four mutineers looked lazily at the sky. After chow, Burnside came into their tent as they moved into their gear for the usual hike.

"I feel I have been hiking you boys too hard," he said.

Their eyes turned to him suspiciously.

"Yes sir," he continued. "I feel kind of bad because you think old Sarge here is more mountain goat than gyrene."

"Aw, Burnside, we was just kidding."

"Shucks, cousin, we love hiking."

"No, no," Burnside said holding up his hands piously. "I want to give you four fellows a rest. You don't have to hike any more."

"Oh-oh . . . he's got a gizmo up his sleeve."

"Happens that the cook was talking to me this morning."

"Looks like we got potwalloping, men."

"Aw, fellows, you don't think that Burnside would make his boys potwallop? Clean out them old greasy pots . . . now do you? You get enough of that dirty work when your turn for mess duty comes up."

"Gee, Sarge, you really giving us the day off?"

"Now, ain't that right nice of Burnside."

"Seems as though the grease trap at the bottom of the cesspool is clogged," Burnside continued, "so I says to myself, now I been hiking them boys too hard. Besides, a day in the cesspool might be refreshing. So I went and volunteered you to bucket the slop out and release the trap. Matter of fact, I'm even going to let you use the communications cart to run the stuff out to the boondocks. But please, fellows, please clean out the cart when you finish."

He went to the tent flap, then turned. "As for the rest of us, I think we'll take it slow and easy to the Little Burma and go out in the woods and just lay by a stream and crap out with a little TBX practice. Ta-ta."

"The cesspool!"

"You're always getting me into trouble, white man. Me and you have split the blanket."

"Go on, you goddam renegade, blame it on me."

"Man, that stuff down there stinks worse than limburger," Speedy moaned.

"Rather spread a ton of manure," Seabags said.

They trudged sadly to the rear of the mess area and adjusted clothespins to their noses. The cesspool was an aged, well-like construction. All the waste garbage and slush was tossed down it. On the bottom, some fifteen feet down, was an iron grate filtering the waste and funneling it to a subterranean runway. Generally, a hosing from above was sufficient to break loose any clogs; however, at the moment it was dammed up tight with gray slop that had backed up some five feet in the well.

They lifted the wooden cover from the opening. The vile odor blasted them back. Bravely they edged forward again and peered down.

"We'll draw straws to see who goes down."

"Shucks, I'm too big to fit in the opening, fellows, so I guess I'll just have to help bucket the stuff off from up here." Seabags smiled.

"To hell with that noise," Speedy cried.

All eyes turned to L.Q. Jones. "Don't look at me that way, old buddy buddies . . . besides, you guys always said I'm a blimp."

"You was the one that dreamed up that bleating at Burnside, L.Q."

"Fellows! Let's be democratic about this. Let's talk this over."

"Sure, we'll be democratic, L.Q.," the Texan said. "Let's vote . . . I vote for Jones."

"Ugh," said the Injun.

"Recktum you're the unanimous candidate," said Seabags, handing him a rubber suit and gas mask.

It was a long day for the cesspool detail. A hundred buckets were raised and run out to the boondocks before L.Q. could pearl dive for the trap. Finally, he sprung it. As he climbed up the ladder triumphantly and took off the mask, the others coughed violently, as though a skunk was loose.

"Clean out the cart," Seabags said. "I got three days service over you. Besides, I'm a regular and you're a reserve. We can't stand the smell another minute." They took off at high port, leaving L.Q. to finish the detail.

The smelly gyrene finally headed back to his tent. As he moved down the catwalk strong men cleared a path for him. He opened the tent flap and stepped in.

"Gawd! Get out of here!"

Someone hurled a helmet in his direction, making him duck out of the tent. In a few seconds, a hand reached out of the tent flap and dropped a towel, soap, and scrubbing brush at his feet.

"And don't come back till you smell like roses!"

Dear Mom,
  I'm not allowed to tell you where I am. However, I find that I have lots of new zeal and energy . . .

"Come in, Pfc. Jones. Did you write this letter?"

"Yes, sir."

"You may go, Private Jones."

2.

ANDY HOOKANS strolled listlessly through the Wellington railway station. He had missed the first liberty train back to camp and it was nearly an hour until the next one.

He walked outside for a breath of air. Across the street he saw a sign: SALVATION ARMY CANTEEN—*Welcome Armed Forces Members*. He entered and seated himself upon a stool at one end of a long counter.

"May I help you, Yank?"

"Coffee, please."

The big Swede eyed her from stem to stern as she filled his cup. Not bad, not bad at all. Tall, slim, not skinny exactly . . . fair skin like most of the girls here . . . short hair, kind of honey blond. She passed the cup over the counter.

"Anything else, please?" she said smiling.

"Yes."

"What?"

"Talk to me."

"Oh, I'm afraid I can't do that, you know. Against the rules to fraternize on duty."

"Doesn't seem like much business tonight."

"Picks up a few minutes before train time. Fast cup of coffee for the Americans, you know."

"Is that so? My name is Andy."

She turned to go.

"Come to think of it, I'd like a crumpet or whatever you call those things."

"You could just as well reach over and get it yourself."

"Nice country you've got here."

"I'm glad you like it, but of course nothing can compare with America."

"Matter of fact, it compares very well."

"Really," she said in amazement. "I say, you *are* a rare one."

"That is correct, but you didn't give me a chance to tell you."

"We do hope you boys like us. We owe so much to you, with the Japs breathing down our necks and our own lads so far away."

"You here often?"

"I do a regular turn twice a week. Now, I told you, no fraternizing."

"No fraternizing *Andy*," he corrected.

"I've another customer. Excuse me please."

"Don't stay too long. I want to tell you about what an amazing fellow I am."

He watched her move on down the counter and serve a Kiwi airman. Andy disliked these opening maneuvers. However, he reckoned they were necessary. He also liked what he saw and there were only a few invaluable moments to try for it. Nothing ventured, nothing gained. As she moved about on her duties, he managed to slip in a word of conversation from time to time.

"What part of America are you from?"

"Washington."

"Oh, the capital?"

"No, Washington State, there's a difference."

"Come now, I went to school, you know. Washington is on the western coast of the United States and produces large quantities of timber," she recited.

"And I cut down half that timber before I enlisted."

"Really, that is interesting—a woodsman."

"Lumberjack." (Now don't flit off again, honey.)

"And you really cut trees at one of those camps?"

"Topped them, cut them, and floated them down the river." (That's right, just lean over the counter and get real interested.) "My name's really Bunyan but modesty forbids so I go by the name of Hookans." (Smile pretty.) "By the way, I didn't catch your name."

"Pat, Pat Rogers."

"I knew a girl by the name of Pat once." (What a dirty bitch she was.) "Heck of a nice girl. Came from Spokane, I had a big crush on her when I was a kid." (Every guy in town was laying her.)

"Yes, there are Pats all over. Small world," she said. (Clever comeback . . . ripping, eh wot?)

"Say Pat, in the interest of harmony among the Allies and lend-lease and my morale, how about a date?" (Close in, boy.)

"I'm afraid I couldn't." (Aw honey, don't make it rough on old Andy.)

"I haven't met anybody since I've been here. I guess I don't make friends easy. I sure would like an evening of dancing and movies. Maybe help me forget I'm so homesick." (To say nothing of a night in bed with you.)

"Thanks very much, Andy, but I'm afraid I'll have to let that part of the war effort down. Nice meeting you." (Boy, she didn't mince words. I'll play it pathetic, then quit.)

He gave a weak smile and grinned like a naughty puppy that was caught in the act and looking for pity. She sighed, shrugged and turned to meet the onrush of Marines pouring in for a quick cup of coffee. He propped his elbows on the counter, put his chin in his hands and looked doleful. Then he spotted the wedding ring on her hand. (Married!) He slipped on his overseas cap, squared away and turned to leave. She met him at the end of the counter.

"Andy."

"Yes?"

"You don't mind if I'm fickle, woman's prerogative. Flickers and dancing do sound nice and I haven't been out in an awfully long time. Could I take you up on it?"

(I've heard everything now, sister. Pining away for your old man in the Middle East? I'll bet you haven't been out since last night.) "You bet you can take me up on it. Just lead the way, wherever you want to go. I get liberty Thursday. I'll be ashore around six, how's that?"

"I'll have to get someone to take my shift, but I'll arrange it." (I'm sure you will . . . old Andy likes married broads, well broken in.)

"Where shall I pick you up?"

"Salvation Army Hotel for Women. On Nelson Square, a bit above Lambdon Quay." (Salvation Army Hotel . . . oh well, I can always get a hotel room.)

"See you Thursday and thanks, Pat." (Yeah, see you in the sack, old bean.)

"I don't give a big rat's ass . . . see, I don't give a big rat's ass." Ski wavered and hit the bar with his face.

"You'd better cut this out, Ski, or you'll get shipped to field music."

"I don't give a big rat's ass. Don't make no goddam difference nohow, any more."

"Are you coming or do I get rough?" Danny demanded.

"You're my buddy, Danny. You're my buddy and you like me even though she don't. A 4-F . . . a stinking 4-F."

"Cut it out. You're going to crack up bigger than crap if you don't quit eating your heart out."

"I don't give a big rat's ass."

"You've been in the brig twice already. Once more and Huxley is going to ship you out."

One day, several weeks after their arrival in New Zealand, I saw my squad in a different light.

Burnside and McQuade had gone on a real pisscutter the night before. The staunch hiker was faltering on his pace. We'd made the Little Burma and pushed halfway up. Then Burny called for a break and sank to the side of the dirt road, under a tree, drenched in sweat.

"Come on, Burnside, getting candy-assed?"

"Yeah, how we ever going to beat Bn 2's record if you quit after four miles?"

"Let's wind it up, Burny, the liberty train goes tonight."

Then it dawned on me. Any man in the platoon could set the pace now. The cumbersome weight he carried didn't mean a thing. Even during the breaks the men no longer bothered to ease the packs from their backs for a rest. And canteens that left camp full returned nearly full. The squad was rugged and hard. Highpockets was getting what he had striven for.

After the hikes we all raced for the ice cold showers. Warm water was a luxury not afforded us. The needles of frigid water washed away the sweat and grim and there was liberty to look forward to. A night at a pub, or with a girl in Wellington. The men drank and slept with their shackups and ran for the liberty train which left at midnight. The train was always overcrowded. Sometimes they had to spend the trip sleeping up in the luggage rack or on the deck. The train stopped at Paekakaraki at two in the morning. From there we hiked the highway for two miles to Camp McKay and fell exhausted on our sacks at three. At six we arose to hike another day and go on liberty another night.

Reveille, roll call and double time a mile before chow. Clean the gear, fall in . . . hike to Little Burma.

We'd communicate. By radio, by phone, by flares, by pyrotechnics, by panels, by semaphore, by air-ground pick up, by runners, by flash guns. We practiced code till we were dit happy.

We broke down and set up the TBXs until we could do it blind-fold.

Pat laughed as they climbed the hill off Lambdon Quay to-wards the Salvation Army Hotel for Women.

"I've had a grand time, Andy. I'm glad I used my preroga-tive on you."

"Me too. We'll do it again, real soon."

"If you'd like. Do you think I'd make a good lumberjack?"

"You'd made a good something," he puffed, slowing her down. "I get winded when I don't have a pack on my back. You'd make a good running mate for Burnside. I think you women hike uphill faster than you do on level ground."

They turned at the gate that led up the path to the hotel. Andy unlatched it, took her arm, and they walked up. Near the entrance to the huge converted mansion she turned.

"Good night, Andy. It was really lovely." She extended her hand to him. He seized her and kissed her. She pushed away from him hard. "Don't ruin it," she said.

"Aw come on Pat, cut the act."

"I beg your pardon?"

He swung her forward again, but she resisted. "Stop it, please!"

He released her and gave a sardonic smile. "You ain't any different than the rest," he said. "Play hard to get . . . oh, really, this is the first time I've been dancing in years . . . baloney."

"I think you'd better go, Andy."

"What have you been doing with the Marines in town? Cry-ing away for your husband while he's sweating in North Africa?"

She arched her back. "My husband," she said, "was killed in Crete two years ago."

Andy sagged back as she walked quickly to the door.

It was a calm, soft New Zealand Sunday. The Second Bat-talion had the camp duty. After chow and church the men wan-dered back to their tents. Gear was cleaned, leather shined, and clothes washed on the laundry racks and uniforms pressed for the next days of liberty. Then came a crap-out session. Talk about home and talk about women. Scuttlebutt on the Marines on Guadalcanal and scuttlebutt about where they were going. Sister Mary went to the Company office to pound out a story. The Injun and Seabags pitched horseshoes down the Company street. The rest, except for Andy, Danny, and Ski, played softball on the rocky diamond on the parade ground.

Finally Danny laced on his boondockers and loaded up a couple of ammo clips.

"What you doing, Danny?"

"Going back in the hills. The farmer on the last hike told me they've got some wild boars back there."

"Oh yeah, how far?"

"About ten miles."

"Christ on a crutch, you hike six days a week. What you want to go back there on crap-out day for?"

"I don't feel comfortable when I'm not hiking."

"You're cracking up bigger'n crap . . . wait a minute, I'll go will you."

They stepped to the tent flap. "Want to come along, Ski?" The Feathermerchant stared idly at the tent top and gave no answer.

"I'd better fill my canteen," Andy said, "and check out with Mac. Christ, I'm worried about Ski."

"Me too. But I suppose time is the only thing."

"Goddam women."

They crossed the open sheds that housed the mess and filled their canteens at a spigot. Then they went to the galley and bummed some sandwiches and soluble coffee from the cook.

"Danny?"

"Yeah."

"Did you ever apologize to anyone?" Andy asked.

"What kind of stupid-assed question is that, of course I have."

"Many times?"

"Sure."

"I mean, be real sorry for something and just go up and say you're sorry."

"Sure."

"Ever say it to a broad?"

"Why the third degree?"

"I just wondered."

Andy Hookans walked into the Salvation Army Canteen and looked about for Pat Rogers. She was at her usual spot behind the counter. He stood and watched some Kiwi's play pingpong until the coast was clear. Then he advanced and took a seat. She saw him and turned away. His face reddened.

"Pat, please," he said, "I want to talk to you for a minute."

"Will you please leave, Yank. I don't wish to see or have anything more to do with you."

"Look," he said, "if you don't let me say what I came in to

say, I'm going to jump this counter and drag you out by the hair and make you listen."

"Be quiet! You're starting a scene."

"In ten seconds I'm coming over and get you. Please, two minutes is all I ask."

She glanced about the room and saw eyes turning in their direction. She sighed disgustedly. "I warn you, Yank, I don't want you to give me any more trouble. I'm just doing this to avoid a scene."

They stepped from the canteen into the shadows cast by a small streetlight. Andy fumbled, face flushed and voice nervous. He lifted his eyes to hers. "Pat . . . I ain't never said I'm sorry to no one as long as I lived. I ain't ever apologized for nothing."

She turned away.

"But I'm saying I'm sorry to you. I ain't ever been sorry for a thing I've ever done or said. . . but I feel bad, real bad, and I couldn't rest easy till I told you." There was silence for many seconds. "That's all I wanted to say," he whispered.

"That was nice of you, Andy, I appreciate it. We all make mistakes, you know."

"I don't expect you'll want to go out with me again and I don't blame you . . . but I'd like you to take this." He handed her a small package. "Don't get the wrong idea . . . I . . . just want to show you . . . well, you know what I mean."

"I accept the apology, but I'm afraid I couldn't take the gift."

"Please take it, I want you to. I won't bother you no more."

She opened the neatly wrapped package and looked at a pair of tiny, well-chosen earrings. "Oh, they are lovely."

"You'll wear them sometimes, maybe?"

"Yes, I'll wear them . . . it's nice of you, Andy. I know this hasn't been easy for you to do."

He extended his hand. "Thanks, I'll shove off now." He walked briskly, half cursing himself for the first honest humility he had ever shown.

"Andy," Pat called.

"Yes."

"Why don't you come in and have a cup of coffee? I'm off duty soon and you could walk me home."

3.

MARION HODGKISS was a happy Marine. A mail call never rolled by without a letter or package from Rae. Mostly books and more knitted stuff than he could ever wear.

We were proud of Marion; it wasn't every outfit that could boast a writer. Each minute off duty was spent in Pucchi's office pounding out stories, and the magazines back home were grabbing them up. We were doubly proud when he turned down a public relations offer in order to stay with the outfit.

Although everything seemed the same between him and Spanish Joe, I couldn't help but feel that in back of his fierce black eyes Gomez kindled and fanned a slow burn. Something told me that there was going to be serious trouble between the two before the cruise was over.

In the half hour before evening chow, we usually played touch football on the rocky parade ground. Sergeant Herman, the quartermaster, had slipped a football in with the gear. It was nice of him to save space for it—along with his five personal cases of shirts, skivvies, socks, and other stuff he had "borrowed" during his tenure as QM. It was scuttlebutt that he planned to open an Army and Navy Store after he mustered out of the Corps. He had a very fine start. Herman, like any good Bn 4 man, literally bled every time he issued a piece of gear. It was like he was losing a son.

Promotions came. All except Spanish Joe and Lighttower were made Pfc and Danny was advanced to corporal. There was the usual ceremony—saluting, reading the long-winded document, cutting corners squarely.

Danny sewed the last stitch of his new chevron and an anxious squad peered over his shoulder. It is Marine custom to "stick on" a new stripe for good luck. Each man in the outfit punches the promotee in the arm, once for each pay grade. Danny being a corporal, had to receive two whacks in the arm to assure his long life in that rate. By the time I got to him his arm was limp. I remembered the time I had made Master Tech and took six raps apiece from the whole company. I took my two swipes at Danny, who took the last two punches with a sigh of relief and, as is the custom, invited us all down to the slop shute for a brew.

L. Q. Jones squared away his field scarf and paced nervously over to Speedy Gray's sack. They were preparing for a double date in Wellington. The Texan brushed his dress shoes with a slow, almost static motion that only he was capable of.

> *"They was a riding down the river,*
> *Jest a settin' on the stern,*
> *She was holding his'n,*
> *And he was holdin her'n ..."*

"Come on, Speedy, get off the pot. Liberty train goes soon."

"Now jest take it slow and easy, pard. We'll meet them hyenas in plenty of time."

"Hey, Tex—same two beasts as last time?"

"Yep."

"I hear they call them sisters the witches of Wellington."

"Now, let's not go into that mildewed routine about old O. and her sister," L.Q. said.

"Man," said Seabags, "I'm getting tired of these foreign women. I had me a broad the other night. Took near an hour to get her damned knee pants off."

"They sure are scratchy."

"What I wouldn't give to run into a nice pair of silk skivvies. Man ain't got no maneuvering room in them long johns."

"Shut up, you bastards," Danny said. "My wife's picture is on the wall."

"How come you ain't going to see old Olga with L.Q., Chief?"

"Last time we stayed after curfew. We hadda sneak all over Wellington trying to get to the railroad yards, then we hadda ride to Paekak in a sheep car. Filled with sheep, yet."

"Hey, Speedy ... you coming or not?"

"Easy, boy, easy."

"Anyhow," the Injun continued, "we hit Paekak a half hour before reveille and it's raining like hell. We hit the parade ground and who did we run into—Sarge Pucchi."

"Yeah, I remember that," Andy said. "L.Q. is wheezing and dripping wet. 'Fine morning,' he says to Pucchi. 'Thought I'd take a walk in the hills.' "

"Yeah, and Pucchi sniffs L.Q. and says, 'Sheep. Why, L.Q. I'm surprised at you.' "

"L.Q., where oh where did you meet them women?"

"Well, he can put a flag over Olga's face and go for old glory."

"O.K.," L.Q. said, red-faced. "What if they are the last roses of summer? While you bastards are wilting away in a pub drinking hot ale, L.Q. Jones is working over Scotch and soda, with ice in it, real ice. Olga's the only broad in New Zealand with an icebox and her old man is loaded. Godammit, Speedy, you coming or not?"

"Don't rush me, boy, don't rush me . . . I'm an artist."

Andy unlatched the gate that led to the Salvation Army Hotel for Women.

"Let's walk up the hill a bit, I don't feel quite like turning in."

They walked the steep hill to a point where the paved street ended for vehicles, then took the zigzag stairway to the top. They came to a rest along a concrete rail guarding the drop. Andy looked down on the browned-out and sleepy city. In the distance they could see the dim outline of ships cluttering the harbor.

"Phew," Andy said, catching his breath. "Pretty up here."

"Softy."

They leaned on the rail and gazed at the view below them. Andy lit two cigarettes and handed Pat one, and helped her to a sitting position on the rail. Her back rested against a lightpost.

"I saw a flicker once where the hero always lit two cigarettes that way. I always wanted someone to do that for me."

"You cold?"

"It is a wee bit chilly."

He opened his green overcoat, which he had been carrying folded over his arm, and put it about her shoulders. "Thanks, now there's a dear."

They puffed contentedly. "Funny," Andy said, "I used to think that New Zealand was right next to Australia. Sure get a crazy idea in your mind of a place. Just like most of the people here thinking America is a place where you just pick dollar bills off trees and everything runs by a motor."

"The girls at the hotel . . . I really shouldn't say this. . . ."

"Go on."

"Well, most of them are hoping to hook a Yank. You boys don't help much either. With our own lads being gone so long, and those uniforms and the way you throw money about."

"I guess we're pretty cocky."

"Too right. We're not used to so much attention, you know."

"Sure is crazy the way everything turns upside down in a war, Pat. People don't realize what has gone on here. We talked about an all-out effort back home. I know what those words mean, now. You people have taken an awful beating."

"It wasn't nice, Andy . . . Crete and Greece and now North Africa. The casualty page was full for weeks when they trapped us on Crete."

"I mean, Pat, everyone here has lost someone. I guess that doesn't come easy . . . but what I like is the guts. The way you accept things, quiet and calm-like, and take in your belt another notch. They're great people here. . . . Pat, what kind of a guy was your husband?"

"Don? Oh, just a plain boy. A distant cousin . . . we had the same name, Rogers. We were only married six months when he shipped over. . . ."

"I'm sorry. I'll change the subject."

"You do like New Zealand, don't you, Andy?"

"Yes, I do. I like the way everybody takes it slow and easy and like they know where they're going and what they're doing. I like it how there ain't no real rich or no poor. Everybody the same, even the Maoris."

"We're proud of the Maoris. After all, it was their country we took."

"Let me tell you something, Pat: it's bad, us being here. A lot of people talk about wanting to be like Americans. That ain't right, you've got the right idea."

"Andy, that's no way to talk."

"Oh hell, I guess I'm proud enough about wearing this uniform. There ain't no guys in the world like my buddies . . . but somehow I just feel like it doesn't owe me nothing and I don't owe it nothing."

"What's the matter, Andy? Sometimes you give me quite a fright, the way you talk . . . the way you think about women."

"It's a long story, and not very interesting." He took a last drag on his cigarette, snuffed it out and knotted the paper in a tiny ball.

"Pat?"

"Yes."

"Am I such a bad guy?"

"Well, I must admit the past three weeks were much better than our first date." She laughed.

"Serious?"

"I'm glad I changed my mind, Andy."

"Look, I want to ask you something. I don't want you to get sore. I mean . . . to ask in a decent way, see?"

"Goodness, what is it?"

"We're celebrating American Thanksgiving Day and I get a pass till Monday. Couldn't me and you go away someplace . . . separate rooms and all that—no funny stuff. I'd just like to get away from camp and Wellington and the Marine Corps, take off a couple days, maybe on South Island."

She smiled. "It sounds nice, Andy."

"Would you? I mean, really?"

"I've been thinking," she said. "I've felt awfully homesick lately. Haven't been home in over a year. My folks have a farm outside Masterton."

"Honest? You a farm girl?"

"I suppose so, at heart. I left when Don died . . . just couldn't seem to get adjusted. Wanted to be off by myself, you know. And when we heard about my brother Timmy . . . well, I just didn't feel like ever returning. . . . Trouble is, Andy, there isn't much of any place to run to in New Zealand."

"There ain't much place in the world to run to from something like that, Pat."

"I'd like to. Yes, it would be nice, Andy. I do want to see them and maybe it would help to have a little support from you. I wonder if Tony and Ariki are still fit?"

"Who are they?"

"The horses—Timmy's and mine. Ariki—that's a Maori name, you know. Papa used to take us to the flickers in Masterton twice a month when we were kiddies. Tom Mix, the American cowboy, was my brother's hero. He named his horse Tony. But goodness, Andy, that won't be much of a leave for you, with my folks and the whole Rogers clan. They're all over the hills down there."

He lifted her gently to the ground.

"No, honest, Pat, it sounds wonderful . . . almost like . . ."

"Like what?"

"Nothing."

"Penny for your thoughts?"

"I was going to say—almost like going home."

Andy fidgeted as the train pulled into Masterton. For the fiftieth time he squared himself and ground out a cigarette on the deck, where a pack had already met its end. He stepped from the car and looked nervously down the long shed over the depot's concrete platform. He broke into a grin as Pat raced toward him. She was dressed in heavy denim slacks, riding boots and a coarse, sloppy man's sweater, probably her father's. Her hair was up in pigtails. She looked fresh and wonderful.

"I look a fright," she said. "Didn't have time to change. Come on, I've been holding up the mail coach. Mr. Adams is in a lather." She grabbed his hand and rushed through the narrow station to an oversized station wagon parked against the curb. The lettering across the top, along the luggage rack, read: ROYAL MAIL. Mr. Adams, the aged purveyor of the King's mails, looked at his saucer-sized pocket watch in disgust. He turned his head and pointed to the official badge on his cap.

"We're exactly fourteen minutes and twenty-two seconds late, Miss Rogers. The bloomin' valley will be up in arms."

"Pay no attention to him, Andy. Mister Adams has been pulling out that watch and grumbling since I was four years old."

Andy flung his haversack on the luggage rack and lashed it down between two large cases.

"Let's be off. My name's Adams, head of the postal service..."

"Hookans, Andy Hookans." They shook hands.

"Humpf."

Pat and Andy climbed over the quantity of crates and grocery sacks stacked all over the car. Mr. Adams quickly checked his lists to make sure he had completed his shopping for the farmers' wives of the valley. His two passengers found an empty space in the rear, near two chicken coops.

"I thought this was a mail wagon?"

"Well, what the deuce does it look like?" she ribbed.

Mr. Adams seated himself behind the wheel and made much to-do over the instruments on the dashboard, checking as though he were about to pilot a Constellation through a perilous sky.

"You should have seen him when he still had the old crank-up Ford."

With a final check of the watch and a sigh of dismay, the Royal Mail coach moved through the streets of Masterton. The town resembled, in many ways, an old Western main street. Shops along either side had built-out upper storeys held up by stout wooden poles, providing a sidewalk underneath. There were few motor vehicles in the streets. Shoppers paced in the quick straight New Zealand stride. There were bicycles all about, the most popular mode of transportation.

Once through the town, they sped along a well-constructed concrete highway into the countryside. There were ever-flowing, soft green hills and gentle knolls with clumps of picturesque trees, sunning themselves lazily in the warm calm day.

They passed miles of farms, herds of sheep. Everything was as tranquil as though posing for a picture, slow and easy. At each farmhouse, Mr. Adams stopped and gave the mail and a shopping bag to the women who awaited him at the gate. Then in his pompous and official manner, he cut short their chatter with a glance at his worthy timepiece. The King's Mail must go through on time.

At a small, one-room schoolhouse they took aboard a gang of screaming, laughing, freckled children. He fretted and grumbled at the laggards, who only giggled at his anger.

Pat curled up in Andy's arm to make room for the children. The flapping feathers of the chickens protruded through the cage and beat against them; a sudden turn in the road sent a barrage of children and luggage spilling over them.

They came to a stop. There was a large swinging gate and a

dirt road worn in double tracks by the wheels that had passed over it for many years. Up the road about three hundred yards was a strongly built, two-storey shingled house sporting a new coat of gleaming white paint and bright trim. There was a huge chimney of field rock running along one side and the windows were graced with the feminine touch of frilled drapes.

A stray goose wandered across the road. In the distance a bleating of sheep could be heard. The area about the farmhouse showed the signs of the life and activity which it served. There was a clump of trees and a tool shed filled with leather harness, plows, and implements. And all around, the scent of fresh-cut hay.

Beyond, a barn and a corral, where enormous draft horses lazed from their chores. The whole place lay on a gently sloping hill.

On the hilltop was a mass of trees which put the area in gentle shade, with a beam of the sun's rays slipping through here and there, casting easy swaying shadows in a mild breeze.

At the bottom of the slope lay the fields, plowed and straight and with a large fenced-in meadow for the flock.

Andy toyed with the hitch on the gate. Above it there was an archway and a painted sign which simply read: *Enoch Rogers*. The gate creaked and swung open.

"Like it?" Pat asked.

"Yeah," he whispered, "yeah."

They galloped over the meadow, bringing their mounts to a halt near the spot where Enoch Rogers had mended the fence. Andy jumped from his horse and helped Pat dismount. He patted Tony briskly.

"Good fellow, Tony. I knew you wouldn't let that filly beat us."

"He must like you, Andy, he usually doesn't take to strangers," Enoch said looking up. He was a lean, rawboned man of six feet or more. His face was wrinkled and leathery, but it still had the fairness of the New Zealand people. A big, ragged-edged straw hat hid an ungroomed shock of graying hair. He took a kerchief from his overall and wiped the sweat from his face. His hands were calloused and the veins stood out on his arms. He stretched like rawhide, wiry as a piece of spring steel, earthy as the hobnailed boots he wore.

"Well now, Patty, have you shown Andy all our trails?" He shifted the curved pipe which hung eternally from his mouth.

"She's been riding my bottom off, sir," he said. "I never was much on horses."

"You do right well, lad."

"Thank you, sir."

"Patty tells me you were a woodsman?"

"Yes, sir."

"Were you now? Come with me, lad. I want to show you something." He placed the pliers and hammer in his pocket and slipped between two strands of the fence. Andy put a hand on a post and sprang over.

"Timmy used to do that," he said softly. "Coming, Patty girl?"

"No, I'll help Mama with tea," she answered, mounting Ariki and reaching for Tony's bridle. "I'll take him back in, Andy." She rode off.

"Mite touchy about this," Enoch said. "Can't say as I blame the poor girl after what she's been through. But she loves the land as all us Rogers do, that I know. This running away to Wellington proves nothing to the contrary."

They walked alongside the fence for a half mile, then down a steep bank to a shallow swift creek. The ancient plank that forded it groaned under their weight. On the other side they came to a small wood of three or four acres. Beyond it lay a grassy knoll, and they climbed it.

From here they could see the quiet land below for many miles.

"This land was bought for my son Timmy," Enoch said, lighting his pipe. "I suppose it belongs to Patty now. I even have some prize rams and ewes and a full rig of tools put away."

Andy was awestruck. From the edge of the knoll he looked up to the sky. A mass of crazy-shaped clouds floated past. Then he had the feeling, as a man does when he stands on the side of a hill and looks up, that the very earth was rushing up to heaven, that nothing was wrong and nothing could ever be wrong. As if in a sweet dream, he let Enoch lead him down to the edge of the trees.

Sunken into a small oak, he saw a rusted axe. It was covered with moss. Enoch looked at it and spoke softly. "My son planted that axe before he went away. He told me that one day he'd return and clear this land."

Andy reached for the handle in the automatic motion of a lumberjack.

"I'm afraid it's frozen, Andy."

He wrapped his large hands about the handle and pulled; it grunted, then gave. Enoch stepped back as Andy ran his fingers over the blade, spat on his hands and swung on the tree. Smooth, powerful strokes and the bite of his axe rang out through the hills, and echoed back like the music he had heard so often in the north woods.

The oak groaned and Andy put his weight behind him and sent it crashing to the ground. He straightened up and wiped the sweat with the sleeve of his dungaree.

"You've got a good pair of hands, lad . . . it's a man like you that will be clearing this land someday."

Andy sunk the axe into the stump and turned and headed back to the farmhouse.

Mrs. Rogers, put the platter, brimming full of fried chicken, before Andy. "Patty told me you were fond of chicken fixed this way, and I suppose you boys are a wee bit tired of our mutton."

"Gosh, Mrs. Rogers, you shouldn't have gone to all that trouble," he said, grabbing a drumstick.

"I hope it turned out all right. I've never made it before. Goodness, I had to phone at least five people to get a recipe."

"Mrs. Rogers," said Enoch, "be getting us some beer, if you please."

"Mr. Rogers," said Mrs. Rogers, "I'll not be going near that closet. Was only this morning that another bottle exploded. It's not safe for body or soul."

"Ach, woman," he grunted, getting up from the table.

The door burst open and six persons entered. A man, unmistakably of the Rogers clan, his rolypoly wife and their four rolypoly children.

"Uncle Ben!" cried Pat.

"Patty, darling, it's been a bloomin' long time since we've seen you, lass."

Mrs. Rogers leaned closed to Andy. "Brace yourself, lad, there's to be a real onslaught tonight."

"Now, where is the Yank Marine you're hiding, Patty?"

Mrs. Rogers rocked back and forth in her aged, creaky chair. Enoch lifted the large ale mug to his lips, shifted his pipe and gazed into the fire. Andy rested on a soft overstuffed chair, Pat curled on the wool rug at his feet. The dancing flames from the open hearth cast flickering shadows about the snug little room. Beamed ceilings, paneling rising from the floor to six feet, then a shelf around the entire room, lined with big pewter mugs, wrought brassware, an occasional oval framed tintype picture of one of the clan. On the rugged stone fireplace, a framed needlepoint picture: *God Bless Our Home*. And mounted heads of the wild pigs that dared endanger his flock. It was sturdy, like Enoch and like his land. He drained his mug and belched.

"*Mister* Rogers!"

"Good Lord, woman, can't a man belch in his own house? As I said, Andy, it's a simple life, not much like your America."

He reached down and gave his dog a comfortable stroke. "A good piece of land, a good woman, and a good dog. A man has his work cut out for him. We Rogers can't understand city folk, we never will. All the rushing and tomfoolery of it. Here, in the hills, is the only way to live."

"I suppose you may find us dull, Andy," Mrs. Rogers said. "I'm sorry that you had to have the whole family barge in on us, but Patty's been gone for such a long time, and sometimes life here is slow and we need a good reason to get together. The women like to talk and the men to have a drink."

"They are nice people. I hope they liked me."

"Ho! The bloomin' lot of them had to take a look at the bloke Patty hooked herself."

"Papa!"

"And an American Marine at that."

"Hold your tongue, Mr. Rogers. You'll be embarrassing the poor lad to tears."

"Nothing of the sort, Mrs. Rogers. When I told Dugger and Ben how this boy fells a tree, they took notice, they did."

The flame fell lower and lower.

"It's not a happy lot for us, Andy. So many of our boys gone, never to come back, and others getting a look at the fast living in London and the likes. They'll not be wanting to come back and castrate the sheep. And some married to them bloomin' Greek girls. Ah yes, we'll be needing new blood out here."

Mrs. Rogers' chair stopped. Enoch stood up, the dog quickly taking to heel beside him. He walked to his wife and gently placed his hand on her shoulder. "Come on with you, old woman, we'd best turn in and give the young folks a turn before the log dies out." They walked to the door and said good night.

"Poor Andy," Pat said. "You did fine. I told you you'd be in for a rough go."

"They're wonderful people, Pat. You're very lucky. I hope they thought I was O.K."

"They like you well enough as long as you can knock a tree down and drink beer with them. You mustn't pay attention to Papa and Mama. They're trying to marry me off before I become an old spinster for good."

He slipped from his chair to the floor beside her and put his arm about her shoulder. She sleepily cuddled in to him. "I never knew there was a place like this or people so nice, like your family." He touched her cheek and lifted her face to his. "Pat . . . Pat, honey, could I?" Her arms tightened about his neck and their lips met.

"Darling," she whispered.

"Pat, honey."

She tugged away, he released her. "We mustn't, we mustn't," she said.

He arose and helped her up.

"Don't be angry with me, Andy."

"It's all right. I understand. . . . Good night, Pat."

I walked over to Andy's sack and jabbed him in the ribs. "Hey, stupid, step outside into my office," I said.

Andy slipped into his boondockers and followed me from the tent. The field music blew recall as we walked down the catwalk to the radio shack and entered. I flipped the light on and sat down on the bench beside the practice key. Almost instinctively Andy placed his finger on the key and tapped out code: .-. .- - .-. -- --. . .-. ... I watched his hand spell out *Pat Rogers*.

"What's the scoop?" Andy asked.

"You fouled up the field problem, like a Chinese firedrill."

"That's a crock of crap."

"And you fouled up the one last week. The Gunner has the red ass and I'm p.o.'d myself."

"Aw, lay off, Mac."

"Lay off, hell. You haven't been right since that seventy-two over Thanksgiving. What's on your mind?"

"I've already been to the chaplain. I'll be O.K."

"Like hell you been to the chaplain. I checked."

Andy sputtered and fumed. I stood fast by the door. I was determined to get him squared away. He wasn't the best operator in the world, but he was reliable.

"I got a broad," he finally croaked.

"So what, we all got broads."

"This is different."

"I know, they're all different."

"What the hell's the use of talking!"

"What's eating you, Andy?"

"You . . . you won't let this get around?"

"You know me better than that."

"Mac . . . I'm nuts about her. I thought I had more damned sense, but I can't get my mind off her."

"Tell me something, Andy, what's your beef against women?"

He got up and walked to the window and slowly lit a cigarette. "It's a long story and it ain't interesting."

"Maybe if you got it off your chest, you'd be able to see things in a clearer light."

He sat again and fiddled with the key, arguing with himself whether he was going to tell me or not.

"My old man died when I was three," he finally whispered. "Got killed trying to blow a log jam." He clenched his teeth and looked away from me. "The welfare people took me away from my old lady when I was four. They found me and my kid brother in a skid row hotel . . . we'd been locked up for two days . . . we hadn't eaten . . . my brother's diaper hadn't been changed . . . they found her, drunk. . . . My old lady was laying every lumberjack in the north woods. . . ."

"You don't have to finish."

"It was your idea, Mac. I ran away from my foster home to the lumber camps. I was twelve then. I swabbed decks, cleaned bunkhouses, waited on tables. I was a twelve-year-old punk listening to those guys cuss and talk dirty about women. When I was sixteen I was topping tall timber and going into town once a month and drinking and shacking up with whores— whores like my old lady."

And then the venom, pent up for years, spat out.

"They'd act like they was having a big time and all they was thinking was how they could roll you and get the dough you beat your brains out for. They'd lay back and tell you what a swell guy you was and groan . . . the phoneys!" he cried. Then he simmered down a bit. "My kid brother wasn't so lucky. He was a skinny kid and had to stay at the foster home . . . but Christ, Mac, that kid had a brain in his head, like Sister Mary. Smart, he was—liked to read and learn new things all the time. You should see what he could do with a motor. I saved a pile of dough so's I could send him to college."

Andy's shoulders sagged and he looked very tired. His voice trembled. "He was a good kid, kept his nose clean. I saw to that, best I could. Then he got mixed up with this broad—a real slut. Somebody knocked her up and she pinned it on him. He had to marry her. And a kid like that with a brain like he's got. Living with her, working for thirty bucks a week in a drygoods store. He's only eighteen, Mac. . . ."

It wasn't a pretty story. I could understand how he felt now. "So what's the payoff?" I asked.

"I don't know, Mac, I just can't put it together."

"Andy, who the hell you think you are—God? You just can't go barreling through life thinking every woman who walks is a pig."

"I don't, I don't," he cut in quickly. "Not about her. She ain't like that, Mac." He looked away bashfully. "I tried making out with her but she cut me down. And I keep coming back for more."

"Nothing I say is going to wipe clean all the things you've got stored up, but if you love this girl you're going to have to lay your cards on the table. Go all the way or pull out."

"I want to tell her what I feel for her, honest. But something inside me won't let me."

"What is it, for Chrisake?"

"I don't want to get hurt, that's what! Ski had a nice girl, didn't he? She loved him, didn't she? Mac, honest to God I want to love her . . . it means more than getting into bed with her. But things like that just don't keep, not for years, they don't. It will end up the same way as all of them."

"Do you think you could sell your story to Danny or Marion? Trusting their women is part of their life. A guy don't go around with a rotten mind. You've got to have trust to live, Andy. Deep down you know she isn't going to hurt you, but you're going to have to find out the hard way."

"I'm scared, Mac."

"What about Pat?"

"How'd you know her name?"

"I read code."

"Aw, I dunno. She's kind of beat out. She's lost a husband and a brother in the war. She's scared like I am, in another way. Mac, did you ever feel this way?"

"No," I said, "not exactly. I've met lots of nice girls. But I guess an old salt like me is married to the Corps. Every once in a while I get a big yen for the pipe and slippers routine . . . Maybe when I finish my thirty years, or when the war is over . . ."

Andy's voice drifted, like he was in another world. "Her dad has a farm up past Masterton. You never met people like them. Funny, Mac, when I walked into the gate from the highway, it seemed like I'd known the place all my life. Like I knew every tree and building. . . . He showed me a piece of land that belonged to Pat's brother . . . I was standing there on a knoll, looking down into the valley. . . . It seemed like I heard a voice saying to me. 'Where have you been, Andy, we've been waiting for you. . . .' "

4.

AS OUR DAYS before combat grew closer, we sharpened our hand-to-hand combat training tenfold. Several hours each day were spent practicing the quickest way to kill with a rifle, a pistol, a knife or bayonet—or a stick or rock if necessary. All field problems included sneak attacks on sentries to sharpen our reflexes and keep us on the alert at all times. Then a picked squad was chosen to roam the battalion and attack us at any time. In the chow line, in the heads, in our sacks at night, they sprang on us.

The use of the flat of your hand, elbow smashes, knees, use of the forehead to butt—nothing was overlooked. We'd get in a circle and face inward and were blindfolded. One man would rove around the edge of the circle and throw a stranglehold on one of us and we had to break it or get half choked.

"You people are bigger and stronger and faster than them Jap bastards. Use your football training, play rough, gouge his eyes, kick his nuts, deck him and finish him."

We were encouraged to attack each other, just for the fun of it. Little fellows like Ski and Lighttower learned their business and overcame, with speed and knowledge of weak spots, their lack of brawn.

We were conscious, at all times, of sneak attack. . . .

December 18, 1942: CAMP MCKAY TO ALL BATTALION COMMANDERS

Inasmuch as the Sixth Regiment will be moving into the field in the near future, the regimental purchasing officer wishes to call attention to the following: several thousand cases of American beer will be surplus at warehouse six, Wellington Docks. It is suggested that said beer be released to the officers and men at cost and that no limit on purchases be made. It is desired that no beer be left when the regiment departs. . . .

You could hardly walk into our tent for the stacks of beer cases. We had utilized every square inch of space, until space and money ran out. We sat about, sipping our brews, and discussed the things that men discuss when they are drinking: women—and women.

Marion entered the tent and deftly dodged and twisted his way to his sack, threw down his manuscript and picked up his Reising gun to clean it.

L.Q. Jones winked at Speedy Gray and Andy, who had already seated themselves alongside Marion.

"Us fellows was having a little talk," Speedy said.

"Couldn't have been anything constructive," Marion countered as he eyed the bore of his gun and ran a thong through it.

"I wouldn't let them talk about you that way, I stick up for your good name," L.Q. said. "I went and bet my last shilling I was going on liberty with you."

"Me and Speedy bet with L.Q. that you couldn't drink a bottle of beer," Andy announced.

"Pay off, L.Q.," Marion said, "you know I don't drink."

I stopped my letter writing as L.Q. went into his act. He pleaded and begged as Andy and Speedy gibed from the background. Marion stood fast. L.Q. fell to his knees and began licking Marion's shoes and at last took his fair leather belt and demanded that Marion hang him from the tent top rather than betray their "friendship."

"Pay us off, L.Q." Speedy winked. "The man's worthless as tits on a boar hog."

L.Q. dug for his wallet with a great show of dismay. We all gathered about, needling Marion into the trap. "Bastard forgets the night he was catting around in Dago and old L.Q. stuck his neck out at rollcall. Bastard forgets that," he moaned, handing a ten-shilling note over to Andy. "Now Olga is going to think I stood her up."

"From what I've heard of Olga, I think it far better this way," Marion said.

"That's the final insult," Jones wept, "our friendship has just gone *pfffft! Pfffft,* do you hear?" He slumped to his sack, muttering.

Marion stopped wiping his gun and sighed. "Give me a darned bottle."

"Old buddy, old bunkmate!"

"I wouldn't do this for anyone else, L.Q. I hope you are happy."

I snatched a bottle, capped it with my belt buckle and thrust it in Marion's face. He had a very sour look. We gathered about, almost falling on top of him as he lifted the bottle to his lips. He took a short sip, his face screwed up in pain.

"He'll never make it."

"Money in the bank."

"Come on, Mary, you can do it."

Marion gulped two swallows and almost choked. He held his breath, closed his eyes and tilted the bottle back. Half of it ran out of his mouth and down the front of his shirt. L.Q. let out a victory whoop as the bottle drained. Marion flung it to the deck, coughing madly. He returned to his Reising gun. Andy and Speedy made an alleged transfer of money to L.Q.

"Now look here, L.Q., only a rattlesnake wouldn't give a man a chance to get his money back," Speedy drawled.

"Never let it be said that L.Q. Jones is a snake. A pound sterling on the corporal, my dearest buddy."

I shoved another bottle under Marion's nose before he could protest. "You guys are in cahoots!" he cried as L.Q. shoved the bottle into his mouth. He finished the second one with considerably less torture and smacked his lips, looked at the dead soldier with smug satisfaction and flipped it cockily to the deck.

"Tell you what I'm going to do," L.Q. said. "I'm going to give you men a chance. I wager the full winnings that Mary can't chugalug one down."

"I'll take that bet," Marion whooped. We all relaxed with great satisfaction. At long last we were going to get Marion drunk. The next four bottles went quickly and Marion was soon embarked on the vivid adventures of Dangerous Dan McGrew in the Yukon.

"Tenshun!" Andy barked as Major Huxley lowered his shoulders to fit through our tent flap. We all snapped up, except Danny, who caught Huxley as he tripped over a beer case. Marion staggered over to Sam Huxley before I could shove him under a cot. He was stinking.

"Well, if it isn't my old buddy, Highpockets . . . what ya doing, slumming?" Huxley nearly fell out of the tent. He caught his bearings and glared down at the wavering genius.

"Now don't give me that goddam holier than thou look . . . you're a man and I'm a man and I got a few little gripes to discuss with you, see?" He emitted a long, loud belch in Huxley's face.

"Hodgkiss, you're drunk!"

"Don't tell me you made Major with such sharp observations." He placed his hands on Huxley's shoulders. "Seriously, old bean," he mumbled, bleary eyed. "You're hiking these men too hard . . . seriously, old bean. Know what they call this outfit? Huxley's Whores—that's a hell of a name." He fell against the Major, who straightened him up at arm's length.

"Looks like this man is the victim of a conspiracy," Huxley said.

"To be truthful, sir, you might say we did uncap a bottle or so for him," Speedy said.

"*Hummmmm.*"

"I'll write a book exposing this goddam outfit!" Marion proclaimed dangling from Huxley's arms with up-pointed finger. Suddenly he slumped to the deck in a peaceful heap.

Huxley tilted his head back and roared, "Sister Mary!" Then he cut us down with a stern look. "If this ever leaves this tent I'll bust you all to privates and ship you to field music and I'll have this guy on piss and punk for the rest of the cruise!"

"Not a word from us," Andy vowed.

"Us guys are all men of honor," Speedy added with reverence.

"Amen, deacon," Huxley said, "and when he gets sobered up, send him to my quarters. Public relations wants him to write a story on the qualities of leadership."

We burped with relief as Highpockets stamped from the tent.

Andy and Seabags lifted the prostrate body and dumped it on his sack.

"Out like a light."

"Well, Sister Mary finally got his cherry busted."

"Hey, Mac, he's puking."

"So what you want me to do? Let him puke."

"But he's puking on his sack."

"So I'll spray him with cologne later."

We sat about, uncorked bottle after bottle with our trusty belts and after two cases had diminished, entered a thick-tongued 3.2 glow. Speedy, the squad ballad singer, broke into song and we joined in.

> *"I've got sixpence, a jolly jolly sixpence,*
> *I've got sixpence, to last me all my life,*
> *I've got tuppence to spend and tuppence to lend,*
> *And tuppence to send home to my wife . . . DEAR WIFE,*
> *I've got no friends to grieve me,*
> *No pretty little girls to deceive meeeeee,*
> *Happy as the day the Marine Corps gets its pay,*
> *As we go rolling rolling home . . . DEAD DRUNK. . . ."*

"L.Q., why don't you keep your fool mouth shut, you was off key again."

"Why bless yo' cotton-picking ass, Speedy."

"No sass, Yankee, or you and me is going to the deck. . . . We'll snap assholes for fair."

"Have another beer and don't talk so much."

"You're a hell of a nice guy, L.Q."

Shining Lighttower began a slow sway on his cot. Ordinarily a man of calm habit, as sweet and gentle an individual as you'd care to meet, he was a human dynamo when crocked. Luckily, he usually gave us a minute's advance warning by swaying and mumbling some ancient Indian chants. Then all hell would break loose. Andy spotted him first.

"The Injun is winding up." Lighttower's chant became louder.

"Oh-oh." The squad backed away toward the tent flap.

"We can't jump ship with Mary out cold there. That redman will have his scalp for sure—besides, he's liable to bust some beer bottles."

"I got it, let's tie the Injun up on his sack."

"A good idea, there's some rope in my pack."

"Hurry, get it."

We fidgeted as Lighttower lifted his head and cast bleary eyes in our direction.

"Andy," Danny ordered, "you go up and coldcock him."

"Like hell, I seen him drunk before."

"Chicken?"

"Yep."

"Oh, well, that makes two of us."

L.Q., who was a little drunker than the rest of us, came up with a foolhardy plan.

"I'll attract his attention. Danny, you're a football player. You tackle him from the rear. Speedy, have that rope ready."

"Good idea," said Seabags, who was omitted from the plan.

We shoved L.Q. to the center of the tent before he could change his mind. He looked at the Injun, then turned and shook each our hands.

"Semper Fidelis," Seabags said. "You'll get the Navy Cross for this, L.Q."

He gritted his teeth and advanced. "On your feet, Injun!" Lighttower sprung up and shrieked like his ancestors as they headed away from a powwow into battle. Danny ran across the deck and took a flying leap. He missed the Indian completely and tackled L.Q. and the pair went flying into a sack, smashing it to smithereens.

"Ya damned fool, you tackled the wrong one," Seabags cried. as Lighttower came out on the warpath full blast after them.

"Quick," Andy yelled, "the rope . . . the rope!"

Speedy cut Andy short by slipping the rope over him and yanking him to the deck. "Not me, not me, get that Injun!"

Lighttower came at me. He howled like a coyote. He sensed the blood of a white man; he was going to avenge the tribe. This called for quick action. I reached down and quickly grabbed a bottle.

"Have a beer," I said.

"Gee, thanks, Mac," the Injun said. He uncapped it and raised it to his lips. By this time, the commandos had untangled and jumped him en masse. The one mouthful of beer he had taken was sprayed all over me. After fifteen minutes of powerful hand-to-hand combat we had him lashed to his bunk. We turned his head, the only movable part of his body, and placed a bottle of beer between his lips.

"When you finish, just sing, old pal," Andy said.

Lighttower smiled and thanked us for our consideration and gurgled away, snug in his bonds.

Next Burnside stumbled into the tent, roaring, "I beat Mc-Quade! Ya hear! I whipped that candy-assed gyrene twenty-eight bottles to twenty-three. . . ." We lifted him carefully from where he had dropped and threw him on his sack.

"Ya know somepin', men," I said, "this is the finest outfit in the Corps. You boys are just like my own kids . . . seeeee!"

"You are my sunshine, my only sunshine," the Injun sang.

"Andy, give Lighttower another bottle of beer, he's singing."

"We oughta land right on Truk with this outfit, right in the middle of the Imperial Fleet."

"Or Wake."

"Or Frisco."

"Get me another bottle."

"Too right for a bloody quid, matey."

"You guys know something?" L.Q. stuttered. "We ought to stick together, even after we win the war."

"Yeah, we oughta stick together."

"I agree."

"Let's make a pact to meet after the war."

"How about it, Mac?"

"Sure."

"Let's put it in writing, L.Q., and the man who breaks the pact is a dirty bastard."

"Yeah."

"How about you, Mac?"

"Count me in, even if I got to go over the hill to meet you." L.Q. took a piece of paper from his folio and sat on his sack. We gathered about him, armed with beer. His bunk groaned under the weight.

"Somebody bring the lantern over here so's I can see."

"When we gonna meet?"

"One year after the war ends—one year to the day."

"Okay with you guys?"

"Yeah."

"I got it," L.Q. said. "We'll all meet in L.A., in Pershing Square, dressed up like fairies."

"Great."

"Yeah."

L.Q. took the paper and pen, and began to write. We crouched over him and belched.

> *DECEMBER 22, 1942. This here is a holy agreement. We are the dit happy armpit smelling bastards of Huxley's Whores. We hereby agree that one year after the end of the war we will meet in the City of. . . .*

"You are my sunshine, my only sunshine . . ."

"Give the Injun another beer."

L.Q. wrote on, stating that each man was to bring a representative animal from his state to the reunion. An Iowa hog, a Maryland terrapin, a coyote, a longhorn, a cougar, a bull for Spanish Joe, and a goat for Burnside because he was a mountain goat. I was to bring a Marine bulldog but we became

"You come with me. I don't want you scalping anybody tonight."

"Aw gee, Mac, I got a little squaw . . ."

"No war dancing for you, you come with me."

"O.K., chief," he said resignedly.

In forty-five seconds flat there wasn't a radio man aboard the *Jackson*. I wished they could set up their radios that fast.

They found a bench in the Botanical Gardens. Andy lit a pair of cigarettes and handed Pat one.

"Not much like Christmas, is it, Andy?"

"I'm used to snow in the States."

She laughed softly. "Here everyone packs up to go to the beach. I suppose we're just plain upside down."

"I'm glad I could see you."

"It was nice of Mac to give up his pass. He's a quaint old duck."

"The old Marine—it's guys like him that's the real backbone of the Corps."

"Where do you suppose you'll be going?"

"Hell, I don't know."

"It was nice, having you Americans."

"Pat."

"Yes."

"Were you . . . were you glad you met me?"

"I . . . don't know, Andy."

He loosened the too snug blouse Mac had loaned him and studied her face. She looked listless that moment, as though her mind were drifting back to other good-bys. Her brother and her husband. She had said farewell to them too, and now she was frightened.

"I mean," she continued, "I like you well enough, maybe that's why I'm sorry we met." She stiffened herself to control the trembling of her body.

"Pat . . . look, I don't know exactly how to say this, but I want you to know I'm glad I came to New Zealand and I'm glad I found you. I'm fouled up inside me—maybe it's a good thing we're shoving off . . . maybe I can get myself squared away."

"That's right, it's best for both of us, Andy. Before we become involved in something we don't want."

"Yeah," he cried, "that's right. Everything is screwy—the whole world. You just can't get tied up when you don't know what's going to happen from one day to the next. Especially in an outfit like the Marines, breezing through."

"Do you suppose you'll ever come back to New Zealand?"

"I don't know . . . maybe when I get away and can think

stymied on Ski because we couldn't think what animal inhabited Philadelphia. Finally we decided on a skunk in memory of the officers.

The document further ordered everyone to dress in the costume of their country. The Injun was to be in war paint, and L.Q. had to wear a beret and dark glasses. I was given dispensation to stay in uniform. L.Q. then concluded the pact with these words: *If any guy gets killed and can't make it, we'll get drunk in his beloved memory. Any guy that breaks this pact is a dirty bastard, on his word of honor.*

We all wrote out our copies and passed them around for signatures.

"Now," L.Q. said, "let's seal the pact in blood." We borrowed Spanish Joe's stiletto and pricked our fingers and put the blood by our signatures. With tears streaming down our faces, we shook hands, vowed everlasting comradeship in this hallowed moment—and still belching, opened another round of beers.

"You are my sunshine, my only sunshine . . ."

5.

WHERE WOULD we go from there? The cold clammy reality fell upon us. The Unholy Four lay at dockside in Wellington harbor, waiting for the Sixth Marines. The transports were dear to the hearts of the Marines: the *Jackson, Adams, Hayes,* and *Crescent City.* The four that had taken the first bunch in to Guadalcanal. The four that had popped Jap Zeros from the skies like tenpins.

The last bottle of beer was gone, the last hangover done. In the hour of breaking camp, you get that restless feeling of wanting to board ship fast and get the hell going so you can stop that queasy feeling in your guts. We weren't there to enjoy the scenery and the women, nor was that the reason we had joined the Corps.

As usual, I had a hell of a time getting my squad out for the working parties. This time they had rigged the tent with cowbells and alarms so that the merest touch of the flap would set off a din. As soon as I would come after them, they'd escape out the back way or through the sides.

At last we strode up the gangplank of the *Jackson,* saluted the watch and the ensign and made our way to quarters. It was a wonderful surprise after the ratship, *Bobo.* Headquarters Company had drawn a place in the first hold, directly across the hatchway from sailor quarters.

"Get a look at this, the Navy sure goes first cabin."

"Sure different than that pigboat."

"Hey, Mac, Seabags is seasick."

"What you mean? We're still tied up to the dock."

"He got sick coming up the gangplank, just like the last time."

"All that farmer has to do is look at a ship and he's puking."

"Say, how about this mattress!"

We settled down quickly for the wait until all ships could be loaded and we would make a sudden sprint to open seas.

Christmas services were held in a warehouse on the Wellington docks. After singing carols, and sermons from Chaplain Peterson and Father McKale, we all came down with a bad case of the GI blues. Andy, Danny, Marion, and the rest, all were quiet and remorseful. I wished the hell I could just wake up and find Christmas had come and gone. No one cared to talk, just sat around, lost to each other, all wrapped in their own thoughts. Danny read an old letter, Marion had his wallet open looking longingly at the picture of the girl with the red hair. Even Ski, with only bitter memories, studied the fading picture of Susan. Thinking was bad, it might wreck the operations. But what else could a man do on Christmas Eve?

The swabbies cooked up a turkey dinner with all the trimmings, but that didn't help much. Food wasn't what we were hungry for. Of course, an old salt like me didn't get homesick. I only wished they'd give the men liberty, so I could get plastered too. L.Q. tried to snap us out of it, but somehow his jokes didn't seem so funny. Times like this you could feel the dirty, rotten, stinking hunger of soldiering.

Ski opened his letter and read it once more. It was the last one from his sister. It told of the complete failure of his dream of only a year ago. Susan had been thrown out of her father's house and was living in a hotel with her husband. His mother's health was failing, mostly out of grief for him. And his sister, only a child, was already dating servicemen and thinking of quitting school to take a high-paying shipyard job.

"Come on, Ski," Danny said, "they just blew chow down. They got a nice dinner fixed, turkey and the works."

The bosun's whistle squealed through the ship's intercom. "Now hear this, now hear this. Shore leave will be granted to all Marines with the rating of Staff NCO and above."

"Blow it out!" a lower pay grade man screamed.

As for me, it was just in time. I was going nuts. I figured that Burnside and me could get drunk enough for the whole squad. I quickly doffed my dungarees and dug up a set of greens from the stored locker. The last button on my blouse was set, when Andy came up behind me with a very soulful look.

"Nothing doing, Andy. I'll blow my cork if I stick around this hole any more," I said.

"I just thought, maybe . . . well, I told you how things were with Pat and me." He turned away. I wasn't getting soft, but after all, I thought, a good sarge has to look after his boys.

"Andy," I called. Andy spun around quickly. There was a big grin all over his face. I peeled off my blouse and threw it to him. Andy threw his arms about me.

"Who the hell wants a musclebound Swede slobbering all over you on Christmas Eve? Go on, get the hell out of here before I reverse my course." I went to my bunk, thoroughly disgusted with my sentimental outburst.

Gunner Keats entered our quarters and summoned Marion and me.

"Seen Gomez, Mac?"

"No, sir, I haven't."

"Have you, Hodgkiss?"

"Er . . . no, sir."

"I thought so, he went over the side. When he comes in, no matter what the hour, I want him sent up to my quarters. He's going to ride this trip out in the brig."

"Yes, sir."

"Corporal Hodgkiss, you seem to be the only man in the company I can trust. I want you to take the quarterdeck watch from twenty to twenty-four hundred," he said. "Here is a list of the men aboard rating liberty and I want each one checked off as he comes up the gangplank. If any of the lower pay grades try sneaking aboard, you are to call the ship's brig."

"Yes, sir."

The Gunner turned to go. I followed him to the hatchway and tapped his shoulder. "I know what you are going to ask me Mac, and the answer is no." Old Jack Keats was a Mustang, u from the ranks, and he knew how an enlisted man felt Christmas Eve in a foreign port. It wasn't so many years that he and I had been corporals together, tossing pisscutter Shanghai. He rubbed his jaw thoughtfully. "For Chrisake, if you take them ashore get them back before Hodgkis off duty or we'll all be up the creek without a paddle."

"Merry Christmas, Jack," I said.

"Go to hell, Mac."

I gathered the squad in the head and locked the do look, you bastards, you all meet me in front of the House at twenty-three fifty, and God help the guy show on time. Remember, Mary goes off the w night and we've got to be back aboard. Lighttowe

"Ugh."

straight and you can too. Maybe we will come back. You never can tell about the Marines."

"Stop, Andy! It's silly talk. We both know you won't come back. . . . War, war . . . damned war."

"Pat, honey, you're all upset."

She closed her eyes. "I'll be all right."

"Would you do something special for me?"

"Yes."

"Look, I know we're just friends and all that. But, would you write me? Regular, you know. I've never got letters regular from a girl like the other guys . . . I mean, nothing to tie you or me down, but stuff about the farm and your folks and yourself. It would be real nice to get letters like that."

"I'll write you, Andy," she whispered, "if you wish."

"And I'll write you too, Pat, and someday. . . ."

"No . . . no someday, Andy. No more somedays for me."

"Jesus! Almost midnight. I've got to shove, Pat, would you please go to the dock with me—or should I ask?"

She nodded and they walked swiftly and silently through the quiet streets. From the tram they walked to the gate by the guard shack on the dock.

"I'm glad I met you, Pat, and I hope inside me that I come back to New Zealand. Maybe we can—" he stopped. "Goodby, Pat."

He kissed her cheek. For a moment he clutched her tightly to him, then drew back.

"Good-by, Yank, good luck." Andy walked through the gate toward the ship. The heels of his shoes echoed through the deserted warehouses, while his form faded gradually from her view.

Pat Rogers clutched the iron fence and sobbed uncontrollably. "Good-by, my darling," she cried. . . .

At five minutes before midnight, my squad staggered up the gangplank. I saluted Marion and reported.

"Master Tech, Mac." He returned the salute and checked me off the list.

"Colonel Huxley," L.Q. snapped.

"Admiral Halsey, *Bull* Halsey," Seabags belched.

"Chief Crazy Horse, mighty warrior massacred palefaces at Little Big Horn—"

"Aw shaddup, Injun . . . you wanna wake up the ship?"

"Yamamoto," Speedy drawled. "I done lost my ship."

"Fearless Fosdick, the human fly," Danny said. The Feathermerchant drew up the rear. "Just plain Bill," he groaned, and passed out.

I herded them below and tucked them in. All were present

and accounted for—all, that is, except Spanish Joe. He had
jumped before the Gunner had given us an O.K.

Marion glanced fitfully at his time piece, only two minutes
to go and Joe was not there. He paced the deck, trying hard to
decide whether or not to have the Gunner send out an alert.
Suddenly a shadow from the dock area caught his eye. It was
flitting in and out of an open warehouse. Marion dropped back
into the darkness to observe. The shadow made a quick sprint
from the warehouse to the side of the ship and fell flat. It
was Spanish Joe! He stood and looked about and then, with the
deftness of a black panther, leapt to one of the huge ropes that
docked the ship. With a slow, steady, noiseless motion Joe
inched up the rope. First one hand reached up and gripped the
rail, then the other. Ever so slowly, the top of his head came
into view. He hooked his nose on the rail and cast his eyes
about. Just about this time Sister Mary made a quick lunge
across the deck, whipped out his pistol, and stuck it right between Joe's eyes. And, as the legend goes in the Corps, Spanish
Joe Gomez threw up both hands and hung from the rail by
his nose.

After the miserable shakedown cruise on the *Bobo*, the *Jackson* was wonderful. Quarters were good and there were three
square chows a day. Solid, well-cooked Navy chow down to the
last bean. There were fresh water showers, a rare luxury, and
everything aboard was run clean and shipshape, as if they
took pride in the ship, like a best girl.

There was a warm bond between the sailors of the *Jackson*
and the Marines. Their task was unglamorous—transporting
men to the enemy. Perhaps they felt like partners in the venture and realized they had lives to protect. The record of the
Unholy Four was great. They were the pioneer U. S. transports of World War II and had stopped attack after attack from
the sky. They had taken the war to the enemy for the first
tottering time on August 7, 1942. And they had a special affection for the Marines. We too felt safe in their hands and no
Marine ever mentioned the Unholy Four without a feeling of
warmth in his heart.

We assigned working parties, chipping paint in the heads,
swabbing decks, doing mess duty and standing guard watches.
The radio squad got the detail of lugging chow up from the
cold storage lockers to the galleys, from two decks down. They
grumbled something or other about being communicators,
but Burnside and I took personal charge and there was no skylarking. For three hours a day we went down the steep ladders
and shouldered hundred-pound sacks of spuds and then worked
them slowly upward.

stymied on Ski because we couldn't think what animal inhabited Philadelphia. Finally we decided on a skunk in memory of the officers.

The document further ordered everyone to dress in the costume of their country. The Injun was to be in war paint, and L.Q. had to wear a beret and dark glasses. I was given dispensation to stay in uniform. L.Q. then concluded the pact with these words: *If any guy gets killed and can't make it, we'll get drunk in his beloved memory. Any guy that breaks this pact is a dirty bastard, on his word of honor.*

We all wrote out our copies and passed them around for signatures.

"Now," L.Q. said, "let's seal the pact in blood." We borrowed Spanish Joe's stilleto and pricked our fingers and put the blood by our signatures. With tears streaming down our faces, we shook hands, vowed everlasting comradeship in this hallowed moment—and still belching, opened another round of beers.

"You are my sunshine, my only sunshine . . ."

5.

WHERE WOULD we go from there? The cold clammy reality fell upon us. The Unholy Four lay at dockside in Wellington harbor, waiting for the Sixth Marines. The transports were dear to the hearts of the Marines: the *Jackson, Adams, Hayes,* and *Crescent City.* The four that had taken the first bunch in to Guadalcanal. The four that had popped Jap Zeros from the skies like tenpins.

The last bottle of beer was gone, the last hangover done. In the hour of breaking camp, you get that restless feeling of wanting to board ship fast and get the hell going so you can stop that queasy feeling in your guts. We weren't there to enjoy the scenery and the women, nor was that the reason we had joined the Corps.

As usual, I had a hell of a time getting my squad out for the working parties. This time they had rigged the tent with cowbells and alarms so that the merest touch of the flap would set off a din. As soon as I would come after them, they'd escape out the back way or through the sides.

At last we strode up the gangplank of the *Jackson,* saluted the watch and the ensign and made our way to quarters. It was a wonderful surprise after the ratship, *Bobo.* Headquarters Company had drawn a place in the first hold, directly across the hatchway from sailor quarters.

"Get a look at this, the Navy sure goes first cabin."

"Sure different than that pigboat."

"Hey, Mac, Seabags is seasick."

"What you mean? We're still tied up to the dock."

"He got sick coming up the gangplank, just like the last time."

"All that farmer has to do is look at a ship and he's puking."

"Say, how about this mattress!"

We settled down quickly for the wait until all ships could be loaded and we would make a sudden sprint to open seas.

Christmas services were held in a warehouse on the Wellington docks. After singing carols, and sermons from Chaplain Peterson and Father McKale, we all came down with a bad case of the GI blues. Andy, Danny, Marion, and the rest, all were quiet and remorseful. I wished the hell I could just wake up and find Christmas had come and gone. No one cared to talk, just sat around, lost to each other, all wrapped in their own thoughts. Danny read an old letter, Marion had his wallet open looking longingly at the picture of the girl with the red hair. Even Ski, with only bitter memories, studied the fading picture of Susan. Thinking was bad, it might wreck the operations. But what else could a man do on Christmas Eve?

The swabbies cooked up a turkey dinner with all the trimmings, but that didn't help much. Food wasn't what we were hungry for. Of course, an old salt like me didn't get homesick. I only wished they'd give the men liberty, so I could get plastered too. L.Q. tried to snap us out of it, but somehow his jokes didn't seem so funny. Times like this you could feel the dirty, rotten, stinking hunger of soldiering.

Ski opened his letter and read it once more. It was the last one from his sister. It told of the complete failure of his dream of only a year ago. Susan had been thrown out of her father's house and was living in a hotel with her husband. His mother's health was failing, mostly out of grief for him. And his sister, only a child, was already dating servicemen and thinking of quitting school to take a high-paying shipyard job.

"Come on, Ski," Danny said, "they just blew chow down. They got a nice dinner fixed, turkey and the works."

The bosun's whistle squealed through the ship's intercom. "Now hear this, now hear this. Shore leave will be granted to all Marines with the rating of Staff NCO and above."

"Blow it out!" a lower pay grade man screamed.

As for me, it was just in time. I was going nuts. I figured that Burnside and me could get drunk enough for the whole squad. I quickly doffed my dungarees and dug up a set of greens from the stored locker. The last button on my blouse was set, when Andy came up behind me with a very soulful look.

"Nothing doing, Andy. I'll blow my cork if I stick around this hole any more," I said.

"I just thought, maybe . . . well, I told you how things were with Pat and me." He turned away. I wasn't getting soft, but after all, I thought, a good sarge has to look after his boys.

"Andy," I called. Andy spun around quickly. There was a big grin all over his face. I peeled off my blouse and threw it to him. Andy threw his arms about me.

"Who the hell wants a musclebound Swede slobbering all over you on Christmas Eve? Go on, get the hell out of here before I reverse my course." I went to my bunk, thoroughly disgusted with my sentimental outburst.

Gunner Keats entered our quarters and summoned Marion and me.

"Seen Gomez, Mac?"

"No, sir, I haven't."

"Have you, Hodgkiss?"

"Er . . . no, sir."

"I thought so, he went over the side. When he comes in, no matter what the hour, I want him sent up to my quarters. He's going to ride this trip out in the brig."

"Yes, sir."

"Corporal Hodgkiss, you seem to be the only man in the company I can trust. I want you to take the quarterdeck watch from twenty to twenty-four hundred," he said. "Here is a list of the men aboard rating liberty and I want each one checked off as he comes up the gangplank. If any of the lower pay grades try sneaking aboard, you are to call the ship's brig."

"Yes, sir."

The Gunner turned to go. I followed him to the hatchway and tapped his shoulder. "I know what you are going to ask me, Mac, and the answer is no." Old Jack Keats was a Mustang, up from the ranks, and he knew how an enlisted man felt on Christmas Eve in a foreign port. It wasn't so many years ago that he and I had been corporals together, tossing pisscutters in Shanghai. He rubbed his jaw thoughtfully. "For Chrisake, Mac, if you take them ashore get them back before Hodgkiss gets off duty or we'll all be up the creek without a paddle."

"Merry Christmas, Jack," I said.

"Go to hell, Mac."

I gathered the squad in the head and locked the door. "Now look, you bastards, you all meet me in front of the Parliament House at twenty-three fifty, and God help the guy that doesn't show on time. Remember, Mary goes off the watch at midnight and we've got to be back aboard. Lighttower!"

"Ugh."

"You come with me. I don't want you scalping anybody tonight."

"Aw gee, Mac, I got a little squaw ..."

"No war dancing for you, you come with me."

"O.K., chief," he said resignedly.

In forty-five seconds flat there wasn't a radio man aboard the *Jackson*. I wished they could set up their radios that fast.

They found a bench in the Botanical Gardens. Andy lit a pair of cigarettes and handed Pat one.

"Not much like Christmas, is it, Andy?"

"I'm used to snow in the States."

She laughed softly. "Here everyone packs up to go to the beach. I suppose we're just plain upside down."

"I'm glad I could see you."

"It was nice of Mac to give up his pass. He's a quaint old duck."

"The old Marine—it's guys like him that's the real backbone of the Corps."

"Where do you suppose you'll be going?"

"Hell, I don't know."

"It was nice, having you Americans."

"Pat."

"Yes."

"Were you ... were you glad you met me?"

"I ... don't know, Andy."

He loosened the too snug blouse Mac had loaned him and studied her face. She looked listless that moment, as though her mind were drifting back to other good-bys. Her brother and her husband. She had said farewell to them too, and now she was frightened.

"I mean," she continued, "I like you well enough, maybe that's why I'm sorry we met." She stiffened herself to control the trembling of her body.

"Pat ... look, I don't know exactly how to say this, but I want you to know I'm glad I came to New Zealand and I'm glad I found you. I'm fouled up inside me—maybe it's a good thing we're shoving off ... maybe I can get myself squared away."

"That's right, it's best for both of us, Andy. Before we become involved in something we don't want."

"Yeah," he cried, "that's right. Everything is screwy—the whole world. You just can't get tied up when you don't know what's going to happen from one day to the next. Especially with an outfit like the Marines, breezing through."

"Do you suppose you'll ever come back to New Zealand?"

"I don't know ... maybe when I get away and can think

straight and you can too. Maybe we will come back. You never can tell about the Marines."

"Stop, Andy! It's silly talk. We both know you won't come back. . . . War, war . . . damned war."

"Pat, honey, you're all upset."

She closed her eyes. "I'll be all right."

"Would you do something special for me?"

"Yes."

"Look, I know we're just friends and all that. But, would you write me? Regular, you know. I've never got letters regular from a girl like the other guys . . . I mean, nothing to tie you or me down, but stuff about the farm and your folks and yourself. It would be real nice to get letters like that."

"I'll write you, Andy," she whispered, "if you wish."

"And I'll write you too, Pat, and someday. . . ."

"No . . . no someday, Andy. No more somedays for me."

"Jesus! Almost midnight. I've got to shove, Pat, would you please go to the dock with me—or should I ask?"

She nodded and they walked swiftly and silently through the quiet streets. From the tram they walked to the gate by the guard shack on the dock.

"I'm glad I met you, Pat, and I hope inside me that I come back to New Zealand. Maybe we can—" he stopped. "Good-by, Pat."

He kissed her cheek. For a moment he clutched her tightly to him, then drew back.

"Good-by, Yank, good luck." Andy walked through the gate toward the ship. The heels of his shoes echoed through the deserted warehouses, while his form faded gradually from her view.

Pat Rogers clutched the iron fence and sobbed uncontrollably. "Good-by, my darling," she cried. . . .

At five minutes before midnight, my squad staggered up the gangplank. I saluted Marion and reported.

"Master Tech, Mac." He returned the salute and checked me off the list.

"Colonel Huxley," L.Q. snapped.

"Admiral Halsey, *Bull* Halsey," Seabags belched.

"Chief Crazy Horse, mighty warrior massacred palefaces at Little Big Horn—"

"Aw shaddup, Injun . . . you wanna wake up the ship?"

"Yamamoto," Speedy drawled. "I done lost my ship."

"Fearless Fosdick, the human fly," Danny said. The Feathermerchant drew up the rear. "Just plain Bill," he groaned, and passed out.

I herded them below and tucked them in. All were present

and accounted for—all, that is, except Spanish Joe. He had jumped before the Gunner had given us an O.K.

Marion glanced fitfully at his time piece, only two minutes to go and Joe was not there. He paced the deck, trying hard to decide whether or not to have the Gunner send out an alert. Suddenly a shadow from the dock area caught his eye. It was flitting in and out of an open warehouse. Marion dropped back into the darkness to observe. The shadow made a quick sprint from the warehouse to the side of the ship and fell flat. It was Spanish Joe! He stood and looked about and then, with the deftness of a black panther, leapt to one of the huge ropes that docked the ship. With a slow, steady, noiseless motion Joe inched up the rope. First one hand reached up and gripped the rail, then the other. Ever so slowly, the top of his head came into view. He hooked his nose on the rail and cast his eyes about. Just about this time Sister Mary made a quick lunge across the deck, whipped out his pistol, and stuck it right between Joe's eyes. And, as the legend goes in the Corps, Spanish Joe Gomez threw up both hands and hung from the rail by his nose.

After the miserable shakedown cruise on the *Bobo*, the *Jackson* was wonderful. Quarters were good and there were three square chows a day. Solid, well-cooked Navy chow down to the last bean. There were fresh water showers, a rare luxury, and everything aboard was run clean and shipshape, as if they took pride in the ship, like a best girl.

There was a warm bond between the sailors of the *Jackson* and the Marines. Their task was unglamorous—transporting men to the enemy. Perhaps they felt like partners in the venture and realized they had lives to protect. The record of the Unholy Four was great. They were the pioneer U. S. transports of World War II and had stopped attack after attack from the sky. They had taken the war to the enemy for the first tottering time on August 7, 1942. And they had a special affection for the Marines. We too felt safe in their hands and no Marine ever mentioned the Unholy Four without a feeling of warmth in his heart.

We assigned working parties, chipping paint in the heads, swabbing decks, doing mess duty and standing guard watches. The radio squad got the detail of lugging chow up from the cold storage lockers to the galleys, from two decks down. They grumbled something or other about being communicators, but Burnside and I took personal charge and there was no skylarking. For three hours a day we went down the steep ladders and shouldered hundred-pound sacks of spuds and then worked them slowly upward.

I for one always liked life aboard a good ship. In the old days, a good deal of a Marine's cruise was sea duty. There was something nice and peaceful about standing by the rail after late chow with a coffin nail. Lots of times I kind of forgot for a minute who I was and where I was going. But soon the squad would edge in by me and I'd look about and see the gun nests and the swabbies standing by the 37-mm's and I'd get back to earth.

When they locked us in at night, we'd start the poker game, the poker game that never really started and never really ended. The deck, the players and the locale might change, but the poker game went on forever. We'd clean gear and write letters; then, before taps, we'd gather on the boarded-up hold and Speedy would start singing and the squad would join in. The bunch sure liked to sing and they made damned good harmony, except for L.Q., who couldn't carry a tune. When it got real soft and quiet-like, Speedy plunked the guitar he had borrowed from a swabby and gave us a ballad or two in that sweet clear voice of his. Kind of made a guy tingle right to his toes when Speedy sang:

> *"From this valley they say you are going,*
> *And I'll miss your bright voice and sweet smile,*
> *But remember the Red River Valley ..."*

"Land!" I jumped from my sack and clambered topside. The morning was steamy hot. The transports cut their speed to almost a drift and edged their way to the baked-out, brown-hilled island dead ahead. It became still as death. We began passing ships, dozens of them, lying anchored and manless. Some were rusted and filling with water, like ghost ships. We wove a course between them toward the lifeless-looking land. A thin fog drifted about us. It was eerie to see the still ships and the background of weird, barren ridges, like we had come to the end of the world.

"Where are we?" I asked.

"New Caledonia. We're pulling into Noumea harbor now. Spooky, isn't it?"

"Like a devil's island, I'd say."

We passed through the mined and netted channels into the harbor. Then I saw it! The United States Navy. All about, battlewagons, carriers, cruisers, destroyers, lay at anchor. So this was where they were hiding.

The bosun's pipe was heard: "Now hear this, now hear this. All Marines return to your quarters. You will square away and stand by for a practice landing with transport packs."

The practice was a mess. We were assigned to the high midship net. It seemed like five hundred feet to the water. Two legs were broken in the transfer to the landing boats below. The heavy load of full upper and lower packs, bedrolls, ammunition, and radios just about sunk us through the boat bottom. We drifted about for a hour and returned to the side of the ship.

Lighttower froze on the net, exhausted, and had to be dragged aboard by Huxley, who was standing on the bridge growling at the mad mess below.

It was brutal and stupid to introduce a green bunch to the tricky nets in such a manner. It was lucky there weren't a half dozen fatalities. After it was over they were all glad, though, because lighter packs and lower nets would seem like child's play after this.

The shower was jammed after the practice so I doused my face in my canteen water and went topside. Some gear was lowered into a barge, then the Jacob's ladder dropped. Two men, a captain and an enlisted man, were climbing aboard. Lieutenant LeForce and Sergeant Paris from Intelligence were waiting to meet them on deck.

"Captain Davis, Division Intelligence," he introduced himself, "and my assistant, Sergeant Seymour."

"LeForce, and this is my chief, Sergeant Paris. When the gear gets aboard arrange quarters for the Sergeant. Please come with me, Captain Davis. Major Huxley is waiting for you."

Paris saw me and came over. "This is Seymour, Intelligence. He's just off Guadalcanal."

"Glad to have you aboard," I said, studying the sallow-faced, rail thin Marine.

"Can't say as I'm glad to be aboard." He smiled a sardonic smile.

"Mac is a communications chief. Do you have an extra sack in your section for Seymour? I'm loaded."

"I think so," I said.

First Sergeant Pucchi approached the Jacob's ladder, muttering to himself.

"Hey, Pucchi, were the hell are you going?"

"Ashore."

"But we're supposed to pull out right after the other ships finish practice."

"Yeah, I know. I'm going to sit the goddam war out on this goddam island."

"How come?"

"The sonofabitches told me that first sergeants aren't expendable. I got to stay here and keep records."

"You lucky bastard," Paris said.

"I feel lousy about this," Pucchi moaned. "First time I been out of the company for six years."

"Aw jeese, don't feel bad. I'll get Herman to save a ribbon for you."

"Cut the clowning, Paris, do you think I want to stay behind?" He glanced at the burned-out, empty hills and winced. "I hope the guys don't think I'm chicken—it wasn't my idea."

"Tough break, Pucchi," Paris said, slapping him on the back.

"Yeah," I agreed.

"Anything on that hellhole island?" he asked Syemour, pointing to the searing mass of land.

"A leprosy colony and a whore. Even got to have M.P.s to keep a line in order—that is if you don't mind laying a whore fifty years old with three kids in bed with her. The place wouldn't be so bad if someone planted a tree."

Pucchi's eyes filled with tears. He swung over the rail to the Jacob's ladder. "Good luck, fellows," he whispered and lowered to the waiting boat.

"Some guys don't know when they're well off," Seymour spat. He was a sarcastic bastard. "Where's quarters, Mac?"

It got hotter as the convoy moved north towards the equator. In the hold, you had to peel to get relief. The convoy plodded steadily and slowly in a gentle sway and continuous whisper of the chugging engine.

The only movement was muffled voice and action of the poker players on the boarded hold at night. I was killing time, waiting for someone to go busted so I could get a seat in the game, when I noticed Gunner Keats standing in the hatchway, trying to get my attention. I went over to him. "What's doing, Jack?" I asked. I always addressed him by his first name when we were alone. Keats moved me over to a dark corner, very quiet-like and secretive. I tried to think what could be wrong. "Did Huxley find out we jumped ship Christmas Eve?" I asked.

He looked about to make sure we were unwatched, then reached inside his shirt and handed me a bottle. "It's for the squad, Mac. Happy New Year."

"Scotch, real Scotch! Christ, I forgot it was New Year's Eve . . . nineteen forty-three . . . thanks, Jack."

"Happy New Year, Mac. I hope the ship's captain doesn't miss the bottle."

I went to my section and aroused my boys and placed my finger to my lips, lest the secret spread. Seymour, the intelligence man, seemed to wake at the first step and spring up with a catlike motion. I asked him to join us. We all moved deftly to the head and locked the door. I broke out the bottle.

"Compliments of the Gunner," I said. "Happy New Year, men."

"New Year's?"

"How about that?"

"Scotch."

"I'll be go to hell."

I passed the bottle. Marion skipped his swig and carefully measured Spanish Joe's, pulling the bottle from his lips and passing it on.

"Aw gee, Marion, I thought you wanted me to drink yours too."

We managed three small slugs apiece. We were all fully awake now and the steamy hold held no invitation for further sleep, so we began shooting the breeze.

"New Year's Eve," L.Q. said. "Know where I'd be now? In my old man's car with a woman, heading for a party. You know, the high school crowd. We'd snitch a drink or two and get a nice warm glow up, then dance and get friendly with our dates. Dance till two or three and then find a nice dark corner and make out. The girls would all go upstairs and sleep and we'd sleep on the couch and the floor. Then around six, get into the cars and head for an all-night beanery and eat big plates of ham and eggs, just when the sun was coming up."

"That's about the way we did." Danny said. "The folks let us get away with it once a year—you know, all being in the same crowd."

"New Year's should be spent in a whorehouse," Spanish Joe said. "The girls usually get good and crocked and you can beat paying them for a couple of tricks."

Marion's face flushed, then Spanish Joe cut himself short and looked apologetic. I wondered whether it was spontaneous or intentional.

"You guys ought to get some hay in your hair. Nothing like a square dance on New Year's," seasick Seabags said.

"We generally get it where we can," Burnside said, "Singapore, Reykjavik, Rio . . . it's all the same to a gyrene."

"I liked mine in a nightclub, a good loud noisy drunken nightclub with a rotten floor show and a ten-dollar cover charge," Seymour said, holding up the last shot in the bottle. "I used to drink this all the time," he said, "but a man should drink it slowly, sip it, get the full flavor. Never mix it. Let it trickle over the ice cubes. Good Scotch is nothing to be devoured like a hambone."

We turned and looked at the thin man with the gaunt face. It was hard to judge his age. Or much else about him, for that matter. His good taste was obvious, but it is hard to tell the rich from the poor or the cultured from the ignorant when they are all in dungarees.

"You're the guy from Intelligence, from Guadalcanal?" L.Q. asked.

"Yes," he almost whispered, "I was just on Guadalcanal."

"How was it, pretty rough, huh?"

"Rough?" he answered, laying the bottle down. "Yes, it was rough."

"Give us the word."

"O.K., I'll give it to you." He perched himself on a sink. His eyes narrowed. The ship speeded her engines, sending a steady vibration through her hull.

"First to land against Japan," Seymour started, "the First Marine Division hit Guadalcanal, and the Second Regiment and paratroopers hit the islands across Skylark Channel—Tulagi, Gavutu, and Tanembogo, all three nestled in a cove of Florida Island. We came in with about twenty hours rations." His voice broke suddenly. "Let me tell you guys something, I studied military campaigns, lots of them . . ."

"You a college boy?" I asked.

"Cornell, class of thirty-eight." He snickered sourly. "There may be bigger and bloodier battles than Guadalcanal, but when the book comes out, Guadalcanal will always be the first one."

Seymour began to tell his long terrible story, which I knew would be part of the folklore of our country for all time. The beginning was sad, with a handful of brave men on a tiny foothold, pitted against the might of the Japanese Empire.

He reached for a cigarette and cupped his hands to keep them from shaking. We leaned forward and hung on his every word.

"The Navy dumped us there and ran. The Army and Dugout Doug sat back and waited."

"To hell with them."

"You can say that again," Seymour snapped. He told of the frantic Japanese efforts to push the Marines into the sea. Gigantic air strikes and but a few crippled Marine planes against them, planes obsolete in everything but the guts of the pilots. Flyers like Joe Foss, Carl, and Boyington's Bastards to stop them. And then came the Tokio Express! The Imperial Fleet to shell them at point blank, with nothing in their way but a handful of plywood PT boats.

Jap reinforcements landed past Marine lines by the thousands as they helplessly sat and watched. And the battles. The Tenaru, the Matanikau—yet their lines never fell. Japs stacked up like cordwood in the rivers but on they came. Marine heroes born each minute. A blind man given instructions where to fire a machine gun by a paralyzed man.

"We scratched back where we could. Sent our patrols to rove and disorganize them. Maybe fifty would start out, maybe five would come back. We fought by night, mostly in the jungle, on the river banks with bayonets and fists. They'd scream for our blood in the dark. Those Marines that didn't get cut down by bullets got cut down by malaria and yellow jaundice and crud."

Seymour smashed out the cigarette and a strange look came into his eyes. "I saw them lying there in the grass near the river with a hundred and four fever, so weak with dysentery they couldn't stand, but they'd stick at their posts as long as they could squeeze a trigger."

At last help came. An Army unit of National Guards who fought like Marines, the never to be forgotten 164th Regiment. Many times when reinforcements came they had to wait for a Jap landing party to unload first.

The Eighth Marines, sick with mumu from Samoa, had been forced to retreat, Seymour told us.

"The Sixth will never retreat," Burnside said.

And then came the terrible night that the Tokio Express caught four cruisers like sitting ducks and sank them all. Seymour related the subsequent caution of our Navy in trying to lure the Japs into open water instead of coming into the Slot. The Japs knew this and hugged land.

"We were up to our ass in blood, and sick and beat out. The Tokio Express was heading in in full battle array, and only the gutty little PTs to stop them." He lit another cigarette. "It was November 15th when the voice from the Lord came. Ching Lee on the U.S.S. *Washington* led the fleet into the Slot and we caught the Japs cold turkey." From a high-pitched crescendo, his voice trailed off. "The Jap navy never came back and we could at last get out of the foxholes and go after them."

There were several moments of silence in the smoke-filled head. Finally Andy spoke up. "What's there now?"

"It's going to be a long war, buddy. Look at the map. It's mean terrain and there'll be Japs there forever. The First Division is either on the way or going to Australia and the Second and Eighth Marines are corked out. You've got thirty miles to go."

"Wake Island, here we went."

Seymour threw his cigarette butt into a toilet bowl and walked to the hatchway and unbolted the door. "Tell your grandchildren the gyrenes were first. Or maybe you won't have to tell them about it. They may be fighting out here themselves."

"They sent for the Army to come to Tulagi," Seymour sang, *"But Douglas MacArthur said no!*

He said, there's a reason, it isn't the season,
Besides, there is no U.S.O."

The battle-happy Seymour turned and left.

6.

THE LOADED landing craft chugged slowly for
shore. The Unholy Four lay at anchor. We craned our necks
and pushed forward for a sight of the island which lay before
us. It looked like a travel poster of the vaunted Pacific paradise. Clean golden beach, miles of neatly planted swaying palms,
backdropped with hills and slopes. Further inland a range of
ragged mountains.

"Sure looks right pretty, cousin."

"Yeah. Wonder if they got a band to meet us?"

As we neared the beach we caught a gimpse of a red streak
dotting through the air, many miles away.

"What was that, Mac?"

"Tracers from a machine gun." The red flash repeated.

"Must be the lines up there."

The boat bumped into shore, the coxswain gunned her hard
to hold her fast and the ramp fell. We were bursting to breaking
point with curiosity and took off straight for a lone Marine who
was standing on shore. His face was yellow with atabrine
and withered from malnutrition.

"Say, what town is this, cousin?"

"You're on the Canal, buster," he answered. "Pardon me, but
I didn't catch the name of the outfit?"

"The Sixth Marines."

The Marine turned and yelled to a couple of buddies heading to the beach, "Hey, Pete, break out the band. The Pogey
Bait Sixth finally got here." He turned and left.

"Now that was mighty unneighborly of that fellow. I wonder
where the nearest ginmill is?"

"O.K., fall in, on the double."

We moved into a fringe of coconut trees near Kokum. The
trees were everywhere. They stretched as far as the eye could
see in neatly planted rows. This must have been the Lever
Brothers' plantation.

Naturally, I had a hell of a time getting the gear ashore and
camp pitched. The squad dropped their packs and took off in
search of scuttlebutt. It wasn't long before the area was swarm-
ing with natives who were as curious as the Marines. They

were long, thin, and extremely black. Their bodies were covered only with a middle loincloth, their arms and chests heavily tattooed with blue markings. Their hair was a black shock of Brillo standing straight up for several inches and dyed red about the roots. They wore earrings and their teeth were filed down to sharp points. They had a weird and shocking appearance.

With a few words of pidgin, bartering began. For a cigarette, a tall palm was scaled in quick monkey fashion and a dozen coconuts dropped. A few pennies, and a dirty wash was hustled to the river.

Speedy handed a set of dungarees to one particularly ugly specimen and indicated they needed washing. The native held out his palm and Speedy dropped a New Zealand sixpence in it. The native took a look at the coin, spat on the ground, and handed it back.

"They don't go for that money."

"Merican, Merican," the native said, "No British."

"It seems," Marion said, "they have no use for their former exploiters."

The bartering continued and we were all soon filled to the gunnels with coconut juice. We were soon tramping to sick bay with stomach aches.

Andy, eying a tall tree, broke out a pair of telephone climbing spikes and soon put the natives out of business. Whenever the word Jap came up in the course of the international trade session, the native would immediately hold up two, three, four, or more fingers, indicating his haul and cap it with a slow motion over his neck, to indicate what he had done to the Jap, and then he'd spit on the deck. The two words they spoke most fluently were: "Can have?" with an extended palm.

As the day wore on, the gear was in and the camp set up, and wild rumors flew.

"They're landing a hundred thousand Japs tonight from Rabaul."

"I heard that Henry Ford is going to give a new car to every Marine on Guadalcanal."

"We're going to hit the lines, end the drive, and go straight back to the States for a parade up Market Street in Frisco."

"The Japs know the Sixth has landed and they're bringing in five hundred planes tonight."

The wonderful strangeness of landing at Lunga on Guadalcanal—Guadalcanal where they first hit. Guadalcanal, the legend. "Look, there's the Slot, there's Skylark Channel, and Florida and Tulagi, over there." Where is Henderson Field from here? Where is the Tenaru? Yes, we were here, right on the spot where history was made. A million questions and wild stories ended any thinking.

∞ Spanish Joe called the squad into a huddle, excepting me and Burnside. "There is an army ordnance shed about a mile from here," he said, "loaded with Garand rifles. Who is with me?"

"How about ammo?"

"There's lots of it."

"I'm for it," Andy said. "Let's dump these goddam Reising guns in the drink."

"Let's go," Seabags said.

"How about you, Mary?" Danny asked.

They waited anxiously as he surveyed the situation. He looked at his weapon, which was rusting badly from a splash in the landing. He looked toward the front lines. "Count me in," Marion said.

By nightfall Burnside and me were about the only two left in Headquarters Company who still carried Reisings. I looked at the rusty barrel and sighed with envy.

Dusk fell on the still-excited encampment. I passed among my squad. "The password for tonight is Philadelphia," I said. A real password in a real battle zone—their eyes lit up. The passwords were picked with two or more of the letter 'l' in it. The Japs supposedly had difficulty pronouncing the letter, as it is nonexistent in their language.

Darkness found the camp still wrapped in nervous chatter. The rumors, the discoveries of the strange new land, and the questions were still on their lips. Soon, exhausted from the day, a fitful hush set in.

L.Q. Jones patted his new Garand rifle and walked to his guard post. It was very dark and very quiet. The sound of the surf on the beach made him uneasy. . . . I wonder how far the lines are, he thought. Any Japs around here? Jesus, it's quiet. What was that! Only Burnside snoring.

He lifted the cover on the luminous dial of his watch. Still three hours to go. He slapped a mosquito, then reached in his helmet and pulled out his headnet and put it on. Another mosquito bit right through his dungarees—then a dozen more. Christ, it's quiet.

Two hours and fifty minutes to go. What was that! Something moving! L.Q. fell on his stomach and edged toward the sound, slowly, carefully. Maybe I should stand up and scream . . . careful, boy, they're tricky. Investigate first, then scream. His hand shot out quickly in the dark and clutched the moving object!

Andy sprung up with a knife in his hand and with the other grabbed L.Q.'s throat. They looked at each other.

"What you grab my toe for, you crazy bastard!"

L.Q. trembled. He managed a sickly grin and mumbled an

apology. They both sighed with relief and said, "I thought you was a Jap."

Two hours to go. They must be crazy to let a guy stand guard alone like this. *What was that!* Dammit, something had moved this time. He slipped quickly behind a tree and lowered his rifle. On a path, heading into the camp, he saw the dim outline of a figure. Small . . . thin . . . look at that silhouette—a Jap!

"Halt," he squeaked. "what's the password?"

"Password?"

"I'll give you three to give me the password."

"Hey, wait a minute, I'm a Marine."

"One . . ."

"It's a city. Dayton . . . Boston . . . Baltimore . . . Florida . . ."

"Two . . ."

"Don't shoot! I'm a Marine . . . San Diego . . . Albany . . . Chicago. . . ."

"Three." BLAM!

Shining Lighttower dropped in his tracks. *"Philadelphia!* That's it, Philadelphia!"

The shot aroused the camp and in a fraction of a second the place was rattling with gunfire. BLAM . . . RAT-A-TAT . . . BLAM . . . POW! Rifle bullets cut the air, grenades exploded and men ran wildly and aimlessly in the dark, their weapons spitting fire in all directions.

"Philadelphia!" Sam Huxley rushed from his tent and blew a whistle. The firing stopped as abruptly as it had started.

"What the hell is the matter with you people? You're acting like a bunch of trigger-happy boots. The front line is ten miles that way. Bryce! Take a check and see if anyone got hurt. Now go to sleep, dammit!"

L.Q. cried apologies a hundred times a minute as they dragged the fear-stricken Injun to his tent and laid him on his sack.

One more hour . . . I don't care if the whole Jap army jumps me, I'm not going to move a muscle . . . what was that! A siren scream pierced the air. "Air Raid," L.Q. screamed, "Air Raid!"

Pencils of light flashed up against the sky as the men huddled in a hastily constructed shelter. They heard the far-off chug of a motor.

"Washing Machine Charley," someone whispered.

"Yeah."

A lone Jap plane was caught in the light. The distant batteries of Henderson Field opened up. Puffs of smoke billowed in the sky above and below the slow lumbering plane.

Hisssss . . . Wham.

"He's dropping bombs!"

"What you expecting, pennies from heaven, maybe?"

"He comes every night," Sergeant Seymour said, "just to keep you new troops from sleeping."

"Ever hit anything?"

"Blew up a head once. But it was an officer's head—not too bad."

Body-weary and angry at their foolish siege of trigger happiness, Huxley's Whores buttoned up and were asleep when the all clear sounded.

The small, thin and graying Army general paraded in front of the large wall map with a pointer in his hand. Brigadier General Pritchard, a fatherly appearing man, was now the commander of all forces on Guadalcanal. Before him stood and sat an array of majors, lieutenant colonels and colonels, cigarette smoking, cigar smoking, and pipe smoking. He laid the pointer on his field desk, rubbed his eyes, and faced the men before him.

"I am extremely anxious to get this drive under way." He turned to the small group of Marine officers near the tent flap. "The Camdiv—combined Army and Marine division—will be unique in this operation. And, I might add, the Pentagon and the Navy are watching with extreme interest. This is the first real offensive of the war. There is much, as I have pointed out, that will be novel and experimental, and it will have a great bearing on future operations. We shall have a testing ground, so to speak. Naval gunfire in support of advancing land troops, flame throwers, close air support and air reconnaissance on short objectives, to name a few new wrinkles." He picked up the pointing stick and tapped it in his hand, restlessly. "Are there any questions? No? Very well, gentlemen. All further information will be relayed through channels. We jump off at zero six four five on the tenth. Good luck to all of you."

A buzz arose from the officers as they filed out and headed for the jeeps. Sam Huxley stood by the opening until all were gone except Pritchard and his aide. Huxley shifted his helmet and approached the field desk. Pritchard looked up from a map.

"Yes?"

"Major Huxley, Second Battalion, Sixth Marines, sir."

"What is it, Huxley?"

"May I have the General's indulgence for a few minutes?"

"Something not clear, Major?"

"Everything is quite clear, sir."

"What's on your mind?"

"General Pritchard, is a suggestion out of order?"

Pritchard put down the magnifying glass and relaxed in his

canvas field chair, tilting it back on its rear legs and swinging it gently. "Sit down, Major. A suggestion is never out of order in my command."

Huxley remained standing. He drew a deep breath and leaned over the desk. "General Pritchard, keep the Sixth Marines off the lines."

The General nearly fell over backwards. He caught the desk and brought the chair to a still position. "What!"

"I said, sir, don't use the Sixth Marines in this operation."

"You're way off base, Major. That is not a matter for a junior officer."

Huxley fidgeted nervously for a moment. "May I speak freely, sir?"

The General tapped his small wrinkled fingers on the field map, eyed the large rawboned man before him and said, "By all means, Huxley, say your piece."

"I believe," Huxley said, "that our senior officers are in a state of constant intoxication and don't grasp the situation. Or, perhaps they do grasp it and have decided to get intoxicated."

"Kindly get to the point."

Huxley clenched his fist. "General," he cried, "the Sixth Marines are too good to waste on this type of operation."

"I beg your pardon?"

"Do you know the history of this outfit, sir?" he rambled on quickly. "General, you command all the forces in the area. You know the situation. They are planning strikes farther up the Solomons."

"What has that to do—"

"You have ample Army forces. Two divisions and the elements of another for this drive on Guadalcanal. I beg you, General, give us an island to hit farther up the line. This Regiment is for assault. We've worked hard and we're well trained. We deserve a better break."

Pritchard smiled softly. "I know the history of the Sixth Marines quite well, Major," he said. "I was captain in the last war. A Marine corporal kept a bayonet up my butt all the way through Belleau Woods."

His appeasing humor did not seem particularly funny to Huxley. "Then give us an island, sir. You can do it. Just recommend that we be held for landing duty in the next operation."

The General's soft mood changed. "Huxley, tell me something. Do you honestly think your men are too good to tramp through the jungle for thirty miles, digging them out of caves, blowing up bunkers, and slushing through the mud? Or isn't there enough glory in it for you?"

"It's not our cup of tea, sir. You have more than enough army. . . ."

"In other words, Huxley, the dirty grind is for the dogfaces. You'd rather have a little more blood."

Huxley turned crimson. The words stuck coming out.

"I'll answer for you, Huxley," Pritchard said. "You think you are too good to fight beside us, don't you? You think that your regiment is worth my division?"

"Exactly! There are a thousand islands out there. If the Army wants to fart around for six weeks, it's their business. We'll never get this war finished, especially if you take one of the few decent outfits you have and waste them. We're fighters, we want a beachhead."

"Suppose we let Washington figure out how long this war is going to last."

"May I leave, sir?"

"No! Sit down, dammit!" The little general drew himself to his full five foot seven-inch height and marched up and down before the chair where Huxley sat. "I've been damned lenient with you, Huxley. You wouldn't be so liberal with one of your own officers. War is a dirty business, Major, and one of the dirtiest things you Marines are going to have to take is orders from the Army. If you are anxious to get your head blown off, we'll get you transferred to assault some choice real estate.

"I do not now, and never will agree with your psychology of fighting this war. By using this Marine regiment, I will save more men, both yours and mine. We are going to drive to Esperance and we're going to do it slowly and surely. We'll not use men where we can use artillery, if we have to wait a month for the artillery to get there. No blood-hungry Marine is going to tell me how to run my campaign. I've warned you, Major, and I warn you again, that I don't want the Marines running a horse race down that coast. You are going to keep your flank intact and you are going to move with us. Now get back to your outfit!"

Sam Huxley arose, trembling with white anger as Pritchard returned to his desk. He glanced up. "You look as if you might blow a gasket, Major. Go on, say it."

"I am thinking, General Pritchard, that you can take the whole goddam Army and shove it you know where." He stormed from the tent.

The General's aide, who had remained silent in the wake of Huxley's anger, rushed to the General. "Surely, sir," he said, "you aren't going to let that man keep his command?"

For several moments Pritchard seemed steeped in thought. Finally he spoke. "If I fire or courtmartial that Marine, there'll be hell to pay. Any co-operation we have or expect to get from the Navy will blow sky high. Thank God, we've only got a regiment of them. There's going to be a real donnybrook before this war is over. Our thinking is too far apart."

"My sympathy certainly rests with the men," the aide said, "having people like that for officers."

"I don't know," Prtichard answered, "I don't know. They're a queer breed. You and I will really never know what makes them tick. But if I was on the lines fighting for my life and I had my choice of whom I wanted on my right and my left, I'd call for a couple of Marines. I suppose they're like women . . . you can't live with 'em and God knows you can't live without 'em."

Major Wellman, the battalion's quiet and efficient executive officer, who usually remained in the background, peered out of the tent anxiously as Huxley's jeep screamed to a stop.

"How did it go, Sam?" Wellman asked.

"We open the drive on the tenth," he answered, attempting to conceal the effect of his clash with the Army. "The Second and Eighth Marines will hold the right flank along the coast while the Army gets into position in the interior. The Army will wheel in against the mountains to cut off retreat."

Wellman quickly opened a map, lit his pipe, and followed Huxley's verbal movements.

"They figure three days before the Army gets into position," Huxley continued.

"Three days?" Wellman shrugged. "What are they using, a regiment?"

"A division."

"A division?"

"Yes, a division." Wellman scratched his head. "They will get to the mountain base. On the thirteenth we will relieve the Second and Eighth Regiments and start driving until we hit the Kokumbona River about ten miles away."

"How about the Japs?"

"Dug in, caves and bunkers . . . battle-happy expendables. Going to be slow."

"Lovely. Any heavy stuff?"

"Some 108 mms. Pistol Pete, they call them. Area is loaded with snipers and machine gun nests."

"Lead on."

"Our left flank will alternate with elements of the Americal Division. Pritchard cooked up a lulu. He calls it a 'combined Marine and Army Division.' "

"Oh, Jesus. I guess we'll have to keep bayonets in their asses to keep them up with us."

"No," Huxley corrected, "we walk, not run to Esperance."

"Wait till the boys hear they are soldiers."

"From Kokumbona we hit for Tassafaronga Point and that's about the ball game. They figure some Army to mop up the rest."

"What does intelligence say?"

"Anywhere from two to ten thousand, they don't know. Most of them are concentrated along our sector, on the coast."

"How bad are they going to try to hold?"

"They might try a landing on us from farther up in the Solomons. We don't know."

"Navy?"

"Might try some of that too. Depends on whether they've marked the island off as lost or not."

"Air?"

"We can expect a lot of action. But our stuff on Henderson Field is good now. We've got F4Us and Army P-38s."

"How long, Sam?"

"Don't know. Maybe a week, maybe a month, maybe more. Call a meeting for all officers fourteen hundred hours. Get Gunner Keats here now. I want to go over the communications setup—issue extra rations and order combat packs in ready."

"How about shaving gear?" Wellman asked, knowing Huxley's insistence on the well-groomed troop.

"We won't have enough water. We'll have to hold a whiskerino contest after it's over."

Huxley lit a cigarette thoughtfully. "The Sixth is a spearhead, Wellman. I hope to God it doesn't get blunted too damned much in that jungle."

We had thrown away our gas masks and used the cases for carrying an extra change of socks and rations. We moved from Kokum at Lunga Point along the road which ran parallel to the never ending coconut plantation. Although the day was hot and the hike would be long, there was a cocky running chatter along the line of march. Huxley, as usual, was at the head of Headquarters Company, overstriding his little orderly, Ziltch. As we passed Army encampments, and the doggies came to the roadside to gawk, we stiffened and cast belittling glares at them. Thanks to the loosely guarded ordnance sheds, the Army had supplied us with all the latest fighting equipment. An Army jeep roared to the head of the column. We halted and the Army colonel went into a conference with Major Huxley.

Gunner Keats moved from the conference area to us. "Somebody stole that colonel's pearl-handled forty-five pistol and they aren't letting us up to the lines till it is returned. Now, I'm not accusing any of you boys but we have been given ten minutes to 'find' it and then there is going to be a shakedown. Now the guy that borrowed it please return it and nothing will be said." We all looked at Spanish Joe. He grinned and turned the pistol over, explaining he had found it, just laying there on the deck. We resumed the march, except for Lieutenant Bryce who had somehow gotten himself into one of the transport jeeps.

Anxiety and growing tenseness mingled with sweat of the hot tropic sun as we neared the lines. Then we saw them—the Second and Eighth Marines coming back. They were kids, most of them, just like our kids . . . but now they were old men. Hungry, skinny, tired old men. As the trucks whisked by we looked into their gaunt bloodshot eyes and at their matted greasy beards. They spoke little. Only a feeble wave or a managed wisecrack.

"So the Pogey Bait Sixth finally came."

"Yeah, you guys can go home now, a fighting outfit is moving up."

"Hope you boys don't mind sleeping on the nasty old deck?"

"How's things up on the lines, got a USO up there?"

"You'll find out, Pogey Bait."

"Hey, what town is this? We must be nearing Hollywood, the Eighth Marines still playing movie actors?"

"I never thought I'd be glad to see the Sixth, but you're sure a fine sight. Hey, look at all them nice clean-cut American boys."

The trucks kept passing. The sallow-faced men with the expressionless look of terror—and a look of nothing. Then we became tired, tired and sweaty. We wanted to go to the beach and wash—but we wouldn't get a bath now for a long time.

It cooled off and the rain came down. The last mile . . . don't look behind or you'll see what you will look like a month from now. Look forward at the grassy slopes, the jungle, the caves. Look forward—there is nothing behind.

7.

January 19, 1943

How long had we been in mud? Only six days? We were up to our asses in mud. It was turning evening and the rain would be coming soon to make more mud. It was nearly knee deep in this ravine. The hills were slick and slimy, the air was heavy and putrid with the smell of dead Japs. You could smell one a mile away. The whiskerino contest was off to a good start, only you couldn't see the whiskers for the mud. Mud caked in so thick on the face and body and the fast-rotting dungarees that it not only seemed the uniform of the day but our very flesh covering.

The drive had been slow, radio operation almost nil. We only used one set, a TBX, to Regiment. Regiment's code was Topeka; we were Topeka White. Due to the snail's pace and the terrain, telephone squad carried most of the load in keeping communications. My boys were used as pack mules. They assisted the telephone men when needed. Mostly, they made several trips a day to the beach supply dump, over glassy ridges, two miles to the coast. Back again in blistering sun, carrying five-gallon cans of water, dragged with curses back to the CP. It was a lifeline. They packed heavy boxes of ammunition, C-ration, D-ration, the chocolate candy bars that tasted like Ex-Lax but held enough vitamins to sustain a man for a day. They walked, limped, and crawled the tortuous miles back and forth to the dump like a line of ants, worn and beaten but coming back again for another load.

At darkness they'd crawl in holes in the mud to sleep until their round of guard duty—attempt to sleep with swarms of bugs all around, and the hated anopheles zinging down and biting into the flesh. And even as the mosquitoes bit and sucked blood, the Marines couldn't raise a dead-tired arm to slap them off.

We hadn't seen a Jap, not a live one. Only the dead with their terrible stench. The riflemen left them there for us to bunk with. But live ones were there. You could feel them all about, peeking at you from the treetops . . . from the brush . . . watching your every move.

In the hole at night you'd huddle next to your mate to stop the shakes. Getting malaria? Hell no, just shaking wet and the mud sliding around in your boondockers. Too beat out to think, even about home. Hard to sleep . . . the jungle was alive with silence. It took time before you could tell a land crab from a Jap. Doc Kyser emptied a whole drum from his tommy gun into a bush one night, and it was a land crab. After a while you didn't mind them crawling over you. You reached automatically for your knife and stabbed it and put it outside the foxhole. If you piled up more land crabs than the next foxhole, you might win a couple cigarettes on a bet.

Thirst . . . always the hunger for water. Our water was salted and made your stomach rebel. Once in a while you got that vision of a long cool beer floating by. Nothing to do but lick your lips with your thick dry tongue and try to forget it.

How long had we been in the mud? Only six days.

We pulled into the new CP and waited for the rain to sink us deeper.

"O.K., you guys, dig in."

"Where the hell we going to dig? We're already in."

"On the slopes where it is dry, asshole."

Lieutenant Bryce approached the Feathermerchant, who was on his knees hacking the earth with a pick as Danny shoveled.

"Ski," Bryce said.

"Yes."

"After you finish your hole, dig me in." He unfolded a stretcher he was carrying. "Fix my hole so this fits in."

Zvonski threw down the trenching tool and arose. "Dig your own goddam hole, Lieutenant. I been lugging water cans for eleven hours."

"Don't address me by rank," Bryce hissed nervously. "There is no rank up here. You want a sniper to hear you?"

"I sure do."

"I'll have you courtmartialed for this!"

"Like hell you will. Sam says we all dig our own holes. So start digging—and don't dig too close around here."

Bryce turned and left. Ski went over to Gunner Keats. "Bryce got a stretcher from sick bay to sleep on, Jack," he said.

"The dirty . . . mind your own business, Ski," he answered and took off after Bryce.

There was a swish overhead of an artillery shell. It landed and exploded on our reverse slope.

"Say, ain't the Tenth firing kind of late in the day?"

"Probably just lining up for effect."

Another shell landed, hitting the top of the ridge some two hundred yards away.

"Crazy bastards, don't they know we're down here?"

Huxley rushed to the switchboard. "Contact the firing officer at once. They're coming too close." Another shell crashed, sending us all flopping into the mud. It hit on our side of the hill.

"Hello," Huxley roared as another dropped almost in us, "this is Topeka White. You men are coming in right on our CP."

"But sir," the voice at the other end of the line answered, "we haven't fired since morning."

"Holy Christ!" the Major yelled. "Hit the deck, it's Pistol Pete!"

We scattered but the Jap 108s found us in their sights. We crawled deep in the mire, behind trees and rocks. Our foxholes hadn't been dug yet. *Swish . . . Whom! Whom!* WHOM! They roared in and the deck bounced and mud and hot shrapnel splattered everywhere.

Andy and Ski spotted a small cave on the hillside and dashed for it. They hung onto their helmets and braced their backs against the wall. There, opposite them, sat a Jap soldier. He was dead. His eyes had been eaten out by the swarms of our goddam pack out of that jeep, Bryce."

am, I was only trying to save a ride for you. You know
e fellows are. Why, I've had a terrible time keeping
ies coming up, the way they hide on working parties
ceful."

your goddam pack out of that jeep," Huxley repeated.
did you get the bright idea you were more important
BX?"

22, 1943

ey calmed the commander of E Company and lifted
d phone. "Hello, Topeka, this is Huxley. Easy Company
ot around K4 on the map. Japs are dug in caves. We
bypass and surround the area . . . Hell no! We can't gun
ut, they're in too deep. E Company's burned up—two
ot killed after the Nips gave them a phony surrender and
ent in to help them out of the caves. . . ."

ll them that—" the E Company skipper interrupted.
e down," Huxley said. "Yes, we need engineers with
hite or something. We'll have to blast. Get them up here
e dark . . . what? Well, O.K., we'll try anything once."

hat did he say, Sam?"

hey're sending flamethrowers up."

lamethrowers? I didn't know we had them."

irst time in the war they're using them. They've been
ng for a situation like this."

en Easy Company riflemen approached the opening in the
with caution. A BAR man sprayed the treetops clean of
ers. They took up positions on either side of the cave mouth.
Come on out," Huxley barked. There was no answer from
blackness inside. "Come on, we know you're in there." Si-
e . . . then a rattling.

Hit the deck, grenade!" They flopped away fast as the mis-
blew.

Lay down a covering fire," Huxley ordered. The Marine
apons blazed into the cave. Huxley signaled the flamethrow-
team to move up. The number one man crawled slowly un-
r the heavy weight of the tank strapped on his back. He took
place between two riflemen. Huxley nodded to him to shoot
will.

The flamethrower man waved everyone back and aimed the
ng hose-connected nozzle. A whiff and a streak of fire shot
ut. It sent a hot breath past the men as it streaked into the
ave.

A shriek! A Japanese soldier ran from the opening, a human
orch. He made five yards, them crumbled into a smoking heap.

maggots which crawled through his body. The stink was excruciating. "I'm getting out of here," Ski said.

Andy jerked him back in. "Hang on, Ski. They're blasting the
hell outa us. Go on, put your head down and puke." A concussion wave caused the Jap to buckle over. He dropped, brok-
en in half by rot. Ski put his head down and vomited.

Spanish Joe crawled through the muck to Sister Mary. He
put his arm about Marion and held him.

"Why didn't you stay where you were? You're safer there."

"I . . . I . . . want somebody to look at," he whined.

Highpockets was on his feet scanning the sky. He was the
only man standing. He waded through the mire as though his
feet were a pair of plungers. "Move over to the other slope, you
people," he shouted to one group. He made his way to the
switchboard, shouting commands as he went. "Give me the
Tenth . . . firing officer . . . LeForce, go to the ridge and see if
you can spot them. Hello, this is Topeka White . . . Pete is
right on us . . . can you give us some help? I'll have a spotter
up there in a minute."

"Hit the deck, Sam!" WHOM!

"Hello, this is Huxley, Topeka White . . . about two thousand
yards to our left. Hello, this is Topeka . . ."

It was dark before we crawled out. Two hours of it. We dug
in and fell off to sleep not even bothering to stab land crabs.

L.Q. Jones crouched down in the middle of a bush and
took a time check. One hour to go. His head nodded; he snapped
his eyes open. Stay with it . . . only an hour and you can go to
sleep . . . only an hour. Jesus, my side aches. . . can't get my eyes
open . . . don't sleep . . . dammit! Snap out of it.

Wish I'd stop sweating and shaking. Must be cold from the
wet. Fifty-eight minutes more. Don't sit . . . stay on your knees,
that's right. You can't sleep on your knees . . . if you doze,
you'll fall over and wake up. Wish my gut would stop
jumping. Crapped nine times tonight. Musta got the crud.

His rifle dropped to the ground, his eyes popped open again.
Can't sleep, dammit, can't . . . Japs all over . . . can't let these
guys get jumped . . . got to guard . . . got to guard. His breath
became heavy and jerky and his eyes swollen from mosquito
bites. He shook his head hard to clear it. His clothing was a
mass of soggy sweat.

Dragging ammo up the hill all day . . . never been so tired . . .
if it wasn't mud wouldn't be so bad. Slopes too slippery . . . how
much longer . . . fifty-two minutes. Hope Danny's watch is
right . . . Oh God. . . .

Forty minutes . . . soon it will be thirty and I can sleep. . . .

Mary had a little lamb . . . its fleece was white as snow . . . no its fleece was black as mud . . . and Mary didn't even know, the lamb had galloping crud. Got to remember that and tell the fellows. I got to . . . "What was that?"

"Halt," L.Q. said. "Who goes there?"

"Marine."

"Password?"

"Lola."

"Who is it?"

"Forrester."

"What you doing? I got thirty minutes more."

"You looked kind of beat out when you fell down the hill with the ammo box today."

"I'm O.K., come back in a half hour, Danny."

"Go on, get some sleep. I can't sleep anyhow."

"Are you sure?"

"Yes."

"Think I'll check in to sick bay, I got the craps bad."

"Twenty-one times today for me," Danny said.

L.Q. somehow managed to reach the battalion aid station two miles in the rear and staggered through the tent flap. Pedro Rojas turned up the dim lantern.

"Christ, L.Q., sit down."

"I . . . I . . . got the shits."

"That hain't all you got, my good friend." He popped a thermometer into L.Q.'s mouth, mopped his forehead with a cool, biting rag of alcohol, and put a blanket over his shoulders. He read the thermometer and wrote out a tag.

"What the hell you doing, Pedro?"

"You got the bug."

"Malaria?"

"Yes."

"You're nuts."

"Hokay, I'm nuts . . . you're going back to the rear echelon."

L.Q. staggered to his feet. "You want the guys to think I'm chicken?"

"I don't care what they think, you are one sick Marine."

"Pedro," L.Q. pleaded, "don't turn me in. Give me some quinine pills, I'll shake it off."

"Nope."

He grabbed the corpsman, tears streaming down his cheeks. "I can't leave my outfit," he cried. "You can't send me back . . . I don't care if I die but you aren't turning me in. We're working our asses off up there. If I go it means more load for them to carry. . . ."

Pedro released L.Q.'s grip and walked him to a cot. "Take three of these now and three every four hours. . . ."

"You won't send me back, will you, Pedro?"

"Hokay, stay here tonight. You ca[n]
the morning."

"Telephone Mac, Pedro. Tell him I[']
back up tomorrow." He downed the pill[s]
and fell into a sweaty, restless sleep.

Pedro covered him and lowered the [
matter with these Marines, he thought.
were they? Did they not know when the[y]
hell with it. If he could sneak quinine pill[s]
give them to L.Q. But why they all pick [
was the fifth man today.

Divito, the little jeep driver, gunned his [
hundred yards from the CP. Where there [
made them. We marveled at Divito and the[
seemed to accomplish miracles with the littl[e]
connaissance cars. It was a lucky break for [
rolled forward another thousand yards and th[e]
command post was sheer murder. The hills [
were knee deep in quagmire and the brush w[as]
gerous. Our new position was closer to the [
mud and graying shroud, but in the baking sun.

The jeep sunk to its hubcaps under the ge[ar]
aboard her. I called Andy and Danny, who w[
the TBX, and went into a conference to de[
they could fit this last piece of gear. By strappin[g]
and generator across the hood, they reckone[d]
Divito room to shift gears, although most of th[
in compound low. As they fitted the battery case i[
Bryce approached "What the devil are you me[n]

"Loading the TBX, Bertram." We called him [
here and it gave us a great deal of satisfaction.

"Well, I'm very sorry, Mac, but I believe I h[
over the radio," he said.

"You mean, Bertram, you want us to carry it[
ride?"

"As company commander it is my duty to see th[at]
reaches its proper destination."

"I know the way," Divito spat.

"You will kindly remove the radio without further [

Ziltch, the skipper's orderly, was standing nearby [
the beef. He paced over to Huxley and on tiptoes whis[
to his ear, pointing to us. As Huxley came over, Bryc[e]
his pack in the jeep and tried to hurry us unloading th[

"Good morning, Sam. I saved a place for you," Br[
Huxley motioned for Bryce to follow him and led him [
earshot.

January 23, 1943

The position of Huxley's battalion was now in the center of the line connecting the Army flank to the interior, with the Marines along the coast. Our command post was inside a horseshoe-shaped ridge and its slopes were rocky and barren. The CP, usually in the rear, this time extended out and was actually the furthermost point towards the Kokumbona River, the next day's objective. Our rifle companies were strung out along a slope some fifty yards behind the bulge of the CP position.

Below us there was a small stream that ran toward the sea. Across the stream was a thick woods which we presumed was infested with Japs. In the CP we had an excellent vantage point. We could look down on the enemy without being seen ourselves.

As the day drew to a close, reconnaissance planes buzzed the woods past us for photos and a destroyer dropped anchor offshore to stand by for additional gunfire support. We set up our radios and dug in on the rocky deck.

I gave my squad the glad tidings. "You guys can take off your shoes tonight."

"Man, that sounds like money from home without writing for it."

As boondockers came off, a terrible smell arose over the bivouac. We hadn't seen our feet in over a week. I tugged on my socks and they disintegrated to shreds. I scraped a half inch of hard caked mud off and looked between my toes. As I had suspected from the pain, they were turning green with fungus growths.

"Don't scrape that stuff off," Pedro warned. "I'll be around to put some joyjuice on them, Mac."

At least we had the jump on the fungus which was growing in our ears, but the feet would be a long time healing. And a long time healing the crud that drained our weight and sucked every ounce of energy until often we ran on sheer will alone. And the malaria which was cropping up, and the yellow jaundice which made our atrabine tans yellower. We were grateful we couldn't see each other's faces under the grizzly-bear beards and layers of hardened sweat and mud.

In honor of the shoe doffing, we all took whores' baths in half helmets of water. It was very refreshing. Burnside and me even omitted the usual growl about wasting the stuff.

"I'd sure like to brush my teeth again before I die."

"Just think, I used to fight with my old lady about taking a bath once a week."

We settled around our foxholes near the radio and batted the breeze.

"I hear say, cousin, that Dugout Doug done reported that all Jap resistance is over on Guadalcanal. Some rear echelon guy heard it over shortwave."

"Mighty nice of Doug. He'll get another medal for that."

"Get any good souvenirs today?"

"Me and Danny went hunting last night but them riflemen don't leave too much."

"I hear some of the guys in Fox Company can shoot a Jap at fifty yards and have him field-stripped before he hits the deck, dead."

"I got mine," Spanish Joe said holding up a bottle of gold teeth.

"If you want to go around with your pliers yanking teeth out of pore old dead Japs, that's your business. They stink too much for me."

"Anybody here got a weed?"

"What do you think this is, a USO?"

"I got one left," I said. "Who's got a match?"

"Not me, gave up smoking, it's bad for my health."

The cigarette lit, we passed it around, each man taking a drag while the others watched cautiously. When it got back to me I had to slip a pin through the end to keep from burning my lips.

"I'd sure like to be in a nice clean bed with a broad snuggled up next to me."

"Knock it off, sex is a reverent subject around here."

"I ain't had one on in a week."

"I hear that malaria will make us sterile."

"I'd sure like to find out."

"You wouldn't know what to do with it if you had it."

Andy broke out a deck of greasy tattered cards. Each one was bent or torn so that even the rankest player could read them. He dealt.

"This is the old legit, gentlemen, five card draw."

"*Hmmm*," L.Q. said, "I'll open."

"Easy, L.Q.," Forrester said. "You already owe me six million, three hundred thousand, four hundred and six dollars and eight cents."

"I guess," L.Q. said, "I'll have to dig into my assets. I'll open for the Golden Gate Bridge."

"The Golden Gate in forty-eight, the bread line in forty-nine."

"I'll call that with the U.S.S. *South Dakota*."

"I call with my cundrum factory and raise you all my whore-houses in South Carolina."

"I think he's bluffing. What you got, L.Q.?"

"A pair of deuces."

maggots which crawled through his body. The stink was excruciating. "I'm getting out of here," Ski said.

Andy jerked him back in. "Hang on, Ski. They're blasting the hell outa us. Go on, put your head down and puke." A concussion wave caused the Jap to buckle over. He dropped, broken in half by rot. Ski put his head down and vomited.

Spanish Joe crawled through the muck to Sister Mary. He put his arm about Marion and held him.

"Why didn't you stay where you were? You're safer there."

"I . . . I . . . want somebody to look at," he whined.

Highpockets was on his feet scanning the sky. He was the only man standing. He waded through the mire as though his feet were a pair of plungers. "Move over to the other slope, you people," he shouted to one group. He made his way to the switchboard, shouting commands as he went. "Give me the Tenth . . . firing officer . . . LeForce, go to the ridge and see if you can spot them. Hello, this is Topeka White . . . Pete is right on us . . . can you give us some help? I'll have a spotter up there in a minute."

"Hit the deck, Sam!" WHOM!

"Hello, this is Huxley, Topeka White . . . about two thousand yards to our left. Hello, this is Topeka . . ."

It was dark before we crawled out. Two hours of it. We dug in and fell off to sleep not even bothering to stab land crabs.

L.Q. Jones crouched down in the middle of a bush and took a time check. One hour to go. His head nodded; he snapped his eyes open. Stay with it . . . only an hour and you can go to sleep . . . only an hour. Jesus, my side aches. . . can't get my eyes open . . . don't sleep . . . dammit! Snap out of it.

Wish I'd stop sweating and shaking. Must be cold from the wet. Fifty-eight minutes more. Don't sit . . . stay on your knees, that's right. You can't sleep on your knees . . . if you doze, you'll fall over and wake up. Wish my gut would stop jumping. Crapped nine times tonight. Musta got the crud.

His rifle dropped to the ground, his eyes popped open again. Can't sleep, dammit, can't . . . Japs all over . . . can't let these guys get jumped . . . got to guard . . . got to guard. His breath became heavy and jerky and his eyes swollen from mosquito bites. He shook his head hard to clear it. His clothing was a mass of soggy sweat.

Dragging ammo up the hill all day . . . never been so tired . . . if it wasn't mud wouldn't be so bad. Slopes too slippery . . . how much longer . . . fifty-two minutes. Hope Danny's watch is right . . . Oh God. . . .

Forty minutes . . . soon it will be thirty and I can sleep. . . .

Mary had a little lamb . . . its fleece was white as snow . . . no its fleece was black as mud ... and Mary didn't even know, the lamb had galloping crud. Got to remember that and tell the fellows. I got to ... "What was that?"

"Halt," L.Q. said. "Who goes there?"

"Marine."

"Password?"

"Lola."

"Who is it?"

"Forrester."

"What you doing? I got thirty minutes more."

"You looked kind of beat out when you fell down the hill with the ammo box today."

"I'm O.K., come back in a half hour, Danny."

"Go on, get some sleep. I can't sleep anyhow."

"Are you sure?"

"Yes."

"Think I'll check in to sick bay, I got the craps bad."

"Twenty-one times today for me," Danny said.

L.Q. somehow managed to reach the battalion aid station two miles in the rear and staggered through the tent flap. Pedro Rojas turned up the dim lantern.

"Christ, L.Q., sit down."

"I ... I ... got the shits."

"That hain't all you got, my good friend." He popped a thermometer into L.Q.'s mouth, mopped his forehead with a cool, biting rag of alcohol, and put a blanket over his shoulders. He read the thermometer and wrote out a tag.

"What the hell you doing, Pedro?"

"You got the bug."

"Malaria?"

"Yes."

"You're nuts."

"Hokay, I'm nuts ... you're going back to the rear echelon."

L.Q. staggered to his feet. "You want the guys to think I'm chicken?"

"I don't care what they think, you are one sick Marine."

"Pedro," L.Q. pleaded, "don't turn me in. Give me some quinine pills, I'll shake it off."

"Nope."

He grabbed the corpsman, tears streaming down his cheeks. "I can't leave my outfit," he cried. "You can't send me back ... I don't care if I die but you aren't turning me in. We're working our asses off up there. If I go it means more load for them to carry. ..."

Pedro released L.Q.'s grip and walked him to a cot. "Take three of these now and three every four hours. ..."

"You won't send me back, will you, Pedro?"

"Hokay, stay here tonight. You can return to the front in the morning."

"Telephone Mac, Pedro. Tell him I'm here . . . and I'll be back up tomorrow." He downed the pills and flopped to the cot and fell into a sweaty, restless sleep.

Pedro covered him and lowered the lantern. What was the matter with these Marines, he thought. What kind of people were they? Did they not know when they were very sick? To hell with it. If he could sneak quinine pills to Huxley he could give them to L.Q. But why they all pick on poor Pedro? This was the fifth man today.

Divito, the little jeep driver, gunned his vehicle to a spot six hundred yards from the CP. Where there were no paths, he made them. We marveled at Divito and the other drivers who seemed to accomplish miracles with the little four-cylinder reconnaissance cars. It was a lucky break for us. The lines had rolled forward another thousand yards and the route to the new command post was sheer murder. The hills out in the interior were knee deep in quagmire and the brush was thick and dangerous. Our new position was closer to the coast, out of the mud and graying shroud, but in the baking sun.

The jeep sunk to its hubcaps under the gear we crammed aboard her. I called Andy and Danny, who were packing up the TBX, and went into a conference to determine where they could fit this last piece of gear. By strapping the antennae and generator across the hood, they reckoned it would give Divito room to shift gears, although most of the driving was in compound low. As they fitted the battery case in, Lieutenant Bryce approached "What the devil are you men doing?"

"Loading the TBX, Bertram." We called him Bertram up here and it gave us a great deal of satisfaction.

"Well, I'm very sorry, Mac, but I believe I have priority over the radio," he said.

"You mean, Bertram, you want us to carry it while you ride?"

"As company commander it is my duty to see that all gear reaches its proper destination."

"I know the way," Divito spat.

"You will kindly remove the radio without further ado."

Ziltch, the skipper's orderly, was standing nearby taking in the beef. He paced over to Huxley and on tiptoes whispered into his ear, pointing to us. As Huxley came over, Bryce threw his pack in the jeep and tried to hurry us unloading the radio.

"Good morning, Sam. I saved a place for you," Bryce lied.

Huxley motioned for Bryce to follow him and led him out of earshot.

"Get your goddam pack out of that jeep, Bryce."

"But, Sam, I was only trying to save a ride for you. You know how those fellows are. Why, I've had a terrible time keeping the supplies coming up, the way they hide on working parties is disgraceful."

"Get your goddam pack out of that jeep," Huxley repeated. "When did you get the bright idea you were more important than a TBX?"

January 22, 1943

Huxley calmed the commander of E Company and lifted the field phone. "Hello, Topeka, this is Huxley. Easy Company hit a spot around K4 on the map. Japs are dug in caves. We had to bypass and surround the area . . . Hell no! We can't gun them out, they're in too deep. E Company's burned up—two boys got killed after the Nips gave them a phony surrender and they went in to help them out of the caves. . . ."

"Tell them that—" the E Company skipper interrupted.

"Pipe down," Huxley said. "Yes, we need engineers with dynamite or something. We'll have to blast. Get them up here before dark . . . what? Well, O.K., we'll try anything once."

"What did he say, Sam?"

"They're sending flamethrowers up."

"Flamethrowers? I didn't know we had them."

"First time in the war they're using them. They've been waiting for a situation like this."

Ten Easy Company riflemen approached the opening in the hill with caution. A BAR man sprayed the treetops clean of snipers. They took up positions on either side of the cave mouth.

"Come on out," Huxley barked. There was no answer from the blackness inside. "Come on, we know you're in there." Silence . . . then a rattling.

"Hit the deck, grenade!" They flopped away fast as the missile blew.

"Lay down a covering fire," Huxley ordered. The Marine weapons blazed into the cave. Huxley signaled the flamethrowing team to move up. The number one man crawled slowly under the heavy weight of the tank strapped on his back. He took a place between two riflemen. Huxley nodded to him to shoot at will.

The flamethrower man waved everyone back and aimed the long hose-connected nozzle. A whiff and a streak of fire shot out. It sent a hot breath past the men as it streaked into the cave.

A shriek! A Japanese soldier ran from the opening, a human torch. He made five yards, them crumbled into a smoking heap.

January 23, 1943

The position of Huxley's battalion was now in the center of the line connecting the Army flank to the interior, with the Marines along the coast. Our command post was inside a horseshoe-shaped ridge and its slopes were rocky and barren. The CP, usually in the rear, this time extended out and was actually the furthermost point towards the Kokumbona River, the next day's objective. Our rifle companies were strung out along a slope some fifty yards behind the bulge of the CP position.

Below us there was a small stream that ran toward the sea. Across the stream was a thick woods which we presumed was infested with Japs. In the CP we had an excellent vantage point. We could look down on the enemy without being seen ourselves.

As the day drew to a close, reconnaissance planes buzzed the woods past us for photos and a destroyer dropped anchor offshore to stand by for additional gunfire support. We set up our radios and dug in on the rocky deck.

I gave my squad the glad tidings. "You guys can take off your shoes tonight."

"Man, that sounds like money from home without writing for it."

As boondockers came off, a terrible smell arose over the bivouac. We hadn't seen our feet in over a week. I tugged on my socks and they disintegrated to shreds. I scraped a half inch of hard caked mud off and looked between my toes. As I had suspected from the pain, they were turning green with fungus growths.

"Don't scrape that stuff off," Pedro warned. "I'll be around to put some joyjuice on them, Mac."

At least we had the jump on the fungus which was growing in our ears, but the feet would be a long time healing. And a long time healing the crud that drained our weight and sucked every ounce of energy until we ran on sheer will alone. And the malaria which was cropping up, and the yellow jaundice which made our atrabine tans yellower. We were grateful we couldn't see each other's faces under the grizzly-bear beards and layers of hardened sweat and mud.

In honor of the shoe doffing, we all took whores' baths in half helmets of water. It was very refreshing. Burnside and me even omitted the usual growl about wasting the stuff.

"I'd sure like to brush my teeth again before I die."

"Just think, I used to fight with my old lady about taking a bath once a week."

We settled around our foxholes near the radio and batted the breeze.

"I hear say, cousin, that Dugout Doug done reported that all Jap resistance is over on Guadalcanal. Some rear echelon guy heard it over shortwave."

"Mighty nice of Doug. He'll get another medal for that."

"Get any good souvenirs today?"

"Me and Danny went hunting last night but them riflemen don't leave too much."

"I hear some of the guys in Fox Company can shoot a Jap at fifty yards and have him field-stripped before he hits the deck, dead."

"I got mine," Spanish Joe said holding up a bottle of gold teeth.

"If you want to go around with your pliers yanking teeth out of pore old dead Japs, that's your business. They stink too much for me."

"Anybody here got a weed?"

"What do you think this is, a USO?"

"I got one left," I said. "Who's got a match?"

"Not me, gave up smoking, it's bad for my health."

The cigarette lit, we passed it around, each man taking a drag while the others watched cautiously. When it got back to me I had to slip a pin through the end to keep from burning my lips.

"I'd sure like to be in a nice clean bed with a broad snuggled up next to me."

"Knock it off, sex is a reverent subject around here."

"I ain't had one on in a week."

"I hear that malaria will make us sterile."

"I'd sure like to find out."

"You wouldn't know what to do with it if you had it."

Andy broke out a deck of greasy tattered cards. Each one was bent or torn so that even the rankest player could read them. He dealt.

"This is the old legit, gentlemen, five card draw."

"*Hmmm,*" L.Q. said, "I'll open."

"Easy, L.Q.," Forrester said. "You already owe me six million, three hundred thousand, four hundred and six dollars and eight cents."

"I guess," L.Q. said, "I'll have to dig into my assets. I'll open for the Golden Gate Bridge."

"The Golden Gate in forty-eight, the bread line in forty-nine."

"I'll call that with the U.S.S. *South Dakota.*"

"I call with my cundrum factory and raise you all my whorehouses in South Carolina."

"I think he's bluffing. What you got, L.Q.?"

"A pair of deuces."

"I guess you weren't bluffing, you win."

Lighttower came running up to us excitedly. "Chow! Hot chow!"

"Hot chow?"

"*Mama mia.*"

"Craphouse mouse, hot chow!"

A mad scramble to the foxholes for mess kits and we soon settled back to our first meal in nine days. Spam, dehydrated potatoes, peaches and hot coffee—real hot coffee already mixed with sidearms. We were overjoyed.

"Peaches—how the hell did they get peaches?"

"I hear that the cook borrowed them from the Army."

"Good old Army."

"Good old cook."

"*Hmmmm*, this steak needs a little tobasco sauce, if you please, Mac."

"Side order of caviar, old bean, and pass the martinis."

"Ya don't drink martinis with steak, ya ignorant crumb."

"Now watch my technique," L.Q. said, holding a forkful of spam. He quickly brushed the swarm of flies off and shoved the mouthful in, then spat out a stray fly.

"Now there's a man with right fuzzy balls, got it down to a science."

"On a good run," L.Q. bragged, "I can get it in without a single fly."

"That will be the bloody day."

"Truth, truth."

Andy slapped a mosquito. "I don't mind sharing chow with flies, but I'll be damned if I'll let these big bastard mosquitoes have any."

"I hear say, cousin, a mosquito landed on Henderson Field and they filled it with a hundred gallons of gas before they found out it wasn't a Flying Fortress."

"That ain't nothing," Seabags said. "Two of them landed on me last night. One of them turned over my dogtags and said to the other, 'Another damned type O. Let's find an A.' "

"Why you dirty bastard, those must be the same two that came after me."

"Say, I got me forty-six land crabs last night. I think that's a company record. Fingerbowl, please."

Tat-a-tat, rat-a-tat, rat-a-tat, rat-a-tat. . . . Dirt kicked up on the rim of the ridge.

"Japs!"

"The dirty no-good stinking sonofabitch bastards . . . I ain't drank my coffee!"

"They must have known we was having hot chow."

We scattered to our foxholes, grabbed our weapons, and dashed for the ridge.

Danny and the Feathermerchant were dug in the rear near one end of the horseshoe, where it connected with a rifle company by a slim file of sentries. They snatched their Garands and wheeled about toward the ridge for the rest of us. Suddenly Ski stopped.

"Look," he said to Danny.

"What?"

"There, coming through the grass."

"Smart sons of bitches—drawing us up to the ridge while they slip one man in on our rear."

They fell to the deck and lay quietly. A hunched figure sprinted through the tall grass a hundred yards from them. Danny felt a weird tingle in his body . . . a live Jap, not dead and rotten. This one was moving, moving at him and Ski. The sweat gushed into his eyes as the man weaved closer . . . two arms, two legs . . . why does he want to kill me? Maybe he has a girl, a Jap girl like Kathy. I'm not mad at him. They raised their rifles . . . fifteen yards . . . got him zero'd in, easy, this will be easy . . . sitting duck, right through the heart . . . Suppose my rifle won't fire? *Crack! Crack! Crack!* The Jap dropped in his tracks.

"You got him," Ski said. "Did you see that bastard fall?"

Danny sprang to his feet and put his bayonet on his rifle. "Cover me, he's probably wired." He paced through the knee-high grass, poised. He moved over to the body of the fallen soldier. A stream of blood was pouring from the man's mouth. Danny shuddered. His eyes were open. The Jap's hand made a last feeble gesture. Danny plunged the steel into the Jap's belly. A moan, a violent twitch of his body. . . . It seemed to Danny that his belly closed tight around the bayonet. Danny tugged at his rifle, it was stuck. He squeezed off a shot, which splattered him with blood and insides of the Jap. *The eyes were still open*. He lifted the gory weapon and with its butt bashed madly again and again until there were no eyes or face or head.

He staggered back to Ski and sat down and wiped his bayonet with his dungaree top.

The firing on the ridge stopped. Andy went to Danny. "I guess this belongs to you," he said, handing him a Japanese battle flag. "He had it in his helmet. Nice going, Danny."

He took the token without words, his eyes glued to the flag.

"What's biting his ass?"

"Lay off," Ski said, "just lay off."

8.

"WHERE is Father McKale? They want him at headquarters," the switchboard operator said.

"Up with H Company, firing mortars as usual . . . I'll send a runner."

"How come we didn't move out this morning, Mac?"

"We can't, the Army retreated."

"What they do, run into a sniper?"

"Two snipers, ran off and left their machine guns and every goddam thing else. They're moving one of our battalions to cover the hole."

"Mail call!"

No, not a dream. Unbelieving, trembling hands ripped at the envelopes. Quiet. Watch the eyes. By now I knew every word their letters said. A grin through a mud-caked lip, a nod of the head, read and reread.

Dear L.Q.,
We put the car up on blocks. We don't mind though, if it will help you come home sooner.

Dear Son,
Mother and I thought it over carefully. We both would like to buy a home in the city and retire. Thirty years of farming is enough. So, when you return, it is yours.

Dear Andy,
We have heard about where you boys are. Believe me, we watch your every move and we are with you in spirit. We are mighty fond of our Yanks. I've been up to the farm twice. Somehow, it doesn't seem so hard to go now. Hope springs eternal.
It is quite hot, middle of summer, you know. . . .

My dearest Sam,
I found out from Colonel Daner where your Regiment is. Please, my darling, try not to take any chances you don't have to. I know your boys will come through with flying colors.

Danny Son,
It just wasn't Christmas at all in Baltimore. I wonder if we really know what you are going through.

243

Dearest Marion,

I've got a job in a department store as a salesgirl. I love it. Your folks have been wonderful to me. . . .

I love you my dearling,

Your Rae

Dear Connie,

I hate to have to tell you this, but we are all afraid for mother. She is sinking fast. The doctor thinks that she might have a chance to live if she really wanted to . . .

We never did have much at Christmas, but at least we had each other.

I've got a boyfriend now, he's twenty-nine and a soldier. . . . I just have to quit school and get a job. Uncle Ed is barely making ends meet and with the hospital bills and you gone it is really rough.

Susan moved from town, no one seems to know where. Frankly, I don't care after what she did to you. . . .

Your sister,

Wanda

"Hey, lookee, Seabags got a carton of cigarettes!"

"Shaddup, you bastard."

"Cigarettes!"

"O.K., don't crowd—I'll keep two packs and you guys can split the rest."

"What you got there?"

"A money belt."

"Just what you needed."

"They're always sending me money belts. What the hell they think I am, the paymaster?"

"A cake!"

"Hard as rock."

"It's better than chewing D-ration. Get the machete and let's split it up."

"Chewing gum!"

"Honest to God?"

"Lookit, a hand-knitted necktie."

"You mean, field scarf, don't you?"

"This one is a necktie."

"What you going to do with it?"

"What you think? I'm gonna wear it."

"Here?"

"Yep, best-dressed gyrene in the regiment."

As the telephone line to Topeka went in, I secured the radio for the night. I made a check call on the other TBX to the destroyer lying offshore and closed that station too. Sergeant Barry, the telephone chief, came up to me.

"Can you spare me a man, Mac?"

"For why?"

"The line to How Company is out. Cassidy is going to trouble shoot and I need someone to guard him."

"Seabags!"

"Yo."

"Go out with Cassidy on the How line and stop spitting that tobacco juice on the deck. It isn't sanitary."

"Sure, cousin," he said as another wad flew out. Brown went to his foxhole, picked up his rifle and hooked a pair of grenades on his suspenders.

"You've got to hustle," Barry said to Red Cassidy. "Get in before dark. The password is Lonely."

"That's the fouled-up line that runs in front of our ridge," I said, "so be careful."

"How the hell did they ever lay a line in front of us?" Seabags asked.

"It isn't easy, but we manage. Keep an eye out for pins, Red. The Japs have been shorting us out with them. I'll be at the switchboard. Give me a test check every couple hundred yards."

Cassidy, a stocky redheaded Irishman, slammed a cigarette between his lips, picked up the wire and went over the ridge. Seabags paced several feet behind him, his eyes scanning the brush and treetops as they moved. They followed the white marked wire of Topeka White and were soon away from the battalion area.

"How in hell did they lay this goddam line out here?" Seabags repeated.

"We overran the objective and pulled back onto the ridge after the line was laid," Cassidy explained.

"Christ, sure is quiet out here, cousin."

Cassidy tested Topeka White and reached them. But he could not get How Company. They moved on till they were at the stream which ran under the reverse slope of the CP knoll. They splashed across and tested once more, then moved for the small clump of trees and brush which lay to the left. Downstream to the right was the big wood full of Japs.

Cassidy raced along the wire running it through his fingers. "I got a feeling we ain't alone, cousin," Seabags said. Another test call. Still no How Company.

"Cassidy, lookit." Seabags pointed to the wire ahead, cut neatly.

"They must have sneaked out of the woods and sliced it."

"Plumb in two." They stood near the small clump of trees.

Cassidy found the cut end and quickly peeled the wire to make a splice.

Crack! Twang!

"Sniper. Take cover!"

Seabags crouched behind a tree. Cassidy dove in after him.

"See him?"

"No."

"I'd better get that line back here so I can splice it." Cassidy took a step and fell to his knees.

"What's the matter, Red?"

"Must have twisted my ankle diving in here." Seabags quickly dragged him to better cover and took off his shoe.

"Hurt?"

"Like hell."

"It's busted. Hold my rifle and keep your eye on them woods."

"Where you going?"

"Got to get that line back here and get it spliced." Seabags dashed out. *Crack! Twang! Rat-a-tat crack!* CRACK! He snatched up the wire and rolled back alongside the telephone man, puffing. "Lousy shots," he wheezed. "Did you see them?" They both looked at the jungle over the stream. It was very still and very quiet.

"You never see them bastards."

"They're there, cousin." Seabags rolled the friction tape over the wires. "How the hell do you test this, Red?"

The Irishman gritted his teeth. "Screw . . . one cap on each wire and hook into the test phone . . ."

"Your ankle bad?"

"It's starting to swell."

Seabags tested into the command post and then into How Company. The circuit was at last complete. "Hold on a minute, Seabags," the CP said, "Sam wants to talk to you."

"Hello, Seabags, this is Sam Huxley."

"Howdy, Sam."

"Where was the break?"

"The little bunch of trees over the stream. They must have sneaked over the creek and clipped it because it's the only part of the line that runs close to them. They can't tap it as long as we're down here—who the hell laid this line here, anyhow? Surer than hell they'll cut it again, soon as it turns dark. You'd better run another line to How."

At the CP, Huxley consulted the Gunner and Sergeant Barry. "We can't get another line laid. It's getting dark and there's a gully between us and How, probably full of Japs."

"Ain't that just peachy," Seabags moaned. "I got a hurt boy here too."

"What's the matter?"

"Cassidy's ankle's broke. The bone looks about ready to bust through the skin. He's in gawd-awful misery."

A wild train of thoughts raced through Huxley's mind. The line had to be kept open. There was no time either now or at dawn to get another one in before the attack on the woods. That wire was to direct a walking curtain of mortar fire from the stream to the woods. At dawn the Tenth Marines' artillery and the destroyer were going to blast the woods apart and planes from Henderson Field would rake it clean. The two boys were only a hair away from the line of fire.

Huxley's eyes narrowed, he clenched his teeth and felt the breath of the men around him on the back of his neck. "Can you guard that line against another break?" he asked Seabags harshly.

"Sure, if they don't slit our throats first, Sam."

The decision made, Huxley quickly followed up. Watches were synchronized and he ordered a test call to be made every half hour. "You've got to stay till the last possible minute. Shove off at zero five five eight—that will give you two minutes," he said.

"We'll never be able to get up that slope, Sam. We'll have to try to follow the stream to the beach."

"Good luck."

"Sam, tell Speedy not to worry about that fin he owes me."

Huxley put the receiver back in its case and turned to the anxious faces about him. "They're trapped," he said, "but they can hold the line open to mortars. . . . Well, break it up, dammit. Don't stare. There's nothing we can do."

"How's the ankle?" Seabags whispered.

"I don't even feel it any more," Red Cassidy answered.

"Sure is still."

"I'm dying for a cigarette."

"Sure glad I chaw tobacco." He spat. "Care for some?"

"Makes me puke."

"Sure is quiet . . . where you from anyhow, Red?"

"Detroit."

"Go on, get some sleep . . . I'm wide awake."

"I can't sleep. Suppose they'll try to jump us?"

"Never can tell about them there things. . . . I'm from Iowa, myself. Black Hawk County, some of the best damned farm land in the world. My old man is retiring after the war . . . turning over a hundred and sixty acres to me. . . ."

"*Owwwwwww*, God."

"What's it?"

"Nothing. I just tried to move my leg . . . it's O.K. as long as I don't touch it."

They propped themselves up, back to back, and cradled their rifles in their laps.

"Yes sir, a hundred and sixty acres. . . ."

"Sure is quiet. . . ."

It was three hours later. "Better not check no more for a while, cousin, they're rustling over the stream looking for us," Seabags said and put the phone away. He helped Cassidy into a prone position. They looked into the black ahead of them. The brush over the stream was crackling with movement. "Don't shoot, even if they hit the stream," Seabags whispered. "I'll try to jump them. . . ."

A high-pitched voice cried out in the darkness, "Marine, you die!"

"Bastards."

"Lay still, Red."

"*Marine . . . you die!*"

"Yellow son of a—" Seabags clamped his hand over Cassidy's mouth.

"They're just trying to rattle you into shooting, now lay still."

"*Dirty Marine, you die, Marine, you die . . . fugg you, yellow Marine . . . fugg Babe Ruth . . . Marine, you die!*"

"I'll show those stinking . . . I'm going after them."

Seabags gripped the pain-wracked boy and pinned him flat. "Dammit, lay still or I'll have to lay you out."

"Sorry . . . I'm O.K. . . . now."

"MARINE . . . YOU DIE!"

Marion gripped his rifle tightly and gritted his teeth to fight back the tears. He could not hear the voices from the stream, but there were other voices calling up to the ridge, "Buddy . . . help me . . . I'm a Marine . . . I'm a Marine . . . help me . . . the Japs got me . . . Yow . . . *Yowwwe.*" Marion bit his lip and trembled.

"Halt, who goes there?"

"Marine."

"Password?"

"Lonely," Spanish Joe said as he slipped in next to Marion. "What are you doing here, Joe?"

"Them Japs are getting my goat with that screaming."

"How do you think I feel?"

"Do you think that is really Seabags and Cassidy yelling?"

"Get back to your post, Joe."

"I'm going to plug the lousy bastards."

"That's just what they want you to try . . ."

"Buddy . . . help me . . . Sarge . . . help me. . . ."

"Get back to your post, Joe."

"I want . . . company."

"Back to your post, dammit," Marion snarled. Joe crept away. Marion edged through the grass. He made out a dim form lying along the ridge back of him and to the left and moved up to it. "Joe, I told you to get back to your . . ."

At this instant the Jap sprang. A knife blade flashed through the darkness. Marion went down, the Jap on top of him. Marion reached up desperately, blocked a thrust, and rolled away. The Jap was on him like a cat. Marion brought his knee up between the Jap's legs. The man grunted and fell back for a split second. Marion tore forward, following up his advantage. They scuffed savagely on the rock. The Jap quivered, pressing his weight behind the knife. Slowly it edged towards Marion's throat. Marion's hand reached out into the enemy's face, pushing his neck back. The Jap sunk his teeth into Marion's hand and he had to open it, bleeding . . . his fingers reached to the Jap's eyes and clawed wildly at them. The knife fell, and the Jap sank to his knees clutching his eyes. Marion pounced on him from the rear, his arm tight around the Jap's neck. The man kicked and twisted in desperation. Marion closed his grip, grunting and straining every fiber of his being. He jerked again and again until the Jap's body finally grew limp and he released a dead man. Then he reeled into the command post switchboard.

"Give me a relief . . . Jap . . . jumped me." He sagged to his knees.

"Your shoulder's bleeding."

"Nick . . . just a nick. . . ."

"Lighttower, take him back to the aid tent on the double!"

Doc Kyser washed away the blood and offered Marion a shot of brandy. "You're lucky, Mary. He just grazed you." Marion managed a feeble grin. The doctor looked at his closed and bloody hand. "Let's take a look at that hand, son."

"What. . . ."

"Open your fist."

It took two corpsmen to pry Marion's bloody hand open. He stared at it unbelievingly. There were shreds of flesh and muscle there. "Wash my hand," Marion cried, "wash it quick."

9.

January 25, 1943

SERGEANT BARRY was standing over me. I
opened my eyes and jumped to my feet with a start. They were
all gathered around the switchboard.

"I must have dozed," I said. "Any word?"

"They haven't answered the last four times."

"Maybe they had to keep quiet on account of the Japs."

"It will be light in a few more minutes," I said, checking
my watch. "The bombardment is due to start in five minutes."

A Navy gunfire observer and the Tenth Marines' observer
went to the top of the ridge. Danny trudged over to me.

"See anything down there yet, Danny?"

"Nothing, at least no Japs in the stream."

"Is the line still open to How Company?"

"Yes."

"Maybe they're just laying low. I wonder how Cassidy is?"

Huxley, followed by Ziltch, raced to us. "What's the scoop?"
he asked.

"The line is still open to How but we can't get Seabags."

"As soon as the bombardment opens, ring them again. Is
the How observer at the observation post?"

"Yes, so are the other two."

"Do you have a phone in up there?"

"Yes."

"I'm going up there. About two minutes before we jump
off I'll phone you. Order the Tenth and the destroyer to hold
fire. If you contact Seabags, have him shag-ass at zero five
fifty eight." Huxley and Ziltch made their way to the rim of
the ridge.

BLAM! BLAM! SWISH, WHOM! BLAM! BLAM!
WHOM!

"This is the observation post. The Tenth Marines are on
target. Have the destroyer lower her fire two hundred yards,
they're in the middle of the stream now."

"Roger," I said. "Crank up the generator, L.Q."

BLAM! BLAM! Smoke began rising over the ridge. The
generator whined. I put my fist to the key, then switched the
dials. The clicks came through the earphones: TOW V DFS
1 0532 K.

BLAM! BLAM! SWHOOSH BLOM!

250

"Crank 'er up." DFS v TOW 2 0533 LOWER 200 SALVO. . . . And the destroyer lowered and came in on the woods.

"Topeka White calling Brown. Are you there, Seabags?"

"Howdy, cousin," a weak voice came through the phone.

"He's there, he's there!"

"Stop yelling and tell them bastards to stop firing at me, they're two hundred yards out of the woods."

"They're lowering now. Are you all right?"

"Why, sure."

"How's Cassidy?"

"Not so hot . . . we got us four Japs and you should see the souvenirs."

"Hang on a minute . . . hello observation post . . . this is Topeka White . . . tell Sam that Cassidy and Brown are still alive."

"Hello Topeka White, this is Sam at the observation post. Call Henderson Field and tell them to call off the air cover. We can't take a chance losing those boys now. All guns are on target. Contact How and tell them we want a machine gun spray before we jump . . . switch me to Seabags."

"Hello . . . Seabags?"

"Howdy, Sam."

"Good to hear your voice, son."

"Good to be talking, Sam."

"How's it look down there?"

"Looks like they're ripping the woods apart, noisy as hell."

"Can you make it up the ridge?"

"Don't think so. I'll have to pack Cassidy . . . never do it in two minutes."

"All right then, hit the stream and run for the beach when the artillery stops . . . take off like a ruptured duck. Topeka Blue has been alerted to look for you. Good luck."

"Ta ta."

"Hello Sam, this is Topeka White. We have Henderson Field on the phone."

"Operations speaking."

"This is Huxley, Topeka White . . . hold off the air cover. We've got some men trapped right in the target area."

"Roger."

BLAM! BLAM! BLAM! BLAM! Shells careened into the woods and burst, blasting apart trees and earth. The roar became more deafening with each salvo. We raced to the ridge top near the observation post and stood by. The jungle was ablaze with smoke and splitting crashes. H-hour drew near. The riflemen lay poised along the length of the knoll awaiting the word to attack.

As suddenly as the noise had started, a quick silence left

the woods panting and fuming. I whispered a Hail Mary. We leaned forward as the time pointed to 0558.

Seabags Brown stepped from a small clump of trees, far below us. A rifle in his right fist and over his left shoulder the body of Red Cassidy. He trotted in jerky, shaky steps to the stream, where he stumbled and fell. He raised to a crouch and darted down the middle of the stream, running directly under us. *Crack! Crack! Rat-a-tat....*

"Goddamit, they still got them in there!"

"Give her the gas, Seabags. Take off!"

He buckled under his load and staggered down the stream, zigging away from the rain of fire from the smoldering woods. We screamed to him from our position.

"He's around the ridge . . . he made it!" A cheer arose.

Huxley grabbed the field phone. "Give me How Company."

"This is How."

"This is Huxley. Give 'em hell!"

With a dim swish the mortars from How arced over us and fell on the stream. Our ridge became alive with machine gun fire. Red tracers crissed and crossed as they sprayed the treetops below. Huxley gave the phone to the How observer who directed the fire in its gradual creep to the edge of the woods.

0600!

The jungle was torn under the impact of the blasting. The machine guns stopped. Only the mortars still roared in. The skipper of George Company arose, his .45 in his right hand. He raised his left hand to his mouth and pointed down to the gulley. "Come on, you Whores—you'll never get a Purple Heart up here. Follow me!"

Along the ridge Huxley's Whores arose with their rifles at high port. The Japs answered with vicious fire.

We poured from the ridge into the gully, our rifles blazing and with bloodcurdling shrieks and rebel yells on our lips. The assault was on! The screams became deafening as we swept over the stream and into the jungle.

January 26, 1943

"I guess there ain't no use of hoping no more."

"Topeka Blue didn't see hide nor hair of them."

"Don't give up hope. They may be lost in the jungle. It's easy."

"Pore damn farmer."

"Oh, well, another day another dollar."

We were on the beach now. There was no trace of Seabags or Cassidy. There was but one chance in a million that they were alive. We had forded the Kokumbona River, about half the drive was over. The Army in the interior held a steel ring around the mountain base, cutting off escape for the Japs. Ten more miles to Tassafaronga Point and we would have the enemy in a vise.

"Jesus," said Lighttower, "I got to crap again."

"Good old dysentery."

"Us Injuns are regular fellows," he said racing for the one-two-three trench.

"I want two volunteers, Andy and Danny, to dig a hole for the officers."

"But we just dug one yesterday," Andy protested.

"It's full, they need a new one."

"I always said it was true about them officers," he moaned as he grabbed his trenching tool.

L.Q. took the message coming over the TBX. He doffed his ear phones and shouted, "Condition Red!"

"Condition Red, air raid!" the word passed along the line.

We propped ourselves comfortably against trees along the beach to watch the show. A far-off sound of motors, and black dots began to appear on the horizon across the channel, over Tulagi. As they became larger, we counted.

"One ... two ... three ... four. ..."

"Twenty-nine ... thirty ... Holy Christ ... forty of them!"

Huxley held his field glasses up. "You men better take cover this time, there's a mess of them."

"Ain't we supposed to shoot at them, Sam?"

"We're not boondocking at Eliot, son. Let's let Henderson Field take care of them."

"Well, where the hell they at?" Speedy asked as the Japs loomed close. We could see the red balls painted on their sides and wing tips. Slow, steady Mitsubishi bombers moving right for our lines, surrounded by quick buzzing Zeros.

"Lookit!"

"Here they come! Gyrene Corsairs!"

"They were upstairs waiting all the time."

Marine Corsairs, the F4Us with inverted seagull wings that the Japs called. "Whispering Death." The sky was soon alive with streaking tracers and snarling planes.

A streak of smoke ... a plane careened and lowered ... another burst into flame. As the Jap craft broke into dizzy whirls and plunged into Skylark Channel a cheer arose from the beach.

An inching bomber burst into flame, disintegrated, and scattered.

"Hit the deck!" A Zero broke and roared in on the beach. Its guns spewing, it zipped by only twenty feet overhead, sending a spray of bullets over us. Our CP machine gun spit back vainly and Speedy emptied his rifle, then defiantly threw it up at the plane as it came in for another pass.

The bombers, now over us, heaved their loads into our midst and the dogfight went on.

"Oh, Jesus—three Japs on that lone gyrene."

"Dirty bastards, three to one ain't fair." A long black line of smoke erupted from the Corsair's tail and it dropped into the sea.

Finally they left. The remnants of the Jap formation limped home, the Army P-38s falling from the sky upon them as they raced back over Tulagi.

Speedy Gray stood up and stretched. Marion put aside his pocket book, adjusted the tape which held his glasses together. "Got to get to the machine gun," Speedy drawled. "Two-hour guard watch."

Marion picked up his book again and nodded as the Texan peered over his shoulder and spelled out the words on the book's cover. "What the hell you reading that stuff for—Oriental Fi-losophy?"

Marion smiled. "One of these days, Speedy, we're going to stop fighting. I'm thinking it might be a good idea then to know how to deal with them."

Speedy scratched his head. "I kind of figured that we'd shoot them all or throw them into stockades."

"Seventy-five million people? I'm afraid that's the wrong solution. We'd be defeating our purpose."

"Aw, they'll probably all commit hara-kiri."

"I doubt that too. Somewhere we must find the answer. It must be something that coincides with their culture. If we used your method we'd be the same as the people we are fighting."

"What culture, Mary? They ain't nothing but a bunch of monkeys."

"On the contrary. Their civilization dates back to a time when all good Texans were living in caves."

"Aw, that there crap is too deep for me. Shoot them all, I say. See you later, I got to take the watch."

Marion turned the page.

Speedy jumped down into the trench that lay in a grove of trees along the rim of the beach. The man on watch hoisted himself out. "Password is Lilac," Speedy said.

"Check."

The sandy-haired lad with the freckled face checked the machine gun. He swung it in an arc aiming his eye through the sight. It commanded any approach up the beach. The dying sun blew up like a leviathan flaming ball. It hit the horizon off Cape Esperance and its mammoth circle silhouetted the curving palms and the gold sand. The water of Skylark Channel was tinged with orange. A quiet and serene beauty like his home back in Texas on the gulf. For a moment he even thought he should like to come back here some day and just lie on the beach and look at it again. His thoughts were broken by a mosquito alighting on his forehead for a drink. He checked his timepiece and settled back.

Down the beach he thought he spotted a moving form. He swung the gun around and strained his eyes. There was something moving! He threw the bolt twice, readying the piece for firing. The form moved slowly and unevenly through the sand. The setting sun made it hard to distinguish. Speedy squinted and waited. It came closer.

"Halt, who goes there?" he barked. No answer. "I said halt, who goes there?"

"Marine, dammit," a hoarse voice croaked from down the beach.

"What's the password?"

"Stop playing dogface, Speedy—it's yer ole cousin Seabags."

"*Seabags!*" Speedy raced faster than he had ever moved in his life. "Seabags, you old fart knocker—we thought you was dead." He took the unconscious body of Red Cassidy from Brown, threw it over his shoulders, and pumped Seabags' hand.

"Pardon my steel grip," Seabags whispered, pitching to his knees, exhausted. Gray assisted him to his feet and half dragged him into the CP, screaming at the top of his lungs: "The farmer's back—ole Seabags made it!"

"Call up the jeep ambulance on the double."

"Doc, Doc . . . get Kyser here quick."

"Seabags!" We clambered all over him.

"Stop kissing me, you goldarn slobbering bastards."

"Seabags is back!"

"You shoulda seen the souvenirs I had to toss away." They laid the two on stretchers. Speedy held Seabags' hand. . . .

"O.K., stand back, stand back dammit, give them air."

"I'm plumb tuckered."

"I told you he'd make it."

Doc Kyser and Sam Huxley leaned close to Brown, whose voice was fading. Kyser studied his exhausted bloodshot eyes and swollen face.

"Water," he whispered.

"Not too much, son . . . just wet your lips."

"Anybody got a chaw?"

"Here, Seabags."

"Hey, Doc . . . I'm O.K. Better take a look at Cassidy. I had to coldcock him. He went loco on me . . . I been carrying him for two days . . . his leg is in a bad way."

Kyser looked at Red's swollen and discolored limb. "Hurry up with that ambulance," he cried. "Phone up base hospital to prepare for surgery . . . hurry, dammit!" The doctor looked up at Sam Huxley. Huxley's eyes asked the question. Kyser shook his head.

"Too bad," Highpockets whispered.

10.

January 28, 1943

THE battalion jeep screeched to a stop. Huxley jumped out and dashed into the CP tent. "Get those men up here on the double." he called to Ziltch.

Paris, Gunnery Sergeant McQuade from Fox Company, Pedro Rojas, and I converged on the tent at the same time.

"Where the hell is that candy-ass Burnside?" McQuade barked.

"In the aid tent," I answered. "Got the bug in a bad way."

"Aw hell, I wanted to hike his ass into the deck," the red-faced gunner moaned.

"Looks like you lost your beer gut, Mac," I said to him.

"Been on a diet, Mac," he answered.

"We'd better report," Paris said. "Highpockets seemed like he was in a real big hurry."

"What's the rush, we been sitting here for four days."

We entered the tent and reported.

"Reporting for the patrol, Sam," McQuade gruffed.

Huxley looked up from his field map. "I told Keats, Kyser, and LeForce to send me four men, not the squad chiefs!"

"I know, Sam," I said, "but my boys are kind of corked out and . . ."

"Er," Paris took it up, "my men are a little beat too. . . ."

"What's the matter with you people? Playing hero? Want me to lose all my squad leaders at once? This patrol too dangerous for your little lambs? Never mind, I haven't time to change now. Who else have you got, Mac?"

"Forrester and Zvonski, the Feathermerchant."

He looked at McQuade.

"A BAR team, Rackley for scouting, two men to help with the radios and a couple riflemen . . . Hawk and Kalberg there."

"Bring them all in. Where's Harper? He's holding up the parade."

"He was taking a crap," McQuade said, just as the hefty little Southerner entered along with the others. Lieutenant Harper of Fox Company reported, a wad of gum bouncing around nervously in his mouth.

"Get rid of that gum," Huxley said.

Lieutenant Harper placed it behind his ear and we gathered about the map. "Here's the scoop," Huxley said. "The Army has a ring around the base of the mountains up to Esperance. Our present position is here." He pointed to a spot about six miles from Tassafaronga Point. "The Japs have all their men concentrated in this area. They are pulling them out by submarine every night."

"I thought we were moving too slow to catch them," Harper said.

"That wasn't our fault," Huxley snapped. "We've got to get in there fast and bottle them before the whole gang gets away. We have a good idea where they are hiding, but we are in the dark as to their strength and armor. You men are to get up there and reconnoiter the area. Pinpoint their position, find out how many and what they've got—especially the heavy stuff."

Harper and Paris nodded. "Look these over," Huxley said, shoving some aerial recon photos at us. "Mac."

"Yo."

"When the patrol nears the Jap area, split into two groups. One stays back and sets up the big radio. The other goes in for observation. Use the walkie-talkies to get the information back to the first group. Transmit it back to us and get the hell out of there. We jump tomorrow."

I nodded.

"All you men, remember: we need this information to set up our air and artillery strikes. Get your asses out of there and don't get into any scraps if you can avoid it. Come back down the beach. We'll be looking for you. The password will be Laughing Luke . . . any questions? All right then. You can deposit any valuables here. Take off all rings, buckles, and any other shiny objects. Report to quartermaster and draw camouflage gear, extra canteens, ammo—and get your faces blacked. You jump in forty minutes. Good luck." We checked in our valuables and left.

"Ziltch!"

"Yes, sir—I mean yes, Sam."

"Get Bryce over here on the double."

"Yes, sir—I mean, Sam."

Lieutenant Bryce entered the tent. "You wanted me, Sam?"

"Yes, Harper is taking a patrol out in forty minutes. I want you to go along."

The blood rushed from Bryce's face. He was very pale. "But the CP, Sam—I've been working like the devil to set up—"

"Sit down, Bryce," he said. "Cigarette?" Huxley offered. "Tell me something Bryce, do you know the difference between a Jersey, a Guernsey, a Holstein, and an Ayrshire?"

"No."

"Seabags Brown does."

"I don't see what that has to do . . ."

"What do you know about Gaelic history?"

"Not much."

"Then why don't you sit down some day with Gunner McQuade. He is an expert. Speaks the language, too."

"I don't . . ."

"What do you know about astronomy?"

"A little."

"Discuss it with Wellman, he held a fellowship."

"This is most puzzling."

"What about Homer, ever read Homer?"

Bryce beamed. "Of course I've read Homer."

"In the original Greek?"

"No."

"Then chat with Pfc. Hodgkiss. Loves to read the ancient Greek."

"Would you kindly get to the point?"

"The point is this, Bryce. What makes you think you're so goddam superior? Who gave you the bright idea that you had a corner on the world's knowledge? There are privates in this battalion who can piss more brains down a slit trench than you'll ever have."

"This is hardly the proper time—"

"It's damn well proper. You're the most pretentious, egotistical individual I've ever encountered. Your superiority complex reeks. I've seen the way you treat men, like a big strutting peacock. Why, you've had them do everything but wipe your ass."

"Major Huxley!"

"Shut up, I haven't finished. I don't suppose it ever occurred to you that a Headquarters Company commander is the most useless command we can find for an officer. You're deadweight, Bryce, deadweight."

"I've done my best," he whined.

"Bryce, we are proud of our officers in the Corps. Our men came up the hard way, through the ranks or Annapolis. I put in eight years of study at Ohio State and Navy to get my bars. It's taken ten years for me to make Major. I'd be a captain yet if we weren't fighting a war. Unfortunately our qualifications had to be lowered due to situations we can't control. Since the outbreak of hostilities we've accepted hundreds of men, such as yourself, and given them commissions. Thank God the vast majority of these people have accepted their tasks, and more, they've found out the spirit that is the life blood of the Marine Corps. They'll make damn fine officers. And the same goes for the thousands of enlisted people. They've all learned there is a price to pay for wearing a green uniform—tell me, Bryce why did you join the Corps?"

"I'd rather not answer that, Huxley."

"Maybe you liked the blue uniform, big social doings—passport to notoriety?"

Bryce puffed jerkily on his cigarette. "I'd like a transfer out of this battalion, Huxley."

"Nothing on God's earth would give me greater pleasure. But who am I going to pawn you off on? What are you good for? Tanks? Artillery? Air? Amphibians? Or maybe a nice soft seat in public relations? Let this sink in. There is no soft touch in the Marine Corps. No matter if you're a company clerk, field music, a cook or what, you are one thing first, last, and always—a rifleman. Shoot and march, Bryce. Our artillery doesn't run when their guns are in danger, they dig in and protect them like any mud Marine. Our tanks are protected by the infantry and not vice versa. Any man in the battalion is capable of leading a platoon of rifles. Why, even our musicians bear stretchers in battle. Shoot and march, and the belief that you are invincible—that's what they call fighting spirit. You wouldn't understand."

"No, I wouldn't understand," Bryce shouted. "Blood, glory, whisky and women. That's the Marine battle cry. The deeper they wade in blood the better. Socially, spiritually, morally, you are nothing but professional killers—against every concept of democratic ideals."

"Bryce, ideals are a great thing. No doubt every man here has some ideals. However, and unfortunately, this war and this island and the next day's objective aren't ideals. They are very real. Killing Japs is real and we are going to kill them and save our ideals for future reference. When we get off this island, Bryce, I'm going to assign you to a platoon of riflemen. You'd better become a good officer. Now, report to Harper at once and join that patrol!"

We fell panting into some brush. The scout, a skinny wiry Tennesseean, held us up. We lay sweat-drenched and gasping for air. Although we were traveling light, the trek through solid jungle had been exhausting. We had steered clear of any paths. The day was broiling and our thick black makeup made it seem hotter. The tension of keeping quiet became greater as we found signs of a Jap bivouac area. We had passed the radios from shoulder to shoulder every few minutes to keep going at top speed.

Even Bryce didn't object when we called on him for a turn. I wet my lips and looked about. No enemy yet. Each step from here on would be filled with anticipation of being cut down by a sniper. The gum-chewing Harper and his scout had chosen their course well. So far we had avoided trouble.

Rackley the scout, three bandoleers of ammo draped over his scrawny shoulders, appeared again. He signaled us to assemble about him. We sank to our knees over Harper's map. The scout whispered, "Thar's a ridge about two hunnert yards up, slopes down to tall grass. Thar's an open field and big field rocks in it. Past it is a woods and cave area, lousy with Japs."

"Can you see them from the ridge?"

"Naw, can't count 'em nohow. We'll have to cross the field and lay in close behind some of them thar rocks."

The gum in Harper's mouth popped as he thought fast. "We'll move to the top of the ridge and split into two parties. Paris, McQuade, a BAR team, and one of the walkie-talkies will go down with me. We'll radio it back up to the ridge, soon as we get our information. Mac, set up the big radio and relay to Topeka White."

"Roger."

"Any suggestions? O.K., let's move up to the ridge." Rackley grabbed his rifle and moved out in front of us, leading the way. We moved forward in a creep. From the ridge top we looked over the field to the woods where the remaining Japs on Guadalcanal were holed up. The slope down the ridge was slick and would be tricky to negotiate. We took position by quiet and quick hand signals. I set up the big radio a way back and then they unzipped the walkie-talkies, screwed on more antennae, and gave each other hushed test calls. I ordered Danny to go down with the observation party, and Ski to stay back with me to relay information.

Rackley crouched low, then went over the top. He lost his footing immediately and slid and rolled over, halfway down the drop. We saw him reach bottom and zigzag through the field from boulder to boulder until he was almost at the Jap camp. He raised his hand and signaled.

Harper lay in the grass. He looked down. "O.K., radio man, over the top." Danny crawled on all fours to the rim. Ski grabbed and held him fast. I went to them quickly to see what the trouble was. Ski, without a word, looked into my eyes. Then he spoke. "Keep Danny up here," he whispered, "I'm shoving," and he dove down the ridge.

"Chrisake, Mac, you assigned me to go down," Danny said.

"It's better this way, he wants it," I said. "Keep in contact with him."

One by one the observation party made the clearing to the edge of the woods. Harper went over last. He called me to him before he went. "If anything happens to us down there, you are in command, Mac." Bryce didn't argue, he was too petrified. "If we get trapped, you get the information back to Topeka White first and then stand by. Don't send anybody down unless you get orders from me." I patted him on the back and he went down.

Harper, Paris, McQuade, and Rackley lay in behind a huge rock.

"Tell the radio man to get his antennae down." Rackley moved back to Ski quickly.

"How many do you see there, Paris?"

"I'd say about six hundred—huh, McQuade?"

"Yeah, crawling with them."

"I count fourteen MGs and two 108s. Looks like a colonel over there . . . must be the big wheel."

"Looks like the whole camp is drunk on saki. They must know they're the chosen ones." Harper opened his map. Paris made an X on it.

"M-7 on the button. Let's get the hell out of here."

They slipped back to Ski. "Are you in contact with Mac up there?"

The Feathermerchant nodded.

"How do you talk into this thing?"

"Press the mike button. Let me know when you want to listen."

"Hello ridge . . . this is Harper."

"Hello Harper, this is the ridge . . . go ahead."

"Six hundred Japs, fifteen machine guns, dozen or so mortars, two Pistol Petes, rest in small arms, plenty of ammo. Colonel seems to be top cheese. Camp disorganized, wide open for surprise attack. Seem to be crocked. Position is exactly M-7."

Danny repeated the message and Harper O.K.'d it. "Get that back to Topeka White and stand by to move out. Keep in contact with us till we get back up there."

It had started to rain, straight down and hard. "Lucky break, gives us cover. O.K., radio man, you go first with that radio."

Ski crouched as he moved out from behind the rock.

Crack! Crack! Crack!

He rolled over and darted back in. His face was screwed in agony.

"Drop!" Harper ordered. "We've been spotted."

In a minute the Jap camp was alive with wild screams.

"Don't fire till they're on top of us." A line of Japs came charging from the woods, led by a saber-wielding officer.

"Banzai! Banzai!"

The marines sweated and beaded in on the horde. "Blast them!" Harper ordered.

"Banzai!"

A burst of bullets came from behind the rocks, cutting down a wave of Japs. Another wave came on shrieking wildly.

"Make every shot count!"

"BANZAI!"

Another volley and they fell back, cursing.

Pedro Rojas, the corpsman, crawled in beside them. His shoulder was bleeding.

"Take a look at Ski, he got hit." Pedro rolled the Feather-merchant over on his back. The rain splattered on his pain-wracked face. Pedro tore up the leg of his dungaree.

"Holy Mother Mary," he whispered, and crossed himself quickly.

"Where did he get it?"

"Right through the kneecap."

"This is the ridge . . . what are you guys doing, playing poker?"

"This is Harper. We're up the creek. I don't think they'll try rushing again though."

"Ridge talking. We can cover you if you break for it one at a time."

"This is Harper. We can't . . . radio man is hit . . . sit tight." He turned to McQuade. "What do you say, Mac?"

"We'll never get him up that hill. It's probably like glass now."

Rackley spoke. "We should better wait for dusk. They ain't in too good a shootin' position and they won't hit us if we lay low."

Harper's gum popped wildly. He looked at each man, then at Ski. "Somebody will have to stay and keep a rear guard. BAR man, give me your weapon. I'll need all the grenades here too."

"Hold it, Harper. Your job is to get the patrol back. I'm staying," McQuade said.

"It's an order and no more talk," Harper said.

"Look here . . ."

"Both you guys stop playing Marine and get the hell out,"

Ski said from the deck. His face was blood-drained but his eyes were open. He trembled. They turned to Pedro.

Pedro leaned close. "Your knee is busted, Ski."

"Don't you think I can feel, you asshole."

Pedro dropped to all fours, shaking his head.

"What's the matter, Pedro?"

"I was hit coming down here . . . just my shoulder . . . put some sulfa and a pressure bandage on . . . I be hokay." McQuade propped him against the rock and went to work.

"The sonofabitches are gettin' loaded on saki so's they can get up the guts to Banzai us again," Rackley said, peering through the rain.

Paris and Harper leaned close to Pedro. "Can Ski hold them?"

"He is in terrible pain . . . he is very fine boy. . . ."

"Can he hold them?"

"With God's help," Pedro said.

The rain gushed. Wild cries beat up from the woods. The trapped men lay close behind their cover and awaited darkness.

Another call came through. "This is the ridge . . . what is the picture?"

"This is Harper. We're waiting for dark. We'll break one by one. The radio man will never make it. He's going to hold a rear guard." Harper bit his lip. Ski winked and smiled, feeling the helpless plight of the officer.

The rain quit. A gray shroud of dusk crept over them. They gently moved the Feathermerchant to a point where he could sit and look through a cleft in the big boulder. Harper handed him the BAR, the grenades, and his pistol.

"Know how to shoot this piece, Ski?"

Ski nodded. He felt no pain. Harper smashed a rifle butt into the radio, then buried the piece. It was near dark now. The cries from the woods grew. The Japs had almost whipped themselves into the frenzy to charge again.

"Anything . . . anything I can do . . . ?"

Ski's lips parted. "Has . . . has anybody got a rosary? Mine's in my pocket. I . . . can't . . . reach it."

Pedro gave him his, kissing it first.

"Thanks, Pedro . . . tell Danny not to be pissed at himself. It don't make no difference to me nohow. Susan . . . Susan . . . aw, you guys better shove. . . ."

"Does it hurt, Ski?"

"Naw, I don't feel nothin'." He clutched the rosary. Beads of sweat popped out on his brow.

"Pedro, move out," Harper said.

"I go last. I want to tell him what to do if the pain comes once more."

Harper nodded to Paris. He slapped Ski on the shoulder, then dropped flat, slid through the mud for a few feet, and sprinted toward the hill. One by one they broke for it—the BAR men, Rackley the rifleman, McQuade.

"They're about ready to charge," Harper whispered. "Dammit, I'm not leaving this kid!"

Pedro grabbed the officer. "Ski ain't scared. Where's your guts, Harper?"

"Oh, God," he cried and dashed toward the ridge.

"You comfortable, Ski?" Pedro asked.

"Yeah."

"I shall pray for your soul each night."

"Pray for your own ass. I know where I'm going."

Pedro disappeared into the black night. Ski was alone.

They must all be safe by now, on the ridge, he thought . . . never fired this damned BAR but once . . . hope I can remember . . . pain coming back. . . .

His wet finger slipped to the trigger as the grass before him began to stir. *Hail Mary . . . Mother of God . . . pray for us . . . now and at the . . . hour . . . of our death. . . .*

"Marine! You die!"

I helped Pedro back in. "Let's get the hell out of here," Harper said.

"They're starting to give him the business."

"Marine! You die!" The haunted echo drifted up to us.

"I hope they don't take him alive."

Danny snatched a BAR and ran to the ridge. I caught him and spun him around. "We can't leave him down there!" he cried. "What kind of chickenshit outfit is this? I'm going down there!"

I slapped his face till it was white. He fell back sobbing. "He knew it, Danny! He knew he wasn't coming back. You're a Marine, Forrester! Act like one," I said quietly.

"Marine! You die!"

"Let's shove, boys."

I turned and looked once more into the blackness below. . . .

PART FOUR

Prologue

IT WAS all over but the shouting. My squad didn't feel much like shouting, though. We didn't have the strength —or the inclination. After Guadalcanal it was never quite the same. They weren't kids any more. They'd seen it and taken it, and they knew there was more to come.

Yet the opportunity to take long baths in the sea pumped new vigor into our tired veins. We just lay there luxuriously and let the surf beat off layer after layer of filth and grime— and the rest did the same for our brains. We washed our ragged dungarees, brushed our teeth, and "borrowed" some clothes from an Army quartermaster. But it was only when we got steaming hot cups of coffee that we knew it was really over.

The men of the battalion adored Sam Huxley. That is, until one day when he canceled the transportation sent by Army and ordered them to hike the seventeen miles back to their camp. But they did it, under the scorching sun, and even managed to look smart when they passed the Army camps. It was anger that did it, anger at Sam Huxley, and the determination not to go down as long as that bastard was still standing and marching himself....

I fell on all fours once, trying to fight off the dizziness that was near blacking me out. I panted and looked at the shade on the other side of the road and tried to crawl over there on all fours—me, Mac, the old gyrene!

Danny took the pack off me and propped me against a tree and wiped my face. We sat there gasping and trying to muster energy to reach for our canteens. There was no cursing—we didn't have the breath.

When we were back in camp, Huxley returned us to full military discipline. Idle Marines make for trouble. We dug ditches, picked up butts, held inspections, practiced code, and did anything we could to keep occupied. We had lived like pigs while we had to, but we didn't have to now.

There was never-ending scuttlebutt, a hundred wild rumors

a day. We heard the Sixth was due to hit another island up the Solomons, although common sense told me we were in no condition to fight yet awhile. We hadn't relished the idea of cleaning up the mess made by the First Division and the Second and Eighth Marines. We felt we ought to have our own island to take, and let them clean up *our* mess. We knew, too, that other outfits would never let the Sixth live it down that we hadn't yet made a landing.

Finally came February 19th and one working party I didn't have to dig my squad out for. All hands turned to. The Unholy Four were lying at anchor in Skylark Channel ready to take us off the Canal. We boarded and shook hands with old friends and heard the wonderful word of hot fresh-water showers below for all troops, to be followed by a big special chow, with all the trimmings.

Then the bosun sounded his pipe. "Now hear this, now hear this . . . the Captain shall read a message to all Marines. . . ." The Skipper read a flock of "good job well done" communiqués from a cross-section of the generals and admirals who wished to express their appreciation to their chore boys.

"Gee, we really that good?"

"Yeah, makes the piss drizzle down my leg."

There was a rumble on the ship, and an excited stir as the *Jackson* weighed anchor. Blinkers on the signal deck flashed to the other ships of the convoy. A little destroyer zigged in front of us weaving her crazy course. (I wonder if a tin can sailor ever sailed a straight line?) There was a tremble and a lurch and the *Jackson* glided into position in the convoy.

My boys lined the rail for a last look at Guadalcanal. She was calm and peaceful, like the day we first found her. Like an exotic Hollywood scene. But she had the body of a goddess and the soul of a witch.

Good-by, you dirty bastard, I thought.

Just then the speakers started up again. "Now hear this, now hear this . . . the Captain wishes to relay the following message: Our destination is Wellington, New Zealand."

Wellington! A roar of cheers. There was a lot of handshaking and back slapping. We were going back to the land we adored. I couldn't help feeling soft about it, even after so many years traveling from pillar to post in the Corps.

I walked up to Andy and put my arm about his shoulder. He looked to the sea, his eyes narrowed, and he was deep in thought. The cool night air came dancing in as we picked up speed. "Just what the doctor ordered," I said.

"Getting chilly, Mac," he answered. "I think I'd better get below."

1.

AGAIN we rushed to the rail like a bunch of excited school kids on an outing and saw her come up on the horizon—New Zealand! Her soft green hills, and the quaint colored houses that graced them looked just the same. Again, she looked like she did that morning the Sixth had seen her from the *Bobo,* as the most beautiful land in the world. The harbor and the surrounding hills reminded us somewhat of San Francisco—not quite, but somewhat. The convoy slipped into Oriental Bay toward the docks, and strains of music drifted out in greeting. The Division Band blared out with *Semper Fidelis.*

Honor guards from the Second, Eighth, Tenth, and Eighteenth Regiments stood stiffly to attention as the rope hit the pier. Then the band played "The Marine's Hymn." Most of the men had heard it a thousand times and it never failed to send the shivers up the spine clear to the stacking swivel. Then the joshing started.

Dock: Well, well, what took you so long? You guys run into a sniper?

Ship: You guys can secure the watch and go back to camp, the Maimas are back.

Dock: I hear the Sixth is going to get a special citation. A box of pogey bait for every man.

Ship: Took a fighting outfit to finish what the Hollywood Marines started.

Dock: 'Fraid all the women are taken, fellows. . . . sorry. You boys better dash off to camp and get your new pogey bait whistles.

We, in the Sixth Marines, had an inferiority complex. We still wore our identification, the *fourragère,* defiantly about our left shoulders, but the Second and Eighth Regiments had seen many more grueling months of combat than we had. We, of course, knew in our hearts that our Sixth was the finest of the three—and of the entire Marine Corps. We didn't accept the ribbing lightly. Many were the lost teeth over the catcall, "Hey, pogey bait!" To worsen matters, the other regiments told the citizens that our *fourragère* was really a V.D. braid.

The Second Marines had taken over Camp McKay, our old billet about two miles past Paekakaraki. The Eighth Regiment was stationed right at Paekak, while the Eighteenth En-

gineers and the Tenth Artillery Regiments were in closer to
Wellington, at Titahi Bay and Plimmerton.

Our new camp, Camp Russell, was directly across the tracks
from Camp McKay. Whereas McKay was on high ground, we
were in the flatlands near the ocean. We debarked from the
train to find that work was still going on at a feverish pace
to complete Camp Russell. Winter and antarctic winds and
rains would soon be on us. But the new camp was neatly laid
out, tailored for the Regiment.

There was much work to do and all hands turned to unloading the trucks which poured gear in from the *Jackson.*
Our seabags were brought in from the warehouse. It was like
greeting old friends. Anxious hands unlocked them and there
were smiles as long-forgotten items popped out. We pitched
tents, drew cots, pads, and extra blankets and squabbled
over placement in the tents.

Chow, a breath of clean air, a smoke and a shower. The
wonderful feeling of solid earth beneath your feet in a place
you almost called home.

The heads weren't covered yet. As we visited them, trucks
of the New Zealand builders raced up and down the road.
Many of them were driven by women. We waved to them from
the sitting position and they waved back.

We gathered up firewood from lumber scraps. The officers
lost no time in placing a guard around the only fuel dump in
the battalion. Combat was over and officers were called Sir
again.

Taps were blown in the still disorganized, but weary and
happy camp. We fell asleep to dream sweetly of open arms in
Wellington waiting to greet us.

Andy opened the door into the lobby of the Salvation Army
Hotel for Women. He was greeted warmly by an Army lass in
uniform at the desk.

"Mister Andy! Welcome back."

"Hello, Mrs. Cozzman," he said.

"We're all excited having our Sixth Marines back. How are
you?"

"Fine, ma'am."

"Praise to God that you are all right. Goodness, those other
Marines we have here now are a gang of rowdies."

"They've been away from folks for a long time, they'll settle
down."

"It seems to me more of them should turn to God instead of
whisky."

"Yes, ma'am . . . is Mrs. Rogers in?"

"Oh, Mrs. Rogers—she moved out last week."

Andy paled.

"She took a flat on Dumbark Street. Right up in the hills near Aota Bay. Only a few minutes tram ride from here. Let me see, what did I do with the address? Ah, here it is."

"Thank you, Mrs. Cozzman."

"God bless you, Andy. Come and see us."

"Yes ma'am, I will . . . good night."

The walk up the hill winded Andy. He caught his breath and plodded toward a big brown-shingled house. He paused for a moment and scanned the row of mailboxes: Mrs. Patricia Rogers No. 3. He felt shaky all over. He opened the door and soon reached Apartment 3. He rapped softly and the door opened. A young New Zealand sailor stood before him. For a moment the two stared at each other. Andy's face flushed in a quick surge of anger and he turned to leave.

"Andy Hookans!" the sailor called.

He spun around to find a hand extended to him. " 'Ow now, of course you don't recognize me in this get up . . . in the King's Navy now, you know."

"I . . ."

"Henry Rogers, Pat's cousin. Met you last summer at the farm. I'm in on a weekend, last one before action. . . . Well, come in, joker. Don't stand in the blooming hall."

They shook hands. Andy felt very foolish. He entered the flat.

Pat arose from her chair as he entered the room. She caught herself by grasping a lamp table. Her face was mixed with anguish, a muffled smile, a verge of tears, and a long, unbelieving stare. Andy lowered his eyes to the floor. "Hello, Pat," he said softly.

"Andy," she whispered.

"Just in from the Canal, eh?" the sailor said. "Bet you jokers had a ruddy time for yourselves. . . ." He cut himself short in the awkward silence of Pat and Andy. "Well, I'd better be pushing off, know you don't need me here." He winked at Andy.

"No . . . don't go," Andy said. "Don't let me chase you out."

"Tsk, tsk. Got to see the mates at the pub. Late now. Thanks, old girl, for the feed. Glad to see you back, Andy."

"Give me a phone if you can get leave again, Henry."

"I'll do that, Patty girl. Ta ta."

"Ta ta."

"See you around, Henry, sorry to bust up your . . ."

"Just stay there—I know the way." He winked at Andy again and left.

"Won't you sit down, Andy?" Pat said. He slipped onto the edge of an overstuffed chair uneasily.

"Nice place you got here, Pat."

"Belonged to a girl friend who lived in Masterton. Her husband was billeted here. He went overseas and she returned home."

"Sure, nice to . . ."

"Would you like a cup of tea?"

"Thanks."

"How did you fare?"

"Ski got killed, Red Cassidy lost his leg."

"Oh. . . ."

"I did O.K."

"You look as though you've lost a bit of weight."

"I'll be all right in a couple of weeks. Heat and all that stuff."

Pat poured the teacup to the brim. He placed it in his lap. As he lifted the cup his hand trembled and the tea spilled on him. "Dammit!"

"Oh, Andy, did you burn yourself? I shouldn't have filled it so full."

"No, I'm just a little shaky. I'll be all right in a few days."

He put the cup aside. They looked at each other, not knowing how to ease the tension. "Let's take a walk or go to a movie or something," he said.

"I'll get my coat."

Once settled, ten-day furloughs were granted in three shifts with permission to travel anywhere in the country. We were warned to conduct ourselves as ambassadors of good will.

Gunnery Sergeant McQuade, Staff Sergeant Burnside, and Private Joe Gomez leaned over a bar in Levin, New Zealand. Their stance had changed little in six days. Seven other Marines, accompanied by girls, paraded in and took a large booth. The three buddies eyed each other's ale glasses, lest they fall behind in the ten-day race.

An exceptionally burly Marine among the new entrants looked toward the bar and noted the *fourragères* on Gomez, Burnside and McQuade. He winked to his buddies. "Say! Anybody got a bar of pogey bait?" he roared.

"How many of them are there?" McQuade mumbled, peering into the mirror on the back bar.

"Seven," Burnside counted. "And they got women with them."

"Say, there's some guys with pogey bait whistles . . . maybe they'll blow us a tune," another in the booth called, referring to the metal ornament on the tip of the braid.

"Sounds like the Hollywood Eighth Marines," Burnside whispered.

"Shall I do the honors?" McQuade asked.

"Aw, lay off them," Spanish Joe said. "We got them out-numbered . . . besides, the poor boys got mumu on Samoa."

The main troublemaker at the booth poured his ale glass full and arose. "I propose a toast to the Sixth Marines. Now, all together, boys." And they sang:

> *"I'm a pogey bait Sixth Marine,*
> *I can't keep my rifle clean,*
> *I don't want a BAR,*
> *I just want a candy bar."*

"That did it," Spanish Joe hissed. He gulped down the re-mainder of his beer, lest Burnside and McQuade filch it. The two sergeants nonchalantly refilled and continued drinking.

"Call us if you run into any trouble," McQuade said.

The seven Marines snickered as Spanish Joe cruised over to the booth. He drew up a chair and leaned on the table with his elbows. "Hi fellows," he said, flashing his big white teeth.

"Shove off, pogey bait."

Spanish Joe reached over to the burly one and straightened his field scarf. "Don't they teach you guys no neatness?" Joe cooed.

"We ain't got no pretty *fourragères*," the Marine answered.

"Aw gee, boys, don't feel that way. You guys are almost the same as allies."

"Look, buddy, we was just having a little fun. We don't want any trouble. We got our girls here, see."

"Oh," Joe said. "All shacked up, huh?"

"Take it easy . . . these are nice girls."

"Ohhhh," Joe said, "nice girls. They do it for you?"

The brawl was on! Spanish Joe landed the first blow. In fact, the first three. He bowled them over quick and cornered the remaining four in the end of the booth where they were unable to unscramble from the screaming girls. It wasn't till a chair fell on Joe's head that Burnside and McQuade finished up the others in quick order. They dragged Joe over the seven prostrate bodies toward the door.

"Jesus, old Spanish Joe is getting soft," McQuade said.

"Yeah, the Canal took something out of that boy."

"Hell, first real fun we've had on furlough."

"Let's bring him to. We got four more days left."

Speedy Gray, Seabags, and the Injun raced from the camp as Gomez, McQuade, and Burnside staggered in.

Speedy propped his back on the end of the aged bed and let an empty bottle fall to the floor. It clinked against another.

Seabags was doubled up in a wooden chair, rocking. He let a wad of tobacco juice skitter over the sill of the half-open window. The sill was brown with missed shots.

"Pig," Speedy said.

"Aw, shaddup, cousin, I'll clean it off before the furlough is up."

The basement room of the large boardinghouse in Wellington was jammed with empty bottles. The bed had been unmade for three days, the men were unshaven. The establishment was "home" for some twenty girls doing war work in the capital. Seabags, through a combination of infallible connections and a winning manner, had been able to promote the basement room for the ten-day leave. They had rented two rooms, the other directly across the hall. It was reserved, however, for after-hours pleasure with one or more of the occupants of the home.

"Sure is a wonderful leave," Speedy said, closing his eyes.

"Yep."

"Hope the Injun gets here with them bottles. We just finished the last one. I'll have to shave and go out after some if they don't come back."

"Yep."

"The Injun said he'd come back before he shoved off for Otaki. I promised old Meg I'd get her an Injun. She'll be mighty disappointed if he shoves."

"Yep." Spit.

"Ya pig."

"Fine girl that Meg, fine girl. Made of iron."

There was a rap on the door.

"Enter our humble domicile."

Shining Lighttower entered, bogged under a burden of bottles. Speedy lifted himself very slowly from the bed and studied the room for a place to set the reinforcements. As he placed the bottles in the sink he read the labels . . . "Bistro's Joyjuice, Manhattan Cocktail . . . is that all you could get? I'm sick of that crap."

"Best we could do."

"Drag up the floor, cousins, and set a spell." Speedy dropped to the bed again.

"Where's the broad, where's the broad?" the Injun asked anxiously.

"Ain't home from work yet. Just take it easy, there's plenty for all."

Lighttower unscrewed a bottle, took a swig, and passed it on. "If she ain't here I got to shove off for Otaki," he said. "I got a squaw all shacked up for the rest of the leave."

"Aw, you just got to stay," Speedy moaned. "I promised old Meg an Injun, she never been laid by an Injun."

"Had just about everything else though, cousin."

"Yeah, but she wants an Injun."

"O.K.," Lighttower said. "For you fellows, I'll do it."

"Now, that's a real buddy for you."

"What time does she get in?"

"Now for Chrisake, will you take it easy."

"Any chance of getting the clap?"

"Damned fine chance."

"Hell, I don't want to go to the clap shack."

"Where's your spirit of adventure?"

"Meg's going to be right happy tonight. I got her an Injun . . ." The half-emptied bottle went to Speedy's lips and he closed his eyes.

Danny, Marion, and L.Q. raced from camp as Speedy and Seabags staggered in.

Their trip north along the Tararua and Ruahine ranges was full of breathtaking sights. In order to make the most of their time, they cancelled their proposed tour to South Island and headed for a place where the trout season was still open. Mile-deep fjords, rushing streams, green mountains, deep-dropping gullies, met their eye as the dinky little train labored toward Hawke Bay. The good Lord had obviously left too much of nature's artwork in New Zealand and too little in some other parts of the world. Sunk in the deep leather chairs of first-class accommodations, they sat with their eyes glued to the panorama of color and shape and splendor that passed by them.

At each stop—Featherton, Carterton, Masterton, Eketahuma, Pahiatua, Woodville, Dannevirke—they rushed from the train, as did the natives of the land, onto the long concrete platforms of the depots. There, lined up along the counter, sat cups of steaming tea and plates of pastry awaiting the arrival of the train. A quick snatch, a sixpence on the counter, and they dashed back to the train. At the next stop the empty cups were returned and fresh ones taken from the waiting counters. It was a refreshing and leisurely custom to travel with tea and sip it in along with the scenery.

They came to Waipukurau, a small town near where the rivers Wiapawa, Makaretu, Tukituki and Mangaonuku flowed. Their streams bulged with brown and rainbow trout and the nearby hills were filled with red deer, fallow, wapiti, virginian, sambur and Himalayan tahr, and chamois. And the game birds in the lagoons and marshes: mallard, shoveller duck, teal, black swan, Canadian geese, Californian quail, pukeko, and chukor. It was March and the air was cool and fresh and sweet.

They put on their packs, shouldered their rifles and, with newly purchased light angling equipment, stepped from the train.

Their accommodation was a small lodge in the hills several miles outside Waipukurau. It was rugged but luxurious and blended with the hills about it. A huge fireplace and a log-paneled wall with a display of mounted heads of fourteen pointers, large quilted comforters over the beds and knitted circular rugs—it was the room of an old hunter's dream.

The fishing season was drawing to a close so there were few guests present. The deerstalking parties and gamebird hunters worked out of camps and used Mr. Portly's lodge as their base. A nearby unit of home guard cavalry patronized the bar nightly. The pub in the wilderness was well stocked with Scotch and aged whiskies and brews not available in the crowded cities. This was of no consequence to Marion who did his toasting in sarsaparilla anyway.

A few miles from the lodge, Hale Hendrickson, a combination farmer, hunter, and pioneer, had carved a small farm from the wilds. His wife, daughter, and small son held forth and awaited the return of the elder son from the Middle East. Two other sons had died in battle. To his new Marine friends Hendrickson made three of his horses available for riding. A man of good tastes, he also loaned Marion his large collection of classical records and some volumes from his well-stocked library.

One evening Danny lay sunken in the deep mattress, reading. Marion adjusted his glasses and crouched over the writing desk. A big stack of papers was scattered over it. The record of the phonograph ended. Marion snapped it off.

"That's a pretty tune. What was it?" Danny asked.

"It's from *The Pearl Fishers* by Bizet."

"What is *The Pearl Fishers*?"

"An opera."

"I thought *Carmen* was the only thing Bizet wrote."

"On the contrary," Marion said, "he wrote suites, symphonies—quite a lot of other music."

"I've got to learn about music someday."

"It was nice of Mr. Hendrickson to lend these records to us. Incidentally, we all have a dinner date at their place tonight."

"Righto, old bean."

"Better be on guard, Danny. I think his daughter has an eye out for you."

"Bully . . . how's the story coming?"

"Fair. I'll let you read the first draft in a few minutes." Marion shuffled through the stack of records.

"Put on that Grieg concerto. I like that. Seems to blend in with the scenery."

"Okay."

"Funny," Danny mused as the first stirring chords came through, "I used to think that Glenn Miller and T. Dorsey were the only musicians in the world. When I was in high school, Glenn Miller came over the radio three times a week on the Supper Club. It was like a ritual, listening to him. We'd go mad when he played 'Volga Boatman' and the 'Anvil Chorus.'"

"I'm fond of Miller, too," Marion said.

"I wonder if I can jitterbug any more. Seems like that was all we lived for, dancing and bowling and stuff like that. Kathy likes classical music. She used to give me a bad time because I'd never get interested in it. I kidded her about it a lot. . . ."

Marion swung his chair around and faced Danny. "Seems like a long time ago, doesn't it?"

"I've had the GI blues bad the last couple of weeks. Guess this has been the first time we've had a couple minutes to think about home."

Marion rose and walked to the fireplace. He ripped some paper and laid kindling on top of it. He struck a match and the paper burst into flame, throwing a mass of dancing shadows on the wall. He poked the crackling wood and put on a heavy log, then stood and brushed his hands, and stared into the flames.

"Marion?"

"Yes."

"Did you ever try to stop and figure out what we are doing here? I mean, halfway around the world."

"Many times."

"I know I'm a Marine and there's a war. But just killing—it isn't right, Marion."

"Seems rather pointless when you say it that way, doesn't it?"

"I only hope I'm fighting for the right thing, Marion."

"You have to feel that way, Danny, or you can't fight."

"I suppose so . . . anyhow, it's too deep for corporals. I wonder if they'll send us home after the next campaign?"

"Things are looking better. Army moving up the Solomons and New Guinea. I suppose the First and Third Marine Divisions will be ready to go soon."

"So many damned islands, so many damned islands out there."

L.Q. stomped into the room and threw himself on a bed, bouncing several times in the deep fluffy down. "Goddammit to hell. That's the last time I ride a horse."

"What happened?"

"I just did it to make time with that Hendrickson broad, I'm scared to death of horses. That damned farmer hasn't got nothing but big dumb plough horses, they're cannibals, I tell you. I got thrown six times. God, I'm sore all over."

Marion and Danny laughed. "Faint heart ne'er won fair lady," Marion said.

"Fair lady, my Aunt Lizzy's butt. These damned broads are like Amazons. Anyhow she's got her meathooks out for you, Danny. What's the matter with me? I got B.O. or something? Hard Luck Jones, that's what . . . all the time I run into crackpots."

"Come on, L.Q., you'd better take a nice cold shower."

"Nuts!" L.Q. said. "I can't stay around this hole another minute. It's too quiet. I'm getting the creeps."

"I thought you wanted peace and quiet."

"Yeah, but not death. Hunting and fishing, the agent said. I ripped my last pair of khakis with fishhooks. One of those homeguard guys told me that a town down the Line, Pahiata, is a factory town and loaded with broads . . . and no Marines there."

"I thought you got fixed up in Wellington with Speedy and Seabags."

"Know what happened? I'll tell you what happened. That Meg liked that Injun so much she wouldn't look at me. What did I wind up with . . . an apple eater. Honest to God, she ate apples in bed."

"So you should be thankful. The other three are in the clap shack at Silverstream Hospital doing G.O. time."

L.Q. hastily loaded his pack. "Can't stand this," he mumbled. "Danny, old buddy buddy, you got to do me a favor. I got a three-pound deposit on this room. I'll act like I got a case of the bug and maybe Mr. Portly will give me my dough back."

Marion turned his head and smiled as Danny shrugged and opened the door.

"Wait a minute, Danny. I'll put some water on my face so it will look like I been sweating."

Danny took L.Q. by the arm and led him into the lobby where Mr. Portly, semi-reclined in an overstuffed chair, was reading the *Free Lance*. He glanced up and saw Danny shaking his head sadly.

"What's up, diggers?" Mr. Portly asked.

"Poor ole L.Q., poor ole L.Q."

"Eh, what's the matter with your cobber, Danny?"

"Got the bug, Mr. Portly."

At those words L.Q. commenced to shake as violently as a man on a D.T. binge faced with a row of full bottles.

"Bug . . . wot bug?"

"Malaria, Mr. Portly." L.Q. chattered his teeth together, setting up a racket that Marion could hear all the way back in their room.

"Goodness!" exclaimed Mr. Portly.

"Guadalcanal," whispered Danny, tenderly patting the pathetic-looking L.Q.

"Poor bloke."

"He'd better get back to Wellington before . . . before . . ."

"Before wot?"

"Before he . . ." Danny leaned close to Mr. Portly and pointed to his head.

The Hendrickson family laughed heartily when Danny told the story of L.Q.'s fake attack of malaria and his hasty departure from the lodge. After dinner the family and their two guests retired to the living room and soon Marion and Mr. Hendrickson were hotly arguing about James Joyce. Danny sat politely as the discussion became more and more involved. It was a welcome break when Nonie Hendrickson beckoned him to step outside for a breath of air.

She threw a knitted shawl over her shoulders and the two walked through the quiet night along the fence which ran from the house to the barn. "Father doesn't get a chance to talk about books and music too much. You must forgive him."

"One of these days I hope to be able to argue with him."

"Poor L.Q. It's a pity he had to run off."

"Maybe if you'd been a little nicer to him he'd have stayed around."

"He's not my cup of tea," Nonie answered.

Danny stopped, put a foot on the split-rail fence, and leaned against it. For many moments he studied the raw, wonderful beauty of the farm in the wilderness.

"It must have been a rough go for you lads on Guadalcanal."

"No worse than for your fellows in Crete."

"Did you lose any pals?"

"One real good one." He lit a cigarette and thought of Ski. "It sure is peaceful around here. I'm glad we found this place."

Nonie laughed. "So peaceful it sometimes drives you mad."

He turned and studied the girl, who leaned her back against a post. She was very light and fair and straight as a ramrod. High and full bosomed, even a little hefty. A woman had to be strong for this vigorous life. Her face, her dress, were simple. It wasn't hard to scratch beneath the sturdy surface and see that she was a bored and lonely girl. Maybe she felt as though she were being robbed. She didn't know how lucky she was, Danny thought.

Their eyes met.

"Well," she whispered softly and invitingly.

"I'm married," Danny said.

"I'm engaged. I've been engaged for three years. He's a prisoner of war."

He turned away from her.

"I'm not very pretty, am I?" she said.

"You'll do."

"But I'm not pretty like American girls. I used to get the magazines all the time before the war. But they have so much. . . ."

"Some people don't know when they're well off, Nonie. They get funny ideas. There are a lot of girls who would change places with you."

He felt her hand on his arm and the warmth of her breath on his neck. He stiffened.

"Kiss me, please," she asked. He felt a surging desire to reach out and take her, but he shook his head.

"I was right," she said. "You see, this is my very best dress."

"You're wrong, Nonie. I want to kiss you very much but I don't think I'd be able to stop."

"I don't care," she whispered.

"I do."

A hurt expression came over her face.

"Look, Nonie, it isn't you. It's every other girl in the world as far as I'm concerned. I want to keep it that way."

He realized that she felt cheap. She had been unfaithful to the boy in the prison camp before. She was trying to be again —he didn't want her.

Milt Norton's words passed through Danny's mind, about wars and women. *It doesn't make any difference what or where they come from . . . in wartime it's an old pattern. . . .*

2.

L. Q. sighed with relief as he stepped to the counter at the railway station and ordered a cup of tea. He looked at the wall clock. The train was due in a few minutes. He glanced over his shoulder and noticed a middle-aged man staring intently at him. The man was neatly attired in a suit of blue with gray pinstripes. His graying temples matched his gray moustache. He wore large horn-rimmed glasses, common in New Zealand, and a squarely placed derby hat. Draped over one arm were a heavy woolen greatcoat and a highly polished cane. L.Q. finally smiled and nodded to the man.

"Evening, Yank," the man said. "Pardon the intrusion, but I don't recognize the braid on your arm, there."

"Called a *fourragère*. The Sixth Marines, my outfit, won it in France in the first war."

"That so? We don't see many Americans out my way. Back from Guadalcanal?"

"Yes sir."

"Bloody awful mess, eh what?"

"Yes sir."

"Busby's the name," he said extending his hand, "Tom Busby, field representative for Dunmore Machinery Company, Limited. We have a new brick-making machine, makes solid or hollow, simple enough for a baby to operate. No tamping, no vibrating." He jabbed L.Q. in the ribs. "But you wouldn't be interested in that, what? What the deuce brings you to Waipukurau?"

"On a ten-day leave, sir."

"Lovely country here, lovely. I didn't catch your name?"

"Lamont Jones. My friends call me L.Q."

"L.Q., that's a good one." They shook hands. "Suppose you're heading back to camp now?"

"No, I have almost a week left. My buddies are at Mr. Portly's Lodge. I'm heading for Pahiatua."

"Pahiatua? What the devil are you going to do in that place?"

"Just looking for a little fun, sir."

"Go to the window and change your ticket this minute."

"What?"

"You're coming home with me, lad. There's nothing in Pahiatua."

"But ... but ..."

"No nonsense about it, L.Q. Have the man give you a ticket to Palmerston North."

"But, Mr. Busby, I can't just bust into your home like this."

"Tommyrot. What kind of a bloke do you think I'd be, letting an American friend go to Pahiatua? My home is yours, son. Now hop to it."

"But ..."

"Come now, lad, there are plenty of Sheilas in Palmerston North if that's what you're worried about—plenty of girls."

"I don't know what to say."

"Tom is the name, L.Q. Now get a move on before the train comes."

The conversation on the long ride to Palmerston North was pleasant. Tom Busby stopped talking and listened intently when L.Q. spoke of Los Angeles. As they came into the station, L. Q. looked worried.

"Now, L.Q., my old woman Grace isn't that bad."

They were greeted by a small plumpish woman in her early forties and a frail-looking boy of about twelve. Tom and his wife exchanged reserved British kisses and the salesman bussed his son's hair as the boy took his briefcase to carry.

"Good trip this round, old girl, got a surprise." He turned to L.Q., who stood awkwardly behind him. "Meet L.Q. Jones, just back from Guadalcanal, that's what. The lad is on a leave and was going to Pahiatua of all places."

"A real Yank!" Ronnie Busby cried. "Is he going to stay with us?"

"Er, this was your husband's idea, Mrs. Busby."

"Well, he does get a good one now and again. Come, you must be starved. The car is just across the street."

"Is old Betsy still running? Having a devil of a time with her, L.Q. Shortage of parts, you know."

"And how do you like New Zealand, L.Q.?" Grace asked.

"Wonderful, Mrs. Busby."

"Can I carry your gun, L.Q.?"

"Sure, kid."

They piled into a Ford of 1935 vintage. Grace pushed the starter button. Nothing happened.

"Damned battery again." Tom Busby sputtered.

"Damned battery again," Ronnie repeated.

"Hush up, both of you."

"Try the horn, Mrs. Busby. Maybe the starter is stuck," L. Q. said.

"Oh, the horn has been gone for almost a year now."

L.Q. found the light switch on the confusing right-hand-drive car. The headlights went on. "It isn't the battery," he said. "Put her into low gear. I'll see if I can rock her loose." They knocked the starter free and the motor turned over.

"Amazing, simply amazing. Are you a mechanic, L.Q.?"

"No, but I guess most of us tinker around with motors now and then."

"Well, this was a good idea. First thing tomorrow I'll let you jump right under the hood and catch up on some of my husband's long lost odd jobs. He's a baby with a hammer in his hand—and to think he sells machinery."

"Hush now, Grace, you'll frighten the lad off."

"I'd be glad to," L.Q. said.

"See, Tom, what did I tell you?"

"I can sing the Marine's Hymn," Ronnie said.

L.Q. opened his eyes and looked about the soft and cheerful room of the cottage on Park Road. The sun streamed in. He sat up and stretched. A rap at the door. "Come in," he said.

Grace, Tom, and Ronnie Busby burst into the room. L.Q. drew the blankets about him. Grace carried a large tray and set it down on his lap.

"Aw look now, Grace. I feel funny eating breakfast in bed, especially in pajamas."

Tom Busby laughed, reservedly.

"You'll have to get used to rhubarb, L.Q., we're right in the middle of the rhubarb season, you know."

"Look, I can get up and eat at the table."

"Nonsense."

"Say, what time is it?"

"Almost one. You slept like a baby."

L.Q. stared at the tray brimming with luscious-smelling food and scratched his head. "You people are sure nice," he sniffled.

"Come now, boys. Let the lad eat, let's get out," Grace said.

"Shake a leg, L.Q. I have a game of bowls on the green at the club in an hour. Great sport, good for the spread," he said patting his stomach. "Phoned up all the boys to let them know I have a Marine. Want to show you off a bit, L.Q."

The door shut and L.Q. Jones sat there for a moment shaking his head.

Later L.Q. looked at the grinning mob of females of the Palmerston North Tennis Club. "Hold my hand, Grace. They look like a pack of vultures."

"See the dark one at the end of the table. She's called Gale Bond. That's the one Tom picked out for you. She'll be over for dinner."

L.Q. lined up the array of children on the vacant lot.

"Now, you guys understand the rules of the game? It isn't like cricket."

"Yes, L.Q."

"O.K., let's choose up sides."

"I want to be the pitcher."

"No, I want to be the pitcher."

"L.Q. says the pitcher is the most important player."

"Wait a minute," L.Q. said. "They're all important. Now we'll see who bats first. Choose up with this broom handle—I mean, bat."

The Marine leaned over and whispered into Ronnie's ear, "Remember what I told you?"

"Yes, L.Q." He wheeled about and faced his team. "O.K., let's have a little chatter in that infield, hustle you, birds," he cried in a shrill voice as he winked at L.Q.

"Play ball," L.Q. ordered.

The Ford was purring, the faucets no longer leaked and the

Busby home sported several rejuvenated lamps and appliances.
Gale Bond and the Busby family stood on the concrete platform with their Marine.

"Now you will write us, L.Q."

"I promise, Grace."

"And remember, any time you have leave, jump on the train.
You don't have to wire or phone, just come on up."

"I will, Tom."

Ronnie clutched L.Q.'s baseball glove and stood behind his
father to hide the tears.

"Thanks for the rod and reel, L.Q."

"Glad to get rid of them, Tom."

"I hope it won't be rhubarb season when you come next
time."

"I'll send some tea up, Grace, and for you too, Gale. We've
got barrels of it in the galley. We never touch the stuff."

"Take care of yourself, L.Q.," Grace said, embracing him
as the train neared. She shook Tom's hand.

"I don't know how I can ever thank you."

"Tut tut, lad, tut tut . . . well, thumbs up, L.Q."

He kissed Gale Bond, and then kissed her again. Then he
knelt before the sobbing boy. "Hey, Ronnie, I thought you
wanted to be a Marine. Marines don't cry."

"I'll . . . I'll practice hard, just like you told me. . . . I'll chuck
for the Dodgers some day."

L.Q. took the boy in his arms and squeezed him hard as the
train pulled in. He boarded quickly and ran to a seat, and
waved as they came to the window.

The train pulled out of Palmerston North. Grace Busby took
her husband's handkerchief and dried her eyes, then Ronnie's,
then passed it on to Gale, who passed it on to Tom Busby,
who blew his nose stiffly and placed it back in his pocket.

Andy stretched in the armchair and put out his cigarette.
"Pat."

"Yes?"

"Do you mind if we just sit and talk tonight? I don't feel
much like going out."

"As you wish."

She entered from the kitchen, drying her hands on a tea
towel. She took off her apron and laid it aside, then turned to
Andy. She frowned. "Goodness, Andy, you look ill."

"I . . . I don't feel so hot . . . I'm a little sick in the stomach."
He rolled his head and opened his eyes. They were bleary.
Perspiration began to form on his forehead.

"You are sick."

He cringed as a chill shot through him. Pat felt his forehead.

"You have a fever. I'll ring for a cab. You'd better report to the hospital."

"Nuts, I ain't going to no hospital."

"Don't be difficult."

"It's just malaria coming on. I seen a lot of guys get it. I'll shake it in a day, soon as the fever breaks." He drew himself close as another cold sensation flashed through his body. Then the sweat poured over his face.

"You've been ill since you've been back. I'm taking you in."

"Pat, I got six days left of furlough, and I'll be go to hell if I'm going to spend it in any hospital."

"You're acting like a hardheaded Swede."

Andy reeled to his feet, catching himself against the wall. "In my blouse," he rasped, "I got some quinine pills. I hoisted them from sick bay . . . get me three of them . . ."

"Andy, you can't."

"Chrisake, woman, stop arguing. I ain't going to no hospital. Get a cab, I'm going back to my hotel. I'll sweat it out . . . be O.K. I'll phone you in a couple days."

"Andy!" He pitched forward into her arms.

"I must've got the bug good . . . I'm dizzier than hell, Pat. Get me to my hotel."

She placed his hulking arm about her shoulder and braced him as best she could. "Come on, I'm putting you to bed."

"Just . . . take me . . . to my hotel. . . ."

"I'll not let you stay there alone in your condition. Won't you please turn in to a hospital?"

"Nuts. I got . . . six days . . . and I'll be damned . . ."

"Very well then."

He flopped to the bed, shaking violently. "Cover me . . . cover me. I'm freezing . . . cover me . . . three quinine every four hours . . . lots of water . . ." His breath was jerky, his eyes rolled shut. Pat struggled to get him undressed and under the covers.

"Ski, run for it, Ski! Ain't no woman worth it." He clutched his knee and thrashed into the blankets. "Don't worry, Ski . . . Andy will come back and get you out of there. Ski! They're coming through the grass!"

The lamp on the bed stand lit the room dimly. Pat shifted her position on the arrangement of chairs and pillows she had set up near the bed. She stretched and looked down at him. He was sleeping peacefully now. She placed her wrist against his forehead . . . the fever was gone. She sat at the bedside and put alcohol on a cloth and gently wiped his face and neck and shoulders. Andy slowly opened his eyes. A sharp ringing buzzed in his head from the quinine.

He propped himself on an elbow, shook his head and slumped weakly back. His face was pale and drained of blood. He reached out his hand and touched the soft down pillow under his head. His eyes turned and surveyed the room. He closed them a second and sighed unevenly and looked again. He saw her. She wore a nightgown beneath her long housecoat . . . she held a cup of tea for him. He rubbed his eyes. There was a stale dry taste in his mouth, everything seemed fuzzed.

"How do you feel?" she asked softly.

"How . . . how long I been here?"

"Almost three days."

He drew a long breath. "I must have tossed a shindig."

"How do you feel?" she repeated.

"Like a million bucks."

"Can you sit up? Drink this. I'll make some hot broth."

Andy came to a sitting position slowly and again shook his head to erase the determined ringing. He instinctively reached for his dogtags. They were gone.

"My tags?"

"I took them off. I was afraid you would choke."

He pulled the covers about him.

"I had to undress you . . . you were wringing wet."

He put the cup to his lips and looked at her. There were deep circles of sleeplessness under her eyes.

"I'm sorry, Pat."

She smiled. "I must say, you did give me a bit of a fright."

"Did I say much?"

She nodded.

"Christ, I bet you hate me."

"I'm glad it's over, Andy. Do you want a cigarette?"

"Please."

"Here."

"Get one of mine."

His senses slowly returned. He drew deeply on the cigarette. Pat sat on the bed's edge. Neither of them spoke. They stared long and hard at each other. Andy snuffed the smoke in the ashtray she held.

"Poor dear," she whispered, "you've been through hell."

"I'm sorry I let you in for it, Pat."

"I'm glad I didn't let you go to your hotel. I'd have lost my mind."

Andy looked at the array of medicines on the bed stand and at the chairs on which she had kept her vigil.

"I'd better make you something to eat," she whispered.

"Wait a minute, Pat. Nobody ever done anything like this for me before. . . ."

"That's all right, Andy," she said softly.

"You look beat out. Have you had any sleep?"

"I caught a wink or two. I'm all right."

"Pat?"

"Yes."

"It seemed like I opened my eyes a couple times, I reached out, and I felt someone . . . warm . . . I felt you. I guess I was just dreaming."

"You weren't dreaming. I was frightened of your chills." Her hand reached out and touched his bare chest. "I was frightened for you." He held her hand and placed it to his mouth and kissed it. And he drew her close and she rested her head on his chest.

"Darling," she cried. "I was so frightened."

He lifted her face to his and kissed her. She closed her eyes as his big hands stroked through her hair and over her cheeks and neck.

"Oh, Andy . . . Andy. . . ."

They kissed again and her arms were about him tightly. He fumbled for the tie of her housecoat. "No, Andy. No, you're too weak."

"I'm all right."

"You're still sick, Andy. . . ."

"Pat, Pat. . . ." She opened her housecoat and embraced him.

He opened his eyes and felt over the bed for her and sprang to a sitting position, then settled back in the pillows as she came into the room with a tray in her hands. She adjusted the pillows for his back and put the tray in his lap.

"You'd best get some nourishment."

He blew into a spoon of soup and sipped it down slowly. The warmth felt luxurious all the way down. She sat on the edge of the bed and cast her eyes to the floor. She reached up and ran her fingers through his mussed hair and patted his cheek. Andy dug his fork into the salad and wolfed it down hungrily.

"I feel awful," she finally said.

He put the spoon down. "Are you sorry, Pat?"

The corners of her mouth showed a small smile and there was a twinkle in her eyes. "Of course I'm not sorry, silly," she said, "but I do feel wicked with you being so sick."

Andy gobbled another bite of salad. "Don't worry none about that. Us gyrenes are tough as redwood trees, specially us Swedes."

She arose and turned partly away from him. "I suppose you think I'm just the same as . . . as those girls you spoke about."

"Aw for Chrisake, Pat."

"I don't really care, you know."

"Don't talk like that."

"Oh, it's quite all right, Andy. You don't have to put up a show for me. I don't expect it."

"That ain't like you and you know it."

"But it is. It is now!"

He wiped his lips and set his glass on the tray, then shoved the tray aside. He reached for her hand and brought her down beside him.

"Listen, Pat honey."

"Really, Andy, you don't have to say anything, really you don't." She kissed his cheek and drew away from him. "I know how you feel about women. Oh, Andy, when you left it was like dying for a second time—only this time it was worse."

"I didn't know."

"Of course you didn't, darling. When the other Marines returned and I knew you were coming back, I . . . I . . . You'll think me horrid, but I don't care. I got this apartment." Pat Rogers stiffened and looked to the window. "I'm not keeping any more lamps in the window or waiting for any more ships to come in the bay. This war has done me in. You are here now and you'll be here for a while. I'll make it plain and simple, Andy. I want you, regardless of what you may think. I don't care. I made up my mind to that long ago. When you go out again, that will be the end of it." She slumped down on the bed and closed her eyes and bit her lip.

"I don't like you to talk like that, Pat."

Her eyes were misty. "I'm propositioning you, you know."

He took her in his arms and held her. Pat's eyes were closed and her lips were on his neck and her arms about him.

"You're like nobody else, Pat, nobody. You got to know that."

"You don't have to flatter me, darling. You're here, you're safe. I'll have you for a while. That's all I care for any more. Today, this minute—to hell with the ships in the bay, to hell with waiting, to hell with living in fear. I'm a sinful woman now and I don't care . . . I don't, Andy, I don't."

"Aw, pipe down." He kissed her and drew the blanket over her. She rested in his arms and sighed contentedly.

3.

OUR TENT flap opened. First Sergeant Pucchi entered followed by a homely, medium-sized Marine. "You check in to Mac, there. He's in charge of communications," Pucchi said. "Mac, this is your new radio man."

I got up and the fellow dropped his seabag. The squad, sitting about, beating their gums and shining gear, looked up. There was a hush. Then the replacement introduced himself loudly.

"Levin's the name, Jake Levin. So this is the accommodations, huh?"

"My name is Mac."

"Glad to meet ya, Sarge." His voice rang with familiarity. "Got a fart sack for me?" He was trying out his Marine lingo to show us how salty he was.

"You can have mine," Speedy said. "I'm going to live with the telephone squad." He left the tent.

Levin shrugged and introduced himself around. Only Marion gave him a warm welcome and handshake. "Welcome to the outfit, Levin."

"Thanks, buster." The new boy sat on Speedy's cot and chattered on loudly.

"Where you from, cousin?"

"Brooklyn."

"I thought so."

"Had a rough trip over. Terrible boat . . . I mean ship. What the hell, I says, make the best of it."

"How long you been out of boot camp?"

"Two months. Like I says," he continued, "I think I'll get along. At least I didn't volunteer into this lash up, so I got my beef all right."

"What do you mean, cousin?"

"I was drafted, that's what, drafted."

"Something stinks in here," Seabags said.

"I got my shoes on," Lightower said as he headed for the catwalk. The others walked out. I followed them.

"Holy Christ, Mac, we got to take that loudmouth bastard?"

"Take it easy," I said. "All replacements make a lot of noise at first. They're just trying to make an impression. They feel uneasy."

"Yeah, but a goddam draftee in the Marine Corps."

"War is hell," I moaned.

"I don't like that Jew boy," Speedy spat.

"I don't like that talk, Speedy," I warned. "The kid might be all right. Don't hang him before he gets one foot in the tent."

"Let's go to the PX, cousin. Got your ration card?"

"Yeah, let's go. I'm sick."

I returned to the tent. Levin stood up from his unpacking. "What's the matter with them guys? It ain't polite they should all take a hike."

"Levin," I said. "this outfit has been together quite a while.

Some of the fellows for ten or more years. It's like a private club."

"I don't get ya."

"Wait a minute, Levin," I said. "I know you hear a lot of Marines bitch. But you've got to earn that right. We like being Marines."

"It ain't my fault I was drafted."

"You're going to make it a lot easier on yourself if you make up your mind not to go around feeling sorry for yourself. I'll give you some gratis advice, Levin. These guys have earned their battle spurs and you've got a lot of proving to do. They're a good bunch of fellows and they're big leaguers and you're just a busher."

Levin clammed up and bowed his head. "I was just trying to be friendly. I ain't no pop off. I was trying to be one of the guys."

"Don't go advertising that you were drafted into the Corps or you'll make your life miserable. I don't like to see you start on the wrong foot," I went on.

"I'll cut the buck," he said.

"I hope so. We're going to work your ass till it drags. If you put out every minute of the day you're going to have one friend in this outfit. If you don't put out, you'll rue the day your mother gave birth to you." I left.

"Jesus," Levin whistled, "I thought I was out of boot camp. What the hell did I get myself into?"

"Don't let Mac scare you, Levin," Marion said. "Besides, you've got one friend already."

"Thanks, Corporal."

"Come on now, snap out of it. It's only that we are jealous. You see, the boy you are replacing was a pretty swell head. He saved a patrol on Guadalcanal."

"Jees," Levin whispered.

"They are sending a Navy Cross home to his sister."

"God."

"Come on, I'll show you around the camp."

"You're a nice guy, Corporal."

They walked from the tent. "Tell me, have you ever studied any of the classics?" Marion asked.

"Levin!"

"Yes, Sergeant?"

"I got you posted for the midnight watch on the switchboard."

"Yes, Sergeant."

"And don't think you can bunk in late. You fall out at reveille for a special detail on a field problem, carrying the generator. And I want you cranking the generator every time it goes into operation for the next two weeks."

"Levin!"

"Yes, Corporal?"

"We got a working party, digging new heads today."

"Yes," he said, heading for the tool shed.

Seabags held a bucket of creosol and a can of lye. He tucked a chaw in his teeth and sat down leisurely. It was an alleged two-man detail. "Let's go," Seabags said, "step on it. You'll never get them there heads clean."

"We'd be finished if you'd help me."

"See this stripe? What does it mean?"

"You're a Pfc."

"Correct. Get busy."

"O.K., Seabags."

"Got a man for a garbage shoveling detail, Mac?"

"Got just the man you want."

At two in the morning a weary private nodded his head on guard over the officer's woodpile.

"*Pssst!*"

"Halt! Who goes there?"

"L.Q. and the Injun."

"What you guys want?"

"We are going to borrow a couple of logs for the stove."

"They'll pull a check and I'll be up the creek without a paddle."

"Nice guy."

"What you expect for a draftee?"

"From Brooklyn, no less."

"Aw, O.K. But hurry before the sergeant of the guard makes a round."

I was determined to work him till his ass dragged, but Levin stood the gaff. After the initial shock was over, the squad accepted him one by one. Spanish Joe's price for friendship was Levin's beer ration card. When I finally let him at a radio, I found him to be an exceptional operator and, of course, we took him in with open arms when we discovered that he was also a first-class barber. Banks, of message center, had been butchering our hair for over a year—and at two bits a crack, yet. As members of the squad, we were entitled to free cuts with a shampoo and shave occasionally thrown in, I explained to Levin.

L.Q. was the first to take Levin to his heart. Levin had been potwalloping on mess duty for almost a month, and they had given him an extended engagement.

"Hey, Levin, you want to get off mess duty?" L.Q. asked.

"I got to do my time."

"Yeah, but they gave you an extra two weeks, just out of spite. I heard the cook say you work so hard he's going to try to keep you there forever."

"I don't mind."

"Tell you what to do. Know that soap they use for the officers' mess gear?"

"Yeah."

"Well, just put a scratch or two on your hand and dip them into a solution—makes your hand get infected and they got to take you off."

"I wouldn't do that."

"You can leave soapsuds on the officers' dishes. They'll all get the trots that way."

"Thanks, anyhow. . . ."

The clincher was when Levin won the Regimental softball championship for Headquarters Company in an epic battle with K Company of the Third Battalion. Three of our guys had folded with malaria, two others were injured, and three were thrown out of the game for calling the umps, Huxley and Chaplain Peterson, dirty names in close decisions in which we were clearly robbed. Levin carried upon his shoulders the honor of Huxley's Whores, to say nothing of the beer we had bet. He pitched us to victory and himself into our hearts.

Only Speedy Gray, the Texan, remained aloof after the game. He went out of his way to be nasty to Levin. But bigotry was something that, unlike the colors of a salamander, couldn't be changed overnight.

L.Q. lay on his sack before reveille. The morning was cold. It was in those last few precious minutes before we fell in for rollcall that we hated the Corps most. In the first chill of being awake and trying to be asleep for that extra minute, nature demanded a duty call. L.Q. cursed to himself. It was no use fighting. He staggered from the cot and lit the stove, a job generally saved for Levin. Levin was on guard duty on this particular day, and L.Q. was the first up.

With his eyes half shut he wended a weary way down the

catwalk through the still dark tents toward the heads. Half frozen and mumbling at his fate he seated himself and nodded his eyes shut. He happened to glance to his left. A shudder of horror passed through him! Seated next to him, almost shoulder to shoulder, he saw a golden bar. He looked to the right—there were the two silver bars of a captain. In the dark he had gone to the officers head.

The two officers looked at the Pfc occupying the center seat and stared arrogantly and coldly. L.Q. grinned and squirmed uncomfortably. The captain tapped his foot restlessly and the lieutenant sighed in disgust. L.Q.'s face reddened with shame. All morning he worried, but the officers chose not to report him for entering their sacred realm.

Sergeant Herman, the quartermaster, bled. All depleted clothing was to be replaced and a complete new issue given. As we drew the new gear we stepped down in a line to a table where two officers checked in our old weapons. They checked off the recorded number of our Reisings. Mac stepped up, turned his in and drew a new carbine rifle, clips, rounds of thirty-caliber shorts and a pistol belt.

Seabags handed the officers Garand rifles.

"Where did you get this weapon, Brown?"

"Lost my Reising in combat, sir."

"All right, next."

Spanish Joe laid a Thompson submachine gun on the table.

"Where is your Reising gun, Private?"

"Lost it in combat, sir."

Danny laid a BAR on the table . . .

"Where is your—don't tell me, you lost it in combat."

"Yes, sir."

The squad fondled the new light carbines. They were beauties. Just the type that had been needed for a long time. Accurate up to two hundred yards, semi-automatic, light and well constructed. A far cry from their infamous predecessor, the Reising. There was a price for the new rifles, however. Huxley decided that too many Reisings had been lost in combat, and all those who had dumped them were charged $64, one third out on each pay call.

Divito, the jeep driver, ran into our tent. "It's here!" he yelled.

We poured out and *then*, we saw her. Our eyes were filled with disbelief as we approached her. Our new TCS radio jeep had arrived. Built into the rear seat of the jeep was a beautiful radio.

"Gawd! Look at that radio."

"Andy!" I shouted, "keep your meathooks off the hood. Do you want to get it dirty?"

We circled the jeep several times, noting that the tires were all right and the paint job was on neat. No one dared to look in at the transmitter and receiver. We feared it would vanish like a mirage. At last we peeked in. My hand was trembling as I reached to set the dials. . . . "Some job . . . some job."

"Jesus, just like the doggies got."

I seated myself, like a king on a throne, in the operator's seat.

"How about this? The transmitter is generated right off the motor."

"Who gets first crack at it, Mac?"

"Er . . . er . . . we go by time in the Corps," I said.

"Dirty poker!"

"Well . . . I got to see if it works."

"Come on, set up the TBX and get in contact with this baby." I lit a cigar, which I always saved for special occasions, and relaxed. "Take her for a spin, Divito . . . want to give her a test," I said.

Dear Marion,

I'm glad you got the package all right. There is another on the way. You're not the only genius. The store was so pleased with my selling that I've been promoted to assistant department manager. It's really a lot better than standing behind the counter for eight hours and I've got lots more responsibilities . . . AND, a five dollar raise.

I tried to read the book you told me about, but honest, maybe I'm plain stupid, but I guess it's not the same without you explaining all the things I don't understand. I wish so much that you were here to read to me. I've played all your records and lots of them a second time around. I like the Romeo and Juliet Overture best by Tschaikowsky (probably spelled it wrong). Only we're not going to have a sad ending like they did. . . .

4.

THE GREEN of our forest greens blended with the green of the meadow. Three thousand men of the Sixth Marines fell in and came to attention. We presented arms as the color guard, followed by the Division band, marched sharply past and took position. We snapped to attention with a ruffle of drums and a flourish of music as Major General Bryant, the division commander, Brigadier Snipes, his assistant, and Colonel Malcolm, the commander of the Sixth, and their staffs took center place before the line of fifteen heroes.

In files of threes, pressed and shiny Marines strung out in rank that ran as straight as an arrow across the field. And there was our Regimental Flag with a silver ring on the staff from each expedition. The rings climbed nearly the length of the pole: Dominican Republic, Shanghai, Haiti, Iceland. . . . The flag was fringed in gold tassel, and red and gold cords fell from its peak. In the center, on a red background, was the golden globe, anchor, and eagle and the words: *SIXTH REGIMENT, USMC.*

From the golden eagle on the top of the staff fell the battle streamers: Nicaragua, Belleau Wood, Chateau Thierry, Guantanamo Bay and a new one, Guadalcanal. They told quite a history, those pieces of cloth and wood.

"Parade, rest!"

In unison we came to the command position. One by one the staff officers of the Second Marine Division stood before her official heroes. The adjutant read the citation of gallantry and General Bryant pinned the medal on with handshake and salute.

"Lieutenant Colonel Samuel Huxley, USMC. With courageous leadership of a battalion of riflemen, against enemy forces on Guadalcanal, British Solomon Islands, he's showed, in many instances, ingenuity and gallantry above and beyond the call of duty. . . .

"Pharmacist's Mate First Class Pedro Rojas, USNR. On a patrol against enemy forces on Guadalcanal he disregarded his own wound and gave aid and comfort to another wounded member of the patrol . . . in keeping with the highest traditions of the Naval Service. . . .

"And we therefore posthumously award the Navy Cross for gallantry above and beyond the call of duty to Private Constantine Zvonski. . . ."

"Regiment, ten shun!"

"Pass in review . . . eyes right! Present arms!"

We marched in tribute past them and the battalion and company standards dipped in salute. They returned the salute. And as the Third Battalion passed in review, marching in precision, the band played the Marine's Hymn.

"Come on," said the Injun after we fell out, "let's go over and congratulate Pedro."

"Yeah," said Andy.

"What the hell for?" Speedy spat.

"He rated it," Andy said.

"Oh sure, give the goddam medals to the officers and the corpsmen."

"Don't be a wedgeass, Speedy," Lighttower said.

"That goddam Mexican didn't deserve it no more than Seabags. What about Seabags?"

"Hell," I said, "if they passed out medals to everybody who rated them, we'd need one for pretty near every guy in the regiment."

"Yeah."

"Yeah, but that don't cut no ice. If the Spik got one, Seabags should have got one. And what about Red Cassidy?"

Seabags walked into our circle. "Come on Speedy," he said.

"Where you going?"

"I'm going to buy Pedro a beer," he said.

Hardly a night passed when I wasn't roused from my sack in the small hours of the morning. "Hey, Mac," a voice would whisper in the dark, "Spanish Joe has got the bug."

"Get a corpsman." I climbed half asleep from my cot, lit the coal lamp and took it over to the sack of the stricken Marine. The scene seemed to play itself over a hundred times.

"Hey, Mac, the Injun has the bug. . . ."

"Hey, Mac, Seabags has the bug. . . ."

"Hey, Mac. Better come quick. Danny has the bug. He's off his rocker now. Screaming something about not liking to shoot rabbits."

Their faces would be sweaty and torture-wracked and they'd roll and groan to wipe out the nightmare. Then came the pain in the guts and they'd start shaking like a dog crapping. They wasted away quick. It was nasty to see and I hated to stand by and not be able to help them. I could only give them quinine and let them lie there, trembling and moaning about home and things like that, till the fever broke. Then they'd be awake with sheet-white faces and black circles under their eyes, too weak to stand up with the goddam bells from the quinine blasting in their heads.

Ninety-five per cent of the Second Division had the bug at one time or another. I had ten recurrences, myself. Most all of us went around with it five or six times.

Each regiment had a small hospital unit but it was soon crowded to capacity, and the division hospital could be used only for a severe case. There was a big base hospital at Silverstream near Upper Hutt, complete with Navy nurses. Silverstream handled casualties from all over the Pacific. It was a beautiful place, the real thing. Big clean wards and a Red Cross and recreation center. You had to be close to dead or an officer to get in, though. I finally made it on my eighth recurrence.

Navy nurses for the most part were little more than orna-mental—pretty social butterflies. The corpsmen did ninety-nine per cent of the work. As a group, they were arrogant and ordered us around more sharply than the officers. But you can't have everything and we all hoped to get sick enough to rate Silverstream in spite of the nurses.

With every hospital bed, makeshift or otherwise, filled with the malaria-riddled division, each battalion set up a shack full of cots to handle the milder cases. Even these facilities bogged down under the capacity load and we were handed some pills and told to go back to our tents and sweat it out.

In a tent, with a hundred and four fever and chills and pains ripping him up, a man finds out what the word buddy means—to bathe a sick kid and feed him and attend to him. Guys that loved each other in a way that no woman could understand. Guys who had been through hell together, and could give a tenderness to each other that even a woman couldn't duplicate. Many a night I lay half shivering on my cot with my head on the lap of L.Q. or Danny or Seabags while they tried to force some fruit juice into me. "Come on, you salty old fart, open up your ugly mouth before I ram it down you sideways."

On nights like that I opened my eyes, still full of the chill, and a fire was going on the potstove, made with stolen wood, and the cold drizzly rain beat a tattoo on the tent and it was good to look up and see a smiling face watching. A cool cloth would be passed over my face and I'd drink some stuff they had swiped for me. Soon Pedro, or one of the other tired, beat-out corpsmen, would check into the tent on late rounds and try to make me comfortable. They worked around the clock, those sailors, trying to ease the suffering of the Marines as best they could.

When quinine in pill form ran out, we were given doses of liquid quinine. It was near impossible to stomach. I some-times thought it would be better to die of malaria than drink it.

On and on it went during those weeks in New Zealand, cycle after cycle of malaria leaving a wake of weak and wrecked men. When we hit the hard training it would be tough-er this time than anything we had ever known before. Home-sickness and loneliness sets in quick when a fellow isn't feeling right. We'd get pissy drunk on a weekend just to bring on the malaria and to be able to escape the drudgery of soldiering. Malaria at least gave us a two-week rest.

Not only were we the best singers and ball players in the regiment but there was never a closer-knit bunch of men in the Corps than Headquarters Company. Sure, we had our inter-platoon rivalry with intelligence and the corpsmen but we stuck together almost to a man. Friendship was infectious. New transferees into the company were astounded by it.

As our company was smaller than the line companies we needed only half the space in our mess hall. L.Q., a great pep boy and organizer, came up with a plan. We put it to the other sections in the company and it was greeted with enthusiasm. He planned to cut the mess hall in half and build a recreation room for our own use. Without bothering to await official sanction, we sent out scouting parties and stole wallboard and lumber wherever we could locate it. The project went into high gear almost immediately.

We all turned to after duty hours. Spanish Joe was invaluable on the "borrowing" parties. He could sniff out a pound of nails or loose lumber in the remotest and best guarded places in camp. When we had walled off half the mess hall we "borrowed" a potbellied stove, and wood from which a ping-pong table, several chairs, and writing tables were built.

Highpockets, at first aggravated over the thefts, finally blessed the project provided we paid for the equipment in the future.

We held a powwow and after a stirring talk by L.Q. decided to build the finest club in New Zealand. Each man would chip in a pound a month from his pay and deposit it in Pucchi's safe. Marion, Paris, Pedro and me were chosen as trustees. The dues were strictly voluntary, but each squad leader was warned to see that his men volunteered at pay call.

After the first pay call any skepticism vanished. A party scoured Wellington for secondhand furniture and the clubroom boasted six overstuffed sofas and a dozen comfortable arm-chairs. A big radio was purchased and we erected an aerial that enabled us to get reception from any part of the world. Next came a phonograph and hundreds of records. After Marion protested and got up a petition from the music lovers, we bought a few albums of good stuff, too. Lamps, rugs, writing paper, footstools, another stove, several handpainted nudes, typewriters, and many other items poured in after each pay call.

L.Q. had an uncle who was a minor-league official in one of the Hollywood studios. From him we received a package of two hundred photographs of almost every star and starlet in filmland, personally addressed to the company. They covered the entire wall space.

We bought oilcloth for the mess tables and set up spice racks. Then came our crowning glory. We cut off a corner of the club and built a bar. It was the best bar in the country, at least it was the only one that had a foot rail. Pine walls, varnished, the biggest and best mirror that money could buy, and a statue of the sexiest broad the country could offer adorned it.

Huxley broke all tradition by allowing the company to purchase its beer ration in a unit. Because there were many nondrinkers and some men were always on liberty a large portion of our allotment was never purchased. By buying all rations at once we benefited by several extra cases. Originally it was feared that unlimited beer each night would lead to trouble. We were anxious to maintain the privilege and we policed each other thoroughly and slapped limits and severe fines or temporary bans on heavy drinkers. The beer was sold at a profit which enabled us to drink in luxury and cut our dues to six shillings a month.

There was nothing like our club in the entire Corps. We guarded it jealously. No men were welcome but our own. A twenty-four-hour guard was posted and a two-man detail was released from duty to clean up each morning. The escape from the drab tents to the warmth of the club gave the company some of the happiest moments they spent in the service. After a tough hike or field problem it was wonderful to clean up and enter this little private domain, built on a rock of comradeship. The men could bat the breeze, write, drink, play cards, listen to command performances from the States, or for laughs, tune in on Tokyo Rose. She gave us some food for thought one night. She said the clock on the Wellington Parliament was two minutes slow. . . . It was.

As the winter bore in there was that warm glow in the club that comes with snoozing in an easy chair by the fire. It helped us forget that we were lonely men. Some nights, though, just before taps, the phonograph would spin some song about home, and the drinking and the talking would stop and the deathly still would hit us. I could see the eyes of my boys, hungry for home, lousy blue and wanting the thing which seemed further and further away with each passing day. They were quiet as the notes and the words knifed in them. Quiet, as they fought off a lump in their throats.

Then, when the field music blew recall, we'd file slowly from the club, through the rain, over the catwalk and into the cold dark tent to get some sleep. Big hike tomorrow.

Every dry day we were in the field and on many of the rainy ones, too. One evening Lighttower and Levin were called to the Special Weapons Company for a pre-dawn field problem. They were interested in the way we worked our walkietalkies. They were assigned to help repel the mock invasion by the First Battalion near the ocean.

The pair put awkward ponchos on over the radios in the still dark, cold and wet morning and hiked to the weapons area at the far end of the camp.

All morning they sat in water-filled foxholes as a chilling wind swept the hills where the 37 mms were set up to repel the invasion. They were ordered to secure and retreat to another defensive position.

"Man, I'm sure one glad redskin that this problem is over," the Indian said, shaking. "I'll get the bug for sure."

"It ain't over, Lighttower. We're supposed to fall back."

"I can see you ain't been on many of these problems."

"What you mean?"

"See that hill?"

"Yeah."

"In about five minutes the First Battalion will be charging over it."

"So?"

"So throw up your hands and surrender and you're a prisoner so they'll send you back to camp."

"But we ain't supposed to do that."

"Look, Levin, my feet are soaked. I'm getting a chill. If you want to run around the hills all day that's your business. I'm getting captured."

"Aw, I'd better not."

"I won't say nothing."

"I'd better not anyhow."

As the officer finally gave the retreat signal, Levin arose and almost toppled over. He had been sitting in the freezing water for nearly three hours without movement. Lighttower wheeled and threw up his hands. "I quit, prisoner." A corporal put a POW band on his arm and he limped through the slush back to camp.

Levin came in four hours later. He threw off his soaked gear, unlaced his shoes, pulled off the saturated socks. His feet were icy and numbed. He held them up near the hot fire going in the stove. He sighed as a tingle of feeling came back to them.

I walked into the tent. . . . "Hey, Levin, what in the hell you doing?"

"Warming my feet, Mac. They're nearly froze off."

"You crazy bastard, get them away from that fire!"

"Why?"

"You'll get frostbite!"

He flopped back exhausted on his cot, drying himself. Then he sprang up and scratched his feet. "They itch!" he screamed and dug his fingers into the flesh. He scratched till tears ran down his cheeks. I helped him into his shoes and walked him to sick bay. He was in agony, begging the corpsmen to scratch them. They stood about dumbfounded; finally Pedro dashed off to get Doc Kyser. "They itch, they itch!" he cried over and over.

Kyser, irate from being pulled away from a poker game, stormed into the aid shack. He bulled through the astounded corpsmen and grabbed Levin's feet and massaged them vigorously until circulation returned to them. The mad itch disappeared and Levin got off the table and pumped the Doc's hand gratefully.

"Minor dose of frostbite," Kyser said. "Called chilblain. Keep him off his feet a couple of days. Don't wear any colored socks and check in tomorrow morning. And for Christ sake keep those feet away from any stoves. You'll feel this for months —just massage when the itch comes."

I helped Levin back to the tent.

"Christ," he said, "I'm sorry, Mac."

"For what?"

"The way I acted. The guys will think I'm chicken."

"Well, quit worrying about it. You should have had better sense."

He sat disgustedly. I offered him a smoke. "You'd better ride the TCS jeep till the Doc okays you to full duty."

"The . . . the guys won't like that. Me working the jeep radio."

"Look, Levin," I said, "if it will make you feel any better I know what the Indian pulled today. Those guys have been getting captured for years. Nobody is griping about your work. You might even get a stripe in a couple of months."

"But . . . but Lighttower and Joe ain't got one yet."

"They probably never will and if they do they'll lose it the first liberty they go on."

He sucked deeply and silent on his cigarette.

"Look, Levin. I know you've been busting your ass to prove yourself. You can ease up. You've made the grade."

"No I ain't. I ain't made it till I been in combat like them. I'll never make it till then."

"In their minds or yours?"

"Just leave me alone, Mac."

"Levin, why are you trying so hard? Is it because you are a Jew?"

He turned pale. I went over to him and put my arm around his shoulders. "I didn't mean to knife you. I guess you can read a guy's mind after a while. Has Speedy been riding you?"

"I don't know why he don't like me. I done everything to make friends. I don't want no trouble, Mac, but honest to God I'm going to clout him if he don't lay off. I don't care if they courtmartial me. I know the rest of the guys are just kidding, but not Speedy."

"Speedy isn't a bad guy. Maybe one of these days he'll see the light."

"He says we're fighting the war because of Jews. He says Jews are yellow . . . I'm going to clout him, Mac . . . I only been taking it because I don't want no trouble."

"Levin, you can't beat a thing like that out of a man. Come on, let's go to the clubroom."

We sat in the middle of the bay and fumed. Morning, noon and night we scampered up and down the nets teaching the swabbies how to run an invasion. Three times a day we charged out of the landing craft into the surf and up the beach. We had a queer feeling that Huxley asked for this detail.

Beyond the narrow beach was a five-foot seawall and past it a street of the town of Petone. On our first landings, we charged up the beach, over the wall and straight for the pubs. We grabbed a fast beer and put in apologetic phone calls to our girls and charged back to the beach again. The natives got a big bang out of us playing like invaders. By the second day the seawall was lined with housewives, children, and a general gathering of kibitzers who shouted and cheered and applauded as we plunged from the boats into hip-deep water and zig-zagged up the sand.

"Thumbs up, Yanks!"

"Up your ass," we whispered under our breath.

Also awaiting us on the second day was a solid line of M.P.'s to keep our invasions limited to the beach. When Marines on liberty came to gawk, it was downright humiliating.

"Hey, ain't that a fine-looking outfit?"

"Fine-looking, fine-looking."

"Hey, how come you guys ain't wearing your pogey bait whistles?"

"Got a number, pogey bait? I'll keep her warm tonight."

That put the M.P.'s into action to keep us from going up after them.

We'd reboard the ship, change our wet and sandy clothes and before a poker game could get going or we could chalk up a few minutes sack drill the intercom would blast general quarters and we were at it again. "Now hear this: Marines, man your debarkation stations."

On the fourth day we tried night landing and rang up a dozen casualties. Three made the grade for Silverstream Hospital. A few others were lucky enough to get malaria and were hauled off. The rest of us went up and down the nets and into the beach with clocklike monotony.

The grand finale on the U.S.S. *Feland* was a full-scale fubard mess. All we had taught the swabbies for a week they forgot. I guess we forgot a little too, for the thought of getting rid of each other for a night in Wellington was what really messed up the landing.

Danny had been packing a heavy walkie-talkie for hours, keeping in communication with Beach Control. He didn't get a chance to lift it off for a single minute to give his back a rest as the officers worked his radio continuously to unscramble the mess on the beach. Landing boats were way off time and course, equipment piled up in the wrong places, and the Heavy Weapons Company landed ahead of the assault troops. The engineers attached to us who were to clear alleged obstacles came in two hours late and the artillery was blowing up our own command post. Air support was shooting the transport in the bay, naval gunfire was hitting a hospital instead of the objectives. C-Ration came instead of blood plasma, and the wounded were dumped in the water instead of empty oil cans. This was typical of a Marine maneuver. Anyhow, the Japs would never outguess us.

Exhausted and constantly on the move, Danny felt his radio cut into his shoulders until they were numb. At last the LCTs and other landing craft made for the long pier a mile down the beach and loaded us up to reboard the ship. Danny sat with the staff officers keeping in communication until the entire battalion loaded up in groups of sixties and sped back to the *Feland*.

The radio had not been off his back for six hours. He had no feeling in the upper reaches of his body. Finally he boarded the last craft still in communication with Sister Mary on the ship. The boat bounced over the choppy waves and pulled up under the bow net. The hated bow net, which was hanging from the highest point of the deck, offered no support as it fell free. The coxswain gunned his boat as Danny, last out, hit the net. The boat pulled out from under him as he started the long climb to deck. He was weak all over. He pushed up a few strands and then made the mistake of looking down to the water. He saw that the boat was gone.

He braced and worked up a few more steps. The weight on his shoulders began pulling him backwards till his body was nearly horizontal. He quickly threw his helmet and ammunition into the bay and pressed every muscle to straighten up.

He broke into a cold sweat as his foot and then a hand slipped. His arms locked in the net and he froze. He looked at the water again and gritted his teeth and shuddered as he realized that his strength was completely gone. It seemed as though the water was rising up to meet him. In desperation he looked up to the deck and screamed, "I'm ditching the radio . . . can't hold!"

"Hang on!" I shouted. "Lock in and don't look at the water!" I raced down one side of the net and Sam Huxley tore down the other. We caught the straps of the radio just as Danny began to slip away. We lifted the weight from him.

"Can you make it now?" Huxley asked.

"I think so. The goddam radio was pulling me backwards."

Huxley and I took the radio and Danny slowly worked up to the deck. As they pulled him aboard he sighed.

"You used your head, son," Huxley said. "Are you all right?"

"Fine, sir, just tired." He caught his breath and looked over the side of the ship once more. Then he turned pale and began shaking all over as he stared into the cold green water far below.

Huxley laughed. "Delayed action. Take him to sick bay, Mac, and get him a double shot of brandy."

Spanish Joe turned his back to the mahogany bar, propped himself up on an elbow and bellowed, "I ain't so tough, even Joe Louis can lick me." He spun about, slamming a large ale mug down. "Survey this!"

New Zealanders about the pub gathered in close around him. Gomez flashed a smile, displaying a mouthful of ivory-white teeth in contrast to his sultry skin.

"Look at the bloke's ribbons, would you," a New Zealander said squinting at Joe's blouse. He thrust out his burly chest to give his admirers a better view of the decorations he had recently purchased at Mulvaney's Army and Navy Store on Lambden Quay.

"Must have seen a lot of action, aye, Marine?"

The spotlight shone on Spanish Joe Gomez. He casually glanced at his fingernails, flicked a small spot of dust from one. "This boy's been around, cobber. Worn out more seabags than you have socks." His fierce eyes cut the enveloping haze of flat-smelling British tobacco smoke and the sharp odor of nine per cent ale. He reached out and clutched an onlooker by the collar. "See this one here, Kiwi?"

"Yes."

"Silver Star for gallantry in action—Guadalcanal."

"Looks bloody impressive."

Joe uncorked a pack of cigarettes and flipped them on the bar. "Have a decent coffin nail, gents." The pack was devoured. "I was on a patrol, see, over the Kokumbona River near Tassafaronga Point, five miles behind Jap lines," Joe said. "They used me as a scout on account of, if I got to say so myself, in all due modesty, I'm a pretty savvy guy."

I was at the other end of the bar and, having heard Joe's routine a hundred times, looked around for Marion. I spotted him alone in a booth and moseyed over. "What's the scoop, Mary?" I asked, dropping anchor opposite him. Marion lay down his book, took off his glasses and rubbed his tired eyes.

"*War and Peace,* by Tolstoy. Very interesting."

"Looks like Joe is really wound up."

"Lost from the patrol five miles behind enemy lines. What a situation. A lesser man would have cracked up right there. But not old Spanish Joe. . . ."

Marion smiled. "He's on the way. Been a pretty good guy though. I've had him in camp for two weeks and that's a record. I suppose he's entitled to a bust."

"I come to this here clearing," Joe went on, "it's burning hot, a hundred and twenty in the shade." Joe dramatized with full sweeping gestures, pointing out his trek with a map of ale bottles and ashtrays on the big black bar.

"By the way," I said, "he hit me for a ten-shilling note and he took one of Andy's shirts." Marion withdrew his notebook and jotted the items down.

"Not too bad this month," Marion said. "He only owes three pounds and eight shillings. I'll take care of you and the boys at pay call."

"Roger."

"The sweat was gushing offa me. I was tired and so hungry I coulda ate the north end of a southbound skunk . . . I peers to the left and what do I see. . . ."

"What was it, Yank?"

"A sniper, had me right in his sights . . . I was like a bump on a log. Makes me shudder to think of it." Joe whipped out a handkerchief and mopped his forehead.

"What the hell happened?"

"I glances around fast like, see . . . and there," he sipped from his glass, "and there, looking down my throat at the edge of the clearing was a Jap machine gun!"

"Blimey!"

"Spanish Joe, I thinks to myself, a hundred broads from Chi to Dago will be grieving this day. I lowered my head and charged bayonet first like a mad bull at them!" He loosened his field scarf and rested back on the bar, leering mischievously at his audience.

"Tell us, man, what happened?"

"What the hell you think happened? I got killed, you damned fool!" He tilted his head back and roared at the stupefied onlookers. "Hey, bartender, survey this ale!"

I always got a kick out of the silly looks of Joe's audience at the punch line of that story. I smiled and turned to Marion. "Heard anything from Rae?"

He nodded. "Look, Mac." He opened his wallet and shoved it over the table to me.

I whistled. "Sharp girl, that Rae, a real lady."

"That's my house in the background, my room is around the corner. You can't see it in that picture."

"You're happy, aren't you, Mary?"

"I'm lucky," he said.

"Tell me something. Anything gone sour between you and Joe because of Rae?"

Marion lowered his head and thought. "I can't help but feel it sometimes, Mac. He tells me to jam it when he gets sore but he always comes back to me sorry. He never mentions her name but I can't help but think . . ."

"What?"

"It's hard to say exactly. But I know he's going to let me down."

"Joe has a yellow streak," I said. "We've all talked about it. Behind all that bluster he hasn't got much guts."

"I don't mean that, Mac. He comes back to me because I'm the only friend he's got."

"Why do you put up with the sneak thief?"

"I don't know. In some ways he's the most rotten person I've ever known. Maybe I'm trying to salvage what little decency he has. I guess, too, I feel duty bound to keep him under control for the rest of the fellows."

"He's slick," I said. "We've never been able to nail a lie or a missing pair of skivvies on him yet."

We looked through the haze to the bar. Joe was swaggering and bleary. "Survey this ale!" he shouted. "I can outdrink any man or beast in this pub . . . any takers? And when I finish I'm gonna get me a broad. They ain't been loved till Spanish Joe loves them."

"Is it true that you were a cattle rustler before the war?" a Kiwi asked.

"Naw, them damned cows just took a liking to me and followed me home."

Marion grinned. "About three more glasses and Joe will be done."

We looked around the room and through the smoke caught sight of Pedro Rojas, who had just entered. "Hey, Pedro!" I called. "Over here." Pedro steered an uneven course around the crowded tables of drinkers toward us. He was half crocked. He slumped down beside Marion, pulled out a handkerchief and wiped the perspiration from his face.

"Ah, my very good friends. Señors Mac and Maria."

"Hello, Pedro."

"I see you are once again babysitting." He nodded toward

Spanish Joe. The waiter surveyed my brew and brought on another round of sarsaparilla for Marion. Pedro's brow furrowed as he sipped from his ale mug. He smacked his lips. "You two are my very good friends. You two are fine understanding fellows . . . for Marines."

"What's on your mind, Pedro?"

"Pedro very sad tonight. Pedro is very sad because he is so happy," the corpsman mumbled.

"Pedro is very drunk," I said.

"Yes, my friend, I am drunk. But I am drunk with great sorrow." He threw up his hands in a disgusted gesture, loosened his field scarf and downed the ale and refilled it from the quart bottle. "I am wishing to hell I have never come to New Zealand."

"I thought you liked it, Pedro. It is a perfectly lovely country."

"It is lovely, Maria, too lovely. That is why Pedro is sad because he is so happy here."

"I don't understand you, Pedro."

Pedro Rojas sighed and looked into the ale mug. He took the handle and spun it about slowly. "I not wish to burden my good friends with my troubles, especially when I am drunk." As he lifted the mug to his lips I reached over and drew his arm down.

"What's on your mind?" I asked. I handed Pedro a smoke and lit it with the tip of my own. Pedro crouched forward, his eyes narrowed.

"You are two fine men. You understand more deeply than most."

"Come on, out with it. You got a broad you want to swap?"

"Nothing as simple as that, Mac." He lowered his head. "Have you ever been to San Antone, Mac?" His face was sad and sullen as his mind drifted back over six thousand miles. "Have you ever been to the Mexican quarters around the city dumps?" He shook his head at us and spoke softly. "Yes, I am sad because I find this country. Do you know this is the first time I have ever been able to walk into a restaurant or a bar with a white man? Oh yes, even in San Diego they look at me like I was a leper. People here, they smile and they say, 'Hello, Yank.' And when I say I am from Texas—well, this is very first time a person he call me a Texan. I am drunk. To hell with it." He squashed out his cigarette and emptied his glass.

"You know what happen tonight? Pedro will tell you. I went to a dance at the Allied Service Club and some colored sailors from a ship come in and the girls, they just dance with them and treat them like anybody else. And then some goddam Texans they go to the hostess and demand the colored boys leave the club. Instead, all the girls refuse to dance with Marines at all and they walk out. I like it here in New Zealand."

Of course there was little or nothing that Marion and I could do. His tongue was loosened now. "Water," he said bitterly to Marion. "Sergeant Mac is always telling you not to drink too much water. I cannot drink it without feeling like a thief. I have been on a water ration since the day I was born. You know, we pay thirty cents for a barrel of water to drink in Las Colonias shacktown. They tell us we are dirty Mexicans. Oh yes, they will pipe us water if every shack pay forty dollar. We got no forty dollar. And, my very good friends, all my life I never see a bathroom . . . my family share a hole with eight other families. A fine way to live, no?"

He clenched his fists. "A man have to pay a thousand dollar for a shack of cardboard and burlap or a chicken coop. For this, he pay twenty per cent interest. And the big coyote, the white fixer, make us pay. He fix a knife fight . . . he fix up the jobs . . . when there is no fixing he make trouble or a riot so he can fix it and take our money.

"Once a year my people get their only work, stoop labor in the white man's field at two bits an hour. And the ranchers, they let thousands of wetbacks from old Mexico cross the border now and they say to us, 'You must work for twenty cent an hour or we get wetbacks for less.' . . . And the poor wetback, he take his money at the end of the season to go home but the coyotes wait for him and kill and rob him. Each year the Rio Grande, she run red with their blood. And many wetback never go back . . . they stay in Texas where there is already no room for them. But the coyote fix it so the immigration people will not send them away." He paused for a swig of the ale.

"My people have much sickness. The babies die of TB and the dysentery and diphtheria. They die like flies. And the coyote fix the funeral. A woman must become a whore to live . . . the coyote fix her up in a house. And the men come like Spanish Joe. Yes, we are nothing but dirty, ignorant, thieving Latinos . . . we live in filth!"

"Get ahold of yourself, Pedro."

"The old people, they have no hope left. The young ones live as the white man say . . . but what Pedro cannot stand . . . is to see the little ones waste away and die. This, he cannot take. Papa Morales, he is one fine man. He is great doctor. He do much to help the little ones. And my dearest Luisa, she is a nurse. She have a very hard time to learn to be nurse. They did not let her in the Navy. Papa Morales tell her not to feel bad. He say we have our own war to fight in Las Colonias. I tell him I go in the Navy and I learn much medicine and I come back to help him to keep the children well. I ask for the Marine

Corps so I can learn many things and my good friend, Doctor Kyser, he let me read his books. They tell great things. Then Pedro come to New Zealand and he does not want to go back to Texas. He wants his Luisa to come here to a land where there is no dirty spik." He guzzled more ale down and shook his reeling head. "I shall never come back here . . . the Holy Mother want me to go to Texas to Las Colonias and make the little ones well." Pedro clutched my arm tightly. "Remember, Mac, I no fight war for democracy. Pedro, he only fight to learn medicine. . . ."

5.

PAWNEE was the new code name of the Sixth Marines. Pawnee red, white, and blue indicated the First, Second, and Third Battalions. On the field problems outside camp, sometimes they laid twenty miles of wire in a single day. The wire was marked in colored stripes of the owning battalion for identification and for reclaiming the next day. Sergeant Barry, the telephone chief, was always moaning about the shortage of wire. Our allotment was divided between the heavy and bulky old type and the new light reels of rubberized combat wire.

Gunner Keats turned his back as they laid down the heavy stuff and sent out raiding parties to reclaim light wire of the other battalions. It was all the same regiment, they reckoned, and they did leave some for the others.

Spanish Joe, needless to say, was the best wire thief in the Second Division. One morning he and Andy were out before daybreak reeling up Third Battalion combat wire. They came to a fence. Joe pulled the barbed strands apart as Andy labored through with two stolen reels. They both looked up and into the eyes of ten communicators from the Third Bat.

"Hello, fellows." Joe smiled sickly.

"So you're the bastards that have been swiping our wire. We should have known it was Mac's crew."

"Plenty for all," Spanish Joe said meekly.

"There oughta be," the sergeant from Third Bat bellowed, "we laid ten miles of it yesterday."

Joe turned to Andy. "Shall we let them have it?"

"Yeah," Andy answered. "It ain't fair sides. There's only ten of them. Besides, they'll probably turn us in." They trudged from the scene dejectedly.

"Jesus," Joe moaned, "Ole Mac is sure going to be pissed off at us for getting caught."

Captain Tompkins, the Regimental Communications Officer, stormed across the mess area heading directly for the battalion command shack. Gunner Keats paced behind him. "But Captain, sir, are you sure it wasn't a mistake?" the Gunner asked.

"Mistake, my ass. I've been suspecting your men for a long time. I got them red-handed this time."

"But, Captain, I'll warn them."

"Nothing doing, Mr. Keats. I'm going to take this up with Huxley." He flung the door open and headed directly for Huxley's office and gave an impatient rap.

"Come in."

"I'd like to speak with the Colonel, sir!" Tompkins roared.

"I can explain," Keats said.

"Take it easy, Gunner. What can I do for you, Captain?"

"The regimental net today, sir. I'd like you to read some of the messages transmitted." He threw a sheaf of message pads on the desk.

Huxley read:

> ENEMY ATTACKING POSITION K-3 IN PLATOON STRENGTH. HAVE WEAPONS BRING UP 37MM'S WITH CANNISTERS.

> 37MM'S BUSY WITH COUNTERATTACK AT POSITION K-5. SENDING FOUR FIFTY CALIBER MACHINE GUNS AT ONCE.

Huxley read several more and shrugged. "I don't see anything wrong with these messages, Captain Tompkins."

"Nothing is wrong with them, sir. They were transmitted by the First and Third Battalions. Kindly look at the messages that your men sent."

Huxley read again:

> THERE WAS A YOUNG MAN FROM BOSTON,
> WHO BOUGHT HIMSELF A NEW AUSTIN
> THERE WAS ROOM FOR HIS ASS AND A GALLON OF GAS,
> BUT THE REST HUNG OUT AND HE LOST 'EM.

"See what I mean, Colonel Huxley? Your men are always sending stuff like that over the air. Thank God, it's in code."

"I see," Huxley said seriously. "I'll take proper measures to see that there is no recurrence of this."

"Thank you, sir. I'd hate to have to report this to Division."

"It won't happen again, Captain."

"May I be excused, sir?"

"Yes, and thanks for calling my attention to this."

Tompkins left, slamming the door behind him.

"*Phew*," Keats sighed.

Huxley fiddled with the message pad for several moments and carefully read the contents. "Dammit, Keats, this is serious."

"Yes, sir."

"They've got to cut this out. It is lucky that Tompkins didn't report this to Division."

"Yes, sir."

Huxley looked at the messages again and up at the red-faced and stiff Gunner. They broke into laughter simultaneously.

"Say, this is a good one, Gunner . . . I mean, for Chrisake warn them to cut it out."

"O.K., Colonel," Keats said, smiling.

"Give them a crap detail, digging ditches or else take away their shore leave."

"Er . . . take away shore leave, Colonel?"

"Well, don't bother. Just rant and rave. You know what I mean."

"Yes, sir," Keats said, heading for the door.

"And for Chrisake, Gunner, tell them to lay off the Third Bat's wire. Colonel Norman jumped me about it yesterday."

Keats opened the door and turned. "They're a fine bunch, sir."

"Yes," Huxley agreed, "the very best."

Seabags and L.Q. laid their meager resources on the cot. L.Q. counted. "Only four shillings. We can't go ashore with that."

"Pretty sad, cousin, pretty sad."

"Did you try Burnside?"

"Yep, he's broke. Got cleaned in a poker game at the NCO club."

"How about you, Marion? Could you spare a bob or two till pay call?"

Marion flipped a half crown over to them. "That's the sum total."

"Jesus, we just got to get finances. A couple of nice broads lined up and everybody suffering from pecuniary strangulation."

"Come again on that last one."

"Everybody's ass is busted, you ignorant farmer."

"Pecuniary strangulation. That's a good one."

"Hey," L.Q. beamed, "I got a sensational idea."

"Well you better give out. The liberty train goes in an hour."

L.Q. walked to Levin's cot and sat beside him. "Levin, old buddy."

"I told you birds I'm broke."

He put an arm about Levin. "Understand, Levin, I wouldn't

ask this of you but this is a dire emergency. How about cutting a couple heads of hair and floating us a small loan?"

"Aw, L.Q., I got blisters all over my feet."

"We'll fix you up a nice comfortable chair, old buddy."

"Well, I don't know . . ."

"The way I figure," L.Q. calculated rapidly, "we'll give a bargain price of a shilling a haircut."

"But . . ."

"That's the only way we can round up anybody this time of the month."

"Yeah, Levin, if we charge two shillings we won't get no customers."

"I ain't looking for none."

"If you was a buddy you'd do it without a second thought."

"Well, cousin, what the hell you expect of a draftee?"

"Fugg you guys and save six for pallbearers," Levin shouted.

"Yep, if he was a Canal buddy it would be different. We'll just have to call off our dates."

"Don't take it so hard, Seabags. We'll see them again. Pay call is in a week. But by then they'll probably be shacked up with Eighth Marines."

"Aw, for Chrisake," Levin said, "get some guys, I'll cut their hair."

"Now that's a real buddy," Seabags said.

"Yeah. Just twenty guys is all we'll need. We'll be able to swing it if we don't have to take them to chow."

"*Twenty haircuts!* Nuttin doin', besides, I can't get them done in an hour."

"Don't worry about that. We'll get them lined up for you, Levin, and we'll collect in advance and shove off. All you got to do is cut their hair."

"Twenty! I'll be cutting to taps."

L.Q. was already on the catwalk running up and down yelling. "Haircuts, a shilling a cut! Nothing on the cuff. Over at the radio shack! Last chance!" The bargain-seekers poured from their tents.

They were indulging in their favorite pastime—trying to give Levin the red ass. Seabags, Danny, Speedy, Mary and me were on our sacks polishing and cleaning as usual.

"Lend me some skin bracer, Levin."

He reached into his handmade locker and passed it over. "Don't forget where you got it."

"Hey, Levin. How about a shirt?" another asked.

"I only got two clean ones left."

"All I want is one."

"Here, and wash and iron it before you return it."

"Hey, I hear the Dodgers lost again yesterday."

"They don't belong in the league."

"They stink."

Levin's face reddened.

"Hey, Levin. Got any Kiwi polish? I'm plumb out."

"You guys is always out of everything."

"What did you say?"

"I said, here is the goddam polish!"

"You don't have to yell, Levin, I ain't deaf. While you're at it lend me your Blitz cloth."

"Did you hear what Noel Coward said about Brooklyn guys?"

"Naw, what'd he say?"

Levin turned purple.

"Can't remember. Hey, Levin, what'd Noel Coward say about Brooklyn?"

"Eat it," Levin spat.

"Hey, Levin, got an extra pair of socks?"

Levin threw open the top of his seabag and dumped it over, the contents strewn all over the deck. "Take it! Take it all!" He stomped towards the the tent flap, leaving us laughing.

"Don't go away mad, Jew boy," Speedy said.

Levin spun and started for Speedy. He cut short and walked from the tent.

"What the hell you have to say that for?" Danny asked.

"Don't look at me," Speedy said. "You guys started it."

"We was just trying to have us a little fun, cousin. You shouldn't of said that," Seabags said.

"What's the difference? I don't like kikes."

Marion put his rifle aside. "I think we'd better have a little talk, Speedy."

"What's biting your ass?"

"What has Levin ever done to you?"

"I said I just don't like Jews. We make it plenty damned rough for them in Texas."

"You're not in Texas," Danny said. "Levin's a nice guy."

"If you don't like Jews," Seabags said, "that's your business. I don't feel one way or the other about it personally. But the guy does a good job and he's an O.K. boy. We got enough hard times without two guys in the squad snapping asses all the time."

"For Chrisake, what is this?" Speedy stammered.

"You don't like Levin because he's Jewish. You don't like Pedro because he's Mexican. You don't like New Zealanders because they talk funny. You don't like colored people—who *do* you like, Speedy?"

"He likes Texans, just Texans."

"What the hell are you guys. A bunch of nigger lovers?" Speedy fumed. "He ain't nothing but a kike draftee."

"What are you acting so goddam important about? You haven't cleaned a head, turned a generator, dug a ditch, or done mess duty since he's been in the outfit. He's done every crap detail for us."

"Let me tell you guys something. They're all yellow. If Levin wasn't yellow then why're you fighting his battle? He's yellow."

I had been trying to keep out of the argument. I didn't feel it right to pull rank in this type of beef. I went over to Speedy, who was enraged. "What you going to do, Mac, order me to love him?"

"No," I said, "I want to try to set you straight."

"You're the one that needs to be set straight. If he had guts then why is he always limping around camp like he was a cripple?"

"Because he has bad feet."

"Sure, he sits in the goddam TCS for a week. Did the Injun get to sit in it? They was both on the same problem. How about sending him to gunfire school. . . ."

"Calm down," I said. "When they asked for Spanish Joe for the Division boxing team, they wanted Levin, too. He was Golden Gloves welterweight champ of New York for two years."

Speedy's mouth fell open.

"But . . . but he don't look like no fighter. Why don't he go on the team?" Speedy said.

"Sure. They're living at the Windsor and touring the country and living like kings. But he wanted to stay for the same reason that Marion turned down the public relations offer. He wants to stick with the outfit. He figures that too many of us got malaria and there's too much work to do. Because he wants to be a Marine like the rest of us."

"If it was me," Danny said, "I'd of clouted you a long time ago, Speedy."

"That's easy for a fighter to do," I said. "It takes guts to take what he's been taking. He hits like a mule. You're lucky, Speedy."

The Texan stomped from the tent followed by his buddy, Seabags.

"Seabags," I called.

"What?"

"Let him sit on it a while. And I don't want you guys taking it out on him. Leave him alone and let him find his own way."

Burnside was slick at beating the ration imposed by the club on nightly beer. He'd first load up at the Staff NCO Club and then tour on to Headquarters Club. Burnside carried it well and I knew he wouldn't make trouble so I never mentioned it to the committee. Burnside pulled in one night under a heavy load. He guzzled his ration down in a few quick swoops.

"Gawd, I could piss a quart," he said.

Pedro was standing next to him. "My good friend, that is impossible."

"Nothing is impossible for Burnside and beer," I said.

"I say it is impossible. The human body cannot hold that much urine. The medical book says so."

"Bullcrap, Pedro. I done it many times," Burnside said.

"You only think you have."

"I know I have."

"It is medically impossible."

"I still say I can."

"You can't."

"Wanna bet?"

"I don't bet when I'm looking down your throat."

"Chicken to bet?"

"No."

"Then bet."

"If you insist."

"How much?"

"Name it."

"Hokay, but you will lose."

"Can I have another glass first?"

"Drink till you bust. I'll still win. I'll get a measure from sick bay."

He left and returned.

"Ready?"

"Any more takers?"

More money showed on the bar.

Burnside won in a walk.

We all held our breath as the night of the company dance approached. Many other outfits in the division had thrown dances but they always seemed to end in a brawl. It seemed that a hundred or more Marines and a load of beer always brought on fireworks. A committee, headed by L.Q., rented the Majestic Cabaret, the finest and only night club in Wellington, with surplus club funds. What funds were lacking for the venture were made up by an assessment and a contribution from the officers. L.Q. did it up right. He hired the club's orchestra, stacked in a hundred cases of beer and coke and set up a free lunch counter of eats prepared by our cooks. He got corsages for the gals and arranged with several cameramen from public relations for mementoes. It was a wonderful evening. Everyone, even Spanish Joe, behaved.

The dancing was soft and smooth and numbers were played on request . . . a nice feed, nice talk, and dancing in the slow, easy atmosphere. The officers made their appearance and took tables we had set aside for them. Generally, at affairs of this nature, the officers and their escorts made only token appearances. However, this particular night was so free of the usual drunks and noise and the dance so pleasant that they decided to squat.

L.Q. had cleaned up several of his skits and put acceptable lyrics to old songs in deference to the ladies. He ran a swell show for an hour while the orchestra grabbed a cup of tea or two. He led some community singing and everyone joined in with the gusto of people nice and tight and enjoying themselves.

Me and my date shared a table with L.Q. and Gale Bond, who was visiting Wellington from Palmerston North, and Pat and Andy. They jumped to their feet as Colonel Huxley approached the table.

"Sit down, please. Mind if I join you?" He pulled up a chair. We were honored at being singled out for a visit. We introduced our dates and poured a long drink for him. "I want to thank you for doing such a splendid job, L.Q. I'm proud of the way the boys are conducting themselves." Everyone agreed that it was delightful and that they were all proud. "It really is swell," Huxley said. "I hope you don't mind the brass hanging around."

"Not at all, sir," I said. "After all, they kicked in their quid."

Huxley smiled. The orchestra began playing. "Er," the skipper stammered, "do you suppose I might have your permission for a dance with Mrs. Rogers, Andy?"

The Swede beamed. "Yes, sir."

He looked at Pat. "I'd be delighted, Colonel," she said, wrinkling the corners of her mouth with a smile. We arose as Huxley gallantly took Pat by the arm and led her to the dance floor. Huxley obviously knew his way around a dance floor. They glided smoothly to the strains of "When the Lights Go On Again All Over the World."

"You dance delightfully, Mrs. Rogers."

"Do call me Pat, Colonel. I'm not in uniform, you know, and I won't whisper it to a soul."

"All right, Pat." Huxley smiled at her friendliness and at being put at ease by her. "I must admit," Huxley said, "I have ulterior motives in asking for this dance. I wanted to meet Andy's girl. I've heard a lot about you."

"Don't tell me you bother yourself with the love affairs of nine hundred men."

"The happiness of every one of my boys concerns me, Pat."

"You know them all, I suppose?"

"Yes, every one of them."

"You are an amazing man."

"I like Andy. He's top stuff."

"And he adores you, Colonel. All your men do."

"Oh, come now, Pat. There is little in the battalion I don't hear."

"Then you must have heard wrong. I don't think any of them would change to another outfit, except . . ."

"Except that Highpockets works them too hard," he said, feeling completely comfortable in her presence. She was clever and had loosened his tongue and he enjoyed the exchange of amenities as they danced. "Don't look so surprised. I don't mind being called Highpockets—just so they don't call me the old man."

"I'd be very angry if they called you the old man."

"Thank you, Mrs. Rogers."

"That is quite all right, Colonel."

The other couples kept a respectful distance from Huxley and his partner.

"I'll wager," she said, "that old Mac put you up to this."

"I'll wager you are right."

"Do I pass the acid test?"

"I don't know how that lumberjack ran into such a streak of luck."

The music stopped. Pat had an intuition that he wanted to say more to her. "Could I interest you in buying me a coke?" she said, taking his hand and leading him toward the bar.

"But . . ."

"Don't worry, Colonel. I'll handle Andy."

"We'll start tongues wagging, Pat, they're starting already."

"Come on, you sissy."

She lifted her glass to his. "To that hardhearted brute with a heart of pure gold," she toasted.

"Here's to the next man that—here's a go." They clinked glasses. Huxley lit a cigarette. "I suppose," he said softly, "they hate me sometimes, Pat. Sometimes I hate myself."

"It isn't too hard when they can see their skipper at the head of the column. I know what you are striving for and it is right. They must be fit or they'll die."

Huxley blew a stream of smoke. "I'm sorry to get so intimate. I find myself babbling like a schoolboy. I certainly don't know why. I've hardly met you, and yet I feel perfectly at ease. I generally don't make a habit of this type of thing, Pat."

"I understand," she said. "Even a colonel has to get things off his chest once in a while. I suppose you get very homesick, don't you? Poor dear. It must be wretched not to be able to sit about as the men do and weep your woes. Keeping up a big front and all that." She spoke as though he were a small lost boy. He opened his wallet and handed it to her. She studied the picture of Jean Huxley.

"She has a wonderful face," Pat said. "I know how you must miss her."

"You are a wise and clever girl, Pat. Do you mind if I say something?"

"Please do."

"Don't be offended. It's strange, but when I walked into this room I singled you out immediately, almost as if I had no choice. I wanted very much to be able to dance with you. It has been a long time since I've spoken to someone as I have tonight to you and I am grateful. In many ways, you remind me of my wife."

She smiled warmly at the lonesome man. "It was very nice of you to say that, Colonel Huxley."

He took her hand between his and squeezed it gently. "I sincerely hope you solve your problem, Pat."

"Thank you very much," she whispered.

Huxley looked about the room and winked. "I'd better take you back to your table. The last time I tangled with a Swede I came out a sad second best."

The alarm went off. Andy lifted himself from the bed, turned on the lamp and dressed. He went to the bathroom and doused his face with cold water and combed his hair and squared away his uniform. He entered the living room. Pat was up and waiting for him. He kissed her.

"Everything is set for Easter. Three days at the farm. I can hardly wait, Pat. I'll see you Wednesday, honey."

"Andy," she said dryly.

"What, honey?"

She paced nervously before him, then took a cigarette from the box on the coffee table. He lit it for her. "Sit down a minute. I'd like to speak to you."

"I'll miss the last train."

"I set the clock up a half hour." She turned away and puffed quickly on her cigarette, sending a cloud of smoke over the room. She spun and faced him and drew a deep breath. The small lines in her forehead were wrinkled in thought. She tugged at the hair on her shoulder in a nervous gesture. "We aren't going to the farm."

"Why? You got to work or something? Won't they give you time off?"

"You don't understand. I'm calling it off between us."

He looked puzzled. "Come again. I don't think I understand you."

"It is over," she said in short measured breaths.

Andy was thunderstruck. He arose. His face was pale and his eyes bore a dazed expression. "What the hell you talking about?"

"I don't want a scene, Andy, please."

"Pat, are you nuts? What have I done?"

After the initial shock she caught her bearings. The pounding inside her slowed. "I know what you must think of me. I can't help that. It's too late. But I'm just not cut out for this sort of thing. I was horribly mistaken to think I could live like this. Whatever you think, you are right . . . it doesn't matter, really it doesn't, now."

The big Swede put his hand on his forehead and tried to clear his brain. "I don't think nothing like that," he stammered. He lifted his face. His eyes were hurt. "I can't think nothing like that about you. I'm crazy about you. . . ."

"Please, Andy," she whispered, "I'm not asking for a showdown. I'm not trying to force anything from you."

"Chrisake," he cried. "You think I can stay in this country and know you're here and not be able to see you? Chrisake!"

"Don't shout."

"I'm sorry."

"Don't make it harder," she pleaded. "You are liable to say something now you will always regret. You are shocked and hurt. But we both know it is for the best."

"I ain't regretting nothing and I ain't leaving you." Andy grasped her and held her tightly in his big arms. "I love you, Pat."

"Oh, Andy—what did you say?"

"I said, I love you, dammit!"

"You mean, do you really? Darling, you aren't just saying it for now, are you, Andy?"

"Of course I love you. Any damned fool could tell that."

"I didn't know."

"You know now."

"A girl likes to be told."

He released his grip and looked into her misty eyes. He repeated the words, but this time he said them tenderly, the words that had been lying dormant in his bitter heart all his life. "I love you, Pat. An awful lot."

"Darling," she cried and they embraced. The room reeled about him.

He held her at arm's length. "Pat, let's get married. I know how you feel but, Chrisake, us Swedes are tough. They ain't made the bullet that can put Andy Hookans away."

"Don't say that, don't!"

"Let's take a chance. We've got to. I'll get through. I've got something to get through for, now."

"I'm frightened," she said.

"So am I."

"But I don't want to go to America."

"Who said anything about America? This is my home and you're my woman. That's all that makes any difference. The rest of the world can go to hell. . . . I think I need a drink."

For the first time since he had known her, the deep sadness was gone from her. Her eyes were alive and dancing. "It's mad, Andy."

"Sure it is. What do you say?"

"Yes, Andy, yes."

She was in his arms again and he felt strong and safe holding her. "I'll see the chaplain tomorrow. You'll be investigated," he said.

"Let them investigate."

"I feel wonderful, Pat."

She drew away gently, led him to the divan, and took her place beside him. "Andy," she whispered, "if we have a little boy would you mind terribly if we named him Timothy after my brother?"

"You mean . . . we're going to have a baby?"

She nodded.

"Why didn't you tell me, honey?"

"I didn't want to use that to hold you, Andy."

He took her hand and kissed it and laid his head on her shoulder. "You . . . you'd send me away? Oh Pat, you'd have done that for me."

"I've loved you for a long time, darling," she whispered. Her arms were about him and she drew him close and he rested his head on her bosom. He closed his eyes as if in a dream from which he never wanted to awake. "I wanted someone," she cried, "that this war couldn't take away from me."

I slapped Andy on the back as we approached Chaplain Peterson's tent. We glanced at the bulletin board outside. In one corner was a picture of a luscious and naked female. Under the picture the words: *No, you can't marry her unless she looks like this. Chaplain Peterson.* The process of getting married involved much red tape and grief and hundreds of men besieged the chaplain. The penalty for failure to go through channels was severe. On several occasions the entire regiment was called out for a reading off of a Marine caught in a bootleg wedding. Dishonorable discharge was often the punishment. I braced Andy again and we entered.

The round-faced man with the crew cut and infectious smile greeted me. "Hello, Mac, what are you doing here? Spying for Father McKale?"

"How's the T.S. business going?" I retorted to my old friend.

"Listen, Mac, do me a favor. I was in the Navy for twelve years but I've never heard anything like the language these Marines use. Talk it up among the boys. I think I'll give them a sermon on it this Sunday. Excuse me, who's your friend?"

"Andy Hookans. One of my squad."

"Sit down, boys. Hookans, huh? Always glad to convert a good Scandahoovian. You a Swede, Andy?"

"Yes, sir."

"Me too, put her there." They shook hands and Andy felt relaxed. The chaplain broke out a pack of smokes. "Hookans," Peterson repeated as he dug through the mass of papers on his desk. "I thought the name sounded familiar . . . oh, here it is." He opened a paper and glanced at it.

"Er, Chaplain, that picture on the bulletin board outside is a dead ringer for my girl."

Peterson smiled. "Looks like you came in well prepared. Matter of fact, you pulled rank on me."

"What do you mean, sir?" Andy asked.

He flipped the paper over to us.

> *Dear Svend,*
> *A big Swede by the name of Andy Hookans will probably come stammering into your sanctuary any day now to pop the question. I've met the girl and she's too damned good for him. She is an angel. I'd appreciate your cutting any red tape in getting them married. If you don't, I'll send all my boys to Father McKale.*
> *Thanks,*
> *Sam Huxley*
> *P.S. (We missed you at the poker game last Friday.)*

"Er . . . the P.S. isn't for publication."

"Yes, sir." Andy beamed. "Yes, sir."

6.

IN RECENT weeks Seabags had been taking his liberty in Otaki, a small town some twenty miles north of Paekakaraki. A yarn spinner, and one with a knack for making friends, he had conquered the place lock, stock and barrel. Seabags Brown became known as the Mayor of Otaki. As he roamed the streets of his favorite haunt the population of the predominantly Maori town would echo a chorus of "Hi, Seabags!"

And he'd answer the greeting between chaws of the eternal plug: "Hi, cousin."

Although the cultures of the white man and the Maori were intermixed, the natives clung jealously to many of their ancient customs and rituals, especially in the smaller towns such as Otaki. Rites of long-gone generations were kept alive in meetinghouses on the outskirts of town and the tribe was ruled by an ancestral chieftain. Few white men ever set foot in the last stronghold of these native traditions. Seabags was one who was always welcomed into the meetinghouses. On the occasion of the aged chief's birthday Seabags was permitted to invite a few of his friends to the ceremony. Seabags, not being able to master the chief's tongue-twisting name, addressed him only as Cousin Benny.

In spite of Seabags' standing in Otaki, I was a bit leery of going to the party. A few days before, a Marine had attacked a Maori girl and tempers in the town were high. Seabags assured us that it was quite safe. Marion, L.Q. and me accepted the invite. Marion was anxious to get a glimpse of the ceremony to use as background for a story. Seabags warned him that it would be an insult to refuse a drink so Marion agreed to try one. Then Seabags said that Cousin Benny might offer one of his granddaughters and it would be a bigger insult to refuse that. Marion turned red and kept quiet.

As we got off the train and headed for the nearest pub I felt as if I was walking on a bed of hot coals. Then started the chorus of old men, young men, old women, middle-aged women: "Hi, Seabags!"

"Hi, cousin."

A dozen small dark children raced up behind us and climbed all over him. "Hi, Cousin Seabags," they cried. He knelt and tussled with them and sent them scampering for the nearest candy store with a handful of pennies.

We entered a bar and took positions at one end to dig in on a couple of quarts of beer, with sarsaparilla for Marion. As we drank time away till the meeting hall opened, an exceptionally large Maori entered. His shirt was open and revealed a burly chest. He was fierce looking and gripped a machete knife in his big brown hand. It was polished and glinting and wicked looking. He strode up to the bar and spotted us. He advanced in our direction with slow, deliberate steps, his machete swinging back and forth in menacing fashion. L.Q. backed up and nearly trampled Marion trying to get out of the way. This guy didn't love Marines. Maybe he was the raped girl's brother.

He came face to face with Seabags and raised his knife! And slammed it on the bar. "Hi, Seabags!" he said, throwing his arms around the farmer.

L.Q. passed out in a dead faint.

"Hi, cousin," Seabags said. "Pull up a glass. I want you to meet . . . funny, I could of swore I brung three guys with me."

At dusk we made our way to the *hapu* house in the flatland outside the city limits. The exterior was carved and painted in a style that reminded me of Indian totem poles. At the door we were greeted by the Ariki of the tribe, Cousin Benny. He and Seabags embraced and rubbed noses, and when we were introduced we followed this procedure. The center room was a big hall. From the raftered ceilings hung a huge raftlike canoe. Perhaps it was the same type of craft that their Polynesian forefathers had used in drifting to this land some eight or nine hundred years before. On the walls were shields and spears. The history of the Maoris has always shown them to be excellent fighters in hand-to-hand combat and masters of ambush and camouflage. In the present war a Maori battalion had spearheaded the Anzac forces in the drive across the deserts of North Africa. Their shrill war cries and anxiousness to mix it up in close gave them many bloody victories.

For the feast a large, low table was crammed with *kumeras*, eels, crayfish, fowl, mussels, *aruhe,* and other delicacies. On the deck, in semicircular fashion, lay sitting-mats woven of *harakeke*. We took off our shoes and took places beside Cousin Benny who was painted, half-naked, and bedecked with feathers and beads. The *rangatira* was seated according to tribal rank with the *ware* or lowest caste at the end of the table.

Seabags joshed with the chief, who was a sucker for chewing-tobacco. L.Q. and me were awed at the whole deal and Marion took notes as fast as he could write. The food was well disguised with a strong flavor of herbs, but the joyjuice was a jolter and I warned the others to take it easy.

We feasted by firelight. Dancers performed in the center

of our big circle. The kikipoo hit me fast and I got a wild urge to grab onto one of the hip-slinging bead-skirted dolls and head for the hills. We knifed and fingered through the never ending courses and drank till we were seeing double. Singing and dancing and drumbeats became louder and more confused.

Then came dart-throwing contests, wrestling matches, top-spinning games, and more drinking. A group of girls seated themselves in the center of the circle, each holding a pair of poi balls. They played a fascinating game, passing the balls to each other in beat to the drums. Cousin Benny arose and walked up and down waving a stick and urging the girls to speed up. A Maori next to me explained that this was a re-enactment of their canoe voyage to the Land of the Long White Cloud, which was the Maori name for New Zealand. The girls flipping the poi balls in perfect unison represented the rowers, and their tempo, the beat of the waves. We three Marines sat and clapped hands while the girls brushed the balls against their beaded skirts and threw them about till they seemed to blur, but never a ball was dropped. The Corps could have used them for drill instructors.

Suddenly the girls fell exhausted, letting out horrible groans. The Maoris explained that this represented a period of starvation on the voyage. Finally Cousin Benny spotted New Zealand and everything ended happily.

Amid howls of delight, Seabags went to the center of the ring and took on the tribe's wrestling champ. Both of them were stewed but the Maori was fast and tricky, and even the Marine's gently applied knowledge of judo could only bring them to a draw. They fell into each other's arms sweating, each patting the other's back.

Just about then I seemed to go blank. All I could recall was the pounding of drums and the chant of voices. I did notice Seabags and L.Q. head for a side room with a couple of girls as the chief nodded smiling approval.

Next thing I remembered, Marion and me were in the center with our trouser legs rolled up, shirts off, spears in our hands dancing with a pair of dynamite-laden hip slingers.

I felt cold water running over my face. I fought my eyes open. Drums were pounding . . . I closed my eyes again. It felt as though someone was shaking my head off. Seabags stood over me. "Come on, Mac, you passed out on the floor. We gotta make a run for the train."

"*Owwww* Gawd!"

"Come on, Mac," I heard L.Q. yell through the fuzz.

"Party still on?"

"It will be on for another week. Can you make it? We got to run for the milk train."

My long years of Marine training brought me to my feet.

"We'll have to carry Marion," L.Q. said.

We bid our hosts a quick adieu and shoved off over an open field toward the depot. The fresh air brought Marion around and lightened the load. As we ran over the field he called to us from some twenty yards behind. "Hey, fellows, wait!"

"Come on, Mary, we're late!"

"I can't run forwards."

We tried to drag him. It was no go. "I tell you I can't move forward!" he screamed. "I'm crippled for life!"

We spun him around and he ran backwards for the depot.

"Fellows!"

"What is it now, Mary?"

"Hold up. I got to take a leak."

He held out his hand to lean against a brick wall. The wall was forty feet away. He fell flat on his face. We lifted him, turned him backwards and lit out again. We hurdled a small ditch and waited for him. Mary took careful aim, jumped and landed in the slush at the bottom of the hole.

"Gawd, what did them drinks have in them?"

The milk train pulled into Otaki and for once some Marines were thankful to the New Zealand Government that the trains ran late. We piled into an open boxcar and fell asleep.

7.

IN THE capacity of best man, I shoved off with Andy for Masterton a day before the wedding. The rest of the squad, under Burnside, would come up the following day. They had been granted three-day passes for the event. Before we left, Andy was presented with a twelve-piece setting of sterling silver from the company. The squad gave him a couple dozen cundrums but we smiled and kept our little secret.

The boys were bush brushing and polishing up. They were to catch a train to Wellington and stay overnight and take the first train to Masterton in the morning. It was the long way around, but they reckoned it was better to stay in Wellington than try to ride the sleeping cars with their beds running crosswise. A night in the sleeping car of a New Zealand train gave you the choice of either smashing into a wall or dangling in the aisle.

As they rushed about, preparing to depart, they made a last minute canvas of the company to secure loans until pay call. Amidst all the bustle, Jake Levin lay quietly on his bunk feigning interest in an already read letter.

"Anybody got an extra battle pin?"

"How about a left ornament . . . somebody got off with mine. Joe?"

"I just borrowed it. I was going to give it back."

"How much loot we got in the kicker?"

"Over twenty pounds."

"Hey, get the lead out of your ass. We got to make Paikak at five."

"Too bad Danny is in Silverstream with the bug."

"Yeah, too bad."

Seabags walked over to Levin and slapped his feet hard across the soles. "Come on, Levin, get your ass in gear."

The homely boy looked up, smiled feebly, and said nothing.

"For Chrisake, Levin, hurry up," echoed L.Q.

"I . . . wasn't invited," he sputtered.

"What do you mean you wasn't invited?"

"Nobody told me I was."

"What the hell you want—a fur-lined pisspot? All the squad was invited."

"Nobody told me."

Burnside grasped the situation and almost barked an order. "You're in the squad aren't you? Better hustle."

"Yeah, Andy will have a hemorrhage if you don't show up."

"But . . . but I got mess duty."

"I already got a guy from telephone to relieve you," Burnside said.

"My greens are messed up."

"You can get them pressed in Wellington."

Levin sat up and looked across the tent to Speedy Gray. Gray turned half away from him. "Better hurry, Levin," he said, "or we'll miss the train."

They found overnight accommodations in a serviceman's hostel, dumped their gear, and headed for the Cecil Hotel. Spanish Joe was sent out to round up bootleg liquor. It was reported that Masterton was dry and Andy could hardly have a dry wedding. Sister Mary escorted Joe to hold the money until a transaction could be made, and then to escort the liquor back to the hostel. He was the only man who could be trusted with a full bottle and was therefore elected as the guardian.

The Cecil Hotel was leased by the American Red Cross for a serviceman's club. The airy old building was across from the train depot. It had been redecorated and converted into one of the finest clubs in the Pacific. A crew of American field workers directed the many activities of the place. The finest thing about it, though, was the lack of that atmosphere of sorrow and self-pity that infested most of these clubs during the war. This place was filled with happy men and a full quota of hostesses. It was a beehive of activity. Physically, it had the same facilities as most USO clubs—lunchcounters, gymnasium-dance floor, hobby rooms, and showers—but it was the mental attitude of the Marine divisions that made it somewhat unique.

The special feature of the Cecil was its restaurant. Here a Marine or sailor could get a plate of ham and eggs and real American coffee for a nominal sum. It was a little corner of America and it was cherished.

The American girls were mostly of the homely variety and were generally bypassed in favor of younger and more comely New Zealand models. It was, however, a ritual to have a word or two with the directors, who spoke a refreshingly unaccented lingo.

The squad entered the Cecil.

"I don't care what they say about the Red Cross," L.Q. said, "they can always come to me for a couple of bucks."

"Yeah, but did we get anything when we were on the lines?"

"Cassidy sure got a lot of blood from them."

"Talk to some guys from the Second and Eighth and see what they got to say about the Red Cross."

"He's right. They ain't no good. One year when we had a flood back in Iowa . . ."

"So what? So they got plenty of faults. If it helps some poor bastard get a free cup of coffee, I say what does it hurt to toss in a couple of bucks?"

They entered the lobby and automatically went to the bulletin board. Their mouths fell open in unison.

"Do you see what I see!"

"Oh, *no!*"

"*Gawd!*"

"Mother, I've come home to die."

On the board were tacked pictures of the newly formed Women Marines.

"Jesus H. Christ. Women in the Marines!"

"The Corps is shot to hell."

"Just the same, their uniforms look kind of pretty."

"But, *women!*"

"You gotta admit they look better than them Wacs and Waves."

"Naturally, but just the same."

It was a bitter pill. They walked away sadly. Of course

they agreed that the uniforms weren't too bad and the girls were most likely a select group and of course superior to the other females in the services. But it was still a bitter pill.

Danny Forrester was asleep in an overstuffed chair in one of the reading rooms. He was quickly hotfooted, and bounced up with joy at seeing the squad after a two-week absence in Silverstream due to a severe case of malaria.

"Cousin, what the hell you doing here?"

"We thought you was going to get a survey to the States when they packed you out."

"Big Dan," Danny answered, "has returned to the living."

"Then you coming back to camp?"

"I'm finished with the bug. I got a four-day leave."

"That is double peachy. Andy is getting hitched and we're going up to Masterton tomorrow."

"What a break. I got two days left."

"Come on, men. Thar's a dance floor full of women awaiting my charms."

They returned to the hostel a few minutes before the midnight curfew. The squad had rented one of the rooms for themselves in the converted mansion. Marion lay on a comfortable bed as the rest entered. He was in his most familiar position—reading.

"Get any stuff?" L.Q. asked.

"Three bottles of gin, three Scotch, and one rum."

"Yeah!" Seabags said. "Let's see them."

"They are under the bed and they're staying there," Marion answered.

"Can't we just look at them, Mary?"

"You can look but no touch . . . see?"

They drooled and fondled the bootleg booze. Under Marion's stern gaze the bottles were handed back to him.

"Where is Spanish Joe?"

"I think he pulled one off on me," Marion said. "After he got a bootlegger he asked me for five pounds. I think he made a deal to meet him later and get a rebate. At any rate he hasn't returned and I doubt that he will."

"We'll never see him with a three-day pass."

"Hey, Mary, couldn't we just have a nightcap? Maybe a little rum."

"No. It's for the reception. We decided that beforehand."

"Where did you get rum?"

"From a British sailor."

"Probably watered. Better taste it."

"No!"

They undressed and went to sleep, thirsty.

The train ride to Masterton was slow and tiresome. The

squad commandeered two double seats across the aisle from each other and each foursome rigged up a makeshift table to enable them to indulge in some poker to kill time. As the morning wore on, more and more glances were cast in the direction of the liquor which Marion was guarding.

"Come to think of it," Seabags said in the course of shuffling the cards, "that bootleg stuff might be poison."

"Correct," L.Q. said. "You can go blind from it."

"Sure might be something wrong with it easy enough," chimed in Burnside.

Marion continued to be enraptured with the scenery and didn't honor their prying leads. Several miles passed.

"There's going to be an awful big reception."

"Hundreds, I hear say, cousin."

"Sure would be terrible if we was responsible for getting everybody poisoned."

"Yeah, I'd feel right bad about that."

"If Spanish Joe got it, there must be something wrong with it."

"Gawd, it's a long trip."

"Yep."

"Never forgive myself if somebody died from it."

Several more miles passed.

"I wonder, Mary, if'n we couldn't just sort of open a bottle and sort of smell it. Just to make sure it's all right?"

"Seriously, Mary," Danny said earnestly, "we'd better check."

With the idea of poisoned whiskey preying on his mind for over an hour, Marion conceded that a spot check might be in order. He uncorked a bottle of gin and a bottle of Scotch as the squad huddled about him. The bottle passed from hand to hand. Each man sniffed and nodded warily. "What's the matter?" Marion asked.

"Don't smell right, cousin, just don't smell right. Where did Joe round this up?"

"What's the matter?" Marion asked anxiously.

"Don't smell right to me," the Injun said, shaking his head. " 'Fraid we'll make a lot of trouble if we bring this in."

"Better throw it away," L.Q. said.

"Maybe I'd better sip it—I mean, just for a double check."

"Well . . ." Marion pondered.

"Think we'd better all take one and get a conclusive result," Burnside said seriously.

The bottle was up before Marion could register a strong protest. It passed from lip to smacking lip.

"Can't tell much from one swig . . . better try another."

The gin went around for the second time, followed by the Scotch.

"Is it all right or isn't it?" Marion demanded.

"Just a minute, Marion, while I offer a drink to these fellows," Danny said, nodding to four Kiwi airmen behind him. "I don't want them to think we're unfriendly."

"Better sample that rum."

"Yeah, I got some British Navy rum and had the G.I. craps for a week."

The rum bottle was grabbed by Speedy as the Injun diverted Marion to some passing scenery. Marion lost control of the situation by trying to look in ten places at the same time. Only by the direct threats did he manage to salvage three of the original seven bottles.

It was a jolly crew I met pouring from the train at Masterton. I hustled them into two waiting cabs and headed for the Red Cross club to clean them up before the ceremony.

As we entered, they were singing at the top of their lungs. Even pie-eyed their harmony was good, but I questioned the choice of lyrics in this public place. The effect of the jump whiskey was hitting home and after I got their faces washed and their greens squared away I herded them into the canteen for a sobering cup or two of coffee.

Andy entered. I had managed to keep him calm but his composure had shattered when I left him and went to meet the squad. Andy was trembling so badly he couldn't light up his cigarette. The sweat was rolling over his face and he could hardly talk. I led him to the counter and patted his back.

"Hey, Andy, you look awful," L.Q. said.

"I feel awful," he moaned. "The whole church is filled up."

"Buck up, old buddy. We're with you."

"What you scared for, cousin?"

"I . . . dunno . . . I'd rather be hitting a beach."

"Shucks, ain't nothing but a wedding. I seen lots of them."

"Got the ring, Mac, got the ring? Sure you got the ring?"

"Yes," I answered for the hundredth time.

"Hey, Andy, you better have a bracer."

"Yeah, I sure need one."

"I don't think that's wise," killjoy Marion said. "I'll order a cup of tea for you. That will be better."

"I need something. I sure need something . . . oh, hello, Danny. I'm sure glad you could make it."

"Had to be in for the kill," Danny answered. That shattered what was left of the Swede's nerves.

As the cup of tea was placed on the counter the Injun deftly replaced nine-tenths of the contents with gin. Andy, under great duress, managed to get the cup to his lips and downed the drink. He sighed and asked for another cup.

"I told you that was what you needed," Marion said smugly.

Two cups later and Andy felt no pain. He clapped his big hands together and his eyes began twisting crazily. I checked the time. "We'd better get to the church," I said. "You guys be there in a half-hour."

Andy turned somberly and faced the squad. One by one he shook each man's hand. As he came to L.Q., L.Q. broke down. "Good-by, old buddy," he said with tears streaming down his cheeks. Andy threw his arms around L.Q. and they both began to cry. I pulled them apart and dragged Andy to the door before he was given any more "tea" to drink.

"And, Burnside," I yelled. "I'm holding you responsible for getting them there."

"Leave it to me," the sergeant answered.

As the cab pulled away from the curb a mood of silent sadness fell over them. "Poor ole Andy. . . ."

"Yeah, he used to be a good man."

"It'll never be the same."

"Time for one quick toast," Burnside said. "For our old pal Andy."

Three rounds later they poured into the cabs and, in a mood of sullen despair over what had befallen their brother, they left for the ceremony. They debarked before St. Peter's Church and mingled with the crowd.

A jeep raced madly up the street and pulled to a stop near them. From it erupted the Gunner, Chaplain Peterson, Banks, Paris, Pedro, Wellman, Doc Kyser, and the driver, Sam Huxley. They had completed a mad dash over the mountains to get there.

Huxley ran to Burnside excitedly. "Did we make it in time?" His hair was windblown and his uniform disheveled from the drive. As Burnside opened his mouth to answer, Huxley fell back under the impact of a powerful whiskey burp.

"They must like the sight of blood," L.Q. groaned sadly.

The squad, on the verge of tears, entered the packed church and filled the last pew. Rogers and MacPhersons of all sizes were there. They turned and nodded and smiled at the new arrivals. Speedy lunged for the Injun's overseas cap and yanked it from his head. "Ain't you ever been in a church before, you renegade?"

A hush fell as the choir took their places. The organist seated himself and the vicar took his place before the altar. Great chords from the organ filled the old stone church and fell sharply into the pits of the stomachs of the drunken members of the radio squad. L.Q., more emotional than the rest, let out a muffled but audible sob as Pat Rogers came slowly down the aisle.

She wore blue and was veiled in ancient lace of the Rogers family. She looked very beautiful indeed. Behind her paraded a half dozen plump little Rogers and MacPhersons. Enoch looked lost in his ancient cutaway. As they passed his wife and as the music swelled and echoed, Mrs. Rogers joined L.Q. in sobs. Next Danny broke down and then the Injun and Speedy. They sniffled and choked with tears as I placed the golden band on the velvet cushion. Andy was feeling no pain. He had a cocky grin on his face and tried to make for Pat and kiss her. I had to yank him back to his place.

The ceremony began. Muffled whispers came from the rear of St. Peter's.

"Poor ole Andy. . . ."

"Poor, poor ole Andy."

I held my breath and cursed them. Andy started to waver like a pendulum as the Anglican vicar babbled on and on. I was glad when he finally got around to asking me for the ring. I took it from the cushion and gave it to Andy, who sighted in on Pat's finger, but saw too many fingers. He closed his eyes and lunged. The ring slipped from his hand and rolled behind the altar. Andy gallantly went down on his hands and knees, crawling after it. Cries from the rear of the church became louder. Andy braced himself and finally found the mark on the third finger, left hand.

He had a silly grin as he accepted the kisses of the many Rogers and MacPhersons who came up the receiving line. Pat was adorable and tolerant as she kissed all the squad. Even though they had loused up the ceremony she was not angry. She radiated happiness and sweetly forgave them. As the church emptied, Sam Huxley brought up the rear. Pat drew him aside.

"It was very nice of you to drive all the way up here, Colonel."

"I'm happy, Pat, very happy," he said.

"You will come to the reception?"

"I'm afraid we're AWOL," he said. "Really, we must return to camp, but we just had to come for the wedding."

"Colonel."

"Yes, Pat?"

"Would you settle for the middle name if we have a boy— Timothy Huxley?"

Huxley put his arms around her and kissed her cheek. "Thank you very much, my dear," he said.

The reception took place in a large banquet room of the farmer's meeting hall in Masterton. If Masterton was dry, it was obvious that the Rogers and MacPherson families had not heard about it. Either that, or they had drag with the local constabulary. The honor table and the two long tables running off either end of it were loaded with bottles of every shape and breed. There were wines, ales, whiskies, rums and mixtures never seen before by the eyes of men, and several cases of homemade beer stood ready against a wall if the other bottles should run dry.

The squad occupied the honor table at the head of the hall with Pat and Andy and her immediate family. At the right table was the MacPherson clan, on the left, the Rogers clan. Scattered tables held the overflow and in a separate little room the children held their own celebration with milk and soda pop. A bandstand held the more talented kinsmen who played dance music.

The photographers in the families dashed about madly posing up, as the entire entourage assembled. Platter after platter came from the kitchen detail of farmers' wives. I had never seen so much food and drink in one place—it looked like the FMF mess hall. For the Marines they brought forth plates piled high with fried chicken and potatoes. The clans knew how to run a shindig.

Harn Rogers, the family elder and toastmaster, babbled through a well-planned speech on the happy union while they all gorged.

"Gentlemen," Harn climaxed the oratory, "charge your glasses. I propose a toast."

All refilled and everyone in the hall arose. The patriarch of the Rogers clan gave a toast to the bride and groom and everyone sang:

> *"For they are jolly good fellows,*
> *For they are jolly good fellows,*
> *For they are jolly good fellows,*
> *And so say all of us. . . .*
> *Hip, hip, hurray!"*

It was the damnedest thing I had ever heard. They downed their drink and were no sooner seated than the MacPherson side of the room was heard from. The elder MacPherson was on his feet. "Gentlemen, charge your glasses. I propose a toast."

And they all went through the routine again. Before I could get my teeth into a drumstick, the Rogers' were heard from. "Gentlemen, charge your glasses."

The MacPhersons weren't going to be outdone by their rivals. I began feeling like an elevator. The only time I got to sit down was about the ninth round when they finally got to toasting the best man. I felt silly as hell when they gave out with that

"Jolly good fellow," but the *"Hip, hip, hurray!"* really made me blush.

My men were close to oblivion even before they came into the hall but they weren't going to be outdone by the hard-drinking kinsmen of the bride. (The ladies had long ago switched to soda pop.) Finally, to break the monotony, the Marines began unlimbering a few toasts of their own.

In the next two hours we drank to Pat, Andy, the Rogers clan, the MacPherson clan, the squad, the Marine Corps, the New Zealand army, navy and air force, Sam Huxley, Chaplain Peterson, the King, the Queen, the Vicar of St. Peter's, President Roosevelt, New York City, Wellington, Masterton, North Island, South Island, Australia, the Second Division, the Sixth Marines, Ginny Simms, Rita Hayworth, Stalin, and all the Allies and dozens of lesser celebrities and landmarks.

By the time the rug was rolled back for dancing there was a bursting frivolity and brotherhood the like of which I had never seen. No wonder the New Zealanders got along so well with the Maoris.

Burnside had ducked the place about halfway through the drinking bout, with a lovely MacPherson maid of honor. Danny and L.Q., recuperating from malaria, were unable to stand the pace and staggered from the hall soon after Burnside and the girl left.

Bleary and wavering, L.Q. and Danny propped themselves against a building and caught their breath, "Shay, Danny, didya see Burny leave with that broad?"

"Yeah," hicked Danny.

"Shay, we better find ole Burny. He's liable to get the shame treatment that ole Andy got."

"Where you suppose he is?"

"At a bar."

"Naw. No bars in this town."

"Anyhoo, we gotta save ole Burnside from a fate worsen death."

"Yeah, we gotta save our old pal, the billygoat."

They hailed a taxi and spilled in. . . . "Shay, where can we get a drink, old bloke?"

"Nothing in this ruddy town, chappies," the cabbie answered.

"Shay, you seen Burnside?"

"The Marine sergeant with the fancy ribbon about his shoulder and the girl, just left the reception?"

"Did he look like a billygoat?"

"Wot?"

"Did he . . . where you take him?"

"Really, lads. I wouldn't butt in."

"What I tell you, L.Q. He'll go like our old pal Andy."

"Speak up, man. This is a dire emergency."

"Well, if you insist. They went over the city line. Only pub and hotel about."

"Be off to the city line."

"Hurry, old bean, or we'll hang you from the highest yard-arm in all Liverpool."

The cabbie's pleas for privacy of the pair were in vain and only heightened the emergency in the minds of Danny and L. Q. After a wild ride the taxi stopped beside a large inn. Danny and L.Q. staggered out, advising the driver to keep his motor running.

They broke into the bar, which was empty save for the bar-tender cleaning glasses for the coming night rush of trade into the wet zone. Danny, with memories of San Diego, sprang over the bar, landing almost on the keeper's back, and de-manded of the startled and mild little man, "What you do with him?"

"Wot is this—a holdup?"

"Where's the Sarge? We know he's here."

"Yeah," bellowed L.Q., helping himself to a quart of ale. "We come to save him from a fate worsen death."

"But ... but ..."

"Speak up, good man. No time for tomfoolery."

"You lads are drunk."

"No."

"Yes."

"He says we're drunk, L.Q."

"*Tsk, tsk,* big Dan."

"But you blokes can't break in on them. Be good lads—he's got a sheila in the room."

"Oh ho, the plot sickens."

"Hurry, where is he? We got to save him. Poor ole Burny."

"Lads, please," pleaded the innkeeper. Danny grabbed him and shook him. "He's in a room at the end of the hall to the left," the little man finally admitted.

The pair wended a wavy course down the corridor and smashed in the door. Sergeant Burnside and the girl were on the bed. She shrieked and fell flat, drawing the sheets over her.

"Sarge! We come to save you," Danny yelled.

"Hey, Burnside, you're out of uniform," L.Q. noted.

"I'll kill you bastards for this!"

The girl became hysterical, but Burnside cursed his way into his trousers. L.Q. and Danny shook hands on the successful completion of their mission.

"Come on, Burnside. Escape while there's still time. We got a cab running outside."

The girl shrieked again and the innkeeper popped his head into the doorway. "Easy now, lads, easy. This is a refined place."

"I'll kill you!"

"Gee, Burnside, we was only trying to save you."

"Get out!"

They staggered out sadly. "Ungrateful bastard," Danny muttered.

I sat in the bus depot and checked the squad as they staggered in one by one, filed aboard the bus, and passed out. Burnside came in raving. "Where's Forrester and Jones? I'm going to kill the bastards!"

It took me several moments to calm the Sergeant and get him aboard, and I had to keep him from touching their unconscious hulks. I left him mumbling to himself and returned to the depot. All were in but Marion. I figured he must have gotten himself tangled up with the public library or some other cultural point of interest.

Pat and Andy were due at the depot to catch a bus north for a two-day honeymoon. A car pulled up. From it debarked four large Rogers kinsmen hauling the stiff, unconscious body of Andy Hookans. Pat comforted her mother as she also directed the "pallbearers" to the proper bus with her luggage and her husband. They spilled the Swede into the long seat in the rear. Pat kissed me and thanked me for my efforts.

"Are you angry, Pat?"

"Angry?"

"I mean about the way the boys behaved and for getting Andy drunk?"

She smiled. "Goodness, no. I've been going to weddings of the clan for twenty-six years. I haven't seen a bridegroom leave sober yet." Enoch cleared his throat as Mrs. Rogers looked knowingly in his direction. "I'm too happy to be angry at anyone, Mac."

"Good luck," I said as she waved good-by to the gathering.

"Fine boy, that Andy, fine boy," Enoch said.

But as Pat boarded the bus, a jeep with three M.P.s pulled up. Sister Mary was between two of them. I rushed up as they dragged Marion out.

"This belong to you?" one of the men asked me. "He was trying to take on everybody at the Red Cross club. Said he wasn't a candy-assed Marine."

"It's mine," I said.

"We should have brigged him, but since he's a Guadalcanal boy..."

"Thanks, fellows, thanks a lot. I'll take care of this."

Marion wavered, brushed off his blouse, straightened his field scarf and turned to Enoch and Mrs. Rogers, "I fear, really," he spouted unevenly, "my conduct has been obnoxious. I shall write you a letter of apology in the morning. I am quite ashamed of my behavior." He pitched into my arms, out cold. I bid a hasty farewell and dragged Marion aboard as the bus gunned its motor, then leaned out of an open window and waved.

"Fine lads, all of them are fine lads," Enoch said as they pulled out of the depot.

8.

HUXLEY propped his feet up on his desk and his long legs pumped the tilted chair back and forth. He studied the bulletin before him intently. Major Wellman tamped the freshly laid tobacco into the bowl of his pipe and lit up. He glanced over Huxley's shoulder. Huxley looked up. "See this, Wellman?"

"I was afraid you'd get around to looking at it sooner or later," Wellman answered.

"Very interesting report, very interesting. How many days did it take that battalion to reach Foxton?"

"Four."

"*Hmmm.*"

"I know what you are thinking, Sam," the exec said.

Huxley ruffled through the bulletin again. A battalion of the Eighth Marines had taken a grueling forced march from camp to Foxton, some sixty odd miles north.

"Let's see," Huxley said. "Concrete highway . . . mild hills . . . two meals a day . . . one ration and one with field kitchen. Bedrolls brought up by motor transport." He rubbed his chin as he opened his map of North Island and ran his finger from McKay's Crossing northward. "Should be an interesting hike."

"It's a rough one, Sam. Cherokee White lost a lot of men."

"Let's see here. Trucks met them at a meadow outside Foxton and drove them back in. Better than sixty miles . . . heavy combat packs." He thumbed through the report. He reached for the field phone, tossed the butterfly switch and cranked the handle.

"Pawnee White," the switchboard answered.

"Get me Colonel Malcolm, Windsor Hotel."

"Yes sir. Shall I ring you back?" the operator said.

"Right. I'll get Malcolm's O.K. Better get Marlin in here to arrange an advance scout unit for bivouacs along the route. Any other battalions giving it a try?"

"Both Pawnee Red and Blue are moving on it."

"You knew about this all the time, Wellman."

"You'd get around to it," the exec smiled. "Incidentally, you won't need an advance unit. We can use the same bivouacs the Eighth used."

Huxley dropped his feet to the floor with a thud. "I don't think so. We are going to beat them up there by a day."

"I had a hunch you'd try to do that."

"Try hell. I'll lay you ten to one we set a record that they won't even bother to go after ... *Ziltch!*"

The little orderly tumbled in the door. "Yes, sir," he snapped.

"Get the staff and company commanders here on the double."

The phone rang three sharp bursts. Huxley lifted it.

"Hello, Colonel Malcolm? This is Huxley. How is everything in Wellington, sir? Fine, glad to hear it. Say, Colonel, I want to take a little walk up to Foxton with my boys. . . ."

I didn't like the smell of this one. Highpockets had been waiting for a deal like this. He wanted some other outfit to set a pace for us to break. Breaking records at the expense of our sweat was his forte. The weather was bad. Gray clouds were blowing in from the ocean and looked like they'd start spilling at any moment. If we were going to beat Cherokee White's mark to Foxton and scare off all other competition, a soggy highway wouldn't make it any easier.

At least we got one break. We wouldn't have to hike with ass packs. We had received a shipment of Army SCR walkie-talkies. They were little hand sets weighing just a few pounds, set to one channel. They were perfect for communications on the march—if they worked. We packed the TBY's in the comm cart, just in case.

The trucks with our bedrolls and field kitchens roared out ahead of us toward the first bivouac. This was a full dress affair. All equipment that would be used in combat was along.

It began to drizzle as we hit the camp gate and wheeled left onto the concrete highway heading north. There was a mad scramble as each man broke out the poncho of the man in front of him and helped him into it. The big rubber sheets with clumsy snaps cramped our gear intolerably. As the rain thickened they threw a hot blanket over our bodies and made us sweat. Under the rain capes the long line of marchers looked like hunch-backs, their packs jutting out in a weird pattern.

We had gone only a mile when the sky opened up for fair. Huxley fumed and sputtered at the rain and ordered the point to quicken the pace. A stiff wind blew the water headlong into our faces in sharp, blinding sheets. The ponchos flapped against our bodies and their bottoms, ending at shoetop level, made perfect funnels for the water running down into our boon-dockers. The morning became almost a night in gray but we plodded on.

The water squished from my shoes, drenching my heavy New Zealand wool socks in a matter of minutes. This was bad. Wet feet and concrete don't mix. The men picked them up and laid them down as water and wind swept the road in increasing fury.

One break, then another miserable one. There was hardly any use in breaking. The cold wet was better controlled with movement than stillness. We couldn't even light a cigarette in the downpour.

Under the poncho it was nearly impossible to make minor adjustments to ease the sore spots that pack straps and pistol belts were cutting into us. We slogged on up and down stiff little hills and the concrete highway was becoming harder and harder with every step. I found myself repeating a little nursery rhyme about rain, rain, go away. . . .

A break for chow. The squad huddled in a small grove of trees off the highway. We labored out of our packs, trying to keep our remaining clothes dry, stacking and covering them with shelter halves. Soggy and too miserable to bitch, we ate the foul hash and stew ration. It was impossible to heat the coffee so we mixed and drank it cold. It kicked us back to life.

Kyser crammed beneath a shelter half that Ziltch and an-other Marine held up over Huxley's head as he studied the field map. The doctor took off his helmet and shook the water from his hair and face. In a second he was doused again. "Colonel," he said, "we'd better call it off and head back to camp."

"We're a mile up on Cherokee's time already," Huxley beamed, not even hearing the doctor's shout against the wind.

"I said," the doctor repeated, "malaria will be dynamite if we don't quit."

Huxley looked up from the map. "What did you say, Doc? I didn't hear you?"

"I didn't say a goddam thing."

The meal was hardly filling and few wanted to relieve them-selves for fear of getting drenched clear through while doffing the ponchos. Our feet were on the way to collecting some juicy blisters even though we all had calloused layers on the soles of our feet now, leathered by miles of hiking.

We staggered back to the hard road again and stepped into the deluge. The short rest had brought out the aches cut in during the first hours of the junket.

A cold, wet numbness set in. We all became void of any feeling except the comforting thought that Hell couldn't be any worse when we'd finally reach it. It was hard to do more than glue our eyes to the man marching ahead, and try to think about the States. As the road cut close to train tracks, a train sped by. We could see the passengers rush to the windows to catch sight of the walking circus and even see them shake their heads. We could almost hear them talking: "Crazy jokers, wot? Don't know enough to come in out of the rain."

I thought the day would never end. Mile after mile fell under the squishing boondockers of Huxley's Whores . . . one hill . . . another. *Pick them up and lay them down.* Dark and wet and cold. A long line of marchers trudged on and on . . . an eerie outline of a helmet and hunched back and a crazy jutting where the rifle poked into the poncho.

The new little SCR radios went out. We couldn't blame them. At least they'd get into the comm cart which slid along the slippery highway under the puffing groans of human oxen. We took a short break and one by one rode in the TCS jeep long enough to convert into ass packs and make room for sixty more pounds of weight on our backs. The extra displacement threw the poncho out of shape, and protection from the wet went out of the window. We got drenched through and through.

More miles fell. Our feeling of blankness gave way to a feeling for blood: Huxley's blood. He just kept glancing at his watch and speeding the pace. I wanted to quit badly. It was the same old game over again . . . I'd have to stay if Huxley did, and he knew it.

The slow grim column slushed through Paraparaumu, Waikanai, and on to Te Horo. The citizens poked their heads through the windows to gawk and the dogs huddled back in the shelter of buildings and thought What fools these gyrenes be. Even our mascot, Halftrack, had had enough common sense to turn back at the camp gate and lie down by a potbellied stove.

Men began dropping. The jeep ambulance raced up and down the line of march sending a stream of water from its tires into our faces. Blubbering hulks sat in the mud on the shoulder of the road, too glassy-eyed and dazed to understand what had happened to them.

We called a halt in a meadow near Otaki. There was work to do. "Get that radio in with regiment . . . run telephone lines to the line companies . . . pitch the shelters . . . dig the one-two-threes." We tried to find our own bedrolls on the trucks. It was a mess. Our area was boondocker deep in water and getting deeper as the rain pounded down. Near the road was dryer ground. We struggled against the lashing gale to pitch shelters. They leaked like sieves. The holding pegs tore out as fast as we pounded them into the soft turf. Mac arranged radio watches and guard details to see to it that no one made for the bridge over the river and a nice dry pub in Otaki.

We slogged over the meadow to the chow trucks. The chow was cold. There wasn't any use trying to eat anyway because the rain filled the mess kits and turned the chow into a soggy mash. The kits couldn't be cleaned as it was impossible to keep fires for boiling water going. Dysentery would follow this meal.

I made the last rounds in a stupor. Miraculously, no one in the platoon had fallen out yet. I crawled into my shelter and buttoned down. The semi-dryness was a relief. I pulled the water-logged shoes and socks off and checked the stuff in my pack. The extra clothes were fairly dry. I wiped my feet and for the first time felt a sharp pain. The blisters were there for good. I was too goddam tired and pissed-off to cut them now. The deck was damp. A streamlet of water had already found its way in. Burnside and me had staked the shelter so the wind hit the middle instead of running over them lengthwise. I felt the whole thing would blow out any time. I fought into partially dry clothes and bundled down as close to Burnside as I could, and fell asleep dead exhausted. Burny was already snoring.

Huxley slogged up to the aid station. Doc Kyser was on duty. He was stripped and wringing out his dungarees when Huxley entered. He put on dry clothes and sat on the deck by the bulky aid packs that the corpsmen had deposited for the night. "Hello, Sam."

"Hello, Doc." Huxley shook the wet from him like a puppy. "How many did we lose?"

"Six men."

Huxley smiled, "We'll beat them in that department, too."

"I wouldn't count on it. Most of them are too numb to know whether they're sick or not. If it's still raining tomorrow, you're liable to be hiking up there by yourself. I'll have business before the night is out. Those tents are going to go if the wind keeps up."

"Dammit," Huxley said, "we're getting nothing but rough breaks. Quartermaster issued new shoes last week. They aren't properly broken in yet. How did blister call go?"

"Like I said, they're too numb to know." Huxley turned to leave. "Incidentally, Sam, your orderly is running a fever."

The lanky man tried to act unconcerned as he buttoned up to head into the storm. "Malaria?" he asked casually.

"I didn't ask. He refused to turn in."

"I'll make him ride the transportation jeep tomorrow. He'll make it."

"Sure, he'll make it," Kyser spat. "They'll follow you to hell, Sam, and you know it." Huxley left.

I thought I'd never see the sun again. After the storm I vowed I'd hike to Auckland if it would only stop raining. Seven hours of sleep and the hot rays filtering down through a clear bright sky next morning made us feel like new men. In lieu of morning chow we were issued D-ration candy bars to nibble on the march. Huxley wanted a fast start and didn't want to waste time on such luxuries as food. We broke communications double time, rolled our bedding, threw them aboard the trucks and fell in.

By 0700 Fox Company was on the road, taking the point of march toward the bridge. It wasn't till I hit the road that I almost crumpled. The pains in my feet were sharp. A Marine has one item that can't be neglected. His feet. They are his wheels, his mechanized warfare. I had babied mine and they had never let me down. I was always careful to keep them powdered and clean and I hiked in broken-in boondockers. Yesterday's rain had brought on blisters, though, that would give me bad trouble before the rest of the thirty-five miles was conquered. Lucky, I thought, that I didn't have new shoes like some of them.

We crossed the bridge of the Otaki River and hit the town as it was awakening. Quickly through, we were on open highway again. The warmth of the sun lessened the discomfort of the men's feet and within a few breaks the clothes were dry, except for the shoes, which were still creaky, stiff, and damp.

After the third break I tried the little SCR radios on a hunch and they went back in as suddenly as they had gone out yesterday. We put the heavy TBY's back in the carts again, gladly.

As the day wore on I could see that Highpockets was really out for a kill. He raced the point so fast the rear company had to run to keep the line from spreading. He pushed us to our peak of endurance. Yesterday's wet was replaced with today's sweat. Fortunately, the mild winter sun played in our favor. Miles fell away. The pace, for a march of this length, was the fastest I had ever seen. With every break I dropped to the roadside for a gulp of water and a quick smoke and eased the heavy pack for a few minutes. It was my feet, though, that worried me. With each break the pain became sharper. When we hit the road it was agony for the first ten minutes.

Then the pavement pounded them into numbness. By noon chow I felt like I was walking on a bed of hot coals.

We gulped the hard biscuits and hash and realized for the first time that we were hungry. We made a fire and heated the coffee. It felt grand going down. I did a quick patch up job on my feet; the two heel blisters were as big as quarters and ready to pop. I cut around them and let the water run off and swabbed them down with iodine, then ripped a pair of skivvy drawers and folded them into small patches to pad and sponge the area. I taped them tight so the pad wouldn't slip, and put on three pairs of dry socks and laced the shoes on tight.

For twenty minutes after the chow break the entire column limped. It was especially noticeable in Sam Huxley. He was a big man and it was twice as hard on him. His feet hurt; I knew it; and it made me happy. Huxley tried to disguise the limp for our benefit by stepping up the pace immediately.

The men cursed and fumed the miles away. Up and down they beat a tattoo on the never ending road. My foot trouble made me less aware of the other pains that were shooting all over my back and hips and neck. Soon they caught up with my feet. I felt like a hunk of raw liver going through a meat-grinder. Another mile . . . another . . . and another. I got short-winded, a thing that rarely happened to me when hiking on level ground. I closed my eyes and prayed. I couldn't quit! What would my boys think? Some were worse off than me and they hung on . . . I've got to hold . . . I've got to, I thought.

Every step became unbearable. I felt like screaming for a halt. After each break I was afraid to stand up. The history of my life came before me. How the hell did I ever get into this mess? They wanted to send me to Communications School as an instructor. Why did I turn it down? . . . I'm an asshole! One more mile gone . . . another . . . Manakau . . . Oahu . . . thank God!

We swung off the road into a big field.

I wanted to drop on the spot but there was work to do. A communicator's work never ends. We had hiked so well that Huxley pulled us in early for a long night's sleep before the final day's push. None of the platoon had fallen out yet but they were a mighty beat-up bunch. It was an effort to cram down chow and set up for the night. The air was calm and the evening mild and peace settled on the shelter halves in the meadow.

An hour and we were rested enough to sit around and bat the breeze and enjoy a late smoke before taps. As we talked I cut blisters and mended feet. The sick bay was overcrowded and I was a blister artist in my own right. I laid out the wet clothes in my pack to dry and buttoned up for some much needed sleep before the big push.

Speedy, on the way to taking over early watch on the TCS, came over to me. "Er, Mac . . ."

"How's it going?" I asked.

"I think that goddamyankee is out of his head. Glad we got only one more day of this."

"Well," I said, "when it is all over we'll be pretty proud of ourselves."

"Tell me, Mac, and be honest. Did you guys ever take a forced march in the old Corps like this one?"

"Lots of times, Speedy, but I guess the one you are on seems like the hardest. I don't think I'll forget this one for a while."

"Look, Mac, I got a few minutes before I take over the watch. Could I fell you something confidential?"

"Sure, I got my chaplain's badge."

"I don't want it out that I said this but I saw Levin pull off his boondockers. His feet are bloody. Maybe you ought to take a look at them."

"He'll come around to sick bay if he needs help," I said.

"Look, Mac," Speedy continued uncomfortably, "I asked Pedro. He didn't check in. Maybe you'd better let him ride the jeep tomorrow. He can have my turn."

"He'll get his own turn and no more."

"Aw, for Christ sake, Mac, his boondockers are soaked with blood. I know about all the trouble, but . . ."

"Speedy. Levin won't quit. He's got something to prove."

"To me?"

"Why don't you just forget it and get on your watch."

Huxley pulled a fast one on us. He cut our sleep short and roused us at four in the morning. It was pitch dark except for the light of a quarter moon and the stars.

Groggy and bitter we broke camp and with a bar of chocolate we were on the highway in less than forty minutes. It was his plan to catch us half asleep so that the pace and pain would only be half felt. It worked. As we passed the town called Levin we were all in stupor, like the rest of the column. There were a few halfhearted cracks about the link between Jake Levin and Levin Township but it was a sad attempt at humor.

Only knowing that the end of the hike was in sight kept me going this day. I felt the most miserable and pain-filled bastard alive and for the first time in my years as a Marine I was ready to throw in the sponge. I just didn't have any guts left. Huxley had pounded them out of me. I was like a punch-drunk fighter, battered and almost out, only staying on his feet because the bell would ring soon and they could drag him to his corner. Foxton might be past the next hill or around the next bend.

For the first time we were not going parallel with the railroad. The route cut into hillier ground past Levin. The rising sun looked down on a gang of dazed zombies tramping and limping up the road.

With each break we gathered our guts for another last surge. Maybe another hour would find us at Foxton. Then another break and another. But Huxley showed no mercy. I pitied any poor bastards who ever set out with the idea of beating our time. And still the miles came and went. The early starting time would cut out the hour stop for noon chow—another Huxley innovation.

Let them try to beat us, crazy bastards, *let* them try. Let the sons of bitches kill themselves out-hiking Huxley's Whores. I don't suppose a man knows how much he can take. Many times in the hours before daylight I had felt I had reached the saturation point. Yet, each crisis passed and I was still half galloping along at the murderous pace—and nearly all of us were still on our feet.

Levin's agony gave me renewed courage. I couldn't order him to stop. The secret had to be kept, even if it killed him.

By 11:00 we began to sense that Foxton was close. The point broke out, almost double timing, in search of the town the name of which was now synonymous with Hell and Heaven. Hell to get there and Heaven to be there. By noon, houses cropped up along the roadside and at last from the crest of a hill we saw her dead ahead. The last two miles meant nothing now. It was almost anticlimax as we trudged through the streets of the sleepy farm town amid greetings from the citizens gathered at the windows and along the sidewalk. We went right through Foxton and were on the highway again.

I was seized with panic! Huxley might want to walk them to Palmerston North! I wouldn't put it past him. The murmur in the column quelled as it swung off onto a dirt road and into a fenced-off field near the ocean.

Highpockets was wreathed in smiles as he checked the time. Of course there was work, but it didn't seem so hard now. It was all over and we were relieved and damned proud. We slowly set up a camp, attended to our dilapidated feet, and a much needed mail call came through.

Aching but happy the battalion settled down. Spanish Joe borrowed a few chickens and a pig from a nearby farm and we had a fine barbecue. A day's rest, a short field problem, and a return by truck to camp were in order. After a songfest around a campfire the boys decided they needed a little liquid refreshment in Foxton. Seabags reckoned it would be mighty unneighborly to walk up this far and not meet the local citizens. Our area was tightly guarded but Seabags was way ahead of the game. He had taken some message center armbands and planned to walk through the gates while "testing" the new SCRs for distance.

I wanted no part of it—only sleep. But I made them promise to watch the Injun and keep him from tearing the place apart. As I buttoned down they were already at the gates, cruising past the guards and giving phony test calls on the radios.

Doc Kyser limped into the command tent angrily. He snarled at Sam Huxley. "Have you lost your mind?" he shouted.

"Come in, Doctor. I was expecting you."

"Huxley! I've sat by before on some of your little expeditions and said nothing. This time I'm putting my foot down!"

"Don't put it down too hard, it's probably sore."

The Doc bent over the table and pointed his finger under the skipper's nose. "Are you mad? You can't hike them back to Russell. We lost twenty coming up—you'll hospitalize the entire battalion. Don't pull any crap on me."

"Don't worry, Doc," Huxley said. "I promised them three-day leaves if we can beat our own time back to camp."

"This is it. I'm going to the top. This is the last torture session I sit by and watch. I'll get you courtmartialed if it's the last thing I do."

"Sit down, dammit!" Huxley barked.

Kyser sat.

"If you can't take it, get the hell out of my battalion, Doc. We're in a war. These boys have to be tough. Yes, I'll drive them and I'll drive myself but I'll see to it we are the best outfit in the Marine Corps. Not a man in the Second Battalion is going to be a straggler, not a man is going to die because he is weak. Get the hell out of my outfit if you don't like it!"

The mild little doctor sagged. "God," he whispered, "what's the matter with you, man? What's burning the insides out of you? You knew all along that we were going to hike both ways, didn't you?"

"Yes."

Kyser arose. "I've got a lot of work to do." He turned for the tent flap.

"Doc," Huxley said softly. The medic turned and lowered his eyes. "Sometimes I don't like myself very much . . . this is one of them. I have to do it for these boys, Doc . . . you understand that, don't you?"

"Yes," Kyser said. "Thank God the Marines are filled with crazy officers like you. Maybe we would never make it otherwise. I'd better go."

We were thunderstruck! The word passed like wildfire. Surely it was someone's idea of a bum joke. We had hiked in the rain for him; we had given him his record—it just didn't seem believable.

Then it dawned on us that it was no joke. Huxley was walking us back and striking for faster time. In the confused shock of the announcement a vicious anger such as I had never seen mounted. Till the last minute I prayed for a reprieve. The men snarled into their gear.

There was only one small compensation: Huxley would walk too. The point vowed to set a pace that would make even the iron man fall to his knees.

This crazy desire to bring Huxley down was just the thing he wanted. He knew that he'd have to throw us into a passionate rage to bring us up to the task.

The first day going back we were so goddam angry that we half ran, throwing all pain and caution to the winds. The pace was brutal and each step was matched with a foul curse along the column. Epitaphs flew, with our feet, southward. I had never seen men drive themselves so hard. Each break stimulated the insane desire to walk . . . walk . . . walk . . . I didn't know if the squad could stay that way. The beat, beat, beat of leather on the paving might well beat our mood to jelly.

The end of the first day found us ahead of our former time. We cursed right through Levin and tramped to a spot between Ohau and Manakau. A brisk evening breeze came up and men began dropping with chills and fever, puking their guts out. Malaria was swooping in wholesale. We walked till dark and finally set up in a meadow outside Ohau.

Our nerve was quelled. A sudden shock of complete exhaustion hit the battalion. The men flopped and floundered and passed out in the shelters like invalids near death. Only a maniac would try to out-hike the miles covered that day—unless they had Huxley's brother for a skipper.

The second day was different. A nightmare. The emotional burst was spent and now there was the reality of water and pack and road and pain and feet—what was left of them. Physical torture such as I had never felt before. Limping and groaning, we hit the bastard road after a breakfast of a chocolate bar. Every man in the Second Battalion called for the last ounce of strength that God gave him. The column began to fall apart. By noon we were moving at a snail's pace.

Several more went down with malaria. Spanish Joe collapsed, done. During the break there was a ghostly stillness as we sat in the shelter of trees eating our ration. Huxley's plan was going to backfire.

Huxley needed a miracle. There was a day and a half to go. At this rate he'd be lucky to walk in with fifty men. His purpose would be defeated.

We hit the road. Huxley limped like a cripple. His body looked all out of proportion and he trembled with each step. The word passed down the line that he was dragging his ass. But the point no longer had the urge or the energy to step up the pace and down him. Maybe he was putting on a show to keep the outfit intact? No, it was no show. He was in trouble and the slow, dragging steps were sending shocks of pain from his feet to his brain, almost paralyzing him with every step.

Highpockets is going to drop . . . Highpockets is going to drop . . . Highpockets is going to drop. . . . This became the cadence as we slugged step after miserable step. A singsong, silent chant was on every lip and every eye was on Sam Huxley, whose face was wrenched in pain. He clenched his teeth to fight off the blackness creeping over him. *Huxley's folding . . . Huxley's folding. . . .* A mile, another. We neared Otaki again. Our pace was almost nil. Five men keeled over in quick succession. We pulled to a halt.

We were finished and we knew it. We'd never make the last day. Fifty men were out now and the time was past for fighting climax after climax. The saturation point was past. No miracle had happened.

Sam Huxley felt nothing in his long legs. He pinched and rubbed for an hour to get feeling back. He looked at his watch like a nervous cat from where he sat propped against a tree. His only order was to get up the galley along the highway quickly. It didn't make sense to put it so close to the road. What was he up to? Suddenly he sprang to his feet and shouted. "Get your mess gear and line up along the road for chow, on the double!"

We staggered up the highway to where the field kitchen was. Eight hundred and fifty men, and the officers at the head of the line. Huxley kept looking at his watch every few seconds. Then he smiled as the sound of motors was heard coming over the Otaki Bridge. Huxley had passed his miracle!

Trucks rolled down near us. In them sat the men of Pawnee Blue, the Third Battalion was coming back from Foxton. On their asses!

"Candy-assed Marines!" A roar went up from us on the road-side, "Candy-assed Marines!" The red-faced men of the Third Battalion held their tongues, ashamed of their position. *"Candy asses . . . candy asses!"*

"Say, what outfit is that?"

"Why that's the Third Battalion, cousin."

"Worthless as tits on a bull!"

"Ain't they sweet!"

"Whatsamatter, candy asses? Road too hard for you boys?"

"Maybe they're Doug's soldiers."

The trucks roared out of sight. I felt wonderful. I felt like bursting inside. Huxley was standing on top of a table, his hands on his hips. "Well," he roared, "shall I call the trucks up for us, or does the Second Battalion walk?"

"The hell with chow!" A cheer went up.

"And when we hit the camp gate," Huxley shouted over the din, "let's show them what the best outfit in the Corps looks like!"

The surge of pride bustled like spring as we pushed south again. It was a fitting climax to the fantastic venture. We realized we were on the brink of a monumental feat that gyrenes would be talking about from Samoa to Frisco for a hundred years. The Second Battalion was near setting a record that would never be equaled anywhere.

As we worked the miles closer to camp, familiar landmarks came into view. We had pounded out the word with our feet that this was the greatest battalion in the Corps.

We passed Paraparamumu and the point gave the word to straighten up and look smart. Eight hundred and fifty men stiffened their backs and L.Q. Jones sang:

> *"Hidy tidy, Christ almighty.*
> *Take a look and see,*
> *Zim zam God damn,*
> *Huxley's Whores are we."*

It made chills go up and down the spine to hear the whole column break out singing. As we swung into the main gate of camp the road was lined with Marines from the Second and Eighth Regiments who had come to gawk at the hiking fools. The highway was filled with jeeps of officers from lieutenants to colonels, from every camp in the division. Their mouths hung open in stunned awe as the files of straight and smart-looking boys marched past them singing at the top of their lungs.

> *"We took a hike to Foxton,*
> *Just the other day,*
> *And just for the hell of it,*
> *We walked the other way...."*

Huxley sat with his bare feet on his desk near an open window. His field phone rang.

"Huxley."

"Hello, Sam, this is Colonel Malcolm. Everyone at the Windsor is talking about it. Your outfit was remarkable. General Bryant is going to congratulate you personally. Remarkable, Sam, remarkable."

"Thanks, Colonel Malcolm. Incidentally I have authorized three-day leaves for my boys."

"Fine, Sam, when?"

"Today."

"But, Sam, that's impossible. You're scheduled to take over the camp guard."

"That's your problem, Colonel."

"What?"

"They've already left camp."

"Dammit. You knew this. Norman will have a fit if I order guard again for his men."

"Forgive me, Colonel, it completely slipped my mind . . . isn't that too bad?"

The beer and ale poured and they verbally walked the miles to Foxton over and over. Some of the squad got so drunk they felt no pain and went dancing the first night of leave. The second and third nights, however, were spent in bed with their women or perched on bar stools high over the deck.

9.

SEPTEMBER and spring. The winter slush and wet gave way. The hikes and field problems increased. Anything that came after the Foxton trek seemed trifling to the Second Battalion. The cycles of malaria lessened in both quantity and quality and new weapons and tactics were being introduced and experimented with.

A restless urge to move out came over the division. Each day brought new ships to Wellington Bay. Then the pot began to boil. The Third Marine Division in Auckland and the First Marine Division in Australia were putting on the final polish for a three-pronged assault into the sprawling dots on the South Sea maps.

Interdivision rivalry was put aside. When the chips were down it wasn't going to make a hell of a lot of difference what outfit you were from as long as you were a Marine.

In the waning days of the stay, more and more Anzac troops began drifting home to New Zealand from the Middle East. The loss of their women, long won over by the Marines after their three-year absence, and the irritation of constant contact with the cocky, smartly dressed, and well-paid Americans who had taken over their country, created an immediate tension. The Kiwis did not get a triumphant welcome; only a shabby deflation as sad as their khakis. Often they were bitter and you couldn't blame them. Of course, the New Zealanders had had little consideration for the men of Greece when they hit Athens, but that was water under the bridge. The Marines were in the saddle and trouble was brewing.

After a few scattered fistfights the situation produced a full-scale brawl one night at the Allied Service Club. The Marines were badly outmanned but still administered a beating to the Anzacs via the buckle to the head route. This only intensified the friction. Word got around that the Maori Battalion of desert legend was going to run the Marines out of Wellington the next weekend.

Major General Bryant, the Marine commander and a man of moderate temper, did not like the threat of the New Zealanders. An immediate order was posted that the entire Second Division was to have liberty to attend the opening day of the races. This was odd because Bryant hated horses. It wasn't hard to read between the lines—every Marine capable of walking or crawling was to get into Wellington with his belt buckle ready.

They prepared for the event. I was content to rely on my belt buckle. Others reinforced themselves with a bar of soap in a sock, buckshot wrapped in cloth, brass knuckles, knives, strangling wires and other civilized incidentals, to cope with the expected situation.

As the Marines hit the city every intersection was guarded by a four-man team of military police, two Marines and two Kiwis. Twenty thousand of us slowly and calmly dispersed into groups of not less than four and awaited the visit of the Maori Battalion and the others. They never came and soon after, the trouble faded.

The squad packed up with sadness for they all felt they would never return to New Zealand. It had been pretty wonderful. They labored to load the trucks that streamed back and forth to the busy harbor. The worst of it was breaking down the clubroom. The furnishings were donated to a group of nuns, former missionaries from the Solomons who had been smuggled out by submarine early in the war. Last, we drew lots for the autographed pictures that adorned the walls. I got Myrna Loy. When the clubroom was finally stripped they all wanted to go fast. They loved New Zealand and hated the thought of a prolonged farewell.

It came quickly. Our ship, the *J. Franklin Bell*, was a hulking affair that fell into a class between the *Bobo* and the *Jackson*. One innovation did appear to us. Instead of nets, many of the new landing craft hung from huge davits and could be lowered to the water with a full load of men.

The ship sped from the harbor at breakneck speed. Then the men learned it was all a gigantic hoax to throw the enemy off guard. In reality, the division was sailing for Hawke's Bay, several hundred miles up the coast, on a maneuver. Whether it fooled the Japs or not is problematical. In any case the landing at Hawke's Bay was the most colossal piece of organized mayhem any of us had ever seen. In the rough surf several boats capsized and men and equipment were lost and damaged. Valuable gear was jettisoned and the attempts at rubber-boat landing proved fatal in many cases. The beach was a disorganized mess and communications were fouled beyond repair. Many landing craft were damaged by the pounding or were wrecked on sandbars and underwater reefs.

As we hit the beach, Brigadier General Snipes, the Division assistant commander, snarled back and forth watching the disaster through his gimlet eyes. Snipes, originally a Raider leader, was a man of stormy action and stony emotion. It was scuttlebutt that no one ever saw his leather face creased in a smile. He had earned the name in the Corps of "joyboy" Snipes. The hefty old campaigner with the flaming red hair cursed his way from one end of the beach to the other as report after report of mishaps and miscalculation rolled in. At last the armada turned and limped back to Wellington to replace lost gear and patch its wounded ego.

The return to the skeleton camp made the Marines edgy. Days straggled into weeks but at last we were once more loaded aboard the *J. Franklin Bell*. The Wellington docks burst with gear and the bay was filled with transports awaiting their turn at an open pier. They loaded and moved into the middle of the bay to await the rest of the division. Seabags, as usual, was rolled into the sick bay the moment he went aboard.

They ran a liberty boat in from the *Bell* nightly. Each day, one of the boys gave up his pass to Andy. As the days came and went with us still in the middle of the bay I became a little worried about him. Andy was getting touchy and unapproachable. I realized the agony he and Pat were going through, expecting each night to be the last. The agony of not knowing how many years it would be . . . if ever, before they would see each other again. When liberty was cut off, Andy began jumping ship by using a message center armband. I held my breath and stayed awake until Andy returned remorsefully, to toss in a fitful sleep, waiting for another chance to go ashore.

One by one the piers emptied. There was little time left, perhaps one more night, before the bolt from the harbor. My concern for Andy was deep. I had a queer feeling in the back of my mind that the big Swede was planning to desert. I decided

to talk it over with him as soon as I could catch him alone. I
found him aft looking wistfully at the city as the sun was going
down.

"Andy," I said, coming up to him, "I want you to take a
detail for me."

"I ain't been feeling so hot," he answered.

"Come on, Andy, you've got to take your turn."

He spun on me, red faced. "Take the detail and shove it."

"All right, fellow, let's have it out."

"Leave me alone."

"Come here, dammit!" I ordered.

Andy sulked up to me, sullen and limp. "I can't take it no
more, Mac, I can't take it. . . ."

"If you got any ideas about deserting, forget them, Andy."

"Don't try to stop me," Andy hissed, "or I'll kill you."

I went to Gunner Keats and pleaded with him to let me go
ashore with the next trip of the control boat. Keats didn't ask
why, but knew from the distress in my voice that it was urgent
and he arranged a special skiff to run me in. As I headed for the
Jacob's ladder, Sam Huxley tapped me on the shoulder.

"Mac," he said.

"Colonel Huxley . . . I'm sorry, sir, you startled me."

"Mac, don't fail. She's too nice a girl. I don't want to have
to take him in irons. . . ."

"I wish to God, sir, I didn't have to do this."

"Good luck."

I was in dungarees but that wasn't out of place in the city. All
about me were Marines in the same dress, walking and talking
slowly with their women, saying bittersweet farewells, trying to
catch a lifetime in each tick of the clock. Wellington was like a
city in mourning. Girls, eyes red from crying, gathered near the
docks to wait for the last liberty boats. Their Marines were
going, never to return. An interlude on an island of beauty in a
sea of war. The lights in the homes of Wellington were dimmed
and eyes were turned to the harbor.

I tapped on Pat's door. It burst open. Pat greeted me with
anguished face.

"I'm sorry to startle you. I should have phoned."

"Oh, come in, Mac," she said. I could see her trembling as
she ushered me into the living room.

"Excuse my appearance. Our dress uniforms are packed."

"Do sit down, Mac. May I make you a cup of tea?"

I tried to start the conversation, then walked over to her and
placed my hand on her shoulder. She sank into an armchair
and whispered, "What is it, Mac? Tell me."

"Andy . . . wants to desert. He's coming ashore tonight."

She sat silently. I lit a cigarette and offered her one. "What do you want of me?" she finally asked.

"You know what you have to do."

"Do I know, Mac? Do I?" she said harshly. "Do I know?"

"Could you ever live in peace with that other boy in a grave in Crete?"

"You have no right to say that."

"Do you want to see that big Swede turn into a shell? It will kill him and you, too."

"What does it matter? At least I'll have him. Oh, Mac, how can you ask this of me?"

"Because . . . you could never betray him."

"Betray him to what?" She rose from the chair. "Oh, God, I knew this was going to happen. Why did I let it? Where is our war, Mac, tell me . . . why does it have to take him, tell me!"

"What do you want me to say? Do you want me to tell you it's all wrong? Do you want me to say, run off and let him become a deserter? Should I tell you that it's time to stop killing each other like animals?" I met her icy stare. "He's a man, he has a job. Don't ask me why. Dammit, Pat, you're no different than a billion women in this war. . . . Go on, run . . . hide . . . take him and live in the shadows. To hell with both of you!"

She walked to the window and clutched the curtains until her knuckles turned white.

"Pat, I often wish I had the courage of a woman. In the long run, I suppose that what a man is asked to do is small beside what you women must bear."

She turned and faced me. Her eyes were closed. She nodded her head slowly.

I walked to the table and put on my pith helmet and folded my poncho.

"Mac."

"Yes?"

"Good luck . . . to all the boys. Write to me and look after him."

Andy rapped on the door hurriedly that night. It opened and they were in each other's arms.

"Hold me, hold me tightly."

"I'm afraid I'll hurt the baby."

"Hold me, darling, hold me."

"Aw, honey, you're all upset. I'm here now . . . I'm here . . . *shhh*, honey, *shhh*."

She regained her composure and went to the kitchen to prepare some tea. He followed her and leaned against the door frame wondering how he was going to say it.

"Pat. I ain't going back to the ship."

She did not answer.

"I said, I ain't going back."

"I expected it." He came to her and put his huge hands on her arms.

"We can do it, Pat. I got it figured. I found a place in Nagio where I can hide out. Then we'll make a run for it. Fly to South Island . . . maybe Australia. Three or four years and we can come back. I been thinking . . . we can do it."

"All right, Andy."

"You mean it honey? You really mean it?"

"Yes."

Her hands fumbled through the cookie jar. She placed some buns on a plate and took sugar from the cupboard. She breathed deeply, afraid her voice would fail. The room seemed to sway. She could not look at him.

"We'll have to pack fast, right away."

"I'd better not bring a radio," she said.

"Why not?"

"Because you'd not want to hear about your battalion."

"Pat!"

She spun about. "What will we name the baby, Andy? Maybe we can call him Rogers—no, even that won't do? Timmy Huxley Smith. That's it. Smith is a good common name." She clenched her teeth. "I hope your buddies come through, Andy."

"You're just trying to get me riled up!" he yelled.

"No, I'll go . . . I'll go," she cried. "Let's run."

"Dammit, what do we owe this lousy war? What do we owe the Marines?"

"Each other," she whispered.

"You don't care. You don't care none for me . . . you'll have your kid—that's all you wanted."

"How dare you! How dare you speak to me that way?"

"Pat . . . I didn't mean to say that . . . I didn't mean it."

"I know, Andy."

"It's just that I'm almost off my nut. I don't want to leave you."

"If you want to, I'll go with you."

He fumbled for a smoke. "I guess I was crazy to ask . . . it . . . it would never work."

She clutched the drainboard for support.

"I'd . . . I'd better get back to my ship."

"I'll get my coat."

"No, I'd better go alone."

His big paws groped through the air as he tried to speak. "Do you love me, Pat?"

"Very much, my darling, very, very much."

His arms were about her and he stroked her hair. "Will you write . . . all the time?"

"Each day."

"Don't worry none if you don't hear from me. Being aboard ship and all that . . . and take care of yourself and the kid."

She nodded, her head on his chest.

"With a little luck we might land here again. Soon as the war is over, I mean . . . I'll be back just as fast as I can."

Her eyes closed. She held him, trying to grasp each second for an eternity.

"You ain't sorry about us, Pat?"

"No."

"I ain't either. Just say once more how you love me."

"I love you, Andy."

Then her arms were empty. The door shut. He was gone.

There were no tears left in Pat. All night she stood vigil by the window which looked into the bay. Then she donned her greatcoat and in the hours before dawn walked aimlessly through the streets of Wellington. The misty sunrise found her in the Tinokori Hills, looking down over the harbor. A cold wisp of breeze rushed past her and she drew the coat over her belly where she felt the first kick of life from her unborn child.

Below her, in the murk, were the gray outlines of ships. In silence one by one they slipped from the bay to open sea until they were all gone and the water was empty.

PART FIVE

Prologue

MAJOR WELLMAN, the battalion exec, entered Huxley's office. He dropped a record book on his desk. "Here it is."

Huxley picked up the hefty record and wrinkled his forehead as he opened the cover and looked at the picture of Captain Max Shapiro. "I don't know, Wellman. I don't know but what I'm making a big mistake." He began to thumb through the pages, which told a story of transfers, demotions, courts-martial, citations for valor, promotions. It was a book of contradictions.

Wellman seated himself, knocked the tobacco from his pipe and placed it in his pocket. "This Shapiro, he's quite a legend. Some of the stories I've heard about him are utterly fantastic."

"Don't discount them," Huxley said. "Don't discount a thing you hear about that man."

"I hope you don't mind me asking a question?"

"Of course not."

"This Shapiro is an obvious troublemaker. He's been run out of over a dozen commands and he's got a list of courts-martial as long as your arm. Why did you grab him out of the replacement pool? Matter of fact, you didn't have to grab for him— no one else wanted him."

Huxley smiled. "The book only tells part of the story, Wellman."

"They call him Two Gun. Is he an expert?"

"On the contrary, he's a lousy shot. Has very bad eyes. The story goes that he sneaked up on a Jap at pointblank range and fired two clips of forty-fives and missed every time."

Wellman shrugged. "I don't get it."

Huxley gazed at the ceiling. His mind wandered back. "The first time I heard of him was . . . oh, let's see . . . must have been ten years ago. His father was a ward heeler in Chicago and got him into West Point. He was low man in his class. One summer he followed a girl to Europe and married her. Her parents had it annulled but he was kicked out of the Academy.

355

The next day he joined the Corps as a private. His career's hardly been illustrious. For six years he went up and down in the ranks from Private to Pfc. and back. Brig time, bread and water, readings off—they never had much effect on such a free soul. He wasn't much with his fists but he wasn't afraid to stick out his jaw in a brawl. In Shanghai in 1937 when Smedley Butler sent the Sixth to defend the International Settlement, Shapiro showed his mettle against the Japs."

Huxley paused.

"The turning point in his cruise came two years later. He had drawn guard duty at a general's home at Camp Quantico. The general's eldest daughter became infatuated with the headstrong little Pfc. who was indeed a change from the big, tanned, well-mannered peacetime Marines she had been in contact with all her life. Well, the inevitable happened. Shortly after, she took the news to her father that she was to become the mother of Shapiro's child. He had performed a feat no other Marine had been able to accomplish. The old general was frantic, of course, but did the only sensible thing. They were married secretly and Max Shapiro was shipped to Officers' Training School to obtain a rank befitting the father of the general's daughter's child. Two years later they were divorced. After that Shapiro was bandied about from post to post and hidden behind obscure desks or put in command of remote details. He's always in debt to his men. They call him Max."

"Sounds like a character, all right," said Wellman. By this time he was deep in study of the fantastic record book.

Huxley turned about seriously. "I'm gambling on him. If I can control him, he'll give me a company of infantrymen second to none."

"From the looks of this, you're chewing off quite a bit, Sam."

"I'll get the drop on him. If I don't, I'll be in for trouble."

"I see here," Wellman said, "he just received a second Navy Cross for a patrol on Guadalcanal."

"It was more than a patrol. It saved the Guadalcanal operation."

Wellman relit his pipe and listened.

"The Japs were putting tremendous pressure on the Teneru River line. Thousands of reinforcements landed. Our beachhead semed ready to collapse. Coleman's Raiders landed at Aola Bay, some forty miles east of the beachhead. They set up a regular reign of terror behind the enemy lines. Broke their communications, razed their supplies, and butchered the Japs till they were half insane with fear."

"I remember it well," the exec said. "It gave everyone in the beachhead a chance to breathe. But go on, where does Shapiro fit in?"

"The Raiders spotted a fresh column of Japs heading for the lines. Ed Coleman sent Shapiro and twenty men up to engage the Jap rearguard while he moved his main forces parallel with their column through the jungle. It was a famous tactic of Coleman's to lull them into thinking that the Raiders were behind them. Actually only a few were behind, Shapiro's group and the rest were right alongside, separated by a few yards of jungle. Coleman caught them during a rest period and inside fifteen minutes killed six hundred. At any rate, Shapiro's unit lost contact with the battalion. They voted to stay out and maraud instead of returning to our lines. They stayed out for almost ninety days, using Jap weapons and eating Jap food. God knows how many times they hit and how many supplies they destroyed. They are credited with killing almost five hundred Japs. Twenty-one Raiders, mind you."

The story sounded fantastic indeed.

"They kept going. Malaria, starvation, Japs—nothing could stop them. Until there were only four men left. Seymour, that battle-happy sergeant who boarded our ship on the way to the Canal—remember him?"

Wellman nodded.

"He saw the four of them come back in. They were naked skeletons. Bloody and inhuman looking. They couldn't even speak coherently."

Huxley arose and walked to the window. "Sure, I know I'm getting a hot potato." He wheeled about. "But I've got a feeling that Shapiro is going to pay off one of these days when the chips are down."

My squad gathered around the large shack which housed the Battalion office. There was rampant excitement. Captain Max Shapiro had been transferred into the Second Battalion to take over Fox Company. The notorious and glorious Two Gun Shapiro from Coleman's Raiders who had earned his first Navy Cross in the Makin raid—and a court-martial. He had more decorations and courts-martial than the next three officers in the Corps combined. He was a legend. As the jeep swung into our street we were bursting with excitement to get a glimpse of him.

The jeep stopped before the Battalion office on the dirt road. Our mouths fell open. There sat a short, pudgy man with ringlets of curly black hair, a heavy moustache, and thick-lensed glasses.

"Jesus, is *that* Two Gun Shapiro?"

"Must be."

"Looks like a rabbi to me."

"He sure doesn't look very tough, cousin."

Shapiro debarked from the jeep ungracefully, buckling under the weight of his officer's bag. He asked for instructions and headed for the office, tripping over one of the steps. Disillusioned, we went back to our tents.

Captain Shapiro set his gear in front of the door marked BATTALION COMMANDER, knocked, and without waiting for an answer entered. Sam Huxley glanced up from the paperwork on his desk. The little man stepped up and thrust his hand forward. "Shapiro's the name, Max Shapiro. I'm your new captain, Huxley." Highpockets was on guard. He had just finished pouring through the Captain's fabulous record book. Max withdrew his hand under Huxley's stern glare, seated himself on the Colonel's desk and threw a pack of cigarettes down. "Have a weed, Huxley. What's my company?"

"Have a seat, Shapiro."

"I'm sitting. Call me Max."

"Let's chat, Captain," Huxley said. Shapiro shrugged. "You have quite a record preceding you into this battalion."

"Don't let that scare you."

"On the contrary. I grabbed you out of the replacement pool as first choice. Seems like I had a clear field. No one else wanted any trade with you."

"Call me Max."

"I think we'd better come to a quick understanding. First, you are not in the Raiders any more. Let me say that no man in the Corps respects Ed Coleman more than I do. However, we aren't a roving band here and we like to play Marines."

"Pep talk, huh? Listen, Huxley, I don't aim to give you a bad time if you don't give me one, so just can all the chatter."

"In this battalion we observe military courtesy. You address me as Colonel Huxley at all times. The only time I want individualism is under fire and that is why I asked for you. You can give me the type of company I want out of Fox. However, as long as you are in my command you will observe all rules and regulations down to the letter. Do I make myself clear?"

"Chickenshit outfit."

"Not quite. I realize that we may never gain the stature of the Raiders, but this battalion will take a back seat to none in the Corps. We can outhike, outshoot, and when the chance comes, outfight anyone. We also know how to behave like gentlemen, something you overlooked in your previous tours of duty."

Shapiro reddened and snarled.

"Don't think, Captain Shapiro, you are going to run a three-ring circus here. I'm not going to get rid of you because you're a hot potato, either. You are going to take over Fox Company and you are going to make them the best riflemen in the world, but under my rules." Huxley drew himself to his towering height over the little captain. "If military discipline holds no awe for you, let's just go to the boondocks right now and see who is the boss here."

Max Shapiro's face broadened in a big grin. "I'll be a sonofabitch. Now you talk my language. You and me are going to hit it off swell. I don't care to fight you right now, but I admire your courage," he said, looking far up into Highpocket's face. "Shake, Colonel, and I'll give you a mean, smelly outfit." Huxley and Two Gun Shapiro clasped hands warmly. "Well, sir, I'd like to get acquainted with my crew."

"Very well, Captain. My orderly will show you to your company area."

"By the way—who is my gunnery sergeant and my exec?"

"McQuade is your gunny—hell of a good man. Fox is being reorganized and I have assigned no new exec officer yet . . . by God, I've got just the man for you. *Ziltch!*" The little orderly tumbled in the door. "Get Lieutenant Bryce over here on the double."

1.

NOVEMBER the first came into being with the dawn. The transport *J. Franklin Bell* drifted from Wellington Harbor into open sea and took its place in the convoy. Each hour the water turned a deeper blue and a new ship appeared on the horizon. The last thought of another maneuver faded by the second day. Warmer air enveloped the ship as it moved north toward the equator.

The initial excitement gave way as they settled down on a zigzag course. It appeared we were in for a long ride on a slow freight. Troopship monotony in the crowded quarters set in by the third day. We exercised topside, played poker, wrote letters, sang, and repeatedly cleaned and checked our already spotless equipment.

The packed holds made it advisable to remain topside for as many hours a day as we could. As we slipped into hotter climates the air below became foul and the dulled senses and sluggishness that always appear on a troopship hit us. So much so that it was a real chore to drag into the crammed head for a sticky salt-water shower and a tortured, scraping shave.

It was impossible to ascertain the number of knots we had put between ourselves and New Zealand on the wiggly course north. Once again the water turned green, indicating land. In a searing noonday sun an island loomed over the horizon. We lined the deck, buzzing thankfully for the break in the boredom of the seemingly aimless and endless journey. The word passed about that we were pulling into the French New Hebrides and the island of Efate, south of the Espiritu Santo. We passed the coast line of another typical "Pacific paradise" baking in the sun and caught a glimpse of Havannah Harbor. I had never seen anything like it. It was crammed with more warships than my seabag held socks. The sailors aboard identified the battlewagons *Colorado* and *Tennessee,* the cruisers *Mobile, Birmingham, Portland,* and *Santa Fé.* There were carriers whose decks bristled with fighter planes and dive bombers and I caught sight of Old Mary, the U.S.S. *Maryland.* It did my heart good to see the old girl. I had done two years aboard her as a seagoing bellhop a long time ago and was glad she had been resurrected from her watery grave at Pearl Harbor.

We dropped anchor in Mele Bay and a wild rash of scuttlebutt broke loose. Foul Ball Philips, Lt. General Tod B. Philips, Commander of the Fleet Marine Force, the big skipper himself, was ashore with Admiral Parks of the Fifth Fleet. The story snowballed from ship to ship that we were going back to Wake Island. There were whoops of joy on the *J. Franklin Bell.* Surely, we reckoned, the Sixth Marines would draw the honor of establishing the beachhead.

With Wake Island and revenge in our minds, the New Hebrides hellhole held little fascination. We wanted to get under way. Even stories of the rare collection of Army nurses there held small interest.

We held maneuvers before departing. A dress rehearsal with Foul Ball himself and his cigar in attendance. I was worried because the landing went off without a hitch. An old super-situation of long-forgotten schooldays in the dramatic club came to mind. Something about a bad dress rehearsal meaning a good opening night. I would have settled at that point for the debacle at Hawke Bay.

As the rest of us pranced about on the beach, Danny, Levin and all the rest of the boys connected with naval gunfire were transferred to a destroyer in Mele Bay to further acquaint themselves with their operation.

The grizzled Marines lifted themselves over the side of the destroyer *Vandervort.* Their week aboard the troopship made them a sharp contrast to the clean sailors in appearance. They were smelly in their stained dungarees. From them hung implements of death: carbines, ammo, assorted knives, and other tools of their trade. The sailors took a step back at the awesome sight of their bearded guests. The Marines looked vicious. At arm's length the sailors engaged them in conversation and showed them through the ship, explaining the complicated mechanisms of gunfire that their messages from the beach would set in motion. The *Vandervort* headed for open sea for gunfire practice. The Marines paraded about the deck like conquering pirates, making no effort to hold their contempt for the Navy's role in the operation.

As the destroyer hit the drink and opened speed, she began a slow roll. As the *Vandervort* rolled, the Marines turned from cocky to green. The awe the sailors held for the nation's finest took a deep dip. They stood by, flabbergasted, as the wicked-looking Marines lined the rail in unison and upchucked into the ocean.

We sailed from Port Efate, an anxious division. It was the most tremendous sight I had ever seen, overpowering. Around the gray transports rode the mightiest armada of ships ever assembled. The *Mary*, proudly to the fore, was our flagship. About her, ten thousand guns of the Fifth Fleet moved steadily north, filling the horizon from one end to the other. Ships everywhere, gray merchants of death inching closer to the defensive outer crust of the Japanese Empire.

Headquarters Company filed into the officers' wardroom for briefing. At last we could get confirmation that we were returning to Wake Island.

Sweaty, dungaree clad, we seated ourselves about the floor, scratching at the raw saltwater shaves demanded daily by Huxley. Major Wellman entered, ordered us at ease, and tacked a large map on one of the walls. We settled back.

"The smoking lamp is lit," he said loading up his pipe. With a bayonet he pointed to the map. My heart sank. It wasn't Wake. Instead I saw a weird-shaped island, somewhat like a seahorse. Above it, in code word: HELEN. A second and larger map showed a string of islands ranging from several square yards to several miles in length. I could count nearly forty of them. Each island bore the name of a girl: SARAH, NELLIE, AMY, BETTY, KAREN, down to the last one, CORA. It was an atoll. Most of us knew little about the atolls of the Central Pacific and were puzzled by the legend on the map which indicated that Helen was merely two miles long and several hundred yards wide. What kind of an objective was that for an entire division of men?

"O.K., men," Wellman said, "everybody comfortable? . . . don't answer that." (Laughter.) "This sexy-looking broad is known as Helen. Don't let her size throw you. We are entering Micronesia, the Central Pacific. This island is a coral atoll. Geologists tell us that these islands were formed by depressions in the ocean. Larger islands have sunk and left these hard-shelled little coral ones above the surface."

"Sir," he was interrupted, "I see that this atoll is just like a circle chain. How deep is the water between the islands?"

"You can wade from island to island when the tide is in. When it is out you can cross without even getting your feet wet. From the lagoon side, that is. Now, there is a barrier reef fringing the entire atoll." Wellman relit his pipe and laid down the bayonet. "The Japs have five thousand hand-picked troops on Helen, or Betio, as it is really called. The Micronesian atolls run in several groups—the Ellice Islands, the Gilberts, and farther north, the Marshalls. As you know, we seized the Ellice group without opposition and our next step up is the Gilberts. The Gilberts will be the springboard to the Marshalls."

He crossed the room, stepping gingerly over several seated men, to a master map of the Pacific. "These chains of atolls stand between Hawaii and the inner Jap defenses. We can cut several thousands of miles by taking this punch right in his guts. I know you boys have all heard the good news about the Third Division hitting Bougainville. You can see that we are coming up from underneath in the Solomons and now this is a center smash in the Gilberts. This operation will put us right within striking distance of the big Jap bases: Truk, Palau, and even the Marianas. Maybe one of these days we'll be up there ourselves."

"How about Wake, Major?"

"I know how we all feel about Wake but the strategy appears to be to bypass it."

"Crap."

"Wake is relatively unimportant to us now. We all want a crack at it, but let's get back to Helen." Wellman went through the plan to strike through the lagoon. Logic of the lowest private asked about Bairiki or Sarah. Wellman told us we were Marines and we didn't fight to starve them out, but to kill them. Then he informed us that an Army division would be capturing Makin at the same time we hit Betio.

"Sir, didn't three hundred Raiders flatten Makin over a year ago?"

"Correct, Coleman's Raid."

"Why the hell do they need a whole division of Army to retake it?"

"Aw, fellows," Wellman said, "they're liable to trip over a slit trench going in. You know the answer." (Laughter and war whoops.)

"Any broads . . . er . . . I mean natives, Major?"

"Yes, several thousand. They are Polynesians like the Maoris. They are friendly and have been British subjects for years.

Missionaries are on the atoll but the chances are that we won't see them. Anyhow, I believe Chaplain Peterson and Father McKale are preparing a booklet about the natives." (More laughter.)

"How about mosquitoes?"

"Not of the malaria variety."

"Phew."

The briefing continued. Wellman related the plans for the terrific shelling the Japs were in for from the Navy and air. He didn't discount the possibility of another Kiska, a dry run. As the meeting wore on, I began to feel as though they were overestimating the Jap strength on Betio. It seemed silly to commit an entire division to this speck of an island. From the way that Wellman spoke and the pulse of the men in the room as he described the softening-up process, I decided this was going to be a cinch. At last the Major got around to combat assignments.

"The Second Marines have been chosen as Combat Team One. They will assault Blue Beaches One, Two, and Three. In case they need help, the Eighth Marines are being used as Division reserve." Wellman braced for what he knew was coming.

"What about us, Major?"

"Yes, sir, did the Sixth come just for the boat ride?"

Wellman threw up his hands in disgust. "We are Corps reserve. Reserve for both Betio and the army at Makin. We'll go wherever we are needed."

"The goddam Second gets all the breaks!"

"We wuz robbed. . . ."

After the outburst, the remainder of the meeting was held in furious silence. We were getting a slow burn at the thought of once more being a bridesmaid. Dejected and cursing, we thought of the long hard months of training for nothing. Humiliated not only by the Marines—the Sixth was going to be reserve for a doggie outfit. We mumbled our way out of the wardroom. Easy Company was lined up to await their briefing.

"Lousy deal," Burnside mumbled as he approached me at the rail. We lit up and scanned the hundreds of ships.

"This is a waste of the taxpayer's money if you ask me," L.Q. said.

"I babied that goddam TCS jeep for six months and now they tell me I got to go ashore with a TBX. Can't take the jeep," Danny griped.

"Crap, piss, and corruption," drawled Speedy.

"Now the Second and Eighth will never let us live in peace. Oh sure, the Commandant is watching *this* outfit . . . bullcrap, little Eva."

"What the hell did Major Wellman say the name of the atoll was?"

"I forget ... Ta ... something ... What was it, Mac?"

"Tarawa," I answered.

"Yeah, that was it. Tarawa."

2.

THE convoy sweltered north. The hot days topside gave way to unbearable nights in the cluttered, humid holds. We were humiliated by our assignment. We hoped that the Second Marines would have an easy time and they would shift the Sixth to an alternate landing. While doing duty in the radio room I discovered another small room that was used for storing surplus kapok lifejackets. I got permission for the squad to sleep up there and it was a wonderful change from the hell-holes below that made sleep impossible. The jackets made wonderful mattresses.

The armada could proceed only as fast as the slowest ship and our course was a jagged line. One transport's rudder stuck and lent a little excitement to the monotony. The ship circled crazily as a score of destroyers swooped in and surrounded her until she untangled herself and caught up with us. Along with cleaning our weapons over and over we memorized our assigned frequencies and codes. The new code name for the Sixth was LINCOLN; we were LINCOLN WHITE. For the greater part of each day my crew stayed on the huge signal deck which gave a panoramic view of the masses of ships that pointed over north. They practiced flag signals and took over watches on the blinker lamps for ship to ship contact. All radio transmission was out since it sent waves which might be picked up by the Jap submarines lurking near the convoy.

With each hour came another rumor. The latest was that the Japs had taken a powder ... an hour later the story circulated that they had moved twenty thousand more men in from the Marshalls. However, up to the last moment none of us held much respect for Helen. The attitude of the convoy was almost an indifferent calm.

Then the calm turned to deadly silence as we came into feeling range of our objective. You could almost tell by the pulse of the engine and the movement of the men that Tarawa atoll was near.

We reduced speed as another convoy equal to ours in size passed us. It was the Army division heading for Makin. Dry run or not, reserve or not, each man cleaned his weapon again, made his peace with God, wrote his letter home and waited. Then a creeping tenseness and flurry of contradictory scuttlebutt began to make us all feel uneasy about the whole operation.

Advance harbingers of the convoy parked out of range of Betio's batteries. Cruisers of the Fifth Fleet opened the shelling on the island, shaped like a sea horse and coded with the name of a woman. It was D-day minus three. Throughout the first night, bursts of orange popped on the skyline. A penciled streak of light sped into the coral rock and spent its venom on the already battered bastion. Next day came more bombers from Phoenix, Ellice, and Samoa, followed by angry little fighters from the carriers which raked the island.

Admiral Shibu and his five thousand little yellow men lay behind walls of concrete and waited angrily. Dug into solid coral behind ten-foot-thick concrete with reinforced steel walls piled with many feet of coconut logs and sand bags, they laughed as ton upon exploding ton of shells blew down the coconut trees. Their ire mounted. They waited.

Levin walked to his beloved TCS jeep, which was lashed to the deck. He inspected it for the hundredth time and sighed at the thought of having to leave it behind when he landed. He seated himself on the hatch and leaned back to catch a glimpse of the dying sun. Speedy came alongside him slowly. Levin got up to leave:

"Levin."

"What do you want?"

"I'd like to talk to you for a minute."

"I ain't looking for no trouble," Levin spat.

"Levin," Speedy continued, "since we're going into combat and . . . well, what the hell, let's shake hands and forget the crap."

A smile lit up Levin's homely face. "Sure, Speedy, put her there." They clasped hands warmly.

"Er, Levin, the guys was talking it over and . . . well . . . we all felt that . . . well here, Levin." He handed Levin a sheet of paper.

He squinted to read it in the fading light: *The Dit-happy Armpit Smellers of Huxley's Whores. . . .*

"It's kind of a club we made up a long time ago. We sort of figure that you are a member now. All the guys signed it. You can sign my copy if you want to."

"Jees, thanks, Speedy. Here, have a cigarette."

We stood topside as the guns of the Fifth Fleet leveled the distant palms and split the dawn with salvo after salvo. Ear-shattering bursts and lines of shells following a red course into Betio. The rest of the troops were locked below but I had my crew in the spare room by the radio room. Hour after hour the battlewagons cracked and thundered and reeled awesomely under the impact of the explosives they were hurling into the tiny coral speck.

"Gawd," Andy whispered, "nothing could live after this."

"The whole island is on fire."

"Gawd."

"Here come the cruisers in closer." A smashing broadside was hurled from the *Portland* and another from the *Mobile*. Little destroyers cockily moved into pointblank range with their five-inchers blazing. Flares of light belched from the guns of the warships with every salvo until the dawn became daylight.

I checked my watch as we dropped anchor in the transport area. The Second Marines awaited word from the *Maryland* whose code name was ROCKY.

H-Hour crept close and every ship of the fleet poured it on except the screening destroyers, which circled the transports on the alert for enemy submarines. Admiral Parks had claimed he would sink Betio. I wouldn't have argued with him.

"Somehow," Danny said, "I can't help but feel sorry for those Japs. Suppose it was us?"

The punishing spectacle rose to new heights until Betio faded from view behind a shroud of rising smoke.

Then it became very quiet.

Excited troops of the Second Marines clambered topside to their landing stations.

"I hope the Navy left some Japs for us."

"Man, what a hammering they gave old Helen."

"Now hear this, now hear this: Team One, over the side."

"Let's go, boys, over the side."

"Man, I bet the pogey bait Sixth is burning up."

"That's us, always a bride, never a bridesmaid."

"Come on, you guys, step it up."

Fifteen minutes before the Second Marines were scheduled to hit Blue Beach, a platoon of picked men, the Scouts and Snipers, was sent in to clear the long pier on Betio. It ran between Blue Beach Two and Blue Beach Three and jutted out from the island for five hundred yards, running over the reef to deep water. The pier had been used to unload supplies and also as a seaplane ramp.

Scouts and Snipers, under command of rugged Lieutenant Roy, closely resembled the Raiders in operation.

The battle plan unfolded in the minutes before H-Hour. The big warships withdrew and left only the relative quiet of the destroyers pounding the immediate landing area. Minesweepers were operating in the lagoon. The Second Marines were in their landing craft and circled the control boat like Indians circling a covered-wagon train. Then they began the perilous transfer to the alligators. The first setback beamed into the operations room of the flagship *Maryland*. The smoke screen had to be called off. The wind was in the wrong direction.

Tod Philips fumed. He wanted smoke cover for the assault wave. He asked for a time check as heavy bombers were due from Samoa to pattern-bomb Betio with daisycutters, missiles which exploded, scattering shrapnel over the ground. The second setback came in. The planes were overloaded and had been forced to turn back after losses while taking off.

As the Second Marines continued their transfer to the alligators the sky became an umbrella of dive bombers and strafing planes which roared in at treetop level, raking and pinpointing Helen from one end to the other. Suddenly, with only half their passes made, the planes returned to their carriers. It had proved impossible to bomb Helen effectively. The flame and smoke were too thick to see targets on the island.

Without a single shot having been fired by the enemy, the operations room of the *Maryland* became uneasy. As the fighter planes moved back, the control board radioed: WE HAVE LOST SEVEN ALLIGATORS AND ALL PERSONNEL IN TRANSFERRING TROOPS FROM LANDING CRAFT.

The shock of the drowning of over a hundred men fell hard on the steamy, smoke-filled operations room aboard the flagship. Foul Ball Philips bit his cigar in half. The confused aides looked to the generals and Admiral Parks for instructions.

"Deploy the remaining alligators and stand by," General Philips ordered calmly.

It was no Kiska! A strange silence fell after the roaring attack and we waited breathlessly as the Second Marines straightened their line of alligators to move in. Then the room shook! I was smashed into a bulkhead. Danny tumbled on top of me. We got to our feet, dazed. The sailors about us were pale and white lipped.

The Japs were firing back!

We looked into each other's anxious eyes. We were shocked out of our complacency. The Division was in for a fight.

"I can't understand it," Admiral Parks complained aboard the *Maryland* at about the same time. "We hit them with everything in the book."

"Goddammit to hell, Parks," Philips roared, "those are eight-inch coastal guns they are shooting at us. Get them out of there before they hit a transport!"

"Move the *Mobile* and *Birmingham* in on target O-T, immediately."

"Aye, aye, sir."

"I don't understand it," Parks repeated.

General Bryant, the Division commander, leaned forward. "I'll explain it to you, Admiral. Naval guns shoot flat trajectories. They don't shoot underground."

Philips banged his fat fist on the table. "Good God, do you realize we may not have killed a single Jap bastard during the whole bombardment?"

"Any word from Roy's Scouts and Snipers?"

"No, sir. They are still standing by."

"We better not send them into that pier until we get those coastal guns out," Bryant said. "British guns they took from Singapore. The British make good guns."

A pale and trembling aide stepped up to the table. "Sir," he sputtered, "we knocked out our own radios during the bombardment. We are out of communication."

"Use flares, anything, man! Use walkie-talkies. But stay in with the control boat."

"We are in for it, Tod," Bryant whispered.

"Sir, the destroyer *Ringgold* has been hit in the lagoon."

"How badly?"

"They said they'll stay in till they run out of ammo or sink."

"Good. Order them to keep firing."

Philips turned to a sweating aide. "Send in Roy's Scouts and Snipers. Have *Wilson* stand by."

"Yes, sir."

"We can't hold off H-Hour forever. I hope to God our boys are right today, Don."

The pent-up wrath of the Japanese burst on Lieutenant Roy's platoon as it hit the end of the pier. They were caught in a murderous crossfire from the bunkers. The Scouts and Snipers dropped like flies as they edged up under the pilings toward Blue Beach. Roy worked like a madman to clear the enemy from their cover. He grenaded and bayoneted with his platoon through waist-deep water. He flushed the Japs from the pilings, put his foot on Blue Beach Two, and ducked behind the seawall. He turned to his radio operator.

"Tell them the pier is clear."

"You're hit," the radioman said.

"Tell them that the pier is clear," Roy repeated as he wrapped a bandage about his shattered arm and deployed the ten remaining men of the original fifty-five.

Finally the signal was given to proceed to the Blue Beaches.

As the alligators filled with Marines neared the edge of the barrier reef where the pier ended, they were greeted with an avalanch of gunfire. A load of men scrambled up on the pier. Inside of two minutes they all lay dead.

A correspondent touched the arm of a young boy and shouted into his ear as the slow, clumsy alligator bumbled its way through the bursting shrapnel. "What's your name, kid?"

"Martini. Pfc Martini from San Francisco . . . I'm a machine gunner."

"Are you scared, Martini?"

"Hell no. I'm a Marine!"

"How old are you, Martini?"

"Eighteen, sir. . . ." The boy grabbed the newspaperman's arm. "I'm scared sick, really, but I can't let the other guys know. . . ."

Those were his last words. The shell of a Jap dual purpose gun exploded inside the alligator.

Four alligators abreast moved in on Blue Beach One creeping up to the barrier reef. One rolled over under the impact of a direct hit, sending bodies and parts of bodies careening over the chalky waters. Another and another was hit and finally all four were gone.

"What's going on in there?" Danny asked me.

"We haven't heard from them yet, we don't know," I said.

Three alligators moved for Blue Beach Two. They became helplessly entangled in the rolls of barbed wire that jutted from the water. The Marines scrambled out and were machine gunned to death before they reached the beach.

"We haven't heard from Colonel Carpe yet," Bryant said.

"Let me see those dispatches," Philips said.

"No word from him, sir, no word."

An aide sprinted in and threw a message down: *Wilson White commander killed.*

"Dammit! What is Carpe doing in there?"

"Sir, the *Ringgold* has been hit again. She moved in almost to the beach, knocking out some Jap 4.7s"

"Any message from her."

"The *Ringgold* says she'll continue firing."

Brigadier General Snipes rushed to the table and placed a message in Philips' hands. It was from Colonel Carpe at Blue Beach Three. Carpe was running the operation from the beach.

OPPOSITION OVERWHELMING. WE CAN'T HOLD. EIGHTY PER CENT CASUALTIES. ARE PINNED DOWN BEHIND THE SEAWALL. SEND REINFORCEMENTS OR ELSE.

"How many alligators do we have left?"

"About twenty-five, sir."

"Get the rest of *Wilson* in. Use the alligators first, then send them in with landing craft."

"Tod!" Bryant shouted. "They'll have to wade in from a mile out."

"We have no choice."

Pfc. Nick Mazoros, a lost radio operator, slushed through waist-deep water stumbling for cover from piling to piling under the pier. He struggled to keep his walkie-talkie above the salt water. A spray from the bullets whining around him sent up a shower. He fell into a pothole, sinking to his knees, then quickly bounced up. A crossfire ripped in. He fought to decide whether to dump his radio and go underwater for protection or try to make it in with her. He kept his radio. Mazoros dropped exhausted on Blue Beach Two dragging his body at last to the cover of the four-foot seawall of logs.

The commander ran up to him. "Is that radio working, son?"

"I think so, sir."

"Sergeant! Take three men and escort this man to Colonel Carpe at Blue Beach Three. Stay close to the wall. We don't want to lose that radio."

"His hand is shot away," the sergeant said pointing to Mazoros' right arm.

"I'll be O.K.," Mazoros answered. "Let's move out."

The Second Marines' desperate toehold on Betio consisted of fifteen yards of sand from the water to the seawall on Blue Beach Two and Three. On Blue Beach One it was twenty yards inland, dug into foxholes in the jagged coral. Carpe's headquarters was behind the concrete wall of a blown-up Jap bunker which had been captured with the sacrifice of twenty Marine lives. The seawall which now protected the beleaguered assault wave might well turn out to mark their graves. To vault the seawall into Jap positions was madness. Every square inch of ground was covered by interlocking lanes of fire from the enemy. To go over the wall meant instant death; to stay behind it meant counterattack. They had only fifteen yards to retreat.

Carpe propped himself against the bunker and gave orders. The blood on his leg had dried and was beginning to smell putrid. He called on knowledge beyond his capabilities to hold off the impending disaster that was threatening the Second Marines.

Men came on to reinforce the slim beachhead. The story of the alligators was repeated. Shelled from the water, tangled in the barbed wire, strafed before they hit the beach . . . but on they came, slushing forward. The landing craft hooked up on the fringing reef a mile out and dropped their ramps. The waves of Second Marines plunged into neck-deep water, their rifles held at high port. They waded in.

A pilot in the spotter seaplane of the *Maryland* landed in the sea and scrambled up the Jacob's ladder to the deck. He was hysterical. "I came right over their heads!" he screamed. "They are dropping in the water like flies but they keep moving in. They keep coming and the Japs riddle them . . . coming through the water with their rifles high!"

On they came. They marched the last mile in the lagoon silently. A Marine folded over . . . a deep red blot of blood swelled from him . . . the body slid down and bobbed in the rippling waves . . . the red faded into a larger pink circle. Yet on they came.

In the searing tropical day the landing craft buzzed to and from the transports rushing another load of lambs to the sacrificial altar. More Marines were dumped a mile out on the treacherous reef and waded into the never ceasing staccato of Japanese guns.

Carpe yelled to Mazoros, the radio man, "Dammit, son, can't you get that thing working?"

"I'm sorry, sir. Salt water got into the battery and it's ruined."

Carpe grabbed his field phone as it rang. "Violet speaking," he said.

"Hello, Carpe, this is Wilson White. The division band is coming in with stretchers and plasma."

"What's the situation over there?" Carpe asked.

"Bad. Our sector is littered with wounded. The corpsmen are doing the best they can."

"How's your ammo holding?"

"We're getting low."

"Have you got any TBY batteries? We can't reach Rocky. I wonder if the dumb bastards know what the hell is going on in here."

There was no answer.

"Hello, Wilson White, hello . . . this is Carpe . . . hello, god-dammit!" He replaced the phone. "Runner, get to Wilson White and find out if their commander has been hit."

A sergeant ran up to Carpe. "We spotted some TBY batteries over the wall, sir."

"Over the wall? How the hell did they get there?"

"Damned if I know."

Mazoros was on his feet.

"Where are you going, son?"

"To get those batteries."

"Like hell you are. Get under cover—there's a shortage of radio operators in these parts."

Before the words had passed from Carpe's lips, seven Marines were crawling up under a Jap machine gun where the batteries lay. Six got killed; one returned with the precious articles.

3.

WE were locked in the hold. No one slept in the crammed quarters. There were whispers in the dim light, of men crouched on the edge of their bunks waiting for word from the Second Marines.

"We ought to be in there helping."

"The poor bastards."

A rifle dropped from an upper bunk startling everyone. A Marine worked his way over a pile of packs and boxes and wiped the sweat from his chest.

"Why can't we make a night landing?"

"Them assholes on the *Maryland* don't know what they're doing."

"Wonder if the Japs have counterattacked?"

I walked into the head and splashed my face with sticky salt water. It gave little relief. I wanted to sleep but there was sleep for no one. We waited sullen and tense for word from Blue Beach. I rubbed the stubble on my chin, thankful at least that I wouldn't have to shave in the morning. If I didn't get out of this goddam hold, I felt, soon I'd be too groggy to walk. I stepped into the hatchway. Andy grabbed me from behind.

"I want to tell you something," he whispered.

"What?"

"I've had the red ass all this trip. I was pissed off because I had to leave New Zealand."

"Shut up."

"Let me finish. I was glad when I heard we were going to be reserve. I wanted to be able to write to Pat and tell her, so she wouldn't worry. I don't feel like that no more, Mac. We should be on that beach. I don't know nothing about farms and wives and nothing like that. I just know I want to get in there and kill some Japs."

"I'm glad you feel that way, Andy."

"I don't know what it is, but I know that sometimes there

is something more important than just two people. I . . . I don't
rightly know what I mean. Only this waiting is getting me. . . ."

On the beach Pfc. Mazoros repeated his instructions for the
tenth time to the rifleman on how to operate the radio. His
voice became weaker. He had been badly wounded and life
ebbed from him. He rolled over to the ground, dead. The rifleman slowly lifted the earphones from Mazoros' head and
placed them on his own.

Over the seawall, thrice wounded Lieutenant Roy was leading his Scouts and Snipers from pillbox to pillbox with
dynamite. At last he fell dead from his fourth wound.

A white moon hung low. It lit up the wreckage. The long
pier shone like a silver ray through the breezeless, sticky
night. The tide crept up on the Marines crouching behind the
seawall until there was no beach left. They lay in water. For a
hundred yards, side by side, the wounded lay, speaking only to
refuse aid or whisper a last prayer. No one cried out. Beyond
the seawall, littered among machine gun nests and bunkers, a
hundred more lay bleeding to death. Yet none of them moved
or cried for help to come and get them. For they knew that a
cry would bring a dozen mates recklessly to the rescue and perhaps to their deaths. No one cried the anguish of the hot burning
in his belly or the unbearable pain of a ripped limb. The
wounded lay in silence with thoughts of a land far away . . . no
one cried.

Landing craft moved for the pier with life-giving blood and
death-dealing ammunition. They dumped their loads on the
pier's edge, five hundred yards into the lagoon. There was no
call for volunteers as each man silently assigned himself to
wade out and bring supplies in through the rattle of sniper fire
from the pilings, and through the storm of bullets and shells
that other desperate men, the Japanese, turned on them from
the bunkers.

Sitting in water, with his back propped against the seawall,
a newspaper correspondent squinted as he held his paper toward
the moon's light and wrote with a pencil stub: *It is hard to believe what I see about me. As I write this story I do not know
whether you will ever read it, for tomorrow morning will find
me dead. I am on the island of Betio, on a coral atoll named
Tarawa in the Gilbert Islands. Like the men around me, I
await a counterattack. We all know we are going to die, yet
there is no confusion, no shouting, no outward sign of nervous
strain or of a crack in our mental armor. I didn't realize that
men could show such courage. Never have men, and boys,
faced sacrifice so gallantly. Bunker Hill, Gettysburg, the Ala-*

mo, Belleau Wood . . . well, today we have a new name to add:
TARAWA. For this is the hour of the Second Marine Division,
the Silent Second.

An aide led a small, dark and grimy sailor into the operations room on the *Maryland*. The bleary-eyed, depressed commanders paid small notice as they waited desperately for word from Carpe.

"Sir," the aide said to General Philips, "this man is a coxswain from the *Haywood*. He has a plan you might be able to use."

Philips looked up at the pilot of the landing craft which had made fifteen runs to Blue Beach during the day. "What is it, son?"

"Sir," the sailor said, "the supplies aren't getting in."

"We know that."

"I have an idea that might be able to clear the snipers from under the pier and let us use it as protection."

Tod Philips had long ago learned that wisdom and improvisation can often come from the lowest ranks. He invited the worn sailor to sit and asked his plan.

"I have found a spot in the barrier reef that is slightly lower than the rest of the reef. I think I can get a shallow draft boat over it if it is lightly loaded. The tide is up to the seawall and that will give an extra lift. If I had a crew of flamethrowers I could make a couple of quick passes right next to the pier, burn the snipers from under the pilings, and give the Marines a chance to move in."

"They'll rip your boat to pieces, sailor. How about an alligator?"

"An alligator would be too slow. If you have an old type Higgins' boat or a skipper's craft with just three or four men in it, sir, I'm sure I'd be able to get enough speed up. With a break we can make it."

"It's worth a try," General Bryant said.

"The ammo and plasma aren't getting in now. We can't gun them from under the pier and they're picking off the Marines as fast as they wade out for supplies," the sailor argued.

"What about the Jap fire from land?" Philips asked.

"It's wild, sir. They're pouring it into the pier but if we have control of the pilings we'll be able to get most of the stuff through underneath."

"Snipes! Get the Eighteenth Marines. Have a flamethrower team stand by. Have an alternate team in ready in case something goes wrong with the first pass."

The sailor arose and extended his hand. "Thanks for the opportunity, sir. I won't let you down."

"By the way," Bryant said, "what is your name, sailor?"

"Bos'n's Mate Herman Rommel, sir."

"Not any relation to Rommel the German Field Marshal by any chance?" Philips asked, half amused.

"The sonofabitch is a cousin, sir." The little sailor left.

For a moment everyone looked at the tired general. The butts of twenty cigars lay dispersed about the table and floor. Tod Philips sat there, slumped down in his chair. Each tick of the clock brought the red-rimmed eyes up for a look. They had been there for six hours.

"No counterattack yet. Carpe has the new radio," Foul Ball spoke. His nervous hands reached for a cigarette.

"They've got something up their sleeve, Tod. Or they are rubbing it in and waiting for the Kill."

"Any report on Jap mortar fire?"

"Sporadic."

Some thought the General had lifted his head and said, "Thanks, God." But it must have been a mistake, for this was Foul Ball Philips and he knew no God except the Marine Corps. He rose and gave an order.

"Contact the Eighth Marines. Have them move in at zero six hundred. Contact Carpe and tell him I want every man to go over the seawall when the Eighth hits the barrier reef. He'll have to move or we'll never make it. Snipes, you go in on the first wave and relieve Carpe. Tell him he's due for a Congressional Medal—come on, you people! I need a cigar."

On Blue Beach One the stench of death was everywhere. No wind, not the slightest zephyr to drive away the smell. The odor of rotted bodies, gangrened limbs and dried blood. Caked with layers of coral dust, cut, bleeding, thirsty, worn beyond endurance, the living clutched their rifles in disbelief as the first rays of a new dawn crept to the edge of the horizon.

The silent wounded lifted their gory heads to the lagoon.

The Eighth Marines were coming in!

Dawn brought new life to the Second Marines. They poised their battered bodies for a surge over the seawall. Colonel Carpe lifted himself, reeling to his feet. His aide phoned the order along Blue Beach: "Fix bayonets . . . prepare to advance."

The Tenth Marines, who still had workable artillery, clattered and rumbled a weak and insufficient covering fire.

Carpe drew his pistol and shouted down the line of men crouched behind the seawall, "Let's get the yellow sons of bitches!"

Like the dead arisen from the graves on Allhallow's Eve, the remains of the Second Regiment burst over the wall to the attack. Admiral Shibu had been killed in the night, his plan of counterattack locked in his mind. After hours of futile argument, the Japanese had been caught off guard. Their fire was concentrated on the reinforcements coming through the lagoon. Before they could shift the hailstorm of lead, the Second had cut across the arced fantail of the island which was designated as Green Beach. With extraordinary energy the Marines slugged forward for a hundred yards and cut off the fortifications in that zone. Then the momentum of their surge petered out and they were unable to advance further. They dug in on the precious new ground and waited for the Eighth to fill the holes in their blasted lines.

A slug had ripped Colonel Carpe's tough hide. This time he dropped, unable to rise. He was dragged back to the CP, protesting. At last he consented to accept aid if it could be given to him near the phone where he could maintain control of the battle. It was in this condition that General Snipes limped up to him.

"Hello, Carpe."

"Get hit, Snipes?"

"Stepped into a pothole coming in, twisted my ankle. What's the situation?"

"We made a few yards, got control of Green Beach. How are the reinforcements coming?"

"Lousy. They're giving them hell again."

By midday, what was left of the Eighth Marines was ashore and only fifty more blood-drenched yards had been gained against the paralyzing fire of the enemy. Reports of stiffer opposition came in to the command post with each grueling yard gained. Locked in close combat, the men of Japan and America fought and killed each other with the fury and hatred and passion of bereaved animals. At last Snipes radioed to the *Maryland*: VIOLET TO ROCKY: THE ISSUE IS IN DOUBT.

The drive had run out of gas. Snipes the ex-Raider, master of hand-to-hand death, snarled and spat at the vicious courage of his foe. Cursing and hoping for a sudden reversal, he finally admitted, "We'll have to ask them to release the Sixth Marines."

A salty old gunner nearby snarled, "Them goddam pogey baits will come in now and swear they won the battle all by themselves."

"Listen, you bastard," Snipes growled, "I don't care if it takes a bunch of Zulu headhunters throwing spears. We need help."

"Have you heard from Paxton at Makin?" Philips asked.

"Yes, sir. They are proceeding slowly against heavy sniper fire. They estimate six hundred Japs."

"Well, we've got six thousand here. Radio him that he's on his own. We're sending the Sixth Marines in."

"Aye aye, sir."

"Tod," Bryant said, "we'd better land them through Green Beach. I'm afraid to try that lagoon again."

"What do you think, Parks?"

"There are minefields and barbed wire and tank traps," the Admiral said.

"If we take another bath in the lagoon we may be beaten," Bryant argued. "This is the last thing we've got. If we don't get the drive rolling quick we're done. We can't count on help from Paxton."

"You're right!" Philips snapped. "The Army will be farting around on Makin for a week. Send Lincoln Red in through Green Beach. Hold Lincoln Blue in ready."

A message from an aircraft carrier fell on the General's desk: AIR TO ROCKY. SEVERAL HUNDRED JAPS SEEN WADING FROM HELEN TO SARAH.

"We'd better land Lincoln White on Bairiki, clear it and set up the rest of artillery. If the other two battalions of the Sixth make a breakthrough, the Japs might pull a retreat to Bairiki. Besides, we'll need every piece of artillery we can get into operation."

"I hope opposition on Bairiki is light. Whose outfit is Lincoln White?"

"Huxley's . . . Sam Huxley's."

"Oh, the hiking fool."

"Right. Contact Lincoln Red. Move to Green Beach at once. Get Huxley and tell him to clean out Bairiki and stop any further retreat. As soon as he clears the island have all remaining artillery move in and set up to blast. Don, this is it . . . the blue chips are down. The pogey baits had better be on the ball!"

4.

"*NOW hear this, now hear this. Marines, man your landing stations.*"

Huxley's Whores scrambled up the ladder topside. Nervous chatter filled the crowded deck of the *J. Franklin Bell* in the high-noon heat.

"O.K., godammit," I ordered. "Fall in and cover down. Answer up when your name is called."

"I hope they saved something for us."

"Did you hear? The First Battalion is going wild."

"Quiet down, you people."

Sam Huxley paced the steel deck to our station. Without a word he looped his long legs over the rail and jumped into the landing craft which hung from the davits. Ziltch, with much more difficulty under the load of Huxley's maps, plopped in after.

"O.K., girls," I said. "First rank move in. Hang on to those guidelines until we are lowered into the water. On the double!"

There was confusion as to our destination. For an hour we circled about the control boat. It wasn't long before the bumpy ride had rocked us green-gilled.

"If you got to puke, puke inside. Puke outside and it blows back in your face."

The landing craft plodded into the lagoon and chopped and bounced over the waves. We huddled in close to try to duck the splashes of spray that splattered over the ramp. It seemed we moved at a drone's pace for mile after mile.

I was in the front of the boat. It continued past the smoking island of Betio till I caught sight of the slanted outline of Sarah or Bairiki, on a downward dip. She was a sharp contrast to the hell in back of me. Palms and white sands beckoned almost lovingly.

Crouched up front, a sudden paralyzing thought shot through my mind. These might be my last minutes on earth. Another ten minutes might find me dead. As the boat dropped I caught a glimpse of the treetops on Sarah and I was struck with a vision of a cross on the coral shore with my name on it. I got queasy all over and for a moment wanted to jump out into the water and get away. I felt the palms of my hands sweat and wiped them against my dungarees just in time to catch a deluge of salt water down the back of my neck. What if a thousand Japs were waiting for us on Bairiki? What if we caught the same thing the Second and Eighth got? We'd be dead ducks . . . we had nothing in back of us!

A crazy thought repeated itself over and over: I hadn't brushed my teeth that morning. I didn't want to die with a bad taste in my mouth. It annoyed me, I didn't know why. I wanted to brush my teeth.

My pent-up tension vanished as our harrowing wait on the landing craft lengthened. I didn't want to avenge any one or any thing. All I knew was that I was Mac and wanted to live. I didn't want to get shot in the water . . . I must have been mad to think of a thousand enemies. I wanted them all gone.

A numbness crept over me. Coward . . . coward . . . coward, I said to myself. After all these years. . . . I tried to shake it off as the boats pushed close to Bairiki.

But I was wrapped in fear, fear that I had never known be-

fore. I felt that any second I would have to stand up and scream
out the horror inside me.

The boat bucked furiously, throwing me flat and sending
me skidding over the slippery deck. The front ramp buckled
with a clang of lead on steel. The Japs were gunning us!

I felt urine running down my leg . . . I was afraid I was going
to vomit. The red glint of a tracer bullet whizzed over the
water in our direction. The boat reared and crashed hard,
flinging me into the ramp. I turned around. Half the men were
puking. Then I saw Huxley . . . he was sallow and trembling. I
had seen men freeze before and had had contempt for them.
But now the stiffening fear was taking me too . . . I must not
let it happen!

"Get the control boat!" Huxley ordered. "Have them contact air cover and get that machine gun."

In less than a minute there was an ear-splitting roar. We
raised our eyes. Navy flyers were swooping in, their wing guns
blazing. I began barking orders automatically. A billow of
smoke rose up from the beach.

"They got them!"

The ramp dropped. I plunged waist deep into the whitish
water and was no longer afraid.

We plodded in. Over the water came a steady whine of rifle
bullets. The lagoon spouted little geysers. The Japs were still
their usual lousy selves at marksmanship. Someone in front of
me suddenly dropped. As a pool of blood formed, for a moment I thought it was Andy. The dead Marine bobbed up and
rolled over. He was a machine gunner from How Company. I
brushed past him as the water dropped to knee depth. I began
sprinting zigzaggedly. My feet suddenly went out from under
me. I had stepped into a pothole. A hand on my back pulled me
upright.

"Come on, Mac, keep your powder dry," Seabags shouted
as he raced past me.

Max Shapiro's Foxes were already inland and at work.
They had moved in quickly and accurately on the enemy. The
Captain had developed a deadly team.

I hit the beach and wheeled about. . . . "Come on, godammit!
Move in and set up that TBX and get in with Rocky."

Spanish Joe, Danny, and me set up the radio hastily between
two palms. A sharp report and a singing whizz peeled the bark
from one of the trees. We all fell flat. I caught a glimpse of a
form racing through the clearing before us, and emptied a
clip of my carbine at him. The Jap dropped and rolled over a
half dozen times. Danny was on his feet. . . . "Cover me," he
shouted.

He ran a couple of steps, stopped cold, and backed up. A vision came to him of standing over a Jap on Guadalcanal blowing loose his bayonet . . . the spray of blood and insides over his dungarees . . .

"What's the matter, Danny?"

"Nothing," he said and continued. He bent down quickly, threw the Jap's rifle away, and frisked him. He signaled us forward.

"He's still alive," Danny said. Spanish Joe leveled with his carbine. I grabbed him.

"Hold it. They might want to question him. Find Doc Kyser and LeForce."

Sporadic rifle fire crackled as our boys went about cleaning up the resistance. We were in a hard, sun-baked clearing. The dying Jap lay flat on his back and the blood spilling from him was blotted up by the coral ground. Danny and I crouched over him. He opened his eyes. There was no look of anger as his hand felt for a hole in his belly. His eyes met Danny's. He must have been a young kid, like some of my squad. His face was round and smooth and he had a short black crew cut. He smiled at me and indicated he would like a drink of water.

Danny's eyes were glued to him. He reached for his canteen, uncapped it and raised it to the Jap's bleeding mouth. The liquid trickled down slowly. He coughed and blood and water squirted from a half dozen holes in his chest. He nodded a feeble thanks and asked with his hands and eyes if we were going to kill him. I shook my head and he smiled and made motions for a cigarette. I lit one and held it as he puffed. I wondered what he could be thinking of.

Danny arose. Somehow he could feel no hatred, though he had wanted to kill, to avenge the men who had died in the lagoon. This Jap seemed harmless now—just another poor guy doing what he was ordered to do.

Kyser, LeForce, and Huxley raced to the clearing behind Spanish Joe. LeForce began pumping questions a mile a minute.

"Hold it," Kyser said. "His larynx has been ruptured. He can't talk, even if he could understand."

"Did you men frisk him?"

"Yes, sir."

"He's just a private," LeForce said.

"He'll be dead in a few minutes," the doctor said.

"Keep an eye on him, Forrester. When he goes out, put a slug through his head to make sure," Huxley ordered and left.

The sun beat down. The Jap waited calmly for death. He

rolled over and went into a spasm. His eyes closed. Danny raised his carbine, aimed a shot carefully and squeezed it off.

The First Battalion of the Sixth had blooded itself badly in its furious drive from Green Beach. Past the airstrip, leaving bypassed bunkers to the engineers, they squeezed the frantic enemy back into the tapering tail of Betio.

There would be no surrender by the fanatic little yellow men. In sheer desperation they hurled themselves at the First Battalion's line in wave after wave of saber-wielding officers. They screamed the old cries: "Marines die!" and "We drink Marine blood!"

As dusk fell on the second day of the invasion, the lines of the First Battalion began to buckle under the repeated onslaughts. They were reinforced by Marines from a dozen different outfits who straggled up and threw a slim picket line across the island. The Japs made banzai charges again and again, each attack coming closer to a breakthrough. *Lincoln White* radioed to *Violet*: WE CAN'T HOLD. Headquarters came back with: YOU HAVE TO.

Those were the orders. From Bairiki, the howitzers of the Tenth Marines pumped salvo after salvo over the water into the compressed Jap area, their guns bouncing with each angry bark. Destroyers entered the lagoon once more and poured their five-inch flat trajectiles into the packed enemy.

The Jap was in a nutcracker. To try to retreat to Bairiki meant to be cut down by Huxley's anxious Whores awaiting them. Only through the picket line of the First Battalion could they possibly break through.

The Marines dug in, fighting fiercely against the waves of human battering rams. When their ammunition ran low, they poised their bayonets and hacked back the wall of flesh. Then the black night came again and the firing faded to a crackle.

Dawn of the third morning ended another suspenseful night filled with cries and trickery. The Marine line held. The first show of light brought the Third Battalion of the Sixth ashore through Green Beach and they raced hellbent for election up the airstrip to reinforce the faltering men embedded there in coral foxholes.

Another wild Jap charge on the line and the fresh new men cut them down. Another and another fell short. Then the Third Battalion stood up and moved in to drive them into the water. With all hope gone, their unconquerable bastion falling, the Japs began taking their lives by their own hand. The battle for Betio was drawing to a close less than seventy-two hours after it had started.

The ramps of our boats dropped at the end of the pier on Betio. We had been wandering about in the lagoon all night awaiting decision as to whether to attempt a night landing to reinforce the hard-pressed First Battalion. Through the dark hours came reports that the line was weaker but still intact. Then, before the decision to send us in, the Third Battalion was on the way to Green Beach. The new day found us still going in aimless circles in the water. We were all dog tired but as we jumped into shoulder-high water, the sight that greeted us rudely awakened us.

It was ghoulish. As we waded in through the potholes from a mile out, the lagoon was filled with bobbing bodies. There were hundreds of them. Marines of the Second and Eighth Regiments. I felt sick and humiliated as I passed. They were bloated and distorted beyond recognition. Many lay face down, their hair weaving up and down on small ripples.

Others lay on their backs stiff with rigor mortis. Their faces were slick from the washing of water and their eyes stared blindly with the wild expression they had worn when the bullet cut them down. And others, whose eyes had been eaten away by the salt, had running, jellied masses over their faces and holes where eyes had once been. It was grisly to be alive in this watery graveyard where lifeless hulks danced on the crests of the waves.

Hundreds of rubber boats were moving in the opposite direction towards the landing craft that awaited them on the edge of the barrier reef. In the rubber boats lay bloody, moaning boys: the wounded. Behind the boats, in the water, shaggy corpsmen and stretcher bearers from the division band passed us by the hundreds, finding sanctuary at last from the island of death.

The stink was rancid as we set foot on Blue Beach. There was no breeze in the humid atmosphere. We jumped to the sea wall and saw devastation to defy description. Rubble on rubble, a junkyard of smoldering brimstone. Every yard brought to light a dead Marine or a dead Jap lying in stiff grotesque pose. I wanted to look up but my foot would touch flesh and I couldn't.

We split up to recheck the bunkers that had held from three to three hundred Japs, working with the engineers to flush out any that could possibly be alive now.

I stood atop some sandbags of a high fortification. From there I could see Betio from one end to the other. It seemed inconceivable that eight thousand men could have died there. I could have walked the length of the island in twenty minutes and could have thrown a rock across a greater part of its width. All that remained were a few dozen cocoanut trees erect in the shambles, standing eerily against the sky. Our victory was complete. There were only four prisoners and three of them were Korean laborers.

A radio was set up. We were all very quiet. Around us sat men of the Second and Eighth and our First Battalion. I wanted to go up and offer them cigarettes or some water or just talk, but I couldn't. On the airstrip the Seabees had already started clearing the rubble with bulldozers to hasten the hour the first plane would touch its wheels on Lieutenant Roy Field.

Sam Huxley was on his haunches, his helmet off, his head lowered and his eyes on the deck. His face was pasty and his eyes brimmed with tears. Colonel Malcolm, the Sixth Marine commander, walked up to him.

"Hello, Sam."

"Hello, Colonel."

"Look, old man, don't take it so badly."

"I can't help it. We were the only battalion in the whole damned—oh, what's the use."

"What is your casualty report, Sam?"

"Four dead, six wounded."

"Would it have made it any better if you had been in the assault wave?"

"I feel like a cheater. I suppose you think I'm a sadist. . . ."

"Of course not. We all wanted the assault assignment."

"I guess I've been a Marine too long. Glory happy. General Pritchard told me I was glory happy. We're laughingstocks now. . . . The hiking fools."

"Sam, the Sixth doesn't have to be ashamed. It was the First Battalion that broke their backs. . . ."

"While we sat on our twats on Bairiki."

"Cigarette?"

"No, thanks."

"Anyhow, General Philips wants to see you at the CP in a half-hour."

"Yes, sir."

"Come on, man, snap out of it."

"I just can't look those kids in the face . . . mine or the others."

Huxley, Colonel Malcolm, and Lt. Colonel Norman of the Third Battalion came to attention and saluted General Philips. He ordered them at ease and they seated themselves about the field desk.

"You people can be proud," Philips said. "Your First Battalion performed magnificently in their charge yesterday. I've never seen them better and that includes Belleau Wood. Does anyone have a cigar? Thank you." He lit up and puffed away contentedly at Malcolm's offering. "You men are about to make up for your light duties."

A smile spread across the faces of Huxley and Norman.

"Colonel Norman, your battalion is to board ship and go to Apamama atoll to the south, immediately. A platoon of Jasco men is already on the way down to scout it for you. We don't know what you are going to hit but we presume it won't be too heavy. As soon as we hear from Jasco we'll arrange for your landing."

Philips opened a large map of Tarawa atoll. "As for you, Huxley, I hear your men have an affection for hiking." Sam laughed politely at the joke. "Well, you might not be laughing when you are finished. Tarawa has forty miles of islands. You are to debark to Bairiki again and move down the entire chain until you get to Cora and you are to destroy any enemy left."

"Aye aye, sir. Any idea of their strength?"

"Hard to say, Huxley, hard to say. We will never get an accurate count of the bodies on Betio. There may not be more than a handful of Japs left . . . again, there may be a thousand. You have the only battalion left that is in condition to handle this assignment. We should get some reports from the natives. Remember this, you are on your own. We haven't a spare bean left. We can give you a dozen planes and one destroyer for support. The supply dump is on Bairiki. We'll assign an alligator to move ammo and medical stuff and rations up to you each day. I want this job done quickly. Travel light—no packs, just water and ammo, period."

"What does the General suggest in regard to heavy mortars and radio and telephone gear?"

"Give the heavy weapons men rifles. Take only enough radio stuff to keep in contact with your support and with Headquarters on Helen. Use light telephone stuff. Move fast. I'm assigning a squad from Jasco to work in front of your battalion. Good luck to both of you."

5.

WE HAD been aboard the *J. Franklin Bell* nearly a month. We were all quiet logy and unsteady at first. It was a blessing to be traveling light. Everything we carried was either in our pockets or on our pistol belts. The romance of the trek was exciting but it soon became evident that Highpockets had no scenic tour in mind.

We assembled and moved out quickly. Captain Harper, the gum-chewing skipper of George Company, took the point of march. He was followed by Shapiro's Foxmen, Headquarters, Major Pagan's weapons company and the rear was brought up by Captain Whistler's Easy Company.

Out a few islands ahead of the battalion a squad from Jasco scouted for us. They were reconnaissance specialists billeted at Fleet Marine Force Headquarters and were sent any place in the theater of war where their talents were needed. Many Jasco men were from the disbanded Raider battalions.

The tide was moving out of the lagoon. The only barrier between islands was ankle-deep water. Harper's boys waded from Bairiki to Belle and stepped onto the path that ran close to the lagoon side of the island.

We moved along the path down Belle at a stiff pace. A few yards from the age-worn path was the still lagoon. On the other side of the path was light brush that sometimes thickened into jungle denseness. Clusters of palm trees were everywhere. They were smaller than the cultivated palms of the Lever Plantation on Guadalcanal.

The tinyness of the islands was amazing. Like their bastard cousin, Betio, the islands were long and narrow, running like a chain with links of water between them. They varied in length from several yards to several miles. The width was seldom more than a few hundred yards. Opposite the calm lagoon side was sharp cragged coral pounded by a heavy surf from the ocean.

The sun was as blistering as Huxley's pace but we necessarily slowed down at any signs of Jap life. First we hit an abandoned fuel dump holding several thousand gallons of high octane gas and oil that the Jap commander had wisely dispersed from Betio to prevent conflagration. Now and then an empty thatched hut cropped into view, deserted and eerie. From bits of information that came in we concluded that these islands had been used as an officers' country club.

The passage from island to island was easy now as the tide completely dried the lagoon to a shelf of glistening moist sand covered with millions of shells and shiny "cats' eyes." The devilish heat soon stirred up a string of bitching down the column. Why the hell, out of the whole goddam Second Division, did the Second Battalion have to get this deal? Destiny, sheer destiny for the Hiking Whores.

In late afternoon we found the first concrete evidence of Japs. When crossing from one island to another, we ran into a Jap truck bogged in the soft sand.

"Don't touch it. It's probably booby trapped." Huxley hurried the pace. We were traveling by then on Karen Island, a long one, running some six miles. As dusk fell it seemed as if we were getting nowhere fast in finding the fleeing remnants of the enemy garrison. The size of their force remained a complete mystery. At any rate, they were running like hell. This gave us little comfort, for the last island on the atoll was still a good twenty-five miles away. It held a leper colony.

We were heading east next day on Karen, the outermost island in that direction, when the middle of the island took an elbow swing northwest. It was here that we ran head on into an abandoned village. From this tip of Karen there was a sweeping view of the ocean. Towers made it obvious that the camp was used for observation. George Company moved past the village and set up a guard line as the rest of us moved in to shake the place down.

We split into parties after a cautioning against booby traps and moved from hut to hut digging for clues. The village lay in a clearing surrounded by palm trees. It showed plenty of signs of a hasty retreat.

The huts were nothing more than long slanting roofs reaching nearly to the ground and supported by short stout poles. They were open on all sides but pitched so low we had to stoop to enter. There were no doors or windows, of course, and the decks were covered with woven mats and small pillows, probably the work of the natives. There was little of intelligence value to us. The stripping had been complete. Here and there were Japanese pin-ups and to our surprise several pictures of Hollywood actresses. It appeared that the Imperial Marines had the same attraction to Betty Grable that we had.

A few moldy pieces of leather, a stray helmet smelling of mustiness—little else was left. An artesian well had been dug into the coral in the center of the village but we were warned to draw no water until Doc Kyser tested it for poison. Spanish Joe discovered a pair of women's silk pajamas, indicating that a ranking officer had commanded the place and had kept a mistress there. We counted the huts to get an estimate of enemy strength and we didn't like the count. It added up to several hundred.

As we swung north on Karen it began turning dark. George Company set up guard and we pulled to a tired stop. As soon as we got into communication with the Jasco squad and the alligator bringing our supplies, we headed down to the ocean for a dip. The lagoon would have been preferable but the tide had taken all the water from it. Swimming was treacherous in the pounding surf and cutting coral. It was icy cold but revived us.

Shivering and blue, we ran around naked to dry off. The alligator pulled into the bivouac and unloaded and rations were doled out. My boys gathered around the radio for chow.

"I'll be a sonofabitch. We got K-rations."

"They must have got us mixed up with the Army on Makin."

"Heah, heah."

"Three boxes. Look at the label . . . breakfast, lunch, and dinner . . . well, kiss my moneymaking ass."

"The old Corps is going first cabin."

"Say, you know what day this is?"

"Sure, Thursday."

"No, I mean what day?"

"So, what day already?"

"It's Thanksgiving."

"I'll be go to hell. It's Thanksgiving . . . Mary, lead us in prayer."

"Go to the devil."

We became quiet as we tore the wax tops from the boxes and pulled out our Thanksgiving meal. The revelation had plunged us all into our own particular memory of what the day meant.

Danny thought of the big football game back in Baltimore. Brisk and cold out and Kathy there on the fifty-yard line wrapped in a blanket, with Sally Davis. . . .

A farmer's table in Iowa is something to behold on Thanksgiving. Seabags' folks didn't just put up a pumpkin pie, they put up a dozen of them.

"Sure is a pretty island."

"Yeah, it sure is."

"Levin, do Jewish people celebrate Thanksgiving?" the Injun asked.

"What you think, we're savages?" Levin answered indignantly. "You should see all the relatives I got. I wanna tell you guys something. You ain't lived till you get a heat on with Manischewitz Wine."

"We always got a good feed in the Corps," Burnside said.

"Hey, you radio men. Put out that fire and turn the smoking lamp off," a security guard called.

"I wonder how many Japs they got left?"

"I don't give a big rat's ass how many."

A mantle of darkness enveloped the little atoll. We downed cold coffee, lit up a king-sized cigarette from the K-ration and hid the tip of it. We looked toward the horizon. Far-off streams of smoke penciled into the orange sky from the ships taking the Second and Eighth Marines away. The Sixth was gone too. Only Huxley's Whores and an unknown destiny remained. The warships and the planes had left for another target. We were alone. An uneasy chill passed through me. On the edge of the world with our battalion . . . what would tomorrow bring?

L.Q. broke into the spell of nostalgia that was enshrouding

us . . . "Hey, Speedy, how about a song or two before taps?"

"Don't mind if I do." He went to his foxhole and got his guitar. We were traveling light but not light enough to leave his guitar behind. We sat in a circle about him as the first stars of night appeared in the still sky. From about the bivouac men gathered to listen.

"I was a-hiking today," Speedy said strumming the guitar, "and I got to thinking about Betio and as we was walking the words just started coming to me . . . you all know 'Old Smokey' . . . well, these here words kind of fit that tune.

> "From out of New Zealand, the Gyrenes set sail,
>   To grab them an atoll where Japs got their mail.
> On an island called Helen, they staked out their claim,
>   And the Second Division, won e'er lasting fame.
> Dug deep in the coral, way under the sand,
>   Five thousand Japs waited for them to land.
> The Second hit Blue Beach, and hit with a thud,
>   The Second hit Blue Beach, all covered with blood.
> The Second hung on to the ground they had made,
>   All night they hid down neath the seawall and prayed.
> The Eighth came ashore, boys, and landed by noon,
>   They waded past buddies, killed in the lagoon.
> The Sixth came through Green Beach, o'er buddies who paid,
>   And killed all the Japs for the mis'ry they'd made.
> Oh one thousand white crosses, to tell of their laurel,
>   There's a thousand Gyrenes lay, asleep in the coral.
> Now listen you mothers, you sweethearts and wives,
>   Shed no tear for the Gyrenes who laid down their dear lives.
> On an island named Helen, they staked out their claim,
>   And the Second Division won e'er lasting fame."

As the freckled-faced boy lay down his guitar, all that could be heard was the pounding of the surf on the other side of the island. I dropped exhausted into my foxhole and drew my poncho over me. A bed in the Waldorf couldn't have felt better. It had been many days since I had slept . . . many days.

"Psssst, Mac."

I sprang up, whipping my carbine out.

"Easy—it's me—Marion."

"What's up?"

"I'm in contact with the Jasco squad. They've spotted Japs up ahead."

I crawled from my hole. It was pitch black. I couldn't find my shoes. I hadn't anticipated this emergency and had welcomed the opportunity of taking them off for the first time in a week. The sharp coral cut me as I held Marion's hand while he led me to the radio. Danny, who was bunked next to the generator, was already up and at the earphones. I held a muted flashlight for him as he wrote:

LW V JAS. LW V JAS. LW V JAS: JAPS ESCAPING PAST US ON NORTH END OF NELLIE K.

"Ask how many. Marion, get the skipper up," I said.

JAS V LW: HOW MANY K.

LW V JAS: APPEAR TO BE SEVERAL HUNDRED K.

Marion stumbled back with Huxley. "What's the scoop?" he asked.

"The Japs are moving past Jasco on Nellie. They say several hundred of them."

The whole camp was now propped up on one groggy elbow.

"Tell them to lay low and not to try anything," Huxley said.

"Crank the generator, Mac," Danny said.

JAS V LW: DO NOT CONTACT ENEMY. STAND BY K.

Danny flicked the receiving switches as Marion held the flashlight close to the message pad. There was a deathly silence in the black night. Danny reached for the dials and gently moved them to catch an answering signal. He turned his face to me.

"Better send that last one over," I said, turning the generator.

JAS V LW: DO YOU READ ME, DO YOU READ ME K K K.

"Maybe they had to quiet down. Their generator would have attracted the Japs," I said.

"Hold it!" Danny crouched over the message pad.

LW V JAS: WE HAVE BEEN . . .

The message broke. Danny dropped his pencil and we all breathed deeply.

"They've been attacked," Marion whispered.

"There is nothing we can do," Huxley said. "Let's get some sleep."

The new day found me aching stiff but well slept out. I fought into my socks which were still damp from yesterday's wading. I had no fresh change along.

The squad huddled around the radio as we ripped off the wax carton tops and dug in for breakfast. There was no time for a fire to warm the coffee so the black dynamite would have to go down cold.

"I hear the Jasco squad got wiped out last night," Andy said.

"We couldn't get them this morning. It don't look good."

"Gimme a cigarette."

"Whatsamatter, you white men never carry your own weeds."

"Butts on that smoke."

"Butts on them there butts, cousin."

"I don't like the smell of this whole shebang. The atoll is wide open for a counterattack from the Marshalls. What's to keep them from coming down after us?"

"What about it, Marion?"

"Counterattack seems rather unlikely but, of course, it can't be ruled out."

"See, what did I tell you? Even Marion says it's possible."

"I doubt if the Japs are in condition to counterattack. We are attacking too many places at the same time," Marion continued. "If they move out of the Marshalls to hit us, they'll leave the door wide open for the First or the new Fourth Division."

"What makes you so smart?"

"I can read."

"Maybe if we get them on the run we'll have a clear field to Tokyo," Speedy said. "I hear that Henry Ford is giving ten thousand dollars to the first Gyrene that sets foot on the Jap mainland."

"Don't discount your enemy," Marion said. "You should see by now that they can fight."

"Yeah, they're a bunch of crazy bastards."

Burnside growled into the session. "Hey, Mac, you bastards going to sit here all day? Crack down the radio. Captain Whistler's already got Easy Company reconnoitering up ahead."

"I hear we're going to run into some native villages today," Levin said, getting up and starting to break down the radio.

"Should be educational," Marion said.

"I wonder if them broads go to the post?"

"I see," Marion said, going to Levin's assistance, "that the conversation is beginning to hit its usual high intellectual level. Excuse me."

"Hey, Mary, wait a minute. Give us the word on the gooks?"

"Yeah, what about these Gilbertese?"

"According to the Encyclopedia . . ." Marion began.

"Listen at him, would you, listen at him," Levin said in awe.

"According to the Encyclopedia," Marion continued, unruffled, "we are in Micronesia. It is one of the three major groups of island people in the Pacific Ocean. The other two are Melanesia and Polynesia."

"Owi, is he clugg."

"Skip all the crap, Mary, how about the women?"

"The Gilbertese are great fishermen. The sea and the palm trees are practically their only means of survival. They have a few chickens and pigs for festive occasions, but, as you can see, the soil is very unfertile."

"Don't much look like Black Hawk County," Seabags spat from his chaw.

"Shaddup, I'm getting enlightened."

"The atoll has been under British control for many years. They export copra and cocoanut oil in exchange for cloth, cooking utensils and other items."

"For Chrisake, Mary. Do the broads go or don't they?"

"Many of the younger generation speak English due to missionary work. They have rigid tribal systems and their own language and customs. Life is simple and remote from Western culture. Few white men . . ."

"Mary, all I asked was a simple question. Do the broads . . . aw, the hell with it."

"Come on, we'd better shag ass," I said, busting up the geography lesson.

"Hey, lookit. Here comes Captain Whistler with a bunch of gooks."

We formed a circle at a polite distance from the skipper and the staff. Whistler and some of his boys had come in with four natives. They were a cross between the light skinned Polynesians like the Maoris and the black Melanesians of Guadalcanal. The young lads hovered on the brink of black. They were handsome men; strikingly so by comparison with other natives I had seen all over the Orient. They stood about five foot nine inches, and were stocky, with well-tapered figures slim in the waist and broad in the shoulders. Fish and copra must have agreed with them. Their clothing consisted of brightly colored cloths wrapped tightly at the waist and falling nearly to their knees.

"I found these boys snooping around camp this morning, sir," Captain Whistler said.

"They are quite friendly," Wellman said, lighting his pipe and joining the group. "Any of you boys speak English?"

"Oh, yes," one said, as he gazed about in childish awe. "My name Lancelot, my good Catholic Christian. Silent night, holy night . . . you want hear my sing?"

"Not just now, Lancelot," Huxley said. "We are more interested in finding Japs. Do you know where they are?"

"Japs bad fellows, very bad fellows are."

"Do you know where they are?"

"They run when you British come." He pointed north, up the chain of islands. The other three natives nodded and pointed north, jabbering.

"How many Japs run?" Wellman asked.

"We no like Japs. They bad fellows. Take chicken."

"How many?"

Lancelot turned puzzled to his friends. They argued for several moments in the confusing native tongue.

"Say again please?"

"How many? Numbers . . . one, two, three, four . . . how many Japs?"

"Oh . . . many thousand."

Wellman coughed.

"Don't get excited, Wellman, they aren't much help."

"Very glad British back," Lancelot said.

"We aren't British, Lancelot. We're Americans."

"No British?" the youth said, becoming long-faced.

"No British?" the other three echoed.

"We good friends of British . . . American . . . British friends," Huxley said, shaking his hands together.

"Like hell we are," Whistler whispered under his breath.

"God save King, no?" Lancelot asked for reassurance.

"God save King, God save King," Huxley repeated. The four smiled.

"We come along no, yes? Help find bad Jap."

Huxley drew Wellman aside. "What do you think, Major?"

"I suppose it is all right. They seem to be O.K. boys."

"All right," Huxley said, "I make you scouts for us. But you must be good boys or I send you home to village. Do you understand?"

"We get coconut for 'Merican. We carry boxes. Jap bad fellow."

"In fact," Wellman said, "they'll probably be quite a help in tricky brush or tides."

"Just be good boys," Huxley said again.

"Oh yes . . . we Catholic . . . Hail Mary, no?"

They eagerly turned about, smiling and nodding to us. We took to them right off the bat. I was glad we were going to toss the Japs off their atoll.

"All right, fall in, goddammit. On the double . . . hit the road."

Without Jasco doing our reconnaissance now, it was necessary to send a platoon from the point company well in advance of the main body. We had moved a few hundred yards when Captain Shapiro and his sidekick, Gunner McQuade, came storming up to Huxley. He literally yanked Highpockets off the side of the road.

"Hey, Colonel," Shapiro stormed, "what's the scoop? Yesterday you had Harper's Company on the point, today Whistler's. Are you saving Fox for the burial detail?"

"Don't get your crap hot, Max."

"My boys are getting pissed, Colonel."

"By my calculations, Max, this hike will last three days before we hit the last island—Cora. It will be your turn to take the point tomorrow." He winked at Shapiro.

"Whistler better not find any Japs today then."

"Don't worry. I think there'll be plenty to go around."

"Well, don't forget it. We get the point tomorrow."

Huxley smiled as the big plump sergeant and the little plump captain stood fast waiting for their rearguard company to reach them. Huxley was confident that Fox Company would be the one to contact the enemy. He had maneuvered the march so it would turn out that way. His gamble on that hothead Shapiro would then pay off, he hoped. The little skipper had the finest and toughest hundred and sixty men he had ever seen, outside of the Raiders. Shapiro turned to him once more.

"Colonel, you got to do me a favor."

"I'm listening."

"Be a good guy and leave that candy-assed Looey, Bryce, in the CP when the action starts or send him to Bairiki for supplies."

"Not so loud, Max."

"I've been a good sport, Colonel, haven't I? I know you palmed the bastard off as my exec just for kicks . . . but be a good guy."

"I'll talk to you tonight about it."

6.

THE scenery was much the same as on the first day, only we found more evidence of Jap flight. Every several hundred yards a group of abandoned huts was spotted in clearings near the path. We didn't stop to inspect them this time. Highpockets was pulling off a Huxley special. The sweat started coming as we turned from east to northwest around the corner of Karen Island. From out of nowhere, more of Lancelot's buddies began appearing at the roadside and joining the march. Alone and in small groups they came until we had over fifty eager beavers prancing up and down the line making friendly chatter, gleeful about the big adventure. With the natives came stray dogs. They looked lean and hungry; their ribs poked against their skins. They soon had themselves a field day with tidbits from softhearted Marines who dug into rations to feed them during the breaks.

Although we weren't burdened with packs, we carried two canteens of water, a first aid kit, a machete, a G.I. knife, a trenching shovel, a poncho, a compass, and two hundred rounds of ammunition and four grenades. Somehow, I just couldn't get the stuff to ride right. We were also burdened with the extra weight of the radios and we switched off the load every fifteen minutes to keep up maximum speed.

We got a lucky break when the natives began insisting on taking a turn in carrying the radios and heavy gear. We were grateful although they couldn't handle the canvas straps on bare skin and Huxley's pace for more than a few minutes at a time. The tempo of their life was much slower than the tempo of Highpockets on the march.

At last we came to an exhausted halt as Captain Whistler raced back to us. We fell to the roadside, gasping, and shared a few gulps of water and cigarettes with the Gilbertese. Jubilant at their reward, they were soon scaling some of the nearby palm trees and slinging down green husked fruit. When the deck was piled high, they cut the tops open with amazing dexterity. The whitish juice was sugary and cool in the natural refrigeration of layers of soft rind. It tasted wonderful.

Whistler, Huxley, Wellman, and Marlin wiped their sweat-soaked faces, doffed their helmets and lit up. "Better come up and take a look, skipper." the beetle-browed Captain of Easy Company said. "We're at the end of the island and there's about sixty yards of water to the next one."

"Did you send any of your boys across?"

"No, sir, we pulled up. I didn't want to commit them without permission."

"I hope it isn't too deep. We're running into a whole string of crossings from here on out. Most of these islands won't run more than a mile. We have to make fifteen of them today. Let's take a look." Huxley turned to the native boy. "Hey, Lancelot! You come with me."

"Yes, sir, yes, sir," Lancelot answered. He was followed jealously by Ziltch who was only waiting for the proper moment to inform the native that he, Ziltch, was number one boy.

They stood looking at the channel that ran between Karen and Lulu. Huxley surveyed the situation. The water was too muddy to see bottom. The book said it wouldn't be too deep but Huxley only trusted the book part way. If any Japs lurked in the thick brush on the opposite bank, his men would make a beautiful target going over. He turned to Lancelot.

"How deep?"

The native went into conference with some others and one pointed to Huxley's chest.

"Close to six feet," Huxley muttered. He unsnapped his pistol belt and looped it around his neck. He took his wallet from his pocket and put it in his helmet.

"Don't you think you'd better send someone else across?" Marlin said.

Highpockets didn't honor the question. He nodded for

Lancelot to come with him and point out the best possible route. The natives cut several long pole markers from the brush.

"When I hit the other side, send one platoon over. I'll move them forward and string them across the island for a covering force. If we hit deep water, send a call for all men over six feet to form a chain over the channel and pass the radios, machine guns, mortars and telephone gear across. All others hold their gear in one hand and swim it with the other. Any boy that can't swim will hang on to the tall boys. We reassemble at once on the other side . . . any questions?"

"How about waiting for the alligator to reach us and take the heavy gear over, sir?"

"Can't depend on it. If we run into Japs we'd better have it ready. Besides, this damned tide is slowing us enough as it is. The alligator may not reach us till late evening. I don't want to give the Japs a chance to dig in too deep. Got to keep them running."

Huxley took Lancelot's hand and stepped into the water. Within several yards he was up to his waist. Two machine guns sat ready to fire on the opposite shore. Huxley plodded about slowly, feeling each step before him. He sank the long poles into the bottom every few yards to mark the shallowest course. At one point he went down to his chin and floundered. Lancelot was ordered to swim back to our side.

Huxley's drenched body began rising. He hit the opposite shore and ran quickly to the cover of a tree, then scanned the brush up ahead. He returned to the water line and signaled to us.

"First Platoon, move over on the double—leave your machine gun."

The riflemen were in the water moving to the first marker. The short men began the torturing one-armed swim, holding their rifles and gear aloft with the other. After several moments they emerged and dashed ashore as Huxley moved them up to disperse a protection picket.

"All men, six feet," Whistler ordered, "Follow the channel markers."

The human chain in midstream grunted under the weight they passed over their heads. Around them, platoon after platoon waded in. A grenade broke loose from a belt held aloft and fell into the water, sending up a muffled spout. No one was hurt. Several boys ran out of gas and had to be towed over by alert men on the other side who had doffed their gear and organized a lifesaving party.

I hit neck-deep water and cursed a blue streak, remembering I had left my cigarettes in my dungaree pockets. I held my carbine and belt up with my left hand and pulled hard against the tugging tide. I was cautious of dropping my feet even by the pole markers. Finally I hit the other shore almost dizzy with exhaustion.

It was a rough go. Each man dragged himself ashore shaking water like a puppy, alternately cold from the dousing and hot from the strain and the sun.

After nearly an hour the wet battalion was squishing uncomfortably down the seemingly never ending trail by the lagoon. The islands ran short now, breaking up into quick sequence. Each hour, or less, found us repeating the water crossing procedure until six more had been made.

High noon found us dripping, exhausted and miserable. The blisters were wearing on at a record pace. Huxley believed that the smaller Japanese must be having a much rougher time of it and he didn't want us to slacken. Our pursuit must not give them a rest or an opportunity to prepare defenses.

"Hey! What town is this!"

The road took a turn from the lagoon to the center of the island and there, straddling it, was the first inhabited village. Our first look at the women started us drooling. It had been a month since we had seen a female of any kind and we little anticipated the luscious sight before us. They were as tall as their men, big hipped and heavy legged, and like the men they wore only bright-colored cloths about their waists. They edged curiously to the road as we passed through. All eyes in the column were glued on them. I had never seen such an array of bare bosoms, all ample, firm and blossoming like tropical fruit.

"Gawd!"

"Cousin, I'd like to walk on a mile of that one barefooted."

The girls giggled and waved and we waved and slobbered.

"Christ, I didn't know that damn thing was still there till now. Guess I'm still a man."

Had the Gilbertese girls known their existence was causing such a ruckus in the ranks they would surely have disappeared in angered shame. As it was, we trudged through giving careful attention to each and every one. Fortunately the girls didn't understand English.

It was mostly the fourteen- to sixteen-year-old jobs that caused the greatest commotion. Apparently the tropical heat withered them at about twenty years of age. A few aged crones were there, wrinkled like rhinos and potbellied, with stone-white hair.

Passing through this village added another twenty natives to our ranks. The pace didn't hurt so much now we could anticipate running into another village. We hit several more ranging from a dozen to a hundred huts. Each time, the Gilbertese came rushing to the road waving, shouting welcome, exchanging smiles and coconuts for cigarettes and gum. Often an older man would snap rigidly to attention and execute a British salute, holding it till the whole battalion passed by. Each new crossing found the tide a bit lower till, at noon break time, we waded in water only waist deep.

We flopped down on the outskirts of a village and word passed down that we weren't to enter huts or touch any girls.

"Where are we, Mac?" L.Q. asked.

"Start of Nellie Island, the government village."

We dumped our belts and helmets by the radio, took our carbines and headed for the lagoon. Marion glanced over his shoulder at the sprawled battalion and the natives dashing up the palms for coconuts.

"Isn't it wonderful?" he said.

I laughed.

"Real adventure, out of a poster. Beautiful place, this atoll."

"Very romantic," I agreed. "How do these girls stack up with Rae?" he teased.

Marion's face turned crimson. I slapped him on the back. "I must admit," he said, "I peeked, but I don't think Rae has anything to worry about."

Near the water's edge by a clump of trees there was a man squatting. On the deck by him lay several fish he was scaling. He looked different from the natives, more like a mulatto, light tan and very freckled, and thin. His hair struggled between red and black and he wore a khaki shirt and faded shorts and sandals. From his lips hung a curved pipe. He had a neatly trimmed Vandyke beard. I approached him as he peeled the fish.

"Mind if we sit here? I mean, you speakee English, no, yes?" I asked with a bevy of motions.

"You may sit," he answered. "It is your island and I speak English quite well, thank you." He spoke sharply without looking up and made me feel ridiculous for my question.

"Er, we wouldn't bother you but we are on the lookout for an alligator."

"You won't find any alligators in these waters," the man said tersely.

"It's a boat—well, like a boat. It goes on land and water . . . we call them alligators." I sat down and opened my ration.

"My name is Marion Hodgkiss. I'm from Kansas. That's a state in America."

"Yes, produces quite a bit of wheat." The man, still squatting, laid down his fish, wiped his hands on his shorts and extended one to Marion. "My name is Calvin MacIntosh," he announced, knocking the tobacco from his pipe and placing it in his breast pocket.

"Glad to meet you, Mr. MacIntosh," Marion said.

"Mac's the name too," I said. "Care to try a hardtack and ham spread?"

"No, thank you," the man said aloofly.

I decided to ignore him. Mary, however, was intrigued with his discovery and anxious to keep a conversation going. "I suppose," he said, "you people are glad to see us?"

The frail man did not answer.

"I mean," Marion continued, "the Japs must have treated you badly."

"On the contrary," MacIntosh answered, picking up a fish and resuming his cleaning. "Admiral Shibu's troops were quite well controlled and disciplined. Oh, they took the pigs and chickens and my books and the white men, but aside from an incident or two we have been treated sternly but fairly. The women they took were more than willing to go."

"I think you'll find that old-time regulars, no matter what army they are in, are pretty decent. These were the best the Emperor had. Damned fine soldiers," I said.

"And not given to committing the atrocities that our good governor warned would befall us," MacIntosh said.

"Very interesting," Marion mused.

"Ethics," I said. "These Japs weren't like those on the Canal. Like the difference between you and a boot or a replacement."

"It certainly is puzzling," Marion said. "I expected to find the atoll raped clean."

"Don't believe everything you read in the papers," I said. Once more I tried to loosen up the dour MacIntosh by offering a cigarette. He raised his eyebrows and looked out of the corner of his eye. He was a tempted but proud man. I shoved the pack under his nose and his pride was outweighed by his obvious hunger for tobacco. He lit up and seemed to relax a bit. He sat on the deck drawing his knees to his chest and placed his arms about them and puffed long and hard on the cigarette and gazed over the lagoon. I shoved the other two cigarettes in the packet into his pocket over a feeble protest.

"American cigarettes are superior," he said. "I've tasted them once or twice before."

"Mr. MacIntosh, I hope you won't think I'm too curious, but you mentioned something about your books."

"Marion is a writer. He's had four stories published."

MacIntosh looked at his sallow, frail arm and spoke softly. "As you see, I am a half-breed. My mother lives over in the village. I have a wife and four children. The children look like me."

"Your father?"

"A Scotsman. A sailor. Before the war the ships visited us every few months for a load of copra. Exchanged it for fishing tools and cloth and the like. We need little here, we give little. There would be quite a celebration when the ships came. It was quite common for a sailor to jump and remain here and marry a native."

"Is he still alive?"

"I do not know. They took the white men when they came. I do not know."

"Perhaps it will turn out all right."

"My father was an intelligent man, a university man. The world frightened him. Being a writer, Mr. Hodgkiss, I suppose you are familiar with the type. I understand there are many books about such men who run off to find a Pacific paradise. A place to escape the strife of civilization."

"Your father picked a beautiful place," I said. "I've seen most of the world and you couldn't have done better."

"My father told me that we were the only civilized people in the world. The past two weeks have proved him righ., I believe."

I had to smile at his reasoning. Maybe he wasn't so wrong. After all, we were on his atoll with guns, hunting other men while he just sat back and scaled his fish.

"Have you ever had a yen to travel? To Scotland, perhaps?"

The little bearded man lowered his head and bit his lip. "My father told me never to leave Tarawa. But I have often traveled to his homeland through him and the books." His hand dropped to the sand and his long fingers traced a pattern. "I am protected here. I know that an Eurasian has no place . . . here, well, the natives accept me as long as I earn my way. I teach English to the boys at the mission, I fish a little. At first I could not understand why the British government people treated me as they did, with contempt. As if I were a leper on Bairiki. My father once told me he was sorry he had brought me into the world . . . a half-breed. I suppose I am happy. To build a house, to eat, I merely have to climb a tree. I have a lovely wife. What more can a man want of the world?"

"You don't know how lucky you are, fellow," I said.

"My father always said that. Except when he was drunk. Then he'd tell me about the Highlands and the pipers and he would hide and weep. Stay hidden for many days. Someday I shall have my books back and they will take me over the horizon again."

"I have some books in my pack, back on Helen."

"Helen?"

"The main island."

"Betio," he corrected. "You are now on Aboaroko."

"I have some books. I'll bring them up to you if I have an opportunity. I'd like to see you again if we remain. Maybe when I get back to the States, I could send you books regularly."

The man's face lit up. "Would you . . . would you really?"

"What do you like?" Marion asked.

"Anything, anything at all. I read German and French too."

Lighttower came up, puffing, "Hey, Mac. The Gunner wants you. We can't make heads or tails out of the alligator. Andy must be sending code with his feet."

Marion and I arose and shook hands with Mr. MacIntosh. "Would you mind speaking to our Colonel?" I said. "Maybe you could give us some information on the Japanese."

"I'm afraid," he said bitterly, "I can be of little use. I was asleep when they passed. I do not wish to take part in your war."

The two Marines walked back over the road to the radio through a mob of natives who were all over the place. Keats was in an uproar. "We can't read the alligator!" he snapped.

"The goddam thing is all metal," I said, "probably pounding the waves all over the place."

The Gunner scratched his head. "We are ready to move out. Mac, you and Marion will have to stay here with the radio and keep trying to reach them. When they catch up, jump aboard and have them ride you up to the next island. We'll be looking out for you. Keep in contact."

In a few moments the battalion had moved out, leaving Mary and me alone but surrounded by a bunch of curious natives. We tried to contact the alligator. The signal from them was weak and Andy kept asking for repeats. I got a volunteer to spin the generator.

Cranking it proved so amusing that Marion had to form an orderly line to let each native have a turn. At last the alligator raised their signal and I gave them directions. They were several miles away and it would be at least an hour before they reached us. Marion and I broke down the set, cased it, waited, and tried to beg off eating the hundred open coconuts which were placed before us.

About fifteen minutes had passed when a small boy burst through the group jabbering wildly and pointing toward the ocean side of the island. "Jap . . . Jap!" he repeated.

We sprang up, grabbed our carbines and waved back the natives who clustered behind us. We dashed the width of the narrow island through some brush, following the swift-running lad. In a small clearing he came to a halt and pointed again.

Three Japanese Imperials were surrounded by a host of

angry club- and rock-wielding natives. The Japs were un-
armed and bleeding from the beating being administered them.
Marion and I shoved a way through the crowd and tried to
quell the mounting ire of the Gilbertese. One native was poised
to hurl a rock. I stuck my carbine under his nose and only then
did they realize we meant business. Slowly, still yelling and
waving their clubs, they widened the circle. We faced the cap-
tives. One was a smooth-faced boy, the other two had straggly
goatees. All three were tattered and evidently fatigued, thirsty, and hungry. They bowed several times to us. Two of them
grinned appeasingly, the other remained sedate.

"Do any of you guys speak English?" I asked.

Their answer was a repeat of the bowing.

"Put your hands on your head," I ordered and pointed. "Both
hands! All right, get on your knees. Cover me, Mary, I'm going
to frisk them."

I ripped the faded smelly jackets off their backs and went
through their pockets. From the corner of my eye I caught
sight of a native waving a Japanese rifle in their direction.

"Get that rifle, Marion." Still covering me, he walked to
the native and asked for the weapon. The native balked. Marion
snatched it away from him.

"We are taking these men prisoner," I yelled to the crowd.
"We must question them." There was a buzz and a few English-
speaking natives nodded and explained to the others.

"Hey, Mary. Sourface here is an officer. I got some maps off
him."

"Good. I hope these people don't give us any trouble till
Danny and Andy get here on the alligator."

"Ask for some rope."

Two small lads were sent scurrying back to the huts.

"All right," I barked, "on your feet. Stand up, keep your
hands high. All right, you people. Clear a path . . . out of the
way."

We edged cautiously into the mob, trying to avoid a clash. I
walked in front of the prisoners, clearing the way, and Marion
behind. Suddenly a young girl burst forth in my direction.
I tried to block her but she shoved past me and threw her arms
about the Jap officer.

I grabbed her and threw her off. She fell to the ground
sobbing and screaming hysterically. The mob turned its anger
from the Japs to the prostrate woman. They jeered and began a
chant which meant no good. Several natives ran up to her and
prodded her with the ends of their sticks. Marion turned to help
her.

"Stay out of it, Mary. It's none of our business!"

"But we can't let them kill her."

I grabbed a native standing by me. "Speak English?"

"Yes."

"Where are the Sisters, the mission . . . do they still live?"

"Sister live. Father die."

"Where are they?"

He pointed north to Taratai Island.

"Get in boat and get Sisters. Bring them here quick or I cut your tongue out. Understand?"

"Yes."

"Hurry then." He scurried off. I wheeled into the mob and picked out two of the largest specimens I could find. "You two, speak English?" One did.

"Put this girl under arrest. Put her in hut and guard her till Sisters come." The natives hedged away. "If you do not obey me, there will be much trouble." I squeezed off a shot into the air. The sudden crack silenced the makings of the lynching.

"She no good. Live with Japanese man. She no good."

"Do as I order. I return tomorrow. She better be alive."

Reluctantly, they dragged her off. She was still shrieking, her face distorted in tortured anguish.

I was relieved when we got our quarry to the beach. The two boys returned with rope and we bound the Japs hand and foot and made them lie near the water's edge. I caught sight of the alligator plodding through the water several hundred yards to the south.

"Mary, there's a blinker gun by the radio. Get it and signal them in."

As Marion dashed away, the officer turned to me.

"You are a sergeant, are you not?" he said.

"I thought you couldn't speak English."

"As one soldier to another, I beg you. Let me have your knife."

"Aren't you a little late for hari-kari? If you wanted to knock yourself off you had all week to do it in."

"I only stayed alive for the sake of the girl. I plead with you . . . shoot me then."

I shook my head. I was sorry that I had gotten mixed up in the whole miserable affair. The iron monster cut sharply toward shore. Its motor roared as it emerged from the water and its knife-edged treads rumbled on the coral.

"Hey, get a look at them broads," Andy shouted as the motor stopped.

"Mac, you bastard. You mean you been going past that stuff all day and you made us ride in this claptrap?" Danny said.

"You guys got a smoke?" I asked.

"Here, Mac," Danny said, jumping to the deck. "We got a whole case. Enough for the battalion. Andy and I already put aside two packs apiece for the squad. What the hell you got there?"

"Prisoners. The natives stoned them out of some trees."

"One is an officer," Marion said.

I cut their leg bonds loose and ordered them into the alligator. "Get in and lay down. If you try a break, I'm not going to shoot you but I'll have to club you unconscious . . . so let's make the trip pleasant." The radio was loaded in after them and Marion and I climbed aboard. "Stay close to the shore, driver. The battalion is up on the next island. Danny, keep a listening watch."

A deafening roar went up as the motor turned over and the alligator made an about face that threw us all to the deck.

"Don't put me on this goddam thing tomorrow. It shakes your guts out," Danny muttered brokenly over the rumbling and bouncing.

I had had many a rough ride in my day. I had even tried a wild broncho once when I was drunk in Oregon at a rodeo. Yet I had never had a ride like this. As the treads turned slowly and rumbled over the rock in shallow water the springless monstrosity pitched and bucked mercilessly. It finally dipped into deep water and churned slowly northward.

On the shore, some two hundred yards away, we caught sight of the natives of the big village lined up and waving. We swung in as close as we could without riding the coral and exchanged greetings with them. Past them, we hit deep water and chugged on.

As the sun was setting I caught a blinker light ashore signaling us in. Huxley had moved the battalion up three islands instead of one. The bivouac was a tiny place, not more than a few hundred square yards. The alligator rumbled ashore and came to a halt. My knees buckled as I jumped down. The ride in the mixmaster left me feeling like a bowl of whipped cream.

"Get that working party going and unload the chow," Huxley greeted us.

"Sir," the driver said, "all we could get was C-ration. Two per man for tomorrow. I'm afraid there'll not be enough for tonight. I did the best I could."

"What's the matter with those people on Bairiki?" Huxley fumed.

"I'm sorry, sir," the driver said.

"It's not your fault, son. Mac, when you get that radio in with Sarah, let me know. I want to talk with them."

"Aye aye, sir." I transferred the prisoners to LeForce, was commended, and wearily unloaded the radios and set out to find the squad.

Right on the water's edge were two small huts. The command post had been set up in them. The radios shared the hut with a message center and the aid station, while Huxley and his staff were in the other. The road ran past the huts, giving little sleeping room near them. Over the road there was a big clearing where the company was digging in on open ground. The ground was dusty soft once the top layer had been pierced. I dug my hole with Burnside and dropped my gear in it, then went back to the radio to see if Spanish Joe had contacted Sarah. Being on the edge of the water and having a clear shot to Bairiki we received and transmitted clearly, five and five.

Highpockets dropped to his knees to get into the low-roofed thatched shelter. He was followed by Doc Kyser, the alligator driver, and Lieutenant LeForce.

"Sorry we couldn't get anything from the prisoners," LeForce said.

"I'd estimate there are three hundred of them," Huxley said.

"We'll find out tomorrow," LeForce answered.

Huxley turned to Spanish Joe at the radio. "Are you in with Sarah?"

"Yes, sir."

"Any chance to talk to them by mike?"

"I think we can reach them O.K.," I said.

"Tell them to get the commander of the island to the radio."

Spanish Joe took off the earphones and Huxley strapped them on. "Give us a signal when you want to talk," Joe said.

"Hello Sarah. Is this the commander? This is Huxley, Lincoln White. What's the matter with you people down there? I asked for ammo today and plasma. I didn't get any."

"Sorry, Huxley. We are all fouled up here. The stuff is going to Helen by mistake. What's the picture up there? Run into anything?"

"We expect to hit Cora by dusk tomorrow. I want to send the alligator back tonight so we can have the stuff up to us when we contact the enemy tomorrow."

"Hello Lincoln White. You will have to hold up your attack till we can get the supplies up there."

Huxley mumbled an oath. He signaled us to spin the generator again. "Hello Sarah. I'm going to make a check of what we'll need and radio it. I want that stuff waiting there when the alligator gets in and you'd better not foul it up, understand?"

"Hello Lincoln White. Who the hell you think you are talking to, Huxley?"

"Hello Sarah. I don't give a damn if I'm talking to Doug MacArthur. Have the supplies ready . . . over and out." Huxley returned the earphones to Spanish Joe.

Sergeant Paris ducked into the hut, breathless. "Sir, we have found the Jasco squad."

"Are they dead?"

"Yes, sir, all ten of them, over by the ocean." We ran out, following Paris over the clearing down the sloping jagged boulders to the surf. He shoved through some brush and we saw them. The Jasco boys lay grotesquely stiff on the deck, like figures in a wax museum, holding the pose they had when they were shot. The radio operator sat erect, his earphones on and his hand on the key of the smashed radio. The generator man stood slumped against a tree, his fingers clutching the handle of the generator. We passed among them quietly.

"At least the Japs didn't cut them up," Huxley whispered. "LeForce, get a burial party organized. Dig graves by the clearing. Make sure they are properly identified. Bring me a list and the personal belongings."

"Aye aye, sir," LeForce said, almost inaudibly.

I walked from the place. I should have been immune to the sight of blood after so many years in the Corps, but whenever I saw a dead man, especially a Marine, I got sick. I took a deep breath and cursed a few times to ease the pounding in my chest. I got to thinking about a bunch of people sitting in a living room, crying and grieving. It always hit me that way.

My eyes turned to the sky. From out of nowhere a monstrous black cloud swept in from the ocean and a swift breeze swished past. Then, as if turned on by a high pressure faucet, the sky opened in a torrent of rain.

"Have Captain Whistler double the guard. This is Jap weather," Huxley said.

Lieutenant Bryce had crouched in the brush and watched as the last shovelful of coral was thrown atop the graves of the Jasco squad, and crudely made wooden crosses were sunk into the ground.

He slumped to the deck, chewed his fingernails and doubled over, sobbing hysterically. It was dark, dark and wet in the rainy night. He looked around. Those dead men . . . those stiff bodies. . . .

I will die . . . we all will die. We will float in the water like the men in the lagoon. Huxley wants me to die . . . Shapiro will kill me! He will kill me! They want to kill themselves like

the men in the lagoon . . . like the enemy kill themselves. I've
got to live . . . I've got to tell the world that Marines live on
blood! Blood! Blood! One island . . . another and another . . .
it will never end. Tomorrow we will meet the Japanese and we
will all kill ourselves. I've got to live. I'll hide . . . yes, that's it.
Run back. The natives will hide me . . . I'll say I was lost.
Huxley can't hurt me then . . . they won't let him touch me.

He crawled to the road on his hands and knees.

"Halt! Who goes there?"

Bryce sprang to his feet and dashed down the road.

Crack! A shot whistled in the air.

Bryce fell to the road, groveling in the mud. "Don't shoot
me . . . don't shoot me!" He pounded his fists into the dirt and
screamed and clawed at the mud as if trying to dig. Doc
Kyser and Huxley raced over to him. The doctor shouted to
the rest to stay back.

Huxley jumped on Bryce and pinioned his arms behind him.
The raving man fought back like a tiger. They rolled on the
ground. Bryce slashed out as if his fingers were claws. Huxley
struggled to his feet. The Lieutenant, his strength spent, crawled
on his knees and threw his arms about Huxley's legs.

"Don't kill me . . . God, don't kill me!"

He rolled over into the mud, emitting little laughs. For several moments Huxley stood over him and stared down. He
shook his head and gritted his teeth.

"He is completely insane," Kyser said.

"Poor devil," Huxley said. "I am to blame."

"Not any more than you are to blame for the war." Kyser
turned to the men. "You fellows get some rope and tie him.
Put him in the empty hut and post a guard. . . . Let's get some
sleep, Sam."

"Yes, it looks like the rain is letting up a little."

7.

NEXT MORNING Captain Shapiro and Gunnery
Sergeant McQuade swung down the road with Fox Company
behind them.

"Hey, candy-ass," McQuade yelled to Burnside. "I'll call
you when we've cleared all the Japs out."

"Blow it out," Burnside called back.

In a few minutes the point had stepped into the channel toward the next island. I limped to my gear, glad that the march
would soon be over.

The natives, who had had the good sense to get in out of the rain and had disappeared into thin air the night before, reappeared in greater numbers as the column rolled on. It was good to have them aboard. This last day was going to be rough. The strain of listless life aboard ship, our skipping from island to island during the strike on Betio, and now this hike from Huxley's pace—it was all catching up with the men. A solemn tenseness came over us as we moved northward along the path that ran by the lagoon.

More villages were passed but the novelty of the bare breasts had worn down to passive admiration. The business at hand was the main concern.

By late afternoon we reached the middle of Molly Island— Taratai. We ran into the Sisters of the Sacred Heart Society. Huxley halted us long enough to receive their blessings and to point out to them the place where we had buried the Jasco squad.

As we crossed over Molly, we caught sight of our objective: the end of Tarawa atoll—Cora, Muariki Island loomed closer, two islands up. Shapiro's company was already working close to the last island. Grim silence set in as Huxley's Whores bent forward to stiffen the pace. The sweat, the weight, were as before. Palm trees floated past rapidly, each step bringing us closer to the fleeing foe. We now had an army half Marine and half Gilbertese. The tingling anticipation of pending action dampened my palms as I plodded on toward the channel which would bring our journey to a close.

A runner from Fox Company puffed down the column to Huxley. "Sir, Cora dead ahead!" The word shot through us like contact with a live wire.

Huxley held up his hand for the battalion to halt. "Have Captain Shapiro report to me at once."

"He's already taken Fox Company over, sir. They're spread out and waiting for you." Highpockets' face reddened.

"I told him not to cross over!"

Wellman smiled. "You knew damned well he would."

"All right. On your feet, men. This is it."

We waded to Cora as though we were walking on hot coals. At last we set foot on her with mixed uneasiness—an island shared by a leprosy colony and the Japs. No fighting had started. Maybe they had decided to swim for it or maybe a submarine had evacuated them. We stood by nervously as Fox Company sent a patrol halfway up the island.

There was no enemy to be found. I didn't like it. Cora was creepy. We moved quickly and quietly up to the narrow waist of the island. At this point it was not more than a hundred yards from lagoon to ocean. The brush was very thick. It showed signs of having been uninhabited for many years. The few huts were filled with holes and smelled moldy and rotten. Past this narrow middle the island suddenly spread to a width of a mile, as the spokes of a fan handle spread to form the fan. The wide part in front of us looked like the Guadalcanal jungle. The hour was late. We halted and set up camp.

A few hundred yards up the narrow waist, before the fan end, Fox Company spread from ocean to lagoon and dug in.

We put all three radios into operation, to Sarah and the alligator, to the destroyer, and to air cover. We set up close to the water of the lagoon. Sarah lay almost due south, twenty-five miles away on a beeline. The battalion had covered better than forty-five miles and crossed twenty-five islands. Still no Japs.

We nervously ate a can of pork and beans, hard crackers, hard candy and cold coffee. Shapiro, McQuade, and Paris ambled into the CP right by us.

"What does it look like, Max?" Huxley asked.

"Beats me. No trace of them."

"I don't like it, I don't like it at all," Wellman said.

"I couldn't find anything, not even footprints," Paris said.

Huxley thought hard as he dragged on his smoke. "How is your position, Max?"

"We're deployed perfectly from lagoon to ocean. Only about seventy-five yards wide there. The island starts spreading just beyond."

"We'd better play it safe. I'll send up the rest of the battalion's machine guns in case they try something tonight. Marlin, have Captain Harper move George Company right in back of Fox. Max, as soon as it turns dark, send out a patrol and probe the fantail."

"How far do you want us to go?"

"Not 'us.' You don't go out tonight, Max."

"Aw hell, Colonel."

"Send Lieutenant Rackley, he's got eyes in back of his head. McQuade and Paris, you go along too. Move as far up as you can. Get the picture of the terrain. As soon as you contact them, shag-ass back."

"Aye aye, sir," McQuade and Paris said.

"We'd better use a password tonight."

"May I suggest *Helen*," Wellman said.

"Helen it is. Pass it on."

The machine gunners of the other companies were already filtering past us for the front. Shapiro put his helmet on over the hair which now looked like a permanent wave and mudpack combination. "If you start fighting, you are not to commit

Fox Company without my orders, understand, Max?" Shapiro nodded. "Gunner, have a telephone line run in there."

"Aye aye, sir."

Dark was coming quickly. We went over our weapons in a final check and then, out of nowhere, native women and children began to shyly edge into our bivouac. At first we were scared that they might be lepers, but were assured that the colony had not been in existence since the British were run off some years back. The natives seemed in a jovial mood. It was really the first time we had had to sit about and exchange chatter. Under the stern eyes of the officers we kept a talking distance from the women. Before long a group of them began singing and the entire camp gathered about. First shades of night were lightened by a huge white moon which dipped low on the lagoon. The sturdy, handsome people sang an ancient song, maybe as old as time itself. Their primitive harmony, born from sheer love of music, awed us. We stamped and applauded for more. They accepted our offerings of gum and cigarettes and sang again. Every new song brought a melody with beautiful harmony. The swelling chorus drifted over the glass-still waters as the group of tattered Marines sat entranced. Then, their voices blended in a familiar tune, and after their own words they sang the words that were known by us:

> *"Oh, come all ye faithful,*
> *Joyful and triumphant,*
> *Oh, come ye, oh, come ye . . ."*

Muffled voices sent me springing up with my carbine. Burnside arose with a knife in hand. I had a hard time opening my eyes, which were puffed shut from mosquito bites. Through the netting I made out Pedro and Doc Kyser coming down the road. Behind them was McQuade and three stretchers sagging. Moans came from one of them. Colonel Huxley jumped from his hole, followed, as always, by Ziltch.

"The patrol," Burnside whispered.

"That's Paris on a stretcher," I said.

"Lay them over there. Pedro, get that plasma." Pedro bent over the moaning Marine and squinted at his dogtag.

"Type O, we have a pint or two, quick."

"Hokay."

"Put sulfa on and dress those other two lads," Kyser ordered another corpsman.

"Aye aye, sir."

I recognized the anguished boy as a corporal, a squad leader from Alabama. He was in bad shape with a hole in his stomach.

Kyser moved him to a place where he could get some light to perform the transfusion. "I hope we don't run out of plasma before we stop the bleeding," Doc muttered.

Paris and the other men accepted their treatment easily. The intelligence sergeant sat up and emitted a shaky smile. Pedro gave him a shot of brandy to steady him.

"Where did you get hit?" I asked.

He held up his right hand. Four fingers were torn away. "Stateside survey," he said, "finally made it."

"Can you talk, Paris?" Huxley asked.

"I'm all right, sir." Highpockets knelt beside the stretcher as Paris gave the story. "We moved out and went up about two hundred yards to where the island starts getting wider. In dead center there is a clearing and a big camp. We counted thirty huts and an observation tower by the ocean. The camp has a lot of big boulders in it and it will make good cover. We went through the camp, it was empty. There is open ground for fifty yards past it, then brush. It's thicker than hell. The Japs were waiting in the brush for us, we didn't even see them." Paris grimaced as Pedro tightened a tourniquet on his wrist. He reached to scratch his beard with the stubs of his fingers, then brought his hand down slowly and stared at it.

"Good work. Take it easy, lad."

"Thank you sir."

"Where is Lieutenant Rackley?"

"Dead," McQuade said. "Right through the head. We had to leave him to help the other three back."

"Too bad. How hard do you estimate they hit you, McQuade?"

"Looks to me like they have a skirmish line in that brush. There was at least two machine guns and they shot like they had plenty of ammunition."

Huxley whistled under his breath. "How wide is the island up there?"

"Big. Five hundred yards maybe. The camp runs from the center of the island to the ocean. On the lagoon side it's like jungle."

Huxley turned to his staff. "Wellman, get Shapiro on the phone. Have him move Fox Company into that abandoned camp and take cover at zero five hundred. Contact Harper and have him move George Company on the flank and move up slowly on the lagoon side and dig in when he straightens his line to meet Fox. Tell him it is jungle thick."

"Suppose they counterattack?"

"I don't think they'll choose to. They are going to make their stand past the clearing of the camp in that brush. We can move to the camp in comparative safety, I believe."

"Got any ideas of how we are going to get at them past the clearing?"

"We'll come to that tomorrow. I want to take a look in daylight." He turned to McQuade. "You'd better stay here tonight."

"I'd better get back up with Max . . . er, I mean Captain Shapiro. He's so mad he'll probably go after them tonight if I don't get him calmed down." Huxley smiled as the large-gutted gunny hitched his belt over his sagging stomach and headed back for Fox Company.

"Gunner."

"Yes, sir?"

"Radio the destroyer. I want them in the lagoon as close to shore as they can get. Radio to Bairiki and ask them to send some landing craft up here so we can shuttle the wounded to the destroyer."

"Aye aye, sir."

Through the night I was awakened by the terrible itching. My hands were swelling fast under the impact of a hundred mosquito bites. With each fitful awakening I sat up, and each time, I caught a glimpse of the gangly skipper still sitting by the water's edge, his knees up, his arm draped about them and his head half nodding. Early in the morning I climbed from my hole and walked over to him. The rest of the camp was asleep except for the radio watch and the corpsman.

"Mind if I sit down, sir?"

"Oh, hello, Mac." I looked about and saw Ziltch propped against a tree ten yards away with his eyes ever watchful on his skipper.

"How did the fellow with the stomach wound make out, sir?"

"Dead . . . not enough plasma to do him any good. He had a widowed mother with three other sons in the service. One of them went down on the *Saratoga*."

It seemed strange that with the burden of eight hundred men in his command he should be so concerned over the loss of one.

"We picked a dandy spot. These mosquitoes are murder tonight, sir."

"Hadn't you better get some sleep, Mac?"

"Kind of hard. I saw you up and I wondered if you were feeling all right."

"I always did say you'd make a fine chaplain . . . go to sleep."

"Aye aye, sir." I returned to my infested hole and snuggled in close to Burnside. For the first time, I felt sorry for Sam Huxley.

Marion and Lighttower were in the aid station. Mary couldn't open either eye and the Injun's face was lopsided. They were assured that the condition was temporary and they would be able to join us by the time we were ready to move up. Marion's eyes were distorted so that the flesh of his eyelids had over-lapped his glasses and cemented them to his face.

They joined the squad around the radios and awaited orders. Up front there was an increased tempo of gunfire as Fox and George Companies were moving out.

"Yes sir, yes sir. We'll have your dress blues when you get to San Diego, just sign here," L.Q. chattered.

"I wish they wouldn't give us so much chow. A man can't fight proper when he's so stuffed up." There had been no breakfast.

"Butts on that cigarette."

"Butts on them butts."

Four walking wounded straggled down the road and asked for the aid station. "How's it going up there?" Andy asked.

"Rough."

Then came a half dozen stretchers straining under their gore-drenched loads.

"Looks like we're getting us a nice casualty list. Another couple hours and we'll be able to rejoin the division."

A white-robed nun stepped up to Doc Kyser. "Are you in charge here?" she asked.

"Yes, Doctor Kyser is the name, Sister."

"I am Sister Joan Claude, Mother Superior of the Mission. I would like to offer our services with the wounded."

The hard-pressed doctor breathed a sigh. "You'll pardon the play on words, Sister, but you are the answer to a prayer. Do you people understand anything about medicine?"

"Nursing is one of our duties, Doctor."

"How many are you?"

"Ten."

"Good, we'll be able to release the corpsmen for line duty. Pedro!"

"Yes, sir."

"Have all corpsmen in the aid station come here at once for reassignment. This is nice of you people."

"We are glad to be of service."

Huxley, Marlin, and Ziltch ducked behind some trees as they approached the Fox Company area. The men before them lay dispersed throughout the abandoned Jap camp, behind boulders, trees, and in protected huts. The air was singing with bullets coming to and from the thicket past the camp.

"Runner," Huxley called.

The call for a runner went down the line till a Marine leapt from behind a rock and zigged from cover to cover till he slid in beside Huxley. A trail of slugs ripped the earth up behind him.

"Where is Shapiro?"

"How the hell do I know?" the runner answered. "He's all over."

"Take us to your CP," Huxley ordered. The runner fell flat and crawled forward to new cover and waved the party up to him. One by one they crawled up behind him. He dashed for a boulder, and a clatter of fire went up from the brush. High-pockets' legs opened as he sprinted to the new cover. It was several moments before Ziltch and Marlin could safely be waved over. Marlin dived head first on top of them, then Ziltch came. The orderly tumbled and fell in the open, and Huxley bolted out and literally threw him to the safety of the rock.

"Damn, it's hot up here," Marlin bellowed.

"There's plenty of them in the brush," Huxley said. The runner pointed to a thatched hut about fifty yards from the ocean. It was hemmed in by trees on the side facing the Japs and offered a natural barrier. Behind the trees a squad of riflemen crouched in protection of the command post. They sprang up for the last dash and bolted across the open ground and tumbled breathlessly into the hut. Gunnery Sergeant McQuade lay flat on his back, his legs crossed and knees up as he enjoyed a cigarette while gazing at the ceiling.

"Sorry to interrupt your siesta, McQuade," Huxley puffed.

"Hello, Sam," McQuade said, dropping military formality in deference to the flying bullets.

"Where is Shapiro?"

"He went to straighten the line, he'll be back in a few minutes."

Huxley impatiently snarled as he peered out of the hut at the brush. Fox Company was pinned down. To rush the Japs when you couldn't even see them might cost the entire company. A runner sprinted toward the hut, fell, arose and skittered in. He held his face.

"Man, I'm lucky. Just nicked me. We're bringing in the telephone," he panted.

"Lay down a covering fire," Huxley shouted outside. "Make them lay low, there's a telephone man trying to get in. Do you people have a mortar here, McQuade?"

"We ran out of mortars an hour after we started."

"Sonofabitch!"

The telephone man ducked with the reel of wire hanging from his hand as he awaited the signal to move for the CP. His covering fire raged. Huxley gave a signal and the man tore across the field like a whippet, with the wire unrolling behind him. He ducked into the safety of the hut, shakily cut the wire from the reel, and unstrapped the field phone from about his neck. Quick and workmanlike, he peeled the wire and screwed the ends under connecting posts of the phone. He held the butterfly switch down and blew into the receiver. He cranked the handle. "Hello Lincoln White, this is Fox CP."

"Hello Fox, this is Lincoln White." The phone man smiled and relaxed as he handed the phone to Huxley.

"Hello, Wellman, this is Huxley. What's the word back there?"

"Hello, Sam. George Company is getting plastered, drawing a lot of casualties. We've got forty or fifty wounded here in the aid station now. Harper says he is ass deep in jungle and trying to move to connect a flank with Fox Company but his position is vulnerable. If Fox can push them out of that thicket, Harper will be able to move forward. Can you move Fox up, Sam?"

"It would be suicide. There's an open field up here and we can't even see them."

"Hang on a minute, Sam. There's a runner from George Company here now."

"Where the hell is Shapiro?" Huxley muttered as he waited for Wellman.

"Hello, Sam . . . are you still there?"

"Yes, go ahead."

"George Company is pinned down. The Japs are picking them off one by one. Do you want me to have Whistler move Easy Company anywhere?"

"Stand fast. Tell Harper to dig in as best he can. I'll call you when we can figure out how we're going to dislodge these bastards. By the way, any word from the alligator?"

"Still a couple hours away."

"How are the wounded holding up?"

"Fine, splendid. No squawks, good bunch. Sisters from the mission are acting as nurses. Doing a good job under the circumstances."

Huxley replaced the phone in its case just in time to see the unmistakable, squat figure of the little captain of Fox walking toward the hut several yards away.

"The goddam fool, he's begging to get hit," Marlin said.

"Take cover, Max!" Huxley yelled.

The men in the CP gazed in awe. Max Shapiro was moving as unconcernedly through the hailstorm of lead as if he were taking a Sunday stroll through a park. Huxley rubbed his eyes as if he thought they were betraying him. The Captain was acting like he was a holy image or something inviolable. The legend of Two Gun Shapiro was no idle slop-shute story, it was quite true. His appearance was like magic and put iron into the embattled boys he led. He walked from rock to rock and tree to tree slapping his boys on the back as if he was coaching a football game. His poor vision through the thick-lensed glasses became alive and crystal clear. Huxley couldn't decide whether he was divine or insane. No mere human could be so utterly fearless for his life. Huxley watched him promenade across the clearing with the bullets singing around him.

"You over there," Shapiro called. "Do you want a purple heart?"

"Hell no, Max."

"Better move your ass then, because there's a sniper fifteen yards from you in that tree. Aim true, son, don't waste any shots."

"O.K., Max."

He strolled into the hut, wiped the sweat from his face, and took a cigarette from McQuade's breast pocket. He pulled the smoke from McQuade's lips and lit his own cigarette with it. "Hi, Sam," he said.

"You may think you're smart, Max, but if I hear of another exhibition like that I'll. . . ."

"Aw calm down, Sam. Them slanteyes couldn't hit a bull in the ass with a bass fiddle."

"Did you see Harper?"

"Yes," Shapiro said, wiping his glasses. "Somebody ought to give him a pack of gum. He's been chewing the same piece for a week. If it gets any harder his teeth are going to fall out."

His irresistible manner seemed to lighten the tension. "Well, how does it look?" Huxley said.

"Not good. We can't get connected with George Company and they're getting cut to pieces. They're like flies in that brush, Sam, maybe a battalion of them, and they're slinging lead like they have an ammo dump of it. I don't like it . . . if we go on trading potshots with them they're going to wear us down."

"Dammit," Huxley said. "We haven't enough ammo to keep this up."

"Maybe we'd better radio for fire support from the destroyer," Marlin suggested.

"No. We are on top of each other now. One bad salvo and we'll fix ourselves up for good, and air support would be even riskier."

Shapiro popped his head outside the hut. "Hey, you people," he called to the riflemen behind the trees, who were covering the CP, "can't you tell when they're shooting down on you? Spray those treetops to your right." He stuck his head back in. "The way it looks to me, skipper, the brush they are in is only about fifty yards deep. If we can bust through it we can make them pull back past the next clearing. That will take the pressure off Harper and get the line connected."

"How?" Huxley said. "We can't rush them."

"Sam," Marlin said excitedly, "why not retreat till morning and let the destroyer have a go at them? Maybe we can starve them out in two or three days and bag the lot of them as prisoners."

Huxley turned purple. He looked for a moment as though he was going to spit at his operations officer. Marlin cowered back.

"Those Nips are as beat out as we are," Shapiro said. "Maybe we can suck them into charging us."

"They won't fall for anything like that."

"They've been pulling it on us the whole damned war. If we quit shooting and start yelling they may whip up into a banzai try. The way we're going now we'll be out of ammo and men before we are able to move. We've got to do something and fast."

Huxley pondered. His line was thin and his casualties were piling up. He had to beat them out of that brush before dark or suffer a night attack. They were simply trying to outlast him and held the superior position. Yes, something unorthodox had to be done. . . . "O.K., Max, we will give her a try."

He cranked the phone. "Wellman, this is Sam. Have Harper hold at all costs. We are going to try to lure the Nips out in the open. If they come out, Whistler is to move his boys right past us into that brush. He is not to come to the assistance of Fox Company but to bypass us and drive forward, understand."

"Yes, Sam. Good luck."

"Funny," Shapiro mused, "Ed Coleman used that same trick, Sam. I underestimated you."

Huxley sluffed off the compliment. "Runner."

"Yes, sir."

"Get out there and pass the word to cease firing except at visible targets. They are to just sit there and start yelling, and tell them to make it loud, clear, and nasty. If the Japs charge, stay put till they reach our position and then use bayonets."

"Aye aye, sir." The runner grabbed his helmet and shot out from the hut. From lip to lip the word soon passed over the field. Behind rocks and trees the men of Fox Company slowly fixed bayonets and their rifles became silent. They grasped their weapons tightly and glued their eyes on the green mass of brush before them. Suddenly, the Japanese rifles stopped firing. The switch had caught them off balance; they feared a trick. A faint jabbering was heard. Max Shapiro stepped from the hut and cupped his hands to his lips.

"Hey Tojo!" he shouted. "You bastards sure are lousy shots. Looks like the vultures will be having a meal of Jap meat tonight!"

"Show your faces, you yellow-bellied bastards!"

"Hey, maggot bait!"

"Have a drink, Jap." A coconut was hurled into the brush, followed by a barrage of them.

"Take a shot, Tojo." A Marine stuck his head from behind a rock. A shot whistled by. "Hey Tojo, three for a quarter."

Huxley watched anxiously as the barrage of words was hurled out. Then, it became very silent. Only the drifting smoke of a cigarette could be seen. A wind rippled through the camp. For ten minutes the eerie quiet continued. Then a weird song arose down the line of Marines:

> *"Did you ever think*
> *When a hearse goes by,*
> *That you might be the next to die. . . ."*

There was no sound of joy in the voices that blended in the chorus that cut the hot afternoon stickiness. It was trembly, sweaty singing from the lips of men crouched low and coiled like rattlers.

> *"The worms crawl in,*
> *The worms crawl out. . . ."*

Captain Shapiro stepped from the hut and signaled for silence. Some snipers blasted at him. He lit a cigarette, spat in the direction of the brush, and returned to the cover of the hut.

"What do you think?" Marlin asked.

"I don't know," Huxley said. "They act rattled, like they're expecting to be hit from another direction and we're stalling for time."

Suddenly a loud jabbering came from the brush, an argument as the Japs spotted Whistler's company moving up behind the camp. They were getting confused! The talk became louder.

"Hold fire," the word passed down Fox Company.

Some bushes separated and a Japanese officer stepped into the clear, staggering like a drunk. He took two slow cautious steps toward the Marines.

"He's loaded on saki," Marlin whispered.

"Good."

The little Oriental's eyes glinted about like a rat's. The deathly quiet forced him to scream to bolster his courage.

"Marine die!" He shook his fist. He got no answer. . . . "Marine die!" he screeched louder. He whipped out his samurai sword and twirled it whistling over his head. He jumped up and down on the ground, cursing and ranting. Shapiro slung a rock at him and he sprang back into the brush. The noise from there became louder and louder. The enraged enemy were unmistakably whipping themselves into a lather.

"They're really getting their crap hot . . . stand ready. Runner, get back there to Captain Whistler and have him prepare to attack."

A violent bevy of shrieks from the brush and at last the outraged enemy poured out over the clearing, their nerves shattered by the chase, the fear, and now the waiting game. They charged behind their officers with their long rifles pointed down and their bayonets glinting, mad yells on their sweaty, hungry lips and violence in their eyes.

Shapiro was in front of Fox Company in an instant. The steps between him and the enemy narrowed. "Charge!" he screamed, firing the two famed pistols point blank into the maddened crowd.

The clamp of inevitable death, closing on them for a week, had turned the Japanese soldiers into young maniacs. With screams of their own the Marines leapt from cover, head on into the charge. The air was filled with bloodcurdling shrieks as the wild melee of men locked in mortal combat. Savage cries, hissing steel, and flesh pounding flesh.

Fox Company worked in teams with each man having a wingman to cover him. The opposing lines buckled a moment under the impact of meeting head on. Gasps, cries, and moans as bayonets found their mark. The flat thud of a rifle butt crushing a skull. Fury heightened as the fighters hurled prone bodies to get at each other.

Captain Whistler's Easy Company raced past the savage combat into the brush. The remaining Japs there fell into wild confusion and fired not only at the Marines but their own comrades.

"Hit the deck, Sam!" Ziltch screamed.

A stray with a knife in his fist flung himself on Huxley's back. The Colonel dived to the deck and rolled the Jap off. The little orderly was on him like a cat, scuffling wildly on the coral earth to hold off the knife point. He pinioned the Jap's arm as Huxley whipped out his pistol and smashed it again and again into the Oriental's face. With a bloody last gasp, the man finally became limp. Huxley flung the body from his sight and shakily helped Ziltch to his feet.

"You hurt, son?"

"I'm O.K., skipper."

"Good lad."

The Japanese fury of the moment before turned into a whimpering slaughter. They were no match now for Shapiro and his Foxes. The Marines waded into them systematically until they were cornered and the butchery was on. They were cut down without mercy. The ground was littered with dead and the moans of the wounded brought only a quick bullet, until the last Japanese was dead.

My squad was still by the radios, ears peeled to every word coming and going over the phone with which Major Wellman commanded the rear echelon. How Company, the reserve, was assembled near us in squads of riflemen. As a tattered runner dashed down the road from the lines and called for reinforcements a squad of How would move up.

"We broke through!" Wellman shouted from the phone. "Move the CP to the abandoned camp."

"Break down the TBX on the double," the Gunner shouted.

Before the words had left his lips a telephone man had cut the lines and moved up. We threw our sets into their clumsy cases and were besieged by native volunteers anxious to carry them.

"Sorry," Keats said, "you can't go up. Too close . . . bang, bang! You stay and get water and wounded, yes?"

We trotted up the road, panting under our loads, and cut into the camp where Fox Company had made its fight just a few moments before. Stumbling over the bodies, we struggled to the former Fox CP hut and set up the battalion command post. There wasn't a single Marine lying in the open, only Japs. Our wounded had all been removed. All around us there was a constant crackle of gunfire and grenades as Easy and George Companies worked through the jungle flushing out the diehards.

"Get that radio in with Sarah and the alligator!" the Gunner yelled.

A set was hooked up in less than two minutes and I signaled the Injun to spin the generator.

"Dammit," Lighttower cried, "the generator conked!"

"Set up another one, quick."

"Burnside," I shouted, "rip the other two radios apart. We'll have to try to piece one together that will work."

"Hurry, dammit, hurry!"

"Lighttower, Levin, Andy, Danny . . . get out there and keep those snipers off our ass. Mary, lend a hand here."

Burnside, Marion and I knocked the cases open and switched tubes, batteries and wiring desperately, trying to find a combination that would work out of the three radios. The Gunner raced from message center to the switchboard and back to us in a crazy circle, prodding us on. At last I signaled for a test and donned the earphones. I said a short prayer as Burnside cranked the generator furiously and beat out a test call to Seabags.

I moved the dials trying to catch something through the static hissing through the earphones. Then a faint flat set of sounds came through. I couldn't read it but I could tell from the spacing that it was Seabags' fist.

"I got them, spin her over again." I repeated the message and asked for a long test call. I could barely make out the call letters.

"Gunner, I only read them one and one. I don't know if we are getting through."

"Hit the deck!"

I knocked the radio flat and threw my body over it just in time to get rocked by the splitting smash of a grenade.

"Get that radio out of here!" Huxley roared.

"We're hitting for the lagoon," I shouted, picking up the battery case. "I'll send a runner back here when we are in contact. Come on men—shag ass." The squad ripped the set from its moorings and packing it under their arms dashed after me through the sniper fire toward the rear of George Company.

At the water's edge we slapped the radio together and made a test to the alligator. It was fairly close and we could read each other clearly. Doc Kyser ran up to me frantically.

"Mac, how close is the alligator?"

"I don't know yet, Doc . . . we can't see them."

"If I don't get the plasma here quick I won't have a boy alive back there. We have nearly two hundred wounded."

"We're doing what we can," I said.

"My hands are tied! I can't just let them die!"

"Quiet, dammit!" I commanded. Levin, at the radio, had caught a call from Seabags.

"They want our position," Levin shouted. "They're only a couple miles south."

"Lighttower!"

"Yo!"

"Get back to the CP and get our exact position."

"Roger." He dashed off.

Wellman sighted us and dashed over the road. "Any word from the alligator? We've got the Japs disorganized but we can't follow through, we're almost out of ammo."

"They'll be in in less than an hour."

"No sooner?"

"I'll have to have those medical supplies before that. . . ."

"I'll have to ask you men to leave the area," I barked to Wellman and Kyser. "We are having radio troubles as it is and we can't do a goddam thing with you poking us in the ass." The two officers, stupefied at first by the terse order, meekly retreated from where Levin labored on the earphones.

"Look! There's the alligator!"

I snatched Burnside's field glasses and focused them on the lagoon. Bogged almost under the water, I caught a faint glimpse of a square gray object moving in slow motion through the water. I judged she was making three knots an hour and was two miles away.

"Runner!" Wellman shouted across the road, "get Major Pagan and have all remaining men in How Company stand by for a working party. I want half of them to unload and the other half to rush ammo up to the front. Have men stand ready to evacuate the wounded to the landing craft waiting at the reef. Kyser, prepare the critical cases for transfer to the destroyer ... Mac!"

"Yes."

"Contact the destroyer and have them prepare to receive the wounded. Have the landing craft get as close to shore as they can."

"Aye aye, sir." I scratched the message out and Levin transmitted it as Speedy and Marion whirled the generator for all they were worth.

"Quiet," Levin demanded. He wrote a message and shouted up to me, "The alligator requests our position again."

"Dammit, where is that Injun?"

In the haste to transfer from the CP and contact the alligator, I hadn't surveyed the new position too well. The radio was set up on the beach near a small clump of brush. I had assumed that they were two hundred yards behind George Company and that the area was clear. I was wrong.

I was electrified by a cracking from the clump of brush. The radio transmitter case split in half and toppled over, then, the generator crashed from its anchor on a tree. The Japs were blasting at the group with an automatic weapon, point blank. We all fell flat and pumped slugs wildly and blindly into the thicket.

"Levin, get the hell out of there!" He sprinted back to cover. The radio was wrecked. I looked over the water. The alligator loomed closer and was making better speed than I had reckoned. Maybe the unpredictable tide was helping. Marion and me crouched behind cover and exchanged fire. I could see nothing . . . the Japs were completely hidden. Out of the corner of my eye I saw Jake Levin up and running away. *Yellow son of a bitch!* Too busy to chase him now.

"Chief! *Hit the deck!*" Danny screamed as the Injun dashed toward us from the CP. He dropped in his tracks behind a fallen log.

"Don't call me chief," he yelled.

Burnside crawled over by me, reloading his carbine.

"They got the radio. The others are no good."

"Tell me something I don't know," I said.

"What we gonna do?"

"Maybe I should stick a tank up your ass and float you over them."

"It's not funny. We're up the creek . . . I crap you not."

"There can't be more than a half dozen of them in there. We'll just have to stand fast and keep them from breaking through to the wounded."

Speedy Gray dived on top of us between bursts of Jap fire.

"What the hell is this, Grand Central Station?" I snapped.

"Had to see you, Mac. The alligator is going too far north. It's heading right for the Jap lines."

"Oh, my God!"

"Burnside, what are we going to do?"

"Close one eye and fart."

"Heads down. . . ."

"We've got to steer them in back of us."

"I can see her now. She's just a couple hundred yards out."

"Quick, where are the semaphore flags?"

"Back in the CP."

"Cover me. I'm going to make a run for the water," I said peeling off my shirt. "I'll try to wave at them."

"It won't work."

"We've got to stop them! They're heading right into Jap territory!"

"Cover me!" a voice screamed behind me. It was Levin. He had gone back to the CP for a blinker gun when the radio was wrecked. He had foreseen the trouble. I closed my eyes, terribly ashamed of what I had thought.

"Levin's coming over the road!"

"Cover him."

Levin hurdled the smashed radio and ducked low under the barrage we lay down for him. He knelt on the beach, pointed the blinker toward the alligator. His finger pulled dots and dashes desperately. He waved the gun back and forth to catch their attention and screamed to them as he did so.

Smoke arose from the brush as the Japs sighted him.

"Levin!"

He doubled over, still pulling the trigger of the light. He lay on his stomach with blood squirting from his face, but he kept signaling. Gunfire ripped his body.

The alligator veered! It cut around sharply. Seabags had the message.

Burnside, Speedy and me sprang up and raced toward the prostrate boy who was lying half in the water. Speedy and me grabbed him as Burnside stood erect and hurled grenades into the brush. We dragged him to cover. I bent down and ripped his shirt off.

"God!" Speedy screamed, turning his face from the sight. "Corpsman! Corpsman! Corpsman!"

Speedy stopped vomiting. "I'll take him back . . ." He lifted Levin in his arms, keeping his eyes raised from the sight of the stomach, horribly torn.

"After them!" I shrieked. The squad was behind me, wading madly into the brush to kill.

The Texan wandered to the place where the long line of wounded lay. A working party unloaded the precious plasma from the alligator near by. A hundred makeshift transfusions were being administered. Other men raced to the lines bogged under bandoleers of ammunition and cases of mortars and grenades. A blood-spattered nun assisted Speedy, laying a poncho on the deck.

"Get the doctor here at once," the Nun said.

When Speedy had returned with Kyser, the Sister was kneeling over Levin's gory body, praying. Kyser took one look and nodded his head slowly and was gone at the beckoning of another nun.

"I'm sorry, my son," the Sister consoled.

"Is he still . . ."

"Yes, but only for a very few moments," she said.

"Look, lady . . . he's . . . he's my buddy . . . could I stay?"

"Yes, my son."

Speedy took off his helmet and sat beside Levin. He emptied his canteen on a ragged handkerchief and wiped the sweat from Levin's forehead. At the touch of the cool rag Jake's eyes opened slowly.

"Hi, Speedy," he whispered weakly.

"How you feel?"

"Don't feel nuttin'. What happened . . . did the alligator get in?"

"Yeah."

"Good . . . that's damned good."

"They'll be evacuating you to the tin can in a couple minutes," Speedy lied.

Levin smiled. He reached out feebly and the Texan took his hand. "Hold my hand . . . will you, Speedy?"

"Sure."

"Speedy . . ."

"Yeah?"

He tugged Speedy close until his mouth nearly touched the Texan's ear. "Don't . . . don't let them guys . . . I want a Star of David . . . My old man would have a fit if they put a cross over me. . . ."

I walked over to Speedy. He was sitting there holding Levin's hand although Levin's face was already covered with the poncho. "We broke through," I whispered. I tried to offer Speedy a cigarette. He looked up at me and tried to speak. His face was grief-stricken. "He wasn't sore at you, Speedy, he never was . . . you were buddies."

Speedy was trembling all over. "Go on, kid. Take off, you'll feel better later." He ran from me toward an abandoned hut.

I looked down the road. Another stretcher was coming in. Burnside lay on it. His eyes were open and glassy.

"Burny," I whispered.

"He dead," the native bearer said, puffing past me.

Less than twenty-four hours after the first shot had been fired on Cora Island, the battle for Tarawa had come to a close.

I slumped down to the deck, too exhausted to think. The battalion sat around me and there were only muffled whispers, like the whispers of the guys who had sat on Betio a week ago. Seemed to me I was on a cloud, hanging on in midair. I heard everything but it was like hearing it through a fog. There was the clanking against the coral of the gravedigging party. *Clank*, then the whisper of sand falling from a shovel to fill a hole . . . and another . . . and another. The sound of the alligator rumbled back and forth on the way to the barrier reef where the landing craft waited to transfer the wounded to the destroyer.

I saw Sam Huxley and Kyser through the haze, haggard, talking to one of the nuns.

"I don't know how we can thank you people enough."

"We are glad to have been able to help, Colonel."

"I don't know what we could have done without you."

"The natives will build a fine cemetery for your brave men and we shall see that it is well kept. I promise you that. And we shall pray for their souls."

"Thank you, Sister Joan. What can we do for you? What do you need here? We will be happy to send anything."

"Don't you worry yourself about that, my son. You are very tired."

"You shall hear from us, I promise."

"Colonel Huxley."

"Yes, Sister?"

"About the Japanese dead . . . would your men?"

"I'm afraid not. I understand your feelings, but this is war, you know."

"Very well. The natives shall dig their graves."

I looked down the road and saw the remains of Fox Company limping back. Shapiro was at their head, a cigar clenched in his teeth and a look of triumph on his face as he went to Huxley to report the end of resistance. McQuade walked by him, his dungaree shirt in shreds and his huge belly hanging over his pistol belt.

"Where is that candy-ass Burnside?" McQuade roared. "He can come out of his hole now, the fighting's over." Gunner Keats went to him and put his arm on his shoulder, led him over the road, and whispered to him. McQuade stopped short and spun about. He stood dazed for a moment. Keats patted his back slowly and then took the helmet from his balding head and walked slowly toward the gravediggers to the long line of bodies awaiting their final sack.

"Mac."

I scrambled to my feet. "Yes, sir?"

"Are any radios working?" Huxley asked.

"The one in the alligator."

"The next time it comes in, send this message."

"Aye aye, sir."

ENEMY CONTACTED AND DESTROYED ON CORA ISLAND THIS DATE. JAPANESE CASUALTIES: FOUR HUNDRED AND TWENTY-THREE DEAD. WOUNDED NONE. CAPTURED NONE. OUR CASUALTIES NINETY-EIGHT DEAD. TWO HUNDRED THIRTEEN WOUNDED. TARAWA ATOLL IS SECURED. SIGNED, SAMUEL HUXLEY, LT. COLONEL, COMMANDER, SECOND BATTALION, SIXTH MARINES.

8.

AGAIN Huxley's Whores were a garrison force. We had no sooner set foot on Bairiki Island, once known as Sarah, than Huxley reminded us that we were Marines. In a matter of a few days we had set up an immaculate camp. Every cigarette butt was up, the slit trenches were dug squarely, we lined up for rollcall, working parties, chow, and inspection. All hands shaved, bathed and slowly returned to the human race. When our packs arrived from Helen it was like meeting old friends. We were the only Marine troops on the atoll and no provision had been made to survey our ragged clothing. We hung our stuff together with sewing kits. The order went out that we were to stay fully clothed at all times as the flies carried a new brand of poison, dengue fever.

We dug a deep shelter for a new radio, organized ball teams, L.Q. put out a daily newspaper made up of armed forces newscasts, and generally we steadied ourselves for the dryrot boredom of inaction.

I was amazed at the speed with which Tarawa was built into a major striking base. The airstrip at Betio was going full blast and installations sprang up daily along the chain of islands.

A lesser man than Highpockets would have had a job on his hands to keep us under control. However, on Sarah we were isolated and left alone to bitch our heads off over the lousy chow, ragged uniforms, and solid coral beds.

This wasn't the case with Fox Company. Shapiro's outfit was dispatched several islands up near a defense battery and very close to the new airstrip and the center of activity. What Shapiro's Foxes did to the Army and Seabees in the next six weeks more than avenged the rest of us on Bairiki.

No sooner was the Fox campsite chosen than the men were over on the Seabees by the airstrip on Lulu. The first things they took were sufficient cots and pads for themselves. In order to escape detection, they cut the legs off and fixed their cots in the deck so that when covered by a poncho it appeared to be nothing more than a hole in the ground. This didn't aggravate the Seabees, they were fond of the Marines, showed them respect and made no effort to locate the missing cots. In fact, they anticipated and encouraged the boys of Fox Company to frequent their mess hall. Their chow call was never held without half of Shapiro's men in line for the fresh juices, vegetables, ice cream, and a variety of meats.

Away from Huxley's watchful eye the Fox Company camp resembled a rest home or sportsmen's club more than a Marine bivouac. Only on rare occasion was the word Captain heard; it was always an affectionate Skipper, or just plain Max. A maximum of leisure and a bare minimum of work was the rule. Just enough work to keep the place going and enough play to rejuvenate the weary minds and bodies of his men.

Shapiro had a strange weakness for radio operators and welcomed part of the squad with open arms. He stole cots from the Seabees, a tent from the Army, and made them a splendid radio shack by the lagoon. A routine check call was made on the network each hour and there was little else to do. Once Shapiro learned that the radio was capable of receiving short wave programs from the States he sent out a squad of his best men to round up an amplifier system and attach it to the radio so that the programs could be enjoyed by all hands.

All supplies to all camps on the atoll came from a boat pool. Like Huxley's Whores, the boat pool was made up of forgotten men. Each ship of the original task force transports had assigned a few landing craft which were to remain after the invasion and be used to run supplies from incoming freighters to the various installations. The coxswains of these boats were homeless men. Max Shapiro found it a good practice to welcome the boat pool to his camp with open arms.

He once more sent out a squad which rounded up several tents and cots and set up a permanent home for the sailors. His mess hall gave them the only hot meal they could find on the atoll and for his efforts the landing craft pilots always saw to it that Fox Company was well supplied from loads destined to Seabees and Army camps.

There were so many choice items destined for the other camps that transport and warehouse space soon became a problem for Fox Company. With each passing day the volume of missing goods from the boat pool's haul became more alarming. The atoll command decided that armed guards would be necessary to see that the landing craft delivered their loads intact. Shapiro quickly volunteered his company to ride and protect the boat pools from these flagrant thefts. Somehow, even the presence of armed Marines riding the landing craft didn't curb the losses—in fact, they increased. It was then that the Army commander discreetly removed the Marines from the guard detail.

This didn't keep the boys in the boat pool from tipping off Max as to the variety and destination of their loads. When the nightly air raid came and all good soldiers and sailors were in their shelters, Fox Company brought forth their well-hidden stolen jeeps and raced to the stockpiles of the other camps.

The mystery of the disappearing goods didn't much bother the other camps. It was when ten thousand cases of Stateside beer was brought to the airstrip on Lulu that the Army and Seabees put their foot down. Food and clothing was one thing, beer was another, and friendship ceased.

It was easy to detect when a load of beer came in, for the landing crafts of the boat pool in the lagoon buzzed around in crazy circles sometimes ramming each other and running aground under the unsteady hands of their drunken coxswains.

They couldn't hide ten thousand cases of beer, so the Seabees constructed a barbed wire stockade and placed a twenty-four-hour guard atop the mountain of three point two. Fox Company found themselves in the embarrassing situation of having to buy the beer or trade it for previously borrowed lots of food-stuffs. Only during their air raids were they able to negotiate the course.

At the first blast of the air raid siren, Fox Company sprang into action. Their alligator roared over the lagoon for Lulu while the four stolen jeeps came from camouflage and raced at breakneck speed through the blackness to the airstrip. The field was the prime target for enemy bombers and there was little chance of interference from holed-up Seabees and soldiers. As the raid progressed, Shapiro's organizational genius came to the fore. The jeeps rushed from the beer dump to the alli-gator with precision that no Marine working party in a hundred and fifty years had accomplished. When the all clear sounded, the alligator spun about quickly for Buota and the four jeeps made a last load and raced southeast back to camp. Then, the jeeps and the beer seemed to disappear into thin air.

All this was very perplexing to the Seabees. Informal calls were made by various camp commanders to Two Gun to re-port the theft of so many hundred cases of beer. With each visit Shapiro became duly alarmed and agreed that something should be done about it. Max would sigh deeply, shake his head and say an oath against the culprits. He suggested that a shake-down raid be pulled on the natives—who after all were the only logical suspects. Many times the other commanders would cast a wistful eye at the Fox Company air raid shelters at which a round-the-clock guard stood behind machine guns. To make a sly implication that the Marines were guilty was one thing. To dare attempt to send a patrol to inspect the shelters could well mean open warfare. So Fox's bombproofs were never inves-tigated.

Baffled and desperate, the Seabee chaplain was sent to Fox Company to have a long heart to heart chat with its curly-haired skipper and to appeal to his finer instincts. Unfortun-ately the chaplain parked his jeep by the lagoon and left the ignition keys in it. He had to walk back to Lulu praying for the souls of the Marines.

Night often found the Marines indulging in prankish games with their confiscated vehicles. The tide usually washed out a major part of the lagoon and left it a glistening sand bed. It was common for ten to fifteen men to pile aboard a jeep, loaded to the gullets with brew. They'd rip out over the misty sand and reach top speed, slam on the brakes and spin round and round sending men and bottles flying to the sand of the lagoon floor. They played other games, too, buzzing down the road and weaving in and out of palm trees. A couple of broken legs ended that. Two jeeps became stuck in the sand of the lagoon during a spinning session and had to be abandoned after they were stripped for spare parts.

Alarmed at the thefts, Shapiro called his crew together in formation and warned them it must stop. However, anything found lying around loose and unclaimed might be taken to prevent it from rotting in the tropical sun. Anything so discovered must be split up and the skipper, naturally, was to get five per cent off the top.

A dozen poker games went on all the time. When Dick Hart, the battalion gambler, snuck into camp, Shapiro promptly ran him out. It was all right for the Foxes to take one another's money but he'd be damned if George Company was going to get it.

It was Shapiro's greed that almost upset the apple cart. He had a tremendous yen to obtain a "duck," a vehicle that ran on both land and water and was very popular transportation over the inlets that blocked island from island. He told McQuade and some of his lads of his yearning, one evening during a poker game. Nothing was too good for the skipper, his lads reckoned, so they set out to get him a duck. If Max wanted a duck, the least they could do was to get him one. They found him the very finest. In fact it belonged to Commodore Perkins, second in command of the atoll. With tears in his eyes, Two Gun received the offering and drove it proudly into its camouflaged garage.

So enraged was Commodore Perkins at the loss of his private vehicle that he cut off Fox Company's movies. It made little difference, for the boys were too busy drinking beer, listening to armed forces radio, playing poker, and chasing native girls to bother with movies. The nightly shows were run almost exclusively with native attendance. It was then that Perkins decided he had had enough and ordered a patrol, to be led by himself, personally to encircle and shake down the Fox Company area, including the vaunted air raid shelters.

Shapiro, however, was not without a spy system. Being extremely liberal in sharing supplies with the nearby village he had hired a half dozen native lads as an intelligence service. His English-speaking spies loitered the days away in a half dozen strategic positions gathering information. Whenever one of them was approached by a soldier or sailor he would pipe conveniently, "No speakee English." Fox's favorite intelligence agent was a young lad of sixteen nicknamed MacArthur and it was he who got the tip on the impending raid. With the aid of the natives of the nearby village, Fox Company removed their entire haul to the village. While they did this, Sergeant Mc-

Quade feverishly typed out orders and posted them all about camp. One said:

> WARNING: ANYONE CAUGHT STEALING GEAR OR SUP-
> PLIES OF ANY TYPE WILL BE SUBJECTED TO GENERAL
> COURT-MARTIAL. MAX SHAPIRO, CAPTAIN, USMC.

Another:

> IT HAS BEEN CALLED TO MY ATTENTION THAT NUMEROUS
> SUPPLIES FROM NEIGHBORING CAMPS HAVE BEEN MISS-
> ING. ANY INFORMATION LEADING TO THE APPREHENSION
> OF THE THIEVES WILL BE APPRECIATED BY THIS COM-
> MAND.

Commodore Perkins' patrol swooped in at daybreak. Jittery over the possibility of having to face armed Marines, they were surprised to find a peaceful little camp of the finest military nature. As they rushed in on three sides, the men of Fox were going through a rigid routine of close order drill and rifle inspection. Perkins left the place, muttering to himself. MacArthur was promoted to corporal and presented with a brand-new machete, something he had always wanted for cutting coconuts down from the palms.

Each day the alligator arrived at the main camp on Bairiki from Buota with new tales of the daring banditry of Shapiro's Foxes. It made good kindling for bull sessions in the monotonous routine.

The first mailcall from the States, bringing in loads of back letters, was a Godsend but at the same time it only made the men realize how lost and alone they were and how long the war was going to last. The G.I. blues set in in a bad way. And there were the neatly wrapped stacks of letters stamped K.I.A. to remind us that so many of our buddies were gone. There was no talk of Levin or Burnside aside from casual mention once that they were up for medals. The rotten diet, alleviated only by Fox Company's packages, did little to build the worn bodies. The searing heat and dryrot monotony was bad for an outfit like Huxley's Whores. We were used to action and life and this sitting on a two-by-four island sucked our vigor. We were listless and soon illness came in the form of dengue fever.

Sam Huxley realized the predicament. He fought hard to prevent demoralization even though morale never seemed to be a Marine problem. Highpockets decided to enlarge the Fox outpost by sending fifty men at a time to Buota for four-day periods. A fill of beer, a look at the women and a chance for atoll liberty did wonders. The four days on Buota rejuvenated them.

Each group returned to Bairiki loaded with beer and Fox Company hospitality, dressed in Navy fatigues and full of tales as tall as the palms. One unfortunate event occurred. The Sisters of the Mission passed the word throughout the villages that all women were to wear halters. They explained discreetly that their exposure caused desires in peoples of Western civilization. A dirty trick! However, a few brave native girls held out for their time-honored bare freedom and it made friendships between them and the Marines much easier, as the unhaltered directly invited establishment of better relations.

As anywhere, the American troops spoiled the natives rotten till the price of services for menial tasks performed soared tenfold.

The jeep stuck in the mud of a rut on the road that ran through the middle of an Army camp on Karen Island. At the sight of a jeep full of Marines the soldiers ducked from sight to protect their belongings. McQuade had made the cardinal mistake of taking a jeep out in the daylight. As its wheels spun about sinking it deeper in the mire, an Army major rushed from his tent.

"Goddammit!" the major screamed. "My jeep!"

McQuade cut off the motor and leaned back. "You say this is your jeep, Major?"

"You're damned right it is. I caught you red-handed."

"Well, what do you know about that," the sergeant sighed. "Found the damned thing abandoned outside our camp. Why, would you believe it, Major, I've been from one end of this atoll to the other trying to find the owner—haven't I, boys?"

They nodded.

"Like hell you have!"

"Gee, I'm sure glad we found it, sir. Here is your jeep."

"Wait a minute . . . come back here, you people."

"Sorry, Major, we got to go gizmo hunting."

"Gizmo hunting?"

"Yep, well, good-by."

The enraged officer looked under the hood and tears streamed down his cheeks. His brand-new car had been battered beyond recognition. He rushed to his superior officer to arrange charges against the Marines. They must have been from the Fox camp and the driver, the fat sergeant, would be unable to hide that stomach anywhere. For several hours the Army staff argued the feasibility of bringing charges. Some feared it would only step up the raids by the Marines. Stouter hearts prevailed and it was decided an example must be made of them once and for all. The Army had the fullhearted backing of Commodore Perkins and again Shapiro's camp underwent a raid. But again the raiders were several hours later than the reliable spy, MacArthur, who had been recently promoted to sergeant.

"Fat boy . . . fat boy?" Shapiro scratched his head. . . . "I haven't got any fat boys in this camp, they're all skinny. If you people gave us a square shake on rations I might have some fat boys."

A mile away in a hut by the ocean, Gunny McQuade lay on the lap of a young native girl who stroked his balding head softly. Another girl brought him a bottle of beer, cooled at the bottom of an artesian well. He uncapped it, passed it about to his friends, guzzled the remains, and gave a long, loud, contented burp.

9.

ON AN exceptionally peaceful evening the men sat about on the beach listening to Command Performance, enjoying the two favorites, Bing Crosby and Dinah Shore. Some lay in the lagoon, floating and cooling from the extreme heat of the day, and others just lazed about with their hands around a beer bottle. During a rendition of the latest song hit, "Pistol-Packing Momma," the air raid siren went off. They doused their cigarettes and settled back to hear the rest of the program. The spotlights and ack-ack made a wonderful show but the bombs falling in the lagoon interrupted the program with their loud bursts.

A Seabee puffed up the road in the darkness from a nearby construction detail. He stumbled into the gathering on the beach as the fire grew intense from the battery of 90's behind the camp.

"Sorry to bother you fellows," the Seabee squealed. "We haven't had time to dig a shelter. Could I use yours?"

"Sure," Shapiro said.

"But skipper," whispered McQuade.

"Aw, it's pitch black and the guy is scared to death. Right over to your left, son."

"Here?" the Seabee called out in the darkness.

"A few yards back."

"But, Max, there ain't no shelter there. . . ."

"Here? By this oilcan?"

"That's right. The can is the opening. Just grab hold of the rope and lower yourself down."

A splash followed as the Seabee dropped to the bottom of the well.

"He's liable to drown, Max."

"Naw, it's only waist high."

"Quiet, you guys. Dinah Shore is gonna sing."

Andy and Danny wandered over to the airstrip on Lulu to scan the planes. They moved about the parking area examining the Billy Mitchel bombers and the names and paintings on the ships' noses.

"Christ, look at that," Andy said. "Seventy-fives right in their nose."

"Regular flying artillery." They walked about the bomber counting the machine guns and 37 mm.s bristling from her.

"We oughta have some of these in the Corps for ground support."

"They're probably still too fast or the Corps would have gotten them."

"Gyrene pilots could really clear the way in these babies."

"I guess you know that gyrene pilots are the best at ground support."

"Certainly, I ain't arguing."

Their attention turned to a Liberator which had just pulled to a stop in the center of the strip and was being surrounded by a bevy of racing jeeps. They went out to the clumsy monster and gazed curiously as the door swung open. Commodore Perkins himself was out to greet the plane which bore the name: *Island Hobo*. Danny and Andy took a respectful step back as a bevy of brass erupted from her.

"V.I.P.s," Danny whispered.

"That's the courier plane," a nearby Seabee whispered. "She transports secret messages, maps, and information to bases all over the Pacific."

"Yeah?"

"She's got a Brigadier General in command of her."

"You mean a Brigadier for just one plane?"

"Not one plane . . . *the* plane. Picked crew too."

Following the high rank with the cute crushed caps, a pair of high and mighty looking sergeants debarked. On their sleeves was a patch which read: *Yank Correspondent*. The two Marines stepped forward and poked their heads into the door. As they did one correspondent bumped into Danny.

" 'Scuse me, soldier," Danny said.

"Watch where you're going."

"Suppose we could go in and take a look around?" Andy

said. "I never seen the inside of a big job like this before. I'd sure like to sit me in one of them there turrets."

The writer spun about and looked at the ill-clad pair before him. They wore blue Navy dungarees, Army shoes, green tops, and battered pith helmets and stood bleary-eyed and bearded, in contrast to the neatly starched men all about. The sergeant lifted his nose and sputtered, "Just shove off. You're in the way. Of course you can't board this plane."

"Don't get unfriendly, dogface, I just asked a simple question."

The correspondent took a step back as if the leprous-looking creatures were going to touch him.

"You boys are Marines, aren't you?" a voice behind them said.

They turned and faced a tanned well-built young man and were amazed to see a silver star gleaming from his collar.

"Yes, sir, we're Marines."

"Kind of hard to tell in that get-up," the general said.

They blushed self-consciously at their tattered clothes. "I'm afraid the sergeant left his manners in the States," the general continued. "You see, Marines, the Yank boys are elite, they like the smell of brass. Real working brass." He turned to the sergeant. "I'm afraid you missed the real story on this island. These Marines took the atoll. Were you in the invasion, lads?"

"Yes sir."

"Well, come aboard . . . Corporal Flowers."

"Yes sir," the corporal said, inching down the narrow gangway.

"These lads are Marines. Show them around the ship. You boys made a lot of noise in the States with this invasion. We are all proud of you."

The red-faced correspondent stood openmouthed as Danny and Andy boarded and were welcomed by Corporal Flowers.

"Say, he's a regular guy," Danny said to the corporal after the general had gone in Perkins' jeep.

"I'll say he is. Most of them are. Young guys, you know," the airman answered.

"Could we go up to the cockpit?"

"Sure, but don't touch anything. Say, were you guys in on the landing? I'll bet it was rough. . . . I can't stand that Yank guy either."

Meanwhile Marion pursued the more cultural aspects of the atoll in his off duty hours. Many times he made the long journey to Aboakoro, Nellie Island, where the largest village was located. He explored the natural wonders, studied the customs, and even made an attempt at mastering the tongue of the

Gilbertese. On occasion he went out fishing in the masterfully handled hollowed-out coconut log canoes and on other occasions he enlarged his friendship with the Eurasian, Calvin McIntosh, and kept his promise by bringing him all the books he could secure. The unhappy halfbreed had a field day when a Fox raiding party stole a case of books by accident and turned them over to Marion.

In the evenings when the tide was low in the lagoon Marion hunted down the million odd-shaped and magnificently colored shells in the sand and dug out the weirdly beautiful cat's eyes to make bracelets and necklaces and earrings for his mother and Rae. Particularly fine specimens he sent back via the alligator to Shining Lighttower. The Navajo was adept in the ancient skill of his tribe, the art of silversmithing. Lighttower mounted the cat's eyes on flawlessly shined and carved bracelets and rings of aluminum which had been secured from abandoned airplanes. He made some sort of memento, a ring, a bracelet, a watchband, for every member of the platoon.

The problem of rotting out the fish life from the cat's-eye shells was solved by MacArthur, the native con boy. Marion dug them into the earth and they were eaten out without the putrid smell they had when left to sun above the ground.

MacArthur grew close to Marion who was generous in sharing the items he craved: chewing gum, knives, cloth, and cigarettes which he did not use. On Marion's roamings, MacArthur generally tagged along to interpret and explain the million oddities he discovered. For many weeks the little native coyly hinted he would surely like to have a very fine pair of shoes such as the Marines wore. He pestered Marion so much that at last he was presented with a pair of brand-new, stiff leather boondockers. MacArthur had not worn them for more than an hour before the novelty wore off and he deeply regretted ever having asked for them. Nature and coral and hot sand had given him his own leather on the soles of his thick flat feet and this Western innovation made the poor boy go through the agonies of a man wearing an Oregon Boot. However, he was afraid of offending Marion and he always appeared in camp smiling sickly and limping in the boondockers.

The day that Marion gave the boy a reprieve and allowed him to throw the shoes away he made himself a lifelong friend.

The nearby village carried on a close and intimate friendship with Fox Company, completely ignoring the non-fraternization order. Shapiro was wise enough to have his officers and NCOs keep sharp watch on the boys who might get out of line. Each evening several men wandered over to the village bearing gifts and settled for a chat, a song session or a round of casino, the mutual card game. The Marines had terrible luck at cards but after a while they learned that the root of their misfortune lay in the tiny native boys and girls who snuggled up to them as they squatted on their pillows. With many displays of friendship they jabbered away, telegraphing the cards to the members of their family. Many packs of cigarettes were lost before the Foxmen learned to cover their hands.

"Pedro."

"Huhhh."

"Pedro, wake up." The corpsman sprung to his feet, tangling in his mosquito net and with a knife in his hand. "Easy, it's me, L.Q. Come to our tent right away."

"What is the matter?"

"Danny's sick, real sick." The corpsman grabbed his aid pack and followed L.Q. through the sleeping, dark camp over the road to the radio tent.

They entered and Marion pumped the Coleman lantern until it lit the place with a bright glow. Andy bent over Danny's cot, rubbing his forehead with a wet rag. He stepped aside as Pedro approached the twisting, moaning boy. Pedro took his pulse and stuck a thermometer in his mouth.

"What is it, Pedro, dengue fever?"

"Yes, but it looks like a very bad case."

"He's been acting groggy for almost a week."

"He should have turned in. I told him to, dammit."

"God! Sonofabitch . . . God!"

Pedro worked the thermometer loose from Danny's teeth and squinted as he held it up to the light. "We've got to get a doctor."

"What is it?"

"He's got over a hundred and five fever."

"Lord."

"Wrap him up, pile blankets on if he gets chills." The three lifted the nets on their cots and took the blankets from them.

"L.Q., get the skipper here quick."

He led the groggy captain into the tent. "What is it, Pedro?" Max asked.

"Very bad Max, very bad. Dengue. Never seen one like it."

"Better get the alligator and move him to a doctor."

"I'm afraid to move him in his condition."

The terrible shakes started under the pile of blankets. The sick boy's face turned soggy with sweat. He gagged and twisted and rolled and screamed as pains shot through his body. Bone-crushing fever, the natives called it.

"He looks terrible," Max whispered. "I don't like it. Is there a doctor on Lulu?"

"I think they're all working out of the base on Helen. Doc Kyser is the closest one."

"Get a jeep and hightail it down there."

"But the tide is in, no can cross."

"Get the duck then."

"But Max, we'll all get courtmartialed."

"I don't give a rat's ass . . . I'll take full responsibility."

"We have to get instructions quicker," Pedro said. "The round trip will take several hours. Radio to Sarah, quick."

They hung on every word as the generator whined out and Pedro's voice skipped down the chain of islands.

I was on watch at Sarah when the call came through and sent a runner to fetch Doc Kyser. I turned the mike and earphones over to him.

"How sick is he?"

"A hundred and five point two temp."

"How long has he been ill?"

"Several days."

"Pains in back and stomach?"

"Seems terrible agony . . . he's delirious now, Doctor."

"It's dengue all right. We can't do a damned thing for him."

"What?"

"We don't know what to do, Pedro. Give him aspirin and take the normal high-fever precautions and just wait it out."

"But Doc, is there nothing . . ."

"We don't know anything about dengue, Pedro. We don't know what to do."

"Can you not get up here?"

"I have fifty boys here full of fever now. I'll try to get up there tomorrow. I'm sorry."

Pedro handed the earphones back to L.Q. and seated himself once more on the edge of the cot and told the others to get some sleep. There was no sleep for Andy, L.Q. and Marion. The three and the corpsman kept a drowsy watch through the night, starting at each new moan and cry of anguish from Danny. A hundred times he called his wife's name, "Kathy . . . Kathy," through lips which turned from cracked dry to sweating wet. His voice moaned weaker as the hours wore on. He would toss and squirm and then make a sudden scream and shoot to a sitting position, his eyes glassy and unseeing. Pedro fought him back down and tried to cool his body before another chill set in.

Dawn found Danny in an exhausted slumber, drained of his strength. Pedro once more worked a thermometer between

Danny's lips. The three buddies nodded in quiet anxiousness as Pedro took the reading.

"It is good. It has dropped to a hundred and two."

McQuade made his way into the tent. He was barefooted and half asleep. "Pedro, can you get over to my tent for a minute. One of my boys is down with the fever. He's trying to make his peace with God."

Pedro arose, wavering, and put his pack together.

"Thanks a lot," Marion said.

"When he come to make him drink plenty juice. He's all dry out. I come back right after sick call." He left.

"Looks like we're in for an epidemic," McQuade said.

Danny opened his eyes. Everything whirled. He tried to speak but it felt as though his throat were caked solid. He raised his hand, then felt his head being lifted by a pair of strong hands and an icy trickle forced its way down his mouth. He gagged and fell back on the cot. He looked up and made out Andy's broad form. It looked like he was standing behind a veil. Danny winced and grabbed his side and rolled and gasped to fight back tears from the knifing pain.

"How's it going, Danny?"

He answered with a mumbled shaking of his head.

"Drink some more juice." He rolled Danny over gently and poured down another few hard-taken swallows. Danny's hand feebly clutched Andy's lapel.

"I'm going to die."

"No you ain't."

"I'm going to die, Andy."

L.Q. was frightened by the terrible change that had come over Danny. "No worse than when you had the bug in New Zealand and they packed you away to Silverstream," he said.

L.Q. didn't like the hollow wild stare of his buddy's eyes. Danny was the kind of guy you had to have in a squad. He never made mistakes. You could always feel relieved knowing he was alongside you.

Danny began crying.

Now, that looked rotten. They had seen him sick before, out of his head with malaria. They had lived through the lonely gnawing at his heart together. But Danny losing his will, lying there and crying? A hulk weeping and groaning with pain, whining like a beaten dog. It scared them all.

"I'm going to die. I never got it like this . . . everything hurts me."

They stood over him awkwardly trying to reach for words of comfort.

"I want to go home . . . I want to quit. Another campaign and another . . . we'll never get home . . . never."

"He's right, dammit!" Andy cried. "When you think they'll send us back—in a box maybe!"

"Be quiet," L.Q. said.

"First the Feathermerchant, then Levin and Burnside. Do you think they're finished? Hell no! The Corps will get us all. If you ain't lucky enough to get a bullet you'll get it the other way—the bug, the crud, jungle rot, yellow jaundice, dengue."

"You're feeling sorry for yourself," Marion said.

"What's the matter? Marines can't feel sorry for themselves? Marines ain't allowed to get homesick?" Andy shouted.

"Why don't you let me write you out a T.S. chit and go over and cry on the chaplain's shoulder," L.Q. spat.

"Sure, Mac sold us a bill of goods. Everybody is selling us a bill of goods."

"Go up to Lulu and cry with some of the doggies. They feel sorry for themselves too."

Danny tossed and clenched his teeth as another pain tore through his body.

"Go on, Mary, tell him something fancy from the goddam books you read."

"Why don't you shove off, Andy?"

"Poor bastard. Look at him . . . you like to see a guy like that cry?"

"Why don't you grab a ship and go down and play with the Kiwi birds, Andy? I think you're getting yellow."

"Stop it, you two," Marion hissed. "We're all in the same boat. What were you looking for when you joined the Corps?"

"Yeah, Semper Fidelis, buddy," Andy snarled and walked from the tent.

For three days they kept a constant watch over the fever-ridden Danny. It seemed as though it would never break. Doc Kyser came up to look at the cases in the Fox camp and removed the less sick to Sarah. As for Danny and other severe cases, he feared the long choppy ride would damage the inflamed, enlarged joints. There was little or nothing known about the virus passed by the flies and mosquitoes.

Danny's temperature hovered between a hundred and two and a hundred and four. In the cycles when it shot up he went into deliriums, calling over and over for his wife. Each day brought a new sign of wasting of what had once been a strong constitution. The siege of dengue fever all but squashed the listless will of Huxley's Whores.

The day before Christmas found the battalion in sadder straits than I had ever seen it. The camp on Sarah was like a morgue. Everyone was touchy and even the comics and the cooks who prepared a chow with all the trimmings failed to lessen the bitterness. The men were too bitter to bitch. A Marine bitches when he is happy. Watch out when he's quiet. Gunner Keats urged me to go up to Fox Company for a few days now that Lighttower and Spanish Joe were back on duty. I was anxious to see Danny and took his offer and set out with the early morning alligator run.

When I landed at the Fox camp, I found it a far cry from the wild stories. It was quiet, too. All about was evidence of the dengue fever epidemic. Any release they had found in their former escapades had been cut off under the stern command of Major Wellman and Marlin.

Sister Mary greeted me like a long-lost father and led me to the radio shack. I entered the tent and dropped my gear. Danny lay with his back to me. I walked to his sack and sat on its edge. The movement of the cot made Danny groan and roll. I was horrified! It had been five weeks since I had seen the lad. He had wasted to a skeleton. His eyes were ringed with thick black circles and his cheekbones protruded from a chalk-colored flesh. A long growth of hair gave his slitty eyes the look of a wild animal. I had known he was sick, but I had no idea it was like this. I wanted to cry.

On the deck lay a stack of neatly tied letters and pinned to the tent side so he could see it, a picture of Kathy, the picture I had seen a thousand times pinned up in the barracks at Eliot, at McKay, at Russell, aboard the *Bobo* and the *Bell* and the *Jackson*, and always beside him in his foxhole or in his pack.

"Hi, Mac," Danny whispered.

I leaned close to him so he could hear. "How do you feel?"

"Not so hot."

Pedro Rojas trudged into the tent and greeted me. Pedro showed the fatigue of working around the clock with the fever-ridden company. "How's the sick-bay soldier today?" he said, jamming a thermometer into Danny's mouth and kneeling to inspect the gallon can of fruit juice he had left in the morning. "Dammit, Danny, how you expect to get better? You didn't drink no juice at all."

"I . . . I can't . . . it makes me puke."

"How is he?" I asked.

"The bastard is goldbricking," Pedro said as he walked out. I followed him. "What's the scoop?" I asked.

"Damn if I know, Mac. The fever goes up and down, up and down. The damn kid won't eat. He hasn't taken solids in a week."

"Isn't there anything Doc Kyser can do?"

Pedro shook his head. "He'd be all right, like the rest of us, if we knew we would ever get home." He smiled weakly and plodded off to another tent.

Seabags approached me with a messkit full of Christmas dinner: turkey, all white meat; sweet potatoes; cranberry sauce; stuffing; peas; ice cream and a cup of eggnog. "Hi, Mac, when you blow in?"

"I'm up for a couple of days," I said. "Danny looks like hell."

"Yeah. Maybe you can help me get him to down some of this chow. He'd be a lot better if he ate."

"Why don't you grab my mess gear and get into line? I'll see if I can feed him."

I went back into the tent. "Hey, Danny, get a load of this. Turkey and all white meat."

He rolled away from me. "Look here, you sonofabitch," I snapped. "You're going to eat this or I'm going to jam it up your ass."

He managed a feeble smile. I propped him up and for a tortured two hours prodded him to take nibble after nibble till the mess gear was half empty. Danny finally lay back and asked for a cigarette and patted his belly.

"That was good. I hope I don't puke it up."

"You better not or you're going to have to start all over, I crap you not."

"I'm sure glad you came up, Mac. Going to take off your pack and stand at ease a while?"

"Yeah, I think I'll stick around a couple days."

He gritted his teeth and closed his eyes. "I don't know Mac . . . I just don't know no more."

I ate the rest of the chow and lit up. Marion, Seabags, and Speedy came back and for a long time we were all pretty quiet. Last year it was in a warehouse on the Wellington docks. This year, in the middle of nowhere. Where would next Christmas bring us? How many of us would still be together? I gazed over the water past the lagoon. It was a big ocean. Every day made the States look farther and farther away. Speedy looked at his guitar but he didn't feel much like singing.

Then we heard voices; softly at first, then louder and louder. I looked out of the tent up the road. It didn't sound real. We saw a flicker of candlelight wending down the road and the harmony of the singers sounded like nothing a guy could expect to hear on earth, it was so beautiful: *"Silent night, holy night, All is calm, all is bright. . . ."*

The natives from the village appeared with candles in their brown hands, their arms filled with gifts of woven pandanus leaf.

"Sleep in heavenly peace. . . ." The tired Marines of Fox Company went up the road to greet their friends and arm in arm they entered the camp.

Marion led a young native and an old native into our tent. I was introduced to MacArthur and his father, Alexander the old chief. We shook hands and went over to Danny's cot. MacArthur put several woven pillows under Danny's head and said, "Cros Alexander want know why friend Danny no come and see?"

"Sick, very sick," Marion answered. As MacArthur relayed the message to the chief the old man nodded knowingly and bent down and felt Danny's back and stomach, making him wince. He placed his wrist on the sick boy's forehead and finally jabbered an order to MacArthur, who sped back to the village.

Several moments later MacArthur returned panting. He held a cup made from a hollowed coconut husk which contained some yellowish liquid.

"Drink," MacArthur said.

Danny propped on his elbows and gazed at the stuff. Alexander nodded and with gestures assured him it was quite safe.

"Make feel better, yes no."

Danny swallowed the stuff with face screwed at the nasty taste and fell back on his cot. He slept.

In a few moments a huge circle of Marines and natives formed in the camp's center and as darkness fell a fire was made. Then East and West joined voices and sang the Christmas hymns.

With wooden boxes used as drums, the native men began beating rhythmically and the center ring filled with grass-skirted dancers. Everyone clapped in time to the beats as the stately bronze girls flipped and swayed in perfect unison. Then a small girl, shapely and young, took the center and the others drifted to the sidelines. MacArthur explained that she was the "sept dancer," the representative of Alexander's clan, an honor that fell only to a direct descendant of the chief. She had been carefully trained in her art since babyhood. The other girls were merely backdrops. With a wad of gum going in her mouth she began her dance with very slow hip gyrations. The young lady must have surely been tutored by Salome, I thought. As the clapping generated steam she flung off her brassière so as not to cramp her style. She glided around the circle's edge, her feet moving as if she were on skates and her hips swinging tauntingly. She swayed back to the center and as the drums beat faster and faster it looked as if she would take off in ten directions at the same time.

"This is dance of chicken," MacArthur whispered.

Wiggling her shoulders, she began a fierce controlled shake that set her breasts shivering. She took short rapid hops with her rear pointing out angularly. Her skirt bounced and swayed madly. The clapping became quicker and quicker, trying to pass her tempo, and she increased her motion until she was a wild flitting blur in the firelight. I thought she must surely shake herself to pieces but she only added more speed as the beats became louder and faster and exuberant shouts arose. She danced until at last she dropped exhausted to the ground. . . . The Marines were no longer so lonely.

The festivities reached a hilarious climax when McQuade stepped into the center of the ring. Around his chest he wore three confiscated halters tied end to end to circle his girth. His monstrous belly hung over a grass skirt and he wore boon-dockers and a big black cigar plastered in his teeth. With the help of the revived village dancer they put on an exhibition of the hula never seen before by the eyes of man. The dance was matched only when Two Gun Shapiro, Major Wellman, and Marlin, similarly attired, tried to outdo them with their native partners.

Suddenly I felt someone shoving through the crowd to the edge of the ring where I sat with my boys. I turned and there, moving in beside me, was Danny. His eyes were bright and some of the color had returned to his face.

"Merry Christmas, Mac!" he shouted. "Anybody got a beer?"

PART SIX

Prologue

OUR SHIP pulled into the lagoon. We took a trip up to Cora to say so long to Levin and Burnside and packed to leave the atoll. Seabags had good reason to get seasick this trip.

The ship, a liberty ship, the *Prince George,* carried no other cargo except Huxley's Whores. The "Kaiser Coffin" had nothing to hold her below her water line and she bobbed like a cork for a slow sickening week at seven knots an hour. Often on the rising swell the *George's* screws came clear out of the water and as she sank she rattled and shuddered till we thought she'd rip apart.

After New Year's she pulled into Hilo on the island of Hawaii with Sam Huxley's beleaguered Whores.

As had been the case on Guadalcanal, we were bringing up the rear. Once upon a time we had believed the Sixth was destined for glory. Two years and two campaigns and we were still cleaning up messes.

The camp was hell. Bitter cold during the night, hot in the day. Very little water and it was rationed. The diet of New Zealand was supplanted by Hawaiian pineapple.

The worst of it was the dust. It choked us by day and night. It was impossible to keep the tents or gear clean. Five minutes after a fresh cleaning the wind blew ancient lava dust around, atop and beneath us.

Liberty in Hilo stank. The island was mainly inhabited by Japanese-Americans. A rumor had been spread that the Second Division were paid killers. Our reception was one of cold hospitality. There were a couple of whorehouses in town but the long, unromantic lines of men being policed by the shore patrol made for the type of love that most of us weren't looking for. Again a smile and the voice of a buddy meant something that none but us could understand.

The grim irony was being so close to the States we could almost touch and taste and smell. It almost drove us crazy hearing American voices over the radio, reading American newspapers, and speaking to American girls at the USO near camp. But we were as far away as ever, perhaps farther, for the

Corps had not chosen this forlorn campsite without reason.

Soon again came the hikes, the drills, the inspections, the field problems—the drudgery of soldiering. New replacements flooded in from the States. Fresh-faced, wisecracking youngsters. We didn't take the trouble to ridicule them, for they stood in awe of the Guadalcanal and Tarawa veterans, now hardbeaten vets of twenty and twenty-one years of age. New equipment and more firepower filtered in.

But the Second Division was listless and tired. We all wanted home now, no bones about it. Yet, there was that inexplicable doggedness that told each man he would stick it out. We hiked the same miles but it was just going through the motions. We were old soldiers with moxey. Yes, even Sam Huxley just went through the motions now.

As weeks passed, again came the hope that this coming invasion would be the last, that they might let the Sixth establish the beachhead. And spirit was replaced by a new driving force. A killer drive. The Second Division, forgotten in the mountains of Hawaii, developed might, power, and the urge to be the professional killers we were accused of being in Hilo.

Then came the news the Fourth Marine Division had hit the Marshalls as a follow-up to Tarawa and that a Fifth Marine Division was being formed.

1.

Dearest Sam,

I am terribly excited. I've just finished seeing Colonel Malcolm. We lunched together at the officer's club and he told me all about you. Oh, my darling, I'm so proud. I got a full account of the wonderful work you have done with your battalion and heard that you are up for another decoration. He also told me, off the record, that you are next in line to succeed him as commander of the Regiment. But darling, couldn't your boys have thought up a better nickname for the battalion? I think it's awful.

I know he shouldn't have, but Colonel Malcolm said that you are in Hawaii. I've tried to think it out clearly but I'm afraid I can't. The thought of you being so close simply overpowers any reason I might master.

Remember old Colonel Drake who retired several years ago? He has a place on Maui and he's asked us time and again to visit him. It is just the next island from Hawaii. I could get over there somehow.

Darling, please don't turn me down on this. I've tried being a Marine wife but I'm going to have to be selfish—as selfish as a wife who longs for her husband. You've had so little time in recent years. It seemed like a few months from the time you returned from Iceland till you went out again. I don't care how short our time, Sam, but I must see you. I had braced myself to see the war through and I've not complained, but it all shattered when I found you were so close by.

I love you, as I've always loved you and I miss you as I always miss you, with all my soul. The thought of seeing you changes everything and has me drunk with happiness.

Your loving wife,
Jean

Jean Huxley's hand trembled as she closed the door of her room and ripped the seam of his return envelope.

My Jean,

You will notice from the postmark that this letter didn't come through proper channels. I had it mailed in the States by a flyer friend of mine.

My life, if ever I've had to make a decision, if ever I've had to find words I didn't want to say, this is that time.

When I read your letter I could hardly believe it. The thought of holding you in my arms again, the thought of loving you, if only for a day, answers the prayer I've said each night for two hungry years.

But, my darling, I must ask you to wait once more. It would be impossible for you to come to Hawaii. Jean, when I returned from Iceland and was given this command I had to whip a green bunch of kids into Marines and it wasn't an easy job. But now my boys are Marines, the finest on God's earth. Perhaps they don't like me, perhaps they hate me. I don't really know but I know we've been through a lot of hell together. These boys are not professional soldiers like I am. This business of saying good-by knifes them more deeply than it ever will us. They want their wives and their mothers as badly as we want each other. But the path is not as easy for them as it has been made for us. They must stay and do their job.

Lord knows I'm not punishing myself for their sake, but what kind of love would it be if I had to face them knowing I'd stolen something that is denied them? Could we cheat? I must see it through with them, Jean. I am their skipper. Darling, you must understand.

I have never written this before but the time has come

now. Since we were kids at Ohio State and you chose to become my wife you must have learned that I am married to two persons, you and the Corps. Many's the time you have had to step back and take it on the chin and you've never complained about it. Many's the time I've wanted to tell you what a brave soldier you have been. You have taken a long hard road—yes, we are always saying good-by.

And many's the time I've cursed myself for bringing you into all this. I have never been able to give you the home and the children I know you long for. It has always been "Take care of yourself, see you soon." But without your courage I never could have made it.

No matter where the call of duty has taken me, no matter what the situation, I can always find comfort in knowing that way back in the States there is a woman waiting for me. A woman so wonderful I surely do not deserve her. But as long as she is there, nothing else matters for me.

And I've thought in anguish of the day I can come back and know I'll never have to leave you again and I can spend the rest of my life making up for every lonely day and every lonely night.

Our die is cast and for the while we must get our bits of happiness when they are doled out to us. I am not sorry for the life I have chosen, only for the misery I've caused you.

And so, once more. Just a little longer, darling.

I adore you,
Sam

The letter fell to the floor and Jean Huxley gazed blankly out of the window. She felt she would never see her husband again.

Something big was brewing for the Sixth Marines. The tip came during maneuvers when the regiment was introduced to the newly developed "buffalo." The buffalo was an amphibious tractor bigger, faster, and more heavily armed than its predecessor, the alligator. The Sixth was drilled in the buffalo while the Second and Eighth Marines drilled in the mountains. This meant the beachhead for us. The big dress rehearsal, as usual, ended in a mess.

Happy with the hope that this would be the last campaign, we prepared to move out again. We were in a fighting mood. Already a rotation plan was in effect for members of the Second and Eighth who had been overseas many more months than we had.

We waited tensely as camp broke and battalion after battalion took the slow torturous trek down the mountain side to the Hilo docks. From Hilo we figured that the transports would proceed to Pearl Harbor, and down the islands for final staging.

Then came shattering news. Five LST's had been blown up at Pearl Harbor. At the last moment we were ordered to stay put in Camp Tarawa. It was obvious that Huxley's Whores had originally been assigned to one of the destroyed ships. Highpockets took a plane for Honolulu while we sat alone in the cold mountains to sweat it out.

The stiff orderly at Major General Merle Snipes' office in Pearl Harbor snapped the door open.

"Sir, Lieutenant Colonel Huxley to see you." He closed the door behind Sam who stood rigid before the General's desk.

Snipes had recently succeeded to the Second Division command. The legend said that no one had ever seen Snipes smile. There is no one to refute that.

"You requested permission to see me, Huxley. I see you wasted no time getting here." His words were always sharp and to the point to subordinates and superiors alike.

"My battalion is still sitting on top of the mountain in Hawaii, sir."

"We won't leave them there."

"General Snipes. I realize I'm stepping out of line but I must ask you a pertinent question. We were originally assigned to one of the LST's that blew up, weren't we?"

"You're quite right. You are way out of line."

"Am I to assume, sir, that the LSTs are to spearhead the pending invasion and that we were selected as one of the combat teams to establish a beachhead?"

"I don't see any reason to carry this conversation further."

"But we're going to."

"What!"

"I further assume that you have been unable to replace all the LSTs and that my outfit has been reassigned to a troop transport."

"For a junior officer, you do a lot of assuming, Huxley."

"Then I'm right. You've changed our assignment. We aren't landing first."

Snipes' words were arctic cold. "You let us do the figuring. You'll do as you're told. Get out of here before I have you courtmartialed." The General began to thumb through the papers on his desk. The tall man before him stood fast. Snipes looked up slowly, his eyes drawn to slits, his face frozen. Tobacco-stained teeth showed between his drawn thin lips.

"Dammit, General! This is the last round. We are getting close to Japan," Huxley went on. "With five divisions of Marines out here we'll never get another chance."

Snipes reached for his phone.

"Go on, call the M.P.s. You and your whole lousy crowd have been shoving the Sixth Marines around too long—you're jealous of us."

Snipes studied the rawboned officer before him. "It is common knowledge that you rode General Pritchard on Guadalcanal. You're getting a reputation as a troublemaker."

"That's a lie and you know it. We've worked hard. You know damned well we have the finest regiment in the Corps."

"All right, Huxley, sit down and cool off. I want to show you something." He walked to a wall safe, spun the dials, and withdrew an immense bound document and threw it on his desk.

"Ever see one of these?"

"No, sir."

He read the cover: *Operation Kingpin, Top Secret.*

"Two thousand pages, Huxley. Tides, winds, expected casualties, rounds of ammo, gallons of gas, topography, native customs, history of the enemy commander, Jap fleet disposition, how many rolls of toilet paper we'll need—name it, we've got it here." He leaned over his desk. "Three divisions are going in, Huxley. Sixty thousand men. We are taking an island to give us a jumping-off place to bomb Tokyo around the clock. Do you hear! So you want to change the entire operation . . . risk a thousand lives and a billion dollars. Who the hell do you think you are!"

Huxley was white faced. "General Snipes," he said slowly, "you can take that big book and you know just where you can shove it. You know as well as I do that you can throw the book away when the first shot is fired. Did the book win Guadalcanal? Did the book keep those kids coming in through the lagoon at Tarawa? This one isn't going to be any different. It's the little bastards with the rifles and the bayonets and the blood and the guts that will win this war for you, General, and by God, I've got the best in the Corps and I want that beachhead!"

"Once upon a time, Huxley, we thought you were a bright young lad. After this campaign you can expect to spend the rest of your life in the Corps inspecting labels on pisspots. I will not tolerate insubordination!"

The color returned to Sam's cheeks and his big fists unclenched. "General," he said softly. "When I came here I knew I was going to leave one of two ways. Either by the brig or at the head of my battalion. I want to resign from the Corps. I want an immediate transfer until the resignation is effective.

If you pigeonhole it you'll have to courtmartial me. I'm not going back to my boys knowing we are going to carry the broom and dustpan again."

He drew a deep breath. Snipes sat down, adjusted his glasses and opened the book, *Operation Kingpin*. He found the page he wanted. "We were unable to replace the fifth LST that blew up. According to the plan the LSTs are to leave five days ahead of the rest of the convoy. The LSTs are to launch their own buffaloes and the transports follow up once the beachhead is firm. I can't get you an LST. However, we have one small supply ship going out with them first. There'll be enough buffaloes on it to take your battalion in. Huxley, in one month you'll wish to hell you hadn't come here, because your outfit is going to be in the hotbox. I'm sending you in on the exposed left flank. You will receive your orders as soon as Phibspac O.K.'s them."

Sam Huxley's lips parted but he could not speak.

"You came here knowing I'm the meanest sonofabitch in the Corps, Huxley. Now you've gotten what you want and you're asking yourself 'why did I do it, and why did Snipes give in?' The first you can answer. I'll answer the last one. It is crazy bastards like you that make the Marine Corps. Well, you should be quite proud of your victory."

"As proud as a man could be when he's dug the graves for three hundred boys."

"You'll be lucky if it's only three hundred . . . now get out of here."

Huxley walked to the door with shoulders stooped. He placed his hand on the knob. Yes, he wondered why. Only that he had known he had to come. . . .

"Sam."

He turned and the legend of Merle Snipes was broken. He had only a slight smile on his lips but his face looked warm and human. "Sam, I sometimes think myself it's a hell of a way to make a living."

Huxley closed the door behind him and walked out.

2.

PROTESTANT services were being conducted on the aft deck. I was oiling my carbine, checking the clips again, and peacefully dragging on a weed when Ziltch summoned me to Huxley's quarters. I climbed the ladder topside and caught a view of the fleet—ships, hundreds of them, moving with serene slowness for as far as the eye could see.

The singing aft seemed to blend with the slow rise and fall of the ship:

> *"Onward Christian soldiers,*
> *Marching as to war . . ."*

I went inside to officers' country, down the gangway, and met Gunner Keats standing before Huxley's door. "What's the scoop?" I asked.

"Beats me, Mac," Keats answered, rapping on the door.

Ziltch ushered us in. Highpockets stood against the bulk-head, squinting out of a porthole eying the great flotilla proceeding majestically to its bloody chore. He turned to us slowly, motioned us at ease, and lit a fresh cigarette with the butt of another. Huxley, the disciplinarian, looked ill at ease for a moment as he beckoned Keats and me to sit and laid his field map on the desk. He rubbed his jaw a second.

"Mac," he said almost bashfully, "and you, Gunner, I've asked you two here . . . well, because we're old shipmates."

"Yes, sir," I blurted out, "since Iceland."

"You've been briefed on tomorrow's operation?"

"Yes, sir."

We could see the dark circles of sleeplessness under his eyes. He pointed a pencil on the map. "There it is, Red Beach One, the hotbox of the whole operation." He walked to the porthole and flipped the cigarette out. "You'll notice that our battalion is to land on the extreme left flank. We will be the nearest troops to the major Japanese concentrations in the City of Garapan. It is a leadpipe cinch that we will be counterattacked and will have to bear the brunt of it."

Keats and I nodded. He strode back to the map. "And right here is Mount Topotchau, a perfect observation post looking right down our throats." He smacked a fist into an open hand. "There are tricky reefs and tides out there. There is a calculated risk that the rest of combat team one might land too far south. That means we will have to stand alone and isolated until they can consolidate with us. The Japs will turn all hell loose to keep us separated." He slumped into a captain's chair and lit another cigarette. "The hotbox," he repeated. "Mac, those radios have got to stay in operation tomorrow."

He half closed his eyes and rested back. "What are the assignments again?"

"Seabags, L.Q., Lighttower, and Andy will be out with the rifle companies. Corporal Hodgkiss will be in the command post on the walkie-talkie team."

"How about the Indian?"

"Not much of a code man but he can work a TBY at the bottom of a well," I assured him.

"The rest?"

"Gomez, Gray, Forrester, and I will operate the sets to regiment and to the flagship."

"Regiment is coming in with Tulsa Blue on our right flank and we've got to stay in with them if they veer south in the tide."

"Yes, sir."

"Whatever you do, don't lose the flagship."

"We plan to use the jeep radio there, sir."

"Good." He folded the map and smiled self-consciously. "Care for a drink?"

I nearly fell over. Huxley opened the desk drawer and withdrew a half pint of Scotch. "I've been nursing this bottle along for six months, but this is an occasion, I believe." He tilted the bottle to his lips. "Good luck, men." He passed the bottle to the Gunner.

"Here's to the next man that . . . er, good luck," the Gunner said.

I took the bottle and held it up for a second. "No offense meant, Colonel, but I want to toast Huxley's Whores, the best goddam outfit in the Corps."

Keats and I stepped out to the promenade deck a moment later and leaned against the rail. The sky was flaming like a bursting fireball as the Pacific sunset turned the death-laden sea to orange. From the aft deck came broken and disharmonized voices drifting through the stillness.

> *"Nearer my God to thee,*
> *Nearer to thee. . . ."*

"Looks like a rough session, Mac. Huxley is really worried."

"Funny," I mused, "he's been living two years to get this assignment. He should be happy if we lose enough for him to get a membership in the butchered battalion club. God knows that's what he wants." I took a smoke from Keats' pack and lit up.

"Maybe now that he's got it, he don't want it," Keats said.

I slapped him on the back. "Services are busting up, I'd better go down and tuck the platoon in. See you in the morning, Jack."

The Black Hole of Calcutta had nothing on the second hold of a troop transport. I held my nose and fought through the mountain of gear to my section. Seabags was tenderly rubbing a last drop of oil on his weapon and patted it. Danny lay on his sack and gazed at Kathy's picture. Andy, L.Q., and Lighttower made chatter over a cribbage board. From Sister Mary's phonograph came the strains of a classical piece of music that flooded the hold. Somehow, none of the boys bitched about it now. It sounded kind of soothing. I climbed up to my bunk on the third tier.

"Sounds nice, what is it?"

"Aren't you ever going to learn? Brahms First Symphony."

"Oh sure, Brahms First gizmo, nice."

Marion put aside his letter. "Rae likes it too."

"Letter to her?"

"Uh-huh."

"Nice girl, that Rae. You're lucky."

"That's what I'm trying to tell her. Mac?"

"Yeah?"

"Are you nervous?"

"Just plain scared."

"Got a cigarette?"

"When did you take up smoking?"

"Just now."

The bosun's pipe whistled through the screechbox: *"Now hear this, now hear this. All Marine personnel will remain below decks. No one is allowed topside for any reason until combat stations are manned at zero four hundred."* The whistle screamed again. We were read a message from the regimental, division, and fleet commanders. Something or other about the glory of the Corps and adding new battle streamers to our already glorious Regimental Flag. We had cheered like boots when we heard this spiel before Guadalcanal; we were rather skeptical at Tarawa. This time it was good for a few laughs.

"I tune in for John's Other Wife and this is what I get," L.Q. said.

"You talk too much, white man, play your cards."

"Turn it off."

I lay back and tried to shut my eyes . . . sleep was impossible.

The hold soon plunged into darkness save for the dim gangway lights. I rolled over and peeled off my skivvy shirt. It was saturated with sweat. I fixed my pack under my head for a pillow. It was quiet, restlessly quiet. I felt a rhythmic tapping. It was Seabags' foot hitting the chain that held his bunk above mine. I wondered what he was thinking.

Seabags' body was slick with sweat. Waist high by the Fourth of July, that's what we say about the corn in Iowa, he thought. Might be cool there tonight . . . before the summer sets in for fair. A man can hear the corn grow in the hot weather . . . just walk through the field and hear it crackling.

I'd sure like to slick up with clean jeans and a fancy shirt and maybe have a little square dance at the courthouse. These guys don't know about square dancing . . . they think it's hick stuff . . . don't know what real living is . . . *Now you aleman with the old left hand and now give out a right and left grand . . . meet your little honey and stomp and kick and now give her a Rocky Mountain do si do . . . give that little girl a twirl and promenade home . . . Swing your partner round and round . . . now do si do your corner maid . . . now form a little circle and come to the bar and let's us have a right hand star. . . .*

Seabags' foot tapped in rhythm to his whispered call on the chain at the foot of his canvas cot.

He lowered himself past me. I reached out and grabbed his shoulder. "What's the matter, Seabags?"

"I'd better see Pedro and get me a little seasick medicine."

Pedro Rojas dozed by the desk in sick bay. The short butt of his smoking cigarette reached his fingers, burned him with a start. He reached for his wallet and withdrew the faded picture of a girl and studied it for several moments. He placed it to his lips and kissed it gently.

I am not so unhappy to come back to Texas now, he thought. I am one fine corpsman . . . the Doc, he is going to make me a chief. My very good friends will not know old Pedro when he get back to San Antone, but they are very nice peoples anyhow. I shall take good care of them.

"Pedro."

"Ho, Seabags. Now what is ailing a big strong gyrene such as you are?"

"You know, the old seasick."

"Seabags! I give you already enough junk to float this ship."

"Aw come on . . . don't give me a bad time. I'm gonna start puking again."

"Jesus Maria! Well, hokay. I hope they send you home on an airplane."

"Don't say that."

He gulped the medicine down and winced.

"Seabags! You make goddam sure you eat one fine breakfast —you hear me!"

"Yeah, I hear you." He put the glass down. "I . . . I guess I better get back and try to sleep."

"Hokay, hombre."

"Hey, Pedro . . . did you ever go square dancing?"

"No, but I do know some very fine Mexican dances."

"Yeah?"

"Ho, Pedro is the finest dancer . . . look, sit down . . . I going to show you something. I show you step that if you can do I give you a bottle of uncut alcohol."

I had to have a cigarette. I lowered myself to the deck and followed the blue light toward the head. I stopped for a swig of water at the scuttlebutt. Someone was behind me. I turned quickly. It was the Injun.

"I didn't mean to scare you, Mac."

"Trouble sleeping?"

"A little. I saw you get up. . . ."

"What's on your mind, kid?"

"Mac, this sounds silly. I want to say something."

"Go on."

"You know how I'm always saying I want to go back to the reservation?" I nodded and saw his grim face through the half shadows. "Mac . . . Mac, I really don't want to go back. I want to stay in the Marine Corps . . . like you. Do . . . do you think I'd make a good gyrene?" There was a strange sad plea in his voice.

"You'll make a hell of a gyrene."

"You mean it?"

"Sure I mean it."

"You know, there ain't really nothing back there on the reservation. I got a lot of buddies here. I like the Corps . . . I . . . want to stay."

I put my arm around the Injun's shoulder. "Come on, for Chrisake, get some sleep. You know, we might be making some new corporals after this shindig."

Marion squinted under the small lightbulb near a sink and his lips moved as he repeated the words he read. Danny walked into the head.

"Hi, Mary."

"Hello, Danny."

"I'm sweating like a pig, I can't sleep. What are you reading?"

Marion handed him the pocket book of poems. *"Under the wide and starry sky. . . . Dig the grave and let me lie. . . . Glad did I live and gladly die."* Danny glanced up and looked soberly at Marion. *"And I lay me down with a will. . . . This be the verse you grave for me . . . Here he lies where he longed to be . . . Home is the sailor, home from the sea . . . And the hunter home from the hill."* He handed the book back slowly. "That's a hell of a thing to be reading now," he whispered.

"It kept running through my mind," Marion answered.

"Home is the sailor, home from the sea, and the hunter home from the hill. It sort of fits, doesn't it?"

"Yes."

"A buddy told me something once about finding peace of

mind. But you can't help wondering. The third time in less than two years."

"Who knows, Danny? Every man on this ship will give you a different answer. His own piece of land, his own dream, his own woman, his own way of life. None of us has the same answer."

"But a guy has got to know. He can't go on forever just being led by the nose."

"This much I can say, Danny: don't let anybody tell you that you were a sucker. Something better has got to come from it all, it has to. Sure, we're going to get kicked around and they'll tell you it was all for nothing. But it can't be for nothing. Think of the guys like Levin. For him, the issues were pretty clear cut. I wish ours were."

"I want to believe that, Mary."

"Don't let them tell you that we are going to hell. If we were, we'd have done so long ago. Just don't forget that this out here is only part of the fight."

Danny nodded, paused a moment, and walked out of the head.

3.

THE bosun's pipe blared through the intercom, shattering the silence: *"General quarters."* Above us we could hear the sailors rushing to their battle stations. I drew myself up: two o'clock.

"Hit the deck, drop your cocks and grab your socks. Half the day gone and not a drop of work done."

"Ah, fair sunrise," L.Q. said.

"Somebody turn on the goddam lights!"

"Lights!"

I laced on my boondockers and shook my head a couple of times to wipe out the clammy stink. *Thump, Thump.* The Navy big guns were pounding the target for the fourth day.

"Sixteen-inchers."

"I hope they knock down something besides coconut trees this time."

"Wait till Spanish Joe hits the beach. I just hope them gook women is the friendly type like on Tarawa," he bellowed. "Stick with me, Marion old buddy, I'll take you over the rough spots."

The mass of sweating humanity moved slowly into their business clothes in the steamy, sealed, dimly lit hold.

THUMP, THUMP. A distant drone, lumbering lazily.

"Heavy bombers."

Screech. *"Now hear this. Chow down in the mess hall, chow down."*

THUMP ... THUMP.

The hours move slowly when you look at your timepiece every thirty seconds.

"They're sure pasting the hell out of them this time. Maybe we'll hit a clean beach."

Speedy began singing:

> *"Send me a letter,*
> *Send it by mail,*
> *Send it in care of,*
> *The Birmingham jail...."*

The Injun joined in another chorus.

"Did I ever tell you jerks about the time I saw a python eat a pig at the zoo?" L.Q. said. "Well, they decided to even the match up, so they greased the pig and gave this snake a gallon of bicarbonate of soda. Damndest thing you ever saw ... this old snake ..."

THUMP ... THUMP.

Hold it! Stop! What's that? We lifted our eyes. We could hear the gentle splash of water against our hull. The high hum of dive bombers streaming in like angry little hornets.

"It won't be long now."

"About that sawbuck you owe me. I'd be willing to make a generous settlement."

I looked at my watch ... THUMP ... THUMP.

"All the gear in order?"

"Roger."

THUMP ... THUMP.

I steadied the Injun's hand so he could light a cigarette. L.Q. moved through the squad slapping them on the back and joking. His eyes met mine. He was very pale but he managed a grin.

"I'm going to puke, Mac," Andy whispered.

"It will all be over soon as they blow the whistle. Say, isn't Pat due to have that baby soon?"

"Jesus, I forgot. Hey, men, I'm going to be a poppa—I forgot to tell you guys!"

"Well, I'll be go to hell."

"I didn't think you had it in you, Andy."

"There goes the old malaria theory shot to hell."

THUMP ... THUMP.

"What's the matter, Marion?" I said quietly.

"I ... I was just thinking ... about the Feathermerchant."

"Knock it off!"

"I'm sorry, Mac."

"Now hear this, now hear this. Marines, man your debarkation stations on the double."

"We been sitting here four hours and now they want us on the double."

Up the ladder quick. The fresh air blasts you in the face, almost knocking you down. Now you see it. Saipan! Laying there smoking and bleeding in the smoky dawn like a wounded beast licking its paws and sulking and waiting to leap back at its tormentors.

I moved the command post men to the rail and made a rollcall. The destroyers streamed in front of the ship, moving close up to the beach. Their five-inchers peppered the flaming shore furiously.

Marion broke rank and came over to him. "See Rae for me, Mac," he said.

I stared at him. I'll never know why I answered what I did. Maybe it was because Marion had the same strange expression the Feathermerchant had when he jumped down that hill on Guadalcanal. "I'll see her," I said.

"Command post, over the side," the Gunner ordered.

The Japs sat on top of Mount Topotchau and had Red Beach One zeroed in. The battalion was snowed under by an avalanche of flying shrapnel. The rest of the battalions were hung up on the reefs and were far off location as the hailstorm fell and kept them cut off. Huxley's Whores were gaining quick admission to the glory club. The blood ran deep under a murderous staccato of careening bomb bursts and geysers of hot metal mixed with spurting sand and flesh. They dug in as the beach heaved and danced in a macabre rhythm.

Marion crouched in a shallow hole and labored over his radio. Fox from Tulsa White: Have you reached your initial objective? Over.

A screaming shell swished its way down, twisting into the open beach.

The earphones of Marion's set clattered.

Tulsa White from Fox: I only receive you two and one. Repeat that last message. Over. Tulsa White from Fox. I don't read you at all . . . Tulsa White from Fox: Can you read me . . .

"Hey, Marion, knock off the skylarking."

Marion felt himself spinning like a man caught in a whirlpool, then was bashed to the sand, his left leg dangling, held only by a stubborn muscle.

Spanish Joe lay on the beach fifty yards away. He heard

an agonized voice crying out between the shell bursts. He rose from his cover. An earsplitting scream, a burst. Joe fell flat.

"Joe, it's me—Marion."

FOX TO EASY: WE NEED CORPSMEN UP HERE . . . HAVE YOU ONE TO SPARE? OVER. The message came through Marion's earphones.

The crescendo rose, jarring men loose from their holes. Spanish Joe crawled back to cover, sweat gushing from his every pore. He clutched the rocks about him so tightly his hands cracked and bled.

"God . . . help . . . help me, Joe."

Spanish Joe pulled his body in closer to the rocks, he shook violently. His eyes were pasted to the spot where Marion lay. The violence of the bombardment grew.

EASY TO FOX: CAN'T GET GEORGE NOW, OVER.

"Oh God . . . I'm dying . . . Joe . . . Joe!" The voice was weaker. Gomez buried his face in his hands and lay cowering and frozen.

Divito gunned the radio jeep into a clump of bushes near the message center. "Mac," he yelled, "I'm going to the beach to help with the wounded."

"Shove off," I said.

"Hey, Mac!"

"What?"

"This TBX is out," Danny said. "Where is Spanish Joe with the spare parts?"

"Sonofabitch, I don't know."

"Mac!" message center called over.

"What!"

"We can't contact any rifle companies."

"Keep runners going to the rifle companies till them phones get in. Barry!" I shouted.

The telephone chief ran up. "Barry, the radio to regiment is out. You're going to have to run a wire down the beach to them."

"Jesus, Mac. They are a mile away and it's exposed beach. The Japs are blasting the piss out of the area to prevent consolidation."

"Hit the deck!"

SSSSSSSSSSSHHHHHHHHH

"I haven't enough men, Mac. They are all out with wires to the rifle companies," Barry continued.

"Message center! Send a runner to How Company and tell them to send two telephone men here right away . . . Speedy!"

"Yo," the Texan drawled.

"Have you seen Marion or Spanish Joe?"

"I ain't seen Mary, and I heard that Joe went berserk and stole a machine gun and headed for the Fox Company area."

"All right, Speedy . . . the walkie-talkie network is busted up. I want you to make a round of the rifle companies and get all the squad back into the CP."

"Roger . . . see you," Speedy said, grabbing his carbine and dashing toward the front.

"Danny!"

"Yes, Mac."

"Get in the jeep and stand watch to Kingpin."

"What about this busted radio to regiment?"

"We'll have to look at it later. I'm going to find Huxley. Barry, as soon as any of your men return shoot them down that beach to regiment. Tell them there's a Silver Star in it if they get that line in."

Barry laughed and slapped me on the back as I ran to the water's edge to try to find the skipper. The deck was still rocked from the steady stream of shells being poured from Mount Topotchau.

I couldn't spot Huxley at first. Then I saw the skipper sitting holding something in his arms. He was crying like a baby. It was his little orderly, Ziltch. He was dead, covered with blood and horribly mangled. Huxley was rocking the body back and forth. He had put over the dead boy's face the faded red handkerchief with the embroidered *Sam Huxley, Ohio State.*

"Skipper, get for cover!" I yelled. He was mute. I dragged him to shelter.

Huxley began screaming. "He threw himself on a grenade! Mac, they're killing my boys! They're killing my boys!"

He was berserk. I straightened him up and belted him in the mouth. The punch knocked him down. He struggled up to a sitting position and sat there shaking his head and blinking. A Jap screaming-meemie whistled down. I threw myself over him and pinned him flat till it passed over.

"Thanks, Mac."

"I didn't want to slug you, skipper."

"I guess . . . I lost my—what's the picture?" he snapped quickly.

"Bad. The rest of the combat team is a mile down the beach and we're out of contact. The network to the rifle companies is busted. All we are in contact with is the flagship."

"Where is Gunner Keats? Have him report here immediately."

"I'm in charge now," I said. "He didn't even get out of the buffalo."

"What are you doing now?"

"Telephones to the riflemen should be in soon. I've called all radiomen back to the CP. We'll try to run a wire down the beach to regiment. But they're really pouring it in on the gap between us."

"You're moving right, Mac. You're a lieutenant now."

"We'll argue about that later."

"Whatever you do, keep the radio in to Kingpin. If we lose them, we're in for it. We'll need naval support when the Japs counterattack from Garapan. Get back to the command post. I'm going to the aid tent to check casualties. I'll be right in."

"Roger." I sprang from cover and sprinted over the sand. Something hissed and arched above and sent me flat. The earth rumbled and then I felt numb as something struck me in the small of my back. I rolled over. It was a man's leg!

"Skipper!"

Huxley was already tying a tourniquet about the stump when I got back to him. "Get back to the CP, Mac. You know your assignment! If I'm not there in ten minutes tell Wellman he's got himself a battalion."

"Skipper, I can't leave you!" I bent over him. The sand was slippery with his blood. Next thing I knew I was looking down the barrel of a .45 automatic.

"Get back to your post, Marine," Huxley snarled as he pulled back the cocking pin.

Up front with Fox Company, L.Q. slammed his earphones to the deck and cursed.

"Hey, L.Q. Max wants to know if you are in with the command post?"

"Tell Shapiro that all I can get is How Company and I can't even get them now."

"Never mind—the telephone line just came in."

"Thank Christ," L.Q. said and dropped back against a tree exhausted.

Out in front a clatter of small arms fire rattled as the company contacted an enemy patrol. "Got a cigarette? I dropped mine jumping out of the buffalo this morning."

"Here, L.Q."

"Thanks." He put the cigarette between his lips. A runner dashed in. A sudden burst of gunfire sent everyone sprawling.

"Come on," the runner panted, "we're moving up to hook on with Easy Company . . . hey, L.Q. . . . . hey, what the hell . . . Jesus!"

"Get a corpsman up here. The radio operator has been hit."

"He won't need no corpsman. He got it right in the head. . . ."

"Come on, move up!"

Speedy Gray dropped to his knees at How Company and fought for breath for a moment.

"Runner!" a man at the telephone shouted. "Get Major Pagan and tell him to get to the CP and assume command of the battalion. Highpockets is dead and Major Wellman has been wounded."

"The skipper! God . . . where is that radio operator?" Speedy asked.

"Over there behind those boulders with the rest of the wounded."

"Hi cousin," Seabags whispered weakly as Speedy knelt beside him.   "What's doing . . . goofing off?"

"Why shore . . . you ain't got a chaw on you?"

"No."

"I didn't think so."

"Look, Seabags, maybe I can help pack you back to the beach and let Doc Kyser. . . ."

"Shucks, Speedy, don't be giving me no snow job. I got a hole in my belly big enough to put my fist through."

"Jesus, Seabags . . . Jesus."

"Hey. . . ."

"What?"

"Did you get the old guitar ashore all right?"

"Yes."

Seabags laughed and then began coughing. Speedy put a canteen to Seabags' lips and laid him back. "This here sounds like that crappy old picture we saw back in Hawaii . . . look, cousin, would you sing 'Red River Valley' over my grave if you can . . . you sing that right pretty. . . ."

The shelling had died to sporadic bursts. I turned up the loudspeaker on the jeep radio so I could catch a signal and walked to message center. Major Pagan paced up and down nervously.

"Well?" he snapped to me.

"Kingpin will call us about naval support against a counterattack as soon as they get unfouled out there."

A message center man came up to them. "All rifle companies consolidated and digging in."

"Good. What about that telephone line to regiment?"

"We've lost four men trying to get it down the beach, Major. Intelligence reports that Japs have infiltrated the gap."

"Can you get that other radio in with them, Mac?"

"We found a piece of shrapnel in it. We'll never get it fixed."

"I guess we're going to have to stand alone," Pagan whispered.

I went back to the jeep and sat down and waited and wondered where Speedy was with the squad. Danny walked up, then fell flat on his face. He dragged himself to the front wheel and leaned against it and took a swig from his canteen. There were deep haggard circles of exhaustion beneath his eyes. He took off his helmet and dropped his head to his chest.

"Did you find Mary and Joe?" I asked.

"Marion's dead," he said. "Spanish Joe is somewhere up around Fox Company . . . they say he's going crazy with a machine gun. They're trying to get the wounded off the beach. There must be half the battalion there."

Several moments passed. Pagan ordered everyone to stand by to move the command post to a safer spot.

Speedy staggered in, glassy eyed. He got into the jeep and laid an arm across the steering wheel and dropped his head on it. I was afraid to talk to him. I was afraid to ask . . . it couldn't be possible . . . it couldn't be!

"Speedy, where's the rest of the squad?" I finally asked.

Speedy did not answer.

"Andy . . . where is Andy?"

"I don't know," Speedy sobbed.

"The Injun?"

"Don't know."

"Seabags?"

"Dead."

"L.Q. . . . did you find L.Q.?"

"I don't know! I don't know! I don't know!"

"Doctor Kyser, four more on stretchers."

"Hold them for a second till we make room."

The long tent was filled with walking wounded who sat about quietly awaiting their turn. Those on the stretchers must come first. Some sat there on the brink of unconsciousness, some agonized with burning pain, but each insisted his wound was small. A long row of the near dead lay on litters on the gory floor.

Kyser took a cup of cold coffee and gulped it down. "Bring in the four new ones . . . lay 'em down here." He walked quickly from stretcher to stretcher. "Those two are dead. Tag them and move them outside." He took the poncho from the body on the third stretcher. "Good Lord, what happened to this boy?"

"It's Spanish Joe, Doctor. He tried to stop a tank. Jumped on it and threw a grenade down the hatch and spun off. It ran over him."

He examined the crushed form and nodded slowly. "Bleeding internally . . . impossible to save him. Move him outside."

Kyser moved to the last stretcher. "He got it in the face and the leg," the corpsman said.

"Give me a sponge." The doctor wiped the caked gore and

dirt away. "The big Swede . . . I was at his wedding." He opened Andy's eye and turned a flashlight on it. "Dilated . . . pulse thready. Rip those dungarees off, I want to take a look at that leg."

He studied the mangled bone and flesh and felt the pulse once more. "Morphine." He flipped the boy's dogtag over and wiped it clean to read. "Pedro, get a thousand cc's of type O ready. We're going to have to cut above the knee. Pedro, dammit, answer up . . . where is he? I sent him out a half hour ago."

"He hit a land mine, Doc."

"Get . . . get . . . this boy ready. Plasma . . . amputation . . ."

"*Hit the deck!*"

Divito dashed into the tent.

"Another buffalo on the beach, Doctor."

"You walking wounded help with the stretchers there. The rest of you get tagged and get aboard the buffalo."

"Doc, let me stay and help you."

"Your arm is in bad shape, son. You'd better evacuate."

"I'll stay on too, Doc. You need help."

"Dammit! You people get out of here! You're just cluttering up the place."

"I'm going back to the front."

"Get to the beach and in that buffalo. That's an order, Marine!"

"Doc, the shelling is starting up again."

"Come on, you people, move out, easy with those litters. Hurry and prep that Swede kid, they'll probably be bringing more in."

Outside the tent there was a wild shouting and ruckus. "Come quick, Doc. Someone's gone loco!"

Kyser rushed outside. Three corpsman clutched the struggling Shining Lighttower. "I'm not leaving! I'm not leaving my buddies!" He kicked and squirmed furiously to break the grip.

"What's the matter with him?" Kyser asked.

"He's stone deaf. Bilateral rupture—both eardrums, from the shellfire."

"Give him a shot of morphine and get him quieted down. If he gives you any more trouble put him in a straight jacket. Get him out of here as soon as you can."

Lighttower broke loose from his tormentors and threw his arms about the doctor. "Don't let them take me away!" A needle plunged into him from behind and the corpsman dragged him loose. Kyser wavered faintly a moment, gripped a canvas flap, steadied himself, and returned to the tent.

Andy was on the table. Doc Kyser reached for his sterile gloves. At the same moment from the other section of the tent he heard a familiar call. "Corpsman, man here in bad

shape." The stretcher bearing the body of Danny Forrester
was lowered to the deck.

Kathy opened the door of the refrigerator and reached for
the bottle of cold water. A shadow fell over the kitchen. She
turned with a start.

"I didn't mean to frighten you, dear," her mother said. "I
saw the light on." Sybil Walker tied her robe, reached across
the table and picked up the small bottle of pills. "How long have
you been taking these?"

"I . . . I saw the doctor a few weeks ago. He said it would be
all right. . . ."

"Kathleen, why didn't you tell me?"

"I didn't want to worry you, Mother."

Kathy stared out the window into the black night. "They've
landed again. I know when he lands. . . ."

"You're just imagining, dear."

"No, I know, Mother."

Sybil came up behind her daughter and placed a hand on
her shoulder. The girl fell into her mother's arms. "I've tried to
be brave," she sobbed.

"There, there, baby," mother soothed.

"If Danny dies, I don't want to live."

"Hush, now, hush. Let's sit down and talk, dear."

"I don't usually let myself get like this," she said as she dried
her eyes. "But when I know he's going in . . . I . . . get afraid. I
dream I see him, all covered with blood . . . trying to reach
out to me. . . ."

"Why didn't you tell me?"

"We promised . . . we'd see it through together."

"Don't you know we love you, that we worry every minute of every day with you? Come on now, how about a nice hot
cup of cocoa?"

"That sounds good."

"Feel better, dear?"

"Uh-huh."

"If you'd like, I'll sleep in with you."

"Would you—please, Mother?"

4.

THERE would be no repetition this time of the miracle that saved the Marines from a counterattack at Tarawa. The Japs were staging at Garapan, bent on overrunning the artillery-riddled troops on Red Beach One.

The remains of the Second Battalion of the Sixth Marines threw up a picket line facing Garapan up the coast. Fox Company was strung out in the brush, behind rocks, straddling the road and running down to the water's edge; it was a slim line, cut deeply by first-day casualties. At dusk the grim horror-filled curtain of dark slowly fell as Shapiro's Foxes, Whistler's Easy Company, How, and Captain Harper's George gritted their teeth and made quick peace with God and waited. Shapiro by understanding and unanimous will took charge of the entire four companies and worked busily over his positions, bucking up the courage of his men.

McQuade and his patrol filtered back and reported to the Captain.

"What's the scoop, McQuade?" Shapiro greeted him.

McQuade sat down and drew a breath and wiped the sweat from his face. "Max, I'm getting too damned old for those patrols, I'm getting a survey after tonight. We're up the creek without a paddle, Max. We got halfway to Garapan, sticking close to the road. The Japs are staging for a pisscutter. We spotted four tanks and maybe two or three thousand of them. They got bugles, flags, samurais, and flushing toilets ready to throw at us." The sergeant scanned the spread of the battalion and shook his head. "I don't see how the hell we're going to hold them. Regiment better get at least another battalion up here."

"I got news for you, McQuade. We are isolated," Shapiro said.

The sergeant tried to act nonchalant. "Gimme a weed."

Shapiro went to the field phone and got Major Marlin, now the battalion commander, at the other end of the line. "Marlin, this is Max. My patrol just reported in. King-sized banzai coming . . . two to three thousand massing with tank support. Can you give us anything?"

"That's great," Marlin sputtered at the command post phone. "Can you use slingshots? Max, you're next in command now. If I'm dead tomorrow I hope you have enough men left for a four-handed poker game."

466

"It's that bad, huh?"

"It's worse than the first night at Tarawa, Max. Worst in the Corps history. I'll get walking wounded and every gun and bullet we have up there. I'll do the best I can. We are trying to get help from the Navy but I hear that the Jap fleet is coming in."

As the moon rose, Max Shapiro called his officers and staff NCOs about him. The harrowing minutes ticked by slowly for the men on the line, their hands clutching their bayoneted rifles and their eyes glued down the coastal road.

Max knelt inside the circle of men about him. "I'm not going to give you people a big Semper Fi talk. We either stop this attack or die. No Marine retreats. If he does, shoot him. Any questions?"

They nodded grimly and returned to their posts. Shapiro then did a very unusual thing. He spread his poncho on the deck and lay down with his helmet as a pillow.

"What the hell are you doing, Max?" McQuade asked.

"What the hell you think I'm doing? I'm going to take a nap. Wake me up when the fun starts."

A wave of laughter spread along the line as the men turned to catch the little skipper feigning sleep. He did a masterful job of acting. It was like a tonic to the tired men.

The Japanese bugles blew. A hundred samurai swords glinted through the moonlight. Down the road the frenzy-whipped enemy charged at Huxley's Whores.

Actually, the Japs were caught in a trap. In the cover of dark they had massed their men in a wedge to overrun Red Beach One. Two Navy destroyers standing offshore shot up a thousand flares and the night turned into a blaring day. The onrushing enemy was caught, lit up, and exposed. The destroyers moved almost on the beach, pumping salvo after slavo into the packed troops at almost point-blank range. Under the calm leadership of Shapiro, who wandered up and down the lines, the Marines directed fire when the Japs were nearly atop their positions. By flare light the enemy was cut down and stacked up like cordwood, and the coastal road soon became littered with a thousand Japs. The attackers fell back, stumbling and reeling over the bodies of their dead in broken retreat. From behind the battalion, a trio of Sherman tanks roared after the enemy tanks and smashed them.

Max Shapiro resumed his nap.

At the break of daylight they came on again. The Japanese command determined to break through the cut-off men on Red Beach One and they had five thousand troops to sacrifice. This time they were sent in in waves to avoid the destroyer fire. A fusillade of death poured from the Marines but that and the cold steel of their bayonets could not stop the enemy. They swarmed into the lines. Fanatic yellow men and fanatic white men locked in hand to hand combat.

The first wave of the battering ram had succeeded in its mission, a breach had been made, and the Second Battalion buckled back over fifty yards of blood-drenched ground. The second wave of Japanese came on to exploit the break. The situation seemed desperate.

As the stunned Marines braced for the death they knew must come, Two Gun Shapiro stepped in front of them, his two pistols smoking. He turned to his Marines and over the din they heard a grisly shriek from his lips. "Blood!" he cried.

Max Shapiro sank to his knees, his pistols empty. He threw them at the enemy. *"Blood!"* he screamed, *"Blood!"*

The men of Huxley's Whores were petrified. A legend was broken! The invincible captain, the man bullets could not touch, the man they believed was almost divine, lay there writhing in agony the same as any human being. The blood gushed from his mouth and ears and nose and he rolled over defiantly, trying to crawl to his enemy to kill with bare hands, the same ghastly word on his lips.

Was he human after all? Did he not realize that something must be done to elevate his men to a task beyond human capabilities? Was it his God that sent him forward to sacrifice himself? Or was Max Shapiro merely a mad dog, full of a glorious madness?

Huxley's Whores rose to the heights of their dead captain. They no longer resembled human beings. Savage beyond all savagery, murderous beyond murder, they shrieked, "Blood!" "BLOOD!" ... "BLOOD!"

The enemy, who were mere mortals, fell back.

HELLO, TULSA WHITE: THIS IS McQUADE, FOX COMPANY. WE HAVE STOPPED THEM. WE HAVE STOPPED THEM.

HELLO, McQUADE: REINFORCEMENTS ARE LANDING ON THE BEACH RIGHT NOW. . . .

After the assault on Red Beach One and the stopping of the counterattacks, the rest of the battle of Saipan was anticlimax for the Second Battalion. After the first twenty-four hours there weren't enough men left to constitute a fighting unit. The rest of the Sixth Marines were in the thick of it all the way. And so, at long last, the regiment had kept its date with destiny and taken its place beside its predecessors at Belleau Wood and Guadalcanal and Tarawa.

On the Second Battalion the fate of the operation had hinged and like a lot of kids on a lot of other islands they had apparently been licked. But nobody got around to telling them so and it was that extra something nobody can explain that pulled them through.

Command of the battalion had changed hands four times in twenty-four hours. Huxley, Wellman, Pagan, and Marlin. But in my book, it was always Highpockets who was the skipper. What he had taught them, what he had half killed them for, was there when it was most needed.

The conquest of Saipan was followed up when the Third Marine Division landed further south and reconquered Guam. Then we pushed over the channel to capture Saipan's neighbor, Tinian. They called Tinian the perfect campaign. But it wasn't quite perfect. I got wounded and was sent back to Saipan for a couple quarts of blood at the base hospital.

I walked into Chaplain Peterson's tent. Peterson arose to greet me. "How's the old salt?"

"They're not going to beat me out of my thirty-year retirement," I said.

"Good. I got your request, Mac. I think it is a fine thing to do. Father McKale is sending Pedro's personal belongings over."

"I'll be shoving off for the States soon. If I knew Gomez's address, I'd visit there, too."

"It's good of you to give up your furlough to visit the parents of these boys."

"It's the least I could do."

"I'll have the things sent over to your camp."

"Chaplain Peterson . . . what about Andy?"

The balding minister shook his head. "Only time will heal his wounds. I've tried to talk to him, as you have. In a little while they will restore his face, but . . ."

"They'll never restore his leg."

"It is a pity. He has a wonderful girl and so much to live for. I took this letter around and read it to him. He threw it back at me." I took the envelope from him and opened it and began to read. *"My Dearest, You have a son. . . ."*

I looked up at Peterson.

"Born on D-day, Mac."

It is rather hard to say what Timmy looks like. Poor little dear, what a horrible mixture he is. New Zealand, American, Scotch, and Swede. At any rate he bellows like a Marine and eats like a lumberjack. I think I'll keep him. You know how happy I am.

*Andy, we know where you are. Our prayers are with
you every second of every minute. I know that it will be a
long long time before you will be back with us but remember that all Timmy and I live for will be the day you return
forever.*

*Mother and Dad have been dears. Dad is already look-
ing about for a pony for Timmy. The poor wee fellow can't
even hold his head up yet. Mom spends half her time digging up American recipes. She says she is really going to
fatten you up.*

*Darling I can hardly wait till the day Timmy is old
enough to walk. I shall take him over to our land and tell
him that some day his Daddy is coming back and clear it
and build us a nice warm little house and we shall live in it
forever and ever.*

*Winter is coming, but soon it shall be spring and we will
be here as always.*

> *Your loving wife,*
> *Pat*

I dropped the letter on the desk.

"He'll go back," the chaplain said. "Love like that girl's is
too strong a magnet for any man."

Speedy came up the road to meet me. "Mac, just got the
word. We're shoving off tomorrow."

"Going home?"

"Yes."

"I think I'll drop over to the hospital and say good-by to
Andy."

Speedy grasped my shoulder. "I was just over there. He told
me to get the hell out."

I walked into the ward, down the row of legless and armless
men till I reached the far end. I opened the screened enclosure
around his bed and drew up a chair. Andy lay flat on his back,
his face invisible under a swath of bandages leaving only his
eyes and lips open.

"Hi, knucklehead, how they been treating you?" He did not
answer. "I was just over to Chaplain Peterson's."

"If you come to preach, pray with somebody that needs it."

"I came to say good-by, Andy. Speedy and me are going
home."

"All right, good-by."

"Chrisake, they'll have that ugly kisser squared away in a
year so there won't even be a scar. I talked to the Doc and ..."

"Sure, I'll get a pretty new face ... a nice leg too. You can
do anything with it. Chop trees, plow a row. Maybe even get a
job in a sideshow."

"Hold on, you're way off base. You've got a home and a wife and son."

"Leave her out of it! I ain't got nothin'! I never had nothin'!"

"She'd want you back if they sent you home in a basket."

"Sure ... sure, after they fit me with a leg, they rehabilitate me. You should listen to them crackpots around here. Look, Mac, want to see me wiggle my stump and show you how funny it is?"

"Cut it out! You're not the only guy in the world that lost a leg. You worked in the woods, you've seen it before."

"I'm glad to give it, Mac. Just ask anybody, we're all real happy to do it. They going to fix up the Injun with a new pair of ears? Maybe they gonna dig up Seabags and the skipper."

"Andy, you're all scarred up inside you. Christ, we can't all just lay down and die. They didn't ask to live when they joined the Corps."

"Get out of here."

"Not before I tell you I think you're a yellow rat. You haven't got the guts to deserve to live. Don't speak about the skipper and the squad. You aren't in the same league with them."

I wanted to take Andy in my arms and tell him I didn't mean it. His hand groped for the air, reaching for mine.

"Mac, I ain't sore at you ... you know that ... I ain't sore at you."

"I shouldn't of said that. It wasn't true." I took his hand.

"Forget it. Look, lots of luck. Tell Speedy I'm sorry. Tell him ole Andy said not to get too much mud for his duck when he gets back to the States."

"So long, Andy."

"So long, Mac, and ... and if you happen to be passing Peterson's tent, maybe you can tell him I'd like him to read them letters to me ... and maybe he could write one for me ... if it ain't too much trouble."

I met Speedy and noticed that he was carrying his guitar. We trudged toward the camp. "Reckon we could stop at the cemetery and say good-by?"

We walked through the white wooden archway where the sign read: SECOND MARINE DIVISION CEMETERY. I supposed it wasn't much different from any other cemetery in the world—except for Speedy and me. We found the Sixth Marine's section and slowly wandered between the mounds and crosses. We stopped for a moment at each grave and for that moment remembered something, the kind of thing a guy remembers about another guy. Some crazy little thing that just stuck in the mind. JONES, L.Q., PFC ... ROJAS, PEDRO, PHM 1/C

... HODGKISS, MARION, CPL. ... GOMEZ, JOSEPH, PVT ...
HUXLEY, SAMUEL, LT. COL.... McQUADE, KEVIN, MGY SGT...
SHAPIRO, MAX, CAPTAIN ... KEATS, JACK, MARINE GUNNER ...
BROWN, CYRIL, PFC. ...

Speedy stopped over Seabags' grave and parted his lips. "I
sort of made a promise, Mac." His fingers strummed a chord
but he could not sing.

Beneath us the ground rumbled and the air was filled with
a deafening roar of motors. We turned our eyes to the sky.
B-29s, flight after flight of the graceful silver birds, winged
over us on the way to Tokyo.

"Let's get out of here, Mac ... why should I be crying over a
bunch of goddamyankees."

5.

THEY stood at the rail of the *Bloomfontein*. They
were all quiet. Silent stares, mouths open as we glided through
the fogbank. And then the two towers of the bridge poked their
heads above the haze.

"The Golden Gate in forty-eight, the breadline in forty-
nine."

The pilot schooner signaled for the submarine nets to be
opened to let us enter. It was chilly.

It wasn't much the way we had thought it was going to be.
Just a bunch of tired heartsick guys at the end of a long, long
voyage. And the Marines were out there yet. The First Division
had landed in the Palau Islands. They were still dying. I remembered how I'd pictured this moment, with my boys alongside me ... wars just didn't turn out that way. Broken and
weary in body and mind ... and the Marines were still landing
out there.

I could still hear my boys singing. They sure sang pretty. I
could hear them plain as day, standing outside the Skipper's
tent on Guadalcanal.

> *"Oh Sixth Marines, Oh Sixth Marines,*
> *Those hardy sons of bitches ..."*

"Hi, Mac."
"Oh ... hi Speedy."
"Thinking?"
"Yeah."
"Me too. Ain't much like coming home, is it?"

"No."

The big bridge loomed closer and closer and then the fog seemed to drift aside and they could see her. Frisco . . . the States.

"Funny," Speedy said. "That bridge ain't gold at all. It's orange."

"Yeah."

"I've been thinking. You got a lot of stops to make on your furlough. Maybe you could give me Pedro's stuff and I could see his family. I don't live very far away."

"But he was a Mexican and you're back home now, Speedy."

"He was my buddy," Speedy whispered.

He took out his wallet and a piece of paper brown with age.

December 22, 1942. This here is a holy agreement. We are the Dit Happy Armpit Smelling bastards of Huxley's Whores. . . . We hereby agree that one year after the end of the war we will meet in the City of Los Angeles. . . .

Speedy tore it up and we watched as the pieces floated slowly down to the water.

Sam Huxley's lady was wonderful. I spent two days at the Base in Dago with her. Afterwards I felt my heart so heavy that it seemed there wasn't any more room for sadness in it. I went to the homes of my boys; it was awkward at first but the folks went out of their way to make me feel at home. They wanted so badly to know so many things.

I wanted to get it over with. I wanted to badly. When I got to Marion's home in Kansas, Rae had left but I felt that one day I'd keep my promise to Marion and run across her someplace again. She had taken the money they'd saved together and bought him a beautiful window in his church.

I caught a train in Chicago with a feeling of relief, knowing I had but one more stop to make. As I neared Baltimore I looked through the window and as the scenes passed before me it somehow felt familiar, the way Danny had told me it was time and again.

It was raining outside. I closed my eyes and rested back. The clickety-clack of the wheels nearly lulled me to sleep and I thought about my boys and about Huxley's Whores. The fresh-faced kids and the misfits that had made the old-timers wince at first sight of them. And I remembered Huxley's words: "Make Marines out of them. . . ."

Yes, they took us back and the roadsigns were white—white crosses. And they were still taking them back, to a place called Iwo Jima. Three divisions of Marines were there, within fighter-plane range of Japan. At this moment they were on the hottest rock of them all.

Like any gyrene I thought there had never been an outfit like mine. But in my heart I knew that we were but one of fifty assault battalions in a Corps that had grown beyond comprehension. There were other outfits that had seen much rougher fighting and shed more blood. Five Marine Divisions, with a Sixth being formed. The Corps had sure grown.

I looked through the rainstreaked window and caught a fleeting glimpse of a wide-lawned street with a set of huge buildings. It must have been Johns Hopkins Hospital. Then the train plunged into a long tunnel.

"Baltimore! There will be a ten-minute stopover."

I nudged the sleeping boy sitting beside me. "Wake up, Danny, you're home."

He opened his eyes and stood. I helped him square away his field scarf and button his blouse.

"How do I look?"

"Like a doll." The train lurched as it braked to a stop. I caught him to prevent his falling. Danny winced. "Hurt?" I asked.

"No."

"How's the old flipper feel?"

He grinned. "It won't be much good for tossing fifty-yard passes. They told me they'll be pulling shrapnel out of my back for ten years."

The train halted. I pulled Danny's gear from the luggage rack and edged to the door. We stepped from the train. I gave the bags to a porter and handed him a bill.

For many moments Danny and I looked at each other. Both of us wanted to say something but neither of us knew what to say. Something had passed from our lives that would never return. For me, just a cruise was over. For me there would be another station, another batch of kids to train, another campaign. Our two lives, which had once been so important to each other, were now a long way apart.

"Sure you won't stay a couple of days, Mac?"

"Naw, you don't want me around. I got to get to New York and see Levin's dad and get on back to the coast. Not much time left."

A crowd surged past us to fight onto the already crowded train. Behind us a gang of kids stood with their handbags. A Marine recruiting sergeant in dress blues paced up and down. "You have five minutes," he barked. Voices rose behind Danny and me.

"Take care of yourself, son."

"Get a Jap for me, will you?"

"Write."

"Now don't worry, Mom, everything is going to be all right."

"They're putting us in a place called boot camp for a few weeks."

"You'll be sorreee," a uniformed Marine sang out as he passed them.

Danny and I embraced clumsily. "So long, you salty old son-ofabitch."

"So long, gyrene."

Danny turned and pushed his way down the platform to the foot of the stairs. I followed, several paces behind him.

A news vendor shouted his headline. "Marines take Sura-batchi on Iwo Jima! Get your latest *News-Post* and *Sun*. Marines on Iwo Jima!" I caught a glimpse of the front page he waved. They were raising the flag on the mountain top in the picture.

Danny fought step by step up the long stairs. Then, he stopped and looked up. She was there. Surely she's the angel I pictured for him.

"Danny!" she shouted over the din.

"Kathy . . . Kathy!" And they fought through the mass of hurrying people into each other's arms.

I saw them move to the top of the steps. An older man was there and a boy. Danny took off his cap and reached for the man's hand. I could see his lips move. "Hello, Dad . . . I'm home."

I saw the four of them fade into the shadows of the barn-like station. Danny turned and raised his hand at the door for a moment. "So long, Mac."

And they stepped into the twilight. The rain had stopped.

"Train for Wilmington, Philadelphia, Newark, and New York . . . Gate twenty-two."

I walked down the steps.

"Read all about it! Marines on Iwo Jima!"

"All right, you people! Get aboard!"

And I remembered the words in the book I had taken from Marion's body.

Home is the sailor, home from the sea,
And the hunter, home from the hill. . . .

ABOUT THE AUTHOR

LEON URIS, born in Baltimore in 1924, left high school to join the Marine Corps. In 1950, *Esquire* magazine bought an article from him—and it encouraged him to begin work on a novel. The result was his acclaimed bestseller *Battle Cry*. *The Angry Hills*, a novel set in wartime Greece, was his second book. As a screenwriter and then newspaper correspondent, he became interested in the dramatic events surrounding the rebirth of the State of Israel. This interest led to *Exodus*, his monumental bestseller which has been read by millions of people. From one of the episodes in *Exodus* came *Mila 18*, the story of the angry uprising of Jewish fighters in the Warsaw Ghetto. *Exodus Revisited*, a work of nonfiction, presents the author's feeling for the land and the people of Israel. Mr. Uris is also the author of *Armageddon*, *Topaz*, *QB VII*, *Trinity*, *The Haj*, and *Mitla Pass*.